Cursebreaker

Book Two of The Heretic Gods

Carol A. Park

Shattered Soul Books

Pennsylvania

Shattered Soul Books
2600 Willow Street Pike North
PMB 259
Willow Street, PA 17584
www.carolapark.com

Publisher's Note: This is a work of fiction. Names, characters, places, and incidents are a product of the author's imagination. Locales and public names are sometimes used for atmospheric purposes. Any resemblance to actual people, living or dead, or to businesses, companies, events, institutions, or locales is completely coincidental.

Cursebreaker/ Carol A. Park. -- 1st ed.
ISBN 978-1-7321491-4-4 (paperback)
ISBN 978-1-7321491-5-1 (e-book)

TO ROBIN

For being a cheerleader, friend,
and all-around awesome mother-in-law.
Given the number of times you've taken the kids so I can write,
I figure you deserve at least one dedication.

Contents

Acknowledgements

Cursebreaker is my first true sequel, though it's my third published book. That presents new and different challenges than writing a first book: How much will people have forgotten? Have I re-explained too much? Not enough? Are the details consistent with the first book? Can I do *that* with the magic system based on the rules I've already canonized?

And that's not to mention that between *Banebringer* and *Cursebreaker,* I decided to write Ivana's backstory in *Sweetblade.* Since I wrote *Sweetblade* with the intent that it could be skipped (or read as a stand-alone), I know there are people who won't have read *Sweetblade* before diving into *Cursebreaker,* and there will also be people who have. Since character arcs are so central to the stories I tell, and since Ivana's backstory is, of course, important to her continuing arc, this presented another challenge. I wanted to write *Cursebreaker* in such a way that wouldn't penalize those who hadn't read *Sweetblade* and yet reward those who had.

The story didn't happen in a vacuum, of course. My husband, Calvin Park, reads all my stories in the earliest forms I'll let him see. It's apparently becoming a time-honored tradition that he tells me I need to change something, I argue with him for a few weeks, and then I cave, realize he was right and change it.

My faithful beta reader, Tam Case, helped me polish up the story even more, and both she and Wes Allen graciously agreed to help me proof the final version. And, of course, my editor, Amy

McNulty, gave it that professional touch.

There's also more than just the story that goes into producing a book. I have the pleasure of continuing to have the very talented Brit K. Caley illustrating and designing my covers. Andrew Park has also provided a few more very cool interior icons to make the inside just that much prettier.

I also must acknowledge some of my fellow authors in the trenches, with whom I have traded advice, stories, laughs, and sometimes whines, in no particular order: Angela Boord, Barbara Kloss, Clayton Snyder, Dave Woolliscroft, Devin Madson, Jon Auerbach, Josh Erikson, Kayleigh Nicol, Phil Williams, Steven McKinnon, and Travis Riddle. I've also interacted with many other lovely people too numerous to list on Twitter and other social media.

Finally, I have to thank my readers. It makes writing that much more fun to know that there are people who are interested in and even excited about the stories I have to tell and who want to come along with me on these characters' journeys.

It's you I think of when I ponder the ultimate question: Will people who liked *Banebringer* also enjoy *Cursebreaker*? Well, I believe so—and I'm very excited to get part two of Vaughn and Ivana's story finally into your hands. Enjoy!

Chapter One

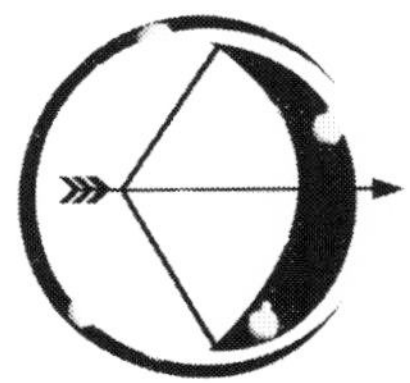

The Shrine

Vaughn stood nose-to-nose with a fire-breathing serpent. He peered into its empty eye sockets, which had once held jade stones, if the illustrations were accurate, and then stuck a finger into a hole in the middle of its open mouth.

He yelped and jumped back as a stream of fire spurted out of the hole and then vanished as abruptly as it had appeared.

Uproarious laughter came from behind him, and he spun around to find Thrax doubled over nearly to the ground.

"Very funny," Vaughn said. "What is it with you and trying to burn off my eyebrows?"

Thrax gained control of himself and straightened up. His exuberance had caused curls of his shoulder-length, chestnut hair, which he kept bundled at the nape, to come loose. It gave him a sort of wild, disheveled look that, in combination with his muscular build, would have been intimidating were it not for the grin plastered on his face. "What in the abyss are you doing?" he asked.

Vaughn scratched at his newly grown beard and then shrugged. "Investigating?"

Thrax snorted. He waltzed over to the same stone relief—carved into one of the shrine's walls—that Vaughn had been examining and leaned in to take a closer look.

While he was bent over, Vaughn promptly dumped his waterskin over Thrax's head.

Thrax flailed and sputtered. "What—?"

Then his eyes went to the empty skin in Vaughn's hand, and he touched a finger to his forehead in a mock salute. "Well played."

"Would you idiots keep it down?" Dax called from the other side of the clearing. He and Saylyn, a researcher Vaughn had briefly worked with back when the Ichtaca still had their base at Gan Barton's manor in Weylyn, were huddled over the book that had caused all this trouble, arguing again. Saylyn's silver-streaked, blond hair and light skin stood in contrast to Dax's dark brown hair and warm beige skin. Both she and Dax, their resident archaeologist, called Cadmyr home, but Vaughn recalled that Saylyn's father was from Fuilyn, where pale, almost white skin was more commonly found than in the rest of the Setanan Empire.

Thrax was from Arlana, another of the three original Setanan regions, and the hue of his skin was closest to Dax's, though it had lost the youthful smoothness of Dax's complexion to middle age.

And then there was Vaughn himself, more bronze than brown. The forebears of his late father, Ri Gildas of Ferehar—

dead at Vaughn's own hands—were originally from Weylyn, and his father's family had remained Setanan through-and-through ever since. His mother, on the other hand, was Fereharian, and Vaughn had inherited her skin tone.

It was a very visual reminder that none of them really had a home anymore. Their little subset of Banebringers, held together by Yaotel, found solidarity in being part of the Ichtaca more than anything else.

Thrax put his finger to his lips and winked.

His merriment didn't last long.

Yasril burst into the clearing. "Soldiers! Coming this way!" The man—even older than Saylyn—doubled over, panting.

Vaughn cursed and scrambled to string his bow. *Not again.* "Go! Go!" he shouted, but the others were already scattering to their predetermined locations.

Yasril stumbled over to one of the walls of the crumbling shrine, right around the corner from the fiery serpent, and leaned against it.

Vaughn joined him. "How long?" He propped his bow up against the shrine, pulled his qixli out of the pouch he wore slung across his body, and held it firmly between two hands. Then, he willed it to find the qixli of Danton, the last and youngest member of their team, also from Arlana.

"Maybe five minutes." Yasril took another gulp of air. "I'm not cut out for this. I don't know why you brought me on this damned expedition."

A seventy-year-old man with a perpetual tremor in his arm would not have been Vaughn's first choice, but he'd wanted another moonblood, and Yasril had been the only one available. "You're doing great. How many?"

A trickle of sweat ran down Yasril's wrinkled, deep brown temple. "Three."

Vaughn scanned the edge of the clearing, where rubble from the shrine's broken stairs turned into natural rock, and then disappeared beneath the undergrowth of the forest beyond. The clearing was silent but for the chirping of birds in the trees around them.

He nodded to Saylyn, who was crouched behind the pedestal where they had been examining the book, which was now snugged safely to her side.

She closed her eyes, and the undergrowth crept across the area they had cleared, hiding their footprints in the dirt, the trampled grass, the ashes of their cooking fire. Vines snaked up the side of the shrine—obscuring the relief Vaughn had been inspecting minutes before—and then across the broken steps to twine around each other until they hung down to block part of the yawning entrance into the shrine itself.

When Saylyn was done, the shrine looked as though it had lain undisturbed for decades—all within the course of a minute or two.

Vaughn exhaled and laid his head back against the wall. Three soldiers.

Thrax hid on the opposite side of the shrine from Vaughn and Yasril, and Dax was inside the shrine itself. Either of them could handle three if need be. And, if necessary, he had his bow.

The silvery, viscous liquid caught between the two glass panes of the qixli—lightblood aether—finally began to stir. It molded itself into the shape of a face, indistinct and featureless because Vaughn wasn't a lightblood. Danton's voice, made tinny by the device, came through. "What's up?"

"We've got company coming from Yasril's side," Vaughn said.

"Got it," Danton said. "Let me know if you need me."

Vaughn slid the qixli back into the pouch and picked up his bow. "Ready?"

Yasril nodded.

Vaughn burned the aether in his blood. He didn't bother with the hardened slivers he had in his pouch; this was too critical a situation to chance having to replenish if he ran out—and he rarely used his own aether externally anymore, anyway. With increased practice and increased need, it had become impractical to harvest all the aether he needed from himself rather than burning it directly.

One by one, the others he could see blinked out of visibility, following his lead. Other than Yasril, they didn't have the option of using their own blood to turn invisible, so they had to use what he and Yasril—the two moonbloods—had lent them.

A flock of birds stirred from the nearby trees. Their wings rustled and their chattering increased until they took flight as one to find a different perch.

Shortly thereafter, three Setanan soldiers stepped into the clearing from the trees, their hands on their swords, their faces wary.

The middle soldier, a middle-aged man who had the stripes of an officer on the shoulder of his jacket, scanned the clearing with a frown on his face. "Nothing here, but let's make sure."

The soldier to his right stared at the ruined shrine, his mouth agape. "I wouldn't say nothing..."

Vaughn could sympathize. He had felt the same way the first time he had seen this place.

The officer gave his men a sharp look. "Search the area—but don't touch anything."

The soldier to his left, the youngest looking of the three, rolled his eyes, but even he skirted the stones of the shrine as they spread out to do as their commander ordered.

It didn't take the soldiers long. The shrine was just that: a shrine, not one of the enormous temples or temple complexes described in some of the ancient texts they had—described but never found.

The officer paused at the entrance to the shrine. He bent and peered beyond the vines into the darkness, hesitated, and then straightened up.

"No signs anyone was here," the officer said as the other two soldiers joined him. "Human or demonspawn." He cast a dark look at the shrine, as if the rocks themselves might taint him.

Hold, Dax, Vaughn thought. He couldn't see the man, but he could envision the hatred burning from his eyes, because he'd seen it before, not that long ago. Vaughn was pretty sure Dax had learned his lesson, considering what it had cost them, but even so.

As an iceblood, Dax could freeze the soldier's blood in his veins if he wanted to.

The officer waved his hand. "Let's keep searching." The three soldiers disappeared back into the trees.

Vaughn counted to two hundred and then pulled out his qixli. "They left," he said quietly. "Status?"

"I see them," Danton said. "Headed away."

"Good. Let me know if that changes." Vaughn released his aether, and soon the others also turned visible again as well.

They met near the pedestal, and Dax's eyes flashed as soon as they were all assembled. "I could have killed him," he said. "I could have killed all three of them myself."

This was an old argument, and Vaughn was tired of it. "No, you couldn't have," he said. "Not unless you wanted to chance suicide in the process."

"Fine." Dax gestured to the group. "But three of them against five Gifted? They would have been dead before—"

"Dax, you know that's not why we're here," Saylyn said.

Dax threw up his hands. "We've been *here* for almost a month, and nothing about this place has helped us interpret *that*"—he pointed to the book, which Saylyn had placed back on the pedestal—"any better."

"I have to say," Yasril put in quietly, "I don't much see the point in remaining here. I don't think we're going to learn anything else."

Saylyn was already shaking her head. "But what if we come up with something, and we're not here to test it out? Then it's another trek back—"

"What if, what if, what if," Dax said. "Every day we're out here is another chance we'll be discovered."

"And whose fault is that?" Thrax asked, rolling a tiny fireball up and down his knuckles.

The group fell quiet. Dax's face reddened, but he made no reply.

Yaotel, the leader of the Ichtaca, had allowed the expedition only under strict orders not to engage any Setanan forces unless it became necessary. Their mission here was supposed to be secret. Dax had ruined that by losing his temper and killing one of a two-soldier scouting party not even a week after they'd arrived, even though they'd known in advance and had hidden themselves well enough. Instead, they'd been forced to eliminate the other scout as well.

They'd hidden the bodies, of course, but the damage had been done. Setanan scouts disappearing without explanation in the southern end of the Fereharian mountains? It was only a matter of time before a search team would be sent out to find the missing men. At least the Conclave's attention was split in a thousand different directions, and to their minds, this was probably a minor annoyance.

A major annoyance to Vaughn's little group, however.

Vaughn put his fingers to his temples. How did Yaotel do this?

He could barely stand three weeks of squabbling among his five-person team, let alone the hundreds of Ichtaca that Yaotel managed.

He sighed and turned to Thrax. "Thrax? You have something more substantive to offer?"

"Eh, as much fun as this has been, I vote we head back to Marakyn," Thrax said. He looked down at the book that had started this whole mess. "Doesn't seem like we're making much progress for the risk."

Saylyn put her hand on the book, almost possessively. "So that's it then? All of this was for nothing?"

Then, as one, they all turned to look at Vaughn. His stomach clenched. *Gods. I hate being the one in charge.*

Which was, case in point, why he *had* to figure this out.

At that moment, Danton strolled into the clearing, his hands in his pockets. He blew his mop of russet brown hair out of his eyes. "So, how'd we do?"

Dax threw his hands up in the air. "Danton, I'll take over for you." He stomped away.

"Just...give me a few minutes to think," Vaughn said. He picked up the book and walked away from the group.

Vaughn wandered over to the shrine's entrance and ducked inside. Yasril had drifted away, but Thrax and Saylyn were still arguing at the pedestal.

He pulled one of the latest Ichtacan inventions out of his pouch. It looked like a miniature qixli, except in place of a round glass panel the size of two palms there was a thumb-sized glass panel cut in the shape of a flame. He touched his thumb to the silvery flame. A few seconds later, it began to glow.

He set it in the middle of the small chamber and sat down

against the far wall amongst their gear.

He laid his head back against a faded mural of blood being collected in some sacred ritual. What would Xiuheuhtli think about his sacred shrine being used as a hiding place for their supplies?

Perhaps he wouldn't mind, considering it was helping one of his Banebringers escape death—or worse.

More likely, if the deity attached to this shrine even existed, he was as indifferent to mortal happenings as the rest of the heretic gods were.

Except, apparently, Danathalt—the god of the abyss. Maybe they weren't *all* as indifferent as they seemed. He had to hope that.

He frowned and flipped through the book.

If it could be called that. It was actually half a book that had been torn in two, and they had the first half. Unlike most of the old texts they had scrounged up through the years, this was not an ancient religious tome. They knew exactly when it had been produced because most of its pages had a date. It spanned a period of several months, over thirty-two years ago.

Far from the crumbling pages of ancient hymns or prescriptions for sacrifice, it appeared to be a diary or journal of sorts recording the details of an archaeological expedition at this very site.

They didn't know what the results of the expedition had been because there was no record of it at any of the three universities in Weylyn, Arlana, and Cadmyr, respectively.

He found the page he was looking for and ran his fingers over the sketch that had been made there. It was of a monument the original archaeological expedition had dug up, mostly still intact. It was, by all accounts, a serpent—a larger replica of the same fiery serpent Vaughn had been studying earlier, except not a relief, but a statue. The author of the book described the monument as being man-high when set upright: one could walk into its open mouth and stand there, as if being swallowed up. Writing had been etched around the serpent's lips—and duplicated in the sketch—in a language none among the Ichtaca could identify, let alone read.

The expedition members had found the serpent early on in their expedition and had spent most of the rest of it puzzling over the language and digging up other artifacts.

He flipped the book over to read the last intact page. The author's excitement was evident:

"Today, we made an incredible discovery: a tablet with text in the mystery language and what we're assuming is the same text translated into Xambrian! I'm certain with this information, we'll be able to make headway deciphering the meaning of the words on the serpent. Of course, I'm the only one here who knows Xambrian, and this is all to be kept quiet—for now. If the Conclave discovered what we found here, let alone that we're working with other languages, that would be the end of this expedition—and probably the end of all of us. They still think we're investigating a site about the ancient Donian nomads. Ha! I'll make a sketch of the tablet later tonight. I'm meeting G in a few minutes."

Except there was no "later tonight." The rest of the book was missing—or had been destroyed.

Vaughn was inclined to think the former. Why destroy only half of it, after all? The Conclave would have no reason to rip a book like this in half and leave the rest to be discovered.

For a while, the initial excitement over the journal's discovery had caused quite a stir. It wasn't a shrine they had run across before—what if there were other artifacts? Sometimes, to their collectors—like Dax—it seemed as though they had exhausted any source of new information about their patrons.

Unfortunately, an initial foray to the site some time ago had turned up nothing. Oh, they had found the shrine all right—completely overgrown. But no serpentine statue, no miraculous second half of the book, and so the interest had died away.

Until Dax had come back from the south with a rotting manuscript that held a rather fantastical story not about the heretic gods, but about Banebringers—and that described a similar-looking serpent. There were no copies of the mysterious language, but there was an explanation as to the supposed function of the serpent: it was a doorway to the gods. The story indicated the serpent harnessed the power of the sky-fire each year to allow Banebringers to travel to, best as they could translate, "the heavens." Why anyone would *want* to visit the gods was another matter.

A shadow fell across the door and Danton poked his head inside. "So...the others want to know what we're going to do."

Vaughn looked up at Danton. "What do you think?"

Danton entered the shrine and settled himself down on the other side of the qixli-light. "I don't know, Vaughn. This has been interesting and all, but I think if there were anything else to discover, we would have discovered it by now." He hesitated. "I think...maybe the resources we're expending here might be better used elsewhere."

"We have the inscription," Vaughn muttered. "We just don't know how to read it."

"And we've found nothing here to help us do that. We haven't even found this supposed serpent-door."

Vaughn waved his hand. The serpent statue itself might be redundant; physical objects were only ever used in their magic as foci. They weren't *technically* necessary components to make the magic work, just to make it work without chancing something unintended happening. Which, admittedly, depending on the type of aether, could be...drastic.

Of course, that all assumed aether was used to make it work in the first place, and *how* it worked was what Vaughn aimed to find out. "A doorway to the gods, Danton. A doorway to the same gods who cursed us. I know Yaotel thinks I'm crazy—but *Danathalt* is somehow helping the Conclave. How are we supposed to ultimately counter him without the help of another god?"

Danton clenched his fist. "Damn it, Vaughn, you know I respect you, but I think at this point you're being stubborn for the sake of it, and it's putting all of us in danger."

Vaughn glanced up at Danton. His normally bright face was shadowed. The last eighteen months—since their plan to expose the Conclave had gone so disastrously wrong—had been difficult for them all, what with the loss of their safe house in Weylyn and the Conclave's redoubled efforts to find and destroy Banebringers.

Vaughn *was* being stubborn, and not without reason. But his personal reason—which Danton didn't know about—for wanting this to succeed wasn't worth risking *all* their lives.

Vaughn stood up and brushed himself off. Time for Plan B. "You're right."

"I am?"

"Yes. There's nothing else for us to do here." He picked up the book and the qixli-light and ducked out of the shrine. The others had scattered. Yasril was nowhere to be seen—probably returned to his post. Dax, likewise, was still gone. Saylyn was standing in front of the pedestal, peering at carvings etched into it. And Thrax...

Vaughn looked up. Just as he had thought. Thrax was twelve feet up, on top of the shrine, playing with fire. As Vaughn watched, Thrax crushed a bit of aether in one hand and turned his little ball of fire into a tiny tornado. It moved toward the edge of Thrax's palm, as if intent on some imaginary path.

"All right, everyone," Vaughn said. "Gather our stuff. We're done here."

Thrax sat up, and the whirlwind sputtered out. "What, really?" he called down.

"Yes. It isn't worth the danger."

There was no argument, not even from Saylyn.

Danton dogged his steps. "Why do I feel like this decision isn't as simple as it sounds?"

Vaughn stopped and put his hand on Danton's shoulder. "Danton, my friend, you know me too well."

Danton groaned. "You're not actually giving up, are you?"

Vaughn grinned. The very thought of Plan B had lifted his spirits. "I think it might be time to look up an old friend of ours who happens to know a lot more than she ought about languages."

"Oh, no."

"Oh, yes," Vaughn said. "And you're coming with me."

"Why in the abyss would I—?"

"Because I need company," Vaughn said. "Anyway, she always seemed a little fond of you. Your presence might soften her up."

Danton crossed his arms over his chest. "Didn't Yaotel gave you explicit instructions to go to Ferehar after you were done here?"

Vaughn pointed the book at Danton. "Exactly. When I'm done here. And I'm not done, am I?"

"I don't think that's what he—"

Vaughn spread his arms to either side of himself. "Look, I *will* go to Ferehar. This is just a slight detour."

Danton gave him a skeptical look.

Vaughn tapped the book onto Danton's chest a few times. "Are you coming with me or not?"

Danton sighed. He glanced around the clearing, where the

others had already gathered most of their things together, as if that would give him some solution. "Why don't you contact Yaotel first and ask—"

"Ask." Vaughn snorted. "Danton, Danton, Danton."

"You're going to be in so much trouble."

"Fortunately..." Vaughn flexed the fingers of one hand and flashed Danton a smile. "I excel at managing trouble."

Chapter Two

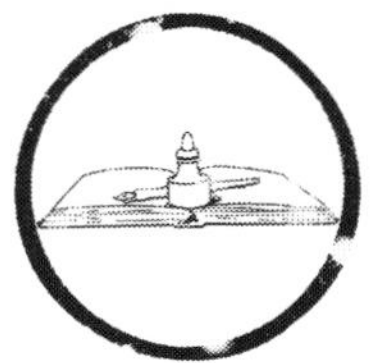

The Donian

Driskell brushed an imaginary speck off his tunic, pushed his spectacles up the bridge of his nose, and snugged the portfolio he held in one arm close to his chest. The double doors in front of him were made of rysta—an import from Cadmyr. The dark, luscious wood was ornately carved and beautifully crafted; the doors were thick and heavy.

The effect was imposing, and even after more than a year of service to the Ri of Donia and his daughter, his stomach couldn't help but squirm a bit before he knocked on these doors.

He knocked anyway.

"Come," a deep voice called from within.

He opened the door enough for him to pop a head through. "Lady Nahua?" he asked, his eyes searching for the Ri's daughter in the midst of the conference room.

Nahua stood at the long table that took up most of the room. She looked up at him and nodded. "Driskell."

The Ri stood next to his daughter. Driskell never noticed how tall Nahua was until she stood next to her father. Ri Tanuac was considered tall, and Nahua almost matched him in height. She always carried herself with a confident grace that belied her relatively few thirty-three years and made Driskell feel all the younger by comparison—at his mere nineteen years of age.

A large map of Setana was laid out in front of the two of them. No one else was in the room, which made his entrance feel like an intrusion into a private conversation. "I'm so sorry to disturb you, but, I have an, ah, unusual message."

Nahua gestured to him. "Come in."

He pushed the door open a bit farther, slid through the crack, and then closed it gently behind him. Even so, the heavy door shut with a resounding thud.

Nahua held out her hand as he approached. "For me?" she asked.

"Oh! No. I was just holding this when..." He faltered. It was an odd message. Perhaps he should have waited. But the man in the vestibule had been so insistent.

Nahua raised her eyebrow. "Can this wait?"

Nahua was kind; she was also efficient.

There was no help for it; he would look ten times the fool if he left now. He cleared his throat. "There's a man by the name of Yaotel in the entrance hall. He's... Well, he's asking to see you."

Nahua's eyebrow rose even higher. "Me?"

"Well, no. Ri Tanuac. But Dal Anwell told him he couldn't see the Ri without an appointment. He was politely insistent that it couldn't wait, so they fetched me. I offered to see if you were available." He shrugged his shoulders apologetically. He hoped that had been the right course of action. "He says he's come with a proposal that, in his words, 'may be of great aid to Donia in the coming months.'"

Nahua exchanged a glance with Tanuac.

"What did you say his name was again?" Tanuac asked.

"Yaotel. He comes representing the..." Driskell pursed his lips. "Ichtaca, I think he said."

Nahua now addressed Tanuac. "Does that mean anything to you?"

Tanuac shook his head. "No." He pressed his lips together. "Well, Nahua. We're done here, anyway. Why don't you go greet our visitor?" The corners of his eyes were already creased by, Driskell suspected, years of quiet amusement suppressed to preserve the dignity befitting a Ri. They crinkled further now—without tugging at his lips. "I trust your judgment as to whether he should be welcomed or ejected."

Nahua inclined her head to the Ri and then strode toward Driskell.

"Come with me," she said. "I hope you have something to write with."

Driskell whipped a notebook and pencil out of the pouch that hung from his belt. "Always, my lady."

She gave him a fond smile. "Well, let's go see what this is all about, shall we?"

Driskell hurried to keep up with Nahua, who strode down the hallway at a purposeful clip. Dal Anwell, Ri Tanuac's steward, was waiting in the vestibule with the man named Yaotel. Yaotel's dark brown skin marked him immediately as Donian or Venetian—in heritage, at least; who knew what region he called home now? A hint of cool undertones pointed to some Fuilynian ancestry, albeit generations back. His coarse, dark brown hair was clipped short, and a neatly trimmed beard and moustache hugged his jawline, chin, and upper lip. With the grey sprinkled through his beard, Driskell guessed him to be about the same age as Ri Tanuac—in his late fifties—but the lines etched into this man's face weren't at the corners of his eyes. Rather, they were at his brow.

In any case, right now he appeared completely at ease, admiring some of the artwork adorning the walls while he waited. Anwell, on the other hand, was agitated. His thin, aging hands were folded politely in front of him, but his eyes kept darting to the clock on a side table.

Anwell was a model steward, but he also didn't like his time being wasted. He lit up when he saw Nahua. "Ah, my lady," he said, meeting Nahua in the center of the room. "I'm so sorry to disturb you. Driskell thought that perhaps if he met with *someone* of importance, he might be mollified..."

"Has he been a nuisance, Dal?" Nahua asked.

"No, my lady. Quite the opposite, in fact."

"Very well. You may go attend to your duties. I'll take care of this."

Anwell bowed and scurried off.

Yaotel had turned toward them, his face placid.

"Yaotel, I presume?" Nahua said.

He inclined his head. "Nahua, I presume?"

Nahua's mouth quirked up. "I'm told you have some matter of great importance to share with us. Ri Tanuac has given me leave to hear what you have to say."

"I'm told you're the Ri's daughter?"

"I am."

"It's been many years since I've been home, my lady, but I hadn't heard Donia had begun to imitate its neighbors in moving to a more hereditary system," Yaotel said. "What role do you play here?"

Driskell's notebook was already out and pencil at the ready, so he made a note of Yaotel's response, which was surely tongue-in-cheek. All Ri were ostensibly elected, and the seven regions varied wildly on how closely they followed the letter of that law. Donia had always prided itself in being the most rigorous in ensuring fair elections when the time came; its neighbor to the northwest, Ferehar, was at the opposite end of the spectrum.

Nahua's face betrayed no hint of offense, however; knowing Nahua, she was probably amused. "I am the Ri's closest advisor, confidant, and legally appointed representative in his absence," she said. "If that does not suffice, you will have to make an appointment."

Yaotel nodded. "It will suffice. Is there somewhere we may discuss this privately?" He raised an eyebrow meaningfully toward an open door to the side of the hall, where the heads of a few curious clerks had popped out of the doorway.

Driskell studied Yaotel. He was not a short man, but Nahua still towered over him by at least an inch.

Most men found this intimidating; Yaotel seemed completely at ease. Worthy of another note in his notebook.

Nahua collected a guard, and the four of them moved down the hall. The guard patted Yaotel down and then nodded him into a small conference room Anwell used to meet with his staff. The guard took up a position outside the door, which Nahua closed after them.

She gestured for Yaotel to sit at the table within. Nahua sat on the opposite side, and Driskell in the middle.

Yaotel looked at Driskell as if seeing him for the first time, but Nahua intercepted his question. "Ri Tanuac's attaché," she said—though in reality Driskell functioned more often as *her* attaché. "Anything you have to say can and will be said in front of him, and he will take notes."

Driskell already had his notebook open on the table and pencil poised.

Yaotel nodded in acquiescence.

Nahua folded her hands on the table expectantly. "Go on, and cut straight to the point, if you please."

"As you wish. The Conclave has seized control of Weylyn City. With the king acquiescing to their demands, they essentially control the United Setanan Army. Of course, they also have at their disposal thousands of what you call Banebringers."

Yaotel was referring to the scandal of the "research facility" the Conclave had been keeping right under the foundations of Weylyn City, the largest city in the Empire. They had threatened to slaughter the thousands of Banebringers in their care if power wasn't ceded to them.

The king had caved, and the bureaucracy—at least in Weylyn City—had collapsed into chaos.

"None of this is new information, Dal," Nahua said.

Yaotel held his hand up. "Donia has never been fond of Setana. As a Donian myself, I know full well we've been biding our time for centuries, waiting for the right opportunity to regain our independence." He spread his hand, palm up, on the table. "Donia is at a crossroads. The opportunity is ripe. My sources tell me you've been laying plans for how best to secede, but so far, all paths have led to too much hypothetical bloodshed, with little assurance of victory."

Driskell followed the lead of Nahua, keeping his eyes up and his face perfectly still. Yaotel was far too well-informed. But at present, it was merely words. Anyone who knew anything about the history of Donia's assimilation into the Setanan Empire could have fabricated such a tale, given the times.

“You have imaginative sources, Dal,” Nahua said.

The corner of Yaotel’s mouth quirked up. “But I haven’t come here to give you information you already know. I’ve come here to offer you a proposal. Aid, if you will.”

“I suppose this so-called aid would come at a cost.”

“Of course,” Yaotel said. “Protection, for myself and my people.”

“These...” She craned her neck toward Driskell’s notebook. He had already written the name Yaotel had given the steward earlier. He tapped his pencil against it, and she repeated the word there. “Ichtaca?”

“Just so.”

“I’ve never heard of them.”

“I would hope not.”

“Very well, Dal Yaotel,” Nahua said. “Let’s say for the sake of argument, we would be interested in your ‘aid.’ What do you have to offer?”

“Extraordinarily effective medicine, medical techniques, and healers skilled enough to use them. Technology that will revolutionize every aspect of your lives.”

Nahua raised one skeptical eyebrow. “Such as?”

“Instant long-distance communication. Light that needs no fuel. Weapons that will cleave through bloodbane with ease. Incredible stealth. And more, waiting to be discovered, with the right resources.”

Driskell took notes as Yaotel rattled off the list, and it looked even more insane on paper than it had sounded out loud. Where in the abyss would he get such innovations that no one else had discovered?

“An impressive list. So impressive as to be almost unbelievable,” Nahua said when Yaotel was done. “What proof do you offer? Did you bring some of this technology with you?”

"I did."

"Where?"

"My associates, who have taken rooms in an inn nearby, have it in their care."

Nahua sat back in her chair and studied the man, her eyes narrowed.

Driskell reviewed the list again. It *was* impressive. How could this even be possible? What was this man's game?

He could tell Nahua was having some of the same thoughts.

She leaned forward. "And what proof do you have of your sincerity? How do I know you're not a Conclave spy?"

At that, Yaotel's face turned grave. He looked down at his palm, still splayed on the table. His jaw worked. Then, at last, he spoke. "I mean you no harm," he said in a low voice. "Please don't overreact to what I do next." He reached into a pocket on the front of his tunic and pulled out a small penknife.

Nahua rose instantly from her seat, and Driskell put himself in front of her, but she didn't call for the guard. Instead she stood, tense and alert, watching Yaotel.

Yaotel pricked his fingertip with the point of the knife and then slid it back into his pocket. "My proof of sincerity is that I'm going to put my life in your hands," he said. "What you do next is entirely up to you. My offer stands, regardless, and I will discuss it with you—and offer you further proof of what I have to offer—when you're ready."

A curious statement.

But Nahua stared intently at his finger. A bead of red blood had welled up and sat on his skin unmoving.

Then, it changed. Like ice creeping unnaturally fast across a pond, the red turned to silver.

Nahua lifted her eyes to meet Yaotel's, but Driskell's were wide. A Banebringer! Right here? Yathyn help them... Was *that* the group of people this Yaotel wanted them to protect? Banebringers? It was insane, it was—

Nahua, after what felt like a tense eternity, finally stirred. She walked to the door and pushed it open to speak to the guard outside. "Please detain our visitor in one of the interior guest rooms at the consulate. He is not to be harmed, but he is to be guarded round-the-clock and is forbidden from leaving his room."

The silver blood had now hardened, and Yaotel picked the dot off his finger and then deposited it into a pocket on the inside of his tunic. He glanced at Driskell and gave him a tight-lipped, sad smile.

Driskell restrained the impulse to scoot farther away. Instead, he averted his eyes and jotted down another stray thought. *Doesn't strike me as threatening.*

Of course, Yaotel would want them to think that. He dared to peek at the Banebringer. He hadn't moved a muscle.

The guard peered into the room curiously. "Yes, my lady. Might I ask...?"

"He is to be considered untrustworthy until I say otherwise, but..." She met Yaotel's eyes. "Treat him with every courtesy." She held up a finger. "Oh. And he has a penknife in his pocket you missed. I suggest you search him again."

The guard's face flushed. "Uh...yes, my lady, I will. I'm so sorry." He took Yaotel gently by the arm. "This way, please."

Yaotel didn't resist; he went with the guard without another word.

When they were gone, Nahua closed the door. She turned to Driskell. "Not a word to anyone," she said.

"But, my lady—" he protested.

"Driskell, I'm asking you to trust me. Can you do that?" She took his notebook from his hands.

His stomach clenched. Rarely did his personal life clash with his professional, but if the relatives of the woman he hoped to marry ever found out about this, that might be the end of their relationship. Tania's family liked Driskell, but this might well change their mind.

"Of course, my lady," he said quietly.

Nahua read over the notes silently. "He doesn't strike you as threatening?" she said when she had finished, tapping the final line of his scrawl with her finger.

"Just a thought that came into my mind." Nahua often asked his opinion of meetings after the fact. She said it was useful to have another point of view from someone who wasn't part of the conversation.

"Explain."

"Well, he told us he was a Banebringer. That seems like a crazy thing to do if he didn't at least believe himself sincere. Also, he seemed resigned at the end. Like he knew what you were going to do. Yet he came here anyway."

"In this case, I agree with you." She gave the notebook back to him. "Gods help me, I agree."

"Then why did you have him detained?"

She leaned over the table, supporting herself on her hands. "Because I need to think this over. He may be sincere, but I have no reason to trust him yet, and I certainly can't let a Banebringer go wandering around. For our safety—and his own."

"Forgive me, but you don't seem particularly afraid. Aren't you concerned he'll summon a bloodbane, or...?" He trailed off, not sure what else.

"Or?"

"I don't know."

"Precisely." She pushed herself off the table. "Driskell, you're an intelligent, reasonable person. Have you ever once read of an eyewitness—not a secondhand account, mind you—who describes a Banebringer summoning a bloodbane—other than, presumably, at the sky-fire or upon their death?" She didn't wait for his response. "Since it is neither the sky-fire nor does Yaotel seem in danger of keeling over, I have little fear of that scenario."

"But they're demonspawn," he protested. "Servants of the heretic gods."

"Yes. So I've heard. I'm going to confess something to you." She leaned toward him. "I'm not religious enough to care." She brushed her hands off, as if such confessions were a matter of wiping a few crumbs away. "Now. I'm going to ask you to do something that isn't quite part of the job you came here to do."

He straightened up, relieved. This philosophical speculation about Banebringers made him uncomfortable. What if someone overheard them?

A task, a nice concrete task. That, he could handle. "My lady, my job is to do what you tell me."

She chuckled. "That's what I like to hear. I want you to find these associates of his. It shouldn't be difficult if he was telling the truth. There are only two inns that could be considered 'nearby,' and his associates are presumably traveling as a group. Don't confront them if you think you've found them—come let me know. Are you up to the task?"

He stifled the urge to sigh. So much for an easy, concrete task. "I'll do my best."

"I know." She winked at him and opened the door. "An interesting meeting with which to end the day, wouldn't you say?"

He swallowed. That was one way of putting it. "Yes, my lady."

She swept out of the room.

Driskell wasted no time in carrying out Nahua's request. The very next day, he stood outside The Silver Nomad—the second possible “nearby” inn. The other, The Black Filly, had turned up empty, almost literally. There were no festivals or events of note going on in the city, and certainly nothing exciting ever happened in the government tier. The two inns on this tier mostly attracted the business of incoming officials and delegates from other regions, or minor nobles who didn't have second apartments in Marakyn in addition to wherever their actual homes were.

He pushed his spectacles up on the bridge of his nose and ambled inside the inn.

The dining room was empty, as he had expected. It was midmorning—too late for breakfast, too early for lunch, and *far* too early for drinking. So he walked up to the bar and caught the attention of the innkeeper, a portly, merry fellow by the name of Tamal.

“Driskell,” Tamal said. “Been awhile. A bit early for gambling, eh?”

Heat crept up Driskell's ears. Tamal knew full well Driskell didn't gamble. However, occasionally, on a day off, he enjoyed a night of friendly, no-betting tapolli... And this particular inn had a beautiful set.

Driskell nodded to Tamal. “Actually, I was wondering if you had a group staying here. I'm not sure how many—it could be as few as two, it could be many more. Possibly not all from Donia, but I'm not sure.”

“Business, then? How droll.” He glanced at his guest book, but Driskell doubted he needed the reference. “Yes, sure do. There's a group of three. Just got in yesterday. Only guests I have right now who came in together, but I wouldn't forget 'em anyway—a Fuilynian, a Donian, and a Setanan. Sounds like the beginning of a joke, eh?”

Driskell shook his head. “Thanks, Tamal.” That had been easy.

Yaotel's associates, whoever they were, weren't trying to hide their presence here. "That's all I needed, for now."

Tamal tipped an imaginary hat.

But before Driskell could leave, a Fuilynian man and a Setanan woman—shorthand for someone from one of the three original regions of Weylyn, Arlana, or Cadmyr—strolled into the dining room.

They both acknowledged him with a friendly nod, but Driskell froze. Banebringers, likely. Both of them!

And yet, as they left the inn together, laughing and talking, they seemed no different from anyone else.

Driskell hesitated. He didn't have to *confront* them. But he could follow them, surely, see what they did, where they went.

No, he told himself sternly. Nahua had said to find out where they were, and nothing more. He was an attaché, not a spy. What if one of them spotted him and did some Banebringer magic on him? Or worse—someone reported him?

He shuddered and strode out of the inn.

Chapter Three

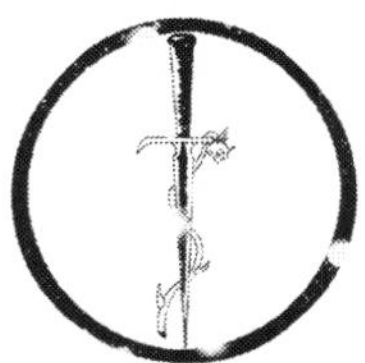

The Journal

The front door to Ivana's rowhouse was unlocked.

She glanced both ways down the dark, empty street and put her key back into her pocket. Had her Fuilynian roommate, Sanca, forgotten to lock it when she'd left for her shift at the inn?

If so, this would be the first time.

Ivana eased the door open, slipped inside, and crept to the short hallway off the front room. Then she peered around the corner.

Light seeped from under the crack of the door at the end.

She might doubt Sanca, but Ivana was certain she had extinguished the lantern in her study.

Her hand went to her thigh.

Of course, there was no dagger there. She had made a deliberate decision to stop carrying one a few months after Sweetblade had died.

Some habits were hard to break.

She slid her boots off, moved over to the dish cabinet, opened the cutlery drawer, and extracted a carving knife.

It couldn't hurt to be careful.

She padded down the hall until she came to the door. She heard no noise from within, but the light wasn't her imagination. She pushed the door open slowly, ever so slowly, and only enough to peek through. It would creak if she didn't. She had deliberately left the creak in the door hinges when she had rented the place, so if someone attempted to enter her study while she was in it, she would immediately know.

She peeked through the crack and scanned for anything amiss other than a lamp she hadn't left burning.

A leather satchel was propped up against the armchair she liked to read in, and a full glass of amber liquid sat on the side table next to it.

The satchel wasn't hers, and she didn't remember leaving a glass on the side table. Even so, there were no visible inhabitants in the room now.

She slipped into the room, put her back to the wall, inched to the side...

"A kitchen knife, Ivana?" a voice said in her ear. "How ordinary."

Ivana whirled around to face the direction of the voice, her knife slashing out.

With a yelp, a man appeared out of the air and jumped out of the way, just in time.

Both relief and irritation spiked through her as she recognized the man—even sporting a full beard. "Damn it, Vaughn, you idiot! I almost gutted you!"

Vaughn shrugged sheepishly. "Nice to see you too."

"How," she asked, her teeth clenched, "did you get in here?"

"No small talk first? I can see you haven't changed."

She strode across the room, tossed the knife on her desk with a clatter, and then whirled to glare at him.

He grinned. "Well, your, uh...*roommate* helpfully stood at the open door rummaging around in her handbag for a full minute before she left. I took that as an invitation."

She exhaled. "Let me try again. How in the abyss did you *find* me?"

"I'll give you one guess."

Damn her. "And how did you find Aleena?"

"Caira's been in contact with her."

Ivana sighed and put two fingers to her forehead. Did no one have any sense that she might not *want* to be found? Caira, at least, she could absolve, since none of her girls had any idea of who she had been. But Aleena? Ivana's old second—and friend—had always had a soft spot for Vaughn. "What do you want, Vaughn?"

His smile grew, and he looked her up and down without shame. "A dangerous question, coming from you."

She snorted. "I can see you haven't changed, either."

He scratched at his chin, drawing her attention to the beard. "Really? Not at all?"

"It doesn't suit you."

"Good. I was hoping that was the case."

She narrowed her eyes at him. What in the abyss did that mean?

The shock of finding him there was wearing off quickly. She pulled a bottle of xabnec, a moderately intoxicating honey-based liquor, from a drawer in her desk and half-filled a small tumbler.

“Drink?” she asked, waving the bottle in his direction.

He walked over to the side table and picked up the glass she’d noticed earlier. “I already helped myself.”

Of course he had. “I thought you didn’t drink.”

He chuckled and settled into the armchair. “I discovered it can be a reliable source of income to bet on out-drinking some arrogant fool.”

She sat heavily at her desk. “Isn’t that cheating?”

“*You’re* going to lecture me about *cheating*?”

Point taken.

“At any rate, the taste has grown on me.” He lifted his glass to her in a mock-toast and threw it back in a few gulps.

For her part, she took a small sip.

He eyed her. “I thought you didn’t drink, either?”

“The taste has grown on me,” she said. Perhaps a little more than she would have liked. “Let me try this one more time. Why are you here, in this town, bothering me again?”

He gave her a wounded look. “*Bothering* you? Can an old acquaintance not stop by for a visit?”

She blinked and pinned him with a level gaze.

He looked at her for a long moment and then sighed. “All right. Down to business it is, then.” He put down the glass, picked up the satchel, and dragged the armchair to the desk. “I need your help.”

She swirled the xabnec in her glass. “I think the person you’re looking for is dead.”

“Not that kind of help.” He reached into his bag and pulled out a rectangular object wrapped in leather. Untying the bindings, he shook the leather off and then pushed a battered book across the desk toward her.

She picked the book up gingerly and turned it over in her hand.

Or half of a battered book. It was missing the backside.

"Careful." He leaned over the desk, took the book back from her, and flipped to a page near the middle. "Take a look." Turning the book to face her, he laid it on the desk, open to his chosen page.

The page had a drawing of a rather exotic-looking serpent. It sported both feathers and scales and what looked like broken flames running from its face down its entire body, which was in the shape of an "S" that had been knocked forward so its head rested on the ground, its mouth wide open. One chunk of the S, at the tail, had been broken off, as well as several of the teeth. Some sort of design ran around its mouth. Was it supposed to be a reproduction of a statue of some sort of bloodbane? She had never seen anything like it.

"All right," she said. "I looked."

"Do you recognize it?" he asked. "The language around its mouth, not the serpent itself." He pointed below the drawing to a few lines of text. "The author reproduced it here, if you can't see it well enough."

Ivana glanced up at him. His voice was taut, the relaxed tone of a moment ago gone, and he now perched on the edge of his chair.

She ran her eyes over the words below the sketch. She turned the book upside down, and then back around again. The script—such as it was—was sharp and angular, at least as it had been reproduced. It literally looked like chicken scratches, and she had never seen anything like it before in her life.

She looked back up at Vaughn. "This is unfamiliar to me. If it's a language I know, it's not in a script I recognize."

He sat slowly back in his chair, looking crestfallen. "Damn."

She flipped absently through the rest of the book. "What is this?"

He sighed. "A vain hope, apparently." Pounding the chair arm, he stood up and paced a few times back and forth in front of her desk. "It's half a book we found in the Weylyn City university library," he said. "Right before the whole city descended into chaos. The book appears to be a personal record of an archaeological expedition in Donia a couple of decades ago."

"Half a book? Recording an expedition that turned up information about the heretic gods? In the *library*?" That was too outlandish to be believed. If the Conclave had known this existed—however little information it contained about the heretic gods—it would have been destroyed, not preserved.

"Well, sort of. It wasn't in the stacks. They were doing renovations on the Weylyn University library. The last time a university library was renovated, we heard of some manuscripts discovered that might have information about Banebringers, but the Conclave got to them first. So, this time, when we heard they were going to renovate the Weylyn University library—this was before I even met you—we planted one of our own people in there. The workmen opened an old wall to look for a leak and our plant found the book shoved in a hollow space that had been covered over. But it looks as though the book was ripped in two, and we only found this half."

Ivana turned to the next page of the book and read the text written there with interest. Once upon a time, this was the sort of thing that would have absolutely fascinated her. Once upon a time, before Sweetblade. "And?"

"He returned to Gan Barton's estate last year, after the Conclave seized control. But it got particularly interesting when Dax came back with an old manuscript containing a myth that describes a similar statue. The myth describes Banebringers using this statue to travel between our world and 'the heavens' at the sky-fire, like some sort of doorway to the gods."

Ivana snorted. "Uh-huh. So what?"

"Well…the myth seems to indicate that the writing around the serpent's mouth tells the would-be traveler how to use it. Unfortunately, the story doesn't relate the instructions, only that they exist."

She finally understood, and she had to laugh. "You think you've found a doorway to the gods? Vaughn…"

"Well, no. We never found the serpent monument. We presume the Conclave destroyed it and any other artifacts once they found out about this dig."

"Let me get this straight. You found a journal that tells about finding some…serpent statue with writing in a mysterious language. Then you found a manuscript with a myth that tells you the serpent-statue is a doorway to the gods, and that the writing around its mouth would tell you how to use it. You also don't know the location of this presumed serpent-doorway. But you feel if you could only translate the writing, you could still use this door and pay the heretic gods a visit?"

Vaughn fiddled with the leather wrapping that had been around the book. "When you put it that way, it sounds rather insane."

"It sounds beyond insane." She flipped the book closed, face-down, so the back page was exposed. "Regardless, if I knew the language, I would translate it for you. Or if I had this tablet the author describes, I could try to translate it via Xambrian. But I don't, on both counts."

There was silence in the room for a moment, and Vaughn slumped back in his chair. "Danton's going to kill me," he muttered.

"Danton?" Ivana remembered him. A friendly, likeable young man Vaughn had rescued from the Conclave.

"Yes. He's with me. We have a room over at the inn." He closed his eyes.

There was silence for a moment. Vaughn showed no sign of moving.

"Even if any of this were true and possible, what precisely were you hoping to discuss with these gods?" Ivana asked.

He opened his eyes. "Not just any god. Ziloxchanachi, the head god—Zily." Wry amusement traced his lips, but it quickly faded. "See, Danathalt is somehow involved with the Conclave. Helping them, goading them, behind it all—I don't know—but I do know his involvement isn't good for any of us."

Danathalt. The new heretic god they had discovered over a year and a half ago. The god—or some sort of entity, anyway—who had appeared to possess his own Banebringer. A god who had been seemingly working with the Conclave, though she never knew to what end.

"Yaotel is trying to figure out a completely mundane, mortal solution to this mess"—he waved his arm wildly in the air, as if the "mess" he referred to were the entire contents of her study—"yet at the source is a *god,* Ivana. We can come up with plan after plan after plan, but in the end, how are we supposed to fight against a god?" He raised a hand, no doubt to ward off any hypothetical response on her part. "I'll tell you how: with another god. Another god more powerful than—or at least as powerful as—Danathalt."

There was a certain amount of logic to that. But... "Instigating these crazy gods to start another war amongst themselves seems like a terrible idea. After spending so long in your ancient texts, I'm now a firm believer that mortals and deities don't mix. I think we've done enough."

Vaughn winced and slumped down. "Don't remind me."

She tilted her head and studied his face. He had shadows and bags under his eyes. He looked...tired. "Please don't tell me you feel personally responsible for destroying the Setanan Empire?"

"You know, it's hard not to."

She rolled her eyes. "Vaughn. Really."

"The whole thing was *my* stupid idea. Expose the Conclave! Turn the people to our side! *That* worked out real well."

"The Conclave *was* exposed," she pointed out.

"Yes. And so some people think they've been working with Banebringers and now hate them *and* us, and others support their efforts, saying they had to do what was necessary for the safety of us all. Whatever divides there were before amongst common people have been sharply accentuated, and neither view helps the Ichtaca. Meanwhile, the Conclave has seized the power they've always wanted, and we essentially no longer have a centralized government."

"Is that so bad? I don't think any of the outer regions ever wanted to be part of Setana anyway." Certainly, Ferehar hadn't.

"Maybe it wouldn't be so bad if the Conclave had seized Weylyn and left well enough alone. But, no, that's not good enough. Ivana, you *know* they won't just quietly cede back the independence of the outer regions."

He rose from his chair, the leather wrapping he had been playing with falling to the floor, and walked to the window. He drew back the curtains a bit and looked into the dark. "Have you heard about the blood tests? Weylyn City, Arlan, Carradon—all the major cities in the three central regions are requiring them entering or leaving. And there's talk that they're going to start enforcing the tests in the outer regions as well. They want the Empire under their control, not just Weylyn, or even only the three central regions. And for the Empire to be under their control, they *cannot have Banebringers around.*"

She was surprised at his vehemence, but she supposed she shouldn't have been. It was easy to forget that he *was* a

Banebringer. The Conclave had given up the pretense of Sedating all Banebringers; as many were killed outright—consequences be damned—as captured or Sedated anymore. And Vaughn, as a Banebringer, would have surely felt that increased pressure.

"This isn't common knowledge yet," Vaughn said quietly into the window, "but there's been talk of Donia and Venetia attempting to secede. Fuilyn might follow if they do." He let the curtains fall and turned to face Ivana. "If they do, there will be war. It's already started. The Conclave knows the danger; they're bolstering the United Setanan with troops from the central regions, just in case. If any of us, not just Banebringers, survive this mess, I can't imagine our new Conclave overlords will be benevolent rulers."

Ivana wasn't surprised to hear that the outer regions were considering withdrawing—a rather mild word for what would ensue, as Vaughn had pointed out. But she also hadn't *heard* that information before.

Vaughn was in the thick of it. She had been hiding in Fuilyn, trying desperately to start a new life for herself and ignore whatever else was happening. She had managed the latter well enough; the success of the former was still up in the air.

And Vaughn was right: If even one or two of the outer regions tried to withdraw, it would mean civil war. If Fuilyn was one of those...

The days of her relatively peaceful life here were numbered.

She looked back down at the book and opened her mouth to tell him to leave it with her till he departed—perhaps something would come to her—but the words died on her tongue.

At the bottom of the page, an anomaly had distracted her.

She peered closer. A series of tiny letters, squished into the thin margin as though they had been an afterthought, had been scrawled along the edge of the paper. *AP. AP. AP.* The two letters were written repeatedly, each iteration slightly different in form. An abbreviation? A code? Probably nothing important.

Except something niggled at her, as though her subconscious mind disagreed with her assessment. There was something *familiar* about some of the pairs of letters. The little swirl at the start of the A, the flourish at the tail of the P.

No doubt alerted by her abrupt silence and sudden attentiveness to the book, Vaughn strode over to the desk and stood next to her, scrutinizing the page as well. "What?" he asked. "What is it?"

She pointed at the line of letters. "What's this?"

His shoulders slumped when he saw what she was pointing at. "Oh. We have no idea. It's the only place something like that is found in the book." He shrugged. "To me, it looks like the author was doodling."

Doodling? She read the rest of the page and then reread the final line. *I'm meeting G in a few minutes.* "Who's 'G'?"

Vaughn shook his head. "Someone else at the dig, apparently. The author mentions them a lot. Colleague? Friend?" He smirked. "Lover?"

AP. G. Doodling. Lover...

A realization crept over her. It couldn't be.

AP. Avira Payiz.

G. Galvyn.

The names of her mother and father.

Chapter Four

Insights

No. That was crazy. It simply couldn't be! What were the odds?

Ivana's heart was suddenly pounding so hard, she could feel it pulsing in her fingertips. "When was this written?" she asked, though the entries were dated. She just hadn't paid attention to the dates as she had flipped through. She didn't want to look now.

"A little under thirty-three years ago." He gave her a quizzical look. "Does this change things somehow?"

She flipped back to the beginning of that last entry. Sure enough, it was dated about a year and five months before she had been born. It was not only possible, but...

She traced her fingers over the letters. She recognized it now.

At least some of them looked like her mother's initials as she remembered them.

Her mother had been playing with her and her father's initials like some love-addled schoolgirl. It would have made her smile, if it were possible for her to resurrect fond memories of her past.

It wasn't.

She splayed her hand over the top of the page, as if to keep the knowledge where it belonged, on this page, thirty-three years in the past—and out of her head.

But the image of her mother writing these very words, some thirty-three years ago, sitting in the middle of an archaeological expedition, pining over her father, stuck fast in her brain.

Where was the rest of this journal? What had happened? What had they been doing?

And why had fate made it so she could never find the answers to those questions?

An uncomfortable ache grew in her chest. A familiar one, but one she hadn't felt in an eon.

The unmistakable hollowness of loss, the knowledge of an empty place that could never be filled.

"Ivana?"

Her palm hurt, and she realized she had clenched her fist, and her fingernails were digging into her hand. She drew in a sharp breath and schooled her expression. She had almost forgotten Vaughn was there; what had he seen played out on her face during those few moments?

"No," she said. "It's nothing." She was dimly aware that too long had passed since he had asked his original question, and her words now made little sense. Control. She had to regain control. She reached for it, but it seemed suddenly elusive, swallowed up in that hole. The ache changed to reflect a different sort of loss.

Where was Sweetblade when she needed her?

Silence. And then, a moment later, he had grabbed her desk chair by both arms and turned it to face him. He crouched in front of her. "*That* wasn't 'nothing.'"

He had seen too much, apparently.

And there, in his deep brown eyes, was that same probing, questioning look that had sought to see beyond her many layers a year and a half ago, sought to know the real person he had insisted existed underneath.

In the short time they had worked together, he had single-handedly breached her walls and shredded her cloak of indifference. The weaknesses in her defenses had never seemed as real to her in the past year and a half as they did now. Panic constricted her throat at the thought that when he looked at her, he might see...her.

She broke the gaze and stood up, unnerved. "It's nothing important," she revised, walking around the chair so it was between them—as if it would somehow protect her from the unexpected assault he had brought with him.

"But it's something," he pressed, straightening up.

"It doesn't matter to your purposes."

He narrowed his eyes. "Perhaps I can decide that?"

She gripped the back of the chair with her hands. *Where are you?* she screamed into the void. "*It doesn't matter.*"

He crossed his arms. "I'm not leaving until you tell me."

She exhaled, and, thankfully, the familiar feeling of annoyance at him washed over her, smothering everything else. "Damn it, Vaughn, why do you have to be so difficult?"

He puffed his chest out. "It's my specialty."

That, at least, was true.

It wouldn't hurt anything to tell him. And then he would take his probing eyes away and leave her in her illusion of peace. That was worth almost anything.

Her defenses had been damaged, but the latter half of her life hadn't been for naught. She gestured toward the book. "My mother wrote this," she said evenly, banishing the encroaching feelings with practiced efficiency—now that she had overcome the initial shock.

His eyes widened. "What? How do you know?"

"Those letters are her initials."

He studied the letters. "Initials? But why should she have written them over and over?"

She snorted. "You've clearly never been a love-addled schoolgirl."

He stared at her blankly for a moment, and then comprehension dawned on his face. "'G' was your father."

"I'm assuming. So, as you can now see, this is irrelevant to—"

"Irrelevant?" He paced to the window and back. "This is hardly irrelevant! Your mother knew how to translate this!"

"Unless you have some Banebringer magic that can speak to the dead, I don't see how that's going to help you."

"Surely, she must have mentioned—"

She cut him off. "She didn't."

"Don't you have anything of hers? You're sure she didn't...bequeath you the second half of this journal or something?"

Ivana couldn't help it. She laughed, and the sound was tinged with bitterness. "Bequeath? What do you think I was, the daughter of a noble, left an inheritance? I have nothing left from that time of my life." Her hand went automatically to her rose necklace, which suddenly felt heavy against her throat, belying her statement. It had belonged to her sister, and the reminder of that now brought back a pang, along with another memory of another item they hadn't sold. "Except..."

He jumped on the word like a bloodwolf on prey. "Except? Except what?"

"My father had a chest. I gave it to an...acquaintance...for safekeeping and never retrieved it." She had intended to. Had certainly wanted to.

Things hadn't worked out in a way that had let her do so when she had left, and she had never gone back.

"What was in it?"

She shook her head. "He kept his research notes and important papers locked in it. What those consisted of, I don't know." Her eyes drifted to the book on her desk. The writing flowing across the pages. And once again that evening, she found herself under assault from feelings she did not want, this time of a different sort. An irrepressible longing to know more, to retrieve that chest—if only to see evidence of her father's hand again as her mother's now lay in front of her.

Vaughn started pacing again, with renewed energy. "If we could get our hands on that chest...it's a slim hope, but who knows? Maybe your father also recorded something of the expedition and kept the notes."

We? *We?* His words drew her back to reality. There was no going back, literally or metaphorically. "There is no *we* in this scenario," she said flatly.

He ran both hands through his hair and left them on top of his head while he stared off into the distance. He obviously hadn't heard her.

"I can send a letter to the woman I gave it to," Ivana offered. "*If* she's even still there, and *if* she still has it, you're welcome to it."

He dropped his hands and waved one in the air. "No, no. That's unnecessary. I'm going to Ferehar after this anyway—for Yaotel. I can do what he wants while also hunting down this lead. It's *perfect.*" He bobbed his head to the side. "Almost perfect. If there's anything to learn, we'll need to be back at the shrine by the next sky-fire, which puts us under a time constraint I'm sure Yaotel didn't have in mind."

There was the *we* again. Did he think she was going to go *with* him? That was absurd. She couldn't go back to Ferehar. She had avoided it successfully for fourteen years, and she wasn't inclined to change that now. *Especially* now. Right? "You seem to be under some delusions about the extent of my desire to be involved in this."

He counted on his fingers. "Two and a half months. There should be plenty of time, if we don't delay."

There was nothing for her there. Even if she did find her father's old chest. What good would that do her? She had buried those memories for a reason.

Her hand went to the rose pendant at her throat. And yet, all these years, she had retained this one thing, this one anchor to her past, despite everything. What did that mean? Had she come full circle? Did she need some sort of closure to find peace and move on with a new life?

She clenched her hand around the rose, and the metal leaves bit into her palm. No. It was a terrible, dangerous idea. Her defenses were too weak; she knew that path too well. It wasn't worth the risk. "Vaughn!" she said, raising her voice. "I am *not* going to Ferehar with you!"

Apparently, her words had finally pierced the whirlwind of his renewed excitement, because he turned to face her, surprise on his face. "But...I'm certain this acquaintance of yours isn't just going to hand over a treasured possession given into her care to a random man she doesn't know."

My life here is fine. "I'll send a sealed letter with you."

"She knows your seal? Your handwriting? Your signature? I can't take that chance."

And that's what you always wanted, was it? Fine? Ivana slammed her hands down on the desk. She would not do this to herself again. *"I am not going to Ferehar with you!"*

Everything on Ivana's desk rattled. Her empty liquor glass. The knife. A pen. Even the book jumped.

Vaughn stared at her. Fury flared in her eyes and then dissipated as quickly as it had come.

Ivana pushed herself off the desk and took a deep breath. "I am not going to Ferehar with you," she repeated more evenly.

"But—"

She cut him off with a chop of her hand. "This is ridiculous. More likely than not, there is nothing in that old chest that will mean anything to you."

"I'll take the chance. If you're right, I'll admit defeat." Do it Yaotel's way.

His stomach soured at the very thought.

"I'm trying to rebuild a life here," Ivana said. "You can't just waltz in and expect me to drop everything to go with you on some fool's errand!"

Was that *desperation* in her voice? "Look, I get it. I don't particularly want to go back to Ferehar, either."

Silence. She placed one hand on top of the book. "I think it's time for you to go," she said, all traces of fury or desperation gone. Her voice was steel, and her eyes were ice.

He knew that voice. He knew those eyes. But they belonged to someone who was supposed to be dead. He met the challenge and dared to push. "Or what...*Ivana*?"

Air hissed through her teeth. Her eyes flicked to the knife still on her desk, to the book, and then to the door. She left the knife where it was, but she picked up the book, strode to the door, and flung it open. She looked expectantly at him.

The hope she had stoked in him fizzled and died. In its place was resignation. This was it. This had been his last hope of escaping Yaotel's plans for him. It had been a stretch, to be sure, but somehow...he had been convinced if anyone could do this, she could.

A month in travel lost—for nothing. Danton wasn't the only one who was going to kill him.

He walked over to the door but hesitated on the threshold. "I'm sorry," he said, "for 'bothering' you up here in your little sanctuary, though I doubt that will last. We'll be off in the morning."

He held out his hand for the book.

She hesitated, then placed it in his hand, but she didn't let go of it when he attempted to take it from her.

He raised an eyebrow.

There was a long pause. "Leave it," she said.

"Pardon?"

"I'll...take a closer look tonight. Perhaps something will come to me."

He let go of it, and she tucked it in close to herself.

"Stop by in the morning," she said. "You can get it on your way out."

He met her eyes. The ice was gone, but her face was tense.

There was a moment of silence while she held his gaze, and he lifted his hand to touch her cheek, much as he had when they had parted last. Her deep bronze skin was warm and soft—like her lips, as he still vividly recalled—her brown eyes dark and inscrutable, as always. "Circumstances notwithstanding, it's...been good to see you again," he said softly.

She reached up to pull his hand away from her face, but unexpectedly, she didn't let go of it.

Neither did he. Instead, he turned her hand over in his and

ran his thumb along her palm, tracing the lines, and then the calluses that were evidence of so long spent wielding a dagger.

She didn't move. He could almost smell that hint of lavender that had clung to her the last time he had held her close, and the longing to draw her into his arms and breathe her in stirred in him once more.

She drew both her hand and her eyes away. "And make sure to bring Danton with you," she said. "I wouldn't mind seeing him again."

He shook himself free of the spell her proximity had laid on him. Right. Danton. Yes. Perhaps Danton could convince her. "I knew he would come in handy," he said.

She shook her head. "Good night, Vaughn."

He grinned at her and inclined his head before he pulled the study door closed behind him.

Ivana leaned back against the closed door, clenching and unclenching her hand to rid it of the tingle that had started when Vaughn had held it. Damn traitorous body. What was it about that idiot man that set her so on edge, in every possible way?

She took a deep breath and stared down at the book in her other hand. Why had she said she would keep it? She wouldn't find anything. Neither of her parents had mentioned this expedition to her, and she had never seen this language before. She was certain of both facts.

She could gain nothing by looking at that book but further erosion of what she had worked so hard to build.

And yet now she had it, and she found she couldn't resist.

She walked over to the armchair, pulled it back into place, and settled down to read.

She opened the journal to the first page.

"Today we arrived on site; there isn't much to see yet, but I'm terribly excited. I'm so glad G convinced the professor to invite me to be the scribe. Now I get to experience one of these digs firsthand. The first step is clearing the overgrowth out of the area. We can barely see the stone of the shrine peeking through the brush; imagine what it will look like when we have it all uncovered. Donian nomads. Ha! The danger of doing this right under the nose of the Conclave is almost thrilling, but for today, it will likely be thankless, tiring work..."

Ivana read on. And on. She jumped when the clock in her study chimed midnight. Had an hour already passed? Sanca would be home soon. She had become sucked into the account of this illegal archaeological dig her parents had been part of. The journal was part official record, and part personal diary. Her mother had made several comments about recopying the official parts when she returned home, leaving out all her personal observations. She never used any actual names, but she often made references to "G." It was clear he was more than a colleague at this point in her life.

That her parents had *had* some life before her had never occurred to her. It was obviously true—but as a child and adolescent, she had never wondered.

She would have probed further eventually. But she had never been given the chance to grow into an adult whose parents had become her mentors, her confidants, her friends.

She curled her hand into a fist again. The sense of loss was back. Not only of the people she had loved, but of the life she might have had if things had been different.

If only she hadn't—

No. She poured herself another glass of xabnec. She would not stray there.

She turned her attention back to the book that held so much of Vaughn's hopes and focused on doing what she had told him she would do.

But, as she suspected, it was no use. As fascinating as it was, both personally and professionally, there was nothing in it that clued her in to what language the writing around the serpent was in. Vaughn would certainly be disappointed.

If only they had one more page. If Ivana had a transcription of this Xambrian tablet the expedition had found, she might have been able to decipher the mysterious language. Perhaps they did decipher it; Ivana would never know since the rest of it was missing.

What had happened? Why had half the journal ended up behind a false wall in the Weylyn City library, of all places? Vaughn had said the serpent had been destroyed. The Conclave had done it, surely, which meant they had learned about the site.

Had the expedition been halted prematurely? Had the Conclave found out who was involved?

Her mother and father had met at the university in Weylyn. She knew that much, and little else. Only that her father had given up his scholarly pursuits to become a private tutor—shortly after her mother had become pregnant with her.

She had thought it was because tutoring paid better, and he had a family. What if that hadn't been it at all?

She slammed the book shut, unsettled, and paced over to the window, unsettled that she was unsettled.

It doesn't matter. Who cared if Vaughn and his friends had happened upon a journal written by her mother? On an illegal archaeological dig, thirty-three years ago?

Who cared that her father had been with her?

Who cared that right in front of her, written in her mother's own hand, were hints as to what her parents had been doing eight months before she had been conceived?

Her father hadn't even been done with the apprenticeship

required during the year after graduation; her mother had made that clear in the journal. Had he not finished? When had they married? In those eight months? And immediately decided to move? Had they already decided to move when she'd been conceived? Why Ferehar? It wasn't as though they had moved closer to family there. Why not? If he was going to give up the university, why not make it easier on the family and go to at least one of their hometowns?

A thousand questions flooded into her brain, a thousand questions her parents had never answered, never talked about. Was that a coincidence? Had they hidden it for a reason?

She couldn't ask them now.

She paced back to her desk, sat down again, and clenched her fists. She was thinking about it again.

She took a deep breath. *It doesn't matter. It isn't supposed to matter!* It was never supposed to matter again.

But that wasn't true. She had always known that the memories hadn't been excised permanently from her mind. If there had been a way to do *that,* she would have found it.

They had just been buried, locked and caged, the key thrown away.

This. Doesn't. Matter!

And yet she found, roiling within her, that it did. Unearthed, they carried with them as much baggage and pain as they ever had.

She picked up her glass, still full of her second helping of xabnec, and downed it. She had to stop herself from hurling the glass across the room in frustration. Instead, she slammed it back down to the desk, her hand shaking.

She dropped into her chair and dropped her head down on her arms, her face to the desk, her fingers digging into her arms, reaching desperately for the numbness she had once had.

It wasn't there. Her armor had cracked beyond repair eighteen months ago, and she had never tried to ensconce herself in a new set.

She had also never had to come face to face with anything resembling her past in that time. Until now.

And she was something she hadn't been in years: utterly defenseless.

Not even when Vaughn had waltzed into her life and chipped away at her walls until the emotions buried deep inside had been given gleeful leave to run free again; not even when Danton had killed Sweetblade, giving her the unexpected freedom to do something else with her life. Her defense, then, had been to run. To forget. To pretend she could just pick up and move on, somewhere else, *someone* else. She had done it before, after all.

Apparently, she had failed.

And no matter what Vaughn wanted or how that tiny part of herself urged her toward it, she was *not* going back to Ferehar.

Danton was lying in his bed on his back, his hands behind his head and his eyes closed when Vaughn returned to their room at the inn.

His eyes opened the moment Vaughn shut the door.

"Sorry. Did I wake you?" Vaughn asked.

Danton sat up and swung his legs over the edge of the bed. "No. I was waiting for you." He leaned forward. "So? How did it go?"

Vaughn pulled his boots off and tossed them in the corner. "Well, I got away without bodily harm, so I think that's a positive sign."

Danton rolled his eyes. "I *told* you she wasn't going to hurt you."

Vaughn sat down heavily on his own bed, facing Danton, and wiggled his hand back and forth. "Eeehhh…it's always a toss-up." There *had* been that moment there when her eyes had flicked to the knife on her desk. And when he had, like an idiot, startled her and she had almost gutted him.

"Hasn't changed, then."

Vaughn had to think hard about that. He had made the quip to her that she hadn't, but there was *something* different about her. She had seemed a little more…uneven in her temperament. Then again, he had just popped in and thrown a piece of her troubled past down on her lap with no warning.

"Anyway," said Danton, "that's not what I meant. Did she know anything?"

Vaughn scratched at his beard. "Sort of." He related his conversation with Ivana. Danton's eyes became wider and wider as he talked until Vaughn finished with his failed bid to convince her to go with him to Ferehar to find her father's chest.

Danton whistled. "Wow. What are the chances?"

"Indeed. But she refused to go with me."

"Can you blame her? I mean, it's not as though you've been thrilled about returning to your old stomping grounds."

Vaughn shrugged and lay back on his bed, mimicking Danton's posture of earlier. He had reasons beyond his past for not wanting to go to Ferehar, but Danton didn't know those. "It's not like I'm going to be knocking on Airell's door."

Actually, the idea bothered him a great deal more than he wanted to admit. To be so close to home and yet know he wasn't welcome.

The word was that, once it became clear Gildas wasn't coming back, Vaughn's oldest brother Airell had seamlessly taken over as Ri without an election. That didn't surprise Vaughn in the slightest. It had been a while since the collective leaders of Ferehar had tried to hold anything more than sham elections. Some of them hadn't even bothered with that; there was no election when his own father had taken over. It had taken political manipulation, important allies, fear, and almost certainly a spot or two of violence to push his way into the position after the old Ri had died. So, there was precedent.

Vaughn had always wondered, though, what his second-oldest brother and mother had thought of his disappearance. Now that they surely knew he was both alive and a Banebringer, did they care? Or did they wish he had stayed dead?

He couldn't risk finding out, even once he arrived in Ferehar. It would be too dangerous with Airell in charge.

And he didn't want to allow himself the hope that they might feel different, lest that hope be shattered.

Danton allowed him his silence for a moment, and then continued. "So...we're headed out tomorrow, then?"

"She has the journal. Said she was going to take a closer look at it and we can stop by in the morning. I'm not ready to give up." He turned his head to look at Danton. "She also said she wouldn't mind seeing you again." He raised an eyebrow. "See?"

Danton grinned and ran a hand through his shaggy mop. "Maybe she does like me."

Vaughn snorted. "She's way out of your league. You never had a chance."

"Oh, and *you* did?"

It had been a near thing. Vaughn closed his eyes, remembering once again the taste of her lips on his, the press of her body against his own. Danton didn't know about that, though.

Ugh. That line of thought wouldn't get him anything other than a perpetual ache in his balls. It had been a really, *really* long time since he'd had some fun in bed, and seeing Ivana again...

He sighed and rolled over. "I'm going to sleep."

Chapter Five

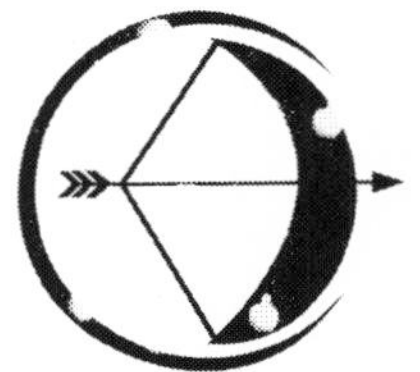

Old Friends

A rapping on the door mid-morning drew Ivana's attention away from brewing a pot of tea for herself and Sanca, her roommate, who would be just rousing herself after working the late shift at the inn.

Of course it would be Vaughn. Why in the abyss hadn't she just sent him on his way with his damned book? It had caused her nothing but consternation and a night of little sleep.

But Danton was the one who had knocked; he wore an easy, slightly shy smile and was as boyish-looking as ever. "Hey, Ivana," he said. "S'good to see you again."

Her irritation melted a bit; it was hard to be annoyed at Danton. She ignored Vaughn, who stood behind him, and gave Danton a warm welcome. "Danton," she said. "It's good to see you too."

They stepped inside, and she closed the door behind them. "Call me 'Serina,'" she said quietly. "Please."

Danton put a hand over his mouth. "Oh. You're in hiding and all that, right?"

"In hiding" might not have been how she would have described it, but she didn't correct him.

She retrieved the book and handed it to Vaughn. "Nothing more came to me."

He took the book reluctantly. His eyes were dark. Frustrated.

She turned away from him and addressed Danton. "You headed out?"

"Soon," Danton said. He looked at Vaughn, uncertainty in his eyes.

So Vaughn had discussed the developments with Danton. She liked Danton, but did Vaughn *really* think Danton would be able to convince her to go with him to Ferehar?

She wouldn't give them the opportunity to find out. "Safe travels," she said, moving toward the door to let them out. She wanted Vaughn and his memory-stirring book out of her hair as soon as possible.

Sanca chose that moment to enter the room. "I thought I heard voices." She was smiling, even though her straight, fine hair hung limp and unbound around her shoulders and she still wore a rumpled dressing gown. "Serina, you should have told me we had guests," she continued, her tone mild and not at all perturbed. She was not vain, and she liked people. It made Sanca's situation all the harder for her, knowing what people would think of her if they knew what she was.

"Old acquaintances passing through," Ivana said. "It wasn't expected."

"How lovely! Why are we all standing around?" Sanca

gestured to the single couch and two armchairs in the room.

"Why, thank you," Vaughn said, taking a seat on the couch, but not without tossing a grin at Ivana.

She suppressed a sigh and had to take a seat herself so she didn't appear rude. She chose an armchair, and Danton sat next to Vaughn on the couch, while Sanca took the other armchair.

"So—old acquaintances?" asked Sanca, leaning forward eagerly. "Serina has always been a bit shy about her past. Where do you come from?"

Vaughn and Danton exchanged a look, and Vaughn opened his mouth to speak—but before he could, there was another knock on the door.

Ivana answered it. Livia, one of the older women from the town, stood on the doorstep wringing her hands in her apron.

"Da Serina," Livia said immediately. "Oh, I'm so glad to find you home. I need a tonic for Thyn. That damned cough has come back, and I do worry."

"Don't, Da," Ivana said. "I'll have Sanca deliver the tonic in a few hours."

"Thank you, dear." Livia curtsied and left.

"Tonic?" both Vaughn and Danton said together.

"Sanca," Ivana said, closing the door and ignoring their question, "do you remember the formula we devised for Dal Thyn?"

"Yes, of course."

"His cough is back. Let's make another batch later?"

Sanca smoothed her dressing gown, glanced toward Vaughn and Danton, and nodded. "Yes, of course," she repeated.

"Wait," Vaughn said. "Are you some sort of *healer* here?"

"Not exactly," Ivana said. Sanca now perched at the edge of the armchair, as if ready to flee. It was best to get it out. "Sanca is the healer. I help her with some of the foci to make the most of her aether-infused tonics."

Sanca gasped and shot out of her chair, her friendly air gone in a moment of terror. "Serina!"

Ivana held out her hand. "Steady, Sanca. Vaughn and Danton are Banebringers as well."

Sanca still stood, trembling, as if hardly daring to believe what Ivana had said was true.

Vaughn and Danton, on the other hand, broke out into simultaneous grins. "Always good to meet one of our own," Vaughn said. "You must be a bindblood."

Sanca's jugular went up and down. "I-I don't know what that means. But I-I can heal." She shifted from foot to foot. "Serina has been so kind to me. When she discovered what I was—after we moved in together—rather than turn me in, she set up a sort of tonic shop in our home. She sells tonics that she makes and that are the marvel of the town. I deliver them. But no one knows they're so effective because I'm providing the aether to make them and activating the medicine when I give it to the patient." She finger-combed her hair a few times. "Wh-What do you two do?"

At Sanca's words, Vaughn's eyes turned toward Ivana again. He studied her as if seeing her anew this morning, but there was also something speculative on his face.

Danton, on the other hand, was full of explanations. "I'm a lightblood," he said eagerly. "And Vaughn is a moonblood."

"I-I don't—" started Sanca.

"Sorry. Sometimes I forget we made up those terms. Vaughn can turn invisible and do some stuff with water. I can manipulate light and, well, here..." He gave a demonstration, causing the armchair Sanca had been sitting on to appear to turn into a small pony, and then back again.

Her eyes widened. "I...had heard rumors...but I..." She swallowed. "I've never met another Banebringer," she finished softly, almost a whisper.

"Gifted," Danton said. "We, uh, we call ourselves 'Gifted.'"

Danton loved to talk, and so did Sanca. Vaughn was watching the two of them, his eyes narrowed.

It seemed Ivana's hopes for a brief visit weren't to be realized. Fantastic. "Danton, would you like some tea? I was just making some." At least it would gain her a few minutes of solitude.

"Sure, I'd love some," Danton said.

Sanca always had a cup in the mornings, so she didn't ask her, and Vaughn stood up when she did.

"I'll help you," he said.

So much for solitude.

But there was a mischievous glint in his eyes that made her wary. What was he up to?

He followed her from the front room through the door that connected it to their small kitchen.

She pressed her lips together and busied herself putting the kettle back on the stove, since the water had long since gone cold. *I'm not going to Ferehar,* she reminded herself. *Absolutely not.*

Vaughn leaned against the counter next to her. "You're sheltering a Banebringer," he said softly.

"So?"

"So, that's...risky."

She gave him a disparaging look and checked to be sure she had put tea leaves in the teapot earlier.

He squinted one eye. "All right. Nice of you?"

"I needed a way to establish myself in a new place. The opportunity fell into my lap. I'm not complaining."

"Mmm," he said. "Have it your way." There was a long pause, and Ivana felt no need to fill the silence with idle conversation.

Vaughn, apparently, did. "So. Roommate?"

"Yes."

Vaughn raised an eyebrow, and a sly grin quirked up one corner of his mouth. "Lover?"

Ivana took the kettle, which was starting to sing, off the stove. "Mmm. Done that. Not my thing."

Vaughn's elbow slipped off the counter. "You've...*really*? Are you trying to drive me crazy again?"

Ivana rolled her eyes and poured the hot water into the teapot.

The tea brewed in silence. Ivana certainly had nothing left to say.

That was not, apparently, true of Vaughn. "I've never forgotten about you, Ivana," he said quietly at last.

She snorted and poured the tea into four teacups. "I'm gratified to know my memory stains the many encounters you've no doubt had since we last saw each other."

"You might be surprised." He helped her put the teacups on a tray and then picked it up before she could. "I'm trying." He shifted so he was in her direct line of sight. "You gave me a lot to think about."

She took the tray back from him. "I don't want to give you anything to think about. I want you to leave, as soon as seems polite. Are we understood?"

What had he been hoping for when he'd come here—other than a lead for his ridiculous plan? For her to embrace him with open arms? Rejoice at seeing him again?

She started toward the door, but he put a hand on her arm. "I thought we parted on cordial terms," he said. "A year and a half ago, and..." He shrugged. "Even last night. I don't understand why you seem to despise me so deeply again."

The persistent questions that had bothered her all night long, keeping her awake and interrupting her dreams when she did sleep, rose back up again.

"I don't despise you," she said, and it was true. But he was a specter. "But I would like to serve this tea before it gets cold."

His hand dropped, and she carried the tea tray out.

Sanca had joined Danton on the couch, and they were engaged in animated conversation.

Ivana set the tray down, selected a cup herself, and sat back down in the armchair.

Sanca turned to look at her and then ducked her head. "Serina," she said, then hesitated.

Ivana raised an eyebrow at her. What was this?

"All right. I'll just come out and say it. Danton has been telling me about the Ich—Ichtaca?" She glanced at Danton for confirmation, and he nodded. "And I..." She took a deep breath. "I think I'd like to join them."

Ivana remained silent. *Damn.* It wasn't that she minded Sanca leaving. She could do whatever she wanted, of course. It was that Sanca was the anchor to her life here. If she left, it would become quickly obvious that Ivana's tonics weren't what they used to be.

If Sanca left, Ivana would have to find somewhere else to start over. It felt like she had only just become settled again.

Ivana felt Vaughn's eyes on her. He would understand what it would mean for her if Sanca left.

She cast him a sharp glance.

The corner of his mouth curled up, and she frowned at him.

And he had known this was likely to happen. *That* was why he had left Danton and Sanca alone to talk. *Not going with you,* she mouthed.

His smile just grew wider.

Sanca, on the other hand, knew nothing about Ivana's past. But she did know Ivana couldn't continue as she had before without her.

Hence, the guilt.

"Serina, you've been so kind to me," Sanca said. "I...I feel so terrible, but this is—" She took a sharp breath, as if still unable to believe it herself. "This is an opportunity I never thought I would have. To be among my own kind."

Going to Ferehar might be your only way of finding out more, a part of her whispered. *And you want to know more, don't you?*

Vaughn had settled back down with his own cup, but he leaned forward now to regard Sanca critically. "Danton has explained to you that things aren't what they used to be? Our old refuge—a manor in Weylyn—is no longer safe for us. We've split up, though we have ways of communicating, and we move around frequently."

No. I do not *want to know more,* she told herself firmly.

Sanca nodded slowly. "I know. But the thought of being among people like me..." Her eyes glistened. "He said they can always use healers—bindbloods."

But what in the abyss was she going to do now?

Vaughn nodded. "That's certainly true."

Should she pick up, find some other small town to settle down in, only to have the inevitable war Vaughn predicted catch up with her anyway?

Danton flopped back and smacked his hand to his forehead. "But she'll need a sponsor, Vaughn. We can't just give her the location where we're bringing new recruits and send her off on her own."

She could feel herself breaking. She no longer had an excuse to stay here. She would have to move again no matter what. Why not go with Vaughn, prove to him there was nothing to find, and then *finally* have him out of her hair?

Vaughn leaned back and spoke slowly. "Unfortunately, I have to go elsewhere. But why couldn't you take her?"

Why not? *Why not?* She could think of a dozen reasons and a dozen outcomes, and none of them seemed promising.

Danton bit his lip, and he gave Vaughn a side-eye. "I'm not even supposed to be here. I was supposed to go to Marakyn, and I still haven't been able to contact Yaotel to let him know why I'm not there yet—let alone to ask permission to go elsewhere."

Sanca's shoulders slumped.

Vaughn rolled his eyes. "I'm certain Yaotel can spare you for a while longer."

Burning skies, why was Vaughn always messing up Ivana's life?

"Excuse me," she said suddenly, leaving them and their arguing behind.

Ivana retreated to her study and closed the door softly behind her. She stood there for a moment in the blessed silence, contemplating, and then did what she had come in here to do.

She opened the bottom drawer of her desk, pried up the false bottom, and lifted out the qixli.

It looked like a small, circular mirror, except upon closer inspection, one could see that the silvery part was viscous and trapped between two airtight panes of glass.

Vaughn didn't know she had it—at least, he wasn't supposed to know. The lightblood who had accompanied her girls back to the estate of Kayden, Caira's now-husband, had insisted on making one for her and one for Caira before he had left. Ivana had relented—after making Caira swear she wouldn't contact her unless it were an emergency.

A couple of months later, she had found the device glowing, and she had been surprised to find Aleena on the other side rather than Caira.

Aleena had apparently stopped by Kayden's estate to visit Caira, and Caira had passed it on to her. Of course, not being a

Banebringer, Aleena couldn't use it without adding her own blood to the lightblood aether within the qixli—which meant she had managed to pry the thing open without breaking it, add her blood, and close it back up again, airtight. Ivana had been duly impressed.

She herself had only used it to contact Aleena since then once—to update her as to her new location in Fuilyn. That had been more than a year ago, and they hadn't spoken since.

Ivana held the device firmly in two hands, willed it to find Aleena, and waited.

A few minutes went by—enough that she was about to give up—when the silver moved, and the vague impression of a face pressed up into it.

"Aleena," she said quietly, by way of acknowledgment. "It's me."

"Ivana?" The voice was tinny and small, distorted by the device and the fact that neither of them were lightbloods—or Banebringers, for that matter. But the distortion couldn't hide Aleena's delight. "Burning skies! How are—what are you—wait. Is everything okay?"

"Yes," Ivana said. "Well, mostly. I just had some questions for you."

It was only then that Ivana realized how much she missed her old friend.

She wanted to chat. She wanted to know what Aleena had been doing. She wanted to fill her in on everything that had happened—or more accurately, hadn't happened—since they had parted ways.

She might even have wanted to ask her advice, which was an odd feeling.

But using the qixli slowly used up the aether that made it work—especially for them—and it wouldn't last forever. So she cut straight to the point. "Have you continued to stay in touch with Caira?"

Aleena seemed surprised. "Well, yes, for the most part."

"How is she?"

"She's doing well. About a month ago she wrote to tell me they were expecting their second child."

"How nice," Ivana said, though the words felt—and sounded—hollow. She wasn't used to sentiment.

And Aleena knew it. Her voice was amused as she went on. "Wynne is still there. She had a bit of a tumultuous relationship with a man, early on, who turned out to be a bit of an ass, but the last I knew, she'd taken charge of the estate's horse breeding and was turning it a nice income."

Wynne, one of Ivana's girls, had stayed with Caira to work with their horses, but Ivana didn't know much more than that.

"Good for her."

So those two were well for now. Unless Fuilyn flipped. Kayden and Caira were nobles. She couldn't imagine *they* would join the Conclave's side.

"In any of your correspondence, has Caira said anything...political?"

"Political?"

"You know. About how sentiments are swaying in Fuilyn—given current events."

"Oh. That kind of political." Aleena paused. "Kayden isn't happy with what's happening in Weylyn. Caira says he's been talking with a few of the other nobles in the area. There's been some unrest. People, overall, don't like what the Conclave's been doing. They don't like that they were lied to all these years. They want the Ri to do something about it."

"Like?"

"I don't know. I just know there've been meetings."

That didn't sound good. Vaughn was right. And this was Fuilyn, which was the least likely of the provinces to rebel without following the lead of one of the others.

With or without Sanca, her relatively peaceful existence here wouldn't last.

"Ivana, did you really contact me only to ask about Caira?" asked Aleena.

Ivana glanced back toward the closed door of her study, the one that led back toward the three people socializing in her front room.

Once again, her life—façade that it had been—had been completely disrupted.

Thanks to Vaughn—though she could hardly blame him for the war.

Then again, *he* blamed himself, so maybe she could too. That would be a convenient excuse to stay annoyed with him.

She was getting distracted. "You're still in Cadmyr?"

"Yes..."

"Are you doing anything important these days? I have a pretty big favor to ask."

Aleena laughed. "You know I'm ever at your disposal—and flexible. What do you need?"

Why in the abyss had she told Vaughn he could drop by this morning? If Sanca hadn't met them...

"Could you escort someone to a group of Ichtaca down in Venetia?"

Ivana could tell by the snatches of conversation she heard as she approached the front room that they had moved on from the possibility of Sanca joining the Ichtaca.

Vaughn was right. Unless something changed soon, war

would engulf Fuilyn sooner rather than later, and then she'd still be stuck deciding what to do.

"Sanca, do you really want to join the Ichtaca?"

Ivana had interrupted, and the voices fell silent as three heads swiveled in her direction.

Sanca went still, as if holding her breath. "Yes—but—"

"I know someone who can get you to them safely. Not another Banebringer, but another ally. Someone used to traveling." She nodded to Danton. "Aleena. As long as you think she could stand in for a Banebringer sponsor."

Sanca rose from her chair, her hands clasped in front of her. "You do? I mean—oh! Would that be…?" She looked first at Danton, and then Vaughn.

Vaughn shrugged, and though he spoke to Sanca, his eyes were on Ivana. "If you can work it out, I'll contact Huiel and let him know I'm sending someone his way. He knows Aleena. I doubt he'll have a problem with that."

In her excitement, Sanca hurled herself at Ivana and wrapped her in an entirely too enthusiastic embrace. "Thank you—thank you!"

Ivana patted her awkwardly on the back, and then pulled herself away. "I can go with you as far as Carradon," she said, "where we'll meet my friend, who can take you the rest of the way."

"And I can go with you as far as Weylyn City," Danton added eagerly.

Initial plans were made. Sanca excused herself to get ready for work, and Danton headed to the inn to reserve another night so they could start fresh the next day.

Vaughn hung back.

He helped Ivana take the teacups and saucers back to the kitchen. "You're going as far as Carradon?" he asked.

Ivana put two hands on the table and leaned on it,

contemplating. She didn't have to go through with this. She could take Sanca to meet Aleena and then go her own way. Searching, yet again, for a place she could settle.

For how long?

This was ridiculous. The questions about her parents had already been let loose. How long would they torment her? Was she afraid of what the sight of a bit of land might to do her? Or an old chest with her father's papers, if they managed to find it? She had been overwrought last night, that was all. Unprepared for what Vaughn had brought with him. She felt calmer today. More in control.

No, perhaps this was what she needed. To prove to herself there was nothing left for her there. To allow herself to move on.

She could face this. For now, she turned to face Vaughn. "And then I'll go on with you to Ferehar. Since you just singlehandedly uprooted my life here and I have no other plans."

Vaughn's face split into a grin. "I knew it. I knew it!"

"You orchestrated this on purpose," she accused.

He held his hands up. "I had no idea your roommate was a Banebringer until this morning."

"But having found out..."

"Did it hurt your decision?"

She grunted. "Don't get your hopes up. It's been over a decade. The chances that we find the woman, that she still has the chest, *and* that the chest has anything of value in it..."

"I don't care," said Vaughn. He spread his hands. "If nothing comes of it, then..." A muscle jumped in his jaw. "I'm out of options."

She eyed him for a moment. Options? There was more going on here than he had told her; he was clinging to this slim hope far too tenaciously. What was the consequence to failing this quest—other than some distant and possibly unrealistic concern that they might need to confront Danathalt himself? "Then I hope for your sake, chance is on your side," she said. "Because I'm going to be disgruntled if I go to all this trouble and you don't even find what you're looking for."

Vaughn grinned. "I'll take that risk."

Chapter Six

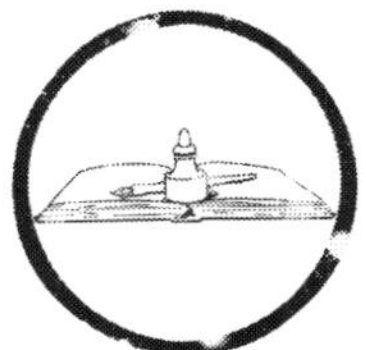

The Xambrian

Driskell's pencil scribbled furiously against his notepad as he tried to keep up with the meeting in progress.

Ri Tanuac was presiding, but right now he sat silent in his chair at the head of the table and listened.

Nahua was beside him, as usual. She, likewise, listened.

The furious scribbling was a result of Driskell recording the comments of the other four people in the room—excepting himself—along with his own commentary for Nahua's later benefit.

"I cannot abide it any longer!" Gan Herne burst out. He slammed his fist on the table with such force that his many braids jumped along with everything on the table. "The arrogance of those dogs—"

H: Conclave = dogs, Driskell scribbled.

"We've tolerated the thumb of the Setanan Empire for centuries," Gan Beatha said, nodding to Herne. "But we will not tolerate the thumb of the Conclave."

B: thumbs = bad, no matter who they belong to, he wrote on the next line. It was a good thing Nahua was the only one who ever saw his originals.

"And what will you do, Beatha?" Gan Dillion spoke up.

Driskell always imagined Dillion as an older version of himself—or at least, what he hoped he might look like, when he was older. Lean, fit, and sophisticated—and definitely having grown out of his long, gangly limbs.

Dillion pushed his spectacles up and offered an alternative. "Take your lands and secede from Donia if we do not in turn secede from Setana?"

D: absurd argument to quell B

Chastised, the heavyset woman sat back, her face heightened in color. She fluffed her luxuriant brown hair, which was almost as full-bodied as she was. "Of course not," she muttered.

B: duly quelled

"I agree with the sentiment," Gan Fiacra said quietly. She, on the other hand, smoothed down her hair, which was cropped short and slicked against her head. "But in the end, the decision is up to the Ri."

F: peacemaker, as usual

"There is no decision. As much as I wish it were different, we cannot win a war against Setana," Dillion insisted.

D: war w/ Setana = certain doom

"If the others could be convinced to join us, they would lose that many more from the United Setanan, and be that much easier to defeat," Beatha said.

B: need allies

Aside from their deep brown skin—typical of most Donians—

the four Gan were as different as night and day, and a meeting with all four of them together never ceased to provide entertaining fodder for Driskell's notes.

Ri Tanuac cleared his throat. "Your Graces. A word."

The table fell silent, and Driskell looked up.

"I am sympathetic to all your complaints. I wish we could simply declare our independence and wash our hands of Setana. But Setana is brutal. History shows us what they did to the Venetians, who dared to fight back."

"Our ancestors were cowards," Herne muttered. "I won't follow their path."

Tanuac silenced him with a glance. "There *is* something else you're forgetting. The Conclave has *them*."

The Banebringers. Everyone knew by now that there were thousands of them under Weylyn City. All the Conclave had to do was slaughter them all, and the land would be overrun.

Beatha sniffed. "An idle threat." She adjusted the necklace at her throat, an ostentatious bit of jewelry featuring at least a dozen polished cualli stones dangling as individual pendants from a single golden choker. "They won't do it. They won't hold power in Weylyn by destroying the capital, after all. The Conclave would be in as much trouble as the rest of us."

"Would they?"

Driskell straightened up. He recognized the change in tone of the Ri's voice. He was about to say something new. He drew a line on his paper and held his pencil at the ready.

"I've just received a report by carrier bird from one of my contacts in Weylyn City, and they've noted something curious."

The table waited, while Driskell scribbled.

"Bloodbane have started trickling toward Weylyn City, almost as if drawn there. And they wait. Already, dozens and dozens of them are swarming about the walls, but they do nothing."

"That's...odd," Beatha admitted.

"An understatement," Herne muttered.

"The Conclave has another tool at their disposal," Tanuac continued, "and *I* believe this oddity is a symptom. They not only have Banebringers, they have their *magic*. Even if we can diminish the numbers of the United Setanan by internal attrition, we have no hope of standing against Banebringer magic wielded by the Conclave against our own people."

Not one of Tanuac's advisors dared to speak after that proclamation.

Driskell couldn't help but risk a glance at Nahua. Her eyes shifted to meet his, but she didn't move her head.

Technology. Weapons. Medicine. Their own Banebringers?

All would be boons to any potential war.

But to ally with them?

It was unthinkable. How did that make them any better than the Conclave?

He didn't write that. He didn't want it recorded on paper anywhere.

Yaotel had been detained now for over two weeks. He had been provided quality food, wine, and any reasonable comfort someone held captive could request.

But still, Nahua had made no move.

Neither had the man's two "associates" tried to retrieve him—or break him out.

Driskell had checked on them occasionally. They were still staying quietly at that same inn, making no trouble.

The Ri hadn't questioned Nahua's judgment when she said she was considering whether Yaotel was trustworthy and was working on an angle she would present to him when ready.

Driskell still couldn't believe she was even considering giving Yaotel a hearing, but he trusted her more than he lent credence to his own misgivings.

A knock sounded on the door to the meeting room.

"Come," Tanuac boomed.

Dal Anwell poked his head into the room. "My apologies, Your Excellency, but a...the...ah...Xambrian ambassador is here to see you."

Xambrian ambassador? They *had* a Xambrian ambassador?

Tanuac stared at Anwell as if uncomprehending. Then he leaned over to whisper in Nahua's ear. She nodded.

Tanuac stood. "Dismissed," he said. "I need to attend to this meeting. Three days from now, same time, we'll reconvene."

The Gan threw curious glances at Tanuac, but they filtered out, all the same.

"Anwell," Tanuac said, when the others had gone.

"Yes, Your Excellency."

Tanuac gestured Dal Anwell into the room, and the steward entered and closed the door behind him. He seemed unusually...frazzled.

"We have a Xambrian ambassador?" Tanuac asked.

"No, Your Excellency." Anwell smoothed an invisible wrinkle out of his tunic. "Well, I suppose the post is on the books, but it isn't filled." He coughed. "The Conclave hasn't allowed foreign ambassadors for decades."

"Yes. That's what I thought. So, who is this man?"

"He's a Xambrian." Anwell looked scandalized at the very possibility of a Xambrian being on the premises.

"And he just showed up?"

Driskell was already intensely curious. For the second time in less than a month, an unexpected and outlandish visitor had arrived. What did this one portend?

"Indeed," Anwell answered.

"Hmm. Curious." Tanuac rubbed at the stubble of beard he

kept on his chin. "Show him in."

Anwell's mouth dropped open. "Your Excellency? But—"

"Well, gather my guards, of course. But this is the first time a Xambrian has shown up in Marakyn for years. I want to hear what he has to say."

Dal Anwell would like to lodge an official protest, Driskell wrote.

"If I may lodge an official protest—" started Anwell.

"You may," said Tanuac. "Driskell? Write that down."

"Already done, Your Excellency," Driskell replied.

Nahua smothered a smile.

"There you go," said Tanuac. "You can take care of the paperwork with Driskell later. Now show the ambassador in."

They didn't have to wait long.

The Xambrian led the way into the room, trailed by two of Tanuac's personal bodyguards and an apologetic Anwell, who closed the door after him, leaving the guards behind to keep watch on their newest guest.

Tanuac, Nahua, and Driskell rose.

Driskell couldn't keep his mouth from hanging open. The Xambrian was a short, squat man, if he could be called a man, with weather-beaten, tanned skin. The rest of them—even Driskell—towered over him. And everything about him was...*squarish*. His head was flat on top—not his hair, but his actual head. His forehead was flat. His stubby nose was squared off. The tips of his fingers were squarish. Driskell had no doubt that were he to remove his boots, his toes would look the same. Even the unadorned cranberry robe he wore hung off his shoulders in a suspiciously squarish way.

His startingly green eyes, at least, were round—almost too round. It gave him a wide-eyed, innocent look that was jarring against his otherwise angular features.

It was...odd. But Driskell looked away before Nahua could cast him a reproving glance. He was here to record and observe, not stare and judge. So instead, he wrote down his observations.

Then, to his surprise, the Xambrian knelt to the floor and bowed with his face to the ground, his back held perfectly parallel to the floor. "My lord Ri," he said. "You have admitted me to your presence. I am indebted by your trust." He spoke in a strange, rough accent, and yet...

He knew Setanan.

Tanuac exchanged a glance with Nahua. "I don't believe I have the honor of your name, Dal."

"Ambassador Mezzo, my lord." The Xambrian continued speaking to the floor. "Forgive me if I am using incorrect honorifics. We have little interaction with your people, you understand."

And he knew it fluently, if his opening statements were any indication. That seemed important, so Driskell noted it alongside his ongoing transcript.

"'Your Excellency,' properly, but I take no offense," Tanuac said. "You may rise."

The Xambrian rose back to his feet.

"Forgive *me*, Dal Mezzo," Tanuac went on, "but I was not aware that we had an ambassador from Xambria, here or anywhere else in Setana."

"Indeed, you did not have one, but you do now. After much discussion, we have taken it upon ourselves to send ambassadors to several of your Empire's regions in the hopes that we may facilitate greater dialogue." Mezzo bowed again, but not to the floor this time. "And thus, here I am."

"Dialogue," Tanuac said, one eyebrow raised. "May I ask which other regions?"

"Of course. Your esteemed sister region—Venetia—as well as Fuilyn and Ferehar."

"Not Weylyn, Arlana, and Cadmyr?"

Mezzo smiled for the first time. And it was, predictably, rather squarish, with the edges of his lips jutting upward at an angle rather than curling, as one would expect. "I hardly think we would be welcome there," he said.

"And yet, you imagine you would be welcome here."

Mezzo gestured around the room. "You have shown me due courtesy in admitting me. Were we incorrect?"

Tanuac inclined his head. "Have a seat, ambassador."

"Before I do, I must ask: are all those in attendance in your confidence?"

Tanuac's eyes rested on Nahua and then Driskell in turn. "Forgive me. This is my daughter, Nahua, and my attaché, Driskell. And yes. Certainly. They may be trusted."

Mezzo seated himself and eyed Nahua. "Your heir?"

"It doesn't quite work that way here, but she's a likely contender." Tanuac folded his hands on the table. "What can we do for you?"

"Direct and to the point. I can appreciate that." Mezzo surveyed the three of them critically. "You have a complicated history with the Conclave here, yes?"

Tanuac was silent for a moment. "You might say that."

"Come. Despite what you may have heard about my people, we're no barbarians. I've read your histories—Setana's bloody battle with Venetia, and your subsequent shame in refusing to fight."

Gan Herne and this Xambrian would get along, Driskell thought, and then on second thought, he wrote it down.

"I would dispute your interpretation of the events," Tanuac said, "but do go on."

"Regardless, we know you have no real love for the Conclave. One might even say, no loyalty?"

A bold statement. It was one thing to hear the Gan argue about this, and even for Nahua to entertain Yaotel's proposal, but a complete outsider?

Driskell hadn't realized events would become so *exciting* when he had been chosen for this post right out of the academy, just under two years ago. His other option had been an internship at a bank—far less prestigious, but closer to home. He might rather have been buried in numbers and ledgers than thrust into the middle of this political intrigue.

Thankfully, his only role was to take good notes, and *that* he could do.

Tanuac's face was carefully blank, but his lips tightened a bit. "You presume much for someone I've only just met...Ambassador."

Mezzo gave his funny, angular smile again. "Keep your own counsels, of course. No matter. I am not here to pry information out of you. Rather, I'm here to make you an offer."

More offers? Burning skies. Would-be benefactors were showing up in droves, it seemed. He glanced at Nahua, whose face betrayed nothing of her thoughts.

Driskell starred Gan Beatha's name and drew a line to a new note: *Potential allies?*

Mezzo tented his fingers on the table, but not in a triangle. No, they were tented in a square, like a flat roof.

Of course they were.

Driskell was noticing a trend. He wrote it down, this time not because he thought it was important, but because it was interesting.

"Not only can we read books," Mezzo continued, "we can also read signs. If I may presume once more, Your Excellency—your

Empire is in chaos. Your Conclave"—the word turned into a guttural growl on the last syllable—"has wrested control of what little centralized government you had, controlling your magicians and controlling your army."

"They don't control Banebringers," Nahua said, voice even. "They've merely squirreled them away beneath Weylyn City."

Mezzo lifted his index fingers from his tent and then put them back. "Ah, yes. Your most wasted resource. A shame." He shook his head.

Driskell eyed Mezzo. He knew other countries had other methods of controlling their Banebringers, but he didn't know all the details. Up until now, the Conclave's most effective weapon had been controlling what people *knew*.

"The way we see it in Xambria," Mezzo continued, "there is both a threat and an opportunity in this chaos. The threat, of course, is that the Conclave will manage to extend its reach beyond Weylyn, beyond the three provinces, and achieve what is most likely its goal: complete subjugation of the entire Setanan Empire—and perhaps beyond."

Under its thumb.

"Indeed, if they are not stopped, that is almost certainly what they will do." Mezzo leaned back in his chair. "Xambria means to stop them."

"You are bold," Tanuac said softly, "coming here to declare your plans for open war against the Empire."

Xambria and the Setanan Empire were not allies. They were not even friendly. Setana had made two bids to conquer the neighboring country in their history, and the Xambrians had retaliated, both times, but the physical geography separating the two countries had made the task of either subjugation or revenge incredibly difficult. In recent history, the relationship had settled into an uneasy truce.

Mezzo didn't respond to Tanuac's comment directly. "What do you think will happen, Your Excellency, when Xambria marches on Cadmyr? Will the Conclave simply let our troops pour through the pass, secure a base position, and sweep through Setana? I daresay they won't. No, they will rally their army and meet us, as they have done in the past. And what will Donia do when Setana calls on the United Setanan army to meet the new northern threat? Will Donian troops respond to the call?" Mezzo leaned forward. "Will Venetian? Fuilynian? Fereharian? Will a common enemy unite you? Or separate you once and for all?"

A tingle traveled down Driskell's spine. If all four outer regions refused to fight, and yet the Conclave was forced to meet the Xambrian threat rather than quell rebellions within their own borders...

They might have a chance.

Tanuac's eyes were narrowed. "You need our withdrawal to succeed."

Mezzo tapped the table. "Not only yours, of course. Which is why three of my comrades are making similar offers to Venetia, Ferehar, and Fuilyn. If all four of you agree, we will graciously extend our offer."

Nahua gestured impatiently. "You've spoken much and made no actual offer. Indeed, from a certain perspective, your words could be taken as a threat."

To Driskell's surprise, Mezzo clapped, seeming dreadfully pleased all of a sudden. "Ah! And they say Setanans have no stomach for this sort of negotiation. You have the right of the situation, my lady. It could be perceived that way. But you are also correct: I have made no offer yet. I will now. If we succeed in our bid, we will leave you alone to rule in peace."

Tanuac leaned back in his chair, folding his arms across his chest. "Or we could refuse, and you would fail to conquer Setana, as you have twice before."

"And our loss would also be yours, for the opportunity to so easily throw off their yoke may not come again."

Driskell had to admit, Mezzo had a point. But no one was asking his opinion at present, so he simply made a note of it.

Nahua and her father exchanged glances again, and then Nahua leaned forward. "And what is to stop you from turning your eyes toward any one of us once you've subjugated the three inner regions?"

"So untrusting!" Mezzo declared. "Your daughter is shrewd, Your Excellency, and I would ask the same. We would not because if you take our offer, you would not only throw off the yoke of the Conclave, but their false religion, and consider then returning to your roots. The Conclave is a plague on the land; their destruction is all we want."

Driskell's eyes grew wide. They wanted them to start worshipping the heretic gods again? *That's* what this was all about?

"But know this: Should you refuse our offer, and we should nonetheless win, with or without the aid of the others..." Mezzo smiled, and this time, it was slightly more sinister. "You are correct. There is nothing that would bar our way." He stood. "I will leave you now to consider. I'm sure you have many advisors to consult. I'm told Setanans enjoy that sort of thing." He bowed. "May your swords ever be bloody, Your Excellency, my lady"

Driskell blinked. He'd never heard *that* one before.

He wrote it down.

Mezzo showed himself out, and after a jerk of Tanuac's head, the guards followed.

There was silence in the room until Nahua finally spoke. "Off the record, Driskell," she said.

Driskell set down his pencil.

Only then did Nahua turn to her father. "All of his posturing aside, surely you're not going to officially recognize this man?"

"Xambrian," Tanuac mussed.

Nahua didn't often disagree with her father in front of Driskell—or anyone else, for that matter. Driskell tried to pretend he wasn't listening, but, naturally, he was.

She waved a hand. "I can't imagine the Conclave would be happy to hear about that."

"No, I suppose not." The corners of Tanuac's eyes creased. "They could lodge an official protest. Driskell has all the paperwork, I'm sure."

"Father," she said, a touch of reproof in her voice. There was a moment of silence, and then Nahua spoke more softly. "Are you truly considering it?"

"It would be an interesting test, wouldn't it? Just to see what they do?"

"If you call poking a sleeping bloodwolf with a stick 'interesting.'"

At that, Tanuac was silent. He glanced at Driskell and said something he didn't often say: "Driskell, thank you. You are dismissed."

Driskell rose, snugged his notebook against his chest, and left the Ri and his daughter to private counsel.

Chapter Seven

Carradon

The capital of Cadmyr, Carradon, made its presence known long before they reached the city proper. The tiny villages that straddled the main road grew in size and number; the sprawl of urban life had long outgrown the city's walls.

The city even stretched across the Tecolti River, which had once been a natural barrier to further expansion. This far north, before the numerous tributaries from the Fereharian Mountains to the west and the Mecatil River from the east joined it, the Tecolti was relatively narrow and swift; even so, the river was navigable, and a ferry now ran regularly from one side to another.

That had not been the case when Ivana had lived here.

Carradon was the first place she had settled after fleeing Ferehar, and though she had been by the city a few times in the years since she had left, she had never again ventured into the city proper.

It was the birthplace of Sweetblade, and she had always deemed it too dangerous to enter.

However, it was improbable that, almost a decade later, she would be recognized by anyone who had been caught up in that transformation, whether knowingly or not. So, for expediency, she and Vaughn would travel through the city the next day, but they wouldn't cross the river tonight. Aleena was to meet them at an inn on this side of the river, where they could plan and prepare for the inevitable blood tests they all would face upon disembarking the ferry to the other side.

Ivana felt as though she might need the night to prepare herself as well.

Aleena stood up when they entered the tavern, a broad smile on her face.

Ivana was torn between wanting to embrace her old friend and feeling awkward about doing so.

Aleena, perceptive as always, solved the problem by meeting her with a firm grasp of both arms instead. "Ivana," she said. "It's so good to see you again."

"The feeling is mutual," Ivana said, and it was.

Seeing Aleena again made her feel...herself again, whoever that was.

After she'd lost Sweetblade, she'd tried to move on. As much as she could, she'd seen to the future of her girls—the disparate group of young, single mothers she'd once cared for under the guise of an innkeeper—and then disappeared. Started over.

Tried to, anyway. She had made a conscious effort to abandon that persona, but the effort had always felt empty. Hollow. Fake.

Even before Vaughn had shown up, she had had the nagging suspicion—perhaps even the dread—that there was no setting aside that persona because it wasn't one. It was who she was now. Anything *else* was the façade.

Except that wasn't true, either, because Sweetblade would have never been so unsettled by finding her mother's journal.

She also wouldn't have felt that discomfort increasing the closer she drew to her past. And now that it had come to it—parting ways with Danton and Sanca and heading to Ferehar with Vaughn, she wondered if she had made the right decision.

Ivana turned toward Sanca. "Aleena, this is Sanca."

Aleena inclined her head. "A pleasure."

She left the two women—and Danton—to become acquainted and ordered herself a shot of lupque at the bar.

Vaughn joined her. "So," he said.

"So what?"

"You ready?"

Ivana exchanged a half-setan for her drink, then downed the tiny glass of milky-white liquor in one draw. The lupque, a particularly strong liquor, burned going down and burned in her stomach as it settled there. She set the glass down with a clunk on the wooden bar. "Ready for what?"

"Ferehar."

She shrugged. "Biggest challenge will be the plateau. But since we can essentially sneak across the entire thing invisible if we need to—"

"I didn't mean that."

She glanced at him and frowned. "Then I don't know what you mean."

"Don't you?"

So he was going to play the concerned friend card, was he? Best to deal with him now. "As I have told you, we're going in, we're seeing if the woman is still there, and when she's probably not, we're leaving, and I'm done. I don't know if there's anything to be ready *for*." She signaled for a refill.

Vaughn watched her as she downed the second shot. "You know, that stuff is pretty strong."

"I'm aware." She could already feel the burn spreading from her stomach and warming the rest of her body nicely. Too much. She knew better. This time, she ordered a bowl of whatever was on the menu that night. Some food to absorb the alcohol a little.

Vaughn's eyes hadn't left her, and it annoyed her.

Did he think she wanted to return to Ferehar, let alone anywhere near her hometown?

Ferehar was the last place in the world she wanted to go. In fact, it was possible she would have more gladly gone to the abyss itself.

Ferehar—and the memories it contained—was her own personal abyss.

She signaled for a third lupque, ignoring the steaming bowl of spiced chickpea stew in front of her.

What had she been thinking? Closure? What in the abyss did that even mean?

She shoved her coin across the table, and before she could down the third glass, she found it being taken gently from her fingers. She turned, a sharp retort on her lips at Vaughn's interference, but instead, she found Aleena standing just behind them. She handed the lupque to Vaughn, who looked at it, shrugged, and downed it himself with a grimace and a shudder. Being a Banebringer, the alcohol wouldn't affect him.

"Three shots of lupque is quite a bit," Aleena said softly. "Perhaps the day before continuing a long journey isn't the best time to give yourself a hangover."

Aleena glanced at Vaughn, and through some unspoken communication, which further irritated Ivana, Vaughn left, and Aleena took his place. She ordered a drink herself, but only cider—her favorite.

They sat in silence until Ivana started picking at her stew.

"You know," Aleena said, "I seem to remember that you used to avoid alcohol most of the time because of how it clouded the mind."

That was when I didn't want my mind clouded, Ivana thought. To Aleena, she offered no response.

That, apparently, was as good as if she had spoken it. Aleena sipped at her—by contrast, mild—drink, and regarded Ivana with those penetrating eyes.

She said nothing more. Just looked at her. Contemplating.

"You know, I was just thinking about how much I've missed you," Ivana said. "I might take those thoughts back if you don't stop looking at me like that."

Aleena chuckled, stood up, and raised her glass to Ivana before walking away, leaving her alone at the bar.

Alone. A state of being she was intimately familiar with. A state of being she had become comfortable with. And yet, that night, it seeped into her in a way it hadn't for a very long time. Maybe it was the alcohol. Maybe it was being surrounded by so many familiar faces after being away for so long. Or maybe it was a signal that she was about to descend into darkness once more. Had she come full circle, then? Had all of it been in vain?

Without a glance back at Vaughn or Aleena to see if they were looking, she ordered the third lupque she had been unable to have, downed it defiantly, and left to go to bed.

———

Vaughn sat at the table with Danton, Sanca, and Aleena, but he didn't participate in their conversation. Instead, he watched Ivana as she sat alone at the bar for a few more minutes, drank a third lupque, and then abruptly stood up and disappeared upstairs—presumably, to her room.

Aleena dropped out of the conversation and nodded to Vaughn, and then toward the stairs. "She all right?"

Vaughn snorted. "As if she'd tell me." He could count on one finger the times Ivana had consciously made herself vulnerable to him, and it hadn't ended well.

"I'm a little concerned. I've never known her to drink much at all, let alone more than she could handle."

And three shots of lupque was more than pretty much anyone could handle. "We all have a vice, don't we?"

"Not Ivana," Aleena said. "She never needed one." She hesitated, chewing on her lower lip, and then spoke again, this time barely audible. "Well. Sweetblade never needed one."

Words Ivana had spoken over a year and a half ago floated unbidden into Vaughn's mind. *"There is no solace for people like me."*

"Maybe Sweetblade *was* her vice," he said, just as quietly.

Aleena's lips pressed together. "Just...keep an eye on her. But don't tell her I asked you that. She'd be furious."

Vaughn saluted. "Yes, Da."

Vaughn took a deep breath and then knocked on the door to Ivana's room. He hoped she wouldn't take this the wrong way.

There was no answer. That could mean she didn't want to be disturbed—which was probably true, regardless—or it could be she was out cold.

He looked up and down the hallway, making sure no one was around, and then called quietly, "Ivana?"

Still nothing. He tried the door handle. Unlocked, which was all the evidence he needed that she wasn't thinking clearly at present.

He hesitated and then, praying her reflexes were too slowed by alcohol to stab him before she knew who he was, gently cracked open the door.

Nothing.

He poked his head into the room.

She was lying on her back on the bed, one arm flung over her eyes, but her jaw was working. She wasn't out.

He slipped into the room and closed the door behind him.

"Did I say you could come in?" Her words were slow and deliberate, as if she were trying too hard to control her diction.

"I just—"

"Wanted to see if you could take advantage of my current state?"

Ha. Not a chance. He'd learned *that* lesson well enough. "In fact, I wanted to see if you were all right."

"That's even worse."

"Three lupques—" he began.

"Did Aleena tell you to check on me? Because if she did, you can tell her—"

Vaughn interrupted quickly. "No. I came on my own."

"Then you can leave on your own." Now there was a definite slur in her words.

"Look—I get it. I don't want to go back to Ferehar, either." Ferehar. Home. The place where he, too, had lost a former life. The place where he might have to start one again. He swallowed and pushed that thought away for tonight.

She lowered the arm from her eyes and looked at him. "Is that what this is? Some sort of attempt to empathize with me?" She laughed, short, cold, and teetering just over the edge of control.

"You don't know anything."

He set his jaw. Was she the only one entitled to wallow in the grief of her past? As if *she* had any inkling of what *he* had been through, either. If there was a medal awarded to the person with the most tragic past, he would hardly quibble about which of them deserved it more—but he understood enough. "I know I'd be drinking too, if alcohol had any effect on me."

"Then how about you go find some naïve barmaid to fuck and leave me alone?"

He flashed her a grin. "Tempting, but I'm trying to cut back."

"Drop dead." She flung the arm back over her eyes. "No, wait. Get out, and then drop dead."

He moved farther into the room and tried one more time, this time, a different tactic. "Is this what you're like now that you can no longer hide behind Sweetblade, then?"

There was a long silence. Then she erupted from the bed, her face twisted in a snarl, and she staggered toward him.

He backed away, his hands up. Anger and drunkenness didn't go well together. Anger and drunk former assassins even less so.

Undeterred by his posture of surrender, she advanced on him until she had backed him against the door. "You think you know me so well?" she hissed, grasping the collar of his shirt.

He never was one for wisdom. "I know this isn't like you."

She growled. "Neither is my having tolerated your presence this long. Get. Out. Now."

He didn't *think* she would hurt him—too much—but then again, the only other time he had seen her under the effects of alcohol, it had been a very little. In that case, it had made her more amiable and talkative.

Apparently, too much made her angry. And violent. "I'm leaving," he said, feeling for the doorknob behind him.

She didn't move, but her arm started trembling. He wasn't

sure if that meant she was fighting the urge to hurt him, or if she had reached her physical and mental limit.

He hesitated, then reached up and untangled her fist from his shirt. Thankfully, she let him. "I'm leaving," he said again, slowly.

Her arm dropped to her side, and she stumbled away from him.

He slipped through the door, closed it, and a moment later, heard a low, feral growl and a hollow *thunk* on the door.

Well. That had gone well.

The nerve—! Ivana rubbed the bottom of her fist where she had slammed it into the door and stumbled back to the bed. She sat down on it heavily and leaned over her knees, her face in her hands.

Her head swam, and her blood was boiling.

She was furious. Furious that he understood even a bit of what was wrong. Furious that he thought he could help. Furious that he had seen her in anything but a state of absolute control.

But most of all, she was furious that, when her mind wasn't at its most optimal, she had fallen back on old habits. What did that say about her?

Her head throbbed already, and she felt like she was going to vomit. She was an idiot. Aleena was right. Tomorrow would be miserable.

The next morning, Vaughn lifted his hand in farewell as a vessel slipped from the docks and into the current. Danton, Sanca, and Aleena stood at the rail, all three waving.

The three had arranged passage to Arlana on a merchant vessel traveling down the Tecolti; it was the fastest—and safest—

way to travel south toward Venetia.

They waited until the ship was out of sight, and then turned back toward the city. Ivana surprised Vaughn by linking her arm through his own and leaning into him. "There's a Watchman on the other side of the docks who's been watching us," she said under her breath. "Fereharian."

He started to look but checked himself just in time. Instead, he scratched at his beard. "What kind of watching?"

"Kind of watching?" she repeated.

"You know. Watchmen specialize in watching, after all. Suspicious watching? Absentminded watching? Curious watching? Ogling watching? Watching of—"

She exhaled. "I don't need a taxonomy of types of watching, thank you."

"You're the one who asked. Also, have I ever mentioned that when you use big words—"

"He's coming this way."

Vaughn grinned. Convenient.

He already had his hand tucked casually in his pocket, a sliver of lightblood aether between his forefinger and thumb.

The Watchman circled them to cut off their trajectory. "Da, Dal," the Watchman said. He produced a tiny cylinder from a satchel at his side. "I'm going to need to do a blood test on you both."

Ivana blinked large eyes at the Watchman. "But, Dal," she protested, the timbre of her voice raised slightly in what Vaughn recognized as her "innocent maid" persona. "We were already tested coming into the city." She extended a finger to show the Watchman where she had been pricked earlier, a slight pout to her lips.

He hesitated and then inclined his head to Ivana. "Random check, of course. Recent change in protocol. Your pardon, Da."

Random check. *Ha. That'd be suspicious watching, then.* It was a bit unsettling, but why would the Watchman have any reason to suspect them? Vaughn had done nothing out of the ordinary, and as Ivana noted, they had already been subjected to the blood test when they had disembarked from the ferry that had carried them across the river.

Ivana allowed the Watchman to prick her finger with the needle hidden in the spring-loaded cylinder. This was not the first time Vaughn had seen one of these; they weren't a new invention, but they were now part of the basic kit for a Watchman when they hadn't been before.

The Conclave had been flexing its newly formed muscles in all sorts of small ways.

The Watchman eyed their packs and then Vaughn's bow. "Traveling?" he asked while he waited to see if her blood would turn.

"Yes," Vaughn said. "Just passing through." He didn't like the way the Watchman was now studying his face. Had he been recognized?

"Where you headed?"

But he had read the descriptions the Conclave had begun circulating of him and other known Banebringers who had been present at that disastrous Harvest Ball. His description could fit thousands of men. And they didn't even have the beard in the description. It was more likely that their little eclectic group had drawn the Watchman's attention early on before the others had boarded their ship.

Ivana broke in, clutching Vaughn's arm closer. "Ferehar to visit family. He's never met them." She gave the Watchman a brilliant smile.

What would it take to get her to smile like that genuinely? An idle thought. One that would probably get him in trouble if he dwelt on it.

Satisfied that she wasn't a Banebringer, the Watchman now turned to Vaughn.

"Hope you've got yourselves in with a good caravan," he said, returning Ivana's smile. "The plateau's been bad lately."

Vaughn pinched the lightblood aether in his pocket and held out his other hand, and the Watchman pricked his finger. Vaughn burned the aether and masked the drop of blood that welled up with an illusion that kept the color of the blood the same. His heart quickened in his chest as it did every time he had to do this. If the aether chose this moment to be unreliable...

"Really?" Ivana asked. "Why is that?"

The Watchman shrugged. "Survivors say it seems like there are more bloodgiants than normal. Even had a couple come down into Cadmyr about a week ago."

Well. That didn't bode well.

The Watchman's eyes flicked to Vaughn's face again, and then glanced at Ivana. "Where are you from? I'm from Ferehar too. Maybe I know your family."

Ivana waved her hand. "Oh, I doubt it. Just a tiny farming village on the southern end." She looked pointedly at Vaughn's finger. "Are we free to go, Dal? We've a long journey ahead."

The Watchman inclined his head and let go of Vaughn's hand, which Vaughn promptly shoved into his other pocket.

"Thanks for the warning," Vaughn said. "We'll be extra careful."

The Watchman jerked his head. "Good luck."

Ivana inclined her head and they ambled away.

Vaughn dared a look back. The Watchman was still watching them.

At the western gates, a short line waited while every person leaving the city was tested.

Vaughn was certain no Banebringer in their right mind would be left in one of the Setanan capitals, if they had a choice about it. Vaughn had lightblood aether at his disposal; that wasn't true of every Banebringer—especially those unconnected to the Ichtaca, who wouldn't have the same resources or information to draw on.

Of course, the lightblood aether Danton had donated wouldn't last forever. A good reason not to tarry in the city for too long.

Their plan was to stop at an inn about seven miles out from Carradon that evening. They wouldn't travel after dark until it was necessary—especially with the report of bloodgiants coming down off the plateau.

They passed through the gate with little fanfare. Vaughn masked his blood again, the guards were satisfied, and they were on their way.

If they hadn't passed through gates and beyond a wall, he wouldn't have known the "city proper" had ended. The urban sprawl of Carradon, much like Weylyn City, was an extension of the city itself, complete with residential, commercial, and industrial areas. The western road out of Carradon was, naturally, lined with shops.

"It's a wonder they haven't started random searches," he said once they were well past the gates. "Or at the least searches at the gates. Surely, someone has realized by now we have ways of subverting their tests."

"I imagine even the Conclave has to close its fist slowly," she said.

Vaughn shuddered. All the more reason to end this sooner rather than later.

Ivana led the way; Vaughn tried to engage her in further conversation about Carradon, but she didn't seem interested. So he tried conversing about plans for crossing the plateau. Also not interested.

He finally resorted to commenting on the weather, and still she remained taciturn.

He lapsed into silence and noted the tension in her shoulders, the way her hands were balled into fists, the slight furrow in her brow.

Huh. She was rarely so transparent.

When they came upon an iron fence surrounding the burial grounds at the outskirts of the city, Ivana's steps slowed—and then halted outside the open gate.

"Ivana?" he asked.

She didn't say anything. She just turned and went through the gate.

Not knowing what else to do, he cast a glance down the mostly empty road and followed her inside.

She wound her way through the graves to a long columbarium and stopped in front of a section that didn't look as weatherworn as the rest of the wall. The newest section, he surmised.

She stood there, staring at the wall for a moment, then reached out and traced the first name on one of the plaques that adorned the stone boxes.

Her hand dropped, and Vaughn peered closer. *Boden,* the name read.

It dawned on him. "You lived here," he said.

"For a time."

"When?"

"It's the first place I lived after I left Ferehar."

He digested that. "And where Sweetblade was born?" he

guessed.

"Indeed."

He hesitated and glanced at the plaque again. "And Boden was…?"

There was a long silence. Long enough that he was certain she wasn't going to answer him. Then, finally, softly, she said, "A friend."

This was ridiculous. Why was she here?

It meant nothing. She didn't care.

She *couldn't* care. If she cared now, what had it all been for?

To buy herself fourteen years of detachment, of death, of numbness? Fourteen years bathed in blood. Fourteen years begun by this one kill.

Oh, she had killed before this one. But there were many points when she could have veered from the path she had chosen.

But this one had been one too many, one too far. The pain of the decision to kill someone who had been a friend—someone who had trusted her—had been too much for her tormented psyche to handle without ensconcing itself in the shield of numbness. She had known there would be no turning back once that decision had been made.

It had been what she had wanted. It was why she had gone through with it.

Only a monster could have killed the gentle young man whose ashes lay behind this wall, so she had become a monster.

She had never wondered before, not even then, what would have happened if she had chosen differently.

She would probably be dead, and he still would be too.

Just not at her hand.

She took a step back and stared at the box. There were no

tears. Not then, not now. There was still numbness. But the quality of it had changed. It was no longer the absence of anything else. She could feel it now, tight and tingly, like fingers exposed too long to the cold but not yet frostbitten. She could prod at them and feel the barest brush of pressure, maybe even a prick of the pain if she dug her fingernails in deep enough.

Her hand drifted to the hilt of the dagger at her thigh—the dagger she had begun to wear again because of this trip.

Why was she prodding? What was she doing here, headed back into the one place that could thaw her out, once and for all?

And then what?

The only way she knew how to live was to be dead inside, yet something deep inside her had started longing for real life again, and the possibility terrified her.

To be truly alive was to feel pain.

Vaughn's eyes were on her, but she didn't owe him any further explanations. "We have six more miles to travel before dark."

"Best get on it then."

Chapter Eight

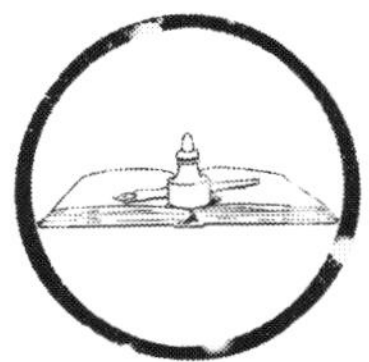

New Enemies

Driskell was the model firstborn child. He had been at the head of every class: well-read, well-rounded in his education, and well-liked on top of it.

He was not, however, well-traveled.

Then again, he wondered how well-traveled a person would have to be to be comfortable with a Xambrian standing at their side.

No matter. Though he had balked when Nahua had originally given him the task, he would be the model guide as well.

He and Ambassador Mezzo now stood at the wall of the eighth ring of Marakyn, the highest and smallest of eight concentric rings that made up the city.

"Wall" was a generous term. It was more like a waist-high

barricade to prevent someone from accidentally falling over the edge and into the seventh ring, thirty feet below.

To Ambassador Mezzo, it was more like chest-high.

Even so, they could both look out over it and into the land beyond. Having exhausted the tour of the city itself over the past week, he had proceeded to give Mezzo a lesson in Donian geography from the highest point in the city.

Driskell cleaned a speck off his spectacles, settled them back on his nose, and pointed across the plains. "Two hundred fifty miles due east is the eastern border of Donia at the Tecolti River," he said. He then traced his finger across the horizon. "Ipsylanti is three hundred twenty-five miles southeast, at the mouth."

Of course, both landmarks were still too far to see; most of the land beneath them consisted of empty plain stretching out to the horizon.

Mezzo, however, turned his eyes to the north. "And your northern border, with Weylyn, is but one hundred miles from here."

"Yes. You...know your geography, I see."

Mezzo gave his strange, squarish smile. "I can assure you, Dal, that I know far more about Setanan geography than you know about Xambrian."

Driskell shifted. Incredibly, after a couple of days of letting Ambassador Mezzo stew in an inn, Tanuac had finally decided to give the ambassador lodging in the consulate. A few days after that, Nahua had charged Driskell with showing the ambassador around, as he had time.

"Your Marakyn, however, is a bit of a wonder," Mezzo went on. "It reminds me more of our own cities than those typically found here."

The ambassador's observation was true, at least as far as the Setanan side of the statement went. Even the Fereharian capital,

Cohoxta, wasn't nestled directly into the side of the mountains the way Marakyn was.

"Well, we didn't build it," Driskell said. "According to the histories, the city was abandoned when our ancestors claimed and settled it."

"A curious location as well," Mezzo continued, as if he hadn't spoken. "And it gains the distinction of being the Donian capital despite being neither the most populous nor the largest of your cities."

No, the honor for both of those titles went instead to Ipsylanti, his own home city.

"Scholars believe it may have been a strategic choice at one point," Driskell said. "It's easily defensible and guards the southern pass into Ferehar. Of course, now, it's important for trade with Ferehar as well as the nomads."

"And still easily defensible."

Driskell eyed Mezzo. He had—inwardly, of course—questioned the wisdom of showing a Xambrian around Marakyn. They weren't exactly allies, after all. "Well. Yes. Though that's not my specialty."

It was Mezzo's turn to eye Driskell. "No? What specialty are you, then?"

"I'm an attaché. So, that's like administrative work for—"

Mezzo cut him off with a wave of his hand. "I'm familiar with the term. But in Xambria, there is no specialty for the knowing of war. We are all trained and ready to fight should the need arise."

Driskell blinked. "You don't have a standing army?"

"We have war leaders—something akin to your Setanan officers. Anything more would be a waste of resources."

Xambrians—or at least this Xambrian—seemed to have a distaste for "wasting" resources. Driskell's hand itched to write the observation down, but he thought whipping out his notebook might be considered rude.

Then again, what did he know about what Xambrians considered rude? It struck him that standing next to him was a wealth of knowledge about a subject he had never tapped. They were forbidden from studying foreign languages, cultures, or anything of the sort. What he knew about Xambria, or Xambrians, could be summed up in a single chapter in their history texts, and it all focused on when they had intersected with Setana.

He hesitated. Mezzo certainly seemed to have no qualms about sharing what he knew.

Driskell glanced around him, but there was no one around. Would it be considered illegal to ask a Xambrian questions about things they were forbidden to learn? It wasn't illegal to *talk* to a Xambrian, after all...

"You have questions, I see," Mezzo said. "And yet fear to ask them. No doubt the work of your Conclave." The last word he spoke as though it were rotten in his mouth.

"What do you have against the Conclave in particular?" Driskell asked. The question popped out before he could stop it.

"They have taken your ancient gods—with whom we share affinity—and defiled them and their places of worship."

Driskell swallowed. No more on this subject. This was a dangerous conversation.

Mezzo, however, had no such reservations. "You are clearly a learned man, Dal Driskell." He spoke the latter syllable of Driskell's name with an odd scratchy noise in the back of his throat. "I would not think someone like you, at the least, would accept so readily the suppression of knowledge."

"Don't be like the Conclave—so xenophobic," Nahua had said. *"This is an opportunity you're not likely to have again. Don't waste it."*

He knew now what she had meant, but had she meant even

more by it than he had considered? He hesitated, and then forged on. "You don't Sedate Banebringers in Xambria," he said. "I know that much."

Mezzo sniffed. "What a waste. Why would we neutralize our greatest weapons? The Godtouched have positions of great honor in battle—at the front."

Driskell blinked again. *Godtouched.* That was a new one. Once again, his fingers twitched on a phantom pencil in his hand. "That's a great honor?"

"Of course it is. Many Xambrians fight long years in the arena to win the honor of being the first to shed blood when the muster is called. Godtouched win it simply by virtue of being touched."

Driskell's head was spinning. *Arena?* "Uh...I'm no war leader, but I'm pretty sure we just throw our most useless soldiers in the front as fodder."

"I will never understand the amount of waste you Setanans tolerate."

"But doesn't having Bane—um—Godtouched at the front mean they might die and spawn bloodbane?"

"Certainly. Both a risk and an advantage, if one knows how to use it properly."

Xambrians—and the Yunqi and the southern nomads, to name a couple more—didn't have the same way of dealing with their Banebringers that Setanans did. But this sounded less like "dealing" with them and more like honoring them. At least in Xambrian culture.

But Xambrians worshipped the heretic gods. Wasn't that what Mezzo had implied? So of course they wouldn't see Banebringers as profane. Even the name he had used—"Godtouched"—seemed to imply that Banebringers were rather highly regarded.

His thoughts turned to Yaotel. What was Nahua waiting for?

A shout rang from the watch tower farther down the wall, and a moment later, a bell rang three times—one long followed by two short chimes—and then a Watchman clattered down the stairs and out of sight.

"Ah," Mezzo said, his eyes on the plains below. "There seems to be an important matter at hand."

Driskell followed his gaze. A single horseman pounded across the plains; the speed at which he rode suggested that his mission was urgent.

"I should get back," Driskell said.

"Of course." Mezzo bowed low again. "Until next time, Dal Driskell."

Driskell hurried through the civic hall toward the conference room, where he guessed he would find Nahua and the Ri.

A servant stopped him on the way to inform him Nahua was looking for him, and he could find her in the conference room, which confirmed his guess.

Heated voices rose from behind the doors. The fact that Driskell could even *hear* them through the thick wood spoke to how heated.

He hesitated only a moment before slipping into the room. Nahua was looking for him. Nahua was in this room; therefore, he could be in the room as well.

No one paid one bit of attention to him.

Ri Tanuac sat at the head of the table in his usual spot, silent while the four Gan stood at the table shouting at one another.

His instinct was to pull out his notebook, but Nahua was in the back of the room pouring herself a glass of wine and gestured for Driskell to join her.

She answered the question that was on the tip of his tongue

before he could ask.

"A messenger just arrived with some disheartening news," she said. "The Conclave has heard of Ambassador Mezzo's presence here and is insisting that we eject him immediately or face the consequences."

Driskell's eyes widened. "And have they spelled out those consequences?"

She gave him a side-eye. "No. But there's a contingent of about six thousand troops headed toward the Donian border."

Driskell took a deep breath. This was bad. This was really bad. "This seems like a bit of an overreaction. I assume we've made no reply yet."

Nahua glanced over at the arguing Gan. "We haven't, but the Conclave isn't stupid," she said. "They know their hold on the outer regions is tenuous. Their best weapon is fear; for us to have openly welcomed the Xambrian ambassador shows that perhaps our fear of them isn't what it ought to be."

Driskell let that sink in. Fear. And now, for the first time since the Conclave had staged their little coup, they were throwing their weight toward Donia. To see what they would do. To see if they would once again bow.

"What about Venetia? Fuilyn? Why us?" Driskell asked.

Nahua shook her head. "Neither of them have, as far as we know, openly acknowledged their ambassadors like we have." She cast a look toward the Ri, whose face was now deeply etched in a frown as he watched his advisors argue. "And, frankly...we already bowed once without a fight. Perhaps they see us as the easiest target."

Driskell found himself indignant at the thought. Just because their ancestors had decided the best answer to the Setanan problem was to give up before a single sword had been drawn didn't mean that, hundreds of years later, they would do the same. "Will they really attack us, or is it a bluff?"

Nahua shook her head. "I don't know." She paused. "Did you learn anything interesting from our friend Mezzo today?"

"They call their Banebringers 'Godtouched,'" Driskell said, "and honor them by placing them on the front lines in battle."

Nahua stared off into nothing for a moment, swishing the wine around her glass. "Interesting. So if it came to battle *against* the Xambrians instead of..."

"Enough." Tanuac's voice boomed out.

The room fell silent.

"I've had enough of all of you," Tanuac said. "You're dismissed. Be back here tomorrow morning, same time, and come prepared with solutions, not bickering."

The four Gan filed out of the room, their expressions ranging from morose to infuriated.

Nahua set her glass down. "I have a task for you," she said quietly. "Retrieve Dal Yaotel and bring him here. You can brief him on the way."

Driskell turned to her, his mouth open. "Here? Now? But—"

"No more questions, Driskell. Just go."

He bit his tongue. "Yes, my lady. Going."

Chapter Nine

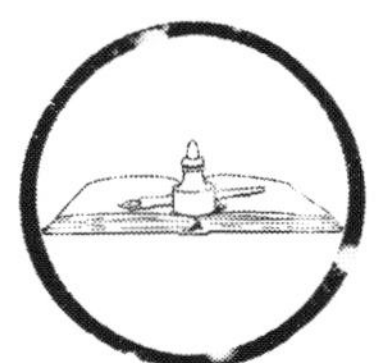

Blood and Magic

Driskell took a deep breath as he stopped in front of the room in the consulate Nahua had given over to Yaotel's house arrest. He had questioned why Nahua had ignored Yaotel for so long; now that it had come to releasing him, he found himself suddenly nervous.

This had the potential to cause a multitude of problems.

Driskell unfolded a release form he had grabbed from his office and held it and a pencil out to the guard on duty. "Lady Nahua is releasing the prisoner into my care."

The guard nodded, signed the form, and unlocked the door.

Driskell tucked the form in his pocket and stepped in. The room was well-appointed. It had a real bed, a soft rug, and artwork adorning the walls. Dal Yaotel had not been mistreated. He was sitting on the bed at present, cross-legged, his head leaned back against the wall.

"Dal," Driskell said. "Lady Nahua requests your presence."

Yaotel shoved himself off the bed and stood in front of Driskell. He said nothing.

"Do you need me, Dal?" the guard asked as Driskell led Yaotel out into the hall.

"No," Driskell said. "I can handle it from here." *I hope.*

After they had stepped through the door of his room and into the hall, Driskell turned to Yaotel. "I *can* trust you not to try to escape, right?"

Yaotel inclined his head.

Driskell took another deep breath and blew it out slowly. "All right. Then let's go."

Yaotel walked alongside him, and Driskell began to summarize what was happening. "I'm taking you to the main conference room to see Lady Nahua and possibly the Ri himself. To my knowledge, Lady Nahua hasn't told him about"—Driskell glanced around to make sure they were still alone—"your...*condition* yet."

"It isn't a disease, Dal," Yaotel said quietly.

Driskell eyed him. The conversation he had had with Ambassador Mezzo was still on his mind. "Did you know the Xambrians call you people 'Godtouched'?" he blurted out.

A smile slid over Yaotel's lips and then faded. "I did know that. I also know they have a higher proportion of beastbloods, which is what I am."

"Beastblood?"

"I think I'll wait to explain until I hear what Nahua has to say."

"Yes. About that." He explained the situation further to Yaotel—the arrival of the Xambrian Ambassador, his offer, the pending arrival of the Conclave army on their northern border.

When Driskell had finished, Yaotel asked no questions.

Driskell was torn between wanting to ask his own questions and being afraid to, so they walked the rest of the way in silence.

They turned down the hall that led to the conference room and stopped in front of the door. Driskell hefted the door open and held it for Yaotel. "After you, Dal."

Tanuac was still in the conference room, along with Nahua, both standing rather than sitting at the table.

They turned to face Driskell and Yaotel as they entered, giving Driskell the impression that they had been talking and had fallen silent.

Tanuac's eyes swept over Yaotel critically. Yaotel's jaw jumped, and his eyes, likewise, swept over Tanuac.

Driskell glanced at Nahua.

She made a gesture with her hand at her thigh, her palm parallel to the ground, like a quick horizontal chop.

She did it to indicate silently to him to wait: say nothing, do nothing, don't even move.

At last, Tanuac broke the standoff. He gestured toward the table. "Dal Yaotel. Please. Have a seat."

Nahua made a circle with her hand to indicate Driskell could go back to business as usual.

Yaotel settled himself into a chair at the end of the table. Nahua did the same, and Driskell sat next to her, pulling out his notebook and pencil.

Tanuac remained standing. He glanced once at Yaotel and then paced back and forth a few times. Finally, he came to a halt at the head of the table and gripped the back of the chair. "Nahua has just informed me of your condition."

Not a disease, Driskell thought, glancing at Yaotel, but the

Banebringer didn't correct Tanuac.

Instead, he folded his hands in front of him on the table. "Has she also informed you of my offer?"

"Yes," Tanuac answered. "And, Temoth help me, I...would like to learn more. Nahua said you can demonstrate some of what you're offering?"

"I can," Yaotel said. "But I'll need my belongings back in order to do so."

Tanuac gave a tight nod to Nahua.

She strode over to the door, pulled it open, and had a brief conversation with one of the guards standing outside. Then she closed the door and returned to her former position.

"While we wait, Dal," Tanuac said, "tell me: Why here? Why not one of the other outer regions?"

Yaotel nodded. "First, because Ferehar, while perhaps the most open-minded regarding my kind amongst the general populace, is politically an untenable option. Fuilyn is too conservative when dealing with Setana; they prefer to mind their own business and hope Setana leaves well enough alone. And out of Venetia and Donia, Donia is the most practical." He trailed off and looked out of the window, which afforded a grand view of the city and plains beyond. "It was also my home, once upon a time."

"And second?" Tanuac prompted.

A satisfied smile flitted across Yaotel's lips. "Second, a so-called Banebringer is already within the upper echelons of your government. I have heard rumors. Talk. Hopes."

Driskell's hand jerked in shock, and a drop of ink spattered onto the table. He hurriedly wiped it up, hoping no one had seen, while his mind spun, wondering who it could be.

Tanuac exchanged a look with Nahua, and his knuckles whitened on the chair. "You've planted someone?"

Yaotel settled back in his chair and folded his arms across his chest. "I haven't *planted* anyone, Your Excellency. Someone already in a position of relative confidence became a *Banebringer* and subsequently learned about the Ichtaca." He raised an eyebrow. "You thought they would confide in you, perhaps?"

One of the Gan? Anwell? One of the Ri's personal guard? While only the Gan knew the specifics of their recent councils, any of the above would know enough to pass on rumors.

Tanuac frowned. "I could order blood tests of my entire staff."

"You could," Yaotel said. "But you won't. Because I happen to know you have expressed a distaste for the Conclave's invasive methods. Or is that distaste only valid as long as the threat is vague and impersonal?"

Nahua's eyebrow quirked up at her father, and Tanuac's frown deepened, but he made no reply.

"Don't worry. The person in question is only tangentially connected to the Ichtaca. I simply know enough that I was willing to take this chance, along with the other reasons I mentioned."

And yet he felt the need to inform the Ri of the Banebringer in his midst. Driskell felt that was somehow important, so he wrote it down.

There was a knock on the door, and one of the Ri's guards poked his head in. He set two bags on the floor next to the door. "Dal Yaotel's belongings, Your Excellency," he said.

"Thank you, Arato," Tanuac said, his eyes on the guard.

Driskell could almost hear his thoughts. Was it this guard? Had he overheard something?

"Please see that we are undisturbed," Tanuac said.

The guard inclined his head and returned to his post.

Yaotel waited until the door had fully closed, and then he stood and walked over to the bags. He opened the smaller of the two and removed an even *smaller* bag from it, and then brought that bag back to his chair and sat down once again. Opening the bag, he removed two items: a small, compact-sized mirror, and a long, leather case.

Yaotel looked up at Tanuac and Nahua. "May I?" he asked.

Tanuac nodded.

Yaotel unwound the string from the smaller leather case and opened the flap. Sewn along the inside was a series of small pockets. Each had a raised symbol embroidered on the outside of the pocket. Yaotel opened the first two and removed fingernail-sized scraps of silver from both.

Hardened aether.

Driskell found himself rising from his chair to take a closer look, his fascination overcoming any fear.

Nahua cleared her throat and looked meaningfully at his notebook.

Oops. Notes. Right. He settled back down and drew a sketch of the pouch, right down to the symbols on the pockets.

"Dal Driskell, was it?" Yaotel asked.

Driskell's head jerked back up. "Yes, Dal."

"May I borrow a sheet of your paper and the lantern from the wall behind you?"

"Uh..." He glanced at Tanuac, who nodded, so Driskell procured both items and pushed them across the table toward Yaotel.

Yaotel nodded his thanks. "I want to spare you a lecture right now, but some basics are in order. First, among the Ichtaca, we call ourselves Gifted, not Banebringers. We do not now and have never summoned bloodbane; the fact that they appear in our world is completely out of our control—as is, in fact, our own existence. But we'll save further education on those points for another day. For now, suffice it to say that I will, from now on, use our preferred terminology." He raised an eyebrow at Tanuac.

"Lest you think the term is arrogant, it is, in fact, a term we resurrected from the not-too-distant past. It's what my kind used to be called before the Conclave."

Driskell leaned forward. *Really?* A dozen more questions popped into his head, but he held his tongue.

Tanuac jerked his head in acknowledgment.

"Second," Yaotel went on, "Gifted have magic; you are aware of this. But there are different types of Gifted, with different abilities. We can't, in and of ourselves, do anything other than the abilities we personally have. We can, however, use each other's aether to reproduce the abilities, to a greater or lesser degree, of that type of Gifted." He held up the first sliver of aether. "This is aether from what we call a fireblood."

He crushed it between his fingers and then touched the wick of the unlit lantern. It flared to life.

Driskell blinked. Had he lit that with his *fingers*?

He then touched the paper, but nothing happened. "The lantern lights because the aether knows it as something that harnesses fire. The aether itself acts as a sort of flint, in this case. We call that a focus. However, if you touch it to anything else, it won't light up. Paper is not an effective focus. I can, however, directly manipulate a fire that already exists." He pointed at the flame and a piece of it tore off and hovered over Yaotel's palm. He then tossed it onto the paper, which, of course, caught on fire. "Harnessing, manipulating, and"—he gestured to the lantern—"in limited applications, even creating fire is one of the more dramatic abilities that our Gifted—those called firebloods—have. You can see immediately the usefulness in a combat setting." He quirked an eyebrow up at Tanuac, who nodded slowly. "Using the aether, I can do some of these things. But our most powerful firebloods can do even more, including creating fire out of nothing."

He smothered the remains of the smoldering paper and picked up the second sliver of aether. "This is aether from what we call a moonblood. The most useful application of this aether, I think you will find, is this." He crushed the aether—and disappeared.

Nahua shot up out of her chair, her mouth open, and even Tanuac made a sound of surprise in the back of his throat.

Driskell stared hard at the place where Yaotel had disappeared. After a moment, he saw a faint outline. It shimmered, and then disappeared again. And then Yaotel reappeared completely.

"An actual moonblood is nigh on undetectable when using their own aether, though it also seems to be linked to the phase of the moon. But others can use it to similar effect."

He opened another pouch and pulled out yet another sliver of aether.

Driskell, again, had to remember what he was supposed to be doing. He scratched down a description of each ability as Yaotel had given it, drawing an arrow to each pouch it had come out of.

"Dal Driskell," said Yaotel, "if I might trouble you again..."

Driskell, once again, looked up.

Yaotel had drawn a penknife, a rag, and a small jar of what looked like a medicinal salve out of his bag. "May I nick your finger?"

Driskell hesitated, and then put his hand out across the table to Yaotel. Yaotel made a short cut, and blood welled up. Yaotel wiped it away on the rag, then tossed the rag to Tanuac.

"There," he said, putting the penknife away and picking up another sliver of aether. "Now you can be confident that your attaché is not a Gifted, Your Excellency," he said, amusement around his eyes.

Tanuac let out a breath.

Yaotel crushed the aether into the salve, and then dabbed a bit on his finger. He rubbed it on Driskell's cut.

His finger already stung less.

"That is aether from what we call a bindblood. It has healing properties, among others. We'll let it sit for a moment."

Yaotel picked up the mirror. "This is a device made from lightblood aether, one of our more ingenious inventions, if I do say so myself. We call it a 'qixli.'" He held the mirror between his hands. "This will allow me to contact any other Gifted with a qixli that I wish and speak to them instantly. If both I and the other Gifted were lightbloods, we would be able to see each other clearly as well."

That was...incredible. Even Driskell had to admit that the ramifications of these abilities were far-ranging. If they could be reproduced on a wide scale, it would transform society.

There was silence in the room, and Yaotel frowned after a moment when nothing happened.

"All right," he said. "I can contact another Gifted if they see the qixli glowing. Let me try someone else."

Finally, the silver in the mirror moved. They all leaned over the table to see better, and even Nahua didn't clear her throat at Driskell this time.

The silver raised like someone was pressing the face of a doll into the back of it: indistinct, but clearly a face.

"Danton," Yaotel said. "It's Yaotel."

And then, a *voice* came through the device. It was tinny, but an understandable voice, all the same. "Hey, boss. It's been awhile. I tried to contact you a few times."

"I've been unavailable; my apologies. I need you in Marakyn. Are you still at the site?"

The person on the other side—Danton—said, "Uh, well, I'm already on my way back. I'd say three or four days out."

Yaotel's brow furrowed. He tilted his head to the side, his eyes searching the air as if calculating or trying to remember something. "All right," he said slowly. "Good. Any word from Vaughn? I tried him first, and he didn't answer."

Danton cleared his throat. At least that was sort of what it sounded like, if a tiny metal man could clear his throat. "Haven't heard from him in a bit, no."

"All right. If you get the chance, try him again for me, and see if you can get an update. I may not be available for a little bit again."

"Got it."

Yaotel put down the qixli and the face disappeared.

Driskell stared at the device in wonder, and based on Nahua's and Tanuac's expressions, he guessed they were feeling the same. Tanuac's face had lost some of its skepticism and was now openly amazed.

Yaotel looked between the three of them, and then at Driskell. "How's the finger, Dal Driskell?"

Driskell wiped the salve on his trousers and looked at his finger. He blinked. "Temoth," he said. "The cut is gone." He held up the finger.

All three of them turned to Yaotel.

"And what do you do? Without the aether of other Banebringers?" Tanuac asked.

Yaotel's jaw tightened, but it smoothed out quickly. "I'm a beastblood," Yaotel said. "Unfortunately, it's not easily demonstrable. My aether allows me to hurt or kill bloodbane more easily. It works wonders for other Gifted when applied to weapons, and I can touch a bloodcrab, for instance, and make the shell explode." He inclined his head. "If I wanted to get close enough, that is."

Driskell felt that if his mouth became any wider, it would

swallow his head whole.

Nahua turned to Tanuac. "The Conclave knows about this, Father. They use this aether. They could have been using it to help people all this time, and instead they've spent it on their own power."

Tanuac's mouth was set in a line. "Yes," he said simply. "How does the Conclave use it, Dal? Are they secretly Banebringers?"

"No," Yaotel said. "It's tedious, but if you were to mix your blood with one of these aether types, and then use that specific mix, you could do this as well. This is something we've only discovered in the past two years. The Conclave has known it for a while; that's how they use the aether themselves."

Driskell was adept at keeping his mouth shut. It wasn't his job to speak in meetings. But this time, it burst out of him before he could help himself. "*I* could do this? If I...do what you say?"

Yaotel nodded at him. "Yes, Dal Driskell. And that's the most far-reaching implication of any of this."

Tanuac, finally, *finally*, sank down in his chair, his steel composure and cynical attitude gone. "I...had no idea."

"Of course not," Yaotel said. "You—generally speaking, of course—have been too busy hating Gifted to consider what we might offer." He tapped his pouch. "There are more than these, but I've given you demonstrations of some of the most obviously helpful applications of our magic—to combat and general society." He raised an eyebrow. "So. Questions?"

"Many," Tanuac said. "First: What are the Ichtaca? Yet another name for Banebringers?"

"No. There are many more Gifted than are under my authority. Most don't even know about us. The Ichtaca are a group of Gifted specifically devoted to researching our magic and everything we can find about Gifted in the past. We've also begun to explore using our abilities for combat, something we've...avoided until recently."

"And in return for sharing all of this with us..."

"Sanctuary, Your Excellency," Yaotel said, sounding suddenly tired. "As you might imagine, the world is a dangerous place for us. Most of us want nothing more than the ability to live a peaceful life like anyone else. Those who have managed to keep their change a secret live in constant fear of discovery."

"So, you want Donia—or at least Marakyn—to provide sanctuary to any Banebringer who asks for it?"

"Not even that much. I can only vouch for those Gifted willing to swear loyalty to the Ichtaca. If they are willing to join the Ichtaca—which would mean willing to cooperate with you—they would be offered safety here in Marakyn." He hesitated. "I won't dissemble. Not all Gifted have our same agenda."

Tanuac rubbed his chin, and Driskell noted Yaotel's qualification. Driskell couldn't help but wonder what other agendas were out there. He wrote both thoughts down for Nahua's later consideration.

"Driskell informed you of the pending Conclave threat, and the Xambrians' proposed alliance?" Tanuac said.

"Yes."

"If the Conclave decides to make use of those troops—and I have no doubt they'll bolster their numbers if necessary—to lay siege to Marakyn, we are well-situated to withstand it, but, of course, not indefinitely. The Xambrians are of no use until the four outer regions—of most importance, Ferehar—agree to their proposal. That's another matter I have yet to figure out, since Ferehar is the one region that will almost certainly refuse. In the meantime, I need to hold the Conclave off—whether by force, diplomacy, or some combination thereof. I don't care, as long as it buys us the time we need. Can you help with that?"

Yaotel didn't waver. "Yes. If you agree to this alliance, I will immediately call any and all Ichtaca scattered around the Empire. There are many already here, or nearby. I will work with your generals to determine the best use of our personnel and abilities. Not knowing the specifics of this army, I can't promise victory, but I can promise our aid."

"I can't make this decision alone." Tanuac jerked his head. "Well. I could. But I won't. That isn't how I do things. I need to discuss this with my Gan, and I want a majority to agree to the alliance before we take such a monumental step. If they refuse, I will see you safely out of the city, and we'll pretend this never happened. Is that acceptable?"

Yaotel stood. "I already determined that I would take this risk, whatever it meant. It's acceptable." He nodded to Nahua. "Thank you, my lady, for giving me a chance, and thank you, Your Excellency, for hearing me. It's more than most would ever do."

Tanuac nodded. "Driskell, show Yaotel back to his room in the consulate. We will continue to keep him under guard until the decision is made."

Driskell inclined his head. "Yes, Your Excellency."

Chapter Ten

Nightmares

Ivana flung herself over her father's corpse, tears streaming down her face.

Gildas spoke from above her, a bloody sword dangling from his hand. "The next time you want to play the whore, girl, at least ask for payment first."

"Monster," she hissed. She lifted her head to look at him, then recoiled. She was staring not at Gildas, but at herself—as a young woman. The sword had become a dagger, and—

The corpse was that of Boden, the friend she had murdered.

She staggered back as the corpse lifted itself off the ground and then rose to its feet. "Monster," it whispered.

Younger Ivana joined it. "Monster," they chanted together.

Only then did she notice that the ground was littered with corpses.

Three more rose: her father, then her mother, and her sister—all leering at her with accusing, hateful eyes. "Monster...monster..."

"No!" she gasped, stumbling back, but they pressed in on her. She fell—

"No!"

Ivana sat up, her heart pounding, her shirt drenched in sweat. She had the vague impression that the exclamation had come from her own lips, and she glanced toward where Vaughn had been keeping watch, near the door of the small shelter.

Now, of course, he had turned toward her. He said nothing, though whether that was out of politeness or discomfort, she didn't know. She couldn't see his face well enough in the dark.

Her hands were trembling while she clutched at her blanket, so she tucked her hands out of sight and glared at Vaughn. She may not have been able to see his expression, but with his night vision—another of his "gifts"—he would be able to see hers.

A few of her harried heartbeats passed, and then he turned back to the door.

Ivana lay back down and turned her back to him. She tugged the blanket back over herself, but she wouldn't be able to sleep now.

At least until her heart stopped thrashing about so wildly.

That had been the third time in the past week and a half. She hadn't had such vivid nightmares in years. Over a decade, in fact.

It was her own damn fault for stopping at the burial grounds on the way out of Carradon. What had she been thinking?

She closed her eyes and breathed deeply, hoping she could trick her body into settling back down.

Her heart eventually did, but she couldn't fall back into deep sleep again. Instead, she drifted in and out of consciousness until Vaughn roused her to take her turn to keep watch. Full wakefulness snatched any other dreams from her memory, leaving behind only the impression that they had been likewise troubled.

It was in that mood that she settled down at the door, where Vaughn had just been, and stared out into the darkness beyond.

And it was dark. Though the night was clear and stars visible high above, the moon was only a sliver in the sky.

Not having Vaughn's night vision, she listened more than she watched; beyond the door-less frame, she could see little other than the hulking shapes of a boulder here or there, and a mass of darkness farther to the north that blotted out the stars: the higher Cadmyrian mountains.

One advantage, if it could be called that, to the barren landscape was that if two luminous white eyes appeared in the night, she would most certainly see them.

She would have preferred a shelter that had a door; this one had been torn off and never fixed.

Thankfully, this was the last night they would have to spend in this place, known interchangeably as the Fereharian desert and the Fereharian plateau. There were no inns here, only a scattering of shelters on the plateau itself where travelers could camp for protection against the elements—or out of the eyes of prowling bloodbane.

They had pushed themselves hard, rising before the sun and traveling well into the night when any caravan or normal traveler would have stopped, and had crossed the rocky wasteland in three days. Another advantage to Vaughn's night vision—and invisibility, if needed.

Tomorrow they would wind their way down the steep path that descended from the plateau and into Ferehar proper.

She inhaled deeply of the night air.

Was that why she had had that nightmare again tonight? They had been on the road from Carradon for a week and a half, but all day that day, as they had traveled, the knowledge that they would soon be back in Ferehar had weighed on her.

She tried to cast it off as nothing, but that wasn't as easy as it used to be.

She had crossed this plateau once before, fourteen years ago, going the other direction. It had not been a pleasant experience. She had followed, unbeknownst to the driver, at the tail end of a large caravan. The rearguard had seen her, but they had ignored her and let her take advantage of the safety of their numbers—and guards—even though she had paid nothing to join them.

But then, it had been late autumn, rather than mid-spring. The pass and plateau were nigh on impassable in the dead of winter, but still treacherous in late fall and early spring, when the weather could be unpredictable and suddenly violent.

And the year she had left Ferehar, winter had come early. While snows hadn't yet blocked the pass, fierce storms higher up in the northern mountains drove down bloodbane that weren't normally seen on the plateau at that time of year. Bitter winds howled across the rocky wasteland, and the wails of bloodbane haunted the caravan. She'd seen one of them once—a monster ten feet tall, clad in hide that looked like chiseled black ice, with teeth and claws to match.

She had been terrified, and rightly so. One of them had attacked the vanguard and decimated the first two wagons before the guards had managed to bring it down—so the word had come back to the rear, anyway.

She had never been more glad to reach the foothills and be on the way to Carradon.

She hadn't known what waited for her there.

Perhaps it would have been better if she had died there on this plateau.

Monster.

She gritted her teeth. She would not question her choice now. It was far too late for that.

A crash sounded in the distance, startling her out of her thoughts. She strained her eyes against the night.

Nothing.

They had been lucky so far. They had seen no bloodgiants, despite the warning the Watchman in Carradon had given them. During the day, the only bloodbane that had troubled them had been the occasional bloodsnake—those liked to lurk in holes in the ground, waiting to dart out and bite the feet or ankles of travelers. However, they had seen several bloodhawks flying far above, and Vaughn had kept his bow—and aether—handy. By night, while they had heard howling in the distance, nothing had ever come closer.

Another crash, this time, closer—and now she saw something large and hulking moving in the dark. She froze. The shape was, for now, moving parallel to their shelter, rather than toward it.

Even so, she crawled back toward where Vaughn slept and shook him. "Vaughn," she whispered, then shook him again.

He started up. "Wha—? Oh." A pause. "It's still dark. What's wrong?"

"There's something out there. I can't see it well. My guess is a bloodgiant."

Vaughn unwound himself from his blanket, crept over to the door, and peered into the night.

Another crash.

"Yeah," he said under his breath. "It's a bloodgiant, all right. It's lumbering around, throwing boulders."

"Wha—why?"

"Bored, probably. Lack of travelers to smash."

The dark shape paused. Another crash.

He leaned over and grabbed his bow from where it lay. "Might be a good time for you to have some of the aether we made at hand. Be better if we can both see—or turn invisible, if need be."

Ivana reached into the pouch at her waist and felt for the final pocket on the right. She fingered a sliver of aether—a mix of her own blood and Vaughn's, so she could use the aether and have the same abilities Vaughn did. It wouldn't last as long as when he burned aether inside or outside his body, and it had a higher likelihood of failure—though she had learned that moonblood aether was one of the less "capricious" of the aethers, whatever that meant.

She had reserved what she had for when it was most needed. "What's the plan?"

"You're asking *me*?"

"You're the bloodbane expert."

Vaughn exhaled. "They have good eyesight, even at night. We should stay put for now. Let's see what it does. It doesn't know we're here, or it'd already be throwing boulders at our shelter. If that changes..." He looked back into the shelter.

There was a back door, of course—no one in their right mind created an aboveground shelter intended partially to shield against bloodbane that one could get cornered in.

"We turn invisible and make for the next closest shelter," Vaughn concluded.

That could be a mile or two away. "You don't want to just try to take it down?"

Vaughn grunted. "I'd rather not engage it if possible. Those things are vicious. And where there's one, there are often more."

Crash.

Ivana grimaced. "So much for an easy passage tomorrow."

"Yeah. If there's one lurking this close to the descent, it

probably means there's a group of them watching the pass. Thankfully, they're also stupid as bloodbane go, and half-deaf. We should be able to slip by without incident, if we stay alert—and out of sight."

Vaughn played the idiot so easily that it was easy to forget he was rather intelligent. He had made bloodbane an area of study. If there was something to know about a bloodbane, he probably knew it.

They fell silent. The bloodgiant seemed in no hurry to leave the area.

Vaughn opened his pack, took out a bowstring, and strung his bow.

Light emitted from the open pack, too bright in the otherwise dark night.

Ivana tugged on Vaughn's arm and jerked her head toward his pack.

Vaughn flipped the flap closed on his pack with a curse and then glanced back out into the darkness. The bloodgiant didn't seem to have noticed.

Then it went silent. The dark form of the monster stopped moving.

Ivana felt Vaughn tense next to him. She held the sliver of aether tightly between her fingers, ready to burn it at a moment's notice.

The lumbering form moved closer and then stopped again. The sound of rock scraping across rock was far too close.

Vaughn pulled Ivana away from the door. "We're out of here," he whispered. "Burn it now, and let's go."

Ivana crushed the aether and willed herself to turn invisible.

No sooner were Vaughn and Ivana out the back than the

bloodgiant hurled a boulder at the shelter. They were built strong for a reason; even so, the sound of stone crashing into the roof of the shelter they had just fled gave him an extra burst of speed.

The shelters followed the road—which was little more than a series of painted stone markers to point the way—so he didn't have to worry about losing Ivana in the dark. He just moved as fast as he could down the road until the next shelter came into view.

He darted inside. "Ivana?" he panted.

"Here," she said, reappearing. Her face was grim. "Did we lose it?"

Vaughn didn't let go of the aether yet. He poked his head out the door and listened.

Nothing... Nothing...

Then there was a thunderous roar in the distance.

"Probably realized we escaped," he said. "But as long as it didn't see us, it isn't smart enough to head toward the next shelter—on purpose, anyway."

He stopped burning aether and sank down on the ground. He didn't, however, unstring his bow yet. He sighed and laid his bow on his knees and his head against the wall. He had been asleep maybe half an hour before Ivana had woken him. "So much for sleeping tonight."

She sat down near him, but she said nothing.

He turned his head to look at her. She hadn't slept well, either. Before she had woken so suddenly with a frightened exclamation on her lips, she had been tossing and turning, and occasionally...whimpering.

It wasn't the first night he'd heard her unconscious mutterings.

He didn't tell her that. A dream that could make *her* so terrified must have truly been a nightmare.

At least she had had a couple of hours before she had woken.

Even as he sat there, weariness tugged at his eyelids. But he needed to stay awake until he was certain the danger had passed.

He bolted upright a moment later at a horrific roar, and then a crash, both far too close to the shelter.

Ivana, too, sat up straight. Had she fallen asleep as well?

"I thought you said they were too stupid to guess where we'd go next?" she hissed.

"They are... Coincidence—has to be." The shelter shuddered. That boulder had connected.

Again, they ran.

Again, they only had a brief reprieve before the damn bloodgiant showed up again.

"It has to be a different one!" Vaughn gasped as they darted into the fourth shelter. This one was right near the beginning—or end, depending on what direction one was going—of the path down off the plateau, which fell sharply away on one side. "There's no way it's following us. The shelters are just boulders sticking up out of the ground, as far as they know!"

Her eyes narrowed. "They aren't intelligent enough to know what the shelters are, yet you're suggesting they've stationed what amounts to guards along the way? It must be the same one."

The slow scraping of enormous feet against rubble that had become too familiar in the past two hours started up again.

"No. No way they have the brains for that, and yet—" He drew a deep breath. "Whatever the case, there are no more shelters. There's nowhere to go but down, and even I don't want to try that descent in the dark unless we have no other option." He dropped his pack and pulled one of his beastblood-infused arrows out of his quiver. "Plan B."

He waited. The bloodgiant lumbered on, throwing boulders

as it moved—in their direction.

Ivana crouched next to him, tense and alert. Her hand was at her thigh, but she hadn't drawn her dagger. She didn't have beastblood aether she could use, so her dagger was nearly useless against these things. She'd be good for a distraction if they needed it.

He sincerely hoped they didn't.

The bloodgiant came into view. It was almost a smaller version of the behemoth he and Ivana had slain in Weylyn City, what seemed now like eons ago, though it hadn't even been two years.

It was brawnier, though. Muscles rippled along its thick arms, and it had huge, clawed hands, if they could be called "hands," that seemed to be custom-made for flinging around boulders. If it didn't manage to kill someone by crushing them with a rock, it could also easily break a neck with a squeeze or disembowel them with a swipe of its claws.

And while a bloodgiant's feet were slow to move at first, its arms and claws were quick enough if one dared to move within reach of them.

He sighted the bloodgiant with an arrow. As with all bloodbane, it had a thick hide, difficult to penetrate with any normal weapon. Certainly, any normal arrow would have bounced off it.

Fortunately, he didn't use normal arrows against bloodbane.

He drew and released. The arrow hit right where he wanted it to: in the soft part of its throat. It stuck there, and the bloodgiant roared. Its white, pupil-less eyes turned in Vaughn's direction, and one clawed hand ripped the arrow from its throat.

Not good.

He loosed another arrow, this time into its knee.

The bloodgiant stumbled and fell. The ground under Vaughn's feet vibrated with the impact, but he didn't waste the moment. He darted out into the night and stuck the monster two more times. Finally, it lay still.

He crept over to its side and yanked out what arrows he could save. He might be able to get another use out of them, and if the aether crafted directly into the heads had been spent, he could still smear them with beastblood aether, like poison.

And then, just as he turned back toward the shelter...

Another roar.

"Vaughn..." Ivana whispered from the shelter behind him.

Vaughn's eyes widened. There were three—no—four—of the hulking figures materializing out of the darkness.

What in the abyss? They tended to congregate, yes, but had they just been *lying* in wait for them? Herding them toward this end? That was *far* too clever for these brutes.

He turned invisible again and backed into the shelter.

"We might have a problem," he said. He looked in his quiver. These weren't the first arrows he'd spent against bloodbane on the trip. If it were just another bloodgiant or two, they'd be fine—but four?

He didn't have time to heat beastblood aether and tip the rest of the spent arrows.

He looked at Ivana. She looked at him. "Not intelligent?" she quipped.

"I swear on the moon goddess herself," he said. "They aren't. They group together, but they don't *work* together."

"We're going to be surrounded," she said. "I can't fight those things."

"No, but you can distract them."

"Oh, no, no. Not that again. Don't you remember what happened the last time I 'distracted' a bloodbane for you?"

He winced. He remembered. Her leg had been almost ripped off by a bloodwolf. "You have my aether this time. You didn't then. Stay invisible. They won't see you. Make noise and draw one or two off. They're slow."

She heaved an enormous sigh, but a moment later, she disappeared.

Vaughn, likewise, disappeared—and stepped back out of the shelter to meet the encroaching bloodgiants.

The four remaining bloodgiants had surrounded the area. Whatever Vaughn might say, Ivana felt that showed a degree of intelligence.

She slipped past their perimeter, invisible. Vaughn's bow twanged, and another one fell to the ground. The second, third, and fourth monsters simultaneously threw the boulders they had been carrying in the direction the arrow had come from. More intelligence.

Ivana heard Vaughn curse, and then the skittering of feet before the boulders crashed into the ground—but there was no scream, so she assumed they had missed him.

Ivana threw a much smaller rock at the closest monster's head. "Rocks for brains!" she shouted. "Come and find me!"

She didn't know if it could understand her, but the one she had hit turned around, its eyes searching the dark for its assailant. It roared, picked up the nearest boulder, and threw it in her direction.

She rolled out of the way.

There was another roar near Vaughn, and a few more crashes.

The other bloodgiants had moved out of her throwing range, so she hurled another rock at the one she had distracted. It was the best she could do.

The monster lumbered in her direction, scooping up another boulder with one hand as it came.

Then the monster threw it. She had already moved, but it was rather disconcerting seeing the boulder crash into the ground where she had been standing not five seconds before.

She circled behind the monster again, and it turned, its white, pupil-less eyes trailing her progress.

Uh-oh.

She plucked another sliver of aether out of the bag and burned it.

The monster ran in her direction.

Now the aether chose to be finicky?

She darted back toward where Vaughn had been. The monster started slow, but as it ran after her, it picked up speed. Soon, its enormous feet were shaking the ground, and for every five of her steps, its long legs took one, gaining on her far too quickly for comfort.

She passed two more bloodgiants lying motionless on the ground, but the last was still searching the area for Vaughn. Its eyes lit on her instead as she ran past.

"What's wrong?" she shouted, zigzagging across the area and then doubling back. The creature, despite all other indications of intelligence, followed her exactly, losing momentum as it slowed to turn. Apparently, coming up with the idea of cutting off her path was a hair *too* intelligent.

"I'm out of arrows!" a voice yelled back.

Great.

"I have an idea," he said. "Make it chase you!"

"Already doing that, genius!"

Another crash, another curse. "Just split—opposite side—try to aim for the edge—and then—boom—crash—"

"Got it!" she said before he could finish his scattered thought. She could see where he was going with it. It was no sure thing—but in lieu of another option—

He reappeared, and Ivana also let go of her aether, though it didn't seem to be doing any good. They took off in opposite directions along the steep edge of the plateau.

Ivana's bloodgiant thundered after her, and Vaughn's after him. They both skidded and turned. The bloodgiants followed and gained speed after they, too, had turned.

Ivana swerved to avoid Vaughn in the middle, and she stopped short, rolled to the side to survey the situation—

The bloodbane were headed toward each other, but they weren't going to crash.

She scrambled up a boulder and hurled herself onto the back of her bloodgiant as it passed.

It bellowed and reached around to try to grab her off its back, staggering dangerously close to the edge of the cliff, but its thick arms weren't quite long enough to reach her.

Vaughn waved his hands at his bloodgiant, and it ignored its spinning and thrashing comrade and headed straight toward him—and into the bloodbane Ivana rode.

She flung herself off as the bloodgiants crashed into each other, a sudden tangle of crashing arms and flashing claws as the two bloodgiants turned their attention toward either freeing themselves from or wrestling one another.

They staggered toward her, and she twisted and inched out of the way—

Just before the two of them thrashed themselves right over the edge of the cliff.

Her ankle caught in the tangle and dragged her over the edge with them.

Chapter Eleven

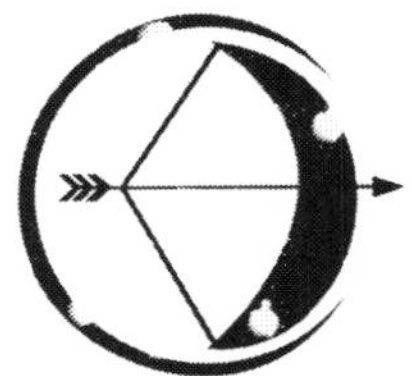

Homecoming

Vaughn hurled himself toward the edge of the cliff just as Ivana disappeared from view.

His heart leapt in his chest. “Ivana!” he shouted. *No, no, no!*

He looked over the edge—only to see her plastered against the side of the cliff about fifteen feet down, one hand grasping a tangle of thorny brambles struggling to life through a fissure in the crumbling rock face, and the toe of one boot tenuously braced against a narrow ledge. Bloody streaks followed the trail of her other hand, the fingers of which were pressed up against the rock, as if trying to find a way to dig in, and her other foot dangled over the open air.

Her face was pale, and her eyes roved the cliff face, no doubt looking for holds that would give her better stability.

It wasn't a completely vertical face, but it was close enough. There were spots where she might be able to climb, either up or down—which was much farther—but given the way that her arm was shaking as she clenched the brambles, he doubted she could manage either.

And if she fell...it was too far to survive.

He swore. "Don't move!" He had rope in his pack, which was still in the shelter, so he ran to retrieve the pack.

She was still there by the time he got back, and, thankfully, hadn't tried to move. He uncoiled the rope and tied one end to a boulder that one of the bloodgiants had thrown nearby. He then tossed down the other end to her.

She pressed her forehead against the rock face. Then she grabbed the rope with her free hand.

She tightened her hold on the rope with one hand and let go of the brambles to grab it with the other, then snaked the rope around her arms. "Brace the rope," she said, her voice hoarse.

He scrambled back and took hold of the rope, just in case.

She heaved herself backward so she could brace her feet against the rock. Together, she climbed, and he pulled, until she was close enough to grab. He tugged her up over the edge, and she immediately tried to stand.

She staggered, and he caught her and pulled her away from the edge.

Sometime along the way, the sky had lightened. The sun hadn't fully risen, but the plateau was no longer shrouded in complete darkness.

She stood there for a moment, her hands gripping the sleeves of his shirt, his own hands on her waist, steadying her.

Her arms were shuddering.

"Sit down and rest for a minute," he said. "They're all gone."

She didn't move. Instead, she muttered, "Burning skies, I'm out of shape."

It was a ridiculous, absurd statement. They had been darting from place to place and fighting for hours—and she had had to dangle by a thorn bush before having to haul herself up over a cliff edge with bloody hands—

He wanted to laugh. He wanted to cry.

Instead, he spread his hands on her waist and said, "I don't know. You still seem pretty shapely to me."

Silence. She lifted her head to look at him. "Really? *That's* the best you've got?"

He looked down at her—and then grinned.

And she laughed. Not a wry or dark chuckle. But a full-throated, full-bodied laugh.

He had heard her laugh like that only once before.

It affected him no differently than it had before.

His arms drew her against his chest almost of their own volition, and she collapsed against him while she continued to laugh. Then the laughter took on the manic edge of over-exhaustion. He himself felt as though he were ready to keel over, so he could relate.

But he didn't allow himself to collapse. He let her cling to him until she stopped laughing. Then she stood there, her entire body trembling.

She had never let him hold her like this before. He didn't think it would be her choice to now, if it weren't that she was using him as a support to stay upright. Stubborn, as usual.

Frankly, he'd rarely held any woman like this. It was too intimate, in all the *wrong* ways.

A year and a half of distance had done nothing to lessen what he felt for this woman—both physically and beyond.

But it was much easier to think about the former than the

latter, so he enjoyed it while he had it.

"Vaughn," she said.

"Mmm..."

"If we don't find what you're looking for, I'm going to kill you for dragging me into this."

He was certain she was kidding, but he couldn't help but feel alarmed. He pulled back to look at her face. "Uh..."

"Figuratively speaking, of course."

"Well. That's an improvement over the last time we traveled together, I suppose."

She flashed him a more Ivana-like smile—a wry smile that didn't reach her eyes. And yet, he detected a hint of mischievousness flickering across her face.

Gods, he wanted her as badly as he ever had.

He couldn't help but look at her lips; she couldn't help but see.

Yet she didn't pull away, and he couldn't help but wonder if she still wanted him as well.

The insane urge to laugh bubbled up in him, probably much as it had her earlier. They were standing on a cliff, surrounded by the dead bodies of bloodgiants, exhausted and battered, and *that* was what he thought about?

If ever there were a bad time, this was it.

He let go of her, and her legs immediately collapsed. He caught her and helped her to the ground.

She drew her knees to her chest and put her forehead against them.

The sun had fully risen by now, and he lowered himself gratefully to the ground next to her. After this, coming on the heels of three days of pushing themselves hard to cross this damned plateau as soon as possible—all he wanted to do was sleep.

They couldn't. They would have to force themselves down the mountain and into Ferehar. The town at the bottom had an inn, and as he recalled, it had good food and clean, comfortable accommodations. They could rest then. Maybe he would even allow an additional day, though he was all too conscious of the passage of time. If there was anything to be found, they *had* to find it and be back at the shrine by the sky-fire.

But they could take a few minutes before they descended to bandage the worst of their wounds.

He opened his pack. "I have some bindblood aether. What hurts the worst?"

Without lifting her head, she held out her hands, palms up. Her fingertips were raw and bloody, her palms scraped and lacerated in multiple places.

He sat back. And she had held on to the shrub that long? And the rope?

He shook his head. *"Out of shape."* He rinsed her hands with a bit of water from his waterskin to get the worst of the dirt out and then dried them on a towel from his pack. Unfortunately, they didn't have enough water to spare for him to thoroughly clean the wounds.

But he did have some salve; they had come prepared for treating minor injuries. So he crushed a bit of the bindblood aether and sprinkled it in, mixing it up and rubbing it on her hands and fingers. He then wrapped both palms with clean bandages several times—though he had to leave her fingers free. She'd have to have use of her hands.

Hopefully, the aether would work quickly and wouldn't give her hallucinations instead. Usually, the salve was good enough as a focus to prevent that.

When he was done, she lifted her head and draped her arms over her knees instead, letting her hands dangle in the air to dry. "Thank you," she said.

"Anything else?"

"I hurt all over. But mostly, I'm exhausted."

"I know. But we're going to have to try to reach the bottom today. Given that we just had to fight off five bloodgiants, I'm not sure it's wise to stay another night in the shelter."

"No. Certainly not." She nodded toward his pack. "Also, your qixli is glowing again."

He sighed and pulled it out.

"Vaughn, it's Danton," a tinny voice said as soon as he had it between his hands. "I've been trying to get a hold of you."

"Sorry. Bad timing."

Danton laughed. "Were you busy with a woman?"

Ivana smirked, and Vaughn rolled his eyes. "*No*. What do you need?"

"I'm almost back to Marakyn, but I heard from Yaotel. Don't know what he's been up to, but he wants an update. Couldn't get a hold of you himself."

He glanced at Ivana. He had yet to tell her why *Yaotel* wanted him to go to Ferehar. "About ready to descend into Ferehar from the plateau, so I don't have an update for him yet."

"I figured. While I have you—watch out for bloodbane acting strange. The few I've seen have been heading single-mindedly toward Weylyn City—and destroying anything in their path that they think might stop them. And then at Weylyn City itself, there were dozens of them swarming around, but not attacking."

Vaughn frowned. "You mean, swarming around, sort of like at Gan Barton's estate?"

"Exactly like that." He paused. "Anyway, I just wanted to warn you not to rely on old assumptions about bloodbane. If they're being controlled again..."

"Right," Vaughn said. Would have been nice to know that yesterday. "Thanks."

Vaughn slipped the qixli back into his pack. "You heard all

that?"

She nodded, her lips pressed together…was that a glare?

He spread his hands. "It's not my fault! How was I supposed to know bloodbane were acting strange?"

She jerked her head and grunted, as if not completely convinced but willing to let it go. "I thought the crazy bug lady was dead," she said.

"She is. Was? But I thought it was more that corpse-thing that was controlling the bloodbane."

She raised an eyebrow. "'Corpse-thing'?"

He shrugged. "Just what I always thought of it as in my head."

She snorted. "I think you need a better name. But didn't you say you saw another one?"

He shuddered, his mind returning to the room under the temple where he had seen the inanimate body of another of those things hooked to the wall like a limp sack. "Yes. Looked like they were trying to make them somehow. But it also sounded like somehow the crazy bug lady—which, by the way, is also a fantastic name"—she eyed him, but the corner of her mouth twitched—"was somehow a part of it."

"So if they succeeded…"

There was silence as they both considered the implications.

It might mean the Conclave had another of Danathalt's Banebringers under their control. Possibly more corpse-things. And, consequentially…all those bloodbane?

The Conclave had threatened to slaughter the Banebringers in their care if the king didn't essentially cede power to them, so perhaps it shouldn't have been so unbelievable that they were gathering an army of bloodbane. But what did they intend on doing with it? And how far did their reach stretch if they were drawing bloodbane this far from Weylyn City?

Yet it aligned with what the Watchman had said about

bloodgiants coming down off the plateau. Maybe the bloodgiant, after having seen Vaughn and Ivana, viewed them as a threat to whatever call had been implanted in their brains.

Ivana pushed herself to her feet, steadier than before, and limped over to the edge of the cliff. She looked out over it into the land beyond.

Vaughn joined her.

The northern reaches of Ferehar stretched out far below, clearly visible under a cloudless sky. "Been a long time since I've seen that sight," he murmured, more to himself than Ivana.

He eyed her. Her face was inscrutable.

She stirred. "What does Yaotel want you here for?"

He chose the easiest explanation. "Basic reconnaissance," he said. "There've been rumors that Ferehar has become unstable now that Gildas is gone. Yaotel wants confirmation of that."

She raised an eyebrow. "And what does he intend to do with this information?"

Vaughn ran a hand back and forth through his hair. "I suppose that depends on what I find." A partial truth.

He felt her eyes on him. She wasn't someone you could dissemble with. He'd have to explain it eventually.

He *really* didn't feel like doing that right now.

Thankfully, she turned away. "Then let's go get this over with."

Chapter Twelve

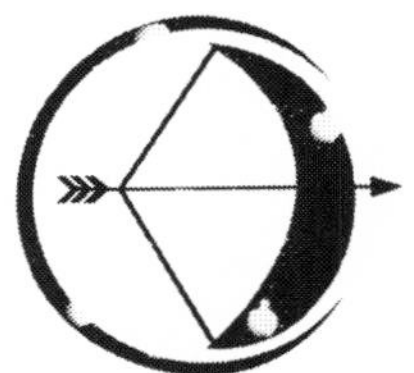

A Moment of Rest

Vaughn and Ivana picked their way down with no further incidents and arrived at the inn in Calqo mid-morning.

The innkeeper surveyed them critically as they stumbled in, but he didn't seem surprised at their rather ragged state. "Had a bit of trouble?"

"An understatement," Vaughn said. "Bloodgiants. Barely escaped."

The innkeeper rubbed at the stubble on his chin. "You're lucky. It's been particularly bad lately."

There was that observation again. Vaughn exchanged a glance with Ivana. "By 'lately', you mean..."

"Last month or so. Last group that came through brought some corpses with them." He glanced once at Ivana and then squinted at Vaughn more closely. "I've been telling people headed up from this side not to bother, even the larger caravans."

"The southern pass through Donia is a long detour to take."

The innkeeper grunted. "That's why most of 'em don't listen. What's so important for you to make the trip this way?"

Ivana put her hand on the small of Vaughn's back and pressed against it gently, as though she were rubbing it. He looked at her quizzically. "Visiting family," she said, offering her feigned shy smile. "They've never met him."

Oh. Right. The same story they'd given the Watchman in Carradon.

"Coming in from Cadmyr?"

"Yes," Ivana said.

The innkeeper grunted again. "What can I do for you? Room? Hot meal? Bath? Healer?"

All of it sounded amazing. "The first three, for sure," Vaughn said to the man. "I think we'll be all right on the medical side." He couldn't remember the last time he'd let a non-Banebringer healer tend to him. The last thing he wanted was a doctor accidentally poking him or insisting they needed to let blood.

"You sure?" He eyed Ivana's bandaged hands. "The town doctor gives folks coming off the plateau who stay in my inn a discount."

"We're sure."

The innkeeper rummaged around under the counter and produced a key, which he slid across the counter. "Down the right hall, third door on the left. Room four. Lunch isn't quite ready yet, so I'll have one of the maids draw a hot bath and let you know when it's ready. The bathing room is right next to yours."

Vaughn took the key and thanked the innkeeper, and then he and Ivana headed to their room.

———

The moment the door was closed, Ivana dropped her pack and turned to Vaughn. "Stay alert," she said, her eyes darting around the room.

Vaughn had just kicked his boots off and was in the middle of a stretch. "Huh?"

"It could be nothing, but the innkeeper seemed awfully interested in our doings."

Vaughn shrugged. "Small talk." Even so, he watched while she examined every corner of the room. It didn't take long; it was a simple, cheap room, much like many of the others they had stayed at along the way. Two single mattresses on low platforms against opposite walls, a narrow rug between them, a washbasin in one corner, and a small round table in the other—and not much room for anything else.

"Don't you think you're being a bit paranoid?" Vaughn asked.

She peered out the sole window and then turned around to face him. "I'm alive because I'm a bit paranoid."

A knock sounded on the door, and after a cursory glance at Ivana, Vaughn opened it. A maid curtsied to him. "There's a bath drawn in the bathing room," she said. "At your convenience."

He inclined his head, murmured his gratitude, and shut the door.

Ivana had pulled a clean set of clothes out of her bag. "I'm going to help myself to the bath first."

He shrugged out of his shirt, plopped down on one of the mattresses, and lay back with a groan. His eyes were already closing. "Go for it."

Ivana took a bath and ate lunch—and Vaughn was still sleeping when she returned.

She sat down on the empty bed and stared at Vaughn's sleeping form. She hurt all over and she was exhausted; she wanted more than anything to sleep as well. She ought to sleep, in fact. If all went smoothly, they still had a five- or six-day journey ahead of them before they reached Eleuria, the town where she had left her father's chest.

But she found that, while her body cried out for rest, her mind was whirling, scattered, going in a dozen different directions.

Five or six days until she was within a few miles of home.

She didn't trust the innkeeper.

What if that nightmare came back when she slept?

Five or six days until home.

She shifted, trying to banish the tightness in her chest, and instead found herself rising to rummage through Vaughn's bag, looking for the journal.

She found it and propped herself up against her pillow to start from the beginning.

"Monster...monster..."

"No!"

Ivana bolted upright in bed with a gasp. She drew in several deep breaths, momentarily disoriented. The room was darker than it had been earlier, and someone had lit the two oil lamps on the brackets on the wall, though she could still see fading daylight on the horizon through the window.

She glanced around the small room. Her mother's journal was no longer in her hands; instead, Vaughn, who was sitting cross-legged on his mattress, had it open on his lap. And he was staring at her.

She clenched her teeth. It was bad enough having nightmares

about this; worse that Vaughn was here to witness it all.

He hesitated, and then he set the book aside. "Everything…okay?"

She glared at him and crawled off her mattress. It had to be close to dinner; or maybe she had missed it altogether.

Every muscle in her body shrieked as she stood, and she couldn't halt the groan that came through her clenched teeth.

Vaughn jerked his head toward the table in the corner. A covered platter rested on it. "You slept through dinner, but I took the liberty of bringing something back for you." He glanced out the window. "There're probably still some hot leftovers, if you'd prefer that, though."

She shook her head and hobbled over to the platter. "This is fine." She removed the lid. A cut of pork, onions, and a thick slice of dark honey bread. Since there was no chair in the room, she took the platter back over to her mattress, set it next to her, and started eating.

"You seem, um…"

"I hurt. Everywhere. I'm probably covered in bruises. I told you I was out of shape."

"You wrestled a bloodgiant and fell off a cliff."

She grunted. "You don't seem any worse for wear."

"I *didn't* wrestle a bloodgiant and fall off a cliff. Anyway, be thankful I don't have any open wounds that might suddenly start bleeding." He nodded toward her hands. She had had to remove the bandages to bathe, of course. They were better than they had been—significantly better, given that not even a full day had passed since Vaughn had bandaged them. The open lacerations and scrapes had mostly closed and scabbed over, leaving her hands looking whole, at least—though not healthy.

If she were being honest with herself, she knew the battering her body had taken the night before had been more than enough to cripple even the most fit person temporarily. A good night's sleep and some exercise would do wonders.

She still hated the feeling. If only she had some starleaf tincture with her. The plant wasn't native to the part of Fuilyn she had lived in, so it wasn't something she had had readily available.

Vaughn lapsed into silence and turned back to the journal while she finished eating.

But the moment she set down her fork, wiped her mouth on the napkin that had been with the platter, and set it aside, he rose from his mattress to sit next to her.

He put his hands on her shoulders and started massaging them.

She stiffened and started to pull away.

"Relax," he said. "I flatter myself that I'm rather good at this."

She wanted to protest, but even his brief ministrations supported his words, and not even half a minute had passed before she turned her back more fully to him.

He worked his way across each shoulder, then her shoulder blades, upper back, and lower back with great deftness, finding and eliminating the knots in her muscles one by one.

"You *are* exceptionally good at this," she said. She was starting to feel sleepy again. "I'm assuming you've had lots of practice."

"I confess, I have found that a massage can be a good way to relax a woman's nerves."

She snorted. "Indeed. Or a man's." She had given her own share of massages in her life. Except hers had usually ended with the recipient dead.

He didn't reply. Instead, he continued to work in silence for a few more minutes until finally, he spread his hands on her shoulders and let them rest there. "Better?"

"Much."

"You know, a salve of bindblood aether rubbed directly into

the skin would do more than loosen your muscles. If you'd like, I could—"

"I think not."

"Come now. I can be professional." He reached around and pulled her hair over her back again, letting his fingers trail across her throat and the side of her neck as he did so.

She caught herself craning her neck to one side in an invitation for him to do it again, and she snapped her head back.

She doubted his words, but she also doubted herself. His suggestion was far more appealing than she wanted to admit, and not because the bindblood aether would heal her, rather than bring temporary relief.

"No," she said firmly.

He stood up and sat back down on his own bed. He looked into the lamplight for a moment, and then back at her. "The offer stands," he said softly, and then he gave her a cockeyed grin, snuffed out the lamp closest to him, and lay back down on his bed, his eyes closed.

She frowned. She wasn't certain which offer he was referring to, and she was positive he meant it that way.

A banging on their door woke Vaughn with a start.

Ivana sat up in her bed, and Vaughn stumbled to his feet, bleary-eyed. "Hold on!" he snapped, pulling his shirt on.

He opened the door to find the innkeeper standing there in his nightclothes, holding a lantern. He bowed nervously. "Ah, pardon the interruption, Dal—"

Vaughn squinted against the sudden light. "Pardon the interruption?" he growled. "It's the gods-cursed middle of the night!"

The innkeeper fumbled for words. "I, ah..."

"Oh, for Yathyn's sake, man," a voice said from behind him,

and then another taller man pushed passed him. The innkeeper himself scurried away, as if relieved to have discharged this duty. "Dal, I'm going to ask you to come with us," the tall man said.

Vaughn's instincts went on high alert. He backed away, hoping Ivana had some trick up her sleeve. "I'm sorry...why? What seems to be the problem?" He scanned this second man; he wasn't wearing a Watch uniform, so whatever this was, it couldn't be official...at least not Watch official.

The man pasted a smile on his face, but his jaw jumped. "No problem, no problem. We just need to ask some questions."

Vaughn caught a glimpse of the hilt of a sword underneath the man's cloak.

Questions be damned. This man could be a Hunter or he could be some other ruffian up to no good. Either way, this meant trouble, and they were cornered.

He bumped into the wall and felt a breeze waft across the back of his neck.

The man looked at the window, which Vaughn suspected was now open behind him. In fact, he suspected that it had been opened before he had even reached the door. With the entire room now in view, he noted that their bags and both pairs of their boots were gone—along with Ivana.

"The innkeeper said there was a woman with you. Where is she?" the man asked, continuing to eye the window.

Vaughn shrugged, feigning nonchalance. "Who knows? I don't keep track of the whores I hire. She got paid. Must have left."

The story blatantly contradicted what they had told the innkeeper upon arrival, but there was a chance this second man didn't know that.

Indeed, he narrowed his eyes at Vaughn and jerked his head in dismissal. "Doesn't matter. It's you I need. Please come with me, Dal, and let's not make trouble."

Vaughn flicked his eyes toward the washbasin, burned aether from his blood, and drew the water out of the pitcher in a silent trickle to gather it in a hovering blob above the man's head. "Yeah," he said to the man. "I think I'm going to decline on both points."

And then he simultaneously let go of the aether controlling the water and burned more aether to turn himself invisible.

The entire contents of a pitcher of water splashed down onto the man's head. He shouted, spluttered, and drew his hidden blade. He charged Vaughn—

But it was too late. Vaughn had already heaved himself out of the window.

Someone brushed against his arm once he was all the way through, and he recoiled, but Ivana's voice came out of the darkness.

"It's me," she hissed. A bag and a pair of boots fell to the ground out of thin air. "Grab your things and run."

He didn't hesitate—didn't even stop to put on his boots. He just yanked on his pack, grabbed his boots, and, still invisible, sprinted down the road.

A man's scream pierced the air behind him, but he didn't stop. He ran until he had left the last of the town buildings behind, and then some—and then he dove into a ditch. He sat there for a moment, panting, and then poked his head over the side of the ditch. No sign of pursuit. Now he just had to find Ivana.

He closed his eyes and strained his ears, listening for anything—the scuff of a boot on the hard-packed dirt road, heavy breathing—

"You might as well put your boots on now," a voice said in his ear.

He bit his tongue to keep from yelping in surprise. Ivana

appeared next to him. He also let go of his invisibility.

"What in the abyss was *that*?" he whispered.

She frowned, looking back toward the town. "Too coincidental, that's what." She watched Vaughn as he pulled his boots on and waited until he had laced them up to drop her casual suggestion. "And I think we should avoid inns for the time being."

Vaughn groaned and threw himself onto his back in the ditch. "I'm never going to sleep again, am I?" They'd finally come back into semi-civilized lands and he *still* couldn't sleep in a real bed each night?

The flat terraces of Fereharian farmland stretched out behind them and on the other side of the road. The hilly terrain and rocky soil made farming many crops a struggle in this part of Ferehar, but as they drew closer to the river that ran from the Fereharian mountains to the sea, easier irrigation meant more arable land—and even more settlements.

As long as they stayed on the road that paralleled the mountains and ran straight through Cohoxta, they ought to find a place to stay indoors each night, even were it only a villager's barn. And indoors would be preferable—because the main road from northern Ferehar to the capital was replete with rocky hills and cliffs on the eastern side that could easily shelter bloodbane.

"Who was it who wanted to take this trip so badly?" Ivana pointed out.

Vaughn threw a hand over his eyes. He hadn't. Not originally.

"We can shelter near villages for safety," Ivana said. "The last thing I want to do is avoid people only to be set upon by bloodbane. I'm not against sneaking into someone's barn. But we should stay out of sight. We don't know if that man, whatever he wanted with you, will continue looking for you."

Well, there was that. But it meant no hot meals, hot baths, soft beds...

He sighed. There was no use arguing. She was probably right. She usually was. "When we get to your town," he said, "we'll have to find somewhere to use as a base. I do have to do *something* for Yaotel while I'm here."

"We can stay in the inn when we get there."

Thank the gods. "So you didn't kill him?" he asked bluntly.

Her forehead wrinkled. "What? Why in the abyss would you think I killed him?"

"I mean, besides the obvious?"

She scowled at him. "A murder in a tiny town like that would have attracted far more attention than our escape."

"I heard a scream."

"I slammed the window on his fingers," she said.

"Oh. Well. That'd do it."

"We need to move. Our best defense now is getting as far away from here as quickly as possible."

"That I can agree with."

Chapter Thirteen

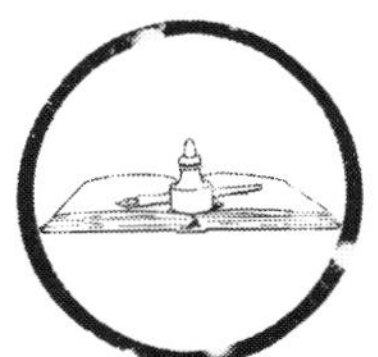

History in the Making

It was a beautiful spring night—not too hot yet, but past the time when the nights were still chilly. Perfect for a leisurely walk with Driskell's soon-to-be fiancé.

He was having a hard time enjoying it.

"You're quiet tonight," Tania said, nudging him in the ribs.

He looked over at her. Burning skies, how he wished he could tell her everything that had transpired the past couple of weeks. He wanted her opinion on it all. But he couldn't. Not a peep. Even more so than usual. "It's just been a hectic couple of days," he said.

She slid her hand into his. "I know. I've hardly seen you."

He squeezed her hand and then let go. "Not here," he admonished.

She laughed and rolled her eyes. "Driskell, I swear on Temoth herself. *No one* believes our relationship is strictly platonic."

"It isn't proper until we're officially betrothed," he insisted.

"Speaking of which..."

"I just want everything to be perfect." Of course, it wouldn't *truly* be a surprise. They'd been talking about marriage ever since Driskell had taken the position with the Ri. They'd been teasing at it even longer.

She stopped and turned to face him, laying slender fingers against his cheek. "And I just want to be with you."

"It won't be long," he said. And it wouldn't be. He'd already received her parents' blessing. His own parents heartily endorsed the union. He'd been arranging it for months, and he wouldn't be hurried along. Not even by those soft fawn brown eyes staring up at him now, or the lower lip protruding slightly—playfully.

He tapped her nose. "I promise."

She heaved an exaggerated sigh. "You have it all planned out on a chart, don't you?"

He coughed. "What? That's ridiculous." He did.

She grinned, as if she knew he was lying. "Come on. My mother will be wondering what's keeping us."

Tania's father, Lasryn, greeted Driskell with a warm clasp of the arms, and her mother, Kiva, ushered them into the kitchen with her usual warm hospitality.

"Dinner smells delicious, Da," Driskell said to Kiva. "Divine, even."

She flicked a towel at him but seemed pleased all the same, modestly smoothing a few stray hairs back into her slicked down, short-coifed hair. "Flattery will get you nothing but help with clean-up."

Driskell smiled. He always helped clean up.

And he always enjoyed dinner with Tania's family. He had met her when his parents had sent him to High Mount Academy—the prestigious boarding school in Marakyn—for further education at age sixteen. She, too, had attended classes at the school, except that her family lived in Marakyn, so she didn't technically "board" there.

The first day of a shared astronomy class, their teacher had engaged the students in a verbal contest to test their prior knowledge of the subject. Driskell and Tania had been the last two students standing. As the questions had become more difficult, Tania had seemed to take great delight in not only answering the questions correctly, but in answering them in words laced with double-entendre. Though Driskell had ultimately won the teacher's contest, he'd felt he had lost whatever secondary contest Tania had started between just the two of them—he stammering over his answers near the end, his cheeks hot, and she looking at him under lowered eyelashes, obviously more and more amused.

Far from offended, he had been instantly smitten by her combined intelligence, wit, and charm. The next day, she'd discovered he was far from home and invited him over to her house for dinner. He'd quickly became part of their family; he now saw them more than he saw his own.

So he settled easily down at the dinner table, surrounded by not only her father and mother, but her two younger sisters and one younger brother, her widowed great-grandmother, and tonight, an uncle, an aunt, and three cousins.

It was noisy, delicious, and a welcome distraction from the burden of silence he was carrying.

At least, it was a distraction until the younger children

finished dinner and scampered off to find other amusement under the watchful eye of Grandma Aya, at which point Tania's Uncle Dayon tossed down his napkin, leaned back in his chair with a groan, patted his protruding stomach, and declared, "I saw that Xambrian down on the fifth tier today."

Driskell's heart sank. *Uh-oh.*

"Funny-looking man," Dayon added.

Xambrian, Driskell thought.

Lasryn nodded. "Can't believe they let him on the temple tier. I'm sure the priests were thrilled."

"There were some dark looks, I'll give you that—and not just from the priests," Dayon said. "The Xambrian gave 'em right back."

"Mezzo," Driskell said, and then flushed as they turned to look at him. "Uh...his name is Mezzo. Ambassador Mezzo."

Dayon stroked his goatee and eyed Driskell. "That's right. You must have a good bit of interaction with him."

"Well, I wouldn't say a *good* bit..." Driskell stammered.

"What were they thinking, letting him come here?" Dayon asked. "You must have some insight. Everyone's been talking about it."

Why in the abyss had Driskell drawn attention to himself?

"Uncle," Tania chided. "You know Driskell can't talk much about his work. He's in a position of confidence."

"He's practically family, Tania," her Aunt Telmi said, winking at Driskell. "Surely, he can share *something.*"

Tania gave him an apologetic look, and he shook his head.

This wasn't unusual. The information he had was just unusually sensitive. He was afraid to say anything lest he say more than he ought. "The position of Ambassador for Xambria is still on the books," he said to Dayon. "It's only been recently that we haven't had one."

Dayon grunted. "*Recently.* Been as long as I can remember, and good riddance." He raised a finger. "And don't mistake me: It's not that I care what those idiot priests at the temple think about it. It's that it just isn't right. We're *Donian,* not Xambrian." He pounded the table. "I always thought our Ri seemed a reasonable man, but it seems he's taken leave of his senses. What next, an alliance with demonspawn?"

Driskell narrowly saved himself from choking on his wine.

"I will say," Telmi said, "given the negative reaction of the temple here, I'm a bit concerned about how Weylyn City might respond. I hope having this ambassador doesn't cause more trouble than it's worth."

And then everyone turned to look at Driskell. Tania's mother, father, uncle, aunt—the only one who wasn't watching for some reaction was Tania, who was biting her lip, no doubt feeling sorry for Driskell being put on the spot like this.

"I have full confidence in the Ri's ability to navigate this situation," Driskell said.

"Ha ha!" Dayon slapped Driskell's back so hard his spectacles slipped down his nose a bit. "That's a line if ever I heard one."

Kiva frowned at her brother. "Dayon, I think you've had too much to drink. Driskell, would you help me clear the table?"

"Of course, Da," Driskell said, flashing her a grateful smile and re-adjusting his spectacles.

As he left the dining room with an armful of plates, Driskell heard Lasryn say, "Leave the lad alone, Dayon. It can't be easy for him navigating this disaster, either."

"I'm sorry, dear," Kiva said to Driskell once the two of them were out of the room. She took the plates from Driskell and placed them in the sink, already full of water. "I know Dayon put you in a difficult spot. I'll have a talk with him."

"It's all right," Driskell said. "I know everyone's eager to know what's going on."

Kiva glanced at him out of the corner of her eye. "Not mere curiosity, dear. They're frightened, too. There's been so much change in Setana lately, and now this..." She shook her head. "It all seems too much, too quickly." She hesitated, glanced back out into the dining room, and then lowered her voice. "And there've been rumors, Driskell. There was an opinion piece in the newssheet just this morning saying we ought to leave the Empire!"

"I saw it," he said. "But forgive me, Da, that's hardly a new or even uncommon opinion."

Her voice lowered again, so Driskell had to lean closer to hear her. "I hate Setana as much as the next person, Driskell. And talk like that is all fine when it's a bunch of grumpy old men shouting into the wind. But now..." A cup slipped out of her soapy hand and into the water. "I fear it may be more than talk. And that makes me afraid for all of us."

Driskell was spared from having to respond by a knock on the front door.

"Would you get that, dear?" Kiva asked.

Driskell put down the bowl he was drying and opened the door.

Standing there was a young man Driskell didn't recognize. He was tall, lanky, and had the warm beige skin of someone from one of the central Setanan regions.

The man inclined his head and then shifted from foot to foot. "I'm looking for a Dal Driskell? I was told if he wasn't in his room he might be here." He craned his neck to look at the outside of the rowhouse. "Assuming *here* is the right place."

"I'm Driskell," Driskell said, startled. "What can I do for you?"

"I, um, I'm really sorry about this." He brushed hair out of his eyes and then spoke as if he were reciting something he had memorized. "Lady Nahua sends her deepest apologies for calling on you during your off-duty hours, but she needs you urgently back up at the government tier."

Driskell eyed the man. "And you are?"

"Oh!" He rummaged around in his pocket, drew out Tanuac's seal, and handed it to Driskell. "Danton. They sent me because, well..." He gave a grimace. "You'll see soon enough."

Danton. Danton. Driskell stared at him. Danton? The Danton Yaotel had contacted through that...device?

Another Banebringer. Yet he seemed so...*normal.*

Driskell swallowed and pocketed the seal. "All right. Hold on."

He ducked back inside and gave his apologies to Tania and her family, and then he went silently with the Banebringer named Danton.

Seven heads swiveled toward Driskell and Danton when they entered the conference room—a place Driskell was beginning to dread having to enter. It seemed every time he was here lately, something else dire or dangerous was happening.

Given the state of the occupants of the room, tonight seemed no different.

Yaotel sat alone on the one side of the table. Three of the four Gan were seated on the other side of the table as though it were some sort of inquisition. Ri Tanuac sat at his customary spot at the head, and Nahua sat next to him closer to Yaotel.

Ri Tanuac sat unmoving, his fingers folded on the table, his face perfectly schooled, and Nahua acknowledged Driskell with a brief nod before returning her attention to the table.

The fourth Gan, Gan Dillion, stood behind the chairs, as close to the wall as he could get. His arms were folded across his chest and his expression stormy. After glancing at Driskell and

Danton, his eyes went back to Yaotel—pinning him with an almost murderous gaze.

Driskell certainly hoped murder wasn't on his mind. Especially of a Banebringer.

Driskell's stomach squirmed, though their attention wasn't on him. Tanuac had had a closed meeting with the four Gan the day before; he hadn't known there would be another tonight.

Tanuac nodded to Driskell and Danton and gestured toward the table. "Dal. Please."

Danton slid into a chair next to Yaotel, and Driskell chose the seat at the other end of the table, across from Tanuac—better to see everyone's expressions. He had a feeling he was going to want to.

He then busied himself with pulling out his notebook and pencil and trying to look like he *didn't* want to slide down his chair and onto the floor.

"To recap for our newest guest," Tanuac said, nodding toward Danton, "the Conclave is moving troops toward our northern border and demanding we turn over the Xambrian ambassador, or at the least, eject him. While they've stipulated no consequences if we refuse, I believe their intent is clear enough. At their current pace, we estimate the vanguard will be at our border in fewer than three weeks. How long they'll give us after that to comply with their demands is anyone's guess. My hope is that their primary goal is to bluff or frighten us into submission. If, however, they truly intend to attack, we're already out of time."

Tanuac cast his gaze around the room, meeting the eyes of each Gan in turn. Herne leaned forward with keen interest. Dillion pressed his lips together. Beatha and Fiacra were both closed, cautious.

"Our weeks of arguing about what to do about the Conclave problem have come to a head," Tanuac continued. "If we eject

Ambassador Mezzo, the Conclave will likely be mollified—for now. But Mezzo has also made it clear that if we eject him, we also reject the Xambrian offer of an alliance when the time is right.

"Unfortunately, that time is not yet right. The Xambrian alliance will only be helpful once the Xambrians themselves attack, and they have made it clear that they won't do so until all the outer regions agree. On that note, Venetia is seriously considering the offer, and though Fuilyn is hesitant, we believe they will come around." He cleared his throat. "Ferehar, on the other hand, is a problem. It is, as you might imagine, of the most strategic importance to this alliance. Due to its geographic proximity to Xambria, Ferehar's failure to comply would mean another flank Xambria would have to defend when they move their troops through the pass. They are, therefore, insistent that Ferehar *must* agree, even if, for instance, Venetia did not. Unfortunately, Ri Airell of Ferehar has made his loyalties clear, though he's sent no official word yet." He glanced at Yaotel. "We are...working on that problem."

Driskell studied Tanuac's face. Driskell hadn't been privy to what solutions they were bandying about to the Ferehar problem, and he was curious as to how they thought they would force Ri Airell to submit—and how Yaotel's Ichtaca could help.

"I know you've been divided over what the best course of action should be, and this new development has swayed some of you to want to resign ourselves to staying under the Conclave's thumb, lest we overextend ourselves. But as you were informed yesterday, the Xambrians aren't our only potential allies."

As he spoke, the four Gan's positions and expressions shifted. Herne now leaned forward in his chair, almost eager. Beatha's eyes shifted back and forth between Yaotel and Nahua, her posture tense. Fiacra looked cautiously intrigued, while Dillion's scowl deepened.

Driskell noted all of this on his notepad—and the silence that followed Tanuac's speech gave him time to do a quick sketch of each Gan.

Driskell then glanced at Nahua. Her hands were gripping the edge of the table, her knuckles white. It was the first sign she had shown of any hesitation or trepidation about the course of action they were proposing.

"I've asked Dal Yaotel to come here in good faith tonight to provide a brief demonstration of what they have to offer. It's my hope that after you see for yourselves what he and his kind can offer, it might change the minds of those of you who were initially set against this option."

Herne burst out, "Well, get on with, Your Excellency. I've heard enough." He turned toward Yaotel eagerly. "What have you to offer, Dal? Let's see it. Anything that we can use to grind these dogs into the mud would be welcome to *me*."

Dillion's gaze turned toward Herne temporarily, his lip curled in a sneer.

But as Yaotel drew out his leather case, even Dillion dropped his crossed arms to watch more closely.

Yaotel looked at Driskell. "Dal Driskell, at your leave, may I demonstrate some of our medical advances?"

Driskell swallowed, and for the second time held out his hand to the Banebringer.

And for the second time, Yaotel went through the demonstration that he had given Tanuac, Nahua, and Driskell. The only difference was that this time, instead of demonstrating the mirror-device—though he showed it to them—he let his associate, Danton, show off what he could do.

Which was pretty incredible.

He made the entire room look like a desert, changed his own

appearance temporarily into that of Gan Herne—to Herne's utmost delight—and showed them a smaller mirror-device that produced light on command.

Danton set the device aside and the light faded.

Driskell swept his eyes over the rest of the observers, gauging their reactions.

All four Gan were staring at the two Banebringers, wide-eyed. Even Dillion's mask of hatred had slipped into astonishment.

Driskell felt strangely smug that he had already seen some of this, and thus was able to, for once, retain a more unaffected air than all of them combined.

Tanuac took back up the narrative. "This is only a small sampling of what Yaotel and his associates can offer us. He's given me a few more demonstrations from a few other associates who are in Marakyn with him, which I would be happy to detail for you. Suffice it to say, I believe they could give us the edge we need to hold the Conclave off—and ultimately win an entire war."

Dillion made a small noise—a grunt, a sniff—Driskell wasn't sure—but it drew Tanuac's attention. "Gan Dillion. You have a comment?"

He rose to his feet, pointedly ignoring the Banebringers on the other side of the table. "Your Excellency, with all due respect, this alliance cannot become common knowledge just yet." He waited for Tanuac to acknowledge his statement with a nod, and then he continued. "Then what good will these *demonspawn* do us in repelling a Conclave attack? You told us yesterday that one well-trained Banebringer of the right 'profile' could be worth a hundred foot soldiers, but how can they be deployed without alerting the rest of the army?"

Yaotel spoke. "May I, Your Excellency?"

Tanuac waved him on.

"Those who would use magic for direct combat couldn't be,

right now," Yaotel said. "However, with misdirection, I have healers who can support combatants and more quickly return injured soldiers to the field. Also, in a relatively short period and with enough concentrated effort and resources, we can provide better weapons and better armor. And we have tools at our disposal that will give your defending force an advantage that will almost certainly ensure a short-term victory—and with it, the additional time you need."

Dillion glared at Yaotel but sat down.

"They offer us all of this in exchange for the small favor of providing sanctuary for them in Marakyn," Tanuac said.

Dillion shook himself. "Small favor," he chided. "Tanuac, you'll doom us all, letting them in here. What if the Conclave finds out? They're already threatening our borders merely for welcoming a Xambrian."

Herne stood, and his chair knocked over backward. "Damn the Conclave," he said, rubbing his hands together. "I don't need to deliberate. Let's send *those* demonspawn back to the abyss where they belong and take back our country."

Fiacra also stood, but with less dramatics. Her eyes were fixed on Yaotel and his friends. "You truly support this alliance, Your Excellency?" she asked softly.

Tanuac's face grew grim. "Setanan ways were forced upon us two centuries ago. Few of us have forgotten that we are not originally Setanan, but it likewise seems that few remember what that really means. I have no wish to waste Donian lives in needless bloodshed, but if, with the Xambrians and the Ichtaca, we can repel Setana once and for all, this may be a chance fate has handed us, and we would be foolish to spurn it heedlessly."

"I will not ally with demonspawn," Dillion spat, trembling.

Danton flinched, and he looked down at his hands, his jaw jumping. Yaotel, however, remained composed.

"Well," Tanuac said. "We know Dillion and Herne's opinions haven't changed. Fiacra? Beatha?"

Driskell watched Beatha in particular. The lands she oversaw contained Ipsylanti, the largest and most populous Donian city. The support of Ipsylanti and its resources would be critical to any war effort.

"When I said we needed allies," Beatha said slowly, "I didn't know it would be Xambrians and Banebringers. The latter, in particular, makes me uncomfortable." She stiffened. "But I've never had any love for the Conclave, and the idea of not only having to live with their temple in our midst but under their thumb as our rulers makes me sick. After seeing what these Ichtaca have to offer, I find myself agreeing that this may well be what could tip this in our favor."

Everyone looked at Fiacra. She was silent for a moment. Her eyes roved back and forth between each of the Banebringer faces, and then Tanuac, and Nahua, and then back on Yaotel again.

She swallowed. "We might muster enough troops to repel the initial force the Conclave has sent our way. Certainly, we would have a chance to do so in Marakyn, or"—she nodded toward Beatha—"even Ipsylanti. But my lands will be overrun. And what then? When the Conclave sends its next, larger army? Can Donian forces alone fight against the combined might of Setana? I think not." She pressed her lips together. "If His Excellency will not eject the Xambrian, then this may be our only hope." She lowered her eyes to the table. "I will accept the wisdom of our Ri in this matter."

Tanuac nodded. "We must decide, or the decision will be made for us. Do any of you require further deliberation, or are your answers tonight firm?" His eyes swept the room, but they settled on Dillion.

"I believe we are decided, Your Excellency," Herne said, and none of the other Gan contradicted him.

"Very well. Dillion, your objection is noted, but in this case, overruled. I will accept the majority opinion." He stood. "Whether you agree or not, I expect complete discretion on all of your parts; this is not to be public knowledge yet." He looked at Yaotel. "Dal, we'll work out the details in the coming days, but we accept your offer of aid in exchange for protection of any Ichtaca who will officially apply for sanctuary in Marakyn." He nodded toward Driskell. "Driskell will draw up the paperwork."

He would? He didn't think any such paperwork existed. He hid a grin. Which meant he would also have to create the paperwork. Tania thought he was strange for enjoying such challenges, but there was something about seeing all those little boxes lined up so neatly, filled in with the proper information...

Yaotel stood up, more slowly. "I'm pleased we could come to an agreement." Then, he held out an arm to Tanuac.

Tanuac looked at Yaotel's offered arm. He flicked his eyes to Nahua, and then Driskell, and then his Gan. Then he set his lips in a line and grasped the Banebringer's arm in a traditional sign of friendship.

Driskell could not tear his eyes away from the sight of their two arms clasped, both brown, but one that would bleed silver and the other, red. He had the odd feeling he was watching a turning point in history as it happened.

He wondered if it would ever be preserved for future generations, or if it would be forgotten—or erased.

Well. He supposed that depended on who won.

Chapter Fourteen

The Chest

Six days after their flight from Calqo, Ivana and Vaughn arrived in Eleuria.

Ivana had had almost four weeks to prepare for this moment, and now that she stood on the main street of the town, she didn't even know what *prepared* meant.

The trip through Ferehar itself had done less damage to her psyche than she had worried it would. Her only previous trip along that route was a blur in retrospect; it might as well have been the other side of the continent. Even the nightmares that had been haunting her had ceased.

But this...this she recognized.

The same stones paved the road, the same shops lined the street.

Indeed, the same apothecary stood on the corner, with the same sign.

Now that she had come to it, she felt...

Numb.

Well. That wasn't so bad. Numb, she could handle. It was everything else she couldn't.

Vaughn was talking to her.

"What?" she snapped.

He glanced at her, his eyebrow raised. "I said, where to now? I've never been in this town before."

She shook herself and glanced at the sun. It was only just past noon, so they had plenty of time yet. "The woman owned the apothecary on the corner," she said, pointing to the shop.

Vaughn held back, waiting for her to move first.

It took her a moment. What if the same woman really was there? What if, after all this time...the chest was there too?

Having her mother's old journal fall into her lap had done enough to unhinge her, though she had recovered well enough. What would finding her father's old chest do to her?

She locked her jaw. She had come this far. There was no turning back now.

She marched down the street, Vaughn trailing behind, and pushed open the door.

Somewhere in the back of her mind, she had expected to find the apothecary exactly as she had left it, almost fifteen years ago.

Her first hint that this might not be as easy as Vaughn hoped was that the entire shop had been remodeled. Even the counter was in a different spot. It was more spacious; rather than shelves and shelves crammed with meticulously labeled boxes and bottles, there were display cases featuring two or three ingredients or tonics at a time, arranged tastefully as though they were decorations, accompanied by lists of other available ingredients, priced by the ounce.

And the young woman who stood behind the counter, an open box and a scale in front of her, was not the same woman.

The woman looked up and then smiled. "Good morning. It's not often we see new faces around here. May I help you?"

Ivana forced her feet forward. "I'm looking for Da Patli?" The eerie similarity to the same words she had spoken so long ago coalesced inside her, sending a shudder down her spine.

The woman's brow furrowed. "I'm so sorry. Da Patli is my mother, but she gave the shop to me and my husband three years ago."

Vaughn shifted. Ivana stole one glance at him, enough to see his own brow furrow. "I see. Does she still live around here?" she asked.

The woman shook her head. "She moved back home to Weylyn with my brothers."

Weylyn. That would take far too long for Vaughn's deadline. If they had gone straight from Fuilyn, yes, but they hadn't. And in any case, she doubted Patli had taken it with her. More likely, she had tossed it long ago.

She exhaled and turned to Vaughn. "Well?"

He scratched at his beard, frustration darkening his eyes, and shook his head.

The woman leaned over the counter to catch their attention. "Is this about a tonic or medicine? She left me with a rather long list of instructions for customers who might come in looking for tonics she had custom mixed. Most of them have come in by now, but if you tell me what you need, perhaps I can help?"

Ivana hesitated. Perhaps Patli had left the chest with her daughter, in the unlikely event Ivana would return. The shop was so neat and tidy, it didn't look like Patli's daughter was the sort of person to hold on to what she would perceive as random junk.

Even so, it couldn't hurt to ask. "I realize this is a stretch. But about fifteen years ago, I left an old chest with her. I always intended to come back for it, but circumstances...changed."

Patli's daughter tapped her chin. "An old chest? Cedar? About..." She mimed the measurements with her hands. "This long, this wide?"

Ivana blinked, hardly able to believe her ears. Apparently, it *was* going to be that easy. "Yes. That sounds exactly like it."

The woman nodded. "I do have it. I was going to throw it out, but my mother insisted I keep it, just in case. It's been tucked away in the cellar for years." She gave Ivana an odd look. "Were you the one who sold her the microscope, too?"

"I... Yes, I was."

Her face lit up. "Then I have you to thank! Mama held on to that old thing for years and years, hoping to have the opportunity to sell it, and one day about seven years ago, a caravan from Donia came up this way, headed to Cohoxta. And—can you believe it—a Donian scholar was part of the group and offered to buy it off my mother! It was just enough to give her the boost she needed to start saving to move home, and three years ago, she finally managed it." She beamed at Ivana. "Never would have happened without you."

Ivana wasn't sure what to say. *My father died to finance your mother's dream?*

That didn't seem appropriate. "You stayed here?"

The woman shrugged. "I always wanted to inherit the shop, and I never minded this 'backwater' place, as Mama used to call it. I made friends, met my husband." She lowered her voice. "Though if I had known that things would be what they are now..." She shook her head. "Maybe I would have made a different decision."

Vaughn, whose attention had drifted to one of the display

cases nearby, focused again on the woman. "'What they are now'?" he asked, repeating her words back to her.

The woman shrugged. "I shouldn't complain, I know. I have it better off than most. But there've been several other shops here in Eleuria that've had to close recently. I had a woman in just the other day from one of the smaller villages. Some of the Ri's men came through and roughed up her place when she couldn't produce the taxes they wanted on demand. Took a beautiful necklace that had been passed down for generations." The woman's face flushed and her eyes flashed. "There's no call for that sort of thing. I never thought I'd say this, but that new fool in charge is worse than Ri Gildas was. He's a bully and a tyrant, and—" She twisted her apron in her hands and glanced around the shop, as if expecting to see one of the Ri's men burst out of the corner. "Listen to me, yammering on. I've let my mouth run away with me again." She cleared her throat. "Let me get that chest for you. Might take me a few minutes—I have to remember where I stashed it." She flashed a sheepish grin at Ivana. "I know it looks organized, but if you saw the cellar..." She shook her head and moved off without finishing the sentence.

Rubbing his chin, Vaughn stared after her until she disappeared into the back and then shook his head. When he turned to Ivana, the frustration on his face was gone. "I told you so. I told you!" He rubbed his hands together.

"All right," Ivana said. "There's still no guarantee that what you want is in there."

"Even so." He started pacing.

Ivana left him to his own thoughts. She drifted around the shop, letting her hand trail along some of the display cases as she went. In a few minutes, she'd have her father's chest back. Only fifteen years late.

Trepidation warred with curiosity. What was in it? Did she

want to know?

Would it answer any of the lingering questions she had about her parents?

What would it be like to read his old study notes again?

Perhaps a quarter of an hour passed before the woman returned. She set the chest on the counter. "Here you go. I'm glad to be able to give it back to its owner."

"Thank you," Ivana said. "If you ever have the chance to pass on the message, thank your mother for me, too."

"I will. Is there anything else I can do for you?"

"No. Have a good day."

It seemed such little fanfare under which to accept an anchor to her past.

She touched her sister's necklace, snugged the chest under her arm, and jerked her head at Vaughn. "Let's go."

Vaughn insisted that they rent the nicest room in the nicest inn. He assumed they would be staying in the town for at least a couple of days, and after the rather rough week they had had, he wanted *comfort*.

Ivana seemed too distracted to argue with him.

The inn was hardly a high-class establishment, but it was clean and the rooms well-furnished. It reminded him of Ivana's old inn, in fact.

"Did you copy this place when you set up your inn?" he asked once the door to the room had been shut.

"I've never been in this inn," she said, setting the chest down on a small desk.

"Oh. I thought this was where you lived."

"No. I lived in Tian, about eight miles from here."

He waited for more—why an apothecary from Eleuria had the

chest, for instance—but she didn't offer it. She had laid her hands on the top of the chest, and she was staring at it. He joined her. "Well? Are you going to open it?"

She stirred. "I have to pick the lock." She rummaged around in her bag, produced a lockpick, bent over, and set to work.

After a minute or two, there was the faintest hint of a snick.

She set the lockpick aside, took a deep breath, and opened the chest.

Ivana stared down at a pile of papers. The chest was crammed full to overflowing; her father had obviously run out of room at some point and just kept trying to shove more into it rather than buying a larger chest or organizing what was in it better.

She shook her head, smiling faintly. Typical.

Was that a fond memory? Was she smiling?

Perhaps... Perhaps there would be something good to come out of this. Perhaps she was right. Perhaps all she needed was some closure.

"So," Vaughn said. "I feel odd about rummaging through your father's things..."

She grabbed a large stack of papers and handed them to him. "Have at it. If you find any of that writing, any translations, anything about a dig...let me know."

He nodded.

She picked up the chest, set it on the floor, and settled herself down next to it.

He sat down at the desk with his papers.

And so it went, for hours.

Ivana read everything. There were a few receipts for major purchases and a haphazardly filled-out accounting ledger. But most of it was his old research notes, pages and pages of them.

The more she read, the more her chest ached. She couldn't help but wonder what life would have been like if none of it had ever happened. Where she might be right now.

Who she might be.

She flipped over a sheet of paper into a "discard" pile—at least as far as what they were looking for was concerned—and lifted another few out of the chest to reveal a bundle of folded sheets of paper, similar in size. Bits of broken wax clung to the top sheet, remnants of an old seal.

She frowned. Correspondence? She untied the string holding the pack together and laid each folded piece of paper out in a line across the floor. There were six of them. She unfolded the first.

The first line was the date of the letter, and her heart jumped into her throat. It was dated about a year after the last date in her mother's journal.

Galvyn,

I hope this letter finds you well. I hear congratulations are in order in regards to your recent marriage to Avira. I take no offense at not being invited to a wedding that didn't happen; I understand the marriage had to be quick.

You'll be sorely missed at the university. I'm still bitter at how things turned out, but I suppose it's better than hanging from a noose, yes?

I'm enclosing the first payment from our mutual associates. I hope it helps to defray some of the costs of the move and your burgeoning family—or perhaps it's Avira who is burgeoning at this point!

Forgive my levity if it's misplaced. If you have the chance, write back. I'd be interested to hear how your new posting with Lord Kadmon is going. I hear he's a mostly decent fellow—for a noble, at least.

Best regards,

V. I.

Ivana laid the letter on the floor in front of her and stared at it. Payment? Payment for what?

It sounded suspiciously shifty; she ought to know.

She shook her head, as if to fling off some sort of strange dream. The thought that her father could have been involved in something less than honorable was, well, unthinkable.

Then again, this was also the man who had been on an illegal dig with her mother, so perhaps she shouldn't make such hasty conclusions.

And about the timing of that dig...

Ivana did some mental calculations and wondered what "recent" meant. She had been born four months after the date of this letter. How recent could the marriage have been? Especially if her mother was already "burgeoning"?

Ivana reread the letter, taking special note of the comment about the lack of a wedding, and then sat back. *Burning skies. They weren't married when I was conceived.*

Why did that surprise her so much? Perhaps because it seemed so unlike her parents.

At least her father hadn't been the type to leave her mother penniless on the streets. A good man who had died for nothing, while the contemptable men who had ensured his death and the destruction of his family lived.

She gritted her teeth, and any sense that she might have found some closure by coming here was erased in a wave of bitterness.

Vaughn happened to glance her way, possibly because he hadn't heard the shifting of papers for a while.

She glanced up at him, and he raised an eyebrow at her. "Find something?"

She handed the letter up to him mutely.

He stared at the letter long enough that he must have read it more than once. "Huh," he said, handing it back to her. "That sounds promising."

"It *sounds* like my father was involved in something illegal."

"Er...well...technically, he was..."

She glared at him.

"At any rate, are there more of these? Perhaps this is related to the dig."

She blinked. Of course. Of course it was related to the dig. At least, the money might have been. Had they found something worth paying them off for? It sounded as though some sort of bargain had been struck.

"Who's 'V.I.'?"

She shrugged. "No idea." The letter was casual in form, so a friend, or perhaps someone else on the dig.

She turned back to the other five letters, and Vaughn turned back to his papers.

Now that she knew they were letters, she opened each of them and arranged them in chronological order. The one she had read had been the second in the set; the first was neatly written onto the letterhead of a solicitor and was dated two months before the second.

I am pleased to report that your appeal has been considered and accepted. All interested parties have come to an agreement I believe you will find suitable.

Given the state of your wife-to-be, an execution order has been generously stayed. In addition, in exchange for your discretion in regards to the matter uncovered at the expedition, you will receive a total sum of 50,000 setans disbursed evenly over the course of the next five years.

In return, you will agree to confinement in your home region of Ferehar for the duration of your life. You will have no contact with any parties involved in the expedition or at your former place of employment, save our mutual contact, nor with any family. Should any evidence to the contrary be discovered, the forbearance on execution will be reevaluated.

Ivana almost choked, and her head was spinning with ten thousand thoughts. The foremost of which was: 50,000 setans? 50,000 *setans*? What in the abyss had he done with all that money?

That aside, this was strong evidence that the dig had been discovered, shut down, and her father had been paid off to remain quiet about their discoveries.

She wondered now if her mother's pregnancy was an accident. Had they deliberately tried to get her with child to make their case more appealing? Would the Conclave really execute a pregnant woman?

Ivana would have said yes, but perhaps not all arms of the Conclave were equally depraved.

The final blow to what she thought she'd known was the move to Ferehar.

It hadn't been her father's attempt to support a growing family at all.

They had been forced into exile as punishment.

It was a rather strange and tenuous arrangement, like two parties pulling on a rope or balancing on a lever; if either side gave an inch, the whole thing would collapse.

The Conclave hadn't wanted what her parents had known to get out, but her mother had been pregnant, so they couldn't just execute her—perhaps the story had become public knowledge. Even the Conclave, at one point in their existence, would bow to poor public perception.

She took a deep breath and read the rest of the letters.

They were more from "V.I.," always one side of a conversation and reported enclosures of payments. The last letter also professed to enclose the final payment; there were no more letters after that.

"Well," she said. "My mother knew something, but it doesn't help with your mystery language." Once again, she handed the stack to Vaughn for his perusal.

While he read over them, she dug farther into the chest. There wasn't much left, and she presumed Vaughn had had no luck with his stacks or he would have said something.

She thumbed through the remainder, finding more of the same—old research notes and accounts, and then just to be sure, she tipped the entire chest upside down and shook it.

Something rattled.

She frowned and set it back upright. The chest was empty, but when she shook it again from side to side, the bottom slid back and forth as well.

A poorly designed false bottom. It wouldn't stop someone determined to find something, but the casual searcher might miss it.

She pried it open and set it aside. Underneath were two sheets of paper, one folded in half and the other a half-sheet upside down. She opened the one folded in half first.

She almost dropped it. It looked like a page that had been ripped out of that same journal. In a bold hand across the top, as if the person were angry or determined, was written:

SO I NEVER FORGET

Sketched beneath was her mother's promised reproduction of the tablet they had found—a text written in the mystery language, with a text of similar length in Xambrian underneath it.

She couldn't believe it. It was here. "Vaughn," she said quietly.

He turned. She held up the paper in the air facing him. "It's the next page from the journal."

His eyes widened.

He took it gingerly from her, as though it might fray into a thousand pieces if he handled it too rough.

And then he set it down on the desk, clapped his hands to his face, and laughed. "I can't believe it. I simply cannot believe it!

"We found it. It's actually here." He put a hand to his forehead. "This wasn't a colossal waste of time."

"You thought it was?"

"Of course I thought it was! This slim chance? I took what I could get, but I never expected to *find* anything!"

She sighed, but even she had a hard time suppressing a smile at his excitement.

"You can translate it now, right? *Right*?" he asked.

"It isn't a lexicon," she said. "But there's a good bit of text here. I can probably translate most of the Xambrian, and assuming the Xambrian is a translation of the mystery language on the tablet, I can then compare this text with the writing on the serpent, and hopefully there will be enough similarities that we can figure some of it out." Exactly what her mother would have done, in fact. The knowledge that thirty-three years ago, her mother had sat looking at this very paper, almost certainly trying to do the very same thing was...

Her throat tightened, and she cleared her throat. "Of course, it would be more helpful if we had more of this language, and more translations. It's always possible there is little-to-no overlap, in which case this will be essentially useless." If still fascinating. What language was it, anyway? Something ancient and long forgotten, if even the people who had originally used the shrine had felt the need to translate it into Xambrian for clarification.

A shiver went down her spine. All implications for trying to use the supposed serpent-door aside—this was a monumental discovery. Was this language the language of the people who had built the shrines to the heretic gods? Official Setanan history didn't stretch back that far. If ever it even had, the Conclave had made sure to erase anything beyond the founding of the Empire itself.

It was no wonder the Conclave had shut down the dig and destroyed what evidence they could.

She couldn't imagine keeping something like this a secret all these years. How it must have eaten away at her mother, knowing she could never speak of it.

Once again, a pang went through her—this time, the ache of loss. That she would never come to know that woman—the adventuresome woman who had risked everything to go on this expedition and summarily given up everything to keep it a secret.

The obstinate woman who had no doubt made her father squirrel away a bit of evidence—out of hope, perhaps? Hope that one day, things would change?

But it hadn't. At least not for her mother. She gritted her teeth, pushed away all thoughts of something she could never have, and focused once again on Vaughn, who had been pacing silently while she was lost in thought.

"And how long will it take you?" he asked. "We're running short on time." Naturally, Vaughn didn't seem at all uneasy by her caution that it might still all come to naught.

She shrugged. "To translate the Xambrian? A solid day of work should do it. The rest? Hard to say."

He started pacing again. "We have about six weeks until the sky-fire, and it's a two-and a-half-week trip to Marakyn, if we push hard. If you think it'll take you longer than a couple of days, we might be better off pushing on. We have time, but I'd feel more comfortable finishing up in Marakyn since it's closer to the dig site."

"I said I'd go with you to Ferehar. I didn't say I'd go with you any farther." She had no problem going on to Marakyn. Indeed, it was a perfect place to settle down for a bit while she figured out what to do next. But he was so earnest, she couldn't help it.

He froze and whirled to face her. "What? But you have to! We're so close. You can't just—" He broke off and studied her face.

She put on her best innocent maiden face and blinked at him.

"You're teasing me," he said.

"Teasing? *Me*? I said nothing that was untrue. I made no promises to go beyond Ferehar."

"But you will. I can tell. You look too innocent. You never put that façade on when you're around me."

It was discomfiting that he knew her well enough to recognize that. She allowed the tiniest of smiles to break through.

He pointed at her and grinned. "See, I knew it! You don't fool me."

She flicked her fingers at him and sighed. "Yes, fine. Whatever. We can keep going and then stop for a more prolonged stay in Marakyn."

He rubbed his hands together and continued his pacing. "Excellent."

While he continued to exalt in their victory, she looked down at the final half-sheet of paper. She flipped it over idly, wondering what else her father had hidden beneath the false bottom that was so important.

Her heart stopped.

Vaughn was still in denial. He had hardly dared hope, and as each slip of paper had held nothing pertinent, his hopes had died a little. Even the letters Ivana had uncovered, while evidence that the expedition had existed and that it had been covered up by the Conclave, had given no progress toward translating that writing.

And then there it was. The gods bless Ivana's mother, that stubborn, wonderful woman who couldn't let it go.

He turned once again to grin at Ivana and suggest a celebratory dinner and drinks, but the expression on her face was unlike anything he had ever seen there before.

Raw, naked shock.

Her face had paled. She held a half-sheet of paper in her hand, and it was trembling.

The smile slipped off his face. "Ivana?"

She didn't respond. She just stood up and stared at the slip of paper.

He moved to look over her shoulder.

It was an unlimited promissory note from the Fereharian regional bank written for 50,000 setans. At the bottom corner, on a memo line that wasn't part of the bank note itself, was written: *Dowry for Ivana and Izel.* The second name was in a different ink, as though added later.

Vaughn whistled. "He never spent it? It's all just sitting in the *bank*? And it was even meant for you, no less. *Damn!* You're rich!" Not that she needed it. She had money squirreled away all over the place from her years in a rather lucrative profession.

Even so.

But she didn't look excited or even mildly pleased. In fact, the shock on her face wasn't that of a pleasant surprise. It was that of learning that someone dear to you had suddenly died.

She looked like she was going to vomit and keel over all at the same time.

"Ivana?" he asked, putting a hand on her shoulder.

She stirred, shaking his hand off her shoulder violently, and took a step backward, the note still in her hand.

Then she turned and fled the room.

It had to be gone. It *had* to be. There was no way he had left 50,000 setans sitting in the bank…how would her mother have not *known* about it? The note was old, after all, dated right after that fifth payment. Maybe the bank had neglected to take it when he had retrieved the money.

She had to know for sure.

She marched directly into what passed for the local bank—little more than a desk with a chair at the other side, a filing cabinet, and a small vault. An older gentleman was sitting behind the desk, pen to a piece of paper, his head nodding to his chest.

She slapped the bank note down in front of him.

He jerked upright. "Wha—What? Who—oh." He cleared his throat. "Yes. What can I do for you?"

"Is this still good?"

He plucked a pair of spectacles off the desk, settled them on his face, and then squinted down at the note. "Hmm… Let's see… Hmm." He held it up to the light, turned it around, and then set it back down and slipped off his glasses. "It appears to be genuine, and there's no expiration date or assignment. So, yes, it's still good. Now, if you're looking to withdraw some of it, I can only do about a fifth here. The rest, I can write you a new note and you'll have to take it to Cohoxta to the regional bank. We don't keep that much on hand here. We're mainly for small business transactions, you see."

Ivana's head was spinning. It was all there. All 50,000 damn setans of it. Nestled away in the bank the whole time. And her mother—obviously—hadn't known about it, or she would have used it to better their lot.

The banker was still talking—rambling on about other options, such as paying a large transaction fee to have the setans brought in, but she stopped listening.

If her mother—if Ivana and her sister—had *known* about this—

She may or may not have been able to save her father. He had known about the money and had *still* demanded support from Gildas for the unborn bastard child Gildas' eldest son had sired on Ivana. It was her father's principles that had killed him.

But everything else, from then on?

Ivana, her mother, and her sister could have moved away from the scandal, somewhere nicer, and found jobs. Her mother would have never become sick and died. Her sister would never have been sold into slavery.

She would have never run away.

And Sweetblade would have never existed.

Chapter Fifteen

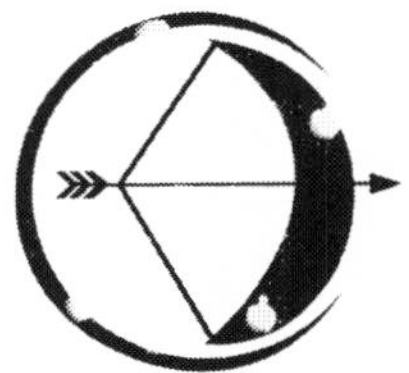

Yaotel's Plans

Ivana walked the streets of Eleuria for three hours before she felt calm enough to return to the room. Even then, she didn't want to talk to Vaughn, but she had little choice, and the sun was setting.

Vaughn was sitting at the desk with a sheet of paper in front of him. Her mother's journal was above the paper to the left, and her mother's key above the paper to the right. He started guiltily when she came in, as though he had been caught doing something naughty.

"I, ah, thought I might give it a go," he said. "Sadly, I'm afraid my Xambrian just isn't good enough."

She yanked off her boots without acknowledging him and hurled them into the corner.

He blinked. “Are we not eating dinner?”

She extinguished her lamp and curled up on her bed, her back to him, hoping he would take the hint.

There was silence for a few minutes, and then he spoke again. “Where were you? I’ve never seen anyone so distressed by finding a ton of money.”

She curled up tighter and stared at the wall. She wished she had never found that money. It could have changed everything, and that knowledge was almost too much to bear.

“Whatever the issue is, it isn’t my fault, so do you think—”

Her stomach roiled. “Not your fault?” she said to the wall, keeping her tone even. “Whose fault is it that I went on this damn trip to begin with?”

“All right—you have a point—but I don’t understand—”

“Obviously,” she snapped.

“Look. I know you find me a convenient target for your anger, but I have no hope of understanding what happened if you don’t just lay it out for me. Did *I* do something, or is this just general rage at life again?”

What she would give right now to just be able to threaten him into leaving her alone. It was so much easier. And right now, it was an extraordinarily tempting option. If she had her dagger at hand, she might have given in.

Instead, she closed her eyes and gritted her teeth, hoping he would just go away.

No such luck. The mattress compressed underneath her. He was sitting next to her. “Ivana. We have weeks ahead of us. Maybe just this once, you might trust me a little?”

She swallowed. In lieu of threatening him with a dagger, perhaps a tall glass of ale might at least take her mind off it.

“Who knows? I might even be able to help.”

She sat up and looked at him. “You want to help? Go hunt

down a pint or two for me."

He narrowed his eyes at her. "No."

"I'm sorry?"

"That is *not* the way to deal with—"

Something inside her broke. She grabbed his collar and drew him close. "I don't need *you* lecturing *me* on the best way to 'deal' with things," she hissed.

Nonplussed, he untangled her hand from his collar and set it back down in her lap. "What is that supposed to mean?"

"You have your vices; let me have mine."

Something flickered in his eyes. His jaw tightened and relaxed several times. Then he stood up and pulled his boots on. "Fine," he said. "I'll find you your pint. But in regards to my 'vice,' would you like to know how many women I've slept with since we parted ways?"

"I have absolutely no desire to hear your count."

"One." He glared at her, threw open the door, and slammed it behind him.

Ivana had risen from bed and was sitting at the desk, by all appearances taking over where Vaughn had faltered.

As promised, he came back to the room carrying not one, but two pints of ale. He also brought back dinner, because *he,* at least, was hungry.

He set the two trays—one carrying the pints, and the other with the platter of food, on a round table in the corner of the room.

He set both pints down in front of her, and then sat down in the single chair at the table and began eating, saying nothing to Ivana.

He was tired of her taking out every little thing on him. He had done nothing to her—he had even tried to keep his tongue in check for her benefit, refusing the temptation to proposition her, whether in jest or in truth, because she hated it—even though in reality he wanted her as much as he ever did.

The mere thought of it made him ache.

And after all this time, *still* she refused to trust him.

The silence dragged on. She didn't touch the ale. It was anyone's guess as to who would break the ceasefire first.

He sighed. Probably him. "There's enough dinner for two," he said at last.

She held the pencil for a moment, staring at the wall, and then set it down. She dragged the chair over to the table, served herself some, and began eating.

Eating was a strong word. She was picking at it, taking a nibble here and there. Finally, after a few minutes of that, she retrieved one of the pints and took a healthy draw.

She did it while looking at him, as if daring him to say something.

He didn't.

"So," she said, "when you say you've only slept with one woman..."

Oh, so they were going to talk about this?

"Were you in a relationship?" she finished.

He snorted. Right. *That* hadn't changed. "No. I was in a bad place right after the Conclave coup."

"I'm amazed you were self-reflective enough to recognize that."

He set down his fork and wiped his mouth. "When I said you gave me a lot to think about, I wasn't lying." He met her eyes. "I've always thought of myself as a decent person, Ivana. Until, in the height of irony, *you* went and screwed with my head." He wiggled his fingers above his head for emphasis.

She didn't look away. She just studied him.

"And it didn't help that every damn time I was tempted to give in, all I could hear was your voice in my head scolding me."

A corner of her mouth quirked up briefly. "I see."

She set her own fork down, though she wasn't anywhere near finished, and looked down at her plate. "That money," she said in a quiet voice, "would have ensured that my mother, sister, and I could have had a comfortable living after my father died. But apparently, my mother didn't know about it."

Oh. *Oh.*

And if that had been the case...she would never have become Sweetblade.

He understood now, inasmuch as he could, what that money represented to her.

She took her ale and downed it in several long chugs.

He didn't stop her.

"There," he said. "Was that so bad?"

She raised an eyebrow at him.

"You know, *telling* me what was bothering you rather than, I don't know, fantasizing about slitting my throat?"

She blinked. "I wasn't fantasizing about slitting your throat."

"Oh." He grinned at her. "That's a relief."

"Maybe just drawing a little blood."

His smile faded. "You're serious, aren't you?"

She shrugged. "Some habits are hard to break."

Dear gods.

There was a long silence while they both finished what was left on their plates, and then she spoke again. "Why is this translation so important to you?"

"What? I told you. Because if we can open a doorway and talk to the gods, maybe they'll—"

She pushed her plate back and waved her hand. "Right, but

no. You're obsessed with this, Vaughn. You just told me you yourself didn't think this was going to pan out. And yet..." She raised an eyebrow. "Here we are. What's Yaotel's alternative plan that you are so desperate to avoid?"

He picked up his fork again and poked at a bit of fat he had pushed to the side, his stomach souring slightly. He'd have to tell her eventually; now was as good a time as any. "If the conditions are right for an easy takeover, as he believes they are, Yaotel wants to oust Airell, put someone sympathetic to us in his place, and, in conjunction with other plans he has, have a chance at resisting the Conclave."

Ivana narrowed her eyes. "He wants you as that replacement."

She didn't miss much. "Yes." Yaotel thought his family connection with Airell—and Gildas before him—would give him legitimacy. Even though the title of Ri wasn't *supposed* to be hereditary, it was a common practice in Ferehar.

She appeared to consider that. "And...you don't want this?"

He gave a short laugh. "Of course I don't. It is literally the *last* thing I would ever choose to pursue." He had hated that life, hated the games, hated being on display. Yaotel might as well slap him in irons and lock him up—forcing him to play that role, to be someone *else* he didn't want to be.

He set his fork down and gave her a bright smile. "So. If I can get Zily to help, none of that will be necessary."

She studied him for a moment longer, and then shook her head. "I'm going to turn in."

"You going to drink the other ale?" he asked.

She glanced at it, then hesitated. "No. I don't think so."

Chapter Sixteen

Lost

The nightmare was particularly bad that night. Ivana's mother, before stalking her down and accusing her of being a monster, started scattering setans at her feet like birdseed. She slipped, and her mother kept piling the coins on top of her until she was buried in them and couldn't breathe.

She couldn't go back to sleep afterward, instead drifting in and out of the same dream repeatedly. When she "woke" in the morning, she felt groggy from lack of sleep. Not a good way to begin a day she'd intended to spend translating Xambrian.

At least translating would keep her mind off the money.

Vaughn was far too cheery for her mood, but he brought breakfast to her and then thankfully left, saying he ought to do what he was supposed to be doing and gather information—as well as restock their supplies.

That left her with a sheet of Xambrian, a few clean pieces of paper, and a pencil.

Truthfully, she couldn't think of a better way to spend a day. She hoped to finish by dinner so they could pack up and head down the road the next day.

Her Xambrian was rusty, but it came back to her quickly enough. Morning bled into midday, and since Vaughn didn't reappear to bring her lunch, she kept working in blessed solitude.

By the time he returned to the room, the sun was low in the sky, she had just finished translating the last sentence, and she realized with a start that she was starving.

Vaughn dropped a bag in the corner. "Any progress?"

She held up the sheet of paper and read aloud: "'And at the time of year when it was appointed that Xiuheuhtli should set loose his serpent upon the sky, to consume its impurities in flame, also would the veil between mortal and divine be at its weakest, and it could be forced to tear, in order to welcome those who should seek the favor of their patrons, even those gifted of divine blood. Thus did the first of our kind, Amatl, gird up his loins to step into the serpent's mouth at the appointed time and by sacrifice of blood be consumed by the flames.'"

Vaughn held up his hand. "Wait. 'Sacrifice of blood'? 'Consumed by *flames*'? Uh...suddenly, I'm not liking the sound of trying out this doorway."

She flicked her hand at him in annoyance. "Quiet, I'm not done." She continued reading. "'Being so purified by blood and fire, Amatl traveled long in the gods' realm—his journeys, are they not recorded in *The Book of Fire*?—and returned to us unharmed and blessed by the gods beyond all mortal measure. They called him *teotontl*, and—'"

"'*Teotontl*'? What's that?"

Ivana sighed. "I don't know. A name or title, maybe? It's not a Xambrian word I know and doesn't sound Xambrian, either, even though it's in the Xambrian script. Now would you let me finish?"

Vaughn waved his hand.

"'They called him *teotontl*, and he became our first mortal king. And Amatl looked upon the rest of his kind with favor, saying...'" She put the paper down.

"'Saying'? Saying *what*?"

Ivana set the paper down. "That's it. That's what the Xambrian says, anyway."

Vaughn walked over to the desk and stared down at the paper, as if he could get it to reveal its secret by looking hard enough. "That's an odd place to leave off. Was the tablet broken off there?"

"Not that my mother indicated, nor does it look that way in her sketch, but then again, we're still missing the latter half of the journal."

Vaughn scratched at his beard. "Huh."

Ivana tapped the paper. "I have a theory. I'm no archaeologist, but I'm wondering if originally this was set up near the serpent as a way of reminding people of what it signified. It's possible what's written around the serpent's mouth is what he said, hence the connection."

"All right. So do you know what the writing around the mouth says yet?"

"I haven't gotten that far. That'll take me a bit longer to work out, as I told you before." She paused. "Is our plan still to leave first thing tomorrow morning and finish this in Marakyn?"

"Yes. I think it's best we keep moving. Especially after the news I heard today."

She raised her eyebrow. "Oh? And what would that be?"

He pulled a sheet of paper out of the bag he'd brought in and slapped it down in front of her. "Well, first, there's this."

Ivana looked over it. It was a notice that there was a dangerous Banebringer thought to be in the area...and a reward was being offered for his capture. Attached was the standard description of Vaughn they'd already seen circulating—not updated to include the beard yet.

She snorted. "Dangerous?"

He folded his arms across his chest. "I'm very dangerous!" He gave her a halfway menacing look.

She raised an eyebrow at him. "What's ironic is that you could be if you wanted to be." His water magic was incredibly powerful, but she had never seen him utilize it to its full potential.

He snatched the paper out from under her and crumpled it into a ball. "I prefer not to reach for *hurting* people as my go-to solution for problems," he said tartly. "I don't see how that's a bad thing."

She grunted, choosing to ignore his implication. "You said 'first.' What else?"

"Apparently, *Ri* Airell just returned to the country estate after being in Cohoxta negotiating with the Conclave. He's ordered increased security measures."

Ivana didn't like the sound of that. Either the name of the man who had once seduced, impregnated, and then left her—or what he was doing. "And what does that mean?"

"First, he's mustering Fereharian troops in response to the call of the United Setanan. Second, he's working with the Gan and local lords to increase patrols on the main roads. We're likely to be stopped on the way if we stay on the main road."

Stopped and tested, no doubt. "How's your lightblood aether holding up?"

"I have enough to get by routine testing on the way. If it turns into something more than routine..." He grimaced, which was enough of an answer.

"Anything else?"

"Everyone hates Airell. More than my father, which hardly seems possible, but there it is." He sighed. "It seems Yaotel was correct in his assessment of the situation here. There's a *lot* of grumbling. Didn't hear one word in defense of Airell—or the Conclave, for that matter. And the frustration is bubbling right beneath the surface. With a pint or two of ale to loosen their tongues, the old-timers were more than willing to wax eloquent regarding their opinions on the change in leadership."

"The apothecary isn't alone in her opinion of their new Ri, then," Ivana said. That would have been gratifying if it didn't mean the hatred was well-deserved—and on the backs of Fereharians, no doubt.

Vaughn shook his head. "No. She's not. And it's justified. Airell's raised taxes to a high enough level that even those in the middle are starting to feel the pinch. The story the apothecary told us yesterday isn't an uncommon occurrence." He paused. "There's been more than one young woman *strongly encouraged* to enter his service."

"Well. He's good at taking advantage of people." She intended it as an offhand, careless comment, but the words struck fire in her bones.

Vaughn eyed her. "At any rate, if the rumors are to be believed, it's not only the commoners who are disgruntled with him. He spends most of his time lazing about at the country estate rather than in Cohoxta doing his job, which has alienated his Gan—and he dismissed all my father's advisors and hired his own, who are, by all reports, nothing more than drinking buddies."

Ivana rolled her eyes.

"There are exceptions, of course. The local lord in charge of this immediate area, Lord Kadmon, hasn't endeared himself to the people in order to earn any supporters, either. He's taken it upon himself to mimic the 'strategies' of his new lord. I overheard the locals grumbling about both him and Airell over their beer."

Ivana stopped listening at the words "Lord Kadmon." How was that bastard still alive? He had been old when Ivana had left.

Left. That sounded so calm. As if she had merely bid farewell one sunny day, instead of having fled with only the clothes on her back, slavers nipping at her heels, and her sister screaming behind her not to leave her.

She couldn't suppress the shudder that went through her.

"Are you listening to me?" asked Vaughn, snapping her back to the moment. "What are you thinking about?"

She was getting bad at masking her emotions in front of Vaughn. "Nothing."

He gave her a look.

She gritted her teeth and sighed. "Lord Kadmon was the noble my father worked for."

"Ah."

"He kicked us out of our home in the middle of winter with pennies to our name, and after my mother died of an illness she probably would never have caught had we had money for better living arrangements, he tried to sell myself and my sister into slavery to make up our so-called debts to him." It was laughable that "V.I." had called him a "decent fellow" in his letter to Ivana's father. He was as monstrous as Gildas in his own way. Despicable, cowardly, greedy man. And yet, he had prolonged his life to above average while Ivana's father, a man who had served him faithfully for more than a decade, had died in his own blood practically on Kadmon's doorstep.

A flame burned in her chest, and try as she might, she couldn't put it out. He was so close. Within a couple of hours' walk. Even in the right direction.

Her eyes flicked to her bag, on top of which she had tossed her dagger in its sheath.

"Ivana?"

She started.

Vaughn folded his arms across his chest. "We're *not* taking a detour so you can wreak vengeance on Kadmon."

She blinked at him. "I'm sure I don't know what you're talking about."

He rolled his eyes. "You know, that whole-innocent-shy-girl routine doesn't work on me. I *know* better. Also, do I need to remind you that Sweetblade is supposed to be dead?"

"I know that. And anyway, Sweetblade never killed anyone unless it was part of a job, self-defense, or to preserve her identity."

Vaughn narrowed his eyes at her, but he let it drop. "Dinner?"

"Yes. I'm famished."

She tried to put Kadmon out of her mind. She really did. But the seed had been planted, and the churning of her own mind nurtured it until it had taken root and sprouted into a plan.

Ivana wasn't going to kill Kadmon. She wasn't. She was just going to scare him a little. Make him nervous. If she could find something she could use to ruin him, all the better.

That was what she told herself when she slipped out of their room once Vaughn was sound asleep, and what she told herself as she hurried down the road, wrapped in a cloak and invisible with the help of Vaughn's aether, and what she told herself when she arrived at Kadmon's estate two hours later and well into the night.

It was what she told herself when she slipped through an

unlocked window to an empty ground-floor room, snuck up the stairs, found Kadmon's study, and rummaged around in file cabinets.

It was even what she told herself when, frustrated in her attempts to quickly find evidence of something she could use to ruin him, she crept into his room, deciding scaring him would have to do.

But when she finally laid eyes on the man who could have helped them but had instead turned a cold shoulder—and worse—to her family's suffering, she knew she had been lying to herself all along. She wanted him dead. She wanted him dead nearly as much as she wanted to see Airell splayed out in his own blood at her hand, but since Airell was a less convenient—and more challenging—target, Kadmon would do.

He lay sleeping amidst more finery than she had ever known. A minor noble, to be sure, but wealthy enough to own a modest estate and employ a dozen servants to maintain it.

And by the state of the grounds, his estate had only grown in wealth in the years since she had last been here.

But knifing him in the dark wasn't enough. She wanted him to know, to see, what he had done.

She made sure the heavy drapes were closed, locked the door, and then lit a single lantern. Then she stood above his bed, waiting until the light and her ambient presence woke him.

It didn't take long. He rolled over to face her and the light, and a moment later, was blinking away sleep from his eyes.

She didn't wait until the confusion turned to fear, and then the inevitable shout for guards. The moment his eyes lit on her, and before he could move another muscle, she hauled him out of the bed, arm around his mouth, dagger to his throat.

He had little meat left on his frail body. She could probably kill him by throwing him hard enough against the wall.

He stopped struggling the moment he felt the cold metal against his flesh.

He tried to say something, but it was muffled against his arm.

"Call for the guards or scream and you die," she whispered into his ear.

He nodded.

She pressed the flat of the blade harder against his neck but loosened the hold on his mouth, just enough to let him talk.

"Who are you? What do you want?" he asked hoarsely.

She pulled him against the wall and then flung him around to face her. With the point of her blade in his throat and the wall behind him, he had no options other than to try to scream for help—and risk her simply killing him before they could come.

He didn't scream. His eyes flicked from her hooded face to the hand pressing into his chest, keeping him against the wall. Old he might have been, but his mind was still there. She could already see it whirring away, considering all his enemies and possibilities and how he could weasel out of this and come out on top.

She hadn't known him well, but she had seen that look on a dozen faces before—especially on those targets who considered themselves shrewd.

"Whatever someone has paid you," he said at last, "I can double it. Triple it, even. Name your price."

She shook her hood back and pinned him with her eyes. "That would only be applicable if I were an assassin and you were some nameless target. You don't know me, do you?"

His face went paler than it already was. Trying to pay off an assassin *might* have worked, though any assassin who wanted to build a good reputation rarely took such offers, or they'd become known as untrustworthy. But someone bent on vengeance? That was another matter altogether—and he knew it.

He studied her face, her eyes, her mouth—and then slowly shook his head. "No. But whatever I did to you, I can make it up to you."

Make it up to her. *Make it up to her?* Could he bring back her mother, her sister, her entire *life*? A strangled laugh left her lips, bereft of anything resembling humor. "I'm afraid there's nothing you could do to make it up to me."

His eyes flashed with despair. "Please, just don't hurt my children—or my grandchildren."

"My, have you grown soft in your much-advanced age? You didn't seem to care about children when you turned my family out into the cold and tried to sell my sister and me into slavery."

His eyes widened. "My gods," he said. "It can't be."

"Much better," she said, and then she pressed the tip of her dagger harder into his throat. "I said this once before, and I'll take great satisfaction in saying it again: Congratulations on creating your own murderer."

He was trembling now. "I can tell you who bought your sister!"

The words were daggers of ice in her heart, reviving the chilling screams of her sister from her nightmares. Did she even want to know? Did she want the possibility to taunt her? Did she even want to find her sister, if she was alive?

A necklace, a journal, a chest. Those were objects. And the latter two had done enough to undo her. What would finding her sister do?

"My sister is almost certainly dead," she said. "And also almost certainly did not stay with the same person you sold her to."

"Perhaps," he said, spreading his fingers wide in what looked like a conciliatory gesture, even as beads of sweat collected on his brow. "But it's a trail to follow."

She wavered. It would haunt her if she didn't at least know, didn't have the option. "I want a name. Now."

"A Lord Paddyn, from farther north in Ferehar. You should also know you're not the first to ask."

She frowned. "What?"

"I..." His voice grew stronger. "Someone else inquired after your sister, maybe a few months back."

Her frown deepened. That was...disconcerting. Why would anyone else care about her sister? "You've been most helpful," she said. "Perhaps that is the only thing you could have done to make it up to me."

He sagged against the wall and his shoulders drooped.

"I didn't say you *had* made it up to me, you bastard."

His head jerked up.

"My father served you faithfully, and you repaid him by destroying what was left of his family. You're a contemptable coward, and if I had time, I'd find a way to do more than take your life. But I don't."

She slammed her hand against his mouth to cover his scream—

Vaughn's voice, soft and low, came from behind her. "Ivana, don't do this."

Damn. "Stay out of this," she snarled. "It doesn't concern you."

"Since when did you become a murderer?"

She laughed again, cold and bitter. "That's cute."

"This is different. No one is paying you to do this. This is nothing but a cold-blooded act. This won't solve anything, this won't change anything, and it certainly won't bring back your family. Let him go."

He was right. But the hatred she had for this man, a poor substitute for the man she most wanted to destroy, but a substitute all the same, was far too strong for his logic.

"It's far too late for that."

"I thought Sweetblade was dead," he said quietly.

"She is." She plunged her dagger under Kadmon's ribs and up into his heart, held it there while the blood ran over her hand, watched his eyes while his life bled out of them.

And the realization washed over her like the blood on her hand: If Sweetblade was dead, then the bloody hand on that hilt was hers. Ivana's.

Sweetblade had last killed a year and a half ago.

As Ivana, it had been a decade.

She yanked the dagger out of Kadmon and stepped back. She expected satisfaction. She hoped for numbness. Instead, her dissipating rage warred with despair.

What she had told Vaughn so many months ago was true: There was no difference.

Vaughn looked away as Ivana stepped back and Kadmon's body fell to the floor.

Silence.

She had done it. He had thought she could be talked out of this.

He lifted his eyes to her, avoiding the sight of Kadmon in a pool of blood.

Her back was still to him, dagger held point down at her side and dripping blood onto Kadmon's fine rug.

"Feel better?" he asked. He hadn't intended for it to come out sounding so accusatory, but it did.

She expelled a low hiss of air. "I don't know who you expected to find when you sought me out, Vaughn." She turned her head so he could see her profile but didn't turn to face him. "But I am sorry that the person you ended up with has disappointed you. I think the woman you were looking for only exists in your imagination."

Vaughn clenched his fists, the emotions of the night roiling through him. "You're wrong."

She did turn, then, and met his eyes. "Discarding an alias doesn't change the core of what I am."

"I know what you are," he replied. His throat was tight. "I recognize it, because I am intimately familiar with the feeling myself."

She snorted. "Please, O Wise One, enlighten me. What am I?"

Monster.

He summoned a single word. "Lost."

She recoiled. Her eyes flashed and her jaw tightened, but he knew her well enough to know the anger was a defensive reflex. If he ignored the obvious, he could see it: The way her lips parted and her chest moved erratically, the tightness around her mouth, the crevices in the skin around her eyes.

He had dealt her a blow with that word, and her agony was leaking out.

He wanted to close the gap between them and draw her into his arms, hold her tightly, and tell her that while he didn't know the way, she would at least not be alone in the journey.

The desire was downright frightening, and she would never accept such a gesture anyway.

Thankfully, she turned away from him and jerked her head toward the bloody corpse on the ground. Her voice was tight. "We should go."

Chapter Seventeen

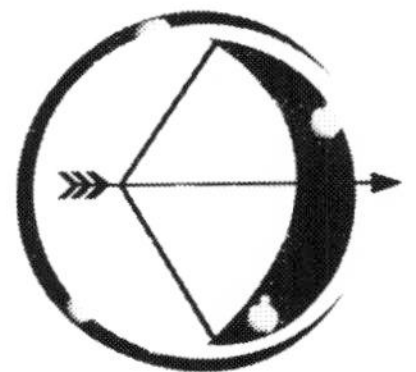

Conclave Lapdog

The return trip to the inn in Eleuria was silent and tense. Vaughn didn't dare speak to Ivana; her face was set in stone.

He didn't know what to make of this woman. In so many ways, she was the same as she had always been. Closed and hard as steel. And in other ways, she had softened. Seemed willing to be, and even desirous of being, someone different than she had been.

And yet she swung between the two extremes rapidly—and as he had just witnessed, rather dramatically.

They were almost to the outskirts of Eleuria, and Vaughn was about to break the silence to suggest disappearing—literally—when a stick cracked in the woods to their left.

Ivana whirled toward the sound, one hand on the hilt of her dagger and the other on the pouch at her belt, where she carried her supply of his moonblood aether.

Vaughn, too, turned to look, already reaching for his bow.

But even his enhanced night vision couldn't reach into the deepest shadows of the trees.

He drew closer to Ivana. "Anything?" he whispered.

She shook her head.

An animal, most likely. It was unlikely to be a bloodbane this close to a small town.

Even so.

He pulled his bow out—

Stars. Blood. Pain.

Vaughn woke sitting on the ground, slumped but not toppled over. He lifted his head and immediately regretted it; it felt as though the world had just tilted, and he suppressed the urge to vomit. He breathed slowly in and out for a minute until he felt right-side up again. His head still throbbed and felt sunken in fog.

And his face was on fire, save his nose. He couldn't feel his nose. He couldn't breathe out of his nose, either.

Yes, something was definitely wrong with his nose.

He tried to reach up to touch it, but his hand wouldn't move. He twisted his wrists and tugged. Manacled behind his back and secured to the wall behind him. Great.

And he couldn't see his surroundings.

At all.

That fact dissipated the fog in his mind more than anything else.

He swallowed and strained again at his bonds to no avail, and then squinted his eyes desperately. There was only one scenario when he could see *nothing* in the dark, and that was when there was not one speck of light to see.

He was either deep underground, in a room sealed so tightly that no light could get in, or someone had physically blinded him.

Or some combination thereof.

But he could move his eyes in their sockets, so they were still there at least—and the movement didn't hurt. He took a few deep breaths and wriggled. Nothing felt broken, but even that bit of movement made his head throb and spin again.

All right. So someone had captured and imprisoned him. But he wasn't Sedated or dead, not yet anyway, so eventually someone had to come to see him. Right?

"Ivana?" he whispered, wondering if she was imprisoned in this tomb as well.

No answer.

He burned a trickle of aether from his blood, reaching out to find any water that might be nearby—

His head exploded with pain.

When Vaughn woke next, it was to the sound of a key turning in a lock.

He blinked and widened his eyes, waiting for the moment when light would come to him again.

A door swung open, and he recoiled from the light that poured in—light that seemed blindingly bright to his eyes, already heightened in sensitivity from sitting for so long in the dark.

Footfalls, and then a voice he hadn't heard in over a decade. "Hello, Teyrnon. It's been a long time."

Vaughn's heart sank. *Airell.*

He squinted up at the newcomer. His oldest brother's face wore a bastardized imitation of Vaughn's best half-cocked grin, full of cruelty and savage delight. It marred his otherwise flawless features—Airell had always been unfairly handsome, and his years of reported excess had seemingly done little to change that.

Vaughn glared at him. "What in the abyss do you think you're doing, Airell?"

Airell's grin broadened. "I knew it was you," he said, not answering Vaughn's question. "Five dead bloodgiants on the plateau? Arrows everywhere? A curious silvery powder when the heads were broken? And then you show up at the inn in Calqo with nary a scratch?" He shook his head and clucked. "Sloppy."

"I'd go with 'impressive,'" Vaughn said. "But I suppose it depends on your perspective."

Airell frowned at him. "You're in no position to brag."

Where was Ivana? He desperately wanted to know, but he didn't dare ask. If she had escaped, he didn't want to draw attention to that fact—and Airell would lie to him anyway.

The thought that she might have escaped and subsequently abandoned him to whatever fate awaited him encroached on his mind. Not that long ago, he might not have considered that she would. After last night...?

He wasn't sure what she might or might not do.

"What do you want with me?" he asked Airell.

Airell wagged his finger. "Ah, ah. That would be telling."

Vaughn gave a perfunctory struggle, and the room turned upside down again. "I could kill you with a thought." Probably.

"Really? Have you not tried to use your demon powers yet?"

The smug look on his brother's face was disconcerting. He had—and he had promptly passed out, hadn't he? But his head didn't hurt *quite* as bad as before, so maybe...

He took the bait willingly. He burned the tiniest stream of aether he could. His head began to throb again, and stars flashed in front of his eyes, but he remained conscious.

He stretched out, felt the water in Airell's body—his blood, in his bones, his organs—and then lost it in a haze of fog—along with anything that had been left in his stomach.

He swallowed, panic rising in his chest. Without his powers, without his bow, he was nothing, had nothing, no tricks up his sleeve, no recourse. "What did you do to me?"

"It's helpful to have friends in the right places," Airell said. "You don't think they haven't spent decades perfecting a perfectly normal sedative to keep the demonspawn they save for harvesting under control?

So the Conclave *did* keep un-Sedated Banebringers. It was a question that had never been answered—how the Conclave was able to use presumably neutralized aether from Sedated Banebringers. "Conclave lapdog," Vaughn spat. "They'll destroy you when they're done using you."

"They'll certainly try," Airell said. "Anyway, just thought I'd stop by to say *hello*." He produced a syringe filled with a clear liquid from beneath his vest. "And give you your medicine."

Vaughn shrank back from the nightmare-inducing implement instinctively, but there was nowhere to go, nothing he could do.

Airell jabbed it into his arm haphazardly, injected the contents of the syringe, winked at Vaughn, and then left.

The door slammed behind him with a resounding thud that made tiny stars explode in front of Vaughn's eyes—and then darkness.

Chapter Eighteen

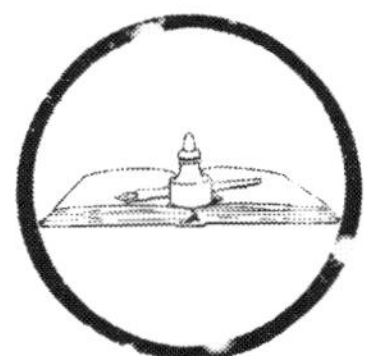

New Friends

Driskell sat alone in the conference room, organizing his notes after another morning-long meeting. Nahua had given him orders to take the afternoon off when she had left, and he intended to follow her orders, truly. But first he had to get his *notes* in order...

The door to the room opened. "Oh, sorry, I didn't realize anyone was still in here."

Driskell lifted his head. One of the Banebringers, Danton, stood at the doorway. He shifted from one foot to the other and then inched into the room, letting the door shut behind him. He pointed to the other side of the table. "I, uh, forgot my jacket."

"No problem," Driskell said, shuffling his papers into a pile and rising. "I was just leaving anyway."

Danton moved around the table toward the chair he had been sitting in earlier, and Driskell tried not to stare at him.

He'd met several of Yaotel's associates by now, including the two whom he had seen at the inn. They all seemed perfectly normal—until they started demonstrating some bit of magic or another, that is.

But they *certainly* didn't seem like the sort who'd be in league with demons—or, more realistically, who wanted to destroy society.

Unless, of course, destroying the Empire *was* destroying society. But then again, he supposed they were all plotting to do that, weren't they?

It was easy to forget what was happening lately. Seceding from Setana and allying with Banebringers and planning how they were going to hold off a Conclave army seemed rather mundane when all it consisted of was meeting, after meeting, after meeting...

Nahua was right. He did need time off. He felt as though he'd barely seen the sun the past few days.

Danton had retrieved his jacket and was headed back toward the door, his head down.

Driskell remembered what it was like to be the odd person out. He hadn't known anyone when he'd come to Marakyn for school four years ago. How much worse would it have been if he had also believed everyone had hated him?

"Have you ever been to Marakyn before?" Driskell asked. Danton's skin was the creamy beige of most Setanans, but that didn't mean he hadn't traveled.

Danton halted with his hand on the door handle. He seemed surprised that Driskell had spoken to him. "No," he said. "I'm from Arlana and, honestly, I've spent most of my life since... Well..." He faltered and scuffed a toe on the floor. "You know."

He cleared his throat. "Anyway, I've been with the Ichtaca in Weylyn since then."

"Have you had a chance to see much of the city?" If he could show a Xambrian around, the gods knew he could show a Banebringer around.

"I haven't wandered far," Danton said.

"Do you have some free time? I mean... I do, right now. I wouldn't mind showing you around a bit. If you want, of course." He flashed Danton a nervous smile.

Danton stared at him for a minute, and then hesitantly returned the smile. "Okay. Sure. I didn't have any definitive plans for the rest of the day. I'd...I'd like that."

"Great. I just want to put my things back in my room."

The start of Driskell's tour was awkward. He pointed out notable locations, gave some history on the city, all the expected actions he might take.

But Danton seemed decidedly on edge.

Which was curious. Driskell felt he ought to have been the one on edge, not the other way around. Then again... What normal person, knowing someone was a Banebringer, would attempt to befriend them?

When they stopped to look over the wall from the eighth tier, where he had brought Ambassador Mezzo on the last day of their more extensive tour, he pointed it out. "You seem jumpy," he said to Danton. "I'm not going to hurt you."

Danton rubbed at a crevice in the top of the wall. "Sorry," he said. "I'm not trying to be rude. I'm just not used to, you know, normal people being friendly." He glanced around, but the tier was empty, as usual. He lowered his voice anyway. "At least not once they know what I am."

Driskell digested that. "What...were you before? I mean, your family. You said you're from Arlana."

"Just a kid from a backwater farming village," he said. "Nothing special. Not like Vaughn."

Driskell raised his eyebrow. "Vaughn?"

Danton cast him a look. "Oh. Right. You don't know Vaughn yet. Vaughn is the son of Ri Gildas of Ferehar. Brother of Ri Airell, I guess, now."

Driskell's mouth dropped open. Talk about a fall from power. "Oh. Wow."

"Yeah." Danton shifted. "But I should probably let him tell you more about that, if he wants to."

"Of course." Driskell hesitated, questions burning in his mind, just as they had with Mezzo. "So...when you were...changed...I'm sorry. I'm just curious. You don't have to answer."

"No, it's okay. If you want to know, I don't mind." Danton glanced at Driskell. "I'd rather people know. That way they know what it is we have to suffer." He pushed himself off the wall and turned to face Driskell, leaning against the wall behind him. "We were huddled in the root cellar—that's the best we have for safe rooms, out in the country—when it happened to me. As far as it goes with my family, it could have been worse. The tear summoned a half dozen bloodrats." A half-smile slid across his face. "My mother went into full battle mode, whacking the things with a broom like she'd been trained in it martially while my father went to throw open the cellar door. The bloodrats ran off." He swallowed. "Once the dust settled, of course, we all knew someone had to have been changed. It was possible that a random tear appeared in our cellar, but that's so unusual...

"So we went around, pricking our fingers. My ma. My da. My three sisters and brother. And there I was, that stupid little dot of silver on my finger." His voice broke, and he turned away, almost angrily. "You come from a nice family, Driskell?"

"Yes," Driskell said. "I mean, my parents are merchants from Ipsylanti. I got the position as attaché because I was at the top of my class." He coughed. "I mean, way at the top. In all areas."

Danton relaxed and grinned. "One of those, huh?"

Driskell flushed and shrugged. "I mean..." He laughed. "Okay. Yes."

"Well, I had a nice family, too. Everyone intact. And I think—you know, I think my parents might have tried to keep the secret. They did, in fact, for a day." He cut himself off, turned around, and looked back over the plains.

"And?" Driskell prompted.

"One of my younger sisters told my oldest sister, who was married and out of the house. And she turned me in." He gave a little half-chuckle. "Just like that. No hesitation. No qualms. When she arrived with the Watchman the next day, it was like I didn't even know her. All I saw on her face was disgust."

Danton lapsed into silence.

Driskell shivered. What would his own family do? Tania's would probably Sedate him themselves, if they could.

"I was so crushed that I didn't even try to run. I was only sixteen. The Watchman just took me into custody while my parents stood by. They tried to hide me, but you know, that was their best effort. When it came to it, they didn't fight for me, either." He drew in a sharp breath.

"Maybe they were afraid," Driskell said quietly.

"I'm sure they were. I get it. If they made a fuss, and the Conclave heard about it, they'd have burned the farm to the ground and had my entire family slaughtered if they were in a bad mood. *I get it.*" His jaw twitched. "Doesn't make it any easier to bear."

A few more moments went by in silence. The sounds of the

factories working five tiers below could be heard faintly on the breeze.

"How did you end up with the Ichtaca, then?" Driskell asked at last.

"A tiny village like ours didn't warrant a Hunter. They packed me up in a cage on wheels and sent me off to the nearest city. Vaughn, the one I told you about earlier, ran across the caravan and rescued me. Brought me to the Ichtaca. The rest is..." He spread his hands. "Well, here I am."

Driskell eyed Danton. He was now looking over the wall, to the tier below them—the government tier. He was so normal. They all were. There was nothing obviously vile or demonic about them. Granted, some people said they *deliberately* tried to appear that way, but...he had a hard time believing this man was in league with evil forces or wanted anything out of life that differed from any other person.

Driskell cleared his throat. "So, you're what they call a lightblood, right?"

Danton straightened up to look at him. "Yeah."

"What can you do? I mean, other than what you've already shown us."

His eyes brightened. "You really want to know?"

Driskell nodded. He really did.

Danton gave the area a furtive once-over. "Not here. Come back with me to the consulate, and I'll give you a demonstration."

"Sounds good," Driskell found himself saying. And, incredibly, it did.

Chapter Nineteen

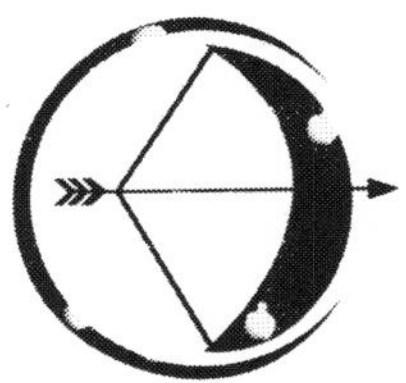

The Widow

Vaughn woke to someone stabbing him in the arm. He recoiled, which was a mistake because it made his head swim and everything else hurt.

"And how are we this evening, dear brother?" Airell's voice came from above him. There were multiple pairs of legs; it seemed Airell had brought backup with him this time.

Vaughn tried to speak, if only to insult him, but his mouth felt like it was full of cotton and nothing came out but a hoarse rasp. He had been given nothing to eat or drink since they had locked him up, and he hadn't eaten since dinner the night he had left to follow Ivana.

Airell leaned down to shove his smug face within Vaughn's sight. "What was that?"

Vaughn closed his eyes.

A moment later, someone had jerked his head up by his hair and was pouring tepid water down his throat.

Vaughn gasped and spluttered, but he managed to choke some of it down. He burned a tiny tendril of aether and reached to gather the water that had spilled—

Gritting his teeth together, he groaned. Terrible idea.

Airell chuckled. "Better? You can have some more if you answer some simple questions for me."

Vaughn moistened his cracked lips. "Rot in the abyss."

Airell's nose flared. "Tell me about the Ichtaca."

"Sounds like a cat hacking up a hairball," Vaughn said.

Pain exploded in Vaughn's side as one of Airell's lackeys slammed his foot into Vaughn's ribs. Something cracked. He gasped with pain, and it hurt; he tried not to breathe, and it hurt.

Airell jeered at him. "Does that hurt? Do you want me to fetch Mama so you can cry in her skirts like you used to?"

Vaughn was still reeling from the blow and couldn't come up with a suitable comeback, which, unfortunately, seemed to satisfy Airell.

"How many of you are there?"

Vaughn managed to eke out a pain-laced response. "Right now," he said, "I feel like maybe...two or three. But pretty...sure that's the drugs you gave me."

Airell frowned. "What's your goal?"

Vaughn was out of snarky responses. His mind already felt as though every thought were being strained through a sieve and, now, talking hurt his ribs. So he chose not to respond.

Airell's eyes glinted maliciously. "You *will* give me the answers I want," he said softly. "One way or another."

"How about...a trade," Vaughn said. "One answer...for one answer."

Airell quirked one eyebrow up. "You think I'm a fool? No matter; perhaps I'll humor you. What's your question?"

"Why me…in particular?" It wasn't as though he were the only Banebringer in the world.

"Because you're a plague on my existence," Airell responded without hesitation. "Ever since you turned into one of those demonspawn, all Father could think about was hunting you down. He was obsessed with it. Instead of preparing me to be Ri, he was out gallivanting trying to find *you*."

Vaughn stared at him. His brother was insane. Absolutely insane.

"Now, I've been generous," Airell said. "Play nice and answer one of mine."

"No…thanks," Vaughn said.

Airell's mouth twisted in a derisive smile. "You amuse yourself, do you? Insulting me? Mocking me? You imagine yourself better than me, I suppose, despite being utterly helpless and friendless? Well, when I'm done with you, the only thing you'll be imagining is the quickest way to die."

Airell spun on his heel and left, and his thugs followed.

Vaughn cringed back as one of the men made like he was going to kick him again as he passed, but the man stopped short, guffawed, and shook his head before following his master.

Vaughn sank back against his bonds and tried to burn aether again.

Pain and darkness.

Ivana sat in the shadows on a rear-facing balcony that overlooked spacious gardens.

It was past midnight, now, and most of the estate was dark—including the room she had been watching for the past couple hours, three stories up in none other than Ri Gildas' country estate house.

Her lip curled into a sneer. Well. She supposed it was Ri *Airell's* estate now. She took a steadying breath. *That is* not *why you're here.*

She'd be fine, as long as she didn't see him. As long as she didn't know where he was, rescuing Vaughn could remain her priority.

Rescuing Vaughn. The irony didn't escape her.

The thought had crossed her mind more than once that she didn't have to do this. The moment Ivana had seen not one, but five brawny men materialize out of the darkness of the woods, she had made the instant decision to disappear rather than fight. Not even one of Vaughn's captors had glanced her way as she had grabbed Vaughn's bag where it had fallen and slipped back into the shadow of the woods to watch what had happened.

It would have been easy to flee.

But it seemed like such a waste to come all this way on Vaughn's little mission, only to leave him in the hands of her own enemy.

And, though she kept swatting at it like a pesky gnat, the thought hovered in her mind that she didn't want to see anything bad happen to Vaughn.

And so, after his captors had slung an unconscious Vaughn over the back of a horse and started on their way, Ivana had slunk along behind, invisible. Once the sun had risen, they had abandoned the main road to cut across the country and marched along for most of the morning until they came to a back door in the wall of Gildas' country estate. From there, Vaughn had been taken by two of the men through a back door in the estate house itself.

She had loitered around, listening to the conversation of the remaining three men as they went on to whatever other duties they had, and gathered that Vaughn had been captured on the order of Ri Airell.

She had then done some light reconnaissance of other servants as they went about their business on the estate grounds the remainder of the afternoon, and she'd begun to formulate a plan.

It was a risky plan, based on far too little information, but Vaughn might have limited time left—if he was even still alive.

Or un-Sedated.

She would take the risk.

The door to the room opened, and Ivana's attention snapped back to the matter at hand. A petite woman swathed in a rich, deep blue cloak and cowl entered and then quickly shut the door behind her. She leaned back against it, her eyes closed, as if thankful to finally be alone.

Ivana could sympathize with the feeling.

The woman moved to her bedside table and set the lamp she held there.

Only then did she remove her cloak.

At first glance, she looked surprisingly young; silver had not yet threaded its way into her dark locks. Ivana wondered momentarily if she had been watching the wrong room.

But then the woman turned to sit on her bed, facing Ivana, and removed her boots.

Her eyes were tired and care-worn, and, without her cloak, the skin revealed by her lowcut dress at the chest and bosom was sagging.

Ivana waited until her back was turned again, and then she slipped through the open window, moved behind the woman, and put a hand to her mouth.

The woman stiffened, but Ivana spoke quickly, using the name she had gleaned from servants. "Askata. Please don't scream," she said. "I won't hurt you. I just need your help."

There was a moment when Ivana thought the woman might fight her—but she relaxed after a few seconds and nodded.

Ivana let go and stepped back.

The woman turned, and Ivana took a deep breath, let down her hood—

And stood face-to-face with Vaughn's mother.

Askata was darker in complexion than Vaughn, if not as dark as Ivana; it was obvious his Fereharian heritage must have come from his mother's side, anyway.

Her eyes raked over Ivana, taking in her boots, the belted sheath at her thigh, and her cloak before coming to rest on her face. "Who are you?"

Ivana walked over to the window and closed it. "Is your room safe for private conversation?"

"The useless widow of a former Ri is no threat to anyone. Of course it is."

Ivana inclined her head politely. "I'm sorry for your loss."

"Why? I'm not."

Ivana blinked. She had heard through snatches of gossip that there was no love between Gildas and Askata. It was what had given her hope that the woman might be willing to help her get to Vaughn. Even so, she hadn't expected such a blatant admittance of it—especially to a stranger.

Askata gave her a wry smile. "I don't recognize you, and it's clear you aren't from close by. Anyone familiar with our family is aware of my feelings regarding my late husband. So I'll ask one more time, before I call for guards: Who are you?"

She wasn't what Ivana had expected, but what had that been, anyway? A gentle, meek woman, frightened at her appearance?

An imperious, cruel noblewoman? Vaughn's mother seemed neither.

There was no ice or malice in her tone, but it was also calm, matter-of-fact. Her eyes were wary, and her body postured to flee, but she evidenced no fear otherwise.

"My name is Ivana," Ivana said. "I'm a friend of your son."

Askata raised her eyebrow. "If you're here seeking payment for a bastard, you've come to the wrong person. Airell cut off my direct access to our coffers as soon as he took on the mantle of Ri. One of the few disadvantages of my husband's death." She looked Ivana over, as if to assess how far along she might be. "I have only a small stipend now."

Apparently, Airell hadn't changed his ways—even married.

"Not that son," Ivana said. "Your son Teyrnon."

The change in Askata's expression so was drastic, it was almost comical. Her eyes widened, and she put a hand to her mouth. "Teyrnon," she whispered. "I-I had heard he was alive. All these years, and Gildas never told me."

"You know he's a Banebringer?"

Askata's jaw tightened. "Yes. I heard that as well. I suppose that's why that bastard kept him from me."

"And you don't care?"

Askata hesitated. "I... I might have, at one point. To preserve our family reputation." She sank down into the chair in front of her dressing table. "But my son was dead, and I grieved for him, along with Teryn—his youngest brother. And now I'm told one of them has been alive all these years?" She stared unfocused into the corner of the room, and tears shone in her eyes. "Do you know where he is? Is he in some sort of trouble?"

Ivana couldn't help but smile. "Always." The tension in her shoulders drained away. "But this might be worse than normal. Airell hunted him down and captured him and now holds him captive here on your estate—as of yesterday."

Askata's expression grew pained. She closed her eyes.

Ivana said nothing. She just waited.

Askata opened her eyes again. "Do you have children, Ivana?"

"No, my lady." She didn't think it was at all relevant that, in fact, she had once borne this woman's own granddaughter, for the short time the babe had lived.

Askata picked up a brush on her dressing table and turned it over in her hand. "They never got along—Airell, and his three younger brothers. Even Glyn, my next oldest, though he tolerates Airell's antics more than Teyrnon ever did, avoids coming home. But this... It breaks my heart. I sometimes wonder..." She shook her head. "But there's no use in that."

"Do you know why Airell might want Teyrnon?" Ivana asked.

"Other than spite?" Askata grimaced. "He doesn't come to me for advice, but it's no secret that he's following in his father's footsteps and ingratiating himself to the Conclave. My best guess is that he hopes to use him as a bargaining token."

That was Ivana's best guess as well. Of course, Ivana also knew that Vaughn was heavily involved with a secret organization of Banebringers called the Ichtaca. Depending on Airell's sources of information, it was possible Airell hoped to torture information out of him he could then offer to the Conclave. *That* was the real bargaining token.

"I can't let that happen," Ivana said. "Will you help me free him?"

For the first time, she saw fear in Askata's eyes—and it wasn't fear of Ivana. "Airell—he has a temper," she said and then she faltered. She pulled back her right sleeve and showed Ivana her wrist. It was bruised black and blue. "I tried to tell him not to raise taxes again, and this is how he repaid my advice." She shook her sleeve down and turned her eyes away. "He is his father's son."

Ivana's jaw locked. Arrogant bastard. Unwed mothers weren't the only women who suffered at the hands of unprincipled men.

She walked over to Askata, crouched down in front of her, and took her hands. "Airell is lost to you. Another of your sons was dead and now lives. Will you lose him again, too?"

Askata met her eyes.

Ivana held them. The seconds dragged by, and still, she held them.

Finally, Askata pressed her lips together and rose. "What would you have me do?"

Chapter Twenty

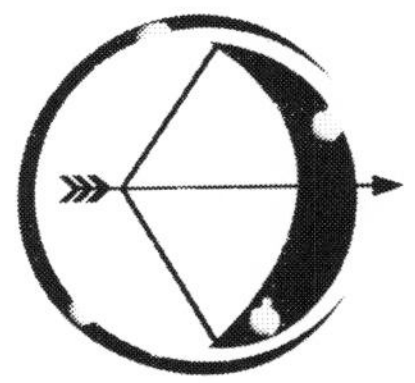

Family

Vaughn lifted his head at the sound of a key turning in the lock on the door.

The door swung open, and Vaughn flinched back from the light. A guard stood framed in the doorway.

He sneered down at Vaughn. "You have a visitor, demonspawn," the guard said, and then he leaned down to unbind Vaughn's manacles from the wall while still leaving his hands and feet shackled together.

The guard immediately jumped back, and it was satisfying to know he was afraid of Vaughn, even when he couldn't use his powers. *See? Dangerous,* he wanted to argue with Ivana.

"Out," the guard snapped, retreating from the chamber. There was the sound of lowered voices, and then the clang of another heavy door closing.

Vaughn stumbled to his feet. He had been forced into this one position for hours—days? He had lost track of time. He didn't think it had been that long, but nonetheless, his knees almost gave way under the weight of his various aches and pains.

He leaned against the wall for support, gaining his equilibrium. The last thing he needed was to trip and fall flat on his face since he couldn't use his hands to catch himself. It didn't help that his head was still spinning. Whatever concoction Airell had been injecting him with made the room sway as he moved.

He shuffled forward, chains clinking, taking short breaths so as not to exacerbate the pain in his ribs.

The moment he left the room, he knew where he was. Airell had locked him up in the safe room at his old home—what was now Airell's country estate. If one was going to imprison a Banebringer, he supposed that made a certain amount of sense—lest the Banebringer die and spawn a bloodbane.

He stood in one of the many rooms in Gildas' extensive cellars; this one was mostly empty and had only two exits: back into the safe room or out into the hallway.

The guard stood in the room with a petite, hooded figure.

Vaughn's heart leapt in his throat. Ivana? But that didn't seem right.

"Leave us," the person said, a feminine voice that sounded vaguely familiar, but definitely not Ivana.

The guard grunted but inclined his head. "You have fifteen minutes, my lady," he said, much more respectfully, and then he left the room through another heavy door.

Only once it had shut did the figure draw down her hood.

Vaughn gaped and sank to his knees. It was his mother.

She looked at him long, saying nothing, while he knelt trembling on the ground. When she continued in silence, he hung his head.

His heart beat wildly. Why was she here? To gaze on her abomination of a son and give personal approval to Airell's plans? As long as he had never seen her again, he could nurture the final hope that she wouldn't reject him the way everyone else had, that—

His mother moved forward. "Teyrnon," she whispered. "It's true. You're alive."

He looked up at her. Tears shone in her eyes, and hope burst out of his chest.

She clasped her hands together in front of her. "I'm so sorry," she said. "Your father—" Her voice broke.

"You don't...hate me?"

She laughed unsteadily. "No. No. In fact—" She turned to look behind her.

Vaughn followed her gaze, and Ivana materialized out of the air, her dagger at her thigh and one of their bags on her back.

His cracked lips curled into a smile—they split and bled as they did so, but he didn't care. His aching head and throbbing side overshadowed any minor pain from cracked lips. "You escaped." And she'd come back for him.

She gave him a curt nod. "We don't have a lot of time." She gave him a critical onceover and then unlocked his hands and feet. "You look terrible. I hope you're up to carrying out your part of the plan."

He shook his hands out and rubbed at his wrists, which were raw from rubbing against the metal. "Which would be?"

"Keeping both of us invisible when we leave with your mother."

His stomach dropped—and his head hurt more even thinking about it. "Damn."

"Damn?"

He started to take a deep breath, and then stopped as pain lanced through his chest. "Could...be a problem."

Ivana paced back and forth along the length of the room while Vaughn sat against a wall, his head in his hands.

"You're *sure* you don't...have enough for all of us?" he mumbled, sounding like every word was a struggle.

"There's no way," Ivana said. "I was concerned enough about what I had lasting long enough to sneak in, let alone get both of us out. But I figured..."

"Of course."

Of everything that could go wrong with this hasty plan, the complication she had been most concerned about was that Vaughn would be unconscious or physically unable to move. That he would be essentially unable to use his powers hadn't occurred to her, but it still resulted in difficulty getting *out*.

If they had more time, they could try making aether that she could use instead, but they didn't. As it was, the guard would be coming back any minute.

"Any chance it's going to wear off soon?" she asked. They both assumed it would eventually since Vaughn had said Airell had given him multiple doses.

He shook his head.

Ivana put her fingers to her temples. Askata was standing quietly in the corner. Her eyes had barely strayed from Vaughn.

And he *was* a mess. His nose was bloody, and the blood had clotted in his beard in silvery clumps—as well as smeared on his face. His lips were cracked and oozing a mix of red and silver—new and old blood. He moved as though he had been beaten, inhaling and exhaling short, shallow breaths, and his clothes were filthy and stained with his own piss.

Frankly, it might have been difficult to get past the guards even invisible. They would have smelled him coming.

"How many guards?" Vaughn asked, lifting his head.

"Four," Ivana and Askata said in unison, and then Ivana added, "Not all together, though."

Vaughn looked back and forth between them, and then his eyes settled on Ivana. "Can you...handle it?"

She sighed. This was *not* the way this was supposed to go. She was supposed to sneak in with Vaughn's mother, who would be let in after appealing to Airell to see her son, however briefly.

That had worked out all right. Askata had said Airell was furious that his mother had found out, but he had also given in to her demand—though he had insisted she wait until dawn.

Ivana hadn't been pleased with that. Sneaking out at night would be better than in broad daylight. But they were to be hidden by Vaughn, using his own invisibility, since her aether was getting low. It would have kept the danger to Askata minimal, though Askata said she was prepared to face the consequences once Airell discovered his prisoner was missing.

If Ivana had to carve their way out of here? There was no telling what might happen to any of them. She wasn't a warrior; she worked best in shadows and stealth, not direct confrontations with household guards.

And on the way were not only guards, but the potential for running into other household staff. Of course, violence was always an option on the table, in *her* mind anyway, but Askata had been dead set against it, unless they had no choice.

It was starting to look like they had no choice.

She stopped pacing and turned to face Askata. "Askata," she said, "I'm afraid our original plan is no longer going to work. We're going to have to fight our way out of here."

Askata's face paled. "Fight? I-I don't fight."

"When I say 'we,' I mean..." She eyed Vaughn. Gods. In his current state, he might be able to handle any vicious mice they ran across. "Me."

"You can't hurt them!" Askata protested. "I've known some of these guards since they were children. They aren't bad people; they're just doing their duty." She glanced at Vaughn, winced, and then looked away, as if suddenly realizing that the very guards she had just called "not bad people" were likely some of the same people who had beaten her son.

Ivana exhaled. "I'll do my best, but I make no guarantees. If you can somehow draw most of the guards away, that will help. Can you do that?"

Askata straightened up, pressed her lips together, and nodded. "Just tell me when."

Ivana turned to Vaughn, but he held up his hand before she could speak.

"Yes," he said, his jaw jumping. "I know. I'll try not to...be a liability."

He hated to be useless. She could see it in his eyes.

She could sympathize.

She closed the safe room door and drew her dagger. "I don't have much aether left. We'll get as far as we can. Who knows? Maybe it'll hold." She helped Vaughn to his feet and took his arm. Then she nodded to Askata. "You first."

Askata banged on door to the hall. "I'm finished," she shouted.

Ivana began burning what moonblood aether she had left, causing her and Vaughn to hopefully wink out of sight.

The cellar door swung open. The same guard who had let Askata in poked his head in the room and looked around.

"He's back in the safe room," Askata said.

The guard nodded, crossed the room, and locked the door. Then he returned to the cellar door and held it open for her.

She marched out of the cellar, and Ivana and Vaughn followed closely behind.

So far so good.

The guard wrinkled his nose as they passed.

Askata sniffed. "The whole room stank," she said. "Send for my maid and have her draw a bath. I want it hot by the time I get back to my rooms."

Her tone had changed to one Ivana hadn't heard her use before. Here was the imperious noblewoman who expected others to come at her beck and call. There was no room for argument in that tone.

The guard blinked and bowed. "Yes, my lady. Of course." He let the door slam shut and then scurried off.

There was a second guard outside the cellar door. He bowed, but Askata had commands for him as well. "And you!"

The guard started. "Uh, at your command, my lady?"

"Go find a bucket and a mop and then a chamber pot. Banebringer or not, there's absolutely no excuse for allowing the prisoner to wallow in his own filth for so long that it offends the nose of anyone who enters. Honestly." She sniffed again. "Men."

The guard bowed and, likewise, scurried off.

Two down, two to go. Ivana was marginally impressed.

Askata led the way down a short dimly lit hall. Both open and closed doors lined the hall—Ivana saw bottles of wine and liquor lined up on shelves in one room, and trays of root vegetables in another.

Ivana fingered the last vestiges of the aether she was burning. She'd be lucky if it lasted another minute.

At the end of the hall, Askata marched without hesitation through an open archway. It led to a final large, open room stacked with crates and barrels. On the other side of the room a stairway ascended to the kitchens and servants' quarters. There were two guards in this room, one short and clean-shaven and the other tall and scruffy. They were sitting at a table that had obviously been erected for their benefit, tossing dice.

The moment they entered the room, Askata crossed her arms and scowled at the guards. "Gambling on duty?"

The guards both shot out of their chairs, guilty looks on their faces. "Ah, begging your pardon, my lady," the shorter one said, "but we're just trying to pass the time. Not much exciting going on down here."

"Do you know what that man at the end of the hall is?" Askata asked, raising her finger slowly to point back the direction they'd come.

The short guard flushed. "Uh..."

"A *Banebringer*, that's what," she snapped.

The taller guard spread his hands. "Well, Arty and Sax are on duty down there. I'm sure we'd hear if—"

"Unacceptable excuse," Askata said, her eyes snapping with fire. "Report immediately to your supervisor and request replacements for the duration of your shift."

"But, my lady," the taller guard said, looking baffled. "We just saw both Arty and Sax go by, saying you had asked them to do something. If we go too—"

"All the more reason you should be on alert! Go, *now!*"

The two guards straightened up and hurried from the room, and not a moment too soon. The last of Ivana's aether ran out.

Askata drew in a sharp breath and looked at them.

"Well done," Ivana said, keeping her voice low. "But that won't hold them long." The last two guards had obviously been overcome by their surprise and a forceful personality; once common sense seeped into their brains they would realize that something was off about the situation.

"No," Askata said. "But we just have to get past the kitchens and out the back. Hopefully, no one will be about."

Askata went first, cautiously, and then gestured for them to follow.

Vaughn stumbled as they began to climb the stairs. He leaned against the wall, taking in staccato breaths.

Ivana halted with him.

"I just...need a minute," he said.

"We don't have a minute." Ivana was beginning to wonder how they were going to get away from the estate without being tracked and caught, let alone out of the house, with Vaughn in this state. He wouldn't be able to travel far.

She hoped she didn't have to make the choice between leaving him and saving herself or staying, fighting, and hoping for the best.

Vaughn grimaced, gathered himself up, and began to climb again.

They joined Askata at the top of the stairs, but now she waved them back. She stepped out into the hall at the top.

"My lady?" a young, feminine voice said. "Begging your pardon, but what were you doing in the cellars? Is there something you need?"

"Oh, Rhianah—I was hoping no one would notice," Askata said, her voice dripping with embarrassment. "There was a particular bottle of wine I was hoping to find and I happened to be nearby and...well, I thought I knew right where it was." A pause. "Never you mind," she said, her voice taking on the air of command. "Just run along."

There was a rustle of fabric, and a few moments later, Askata came back to the stair and waved them on.

She's good, Ivana thought. She tugged Vaughn on.

They emerged into a bright hallway. At the end was the door leading out—but before that, to the left, the noise of pots and pans banging together and the chatter of gossip floated through an open door. This they hurried past, Askata keeping the closest to the door.

They almost made it.

Just as they reached the door leading out, it flew open, and standing in the frame was one of the guards Askata had shooed away from gambling.

They all froze.

Then, his eyes widened and he drew his sword. "Noxtl!" he shouted through the open door behind him. "The pris—"

Ivana grabbed Askata, hurled her around, and put her dagger to her throat. "Let us go, or she dies."

The guard's knuckles were white as he clenched the hilt of his sword with both hands. He was young and likely hadn't seen much, if any, action. "I-I-I can't do that," he stammered, moving to block the way out.

She pushed Askata toward the guard, and, startled, he dropped his sword in an instinct to catch her.

Ivana lunged at him and kicked him in the groin. He crumpled and stumbled to the side, and she shoved him into a shelving unit full of supplies behind him. The entire contraption came raining down on his head.

As he flailed, Ivana pushed past him, and then pushed open the outside door. Vaughn staggered out, followed by Ivana and Askata.

Thankfully, the aforementioned "Noxtl" didn't appear to be nearby—nor was anyone else.

"The gardens." Vaughn panted. "There's an exit there. Our best bet. I have...an idea where we can go from there."

But Askata pulled back. She was trembling.

Ivana turned to face her. "You could come with us," she said.

Askata shook her head. "I can't."

"What will he do to you?"

"He—I'll be all right. He won't dare tarnish his reputation letting it be known his own mother helped a Banebringer escape." She gave Ivana a weak smile. "Go."

Vaughn grabbed Askata's hand. "Thank you."

Ivana was surprised to see that his cheeks were wet, but whether they were tears of sentiment or pain, she didn't know.

Askata squeezed Vaughn's hand. "Go," she repeated.

There were shouts in the distance, and thuds coming from the other side of the door.

Askata didn't have to tell them again.

Chapter Twenty-One

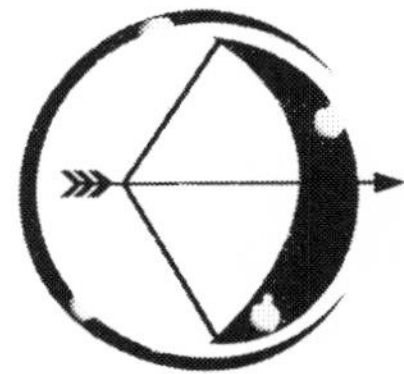

Wounds

Vaughn was flagging. The world seemed permanently off-kilter, every breath was agony, he was dehydrated and hungry, his head still throbbed from Airell's concoction, and he hadn't had any restful sleep since he had awoken to follow Ivana—and that had only been half a night.

About ten minutes into their flight, he had tripped and fallen and almost hadn't gotten back up—but Ivana had shaken and slapped him until he was annoyed enough to find the strength to keep moving.

So he pushed himself on. There was no stopping until they could find somewhere safe to rest; there would be dogs after them soon enough.

But fate was kind, for once; this early in the morning, they passed only the gardener, who, hunched over a line of shrubs and elbow-deep in weeds, hadn't even looked up.

Vaughn had roamed these lands once, as a boy and adolescent, and they were still familiar to him. And this wasn't the first time he had sought to hide from Airell.

Once they had left the estate grounds proper, he found the path he was looking for. It ended in a tangle of bramble at the side of a creek that ran through a shallow ravine.

They wrestled aside the brambles, skittered down the slope, and splashed into the creek, which only came up to Vaughn's thighs.

Funny. He remembered it as deeper than that.

He stopped only to fill his stomach with water to quench his desperate thirst, and then led Ivana farther down the creek until the ravine grew wider but deeper. There would be no climbing back to the top of the ravine other than the way they had come.

He put his hand up, halting Ivana, and glanced around.

This was the place. He was sure of it.

He trudged out of the creek to the opposite bank and poked around in the man-high stiff bushes and brambles there.

After pulling aside a few branches, he relaxed. It was still there. The fort he and his brothers—less Airell—had made, tucked underneath the side of the embankment where the creek had eroded the rocky hillside at some point in the distant past.

The roof was comprised of dirt and rock, but they had reinforced the fort with planks of wood for walls.

It was overgrown—he could see plants peeking out of the one window they had cut—but it still stood.

He dropped to the ground and hobbled on hands and knees through the door—also lower than he remembered. The moment he was inside, he collapsed to the dirt and closed his eyes, laying his cheek against the ground.

He heard the rustle of the branches as Ivana followed him in. "What is this place?" she asked.

He didn't open his eyes. His eyelids hurt. Now that he had closed them, he wasn't sure if he could open them again. "A fort...my brothers..."

He couldn't seem to continue, but Ivana apparently got the gist. "Airell doesn't know it's here?"

Vaughn shook his head—and even that movement hurt. "Impossible to see from the top of the creek."

"So we're relatively safe, for now."

Most likely, he thought, but the words wouldn't come out. Safe or not, exhaustion was already claiming him. He curled up on the moss-covered ground and fell asleep.

Amber light filtering through the green of the shrubs hiding the entrance to the fort played on Vaughn's face, waking him.

He opened his eyes.

He could see the creek from the spot where he lay. He also heard splashing, and since he *didn't* see Ivana, he assumed she was cleaning herself up in the creek. Something he also badly needed to do.

It took three tries to get himself upright; every time he twisted wrong, his chest protested painfully. So *that* hadn't improved. He swallowed; his throat was still parched. He turned his head from side to side; it felt marginally better than it had that morning, if not completely well, and the world had stopped acting as though it were on a pendulum. But he could barely sit up, let alone bathe without managing to drown himself.

But there was one thing he had to know that was more important than anything else. He burned aether, reaching for the water just outside.

To his utmost relief, the action caused no additional pain. Soon, the water responded to his call by way of a trickle floating through the doorway, and he directed it into his mouth. It was sloppy, and half of it ran out of his mouth and down his chest, but he didn't care. He could use his magic again.

He never thought he'd be so happy to have his magic fully back. He'd grown used to it always being there over the years; he'd also grown used to hating it.

Maybe he didn't hate it as much as he'd thought he did.

He drew more water from the creek and splashed it over his head; the water was cold. One summer, he and his brothers had attempted to build a dam to make a swimming pool; it had worked for a few months and then fallen apart. The water had been warm that summer.

He closed his eyes and lay back against the dirt wall. He needed to move. That was what he needed most.

The rustle of branches told him Ivana had returned.

She nudged his shoulder. "You alive?"

He grunted. "You'd have known it if I weren't." He took a deep, painful breath and gingerly pushed himself to his knees. He'd probably fractured a rib or two.

He glanced around the little hut; sure enough, the bag he'd seen Ivana carrying earlier was propped up against the wall. It had to be his; he'd shoved what he could in it before leaving the inn that night he'd followed her—in case things didn't go well and they couldn't get back—but she hadn't had hers with her.

He was glad she'd been able to retrieve it. There was bind-blood salve in it. It would speed the healing, but he ought to bathe *before* using it, or he'd just wash it off.

"Going to bathe," he said. He tried to peel his filthy shirt off and stopped short as pain lanced through his chest when he raised his arms. He lowered them again, trying to force himself to take slow, steady breaths until the worst of pain went away. *Forget the shirt. I'll just hold my breath and lie in the water until the grime washes away or I drown, whichever comes first.*

To his surprise, Ivana sighed and crawled over to him. She jerked her head. "Pull your arms in, one at a time."

He did as she asked, and when he was done, she helped him gently pull the shirt over his head without him having to contort his body.

He gave her a hopeful smile as she tossed it aside. "Don't suppose you want to help with any other articles of clothing?"

She looked at him askance. "Really? Broken ribs, and *that's* what you're thinking about?"

His smile grew. "Not *everything* is broken..."

She snorted.

Ah, well. He grabbed what he needed from his bag and crawled out of the fort straight into the cold creek.

Being clean again seemed to improve Vaughn's condition considerably, Ivana noted. He still moved slowly, a perpetual grimace on his face, as he returned to the fort, but the filth of being held over a day as a prisoner with no comforts had been washed away, and the silvery blood that had clotted his nose, smeared his cheeks, and congealed in his beard was all gone.

Actually, his beard was gone. "You choose now to return to your former look?" Ivana asked.

He settled down, cross-legged, and pulled the salve and bindblood aether out of the bag.

He rubbed his newly clean-shaven jaw. "I had a beard when Airell caught me," Vaughn said. "He'll be putting out word for someone with a beard for sure now."

Ivana grunted and continued to finger-comb her wet hair.

Sound enough logic.

He had managed to put on his one clean pair of pants, but he left his one clean shirt off, leaving plain-to-see the ugly black-and-blue splotches on the right side of his lower chest. "That looks pleasant," she said.

"It feels about as pleasant," he said. He mixed the aether and the salve and started rubbing it over the area. Once he had finished, he rubbed some over his nose, which she could see, now that the blood was gone, was swollen.

"Did they break your nose, too?" she asked.

He prodded it gently with a finger and winced. "I don't know. It's not crooked, is it?"

"I don't think so."

He let out a breath of air. "Temoth. I'm a mess, aren't I?"

She sat back. "At least you had a set of clean clothes." All of hers had been left behind at the inn, and while the clothes she wore were mostly dry, now, they were also bloodstained.

Vaughn glanced just long enough at the large patch of dried blood on the sleeve and torso of her shirt for her to see that his eyes were rife with disapproval, just as they had been that night.

Her nostrils flared at the look. "You have no idea what I went through because of that man. So you can keep your opinions about my actions to yourself."

He pressed his lips together. "If you hadn't run off on some decade-old quest for vengeance, we might not have been caught unaware and I might not have been captured."

"You didn't have to follow me."

"I couldn't just let you *murder* someone!"

"Well, bang-up job you did of stopping me," she snapped.

He rubbed the back of his neck. "You don't even care, do you?"

Her throat squeezed tight. *Monster*. She set her jaw, refusing to submit to the terror of her nightmares—at least in front of him. "Is that a surprise to you, after all this time?"

He held her eyes for a moment, and then looked away, his jaw clenched.

She folded her arms across her chest. *I know what you are.* The words Vaughn had spoken to her came back, unbidden, despite her attempt to shove them away.

Lost.

Her jaw jumped. Which was better, she wondered? A monster, or lost? She didn't want to be either. She wanted...

Her chest ached, and she dug her fingernails into her arms. *No more.* Thoughts about what she wanted were dangerous. All that led to was disappointments.

Impossibilities.

"Thank you," Vaughn said quietly. "For coming after me."

She didn't tell him she had considered leaving him. "You thought I wouldn't?" she asked instead.

He glanced back. "Honestly? I had no idea."

Something inside her squeezed. Was it ironic that when she was Sweetblade, he had seemed to have some sort of unswerving faith that she would do the right thing, and now that Sweetblade was dead, he didn't seem so certain?

She had never deserved his trust. She certainly didn't now. It had never bothered her before. But she also didn't tell him that for some reason, it did now.

He dragged a hand over his face. He seemed like he wanted to say more, but instead, he shook his head slightly and lapsed into silence.

Vaughn had never wished more than he did right now that he could crack Ivana's shell. There were thoughts shifting behind her eyes, far more than she let on, and he wanted to know what they were, and what she was feeling.

He wanted to feel, for once, as if there weren't a constant barrier between them, of her making.

Then again, was it *all* of her making?

Did he really want her to *tell* him those things, or did he want to know because he was nosy? Did he want to take without having to expose himself?

He met her eyes again, and he remembered how, in the moments before she had killed Lord Kadmon, he *had* exposed himself in his desperate effort to find a way to stop her.

Are you lost, too, Vaughn?

He had the urge to laugh. The pair of them were a complete mess. But wouldn't it be better to be a mess together, rather than alone?

But there was danger in such intimacy; there was danger in even extending the offer.

He broke the gaze.

There was silence but for the chirping of birds in the woods outside the fort. Vaughn focused on the sound. Birds tended to be the first to notice when a bloodbane started prowling around. The more vicious ones didn't come this close to the estate and town, but there was always the chance of running across a bloodsnake that had holed up somewhere.

"What did he want with you? Did he say?" Ivana asked at last, quietly.

Vaughn laughed, thankful for the change of subject. "He wanted to torture information about the Ichtaca out of me, but thankfully, he hadn't set to real work on that yet. He was weakening me with dehydration and hunger and a few light beatings first, I think."

Ivana frowned. "How does he even know about the Ichtaca?"

"That's a good question with disturbing implications, and I

don't have the answer," he said. Yaotel would surely want to know about it, though, if they ever managed to make their way to Marakyn.

She shook her head. "But why go to so much trouble to find *you*? Why not some other Banebringer?"

Vaughn rolled his shoulders. "He's insane, Ivana. He hates me because our father became obsessed with hunting me down." He leaned forward and raised an eyebrow. "And so didn't give him enough attention afterward."

Ivana snorted. "Gildas' son, that's for sure."

"The power's gone to his head. He gained it sooner than expected, and now he's terrified of losing it."

"He needs to hire better guards, then. They were persuaded *way* too easily to leave their posts."

Vaughn shook his head. "Nah, it doesn't surprise me. My mother..." He thought for a moment. "She's perplexing. She could be the gentlest woman in the world one moment, and then the next issuing commands like a general. She was highly respected by the servants, the guards—far more than my father ever was. People feared rather than respected him." He glanced at Ivana. She hadn't had the best experiences with nobles. "I won't pretend she was perfect. She had her flaws—a certain sense of entitlement typical of nobility, though I'd say it was more subconscious with her—but she was kind when it counted." He paused and laid his head back against the wall. "And her marriage to my father was political. She hated him."

"I picked that up."

"Even so, she seemed different than I remembered. I..." He hesitated. "I was never certain if she would accept me. When I saw her..." He swallowed, glanced at Ivana, and looked away. He had been terrified.

But he didn't tell her that. That was a step too far, wasn't it?

“I’m assuming you’re going to want to leave sooner rather than later,” Ivana said, changing the subject.

He breathed out. “After this? I don’t think I have a choice. Tomorrow morning, if I can manage it.”

“Then we should rest. You especially.”

“Gladly.”

Chapter Twenty-Two

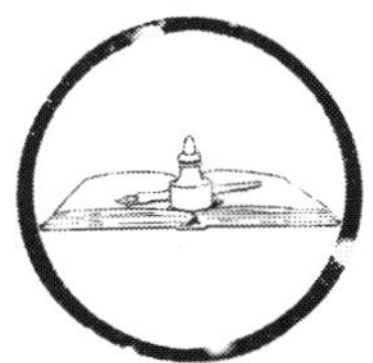

Demands

The door to the conference chamber swung open without even a knock a mere five minutes into this latest meeting. One of the Ri's couriers stood there, panting. "Your Excellency," he said, sketching a bow to Ri Tanuac. "We've just received word. The Conclave vanguard has arrived at the northern border. I've a message from...their leader." The courier held out a sealed envelope.

Driskell looked at the envelope with trepidation. Inside that slight piece of paper could be their doom.

Tanuac stood and took the envelope from the courier. "Thank you," he said. "No return message yet."

The courier bowed again and left as quickly as he had entered.

The entire room was silent. Yaotel, Danton, the four Gan,

Ambassador Mezzo, Nahua, and General Gyano—Tanuac's military advisor and head of the Donian reserve—stared at the letter. There was also a new face there, a plain but pretty woman with, like Danton, the creamy beige complexion of a Setanan. Even she seemed to know what it portended.

Tanuac broke the seal, removed the folded sheet of paper from the outer envelope, and unfolded it. He read it silently first.

"Well, go on," Gan Herne said with a wave of his hand. "What do they have to say?"

Tanuac cleared his throat. "The Conclave," he said, "observes that we have yet to remove the Xambrian from our borders. They insist that we eject him to prove our loyalty to Setana. They demand a meeting at the border in three days' time to discuss the details of our compliance."

Herne snorted. "Some discussion, with an army at their backs."

Tanuac handed the letter to Nahua, who read it and then passed it down the table for each of Tanuac's advisors to read for themselves.

The room was silent as the letter traveled. It reached Driskell last, and he read the message, which said exactly what Tanuac had said it had.

He transcribed the contents of the message into his notebook and then handed the paper back to Tanuac.

Ambassador Mezzo stood and folded his hands together across his mid-section. "It seems you have a decision to make."

"The decision has already been made," Tanuac said.

Dillion scowled, but the other three Gan nodded in turn.

Driskell noted all of this in his notebook as well.

"I might remind you that until you have Ferehar's agreement, we will not attack Setana," Mezzo said.

Ferehar hadn't even allowed the Xambrian ambassador in to

see the Ri, and so the ambassador had returned to Xambria. In turn, Ri Airell had ignored any messages from Tanuac.

It was clear to all involved that Ferehar could not be cajoled into cooperating via normal means.

"I'm aware, Ambassador," Tanuac said. He looked at Yaotel. "Where are we on that front?"

"I'm still working on it," Yaotel said. His eyes flicked toward the new woman.

"That's all well and good," Beatha said, "but the Conclave is on our doorstep *now*."

"Which is why we still need to buy time," Tanuac said. "And that is why we're going to meet with the Conclave and see what they have to say. While we're there, we're going to take the opportunity to find out what we can about their army."

General Gyano folded his grizzled hands on the table and took the narrative over. "Depending on what we conclude about the Conclave's intent and resources, we will formulate an appropriate plan to meet them. Meanwhile, the Gan have sent word to their respective quarters to muster the reserves. Those under Gan Herne's purview are at the ready, and we expect others to be trickling in soon."

"If we're forced to fight the Conclave army," Fiacra said, "that will be the end of any façade of cooperation with the Conclave."

There was a heavy silence in the room.

"I know," Tanuac said softly, but his jaw was firm. "I'm sending Lady Nahua to negotiate on my behalf and Driskell as her scribe. A retinue of those deemed best able to assist with this mission will also go with her."

Driskell started. That was the first he'd heard of his extended involvement.

He jotted down the additional note with an unsteady hand and tried to look like the prospect of meeting with the Conclave *didn't* terrify him.

What if it was all a trap? What if the Conclave realized they weren't going to cooperate and killed them all? What if Driskell screwed it up and gave something away? He was only a simple attaché, after all.

"Dismissed. Yaotel, you and yours—remain for a moment. I have a few matters I want to discuss with you. You too, Driskell."

The others filtered out of the room, leaving Yaotel, Danton, Driskell, Nahua, and the new woman—and Tanuac himself.

Tanuac waited a few beats after the door had closed all the way and then looked around the room. "Dal Yaotel. I believe the time has come for you to gain some trust. You have people who can move invisibly?"

"Yes," Yaotel said. "We call them moonbloods. The only one I have available right now is Yasril. What do you intend?" He nodded to Danton. "A lightblood could also be helpful if you're just looking for some subtle reconnaissance."

"Yes, that's all," Tanuac said. "No fighting, no interaction at all with the Conclave if they can help it. Just find out the exact makeup of the army and what we're going to have to contend with while Nahua and Driskell attend to the negotiations."

"I think they can handle that."

Tanuac nodded. "Good. They'll leave in the morning. Now, as to the matter of Ferehar. Updates?"

Yaotel's brow creased. "Unfortunately, no. I've tried contacting the man I have there a few times in the past two weeks but haven't been able to get a hold of him. Frankly, I'm becoming concerned something may have happened." He nodded toward the woman. "This is Da Aleena. She just arrived in Marakyn yesterday. She's not Gifted, but she's an ally who's helped us in the past. When I found out she had recently been in contact with Danton, I asked if she'd be willing to come to Marakyn to lend whatever assistance she could, and she agreed."

Aleena inclined her head toward Tanuac, and he nodded in return.

"Since I've been unable to get a hold of my man, I've decided to send her on to Ferehar to either find and meet my contact or pick up where he left off, if necessary."

Tanuac drummed his fingers on the table. "That's all fine and good," he said, "but I confess that I'm a bit in Beatha's camp here: time is a precious commodity and we don't know when we may run out."

Yaotel's face was grim. "I'm aware, Your Excellency." He hesitated and then pulled out his communication device—the qixli. "If you don't mind, I can try contacting my man one more time right now. Perhaps I'll get lucky."

Tanuac waved his hand. "Go on."

Driskell leaned forward again. The devices were fascinating to him. Somehow, creating fire and turning invisible seemed less impressive feats—however fantastical—than being able to communicate with someone instantly across a great distance.

Yaotel held the qixli in both hands.

A few silent moments passed before the vague impression of a face appeared in the silvery aether inside it.

"Vaughn?" Yaotel asked.

"Yes. I'm here," a voice said. It sounded tired; then again, it was hard to tell with the distortion the device caused.

Yaotel's face smoothed. "Thank the gods. I've been trying to get a hold of you for almost two weeks."

"Was that concern for my welfare?" the man on the other end—Vaughn—asked.

Yaotel grunted. "Any information yet?"

"Enough to confirm what you already thought," Vaughn said. "But I have bad news. I ran into trouble that made it hard for me to stick around, so I'm already heading to Marakyn. I'm about three days out. You want more now or when I get there?"

"You can give me a full update when you get here," Yaotel said. "But when you arrive, come directly to the consulate in the government ring. Ask for Lady Nahua if you can't find me."

"Got it."

Yaotel put the qixli down and looked up at Aleena. "Meanwhile, can you be ready to head to Ferehar in the morning? Sounds like we'll need someone to take over, so this is perfect."

Aleena saluted. "Sure thing."

"Good luck to all of you, then," Tanuac said, standing. "The gods know we'll need it."

Driskell's hands were sweaty on the reins of his horse. Their small caravan included Nahua's personal guards and Yasril and Danton masquerading as two more of Nahua's personal guards—though if all went well, no one would ever notice them. They had almost reached where the Conclave army was camped.

It had been a long two days for Driskell—each day another day closer to an unknown ending.

The worst part was he couldn't even say a proper goodbye to Tania. He had said he had been called upon to travel with Nahua on government business; he couldn't tell her this government business was potentially dangerous.

"Nervous, Driskell?" Nahua asked. She rode on one side of him in the middle of their small caravan. "I hope your horse doesn't bolt."

Driskell looked down at his hands and unwound the reins from around his wrists, where he had unconsciously wrapped them until they were far too tight. "What if something goes wrong?" he asked, his voice low.

"This is a peace-keeping mission, Driskell," Nahua said. "They won't attack us unless they feel threatened."

He pushed his spectacles up the bridge of his nose. "But what if they aren't fooled? What if they somehow *know*?"

"What are you fretting about?" Danton put in from the other side of Nahua. "All *you* have to do is stand next to Nahua and look pretty."

Driskell looked over at him dubiously. "Are you sure you can do this?"

Danton did a fancy wiggle in the air with his fingers, and a moment later, he transformed himself into a Conclave priest and then back again.

"All right," Driskell said. "But how long can you hold that for?"

"Long enough," Danton said.

"What if you can't?"

"Driskell," Nahua said, "*stop worrying*. Everyone knows the risks."

The other Banebringer who was with them, Dal Yasril, a so-called moonblood, was silent at that. His face was pale and his eyes aimed straight ahead.

The reaction did little to comfort Driskell. "What do we know about this commander we're meeting with?" he asked.

Nahua wrinkled her nose. "His name is Bherg. I've never met him before, but I've heard of him. He's part of one of the higher circles of priests in Weylyn City—the one who suggested the blood tests, actually."

Yet another soft mandate from Weylyn that Ri Tanuac had balked at. The little cylindrical blood testing devices were now part of the standard issue Watch kits, which Tanuac could do nothing about. But since, so far, the Conclave had only been enforcing the blood tests in the three central regions, Tanuac had gotten away with failing to implement the tests at the gates of

Marakyn or including the random tests as part of their own Watchmen's regular duties.

If the opinion pieces in the newssheets were anything to go by, the people's overwhelming opinion of the tests was negative.

"They have a priest in charge of an army?" Driskell asked. "Does he *know* anything about leading an army?"

"Your guess is as good as mine," Nahua said.

Not long after, the caravan stopped.

They all dismounted and led their horses on foot.

Another few minutes brought them to the top of another hill and out of the woods—in sight of the army.

They stopped to survey the encampment.

There were more soldiers scurrying around than Driskell had ever seen in his life. It wasn't that many, relatively speaking. He knew that, intellectually. But the sight still made a pit open in his stomach.

"Looks like only about half of the army is here," Nahua said, nodding toward the northern side of the encampment, where there was a line of men and supplies trickling in.

Half? Burning skies. It already looked like enough to raze Marakyn to the ground.

"Marakyn is well-fortified," Nahua reminded him, as if reading his thoughts. "It would take more than this to threaten it."

"But what of all the towns that are unfortified?"

"That's why we're here, isn't it?"

One of Nahua's guards lifted a flag into the air with the symbol of Donia on it. Underneath, a white cloth had been tied as a symbol of peace.

A handful of men detached themselves from the encampment and headed their way. Three of them were soldiers, but the fourth was attired as a Conclave battle-priest: a brown robe, belted at the waist as usual, but sleeveless and split at the front from hem to thigh—presumably to allow freedom of movement—with a tan shirt and brown trousers underneath. An ornate silver amulet rested atop the Conclave symbol embroidered in cream onto the chest of the robe—a glittering adornment against otherwise modest garb.

Bherg, no doubt.

"Here we go," Nahua said. "Everyone ready?"

No, Driskell thought. But he had no choice.

The Conclave priest strode ahead of his guards to meet Nahua's entourage. One of the priest's guards carried a flag with the symbol of the Conclave, also tied with a white cloth.

The priest approached them, his hands spread out, palms up. "Emissaries of Donia," he said, "we greet you in peace."

Nahua dismounted, and Driskell followed suit. She, too, showed her empty palms. "Peace, brothers," she said. "I am Lady Nahua, Ri Tanuac's daughter. I speak on his behalf. This is my attaché, Dal Driskell." She then gestured vaguely to the guards behind them. "The others are my personal guards." Yasril and Danton, exactly according to plan, were nowhere to be seen.

The priest's eyes flicked toward the guards and then back. "Very good," he said. "I am Bherg. I have hopes that we can put all this unpleasantness behind us."

Nahua bowed. "We certainly wish no further unpleasantness, Holiness," she said.

Which was entirely true. They didn't. That didn't mean there wouldn't be.

Bherg gestured widely to their group. "I've ordered refreshments while we wait for those who are to be in attendance to assemble; I'm sure you would welcome the chance to rest for a while, yes?"

"Indeed, Holiness," Nahua said.

"Then follow me."

Refreshments turned out to be a limited spread of salted meats and cheeses sheltered in a large tent arranged with two opposing lines of chairs, but there was wine at least.

From the latter, Driskell regretfully abstained—following the example of Nahua, who graciously declined anything stronger than cider.

Bherg was over-generous in his estimation of the amount of time they would have to rest. "A while" turned out to be not more than a quarter of an hour, when he returned to the tent with two more priests and two soldiers—officers, by their uniforms.

All in all, the assembled company consisted of five from the Setanan side and four from the Donian—if Driskell didn't include Danton and Yasril, which he didn't, because they were supposed to be sneaking about the camp by then—or the rest of Nahua's guards, who were outside the tent.

Driskell didn't like being outnumbered. It was foolish, of course. They were *vastly* outnumbered by the thousands of men arranged about their central position in the camp. Even so, it felt like a deliberate move on the part of Bherg. A way to have the advantage over them from the start.

Bherg moved to the middle of the chairs. "I count this meeting as a success already," he began, offering a diplomatic smile that didn't reach his eyes, "since you showed up."

The other priests and the officers chuckled politely.

Nahua gave a brief, polite smile.

Bherg gestured to the group. "Please. Have a seat."

Nahua and Driskell were already sitting, but he pulled out his notebook and pencil.

Her two guards stood behind her.

Likewise, the two other priests sat, and the two soldiers stood behind.

It felt like a standoff to Driskell. He didn't like that feeling, either.

He made a quick note of his trepidation, as well as his earlier observation about the number of people there.

Bherg introduced his associates—the older officer, Commander Natryk, was one of the commanders of this contingent—and then rambled on about the necessity of cooperation in troubled times.

It was a pretty speech, obviously written ahead of time, and obviously a load of manure.

By the time Bherg got around to presenting Nahua with their terms, Driskell was hot, sweaty, and desperate for an excuse to escape the stuffy tent.

Bherg made a great show of excusing their half of the party for a break while Nahua "thought it over."

Once they had left, Nahua held out the parchment so Driskell could see it. "Thoughts?" she asked softly.

Driskell studied the document. "It's not a draft. It's official," he said. "Even has lines for signatures."

"Yes. This isn't a negotiation, but that much was clear before we set out."

They would eject the Xambrian ambassador immediately upon returning home. They would consent to a representative from the Conclave being present during all meetings from now on. Said representative would be given complete access to all records and files.

Said representative would only serve in an advisory capacity, of course, and would only serve until the Conclave was satisfied that Donia intended no trouble.

Said representative would accompany them back.

It was outrageous. Never had Setana meddled so directly in the affairs of its outer regions. Oh, the Conclave had its eyes and ears, but under the old regime, they had no *official* role, and so could be legally kept out of local government business.

As long as the outer regions paid their taxes, upheld the Conclave's admittedly pervasive religious restrictions, contributed men to the United Setanan, maintained their arm of the ubiquitous Watch—and generally caused no trouble—they had relative freedom to order themselves the way they wanted.

"I wonder if they've presented a like document to the other regions," Driskell said.

Nahua shook her head. "All indications are that we're the test," she said. "If we comply, I'm almost certain the rest of the regions will be similarly served."

She stood and placed the parchment back on the table. "That I'll sign it is a foregone conclusion, of course, unless we'd like an army four-thousand strong chasing us back to Marakyn." She gave him a wan smile.

Both of them knew that her signature on the document was meaningless. Tanuac had no intention of doing anything the Conclave wanted. They had bought Donia a few weeks—perhaps more, depending on how long they could successfully feign compliance.

"Shall we get some fresh air? I find this tent rather stuffy," Nahua said.

Driskell couldn't agree more. He also could use a trip to the latrines.

His trip to the latrines was unfortunately delayed by a sudden voice in his ear.

"Keep walking. Act natural. Don't speak."

It was Danton's voice, but Driskell couldn't see him. Regardless, the voice kept pace with him.

"There's something you need to see, but your escort will almost certainly prevent you from going where you need to go."

Driskell refrained from looking back at the soldier who was trailing him. They had no intention of letting Nahua or himself roam freely, of course.

"So when you come out of the latrine, your guard will be different. You won't recognize him, but that's all right, because it's going to be me. Just follow him."

Danton didn't speak again, and a few moments after Driskell walked behind the hastily erected wooden wall that served as privacy for those using the pits in the ground—thankfully, leaving his escort temporarily behind—he heard voices on the other side.

He couldn't make out the words, but one was Danton's, he was certain.

When he walked back around, his guard had indeed changed.

Driskell swallowed and wiped his hands on his tunic. This was a bit too risky for his liking, but what else could he do but follow the new guard?

The guard led him down another path and then stepped into a small tent.

Driskell halted, uncertain, but no one was around, so he, too, ducked into the tent.

Danton and Yasril were both inside.

Driskell blinked. "What's going on?" he whispered. "I need to be back with Nahua soon."

"This won't take long, I promise," Danton said. "But you can't be seen waltzing over to the part of the camp we need to go to, so Yasril's gonna have to take you." He pulled out a pouch and extracted a silvery chunk. "I'll take care of myself, but I'll be with you."

Yasril held out his hand. "Just take it," the older man said. His face was pale and his hand trembled, but he seemed to know what he was doing, so Driskell did as he asked.

Danton disappeared.

"Don't let go of my hand," Yasril said, and then he ducked out of the tent, dragging Driskell along.

"I thought you said you didn't want me to be seen?" Driskell whispered.

"You're invisible," Yasril said. "We both are. Now be quiet. It doesn't mask sound."

Driskell looked down at himself, but all of himself appeared to be there, as did Yasril. But as the man pulled him through the camp, Driskell had to admit the veracity of his claim. Not a single person looked at them. Even once when they had to dodge a man who suddenly exited a tent in their path, the man didn't even glance their way.

They walked for about five minutes to reach the other side of camp. There, it looked like a smaller secondary camp had been set up on the outskirts of the first. And within that camp wandered not soldiers, but priests.

Lots of them.

Driskell blinked.

There had to be another hundred men there—all in robes like Bherg, all bearing the symbol of the Conclave.

But Yasril pulled him on, skirting the edges of the camp until they ended up hiding behind a tall stack of crates and barrels. Yasril pointed to a man dressed in neither battle-robes nor the leathers of the soldiers, his back to them. His hair was black and hung to his waist, tied back at the nape. His hands were clasped behind his back. No one spoke to him. In fact, any passersby appeared to go out of their way to avoid him.

He said and did nothing. Just stood there.

Yasril appeared to be waiting for something, and despite being invisible, he hunkered down, out of sight, and peered through a crack between the barrels.

Driskell did likewise, watching the man.

Then the man turned his profile to them and walked forward. But before he went too far, he glanced in their direction.

Driskell ducked down instinctively, even though they were both invisible and hidden, but kept his eyes on the man.

Driskell's eyes widened.

The man's skin had the pallor of a corpse, and his eyes were white. Pupil-less. Just like a bloodbane. He shrank as far down as he could.

"It's gone," he heard Danton whisper, and Yasril tugged him up. They hightailed it out of the camp and back to the latrines, where Danton reappeared—briefly—before he turned himself back into a Setanan soldier again—and Yasril let go of his hand and disappeared.

"Who in the abyss was that man?" Driskell asked, his voice hoarse.

Danton shook his head. "An apt choice of words, but later," he said. "I just wanted you to see. I'll take you back to the negotiations."

Those in the meeting had already returned by the time Driskell slipped back in.

"Ah," Bherg said. "Dal Driskell. Excellent. We were waiting on you."

Nahua looked at Driskell as he settled back into his chair and picked up his notebook. He splayed his hand on the paper, trying to stop it from trembling.

Nahua's eyes narrowed, but she said nothing.

Driskell could hardly pay attention to the rest of the meeting. Nahua wordlessly signed the parchment and handed it back to a triumphant Bherg, who gave another pretty speech about future cooperation, and at some point Nahua begged off staying longer in the camp, citing the need to get back home as soon as possible. His aching bones were back in a saddle far too soon, and this time they had to be on their best behavior under the watchful eye of their new Conclave minder.

Beyond that, all he could see was the image of that *thing* haunting his mind.

Dread chilled him, remembering that face, those *eyes*, and he felt he saw it hovering in the shadows of the trees the entire trip home. He didn't know what it forebode, but Danton and Yasril seemed to think it a critical discovery.

He only hoped it was a critical discovery that would allow them a victory, because within a few weeks' time...

Everything was about to go to the abyss.

Chapter Twenty-Three

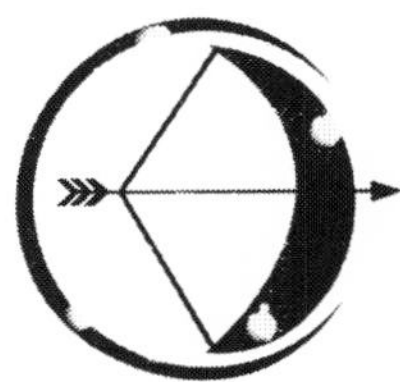

Marakyn

The sun was creeping toward noon when Vaughn and Ivana crested the final rise of the southern Fereharian pass.

Vaughn inhaled deeply as the city of Marakyn became visible in all its glory to the south, eight concentric tiers nestled into the mountainside. There was nothing else like it in all Setana. There was also nothing like being able to take full breaths again.

Their progress out of Ferehar and toward Marakyn had been slow, partially because of Vaughn's injuries. But even once his injuries had mostly healed—more quickly than they would have without bindblood aether—they had abandoned the main road in favor of slinking through rocks, fields, and forests, in case Airell decided to pursue them.

But they'd made it at last. The southern end of the Fereharian Mountains wasn't as high as the northern side, and the mountains ended rather abruptly in a steppe of rolling hills. Even so, at this altitude, Marakyn stretched out below them.

Not that they hadn't seen signs of the city before now. Unlike the northern plateau, which was primarily controlled by Ferehar, the southern pass was primarily controlled by Donia, and there were guard towers evenly stationed from about the midpoint of the much narrower passage. There was no sneaking by through that pass—unless, of course, one could literally turn invisible.

Ivana stopped beside him, also gazing at the city.

"When Yaotel had some of us gather here, it was only the second time I'd been to Marakyn. The first was long ago, before I had to flee home. You?"

"Twice," she said but offered nothing more.

Probably jobs. He didn't ask her to elaborate.

It took them another hour to pick their way down to the city gates. Vaughn fingered the little lightblood he had left, waiting to be tested at the gates—but the gates, while under guard, were open to all traffic, and no one questioned them.

"Refreshing," he muttered to Ivana.

"From what I remember," Ivana said, "Marakyn simply seems more *civilized* than what we're used to."

She remembered correctly. The streets of Marakyn, even in the lower tiers, were clean, the buildings well-maintained, and it felt overall more *safe*. Even so, most people would still turn on a Banebringer—and the guards still wore the standard-issue Setanan Watch uniform.

"Have you been to Ipsylanti?" Vaughn asked. He had never made it that far south and east.

"Yes. It's not as bad as, say, Weylyn City, but it's also enormous and sprawling—and thus not nearly as easy to keep in order."

He supposed that was fair. Marakyn, unlike most Setanan cities, was built like a fortress. The city stopped at its formidable walls, and what its walls contained was limited in space. There was no urban sprawl, there were no unaccounted-for abandoned buildings in crooked back alleys—and it probably helped that its prime location for trade with Ferehar and the nomads to the south kept the city reasonably affluent.

They wound their way back and forth through the tiers until they reached the seventh tier: the government tier. They entered the tier itself with no trouble, but at a second set of gates that led to the consulate and civic hall, they were stopped.

A single Watchman stepped forward. "Please state your name and business." He didn't seem concerned—just doing his duty. He flipped open a slim book, pencil at the ready.

Vaughn exchanged a glance with Ivana. "My name is Vaughn. We've been told to meet Dal Yaotel or Lady Nahua in the consulate."

The guard flipped a page in his book, made a mark, and then looked at Ivana. "Name?"

"Ivana."

The guard frowned and then shook his head. "I don't have your name down."

Uh-oh. Vaughn had neglected to mention to Yaotel that Ivana was with him, and apparently Danton hadn't informed him, either.

"Guest of yours?" the guard asked Vaughn.

"Yes. She's with me."

The guard made another mark. "I'll let you through for now, Da, but please be aware I'll have to send word on ahead to double-check. If you're not cleared, you'll have to wait outside with the others." He inclined his head to Ivana.

She returned the gesture. "Of course."

"I'll need you to leave any weapons with me. They aren't allowed beyond these gates."

Vaughn held out his hands. His bow, quiver, and, sadly, even his weaveblood-made bowstring had been lost when he had been captured by Airell; purchasing a new bow had been at the top of his list of things to do when they reached Marakyn. The guard patted him down and then turned to Ivana.

Perhaps it was his imagination, but he could almost *feel* the wave of tension beating out from her. Her face, however, remained perfectly calm. She unbuckled the dagger, sheath and all, from her belt, removed a small knife from her boot, and handed both to the guard.

He took them, set them aside, and patted her down as well. Then he rummaged quickly through their one remaining bag, and, finding nothing more, waved them both through.

"'Others'?" Ivana asked once they were out of the guard's hearing.

Vaughn shrugged. "I have no idea. I don't know what Yaotel's been doing or how he's managed to get himself admitted to the consulate. He didn't tell us much before we left on our expedition to the shrine." He squinted his eyes against the glare of the sun. There were two large buildings ahead of them, separated by an ornate garden. The one on the left was a square stone block three stories high, while the one on the right was a single level and sprawled across a greater area. There was a smattering of smaller buildings as well.

Vaughn slowed, uncertain. "Maybe we should have asked which one is the consulate."

But as it turned out, he didn't need to. A familiar figure came out of the door of the single-level building and turned in their direction.

Vaughn recognized his goofy grin at once and stepped up his pace to meet him.

"Danton!" he said, gripping the young man's arms. "When did you get here?"

"Almost a month ago originally and only yesterday, from...well. You'll hear all about it soon." Danton rubbed the back of his head and smiled at Ivana. "Ivana."

"Danton. Sanca make it okay?"

He nodded. "Huiel contacted me about a week ago to let me know she's integrating well."

She returned Danton's smile. "Good."

Wish she'd smile at me that way. Vaughn cast Danton a side eye. "So...you don't have to wait with the 'others'?"

Danton laughed. "Oh, no you don't. Yaotel will explain everything. It's a good thing you arrived when you did—we only have a few hours before the council meeting this afternoon and I'm sure you'll want to settle in, freshen up, and be briefed."

Vaughn groaned. "I don't know what's happening, but if it involves a meeting important enough to be called a 'council,' *I* may go wait with the 'others.'"

Danton slapped him on the back. "Sorry, friend. You're not getting out of this one. Now that he knows you're not dead, Yaotel's been frothing at the mouth that you've been out of touch for so long."

Ugh. Ugh. Ugh. Talking to Yaotel was the last thing he wanted to do because he knew where it would lead. If only he could report that Ferehar was perfectly stable and everyone loved their new Ri.

Danton hesitated and glanced apologetically at Ivana. "Uh, I didn't tell him Ivana was with you. Or what *else* you were doing. So, not sure if—"

"I'm more than willing to stay elsewhere," Ivana said, cutting in.

"That won't be necessary," Vaughn said firmly. "What *else* we've been doing is important too, so Yaotel has me until approximately three days before the sky-fire." It would work. It *had* to.

Danton's eyes widened. "Did you...?"

"Maybe." He glanced at Ivana. "We're still working on it." He jerked his head. "Why don't you show us where we're staying? You wouldn't *believe* what happened..."

Danton showed them back to the one-story building he had exited from, explaining their accommodations as he went. "Ri Tanuac's been generous enough to give us an entire wing, such as it is, of the consulate, for now. It's basically a common area with four sleeping rooms around it." He pulled open the door to the consulate and led them into a long stone hallway, and then through another door into a small entryway.

Vaughn glanced around the room curiously. Within this section of the consulate, the walls were made of long, wooden poles secured together and to the floor and ceiling. There was no door at the end, only a cured and dyed animal hide that stretched from ceiling to floor. "What is this?" he asked.

"This used to be the section of the consulate where important visitors from the southern lands would stay—they even had an ambassador from there once." He paused before the hide. "I think they were trying to make it more like home."

"Ah. I see." That made sense. The southern lands below Donia were populated by a semi-nomadic group of people; Setana had never bothered with them or their land because there had always been "better" opportunities. Vaughn didn't think any Setanans were interested in settling the sometimes harsh wilderness anyway.

"Of course," Danton continued, "there are no ambassadors anymore. Except—" He halted. "Well. That's not my place. I'll let Yaotel and Driskell explain everything to you."

He held back the hide for Vaughn and Ivana.

They ducked into the room, which was a large, circular room made of the same stick-like walls. Four hides covered door-sized gaps in the walls, and in the middle of the room, on cushions around a low, round table, sat Yaotel, Linette—one of their best bindblood healers—Thrax, and a young, spectacled, Donian man Vaughn had never seen before. Presumably, he was the aforementioned Driskell.

Danton let the hide fall closed, and Thrax gave them a grin and lazy salute and opened his mouth, but Yaotel was on his feet before Thrax could speak.

"What is *she* doing here?" were the first words out of his mouth.

The *she* he referred to was, of course, Ivana.

Vaughn shrugged. "You *did* tell me a full update could wait until—"

"Danton, I note that you conveniently neglected to mention this."

Danton took a step away from Yaotel and toward the wall, as if he was thinking of blending in. "Uh, I... Well—"

"Ivana is helping me with the shrine mission," Vaughn said. "And therefore also helping *us*."

Yaotel locked eyes with Ivana, and his gaze wasn't friendly.

Vaughn had halfway expected this. Ivana had killed Yaotel's sister in the course of a job a couple years back, and it seemed Yaotel was still bearing a grudge. That didn't surprise Vaughn, but he did wish Danton had prepared Yaotel.

Ivana had stayed near the door and was now leaning against the wall, her arms folded across her chest. She didn't flinch back from Yaotel's gaze. "I would be more than happy to leave."

Vaughn gritted his teeth. His reason for wanting Ivana to stay nearby was partially because he wanted to be able to easily check in on her progress, partially because he liked having her around, and partially because... Well, he was afraid if he let her out of his sight for too long, she might disappear again.

Linette looked on, her brow furrowed, Thrax had one eyebrow cocked, and Driskell fidgeted with his fingers uncomfortably—none of the three had any idea what the conflict stemmed from, of course. "If you would let me explain," Vaughn said to Yaotel, "I'm sure that—"

The hide opened, and a Donian servant bearing a tray of food walked in. He bowed over the tray. "Pardon me," he said. "I was told to be sure you had adequate refreshment before the meeting this afternoon."

No one said anything. The servant set the tray of food down on the low table, next to where Yaotel stood, and then straightened and turned to go.

As he did, metal flashed.

Ivana sensed the attack before she saw the knife.

The flick of servant's eyes around the room, the way he had turned, the movement of his arm—

She hurled herself into him just as he slashed toward Yaotel.

His strike went wild, his arms flailing out as Ivana knocked him off-balance. The knife grazed Yaotel's chest, and he bellowed and staggered to the side.

Ivana grabbed the servant's shoulders before he could recover from his surprise and kneed him in the groin. He groaned and stumbled backward, but he didn't fall. Instead, incredibly, he ignored her and lunged once more toward Yaotel.

She threw herself to the side, grabbed his knife arm, and used his own weight and momentum to hurl herself around him and into his back.

He grunted, and she jumped up, wrapped her arms around his neck, and lifted her legs off the ground so that her entire weight hung off his throat.

He dropped the knife and staggered backward, grasping at her arms, trying to pull them away, and then, failing to do so, hurled himself backward.

His full weight landed on top of her—a cushion for him, a painful impact for her.

But she didn't let go. He tried to get free by rolling over her, so she wrapped her legs around his waist and kicked her heel back into his groin, multiple times, until his soundless attempts to scream finally failed him, and he slumped back to the ground, motionless.

Chapter Twenty-Four

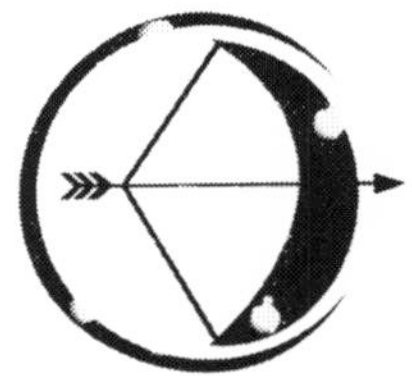

A Grumpy Old Man

Vaughn winced with every one of those kicks. *Damn.* What a way to go.

Ivana shoved Yaotel's would-be assassin off her and sat up, rubbing her shoulder.

You okay? Vaughn mouthed when she glanced his way.

She just shrugged.

He'd ask Linette to check over her after things calmed down.

He looked around. Not that it was chaotic. In fact, the rest of the room seemed to be in a state of shocked silence.

Yaotel held a hand over a bleeding gash in his chest, the blood trickling down his hand in a mix of silver and red.

Linette and Thrax stood slightly in front of him, as if ready to defend him should Ivana have failed.

Dal Driskell was pressed back against the wall, his eyes wide and flicking back and forth between Yaotel and the "servant" on the floor. Danton stood next to him.

Driskell ran a hand down his face. "Are you all right, Dal?" he asked Yaotel, a slight tremor in his voice.

Linette stirred. She turned toward Yaotel and pried his hand off the wound. "It's not deep," she said after examining it for a moment. "He's lucky." She placed her hand on his chest.

Vaughn snorted. "Luck has nothing to do with it." He looked pointedly at Yaotel and then at Ivana.

"Who is he?" Driskell whispered, looking down at the man.

"If you don't know," Ivana said, "then you're probably asking the wrong question." She pushed herself to her feet. "The question should be: Who sent him?"

Driskell had begun shaking his head before she finished speaking, as if he anticipated her response. "No, no, no. You're suggesting someone tried to have Yaotel assassinated? There aren't *that* many people who know about what's going on. The four Gan, the ambassador, the Ri, his daughter, a few military personnel... None of them would have done this."

As of yet, neither Vaughn nor Ivana knew anything about "what was going on," nor were they acquainted with any of the people Driskell had listed, but Ivana answered as if it were immaterial. "And yet," she countered, "if that's true, one of them must have—or they told someone else who turned out to be untrustworthy."

Driskell pushed his spectacles up his nose. He opened his mouth to say something more, then shook his head.

Yaotel frowned. "Might have been nice to be able to interrogate him."

Vaughn gritted his teeth. Never mind that Ivana had just saved Yaotel's life and consequentially the rest of their lives. His first thought was to lay blame at her feet for not being able to *question* the man?

Ivana's face was granite. "He's not dead," she said, her tone clipped. "But that probably won't last."

Yaotel glanced at Linette, who immediately knelt at the man's side. She put her fingers to his bruised throat. "She's right."

Ha. So there.

Yaotel pressed his lips together. "Can you save him?"

"Probably," Linette said, rising again. "But it might take a few days to get him to the point where he'll be able to talk."

Yaotel then looked at Driskell. "Dal Driskell," he said. "I have no authority here."

Driskell, who still looked rather shaken, blinked. "Oh. *Oh!* Right. Of course." He smoothed his tunic, pulled a pencil and notebook out from a pocket, and flipped the notebook open. "I'll report this immediately to the Ri himself and, of course, I'll pass on your request...and...um..." He faltered, looked at the unconscious man, and bit his lip. "I guess...we need guards..."

Vaughn felt a stab of pity for this Driskell. He didn't know who Driskell was, but given the context, he assumed he was someone official, perhaps a liaison for the Ri. Either way, he was young and obviously out of his element.

A small sigh issued from Ivana's lips. "Have him taken to a secure location," she suggested. "And make sure that whoever gets him there is someone you trust, lest whoever sent him find out you have him alive."

Driskell swallowed, but he gave Ivana a grateful look. "Right. Of course. I'll be back as soon as I can to get him out of here." His eyes skittered across Yaotel's chest, now stained with silver. "Uh...you might want to...clean up, just in case, before I get back." He scratched out a few notes and then moved toward the door with purpose, as if making a to-do list had given him an anchor.

He bowed generally in the direction of the room and ducked through the hide.

Vaughn took a deep breath. "All right. I think it's time you told us..." He gestured to himself and Ivana. "What in the abyss you've gotten us into."

Yaotel's lips pressed together. "After Dal Driskell has made arrangements for our uninvited guest, I will explain everything. To *you*." His eyes flicked to Ivana.

Here we go again. "She just saved your life, Yaotel."

"This is highly sensitive, need-to-know information. And if I decide she needs to know, I will tell her then."

Oh, for the love of—

Ivana held up her hands. "You know what? I don't *want* to know." She glanced at Vaughn. "I'm going to take a room at that inn we passed, The Silver Nomad. If you need me, I'll be there, working on *your* project." Then she stalked out.

Thrax whistled. "Yikes. Not getting in the middle of that one."

Yaotel glared at Thrax, and Danton backed away and pretended to be incredibly interested in a spot on the wall.

Linette cleared her throat and knelt back down by the unconscious man. "I'll make sure he stays stable."

Vaughn took a long, controlled breath in, and then let it out again, just as slowly. *She killed his sister,* he reminded himself. "So, does this mean I don't have to go to a council meeting?"

Yaotel let out an exasperated huff and sat down heavily on one of the cushions at the table. He waved his hand at another cushion, and Vaughn cautiously joined him.

"What in the abyss have you been *doing*?" Yaotel asked.

"What you asked me to do!"

Yaotel looked at him askance. "Danton told me that you didn't go directly to Ferehar, though he's been vague on the details. Then I couldn't get a hold of you for an entire month. *Then,* when

I finally do, you tell me you're done in Ferehar and on your way back to Marakyn."

"Look—I had some things to follow up on with the shrine mission first, and that involved finding Ivana. In, uh..." He cracked his neck from side to side. "Fuilyn."

Yaotel pressed his lips together.

"You *did* give me permission to work on that project," Vaughn reminded him.

"I gave you permission to check out the site, not go gallivanting across Setana."

"Eh," Vaughn said, wiggling his hand in the air, "that's not how I interpreted it."

Danton edged toward one of the adjoining rooms.

"Danton!" Yaotel snapped.

Danton froze.

"Sit."

Danton's shoulders slumped. "I told you so," he whispered to Vaughn as he plopped down next to him.

"Bah," Vaughn whispered back. "He's just a grumpy old man."

"I can hear you."

"Not old enough, apparently," Vaughn whispered again.

Vaughn was sure, for a moment, that Yaotel's head was about to pop. "Everyone else did what they were supposed to do," Yaotel said evenly. "Yasril came back. Saylyn came back. Dax came back. Even *Thrax* came back."

"Hey!" Thrax protested from the other side of the room. "Don't make me out to be the responsible one now."

"Thrax, out," Yaotel said.

Thrax crossed his eyes at them and disappeared behind one of the hides to an adjoining room. Danton looked regretfully after him.

"I don't understand what the big deal is," Vaughn said,

plucking a grape off the platter the servant had brought.

"The 'big deal' is that I had a job for you to do, and you dragged your feet doing it. And then you dragged Danton along with you."

"Uh, did that come from the tray the assassin brought in?" Danton interrupted, just as Vaughn was about to pop the grape in his mouth.

He dropped the grape. "See," he said, "*that* is why Ivana's useful to have around. If Danton weren't so smart, I could have died."

Yaotel's eye twitched.

All right. Too far. He spread his hands. "Look, I'm *sorry*, okay? I didn't realize the job was so time-sensitive. I'm here now—for now."

"For now? You have plans to go elsewhere?"

Vaughn raised an eyebrow. "Yes. I have an appointment with the heretic gods in about, oh, two and a half weeks?"

Yaotel just stared at him, unblinking.

"You...do know what I was doing at that shrine, right? Remember, fascinating journal, mysterious portal to the heavens..."

"Yes. Another of your wild schemes, no doubt to get out of doing what you should be doing. And everyone else came back and said you learned nothing."

Vaughn raised a finger. "That is..." He thought about it for a moment and then shrugged. "All right, technically true. Which is *why* I tracked down Ivana, because I needed someone who was good with languages."

"And that then required you to drag her through Ferehar and back to Marakyn?"

Vaughn hesitated. He doubted Ivana would want her personal connection with the journal shared with anyone else, let alone Yaotel. "Yes, in fact. But what's important is that in the end, she was able to translate the page out of the journal that we needed translated, and she's working right now on translating the inscription on the serpent. After all I went through to get back here, I need to at least give it a try."

Yaotel closed his eyes.

Vaughn glanced at Danton. He shrugged.

After what seemed like an eternity, Yaotel opened his eyes again. "I'm hoping," he said calmly, "that after I'm able to explain to you the situation here, you'll realize how inconsequential your plan sounds in comparison. But *I* realize that's probably a vain hope, and I also realize that you've never taken direction particularly well. I've got Aleena taking your place in Ferehar for now, so go do whatever it is you think you need to do. As long as you promise me that after you're done standing in the middle of the forest reciting ancient incantations, or whatever it is you're planning, and you're feeling like an idiot, you'll get your ass back here and do what I tell you?"

Vaughn held his hands up. "Sure, fine, whatever." There had to be a way out of this. He didn't *want* to be Ri. The translation, the doorway, it had to work. The gods *had* to help.

Yaotel exhaled.

"Might it interest you to know that my brother was asking about the Ichtaca?"

Yaotel's eyes sharpened and he sat up straighter. "What?"

"I had a run-in with him. Nothing much, just some mild torture and—don't worry, I didn't *tell* him anything—questions. But he knew the name 'Ichtaca.' You have some loose lips somewhere?"

Yaotel's brow furrowed. "That's...disturbing. How did you escape?"

"Ivana"—he snapped his fingers—"*again*, I reiterate how she comes in handy—rescued me." He paused. "With the help of my mother."

Yaotel narrowed his eyes. "Your mother helped you?"

Vaughn shifted. All wisecracks left him. "Yeah."

"Interesting. Good to keep that in mind."

Vaughn had the sudden urge to get up and start pacing. He didn't want to hear any more about plans for Ferehar right now.

The hide slid aside and Driskell popped his head in. "Pardon the interruption, but we have a place to hold him," he said, nodding at the still-unconscious man. "Danton, would you mind sort of...concealing him while we get him there?"

Danton popped up off his cushion before Driskell had finished speaking. "Happy to help."

"And then, Ri Tanuac wants to see all of you," Driskell continued.

Damn. Guess Vaughn was going to have to go to a meeting after all.

Chapter Twenty-Five

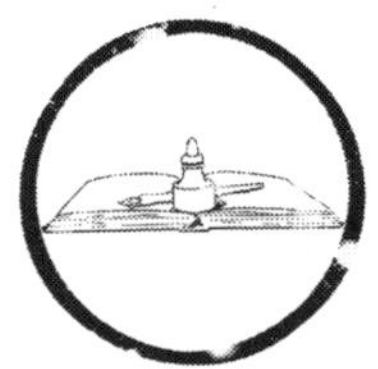

A Friendly Game

Driskell shivered in the night air, and not because it was cold. No, every empty street, every shadow, every nook and cranny could hold a knife in the dark.

Not that he flattered himself that *he* was important enough for someone to want to eliminate, but never in his life had he witnessed someone attempt to *kill* someone else in front of him. It left him more shaken than he wanted to admit.

He turned the corner and quickened his pace, relieved to see light and hear music flooding out of the building he was headed for: Tamal's inn. He thought maybe a night of tapolli and a mild drink or two might take his mind off work.

Had he realized when he'd accepted this position that in less than two years he'd be embroiled in the middle of a revolt, on friendly terms with Banebringers and Xambrians, and watching people get strangled in front of him, he might have settled for that desk job at the Donian regional bank.

The assassination attempt on Yaotel was also a sobering reminder to Driskell of what having Banebringers around meant for the rest of them, should one of the Banebringers die.

With the amount of time he had spent with Banebringers lately, Driskell had found himself relaxing. They seemed like perfectly normal people—most of them perfectly likeable people, in fact—and it was easy to forget what they were.

Until one of them was bleeding silver all over himself.

Thankfully, the rest of the afternoon remained incident-free. Tanuac had a rather brilliant idea for where to hold the man *and* a place to move the Ichtaca—all of them, not just Yaotel's inner circle—where they would be safer for now. The man had been successfully moved in secret and the Banebringer healer, Linette, was working on reviving him as soon as possible so he could be questioned.

And the sooner, the better. There was a traitor in their midst—or at least someone who had broken confidence. Either way, their planning for how to deal with the impending Conclave threat had come to a grinding halt until the culprit could be identified and dealt with because Tanuac could no longer trust his own advisors.

And that fact smarted. Both Tanuac and Nahua had been deeply disturbed by the assassination attempt, and, frankly, he had been too, beyond the obvious reasons.

Donians had always prided themselves on the relative purity of their interpretation of the Setanan political system. They held fair elections when the Ri died or decided to retire. Though connections didn't hurt, ultimately the Gan were selected for their abilities and character. And even though it wasn't strictly necessary, the Donian Ri had always striven to involve their Gan in the process of governance to a greater extent than other Setanan regions.

There were not assassinations, back-room politicking, and under-the-table deals.

In short, they prided themselves in not being Setanan.

In light of the assassination attempt, Tanuac had canceled the meeting scheduled for that afternoon. He had intended it as a brainstorming and planning session with the Ichtacan inner circle, his Gan, and General Gyano. Instead, he met only with the Ichtaca. It was a strange reversal that Banebringers were suddenly the only people they could trust.

Enough of that, Driskell thought, pushing open the door to the inn.

Tamal gave him a cheery wave as he entered, and Driskell felt some of the tension drain from his shoulders. Part of him wished Tania could be here with him tonight—she had work obligations—and part of him was glad she couldn't, because there was no way he'd be able to hide his tension from her, and she'd be too concerned to let it go.

"Driskell!" a voice called from across the room, waving him over to one of the tapolli tables.

Driskell recognized two of the four men seated around the table, and neither of the women. The first whom he recognized, the one who had called to him, was a friend and co-worker—a clerk from the civic hall by the name of Deloro. The other was an older minor noble Driskell had seen on occasion but didn't know well named Lord Grinya.

Driskell wandered over to watch the game in progress. He didn't know the two men playing. One of them tossed a setan into the hole at the end of his board—already almost full—and his opponent groaned, while Lord Grinya banged his empty mug on the table loudly.

"Come on, Klai," he said, "one more."

Klai frowned. "That's what you said last time, Grinya, and I'm already in the hole." But he matched his opponent's wager, took a deep breath, and tossed his five stones.

Only two landed with the white dot up.

His opponent moved his red marker forward a space with a triumphant shout while Klai cursed under his breath.

"You want to play the winner?" Deloro asked Driskell. He winked. Deloro knew Driskell didn't bet.

"Ha. No thanks."

Grinya overheard them. "Ah, Driskell," he said, putting a hand a little too heavily on his shoulder. "Live a little. Drinks on me!"

Driskell slunk away from him as politely as he could manage, but Grinya only leaned closer, so much so that Driskell could smell the alcohol on his breath, and jerked his head toward the woman at his side. "I'll even share Deiya here if you win."

Driskell glanced at the woman, who gave him a sly wink. "Er..." He stammered, feeling his cheeks heat. "I'm not really—"

The hand on Driskell's shoulder tightened. "Come on, boy. You're being awfully impolite to your betters, don't you think, for someone angling for promotion himself?"

Driskell glanced at Deloro, who gave him a sympathetic look. Ri Tanuac's noble appointees were generally good people, but some of those born into it thought a little too highly of themselves. Of all the nights to run into this crowd...

"Are you ready for our game?" a woman's voice said impatiently from behind him.

Driskell spun around and blinked at the woman who stood there—staring at *him.* The same woman who had saved Yaotel from the assassin earlier that day. He searched for a name—he knew he'd heard it... There. "Da Ivana. Uh, yes," he said, though he had no idea what she was talking about, it was as good of an excuse as any. "Of course."

He sketched a quick bow to Grinya. "Prior engagement, my lord. So sorry."

Grinya frowned at him but said nothing more.

Ivana led him to the other side of the room, where there was an empty tapolli table, and sat down on one side of it.

He cautiously joined her on the other.

"I apologize if I misread the situation," she said, picking up one of the silver stones in the groove on her side of the table. "But I happened to notice you come in, and you looked like you needed an excuse to escape."

He relaxed a bit. "Ah. Yes. You had the right of it." He glanced back at Grinya and then gave Ivana a grateful smile. "It seems, once again, I'm in your debt, Da."

She returned the smile. "I don't keep a tally of debts. Is he going to be a problem later?"

"No, I don't think so. He's just half-drunk."

She made a noncommittal noise. "Dal Driskell, was it?"

He nodded.

"I don't think we were ever formally introduced."

"No...I suppose not." He took a deep breath. "I'm Ri Tanuac's attaché—though in reality I work with both him and Lady Nahua, his daughter." He paused. "Not to pry, but you weren't with the others this afternoon. And...you're not with them now?"

She set the silver stone on the opening space. "I'm not part of their *group*."

He blinked. "Oh. When you came in with Dal Vaughn, I suppose I assumed you...were," he finished lamely since he couldn't be more specific in public.

"No. Just a friend of Vaughn's." She gestured toward his side. "Now, Dal, I confess, I don't remember how to play this game.

It's been a long time."

"Oh! You really want to play? Sure. That's why I came here tonight anyway. But I don't bet."

"Wise choice," she said.

A crash sounded from somewhere in the vicinity of the kitchen, and Driskell jumped, scattering across the floor the pieces he had just laid out.

He clenched his fist and bent down to gather the stones, embarrassed. "I apologize. I've been jumpy today." He lowered his voice. "I...think I'm seeing assassins around every corner now, you know?" He straightened up.

She didn't reply; instead, she flicked her eyes behind him.

He turned to find Gan Dillion coming their way. "Driskell," Dillion said, nodding to him. "Been a while since I've seen you in here."

He rose from his chair, dropping the stones that he had just put in his lap.

Burning skies, what was *wrong* with him tonight?

"Your Grace," he said, inclining his head. "Am I needed?"

"No, no," Dillion said, waving his hand. "I'm sorry to interrupt you. I just thought I'd say *hello*. I'm picking up one of Tamal's famous tarts for Keita on my way home...since it turns out I wasn't needed this afternoon after all, eh?"

Driskell swallowed. This was...awkward. "Indeed, Your Grace."

Dillion hesitated. "Any idea what that was about?"

"I'm sure Ri Tanuac had his reasons for canceling."

Dillion proffered a tight smile. "I'm sure." He inclined his head. "Have a good night."

Driskell sank back into his chair, watching the Gan's back as he made his way to the bar to talk to Tamal.

Ri Tanuac had asked Driskell's opinion on his four Gan that

afternoon, after they had met with the Ichtaca. Driskell had been forced to admit that Gan Dillion seemed the most obvious suspect.

Tanuac preferred that all his advisors come to an agreement on pivotal decisions, but in this case, he had ruled that they would make both alliances without Dillion's support. Could Dillion have really been that angry?

The truth was, Driskell had always rather liked Dillion. He was brusque, attentive to detail, and a master administrator. He was proof that one didn't have to be charismatic or have much to offer other than his own skill to be appointed as a Gan. It meant that Driskell might one day aspire to such an appointment, despite not being connected to nobility himself. The man had even given him a few pointers here and there.

Driskell *really* didn't want to believe Dillion was a murderer—or even untrustworthy, however outspoken he was against Tanuac's plans in their private meetings.

But Driskell had also said to the Ri that if Dillion wanted to subvert their plans, it seemed he would be less vocal about his disagreement—since it *did* too obviously point to him if anything went wrong.

Both Tanuac and Nahua agreed with him on all points, which still left them with no clear suspects. Herne, unless he was an incredible actor, was by all appearances fully supportive of both alliances. Both Gan Fiacra and Gan Beatha appeared to Driskell to have submitted to the Ri's will and reluctantly agreed that this was the only way to accomplish their goals.

"Dal, it doesn't appear that you *really* want to play tapolli tonight."

Driskell jerked his eyes back to Da Ivana, who was patiently waiting for him to return his mind to setting up the game.

He swallowed. "No. I...actually, I think I'm going to head

home and turn in. This has been a..." He shook his head and stood. "My apologies. Maybe another time?"

Ivana stood and inclined her head. "If you'd like."

Driskell gave her a short bow and headed back to the dormitory. It felt as though the entire city of Marakyn were balanced on a precipice, instead of beneath it. One shove and the whole thing would come crashing to the ground.

Ivana returned to her room after Dal Driskell left. She had only gone to the dining room to bring something back for dinner—and had happened to see the young man walk in.

When he obviously hadn't been enthused about the group of people he'd joined, she'd taken the opportunity to seize him up.

He was certainly not a threat, unless he was an excellent actor. No, rather, Ri Tanuac's attaché was very young...and very, very stressed.

Chapter Twenty-Six

Puzzles

Ivana spent five days alone in a room with a mysterious language to puzzle over.

It was glorious.

No bickering with Vaughn, no daggers of hatred from Yaotel, no polite conversation with people she'd rather not talk to, no bloodbane to slay, no murders to stop or commit, no ghosts from her past...

Well, aside from the journal lying on the corner of the desk, of course. But she had *almost* grown used to the sight of her mother's neat script staring at her every time she looked at it.

She was glad that Yaotel hadn't seen fit to include her in whatever plots the Ichtaca and Donian government had going on. She could do this translation for Vaughn and be done with all of them.

Then what?

Well. Her solitude was glorious aside from that nagging thought.

She pushed aside a piece of paper—and the thought.

She was just starting to wonder if Vaughn had forgotten about her—or if what Yaotel had told him had pushed everything else out of his mind—when he finally showed up at her door again.

She let him in and went to sit back at the desk.

"How's it going?" He closed the door after him and then wandered over behind her at the desk.

"Surprisingly well," she said. "There's a lot of vocabulary overlap, which is what I was hoping for."

"So you're almost done?" he asked, craning his neck to look at her translation work.

"I'd give it another couple of days for a finished product. Or at least as finished as I'm going to get it."

There was a long silence. "There still seem to be an awful lot of questions marks..."

She shuffled her papers around to hide the one with her marked-up, rough translation. "It isn't as simple as plopping one word in the place of another. For one thing, the Xambrian order isn't necessarily the same as the word order of this mystery language. So I have to figure out *which* vocabulary the words in this script are supposed to represent from my own translation of the Xambrian, already a translation of a mystery language."

She tapped her pencil on what was now the topmost paper, which was her mini-primer on the mystery language, so far as she could figure out from the miniscule sample she had to work with. "Secondarily, just because a vocabulary word is similar doesn't mean it can be translated the same. The language appears to be marked for gender and plurality, but only partially for case? I'm not sure on that one—I think my sample size is just too small to say definitively. And then, the verbal system is...different. Tense doesn't appear to carry the same meaning that it does in Xambrian and Setanan, so the verbal forms are confusing me, even when they're consistent. And then again, maybe I'm completely wrong—maybe this sample isn't representative. Maybe monumental writing had different conventions—"

"Ivana."

She turned to look up at him.

He was smiling slightly. "I was teasing you. I get it. I think. It's fine. Just do the best you can."

She exhaled, stood up, and stretched, rubbing her right shoulder blade—which was still sore after five days. "Why are you grinning at me like that?"

He shook his head. "You should have been a scholar. When you get like this, it's like nothing else matters."

Yes. Well. Perhaps she could have been if things had turned out differently.

One single comment, and she felt the peace of the last few days slipping away.

"I so rarely get to see this unfiltered *you,*" he continued.

You. She turned away to shuffle her papers into a pile. "Was there something else you needed?"

"And then that happens," he said softly.

She straightened up and clenched her teeth together. And apparently, also her back muscles, because the ache in the right blade came back.

She rolled her shoulder and rubbed at it again.

"Back bothering you?" he asked. "Is that from—?"

"Yes," she said, sliding past him and over to the bed. She sat down and leaned back against the wall.

“Do you want me to have Linette—”

“No.”

He held up a finger. “I anticipated that.” He pulled a jar of what looked like salve out of his pocket, held it up, and raised an eyebrow.

She started to shake her head, but he held up a hand. “Don’t be so stubborn. This will *help*. Perhaps you remember the broken wrist that healed in a few days’ time, once you let me help you? Or the leg that didn’t have to be amputated? Or—”

She held up her hand. Burning skies, that seemed like eons ago. “Fine. Just—fine.”

She scooted to the edge of the bed, and he sat down next to her and opened the jar of salve. “Glad to see you can still be reasoned with.”

She undid the top several buttons of her shirt so she could shimmy it down to bare her upper back.

His eyes slid over her skin and then flicked back up to her face. The pang of desire she saw there only lasted a moment before he schooled himself, but it was enough.

Enough to stir the same momentary pang in herself.

She turned on the bed so her back was to him.

He brushed a few locks of hair that had fallen out of her hair tie away from her back and across to her other shoulder, and then let that hand rest there while he rubbed salve into the muscles around the opposite shoulder blade.

His hands were warm. She closed her eyes and swallowed.

“Burning skies, Ivana,” he said. “It’s a wonder you don’t have a constant backache, as tight as your muscles are.” He trailed his other hand down her left shoulder blade. “*Relax*.”

She tried. She really did. But it was hard to relax when she was fighting with herself about enjoying the touch of his fingers on her bare skin. When she was trying to stop herself from fantasizing about what might happen if she unbuttoned a few more buttons and let her shirt slip away entirely, if she invited him to give her another full back massage. It would be so easy to do, wouldn't it? Just a few more buttons...

He dropped his hands. "Done," he said, wiping his hand on his trousers and then sealing back up the jar of salve.

She pulled the shirt back over her shoulders and buttoned it back up. Admittedly, her back felt better already.

He folded his hands in his lap. "So, now's the part when I have to pass on the message from Yaotel."

"I'm almost afraid to ask."

"He wants you to try talking to the man who attacked him," Vaughn said. "They can't get anything out of him."

Cold ran through her. "What in the abyss does he think *I* can do?

"I think his logic is—"

"Takes one to know one?" she snapped.

"Ivana—"

"The person he's looking for is dead."

There was a heavy silence. Vaughn met her eyes. He hesitated. And then he said quietly, "Weren't you the one who told me discarding a name didn't mean the core of who you are had changed?"

Hearing her own words repeated back at her cut deep.

No matter how many days she sat in a room translating a text, she would never escape this. Never.

"I see," she said. "Glad to know you agree with me now. Now you can go tell Yaotel—"

He put a finger on her lips.

She halted, more out of surprise than anything else.

"Yes, I do agree," he said firmly. "But only because you have it reversed. You think Sweetblade was your core. One and the same with Ivana. But she wasn't, and she never was. She was a mask you wore so often, you lost track of the real you."

He was wrong on both counts. Sweetblade was neither the same as the person who had once been Ivana, nor a mere mask. She was a suit of armor, a prison, a grave. Now, she was gone, and what remained was the detritus of three shattered lives—not some abstract "real her" that had been floating around waiting to be found again.

"But she *did* teach you an awful lot," he continued, "and her loss doesn't mean you've lost the skills and memories that could enable you to help us."

"Not that long ago," she said tightly, "Yaotel's needs and wants didn't seem that important to you. What changed?"

Vaughn exhaled. "Well. Turns out things here are..." He bit his lip. "Way more dire than I thought."

She didn't want to know. But what was the alternative? Retreating to the other façade, that of a peaceful life never marred by the things she'd seen or done in her past life, or the one before that?

She sighed. "I suppose you're going to tell me, aren't you?"

"Yes. He's decided you need to know."

Ivana listened, dispassionate, to Vaughn's relation of what Yaotel had told him. She didn't even flinch when he told her that the Conclave army had an entire unit of battle-priests—and apparently a corpse-thing.

"Ri Tanuac's plan," Vaughn said, "is to continue putting off the Conclave with misdirection as long as they can. Three days ago, they made a big show of kicking Ambassador Mezzo out of the city. It was actually Danton, disguised as Ambassador Mezzo. Mezzo himself has agreed to stay hidden for now. As far as the so-called Conclave representative, they've put off 'official' meetings until they find out who talked. Tanuac doesn't think they'll move against Donia until after the sky-fire since it's so close. He's hoping to continue to put them off even longer. But it won't last forever." He ran a hand through his hair. "As soon as we get word that they're marching toward Donia, Tanuac plans to send in a team to steal all their aether so the battle-priests are rendered ineffective."

Ivana grunted. "Makes sense. What about the...corpse-thing?" she asked, the slightest of smiles twitching her lips, gone almost before it was there.

"A prime target, obviously, if they end up skirmishing with them. We've informed Ri Tanuac what we know about those things, assuming it's anything like the other one we encountered—and to be prepared for the possibility of the Conclave using bloodbane in the assault." He shuddered. "We're all hoping that doesn't happen. Frankly, I think Yaotel is hoping we can get Ferehar on board before it comes to anything so drastic."

He understood why the mission Yaotel had sent him on had become so critical now. They needed Ferehar for the Xambrians to fulfill their part of the alliance—though, of course, Yaotel hadn't known that when he'd first tasked Vaughn with reconnaissance.

Vaughn just wished he didn't have to be a part of it. He never thought he'd miss his solitary days of roaming around hunting bloodbane. He'd wanted a normal life, and he was pretty sure this didn't qualify.

Ivana sat silently, studying his face.

He rubbed his jaw and tried to push aside the gloom that encroached every time he thought about what Yaotel wanted him for. "Thankfully, I've got some time. He sent a friend of yours to Ferehar to continue laying some groundwork before we need to take any action."

Ivana stared at him. "A friend of mine?"

"Aleena."

"*What?*"

Vaughn nodded. "Yaotel apparently contacted her and asked if she'd help us. She should be there soon."

Ivana seemed annoyed at that, though Vaughn wasn't sure why. "Shouldn't we have seen her on our way in?" she asked.

"Why? She wouldn't have seen us. Yaotel gave her resources."

Ivana shook her head.

"So. Will you talk to the man?" Vaughn asked.

Ivana closed her eyes.

Vaughn fidgeted with the cuff of his sleeve. Tanuac had forbidden the use of torture, and Yaotel had said it wouldn't work anyway—he'd just lie. Even the offer of some sort of eventual clemency for good information hadn't swayed him.

Vaughn didn't know if Ivana could get him to talk where others had failed, but if she could...

He hated to admit it, but what was happening here *was* important. If they could *win*, this could be the turning point for the Ichtaca—for all Banebringers.

But winning would involve more than keeping the Conclave at bay, or, if it came to it, winning against them in battle. Ultimately, it meant winning the Donian people over to their side. That wasn't an impossibility, especially once they could oust any official Setanan influence, but it would still be a long road fraught with plenty of internal conflict. And the danger of outright revolt always existed so early on if the news leaked out that the Ri was working with Banebringers.

They had to find out who among the Ri's advisors could no longer be trusted.

Ivana opened her eyes. "Don't you have people who can do this sort of thing? Persuade with your Banebringer magic?"

"Charmbloods?" Vaughn asked. "Yes, but not in Marakyn right now. And, the way I understand it, their powers work best on people who aren't already on guard, and it's hard to use them to simply force someone to do what you want."

She sighed. "I'll talk to him," she said. "With conditions."

Vaughn had a feeling this was coming.

"One, no one other than you or Yaotel is to be within hearing distance while I'm speaking with him. Two, if I have to reveal my former identity to get him to talk, he dies when I'm done. Immediately. I don't care if he's destined for the noose anyway."

Yaotel wasn't going to like that, and Tanuac certainly wouldn't—especially without knowing the reason. "I'll...pass on the message."

"Fine. If he decides he wants me to try, you know where to find me."

Chapter Twenty-Seven

The Assassin

The lanterns along the wall of the tunnel flickered with the passage of Nahua, then Yaotel, and then Vaughn and Ivana behind. The dank passage smelled of lichen and moss, and the air was heavy with little circulation.

Danton had told Vaughn—passing the information on from Driskell—that the vast network of tunnels and rooms beneath the mountain that overlooked Marakyn had been used for many purposes over the centuries. Dungeons, safe rooms, storage—even barracks.

Ultimately, it was the final purpose they intended to return it to. At the first branching corridor they had come to, the left passage had led to the area into which, even now, Ichtaca were moving their supplies and gear. What Ri Tanuac called "the inner circle"—those of the Ichtaca who had joined Yaotel in meetings with the Ri already, including Vaughn—had already settled into their new, if hopefully temporary, home. The rest, some of whom were still scattered throughout Marakyn, and some of whom hadn't even arrived yet, were following in a trickle of one or two at a time, so as not to attract attention.

They had taken the right passage, which was narrower and empty of people.

Nahua stopped in front of one of the many doors that lined the passage. She pulled a key out of her pocket and handed it to Yaotel. Her eyes flicked to Ivana and then back. "I'm going to go see how the latest batch of Ichtaca are settling in. Let me know when you're...done."

She turned and walked back down the passage.

Vaughn took a deep breath. Yaotel hadn't liked Ivana's conditions, but he understood them. Tanuac hadn't liked or understood them since Yaotel couldn't explain who Ivana was or why she might be effective when others could not be. But after another few days of attempting to coerce, cajole, or bribe the attacker into giving them *anything*, and still, the man had remained silent, Tanuac had finally given in to Yaotel's odd request.

When Nahua had disappeared, Yaotel unlocked the door and pushed it open.

Ivana's face was stone. She glanced at Vaughn, jerked her head, and entered the door.

He closed it behind her, stepped into the corner, and folded his arms across his chest. He was here both to hear what the man had to say and as an extra precaution if the man tried anything.

Ivana stopped to survey the room where they were keeping Yaotel's assailant.

It was empty other than a bedroll, a chamber pot, a plate, and the man himself.

He sat cross-legged on his bedroll, a vaguely bored expression on his face. His ankles had been slapped in irons and chains and one ankle had a chain leading to a bar on the wall—long enough to allow him some freedom of movement, but not long enough to get close to the door.

He took both their measures quickly, his eyes flicking once to the dagger at Ivana's thigh, and then he leered at her as though she hadn't recently bested him in a hand-to-hand contest. "Is this the part where they send in a whore to seduce me so I whisper secrets in the throes of passion?"

Vaughn frowned, but Ivana ignored his opening volley. "I hear you're being uncooperative," she said. "I went to the trouble of keeping you alive so you could be questioned, only to have you refuse to talk?"

She had? Vaughn hadn't known that she had *deliberately* kept him alive. Then again, she could also be lying.

Ivana drew her dagger and walked closer to the man.

He eyed Ivana's dagger, but his expression didn't change.

"Here's the deal," she said, tapping the dagger against her thigh. "I don't want to be here. I'm not going to waste my time asking you questions we both know you won't answer. So instead, I'm going to tell you why you *should* spill what you know."

Vaughn hadn't had the faintest idea what she'd planned to say to the man, so now he found his curiosity piqued.

"Because, now that I *am* here," Ivana continued, "you have exactly three options remaining. First, I heard they offered the possibility of clemency if you give good information. You could still take them up on it, but I sense that you didn't like that option for some reason."

The man rolled his eyes.

"As I thought. You know that if you do that, at best, you're a free man with a ruined reputation and a target on your back."

The man's eyes narrowed.

"Still, until that hangman's noose is around your neck, there's time to think it over, time for certain types of clients to rescue you, maybe even time to orchestrate your own escape and deal with the client on your own terms."

She crouched down to his level. "This isn't a job given to second chances. Most of the time, the only way you leave it is in a grave. I'd take the chance they're giving you. It's slim, but if you don't agree to it now, it will no longer be an option on the table."

Vaughn studied Ivana's profile. She was perfectly calm and her expression schooled. Was she was listening to her own advice? Was it all an act, or did the words come from something deeper? *She* had been given a second chance and yet seemed to struggle with embracing it fully. Not that she'd ever *admit* that to him...

The man leaned forward, inches from her face, and sneered at her. "Who in the abyss do you think you are, wench?"

Vaughn bristled; he had to restrain himself from jumping forward and threatening to throttle the man until he rephrased that.

And then he wondered at his own reaction, toward protectiveness, toward offense on her behalf. That was not...normal for him.

For Ivana's part, she merely straightened up, looked down on the man, and answered his question. "I was once known as Sweetblade."

Vaughn had to restrain a wince. So much for clemency.

There was a long pause. The would-be assassin looked the former assassin up and down again, a little less smugness, a little more disbelief.

"I see you've heard of me," Ivana said. "Good."

"Sweetblade is dead," he said.

"So they say," she said. "And yet."

And yet. It seemed an apt description of his observations of the woman Vaughn had traveled with these past months. Sweetblade was dead. And yet.

The man swallowed, but still, he sneered at her. "You're lying."

She shrugged. "All right. You can believe that. Doesn't change the fact that now that I've told you that information, I cannot possibly let you walk free, whatever the Ri may have promised you. Option one is now off the table."

In one quick motion, she had her foot on the chain between his ankles and her dagger against his throat. "Now you have two options left. You can tell them what they want to know, and then I'll give you a nice, quick, painless death. Or you can refuse, and when I'm done with you, your mind won't be intact enough to tell anyone what you know, let alone what *they* want to know."

He swallowed again. "They haven't tortured me yet—"

"Do you think *I* care about *their* standards?" she asked.

Vaughn bit his tongue. She wouldn't *really* torture him, would she?

Okay, she probably would. But he couldn't imagine Tanuac being happy with that outcome...

The man stared at her. And then his shoulders deflated. "Fine."

Ivana stood up and sheathed her dagger. "Then talk."

Vaughn quickly pulled his qixli out of one of the pouches at his waist. He held it down at his thigh and clenched it tightly in one hand, activating the aether, and connected to Yaotel's qixli just outside the door. Not a sound came out. Yaotel should be ready.

"I don't know the client's name," the man began. "But he wasn't Donian. Setanan."

"And what were the terms of the job?"

"Eliminate first and primarily the man named Yaotel—and then anyone else in the room I could, if I had the chance."

That was unexpected—and disturbing. The person who'd hired him presumably knew there'd be a room full of Banebringers. Killing Yaotel *would* likely have meant more deaths, which would have compounded upon itself. So that *had* to be intentional, right? It was targeted at Yaotel but intended to take out as many of them as it could, consequences be damned—maybe even consequences be desired.

The assassin couldn't have known they were Banebringers. Or that the job he had accepted had been near-suicidal.

"Ambitious," Ivana said. "The payment must have been especially generous for such a risky job."

The man shifted. "What he offered was more valuable than money." He leaned forward. "He offered me *magic*. He was a Banebringer."

Vaughn started. *What? No.* That was impossible. That was... He struggled to school his face, lest the assassin notice his disconcertment.

There was a long pause. "And how would you know that?" Ivana said evenly after a moment.

The assassin seemed to sense that he had surprised even Ivana because at this point some of his smugness returned. "He showed me his blood. And then he showed me a trick so I could use it, same as the Conclave. And demonstrated a bunch of others too."

Vaughn wanted to take over the questioning. There were far too many questions, new questions, running through his mind, questions he wanted to be sure Ivana asked the man. But he didn't dare interrupt. He had to trust she would understand what they might need.

"And what sort of magic did he offer?"

Good.

"Stealth, healing, manipulation, a few others. Stuff that would have come in handy, ya know?"

"And did he show you what *he* could do?"

Even better.

The man shrugged. "Yeah, wasn't as useful to me. But he did some stuff with ice."

An iceblood.

"Did this Banebringer happen to say *why* he wanted Yaotel and the rest of us dead?"

The man shook his head.

Ivana drew in a slow breath through her nose. "Anything else you can think of? Distinctive features on the man's face?"

The assassin snorted. "I'd think being a Banebringer ought to be distinctive enough. He was Setanan, knew from his hands. Wore a hood and a mask and it was dark, so I can't tell you much more than that."

"Where was pickup once the job was done?"

"Same place I met him. Down on the first tier, behind one of the factories—after hours."

Then, at last, Ivana turned to glance at Vaughn.

At the same moment, the door to the room opened, and Yaotel slid in, his face grim. He closed the door behind him and then looked at Ivana. "Finish it."

"You know you're working with a notorious assassin, right?" the man said to Yaotel. "Her real name is Sweetblade. Don't know what agenda she has, but—"

"You don't think I'm that stupid, do you?" Ivana asked. She knelt in front of him and took a clear, finger-nail-sized disc out of her pouch. "If it's any consolation, you got mixed up in the wrong job this time. There was never any other end for you." She handed him the disc. "Dissolve it on your tongue. It won't hurt, and you'll be dead in less than a minute."

The man took the disc, but then he leered at her again, his eyes lingering on her breasts. "So. Is it true what they say? That you're as sweet as you are sharp?"

She gave the man an icy look Vaughn well remembered because he had received plenty of them himself during his initial acquaintance with her. "I think you misunderstand the name. The two aren't meant to be separated."

He held up the disc to her, as if to make some sort of morbid toast, and then put it on his tongue. A few moments later, he stilled, dead eyes still on her chest.

Ivana closed his eyelids and stood up to face Vaughn and Yaotel. "Well. It looks like your traitor is in your own camp."

Yaotel didn't say anything. He just opened the door, and the three of them filed out, leaving the corpse of the assassin behind.

"Do you need me for anything else?" Ivana asked.

Yaotel pressed his lips together and waved her off with nary a word of gratitude for her help leaving his lips.

"I'm done with your translation," she said to Vaughn. "So if it still matters...you know where to find me."

He nodded, and she retreated down the tunnel.

Then he looked at Yaotel. "How many icebloods do we have here in Marakyn?"

"Three," Yaotel said immediately. "But only one who's Setanan."

Vaughn was afraid that was going to be the case. It made it incredibly easy to identify the culprit, but not easy to accept.

Dax.

A rap on the door to Ivana's room at the inn made her start

awake, echoes of *whore* still playing in her mind. She rose to her feet and retrieved her dagger before going to the door.

She cracked it open, and Vaughn's eye peeked back at her through the crack. "It's just me," he said.

She was clearly on edge; she knew he'd be stopping by. She let him in.

Vaughn was unnaturally subdued once she closed the door behind him. He glanced at the rumpled sheets on her bed and then at her clothes—the same she had been wearing earlier, not a robe or nightshift. "Did I...wake you up?"

She glanced at the clock. Only nine o'clock. It felt later than that, but she had no desire to return to her troubled dreams, so his presence wasn't wholly unwelcome.

She shrugged and laid the dagger on the desk. "I hadn't gone to bed," she said, which was true. She had fallen asleep lying on her bed, staring up at the ceiling, rehashing the scene from earlier that day. Remembering how easy it had been to slip back into that role, and yet somehow different—because her internal monologue about it had changed.

Sweetblade was dead. *And yet.*

He sat down on the bed and ran his hand through his hair. "The translation is done, you said?"

She walked over to the desk and picked up her clean copy of the translation, and then she turned to face him. "You're still planning on trying this?"

He gave a short laugh. "After everything I went through to get to this point? Yes. Absolutely."

"I'm surprised Yaotel is letting you go after today."

He grunted. "Yaotel isn't *letting* me do anything. I'll damn well do what I want."

Ivana had a feeling this had less to do with his actual belief that he would accomplish something at that shrine and more with his last fling with self-determination before he had to submit to Yaotel's command. "And that's why you're going to overthrow Airell and become Ri of Ferehar? Because it's what you want?"

Vaughn pressed his lips together and scowled at her.

A smile tugged at the corner of her mouth, but she tamped it down. "So, do you know who the traitor is?"

The scowl melted off his face, and once again, he just looked worn. "There's only one option. It must be Dax. Doesn't help his case that no one now recalls having seen him since just after the attempt on Yaotel's life failed."

She shook her head. "I don't think I know him."

Vaughn sighed. "He's helped me a few times. He's also the one who found the evidence that corroborated what was in that journal." He waved his hand in the direction of her desk, where the object in question sat. "As well as a ton of other manuscripts, codices, and scrolls over the years. *Seventeen years,* Ivana. That's how long he's been with the Ichtaca. Way longer than me."

Even Ivana could appreciate the wound of that betrayal. For Yaotel, especially. "Yaotel have any idea why?"

Vaughn shrugged. "Best guess? He hates non-Banebringers, without exception," he said simply. "He didn't try to hide his opinion that the alliance with Donia was unwise. He told Yaotel they'd use us to accomplish their goals and then turn on us when they were done." He looked down at his hands. "Honestly, he's not the only one with reservations. But I had no idea Dax would go to such an extreme to try to stop it. None of us did."

"And what does Ri Tanuac think of all this?" Ivana asked.

"He's relieved it wasn't one of his own advisors and glad to be able to get back to the task at hand."

"Not worried about the apparent fragility of this alliance?"

Vaughn snorted. "There's nothing apparent about it. And,

anyway, Yaotel said he warned Tanuac from the start that we were hardly a unified group. Perth—remember him?—he's still out there doing the gods know what. Never came back after the Harvest Ball."

Ivana remembered him. Vaughn had gotten into a verbal sparring match with him about Ivana's fate after that final bloodbane battle at Gan Barton's estate. Too handsy for her liking.

Vaughn shifted. "Yaotel isn't ever going to express his gratitude to you for helping us out, so I will. Thank you. I know it can't have been easy."

"On the contrary, it was quite easy," she said.

He studied her with narrowed eyes, as if suspecting she was lying to him.

She wasn't. As she had already reflected upon herself, it had been far *too* easy to be *her* again.

Sweetblade was dead. *And yet.*

"All right. Have it your way," he said. "But I also wanted to—" He bit his lip. "That man. Some of the things he said to you. Insinuated about you."

She raised an eyebrow at him. Where was he going with this?

"You looked at him the way you used to look at me."

Ah. "Yes. Well. I'm certain some of his comments were similar to things you've said to me. What did you expect?"

He visibly winced. And then he seemed to find whatever reserve of words or perhaps courage he was looking for. "I don't ever want to say or do something to make you look at me that way again."

Amusement and discomfort warred in her. This felt far too intimate of a conversation for her liking. What in the abyss did he think he was *doing*? "As touching as your sudden display of contrition is, you can be comforted to know that I haven't found you nearly as distasteful this time around."

"Oh. Well that's goo—wait, *nearly* as *distasteful*?"

She shrugged.

He let out an exasperated breath. "The point I was trying to get at was: I'm not perfect. So if I screw up, feel free to tell me."

"Noted." She moved over to the bed and handed him her translation. "I won't pretend this is perfect, but I think it's the gist of it."

He took it and read it silently to himself while she also read it over again, upside down:

"When the serpent [v. 'loose' perhaps, 'is loosed'?] upon the sky
All who seek the favor [of?] the gods
Even those gifted of their blood
[Shall?] at the appointed [?]
By sacrifice of blood
[Be?] purified by the flames [of?] the serpent
And [?] divine [blessing?] and [?]
Beyond all mortal measure."

He squinted one eye at the words. "There are still an awful lot of question marks."

"I'm fairly confident where I've supplied a guess. If it's *only* a question mark, it means I haven't the faintest idea what the missing word is."

"I guess that's not so bad, then. Thoughts on what this might mean we need to do when we get there?"

She plucked it out of his hand and returned it to the desk. "My working theory is that the person wanting to travel to 'the heavens' stepped into the mouth of that serpent at the sky-fire, and fire and blood were used to activate it."

"Fire and blood," Vaughn said. "That's still so...vague. What do we have to do? Sacrifice someone in flames? Set *ourselves* on fire? Or did the serpent just magically shoot flames out?"

Ivana shook her head. "This is the best you're going to have by way of explanation. I think the only thing left to do is experiment." She paused. "Do you not think it's possible that even if you knew exactly what to do, it wouldn't work because it needs this serpent door?"

"If this were a magical door that worked anything like our own magic, then it must have used aether to activate the door, which acted as a focus to tell the aether what to do. I'm thinking that's what it means by 'blood.'" He stood and paced the small amount of floor in the room—to the door and back to the bed again. "Xiuheuhtli—the deity that shrine was dedicated to—is the firebloods' patron deity, so perhaps a fireblood or at least fireblood aether is involved somehow. Maybe there was a receptacle for it, in the same way we power some of our devices, like the qixli and light panels? At any rate, if it was only a focus, we should still be able to take advantage of the weakness in the veil at that place and time, even without the advantage of a focus."

"Or," Ivana said, "maybe the door has nothing to do with your magic, and the gods made it work. Or maybe none of it is real in the first place, including the gods." She raised an eyebrow. "That's my current theory."

"Always the skeptic. But what if it *does* work?"

"I think you just want to get out of having to do what Yaotel tells you."

He spread his hands. "I mean, having Zily on my side would change everything, right?"

She rolled her eyes.

"Look—I know you and everyone else think this is a lost cause—and I'm not saying it isn't...but if by some slim chance, I can make this thing work—"

"And survive such a trip," she interjected.

"Find Zily—"

"And he cares."

"And get him to help somehow..."

"In a way that doesn't destroy the world or kill half its population..."

He halted in front of her and crossed his arms. "You know, you could be more positive here."

She almost laughed at that. And he could be reasonable. "Have I ever pretended optimism is an attribute of mine?"

He grunted. "That's an understatement."

"I prefer to be realistic."

"Which is just another way of saying 'pessimistic,'" he said.

She shrugged. Such was life. "At least I won't be disappointed."

He started to say something, then halted, then finally spit it out. "All right. You have a point." He lifted a finger. "But that also seems like a terrible way to live."

He assumed she was *living*. "Now you sound like Aleena."

"I've always thought she was a pretty wise woman. Anyway, whatever the result, barring the Conclave moving before then, we're leaving in about a week."

"First-person plural pronouns seem to be a perennial problem with you. I hope your *we* is exclusive of *me*."

He seemed momentarily stymied, and then he spread his hands. "Aw, aren't you going to come with me? I do need a small team..."

"Vaughn. I'm not a Banebringer. I couldn't come with you even if I *wanted* to, at least if the inscription is at all accurate."

"I just meant to the shrine. In case of a, uh, last-minute language crisis."

She couldn't keep a smile from breaking through. He was so ridiculous. "Last-minute language crisis?"

He looked at her. Just *looked* at her. That look she had once despised and yet at the same time longed to embrace. The look that sought to see her beyond what she wanted to show, even now. Then he gave her a lopsided grin. "All right. I confess. I just like having you around."

Ivana wasn't entirely sure what had happened. His smile, their banter, his company.

Whatever the case, his words did something to her. She had never wanted to be missed before, and yet his casual uttering of the words made her ache inside at the sure knowledge that once this was over, she would be alone.

Again.

She had been alone since she had left Ferehar, even when surrounded by her girls, even in the cautious comradery she had with Aleena. In shutting out the despair and darkness that fed off, in part, her loneliness, she had also shut out her ability to truly connect with someone else again.

That long-silenced part of her had been rattling the bars on its cage since Vaughn had stripped her outer defenses, and since he had pushed his way back into her life again, it seemed positively determined to escape at all costs—even her own sanity.

Right now, it sensed her weakness—her longing—and it reached out, as it had so long ago, to grasp what was right in front of her—that tendril of connection.

And so, yes. She looked into Vaughn's eyes, and she wondered if it would be so bad to let go of herself just once. She looked at his lips, and she wondered what it might be like to give that part of herself a taste of anything that looked and felt like what she had lost, what had been taken from her, and ultimately what she had given up to become what she needed to.

Yes, it eagerly whispered, goading her on.

Why did she insist on holding back? Sweetblade was dead. What did *Ivana* want?

Vaughn was silent. He watched her, oblivious to her tangled thoughts, but that he sensed a change was obvious.

She reached out her hand, hesitant, and traced a finger down his cheek, across his jaw, over his lips.

He didn't move, other than to softly kiss the fingertip she had placed there. The simple gesture set a fire burning in her.

To the abyss with it. She dropped her hand to his waist, pulled herself close to him, and kissed him.

The moment her lips touched his, he inhaled sharply through his nose, moved his hands to cradle her head, one on either side, and kissed her back.

She met his lips again and again, savoring the taste, then opened her mouth to find his tongue, drowning herself in the cascades of longing that washed over her body until finally she pulled back with a gasp, needing to come up for air.

Vaughn hadn't moved his hands from her head. He leaned forward to put his forehead to hers and held her there.

She didn't move, either. Her body was trembling like some young, untested virgin.

Fear, desire—she didn't know what, only that it beat against her until she thought she would go mad.

Finally, Vaughn spoke. Only one word. A question. "Ivana?"

She swallowed. *Ivana. Ivana. Who is Ivana?* Sweetblade was dead, and in her place was a void, an emptiness in which memories and feelings and faces swirled and then disappeared, snatches of light in overwhelming darkness. The Ivana she had been was gone, and yet here she was, Ivana again.

She pulled away from him, and he let her go, his hands sliding down her face and then dropping to his sides.

She couldn't meet his eyes. She didn't know what to say, how to answer his implied question, because she couldn't explain her actions in simple words.

She was both shocked and grateful that he hadn't asked more of her, if not with words, than with his body.

After a few moments of silence, she forced herself to speak. "I'll go," she said. "Might as well see if all my work comes to fruition or not." And put off answering the inevitable question of what to do afterward.

He rubbed his jaw. "Good. Well. I'm going to head back to our barracks. Let me know if you need anything."

I need you to stay with me, wrap your arms around me, keep the darkness from swallowing me whole. "I'll be fine. See you in a week."

Vaughn closed the door to Ivana's room, but he didn't immediately move on. Instead, he leaned against the wall and stood there for several minutes, reeling from what had just happened.

Ivana had kissed him. He had kissed her back. And then he had let her go and left.

He couldn't remember the last time an encounter with a woman had gone that way.

Had it ever?

It wasn't that he didn't *want* more; the gods knew he had wanted Ivana since almost the moment he had met her.

But it hadn't felt right. And for once, he had listened to something other than the brain between his legs.

He hadn't the faintest idea what had spurred her to kiss him, what had been going on in her mind—but for his part? He was terrified.

He was terrified because today he realized for the first time, in a concrete way, that he had changed. And having changed, he was terrified because there was no going back. He could have once claimed ignorance, but he would not be willfully ignorant. To do so would either make him egotistical or a coward, and he wanted to be neither.

He was terrified because his old defenses, his old vices, would no longer suffice to hide behind or find solace in, and he had nothing else.

But mostly, he was terrified because he had no doubt that he had fallen in love with Ivana, and he also had no doubt that loving Ivana would one day, sooner or later, leave him with a broken heart.

Well. There certainly were plenty of things to be terrified of lately, not least of which was the possibility of stepping through a portal into a world inhabited by seemingly capricious gods to beg their favor.

He could focus on that. What was the terror of coming to care for a woman compared to facing the divine?

He thought on that for a moment. The former was worse. Way worse.

Chapter Twenty-Eight

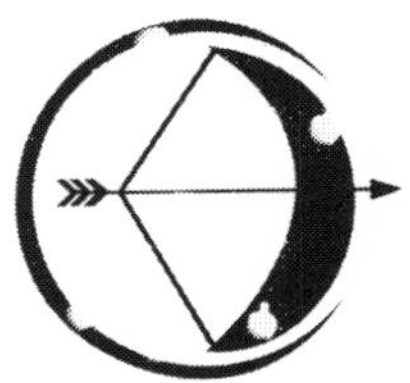

Purified in Flames

"Vaughn." Someone was shaking him. "Vaughn!"

He sat up with a start. Danton loomed over him.

"The sun's setting," Danton said.

Vaughn rubbed his eyes and took a deep breath. "Thanks. Thrax up already?"

"Yes. He's already filled the bowl with some of his blood."

Thrax, their requisite fireblood, would be joining Vaughn in his theoretical journey through the portal. He figured he couldn't go wrong with a fireblood, since Xiuheuhtli was their patron, this was his shrine, and apparently, the sky-fire also belonged under his purview. He needed one anyway, for the best results in manipulating fire.

At least, he assumed he did.

There was a lot they still didn't know for sure, but they had all night to experiment. If they hadn't figured it out by then, Vaughn's entire mission ended here. They'd have to wait until next year—or more likely, never try again, since he'd have more responsibilities than gallivanting around Setana, as Yaotel had put it.

His throat tightened. *Not gonna think about that.* As long as it was all theory, he was fine. Vaughn grabbed his pack and the new bow he had bought and followed Danton out of the tent they had set up. Danton was with them to cover their tracks if need be.

Ivana ducked out of the shrine. And she was with them in case of...

Ha. *Last-minute language problems.*

Really, she was the closest expert on this journal and inscription that he had—and likely the only living person who knew anything about the mysterious language.

Seven days after he had left her room at the inn, he had collected her. She had said nothing about their kiss, so neither had he.

Perhaps it was his imagination, but she seemed more aloof than she had recently. More curt and clipped.

He took a deep breath and met her in the courtyard before the shrine.

"Anything new strike you?" he asked.

She shook her head. "Do you want the journal with you?"

"The copies of the relevant bits are good enough," he said, adjusting the flap on the pocket of his pack where he'd tucked said copies. "I don't want to chance the journal itself getting lost."

He turned toward the spot they'd chosen to try their first experiment. It seemed like the spot where the serpent monument would have once been, both from the description in the journal and the layout of the small shrine area itself.

Thrax had his pack on as well, while Danton and Ivana stood off to the side. They watched in silence while the sky slowly darkened until the last vestiges of the sun had disappeared.

The first burning ember streaked across the sky. They all stood for a moment, transfixed. He had to admit, it was a breathtaking sight. Nonetheless, any sane person was in a safe room—or at least inside, on a night like tonight—not standing in the middle of nowhere.

But the chances of a bloodbane appearing nearby were just as high as in the city—perhaps higher in the city—and out in the wilderness, unless it appeared literally in front of them, all but the most vicious would run away.

More likely than not, they'd have no issues.

Vaughn looked around. "Ready?" he asked Thrax.

Thrax snorted. "Ready as I'll ever be. So what's your first idea?"

Vaughn stepped toward the stone bowl full of Thrax's blood, now solidified into a bowl of aether. "Um. So, fire and blood. We've got blood. We've even got blood from a fireblood. Try setting it on fire?"

Thrax reached out with his hand and made a clenching motion toward the lantern that Danton held. Fire trickled out from it like water had from the creek for Vaughn not that long ago.

Thrax was becoming more skilled.

He directed the gout of flame to the bowl and then let it go there.

It caught the aether but burned through it like kindling and then went out.

Nothing happened. Of course, it wouldn't be *that* easy.

"Next," Thrax said.

Vaughn turned toward the small campfire they had set up behind the bowl. "Light the fire."

Thrax used his magic to goad the logs into flames. They

caught and burned, and before long, they had a roaring fire.

"Anyone have some meat they want to roast?" Danton joked.

"Now try your blood on top of it," Vaughn said.

Thrax ran a knife over one of his palms and held it over the fire, letting drops of blood fall into the flames.

They sparked and sizzled, but again, nothing apparent happened.

Vaughn sighed. "Okay. So those were the two easiest options. Next..." He grimaced. "The inscription talks about the traveler being purified in flame. I was hoping it was a metaphor, or maybe a description of the portal itself when it formed, but I suppose it's possible we have to step into a fire."

"Oh, that's rich," Thrax said. "Maybe we *will* be roasting some meat."

"Easy enough for you," Vaughn shot back. "You can shield yourself."

Thrax tossed him a pouch. "So can you."

Vaughn eyed the pouch dubiously. Fireblood aether was some of the most volatile. Firebloods could control it easily enough from their own blood, but Vaughn would never attain the level of precision over it that Thrax had.

He had shielded his hand before but never his entire body. "You first," he said, grinning at Thrax.

Thrax shrugged and stepped into the flames.

Vaughn had to restrain himself from pulling the man back.

"I'm good," Thrax said, shaking out his hands. "Just feels a bit ticklish."

"Any...tingling in your fingers? An insatiable desire to step toward a certain spot or do a little dance? Anything at all?"

"Nope." Thrax cracked his neck, waited another few moments, and then stepped out of the fire.

Well, at least that meant there was no point in Vaughn trying it. He hooked the pouch of fireblood aether to his belt and tapped his fingers against his waist. "Maybe you're not pure enough," he said.

Danton snorted and Thrax barked a laugh. "Look who's talking!"

Even Ivana sniggered at that.

Vaughn frowned at all of them. "All right, all right. My next idea is to offer up a human sacrifice. Any volunteers?"

Thrax stopped laughing. "You're joking, right?"

Vaughn raised an eyebrow at him, unsmiling.

"Uh...Vaughn..." Danton said.

Vaughn rolled his eyes. "Yes. I'm joking. Sort of. I mean, I suppose it is possible that the doorway requires a human sacrifice, but I'm not willing to go that far." He sighed and ran a hand through his hair.

"There we go," Thrax said. "That's what we could have used that assassin for."

Ivana licked her lips, not seeming at all amused.

The sky was ablaze now, so much so that their little fire hardly seemed to make a difference to the amount of light in the area.

"Maybe we started too early, or there's something else we missed. Ivana, let's hear the inscription again."

She held out a piece of paper in front of her and read: "'When the serpent is loosed upon the sky, all who seek the favor of the gods, even those gifted of their blood, shall at the appointed...'" She waved her hand in the air. "'*Blank*, by sacrifice of blood, be purified by the flames of the serpent, and *blank* divine blessing and *blank*, beyond all mortal measure.'"

On the word "measure," the fire chose that moment to send up a flare.

Ivana lowered her hand and stared at the fire.

"Was that coincidence, or did reading that make something

happen?" Vaughn said eagerly. "Read it again."

Ivana obliged him, and again, at the end, the flames seemed to dance a little more.

"Anyone else see that?" he asked, looking around.

Danton nodded. "It did seem to get a little more vigorous there at the end."

"Didn't you say this was originally written in some ancient dead language?" Thrax put in. "Maybe it needs to be read in the original language."

"Can you do that?" Vaughn asked Ivana.

"No. I have no idea how it's pronounced."

Vaughn pounded his fist against his thigh. "Well, damn."

Ivana pursed her lips and stared into the flames. "I don't think the language has anything to do with it."

"No?"

"When has speaking words ever made your magic work?"

Vaughn rubbed at his jaw. "All right. You have a point. But—"

"What are you missing?"

Vaughn's heart sank. "The serpent," he said. All this, and the serpent *did* matter? He had been banking on the idea that it didn't.

"Not exactly. You're missing a focus. Could you use something else?"

Vaughn scratched his head and turned to Thrax. "Thrax? Any recommendations?"

Thrax tapped his chin. "I mean, for lighting a fire to be used as a light, an unlit torch or even the wick of a candle helps. Or a campfire, the wood itself." He gestured toward the burning fire for emphasis. "But what kind of focus does one use to tell the fire to open a doorway to the gods?"

"A door?" Danton suggested.

It sounded stupid on the surface, but if aether could be

encouraged to heal because it was sprinkled in salve, or encouraged to light up a room because they trapped it in a panel that they decided would light the room, maybe it wasn't such a dumb idea after all.

Thrax snapped his fingers. "Crap. We forgot to haul a door with us."

"Thrax," Vaughn said slowly. "Find some more wood and set it out in the shape of a literal door on the ground."

They all stared at him. "Look, I know it sounds dumb, but who knows? I'll try anything." He thought about that, and then he revised his statement. "*Except* human sacrifice. I won't try that."

Thrax was already building a rectangle with sticks on the ground nearby. "Shall I light them up?" he asked when he was done.

"Wait," Vaughn said. "Add a few pieces of kindling in the shape of a snake in the middle. Maybe it'll get the idea of what type of door then."

"What in the abyss is the shape of a snake?" Thrax demanded to know.

"I don't know! Make it...snakey-like!"

"Snakey-like," Thrax muttered, but he complied, creating a line of smaller sticks that waved back and forth.

"Now try," Vaughn said.

Thrax carefully lit the sticks on fire, and then the "snake," so that before long, a burning rectangle lay on the ruined stones with a long, wiggly pattern in the middle.

Vaughn cut his hand and sprinkled more blood on it.

Still, nothing happened.

"Wait," Ivana said. "I just remembered something."

"What?" Danton, Vaughn, and Thrax said as one.

"You know how the Conclave priests chant words, sometimes music, when they use their aether?"

"Yes..." Vaughn said. He had witnessed it firsthand, on many occasions.

"What if the words aren't nonsense, smoke and mirrors? What if they act like a different sort of foci?"

Vaughn looked back at the flickering rectangle again. "All right. I'll buy that. Can't hurt to try it."

Ivana read the inscription one more time. And as she spoke, something changed.

The fire burning on the stick-door burned brighter and then hotter, turning into the blue-white flames of the center of the hottest fire. Vaughn could feel the heat intensify from where he stood; and even Danton, already a few feet away, took a couple steps back.

Ivana lowered the paper and stared at the door. The sticks were no longer being actively consumed by the fire. "My gods," she said. "It's actually doing something."

"This is it," Vaughn said with certainty. He nodded to Thrax. "I'll go first this time." He plunged his hand into the bag of fireblood aether and crushed a handful, willing it to shield him from the flames.

Then he closed his eyes, took a deep breath, and stepped into the rectangle.

The flames leapt out to meet him, almost eagerly, and then writhed around him, within him. He clenched the fireblood aether in his hand and gritted his teeth. It was hot—painfully hot—

"Get him out of there!" he heard distantly, and it sounded like Danton's voice.

"No!" he shouted through clenched teeth. "It's painful, but I don't think it's hurting me! Thrax!"

But Thrax didn't join him. Vaughn heard shouting, but it faded, and he could no longer hear anything but the roar of flames, or see anything but the blue dance in his eyes—even his lungs seemed to breathe only hot, burning air—until he was certain he was going to be torn in two from the inside out.

He fell to his hands and knees, the heat vanished, and everything went black.

Literally.

He knelt for a moment, feeling a bit dizzy. He waited, and the feeling eventually dissipated. He sat back on his heels and waved his hand in front of his face.

He could see its outline, so it wasn't pitch black, then.

"Thrax?" he whispered, though he wasn't sure why he was whispering.

Nothing.

He hesitated. "Danton? Ivana?"

Silence.

He looked around, straining his eyes into the dark. His eyes were already starting to adjust, just not in the way they did for his night vision.

His heart sped up. That was...disconcerting.

He burned aether to turn invisible, but he had no way of confirming whether it worked without someone else—or a mirror. Even so, he could *feel* aether when it burned in his blood—it was difficult to describe, but he knew it was happening.

He felt nothing.

He swung his pack off his shoulders and fumbled in it until he found his portable light panel, then pressed his thumb against it and held it up.

Nothing.

Feeling a bit panicked, he jerked the hunting knife he'd brought with him out of the little sheath at his waist and pricked his finger with the tip.

He had never—*never*—been so glad to see his own blood turn silver.

So he still had aether in him. Why couldn't he use it?

He could now faintly see his immediate surroundings, empty shapes and lumps in the darkness. There was one such shape nearby, and it reminded him a bit of a prone human body. Thrax?

He crawled toward it. The ground was dry dirt and rock, hard and unforgiving, and shriveled clumps of brown and sometimes blackened grass crackled against his hands and knees.

He reached the shape, leaned over it, and looked down in shock.

It wasn't Thrax, but *Ivana.*

How in the abyss—

Blood trickled from her nose and the corner of her mouth, and her eyes were closed. Panic rising in his chest once more, he felt for a pulse at her throat...

He breathed out in relief. Her heart still beat, strong and healthy.

He put a hand on her chest, and it rose and fell.

She was alive. Just unconscious.

He glanced around once again. The landscape was becoming easier to see, his eyes having adjusted as much as they were going to. The sky wasn't truly black, but rather dark red, like the color of drying blood. There was enough light to see now, but he didn't know where it was coming from. There were no stars, moon, or sun in the sky. Most of the dark shapes were rocks and boulders: large, jagged formations sprinkled across what appeared to be an otherwise flat, brown plain—pitted occasionally with craters—as if some angry deity had picked up a handful of stones and hurled them there in a fit.

He swallowed. Maybe they had.

He turned back to Ivana and shook her. "Ivana!" he whispered again, not daring to speak louder, due to the terrible suspicion growing in his mind.

Still, she didn't move.

He rummaged around in his bag again, looking for one of his two waterskins. He found one and dribbled water over her face.

A moment later, she gasped, as if she *hadn't* been breathing, and sat up, her hand immediately moving to grasp the hilt of the dagger at her thigh. "What in the—?" Her eyes flicked around the landscape and then came to rest on Vaughn.

Her hand relaxed. "Where are we? Why am I here?" She wiped her nose on the back of her sleeve and looked at the blood. "What happened?"

"I don't know, I don't know, and I don't know," Vaughn said, answering each of her questions in turn. "Though as to the last, I was hoping you could tell *me*."

She wrinkled her nose, as if trying to remember. "You were in the fire. It turned blue, then white, and the flames looked like they were beginning to consume you. You started screaming—"

"I did *not*!"

"You started screaming, and Danton panicked. He tried to drag you out but couldn't get close enough. Thrax leapt in after you, but it was too late. You were gone."

"And Thrax wasn't?"

She shook her head. "As soon as you...I don't know. Disintegrated? The fire started dying back down."

"And so how did *you* get here?"

"I'm... Well, I'm not sure. Thrax stepped out of the fire, and then it just...exploded."

"*Exploded*?"

"That was the last thing I remember. I woke up..." She gestured around them. "Here."

Vaughn stared at her. "I didn't think you'd be able to come here. You're not a Banebringer." His eyes widened. "Are you? Did a bloodbane get summoned? It *was* the sky-fire—"

She held up her hand. The smear of blood from her nose was still red.

Vaughn scratched his head. "Okay, let's forget about that for now. You *are* here. Somehow. And—" He looked around. The landscape was as desolate and empty as before. "Unless Danton and Thrax got, I don't know, thrown somewhere else, they aren't."

"Vaughn. Where is *here,* exactly?"

"I...guess we made it. To the...heavens." But his stomach felt sick as he said it. That didn't seem right. Something had gone wrong. He could feel it in his blood.

Ivana's gaze slid over the barren plain, taking in the rock formations, the blood-red sky.

In the distance, Vaughn heard the first sound other than their own conversation.

A wolf howled. Distorted. Strangled. And then another. Something crashed.

Dark shapes began to move against the blood-red sky.

Vaughn met Ivana's eyes, and he could tell she had the same thought he did.

This wasn't the heavens.

It was the abyss.

Chapter Twenty-Nine

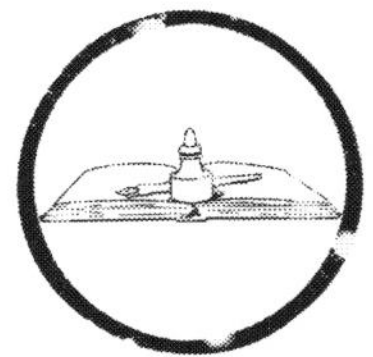

Sky-Fire

Driskell hurried through the empty streets. He glanced at the sky overhead, anxiously searching for any sign that the sky-fire had begun.

No streaks of fire yet. He still had time.

Ugh. What had he been thinking, going to visit Tania tonight, of all nights?

But she had insisted since he hadn't been to see her in several weeks. Of course, he hadn't intended to stay this late tonight of all nights—and then he had been drawn into a mock tapolli tournament and completely lost track of time.

He should have just stayed with her family, but every moment spent with them as of late had been more than uncomfortable. He had wanted to be back in his room, away from their prying questions about the Xambrian ambassador and secret meetings and rumors of a Conclave army on their border. They knew he had to know something, and even Tania, who was usually so understanding of the sensitive nature of his job, was becoming annoyed that he wouldn't tell her *anything.*

He was sure he could make it back in time if he used the guards' stair. It was carved into the inside of the mountain, reserved for the Watch and those few with unrestricted access to all eight tiers.

His hands shook as he unlocked the gate to the entrance on the fourth tier and then shut it firmly behind him, but his long legs carried him swiftly up. He paused at the opening to the fifth tier—the Temple tier—to peer through the gate and check the sky one more time.

His heart sank. The first embers were streaking across the sky.

He swore and increased his pace. The sixth tier passed, and then somewhere between the sixth and seventh, his destination, he turned a corner—

To find a tear forming directly in front of him.

He tripped in his shock and banged his knee on a step. *Temoth, have mercy!*

A shiver ran through his body, cold followed by a rush of warmth—a strange feeling, but he chalked it up to the terror of staring at that horrible tear, waiting for the inevitable.

He shook his head, flinging off the paralysis. *Why wait for the inevitable, idiot?*

The government tier was but a few paces beyond the next corner.

He took a deep breath and raced past the tear as it continued to lengthen and then open, the black flames almost brushing against his sleeve as he scooted by.

Ignoring the smarting of his knee, he fled up the final flight of stairs. His heart thudded in time with the slap of his shoes against the steps, every sense vigilant as he listened for some sign that there was a bloodbane behind him, chasing him, about to tear his throat out...

A cold, shrill shriek knifed through him, but he didn't look. He couldn't look, or he'd freeze again.

He wasn't cut out for this sort of thing.

He reached the gate at the government tier, flung it open, and then slammed it shut behind him.

The lock clicked into place, and only then did he dare to glance behind him.

A bloodhawk hurled itself against the gate. He stumbled back, holding his hands out as if to stop the creature if it charged him, but though the gate buckled, it held—for now. The bloodhawk screeched in rage, retreated, and then tried again.

Crash!

He heard the shouts of nearby Watchmen already, waiting for trouble, so he did the only sensible thing one could do: He ran.

He passed the Watchmen on the way, but he didn't stop. Instead, he sprinted until he reached the small government dormitory, wound his way through the corridors, and burst into his room.

He slammed the door behind him, panting.

He could have gone to the safe room in the Ri's manor, but his own room was closer, and they would have already locked and closed it by now.

Besides, his own quarters were buried deep enough within the stone building that it was an unlikely target for a roaming bloodbane.

He slumped into his armchair, willing his heart to stop pounding so fiercely, and wiped his sweaty hands on his trousers.

Only then did he see his knee.

His trousers had torn, and there, shimmering in the dim light, was a patch of silver, sunk into the scrape on his knee like a metallic scab.

He stared at it, uncomprehending.

He touched the wound and rubbed at the silver. Some of it flaked off under his touch.

Only then did he understand.

He shot out of his chair, knocking it over backward. *No,* he thought. *No!* It couldn't be.

Papers and pens and inkwells scattered before his hand as he groped unseeing for his letter opener.

Finding it, he scraped the rest of the silvery scab away from the wound on his knee.

Fresh, red blood seeped up beneath, and a shock of relief passed through him. His imagination—maybe the bloodhawk had bled on the stair and he had landed in it, maybe—

The blood shimmered, and, just like Yaotel's, it turned into silver.

He dropped the letter opener with a clatter.

He...He had been changed. He was a Banebringer.

He righted the chair and sank back down into it, one hand pressed to his forehead, his mind spinning with the implications.

I'll have to fill out my own form, was the only coherent thought that would come to him.

Then the rest rushed in.

Would he have to give up his post as attaché? Would he be forced to join this group—these Ichtaca? Did he ever have a hope of being appointed Gan? If ever there was a good time and place to be changed, this was it—but their alliance was only known to a few. He could still be arrested if caught.

He shuddered. Dealt with. Sedated. And he didn't know if Tanuac or Nahua would—or could—come to his rescue.

His heart thudded once and then twisted inside him. And Tania. Would she...?

He had already planned the proposal. Her family had already sanctioned the union. Everything was in place; he had merely been waiting for the day to come.

Now her family would never continue to sanction the union. Tania herself might well hate him, might even turn him in. But she wouldn't do that, would she? She *loved* him.

And yet, he had heard enough stories from the Banebringers in Marakyn to know that it wouldn't be unheard of.

He felt sick. No. No one needed to know. Even the Ichtaca, even Nahua. He would hide it as long as possible, hoping that the Banebringer plight would soon improve in Marakyn.

Yes. That was the right course, for now. He would hide it. Maybe, *maybe*, when Danton got back from wherever he'd gone, he could ask his advice.

He stood up and went to the washbasin, poured water on a rag, and scrubbed furiously at his knee, removing all the evidence.

He'd burn the trousers. Scrub the carpet.

He looked frantically around. He could do this. He. Could. Do. This.

He had to.

Chapter Thirty

God of Fire

"I'm going to kill you," Ivana said through clenched teeth. "I am—I am literally going to kill you."

Vaughn seemed justifiably alarmed. "All right. Let's calm down and think this through."

"This is *your* fault! Go visit the gods, you say, like it's a merry jaunt to your gods-damned kindly grandmother's house!"

Vaughn spread his hands. "How was I supposed to know it would take us to the *abyss*? None of the texts said anything about that! In fact, quite the opposite—"

"I'm not even supposed to be here!"

"That's not my fault, either!" Vaughn protested.

The howling drew nearer.

Ivana drew in a deep breath. *Calm.* They could worry about

the details of *how* and *why* later. For now… "Why don't you make us invisible so we can figure out where in the abyss we're supposed to go now?" She paused, realizing what she'd just said. "And that was *not* supposed to be a joke."

He didn't smile. "I can't."

"What do you mean, you can't?"

He held out his hand. "I'm trying again right now. It doesn't work. Not like when I was in Airell's dungeons. It just…doesn't work at *all*."

"Oh, gods," Ivana muttered, running a hand through her hair. All the ways she could have died in her life, and she was going to be torn to shreds by a bloodbane in the abyss itself.

She eyed the approaching shapes. But she wasn't going to go out without a fight. "Well, we're certainly not going to accomplish anything by standing around in the open—except dying." She pointed toward a particularly large boulder. "Maybe there's a crevice we can hide in."

They jogged over to the rock formation. It was lumpy, mottled brown and grey with red mossy growths all over it, and it was the size of a modest house.

She shoved him in the opposite direction. "Run around that way and meet me on the other side."

He obeyed, and she darted around, looking for anything that might hide them.

"Over here!" Vaughn shouted.

She turned and joined him on the other side of the formation. The rock rose at one side, leaving a hole that someone might be able to squirm their way into, underneath the rock, out of sight. Or two someones, though it would be tight.

"Go on," Vaughn said, looking behind them. The shapes in the distance had disappeared behind the bulk of the rock, which was good. Maybe the bloodbane wouldn't see them trying to hide.

Ivana turned, dropped to her stomach, and squirmed her way under the rock, feet first. Vaughn dropped beside her and did the same, and then pulled his pack and bow in next to him.

They managed to squeeze themselves far enough back that no body parts were hanging out, but it was by no means perfect.

The howls sounded closer, and Ivana peered out into the gloom. She was certain she saw a bloodhawk circling in the sky on the horizon.

Then the thudding of feet. Many feet. The ground began to tremble.

Then the feet of a bloodwolf charged around the edge of the rock and came to a halt near where they hid.

The bloodwolf's nose dipped to the ground, and it snuffled around the rock, coming closer to where they lay, closer...

It stopped right at the crevice, long, sharp teeth clearly in view, drool dripping off its fangs, down its jaw, onto the ground. *It knows we're here. It can smell us.*

Then it turned its head, and one white, pupil-less eye came into view.

"Damn," Vaughn whispered.

The bloodwolf lifted its head and howled. The ground trembled again, and a few moments later, half a dozen more bloodwolves burst out from around the rock.

The first one stuck its head into the crevice and wriggled toward them.

Ivana lashed out at it with her dagger, even though it was ultimately futile, and Vaughn hurled a rock at it.

She nicked its nose, and it snarled and snapped its teeth.

She had vivid memories of those same sort of teeth impaling her thigh and nearly ripping off her leg.

They didn't stand a chance.

Beside her, Vaughn caught her other hand, intertwining his

fingers in hers, and she didn't think twice about grasping it back.

The other bloodwolves now crowded behind the first, snarling and snapping at each other as they jostled to be the next in, while the first drew closer and opened its jaws.

Ivana threw her arm in front of her face and cringed back—

And then the rock above their heads heaved.

Ivana put her arm down, astonished. "What in the—?"

It heaved again, and then it *groaned*—like the long, loud creak of a rusty door being slowly inched open.

The bloodwolves now fought with each other to retreat, and the moment they had space, both she and Vaughn scrambled out of their hole. The rock unfurled itself until it stood on two gigantic legs, now much taller than a modest house. A misshapen head sat on top of what she supposed was its neck, and two burning, white eyes flared in the depths of two deep sockets. It cocked its head and looked down at them, as if considering what sort of curiosity they were before crushing them to death.

Vaughn slung his bow off his back and started stringing it.

Ivana admired his effort, but she didn't know what they could do against such a hoard, without even Vaughn's magic at his disposal. The bloodwolves had backed away, true, snarling and shaking their heads at the rock creature, but there were at least a dozen of them, and they had surrounded Vaughn, Ivana, and the rock monster. Four bloodhawks also circled in the sky overhead, and the giant rock monster loomed over them.

Vaughn loosed an arrow at the thing's chest, but the arrow bounced off.

"Damn," he muttered. "Even with beastblood."

"The beastblood probably isn't working..." Ivana reminded him.

"Damn," he said again.

It didn't seem bothered by the arrow at all. One enormous

hand reached slowly down toward them, whether to grab them, smash them, poke them—Ivana didn't know, but no option could be good, and they had nowhere to run, couldn't even back away without backing into the waiting bloodwolves.

The hand paused. The bloodwolves stopped snarling and began to whine.

Then a giant, flaming sword arced through the air from behind them and sliced the rock monster's arm clean off.

Ivana swore and yanked Vaughn back just as the arm fell with a crash right where they had been standing.

The rock monster howled, picked up its own arm, and shook it at something beyond Vaughn's and Ivana's shoulders. Then it turned and stomped off in an almost comically human gesture of offense, kicking one of the lingering bloodwolves out of the way as it went.

"Well, well, well. What have we here?" a deep, booming voice said from behind them.

Vaughn turned, looked up, scrambled backward, and then promptly fell onto his rear. He shielded his eyes against the sudden brightness of the being in front of him.

Ivana crouched next to him, also squinting, and he lowered his hand, gaping at their...rescuer? Or did this just mean a worse fate?

He'd never seen or heard of a bloodbane that looked like this; it looked human—a human that stood at least as tall as the rock monster—perhaps twenty feet—and was clothed in blue, white, and orange flames.

A feathered serpent was wrapped around its neck—a live one, by the looks of it—and the creature stared at them curiously, its tongue flicking out into the air in their direction.

A flaming hand rose to stroke the serpent's head. "Lohti. You'll scare our guests."

The flames diminished slowly until they were merely a subtle orange-and-yellow flicker around the giant flaming man's feet. Now that most of the flames were gone, Vaughn could see that the man wore little more than a loincloth—if a handsomely embroidered one—and an odd sort of short cape draped around one shoulder and tied at the neck. His no-longer-flaming sword was back in its sheath belted at his waist.

"My gods," Ivana whispered.

The man tilted his head and pinned her with flickering orange pupils. "Yes. Yes, that's what they used to say, anyway." He frowned.

It couldn't be. It—this—man—being—was one of the heretic gods?

Vaughn's head was spinning. He was dreaming. This was all a dream.

The bloodwolves were still hanging nearby. One darted toward Vaughn, and the man, with a single heavy kick, punted it, causing it to yelp as it soared fifty feet across the plain. The rest of the bloodwolves slunk away one by one.

An irritated look flashed across the man's face. "Let's go somewhere we can talk without these annoying creatures nipping about our heels, shall we?" He waved his hands in the air at the bloodhawks. "Shoo. Shoo!" He began to stride off, and then turned back toward Vaughn and Ivana when they hadn't moved. "Well? Follow me. They'll return if you tarry."

Vaughn and Ivana exchanged a glance.

There was no decision to be made. They had no choice.

They followed him.

The flaming man led them on at a steady clip. They had to alternate between running and walking to keep up with him, and it seemed that he was still walking slower than he might have normally.

They traveled across miles of the same featureless, barren plain, though now and again they saw it pockmarked with black, burned circles.

Bloodbane of varying sorts lurked within sight the whole trip, as if waiting for the god to abandon his charges so they could tear them apart. By the time they reached their destination, they had gathered a large entourage.

That was enough to spur Vaughn on, despite his growing exhaustion.

Just when Vaughn thought he was about to collapse, a large building came into view.

It looked exactly like one of the ancient shrines to the heretic gods—only larger and longer. The flaming man was able to walk into the rectangular opening without ducking, and Vaughn felt like an ant in comparison. Before following him in, Vaughn looked back—and all around, he noticed slightly smaller versions of the shrine scattered about in a pattern that almost seemed city-like.

The inside of the shrine was alight with flame—but this time from lanterns hanging on every wall. The flaming man led them through a cavernous stone hall three times the height of the man himself, and into another opening, and only then did he stop.

The room was, by all appearances, a large dining hall. A long, low table took up the middle of the room, and a feast was laid out on it.

But there was no one in the room to feast.

"Please," the flaming man said, gesturing toward the table. "Have a seat. You must be tired from your journey."

Vaughn sat down cautiously next to Ivana, but neither of them dared to eat. Who knew what kind of cursed food was found in the abyss?

The man watched their hesitance, and then sighed. "I supposed it's only to be expected," he murmured, as if to himself. He clapped his hands. "Friends, come out. It's all right."

And then, out of crevices in the walls, from the doorway, and some, out of thin air, other creatures began to appear. Some were more beast-like, and some more human-like—with orange skin and orange eyes. These joined Vaughn and Ivana at the table and began to partake of the meal.

The flaming man sat himself, but he didn't eat. Instead, he studied Vaughn and Ivana. "It has been...centuries...millennia, perhaps—it *is* hard to keep track of time by your standards—since your kind visited us here," he said.

Vaughn took a stab in the dark. "Xiuheuhtli?" God of fire. God of serpents.

He sat back. "Yes. Yes, that is one name I was known by." His eyes roved over Vaughn almost greedily, but Ivana he ignored.

Vaughn didn't like the look. While this...god...had rescued them from bloodbane, Vaughn now wondered if there was going to be a price for his assistance. He had read enough myths to know that he shouldn't assume these gods were all—or even mostly—benevolent.

"How did you find us...?" Vaughn hesitated. How *did* one address a god? "Your Worship"? "Your Dieficness"? "Great God of Fire"? He settled on something that seemed safe. "My lord?"

Xiuheuhtli waved his hand. "Oh, the portals have always been under my purview. But it has been so long since one opened, I stopped keeping watch long ago. But I still knew." He shrugged. "Even so, I was almost too late." A dark look crossed his face. "Danathalt's dogs nearly got to you first."

All right. He wasn't a fan of Danathalt. That was good, right?

But that spawned a different question. "Isn't this Danathalt's realm?" Vaughn asked. "That is where we are, right? The abyss?"

Xiuheuhtli tilted his head again. "Why, yes. And yes."

"We thought the, uh, *portals* led to the heavens."

He seemed confused. "The...heavens?"

"You know. Where...all the *other* gods live."

Understanding flared—literally—in his orange eyes, and he stroked the serpent around his neck again. "You mean you don't know."

"Know?"

Xiuheuhtli unwound the serpent from around his neck and set it on the ground. "The portals are locked to the abyss—and have been ever since the Great Father's damn curse."

Great Father. *He must mean Zily.*

"Well *that* would have been useful to know," Ivana muttered beside him.

Xiuheuhtli flicked his eyes toward Ivana, frowned, and then looked back at Vaughn. "Why are you here?"

"We need to speak to Zily. Uh. I mean, your Great Father. Ziloxchanachi. We, um..."

Ivana nudged him and he turned to look at her. "Perhaps," she said quietly. "The details might be left for Zily?"

"Oh. Right." Until they knew if Xiuheuhtli's interest would help or hurt their quest, it was best not to say too much.

The serpent began to slither toward them. Vaughn swallowed and watched it as it came, its tongue flicking out again and again.

Xiuheuhtli folded his hands across his chest, fingers intertwined. Something glimmered in his eyes. "You wish to see Ziloxchanachi? Not your patron?"

Vaughn blinked. "Thaxchatichan?"

"I'll send word for her to collect you and your *xchotli*."

"My—what?"

Xiuheuhtli looked at Ivana. "Your *xchotli,* your bound servant. Is that not whom you've brought with you?"

"No, no," Vaughn said. "She's not my servant, and I don't know what that other thing is. This is Ivana. She's my, um, friend. We're here together. To see the Great Father. I don't need to see Thaxchatichan at all, actually. Just show us the way to Ziloxchanachi, and we can—"

Xiuheuhtli frowned. "But that cannot be."

"I'm sorry?"

He was looking at Ivana. "She doesn't have our blood."

He could tell that by looking at her? "Well, no. But—"

"Then she's your *xchotli,*" Xiuheuhtli said firmly. "No mere human can pass through the portals. It's impossible."

"I beg your pardon, my lord," Ivana said, speaking directly to Xiuheuhtli for the first time. "But I am not a servant or a *xchotli,* I am most definitely a human, and I passed through the portal."

The serpent had drawn closer to them. It slithered up Ivana's arm and tickled her ear with its tongue. To her credit, though her eyes shifted to look at it, she didn't flinch.

"Look, Xiu—can I call you 'Xiu'? I think that maybe some things have changed since Banebringers last visited you all. But what I need—"

"Banebringers?"

"Yes. It's what the non-Banebringers call us. Because...our existence draws bloodbane."

Xiu exhaled. "Ah. Of course. What a nuisance Great Father's curse was all around."

Good gods. A nuisance? That was all they saw it as? "I'd call it more than a nuisance—"

The serpent hissed. It had coiled itself around Ivana's

shoulders, and in so doing, had covered half her body. Its head was level with hers, looking into her eyes.

"Um...your snake isn't going to eat my friend, is it?"

Xiu ignored him. Instead, he rose and lifted the serpent off Ivana. It hissed again, and Xiu tilted his head. "Interesting." He looked at Ivana, something glimmering in his eyes again.

"What's interesting?" Vaughn was becoming frustrated at getting so few answers.

Xiu waved his hand. "You say you want to see the Great Father?"

"Yes!"

"That may be more difficult than you imagine. My brothers and sisters can travel back and forth between his realm and the abyss at will, but you will need an invitation. And if you get there, he will not see you."

"But...don't you all—other than Danathalt—live there? Didn't our kind used to go there?"

"We do, and they did," Xiu said gravely, giving him a straight answer for the first time.

"Then what are you doing here?"

"Fighting," Xiu said simply. He rose. "Thaxchatichan is currently at her residence in the Great Father's realm. I will send a message that one of hers is here. If she wishes to claim you, she will issue the invitation." Again, he eyed Vaughn, and again, Vaughn's skin crawled. "As much as I would like to keep you, you are hers; therefore, I cannot." He strode toward the door. "Until then, you may eat and rest here."

"Wait," Vaughn said.

Xiu paused and raised an eyebrow at him.

"Why doesn't my magic work here?"

At that, Xiu laughed. "You amuse me, *teotontl*. You can only claim divinity in your own world, I'm afraid. Here, that spot is already taken."

And then he left.

Chapter Thirty-One

The Xchotli

After Xiu departed, his "friends" departed too, filtering out one by one until Vaughn and Ivana were left alone.

"This went from being one of the worst days of my life to one of the strangest," Ivana said. She looked out over the table. Much of the food was gone, but there were still platters of meat, fruit, and sweets enough to tempt anyone.

Her stomach grumbled, but she still hesitated.

Vaughn seemed to have lost any previous qualms. He helped himself to a thick cut of beef—or what looked like beef, anyway—and a sprig of grapes. "Aren't you going to eat?"

"I question the wisdom of that," Ivana said.

"Me too," Vaughn said, cutting a piece of the meat off and popping it in his mouth. "But I figure we can starve to death for sure, or we can eat and *maybe* not die."

She gave the food a suspicious look. "Where did it come from? It certainly doesn't look like anything could survive around here."

"Ivana, we're literally eating the food of the gods, and you're going to question how they farmed it?"

She sighed and finally filled her own plate.

"So I was right," Vaughn said around the mouthful of meat.

"I'm sorry?"

"They do exist."

Ivana grunted and tentatively tried a grape. "Fantastic. The psychopathic deities found in all those myths are *real*, and we've met one of them. That's reassuring."

"I didn't say it was reassuring, I said I was *right*."

She shook her head. "Look, I don't even know why I'm here or how it happened. Even Xiuheuhtli seemed mystified. But I'm here, and I doubt I'm getting home without you, so let's just do this thing."

"I think to do it, we're going to have to figure out what's happening here. There's a lot we don't know, it seems. It sounds like some things have changed. Some things that aren't reflected in the myths."

Ivana paused in buttering a roll. "Yes. It does sound that way." She frowned and tucked a piece of hair behind her ear. "Xiuheu..." She sighed. "*Xiu* made it sound like once upon a time, there were no bloodbane coming through at the sky-fire. And that the reason they do now is because of Zily's curse."

"I'm beginning to think that a lot of things are because of Zily's curse," Vaughn said. He rubbed at his jaw. "The portal connecting to the abyss. The other gods, apparently, aren't living full-time in the heavens, but are waging some sort of war here in the abyss?"

Ivana mulled on that for a moment. "What if the part of the curse that led us to discover how aether interacts with its rival is more than what we thought? What if the curse was that the gods would literally fight with their rivals? What if that's why the aether works the way it does?" She stood up and started pacing. "What if, all along, the curse had nothing to do with us, except that Banebringers are affected by what their patrons are doing?" She stopped pacing and looked at him. "What if we don't need to get Zily to intervene—what if all we need to do is get him to lift his curse?"

Vaughn frowned. "But...doesn't that free Danathalt up to try his tricks again? Why would Zily do that?"

She shook her head.

They tried to take Xiu's advice and rest. Ivana was certainly exhausted, but any sleep she found, curled up in the corner on cushions stolen from the table, was restless. Given Vaughn's tossing and turning, she guessed he fared about the same.

Even so, she was startled out of a half-wakeful state by a *boom* from outside, which vibrated the shrine.

She sprang to her feet. Vaughn rose as well.

There was another thud, and then a shower of dust.

That didn't bode well.

The next thud shook the ground so hard, she staggered to the side. Vaughn caught her arm, and they stared at one another.

She was out of her element. She had no idea what was normal or not in the abyss, and she had a feeling that even what was normal could kill them in an instant.

Before they had a chance to say or do anything else, Xiu rushed back into the room. One of his almost-human, orange-skinned companions trailed in his wake.

"You must leave—now," Xiu said, his voice stern and brooking no argument.

"What's happening?" Vaughn asked.

Xiu's eyes flashed—literally. Sparks flew out of them. "Chiquoxetlaz found out you're here and is using it as an excuse to attack my base directly."

Chiquoxetlaz. Ivana racked her brain. The patron of charmbloods, perhaps?

Xiu gestured toward his orange companion. "Azaz will take you to the river, where you may apply for entrance to the Great Father's realm."

The walls shuddered again.

"Go!" Xiu said. "Now!"

Ivana didn't trust Xiu or his servant, but they didn't stand a chance out on the plains of the abyss on their own, so they had little choice.

They followed Azaz.

Azaz silently led them through a winding passageway, not the way they had entered Xiu's home. The booms and thuds continued to shake the walls and vibrate the clothes on their back. It was unnerving, and Vaughn was relieved when they emerged on the backside of the shrine.

Until, of course, he realized that meant they were back out on the plains.

Against the backdrop of the blood-red sky, giant fiery boulders flew. So far, most seemed to land outside Xiu's "camp," but one came too close for comfort, knocking Vaughn off his feet again.

So that was what had caused the pits in the terrain.

Up until now, Azaz hadn't spoken a word. Now, he hissed at them—his voice the sound of a fire being quenched with water. "Get up," he said. "Hurry."

And with that, he hurried on, away from the camp, in the direction opposite the one they had come from.

Vaughn glanced back to see Xiu marching out of his camp onto the plains, wreathed in flame again. Another figure came from the plains to meet him, just as tall as he was, but Vaughn couldn't get a good look before Xiu lifted his enormous fiery sword and brought it down toward the other figure's head. The other figure lifted a staff and caught the strike. Flames erupted from the sword and encircled both of them, and the impact of the block sent a shockwave through the earth under Vaughn's feet.

Maybe Ivana was right to be concerned about any potential intervention by Zily destroying the world...

"Hurry, hurry!" Azaz said, glancing back. "We're almost there."

Almost where? Vaughn thought. While the battle behind them was retreating, in front only seemed to be the same, dreary, trackless plains of before. Azaz knelt on the ground.

Vaughn and Ivana came to an abrupt halt behind him.

He threw Ivana a glance, and she just shrugged.

Azaz pressed his hand into the ground, and when he lifted it, the ground began to rumble again, and then the dirt cracked, and a hole gaped in the ground.

Vaughn backed away, his heart pounding. *What in the—?*

A giant rock unfurled itself, ten-, twenty-, then thirty-feet high—even larger than the other one.

Vaughn's neck craned to look up at it as it stretched and stepped out of the hole it had come from.

Even the otherworldly Azaz seemed small and puny.

"Uh, not that I want to question your methods," said Vaughn, "but the last one of these we ran into—"

Azaz swatted his hand in the air, as if to smack a pesky bug, and cut Vaughn off. "This is one of ours," Azaz said. "Not all the creatures in the abyss belong to Danathalt."

The rock looked down at them and rumbled, and that was when Vaughn noticed that the rock's eyes were glowing orange, not white.

"We require transportation to the river," Azaz said.

The rock rumbled again and slowly bent down. It placed its hand flat on the ground, and Azaz climbed up into it. Then he turned to look expectantly at Vaughn and Ivana.

"This is a dream," Ivana muttered, climbing up first. "I'm going to wake up and find out this was one long, insane dream."

Vaughn climbed up after her and then pinched her arm.

"Ouch!" she cried. "What'd you do that for?"

"Not a dream."

The rock hand rose. Vaughn braced himself against what he supposed was a thumb. When the rock creature had stood erect again, it began to move: slowly, at first, and then more quickly, until the plains moved by in a blur in its long strides.

Azaz stood perilously close to the edge of the hand, bracing himself on the thumb, looking out over the plains. His fire-orange hair whipped out behind him like flames—in fact, it was possible Vaughn saw a real flame or two.

"You realize that a pinch hurting doesn't mean something's not a dream, right?" Ivana said.

"What? No. Because unless you pinch yourself in your sleep—"

"You'll just dream that it hurts. Trust me." She turned her face away from him. "I know."

Her hair had been tied back, but the loose strands whipped around her face as well.

She said nothing else, just stared across the broken landscape.

Vaughn glanced at Azaz. The creature didn't appear at all interested in Vaughn or Ivana, but perhaps it would answer some questions.

He edged closer to Azaz and cleared his throat.

Azaz turned his head to look at him, unblinking.

"So," Vaughn said. "Would it offend you if I asked what you are?"

Azaz blinked at him. "I am a *xchotli* of Xiuheuhtli."

Vaughn waved his hand. "Wait. That's what Xiu thought my friend was." He nodded toward Ivana. "And she looks nothing like you."

Azaz studied Ivana. "If she were a *xchotli,* she wouldn't reveal her true nature in your world," he said.

Vaughn frowned. "There are beings like you in our world?"

"I would say no, not any longer," Azaz said. "Xiuheuhtli is so old, he loses track of time, but I know that it's been too long since the portals have been used. We are not immortal."

It took Vaughn a moment to digest that, and then he moved on to the next question Azaz's comment had spawned. "You can change your appearance?"

"After a fashion. We can change to match your expectations of us."

"Like...you'd look Setanan if you were in Setana and a Xambrian if you were in Xambria?"

"Possibly."

Vaughn thought about that. "So...do you really look like what you look like right now, or do you look like that because I think you ought to look like that?"

"Yes," Azaz said, then turned away.

Vaughn was starting to get a headache. "All right, let's backtrack. I can assure you Ivana is human, not a...*xchotli.*"

Azaz glanced at Ivana, who could surely hear their

conversation, and was choosing to ignore them. Or at least choosing to pretend to ignore them. "Agreed. She's human. I would know if she weren't. Which is curious, since those who have not been gifted of the blood have never been able to cross into our world."

"I'd welcome any theory you had on how she got here, then..."

Azaz shook his head mutely.

Vaughn frowned. "She read the inscription...maybe that had something to do with it."

Ivana joined the conversation, confirming his guess that she *had* been listening. "But our friend here just said if I don't have Banebringer blood, it shouldn't matter."

"Were you using aether at the time?"

She shook her head. "The only aether mix I had on me was moonblood, and I wasn't touching it."

"Pardon," Azaz broke in, "but what do you mean, was she *using* aether?"

"We can mix normal blood with that of a Banebringer, and then that person can use that particular aether."

Azaz stared at him, his mouth agape.

"You knew that, right?" Vaughn asked. It seemed inconceivable that the gods—or at least whatever this creature was that worked for the gods—wouldn't know that.

Azaz blinked slowly. "I...can see how that might work, in theory. But *why* would you do that?"

Vaughn scratched his head. "Why not?"

"You are a *teotontl.*"

Xiu had called him that, too. In fact, wasn't that the word in Ivana's first translation that she had no knowledge of, had said probably wasn't even Xambrian? "I have no idea what that means. Is that, like, 'Banebringer' in your language?"

"Teotontl," Azaz repeated slowly, and then he hesitated, as if

trying to find the right words. "'Little god.' Why would you contaminate your blood with that of a lesser creature?"

Vaughn burst out laughing. "Little god? Me? You must be joking. I'm despised and cast out—hunted, even. All of us are."

Azaz said nothing, but the orange in his irises began to bleed into the whites.

"You didn't *know* that? How would you not know that? And does that mean at one point my kind were considered…little *gods*?"

Azaz pressed his lips together. "I am out of place," he said. "These are not questions that are mine to answer." And then he turned away again, his face set into stone. Glowing, hot stone.

Vaughn carefully moved back toward Ivana. "Did you hear the rest of that?" he whispered.

"Yes. But in Xambria and Yunqi, they treat their Banebringers differently. I'm almost certain in Yunqi they are, in fact, highly revered."

He knew that. He did. But it still struck him as insane.

"*Highly revered* is different than being so…superior that to even mix our blood with someone normal would be abhorrent."

She cast him a wry look. "Apparently, Banebringers were once the nobles of the world."

Vaughn pondered this. It seemed so incredible to him. And arrogant. And how had Azaz not known about Banebringers' current plight? He'd seemed surprised and perhaps even put out by the information.

Azaz had moved farther away from them, making it clear he had no intention of answering any more questions.

Which was too bad. Because Vaughn had a least a hundred more.

Xiu's rock giant carried them for what seemed liked forever before it slowed again. Vaughn had settled himself down in a nook that seemed safe and fallen asleep, when suddenly, the change in speed roused him. He poked his head back up again.

The terrain had changed. Behind them lay the pockmarked plains. To their right, the beginnings of mountains rose from the horizon. And directly in front of them was a wide river of tumultuous black water.

A few dozen feet past the opposite bank, the land disappeared into a heavy white fog. Vaughn could see shapes in the fog, shifting, growing, shrinking, but he couldn't make out what any of them were.

Azaz made his way over to where Vaughn and Ivana stood. "We're here," he said.

"Where, exactly, is that?"

Azaz gestured. "The final divide."

"Wait... There really *is* a river?"

Azaz didn't respond. "Wait here." He catapulted over the edge of the giant's hand.

Vaughn looked over the edge. Azaz was striding toward the edge of the river. The already churning water swirled and eddied, and a moment later, a creature began to emerge from the water.

It looked like an enormous, distorted dog. It stood, dripping on the bank, its head bowed to the shorter Azaz.

Vaughn couldn't hear any words pass between the two creatures, but after a few minutes, the dog turned and bounded back into the river, disappearing under the surface again.

Azaz returned to the giant. It picked Azaz up and placed him back in its hand.

"We will cross," Azaz said. "As Xiuheuhtli anticipated, Thaxchatichan will gladly receive you."

Vaughn breathed out. "Great. Progress." He flashed a smile at Ivana, but she didn't return it.

True to Azaz's word, the stone giant waded slowly into the river. At the center of the river, the water rose to the giant's waist, and Vaughn was afraid that even this giant would be swallowed. But from there, it pushed on, and the water remained level.

Vaughn couldn't help staring down into the depths of the water. Something black and spiny crested the surface and then disappeared again. "Is there something in the water?"

Azaz looked amused. "There are many somethings in the water. Please don't fall in. You are not meant to be in this land—to traverse this test or any other. You would fail."

Vaughn glanced at Ivana, and she shrugged.

It didn't take the giant long to cross the raging river, though the current was so strong that even the giant had to push against it. Vaughn couldn't imagine anyone less than a rock giant traversing it.

The rock giant reached the other side and stood at the edge of the fog. There, it lowered its hand for the three of them to climb out.

Azaz pointed toward the fog. "You are beyond the dangers of the abyss now, and the fog will not hurt you as long as you keep moving forward." He paused. "I will offer you one word of advice: Stay alert. Once you step through, you are not beyond all danger." He bowed. "A *xchotli* of Thaxchatichan will meet you on the other side. There, you will be on your own to accomplish your goals. Good luck."

Not beyond danger? On their own? Good luck? That sounded ominous. "Will Thaxchatichan not help us?" he asked. "I *am* one of her Banebringers, after all."

Azaz didn't answer. He merely climbed back into the giant's hand, which turned and splashed back into the river, crossed, and disappeared into the distance.

Vaughn glanced back into the depths of the black river. Then looked ahead into the fog and shivered. "Well." He held out his hand to Ivana. "Shall we?"

Ivana took Vaughn's hand; she had no desire to be lost in this ominous fog. They stepped into it and immediately sight and sound were lost to her. She could feel the press of Vaughn's hand, for which she was grateful, but otherwise, the deceptively bright fog felt oppressively dark. She could see nothing beneath her feet, nothing to either side, and she heard nothing other than the hollow thud of her own footsteps and the beating of her heart.

They walked on.

She wasn't sure how they would know they weren't just walking in circles, but Azaz had seemed sincere enough in his duty to deliver them to their next guide, so she tried not to think about it and kept moving forward, as he'd suggested.

Mist clung to her hair, and her shirt dampened. Dark shapes swirled around her, and after a time, she was certain she heard whispers.

Vaughn's grip tightened, and she put her other hand on his arm, just to be on the safe side.

They didn't speak. She wasn't sure if he could have heard her if she tried.

The whispers grew louder, as if an initial dozen had been joined by a hundred more whisperers. She felt, somehow, that they were whispering about her, but the words were unintelligible.

Ivana.

She almost stopped, but remembering Azaz's words, she pressed her lips together and kept walking.

Monster... the darkness hissed. *Monster.*

A thousand more joined the chorus. *Monster. Monster. Monster.*

Her heart started beating harder and faster. She willed her eyes forward, though the shapes now seemed to take human form around her. She would not live this nightmare.

Vaughn faltered, tugging her back.

The shapes loomed in closer.

"Keep going," she hissed, yanking him forward.

He started walking again, but his hand trembled under her grasp.

She wondered what the darkness was whispering to him.

The face of her father appeared in the air in front of her. She started, and then closed her eyes. She didn't need to see in this place anyway.

So they continued until their steps began to falter from exhaustion. Neither of them had slept much since the night they'd entered the portal—and though Ivana had no sense of how much time had passed, they had hardly been idle.

Perhaps Azaz had been wrong. Perhaps they would wander in this fog forever.

The fog lifted.

Chapter Thirty-Two

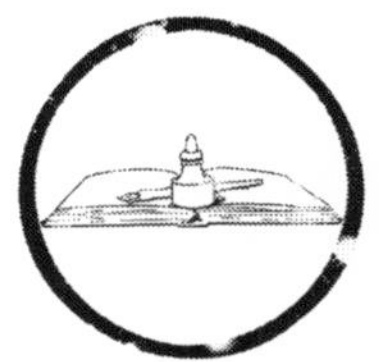

Helpless No More

"Driskell."

"Damn demonspawn caused all this ruckus. They ought to round 'em all up and drown them in the ocean."

"Driskell!"

"Bloodbane can drown right? Take 'em out on a boat. Why has no one thought of that yet?"

"Driskell!"

Driskell's hand jerked across the page, leaving a jagged line across the notes he was supposed to be taking.

He cleared his throat and looked up, trying in vain to clear the vestiges of the conversation he had just overheard at Tania's house from his mind. "My lady?"

Nahua was staring at him. The meeting was over, and the

room was empty of all but him and Nahua.

He looked down at his notes. And he had recorded barely a page.

His face heated and he spread a hand over the notes, though she had surely already seen his meager offerings.

Nahua sat on the edge of the table. "You've been distracted the past couple of days." She nodded toward his notes. "This isn't like you. Anything you'd like to share?"

He swallowed. "I'm so sorry, my lady. It won't happen again."

She studied him for a moment. "I know it's been difficult, keeping this all so quiet. Tania's family must be frothing at the mouth."

Yes. Yes, that was it. The perfect excuse. Besides, it wasn't *completely* a lie. They were. It just wasn't what was bothering him so much that he couldn't do his job.

So, he hesitated, then nodded. "I was just thinking about the last conversation they had around the dinner table. Her uncle suggested rounding up all the Banebring—I mean, Gifted—and tossing them in the ocean, so the bloodbane would drown too." He looked down at his hands. "I'm afraid when they find out what's happening, they're going to disown me for being part of it."

There. That was close enough to the truth.

"You're just doing your job, Driskell," Nahua said gently. "If it comes to it, those of us in charge will be the ones to blame. The ones to face the worst consequences."

He felt sick to his stomach, deceiving Nahua like this. What if he just told her? She...She wouldn't care, right? She seemed to be rational about the others. Maybe—

"Perhaps remind her uncle that you certainly won't earn any points toward advancement if you're proven to be untrustworthy," Nahua added. "He'll respond to that, I'd wager."

He looked up at her, and she winked at him.

His stomach was in a full-out revolt now. Three days ago, he would have given anything to hear those words drop from her mouth. How could he tell her that now, it didn't matter?

She furrowed her brow and put a hand on his shoulder. "You're taking on a distinct green hue," she said. "Perhaps you should go home and lie down. Any tasks you have for this afternoon can wait. This has been an understandably stressful time for you—for all of us."

He nodded mutely. She gave his shoulder a squeeze and left the room.

Driskell slumped down in his chair and buried his head in his arms on the table. He was doomed.

Finally, he roused himself. He'd take Nahua's advice. Go back to his room, take a nap. Or better yet, maybe he'd go have a nice game of tapolli at Tamal's.

His head was down all through the hall, down the steps of the civic hall, and out the second gate, deep in thought, so he didn't see Danton when he ran into him from behind.

"Oh!" Driskell said. "I'm sorry—you're back?"

Danton turned and blinked at him, as if surprised to find him there as well. "Yeah," he said. "A few hours ago. Just got done debriefing with Yaotel. It's..." He shook his head. A shadow passed over his face, but it brightened again. "I was going to grab a pint. Want to join me?"

Driskell hesitated. He could tell Danton. He'd already thought about it, even. Maybe Danton could help him somehow. Give him tips as to how to hide it. It would...just be good to tell *someone*. "I don't want to stop you from getting a drink," he said, "but do you have a few minutes? I have a question for you. A, uh, sort of...confidential question."

Danton didn't miss a beat. There were certainly enough

confidential events transpiring that such a request wouldn't seem strange. "Sure thing. I can get a drink later. Want to go back to the civic hall, then?"

"It's more of a personal question. Maybe...your barracks?"

That did prompt a raise of Danton's eyebrow. "No problem."

Danton dragged a chair into his small room, shut the door, and then sat down on his bed.

It was the first time Driskell had been in one of the rooms set aside as private chambers for the Banebringers since any of them had moved into them. Danton's had two cots and a small table holding a washbasin and a ceramic pitcher—and that was about it.

It was sparse. An inn would have been nicer.

"I'm sorry," Driskell said, settling into the chair and feeling guilty for his small but comfortable room in the government dormitory. "I know this isn't exactly the lap of luxury, but..."

Danton shrugged. "I've slept in a lot worse for a lot longer," he said. "Besides, it's only temporary, right?"

That was the idea, anyway. "Right. But I mean, if you need anything... Maybe we could get you all some rugs or something."

Danton scratched his chin. "Is this what you wanted to talk about? The furnishings in the new Ichtacan headquarters?"

Driskell rubbed his thighs with sweaty hands. "No. I'm stalling. Where's Vaughn? Aren't you rooming with him?" He didn't know Vaughn as well as Danton and didn't want a surprise visit in the middle of his confession.

The shadow passed over Danton's face again, and he bit his lip. "He... I don't know, for sure. He disappeared. I mean, in a less conventional way, for him."

Driskell was momentarily caught off-guard. Yaotel had

briefly explained Vaughn's side mission to Tanuac in a semi-private meeting—Driskell thought mostly so Tanuac wouldn't be worried about yet another Banebringer going missing. Yaotel had seemed dismissive of the idea that Vaughn's plan would work. "He disappeared? You mean, he really went through that doorway or whatever it was?"

Danton spread his hands out to his sides. "Maybe? Who knows? But there was no body, and no bloodbane summoned, so I guess we can hope. Yaotel's...well, I don't think he's pleased. He has some important task for Vaughn, and now we have no idea when he'll be back." Danton swallowed. "But anyway. What did you want to ask me, then?"

Now that it had come to it, Driskell didn't know how to say it. He wrung his hands together, took another deep breath, and then exhaled.

"Driskell," Danton said. "What in the abyss is wrong?"

"The sky-fire," Driskell began. "I...I think I..." He rolled up the leg of his trousers; easier to just show him. The scab had shrunk in the couple of days since the sky-fire, but it was still a visibly silver-ish patch on his knee.

Danton looked at his knee while Driskell's heart pounded wildly. Why was he so nervous? Danton was a Banebringer. He wasn't going to reject him or judge him or tell someone else. Right?

"Oh," Danton said softly. "Well, damn."

Driskell swallowed. "I don't know what to do. I'm sorry for bothering you. I-I didn't know who else to go to." And he had felt about ready to burst if he didn't tell someone.

Danton leaned back on his hands and studied Driskell's face. "Anyone else see?"

Driskell shook his head. "I was alone."

"So you're lucky. You don't have to run or abandon your

current life. You just do everything you can do to hide it and hope no one finds out."

Driskell rubbed his hands on his trousers again. "I-I was planning on proposing to Tania in only a few weeks. I have everything planned. Her entire family already knows. My family knows. *She* knows it's coming; she just doesn't know when. Do I still do it?" He licked his lips. "Do I tell her beforehand, if so? If I don't, how could she ever forgive me if..." He pressed his lips together, feeling like he was going to vomit.

Danton rose and poured a glass of water, then handed it to Driskell and sat back down. "I hear you. But I don't have an easy answer for you," Danton said. "There *are* people who take it okay. And then there are other people, people you think you know, people you thought cared about you, and they turn on you." He looked down at his hands.

Danton's family had betrayed him, Driskell recalled.

"You tell them, you take a chance. Maybe they keep your secret, maybe they even become an ally. Maybe they turn on you. And if they turn on you, your chance at hiding it, at a relatively normal life, is gone. You have to run."

"But I can't marry Tania without telling her. I can't." It would be wrong.

Danton looked up. "Look, I don't know your girl, and I'm hardly an expert on that sort of thing. But if that's the case, you have two options: you take a chance and hope for the best, or you break it off and say nothing."

Both of those options made him feel like a pit had opened under him. "And what about...?" He bit his lip. "Do I tell Nahua? The Ri?"

Danton's face took on a curious expression. "I mean, given the current situation, why does it matter? Of all the times and places to become Gifted, this has got to be one of the best circumstances you could find yourself in."

"I know. That's not lost on me. But I'm afraid that while I might not lose my job, or they might be...*okay* with it, any chances of advancement will be gone." His shoulders slumped. "Should I join the Ichtaca? Do I have to?"

"Nah, you don't have to. But, if you do, you'll obviously have to tell Yaotel, and then Nahua and Tanuac will find out. Do you *want* to join?"

"I don't know. What does that even mean? Do I have other options?"

Danton scratched at his chin. "There might be other groups like ours out there. Given how secretive we are, it's hard to say. If Yaotel knows, he keeps the information close to himself. But I can tell you that the Ichtaca, in the past, had been about finding a diplomatic solution to our problems. Yaotel and his non-Gifted allies poured a lot of resources into researching our abilities, researching ways to subtly thwart the Conclave, searching for and gathering together anything left out there about Gifted or the heretic gods, before the Conclave could get to it and destroy it."

"And that's changed?" Driskell asked. "Seems to me this was still an attempt at diplomacy on your leader's part."

Danton gave him a side eye. "I mean, sure. In theory. If the alternative is gathering an army and attacking Weylyn City. But I don't know in what history books planning a coup counts as diplomacy."

Driskell took a deep breath. He had a point. It was hard to see that right now when the only results of their quiet rebellion so far had been a bunch of meetings and some nerve-racking evasion of the Conclave representative.

He'd rather not think about how that might change in the near future. His personal problems were enough for today.

"If you decide you want to explore the idea of officially joining us, Yaotel *will* put you to use. That's sort of part of the deal. What can you do?"

Driskell blinked. He hadn't even thought about it. "I have no idea."

Danton grinned. "Oh, that's fun, at least. Wanna find out?"

"How would I know? How do people usually find out?"

"It varies. Some people come to us having no idea. Some people figure it out on their own, by accident—it's possible, because you don't *need* to know what you're doing to make your powers work. It's just not efficient—and can be dangerous."

Driskell swallowed. *Dangerous?*

Danton seemed not at all concerned. Instead, he rubbed his hands together. "You have your notebook on you?"

Driskell gave him a sheepish smile. "Of course," he said, drawing it out of his pocket and handing it to Danton.

Danton made a list and handed it back to him.

Driskell read over it. *Lightblood. Moonblood. Fireblood. Iceblood. Windblood. Bindblood. Sunblood. Charmblood. Darkblood. Weaveblood. Beastblood.* The terms were familiar by now, but there were a couple he didn't recognize. "Is this a list of all the types of Banebring—sorry—Gifted?"

"It's not necessarily complete. We've discovered new profiles before. But these are the ones we've run across in the Ichtaca. I put them in order of the easiest to identify with a few tests and the hardest to identify." Danton raised a finger. "But first, you need to know how to burn your own aether. It's not hard, but it takes practice to do efficiently. Fortunately, we don't need efficiency yet; we just need to find out what profile you are."

"Aether. The silver stuff," Driskell said.

"Yes. The silver stuff you're now bleeding. Did you feel any different when the change happened?"

Driskell thought back to that night a few days ago. "I'm not sure if I could pinpoint *when* it happened, exactly..."

"Did you see a tear? A bloodbane?"

"Yes. A bloodhawk came through. I thought I was dead."

Danton nodded. "That's when it happened. Right around there. What did you feel?"

"Abject terror."

Danton chuckled. "Fair enough. Anything more?"

"I guess—" Now that he thought about it... "I did feel this sort of cold sweep through me, followed by warmth. I chalked it up to fear."

"Good. Best as we can tell, that's what it feels like when your blood changes." Danton held up a hand. "Don't ask me why. That's not my area. But it feels similar when you burn aether—at least, it does at first, before you get used to it. I don't notice it anymore unless I'm concentrating."

"I don't feel anything," Driskell said. "I feel normal."

Danton waved his hand. "That's because you're not trying to do anything. So, close your eyes..."

"Really?"

"It's easier this way. Just trust me."

Driskell sighed and closed his eyes, even though it felt awkward.

"Now, I'm going to give you a list of things to try doing. Think hard about doing those things and tell me if you feel anything like what you did before."

"All right."

"Make light."

Driskell opened his eyes. This was crazy. "I can't make light!"

Danton snapped his fingers and held out his hand, which was now lined in bright white light. He clenched his fist and it disappeared. "I'm a lightblood. It's about the most basic thing I can do. You don't need to worry about *succeeding* in doing anything right now. Just concentrate on what you *feel*."

Driskell sighed and closed his eyes. *Right. Make light.* He imagined himself making his hand light up like Danton had.

"Still feel normal," he said.

"All right, so probably not a lightblood. I'm going to go quick here, so don't protest again. Just do what I say."

"I'll try."

"Turn invisible."

Driskell opened his mouth to argue, but he shut it just as fast and wished he were invisible. "Nothing."

"Make fire."

"Uh..." He imagined setting something on fire. "No."

"Freeze the water in your glass."

"Nothing."

"Make wind blow."

"Nothing."

"You can open your eyes. Assuming you were following my instructions, that rules out lightblood, moonblood, fireblood, iceblood, and windblood."

Driskell couldn't help but feel a little disappointed. All those powers seemed... Well, if he could set aside the implications of having them, they *were* sort of incredible.

"Roll up your trouser leg again," Danton instructed. "Look at that scrape and heal it."

Once again, Driskell had to bite back a protest as he did what Danton asked. No funny feeling. "Nope."

Danton sighed. "Ugh. Okay." He stood up. "Come with me."

Driskell trailed behind Danton as they left his room and went out into the larger chamber that a dozen rooms connected to. There was no one in it at present. The Banebringers had tried to make the dank stone area more homey by throwing some rugs and cushions on the floor, and someone had even potted a flower and set it on a table.

It was the last that Danton led him to. He folded his arms across his chest. "Make it grow," he said, nodding toward the flower.

"Er...nothing. What was that?"

"Sunblood. We don't know that much about them, unfortunately, other than that they seem to have a way with vegetation. The next one is going to be tricky, and the last three nigh-on-impossible to test right now, so let's hope this does it." He pointed through the archway back into the main tunnel. "Now listen carefully. We're going to head to the main chambers. Hopefully, someone will be around. Concentrate on someone—someone other than me—and try to will them into saying or doing something."

Driskell blinked. "*Will* them...?"

"You probably won't be able to. But try anyway."

Driskell humored him.

In the main chamber, they found Linette, the bindblood healer, talking in the corner to a woman Driskell didn't know well.

The two women glanced Driskell and Danton's way as they entered and gave a wave, but then went back to their conversation.

Danton nodded at Driskell.

Driskell focused on Linette. *Stop talking*, he told her in his mind.

Nothing happened to Linette, but Driskell...

Burning skies. He *did* feel something. He frowned and tried again. *Stop talking*, he told Linette again.

There it was again. A peculiar sensation, almost like he could feel his blood moving or maybe bubbling in his veins—but Danton was right. It was warm and cold at the same time, not exactly the same as the night he had been changed, but similar.

Intrigued, he tried one more time.

Linette broke off for a moment. She shook her head and then started the conversation again.

Had *he* done that?

Driskell looked at Danton and nodded.

They returned silently to Danton's room—silent until the door closed, at which point Danton turned to him with a huge grin. "Congratulations. You're a charmblood."

"Charmblood?" He didn't think he'd met one of those yet.

"Yes. That means you have the ability to exert influence over people." He winked. "You know. Charm them."

Driskell stared at Danton, horrified. "I don't want to make people do things! That's just...wrong."

Danton quirked an eyebrow up. "Well, as I understand it, you can't *make* people do things. Not like you're thinking anyway. It's more influence or goad them, under the right circumstances. Unfortunately, we don't have any charmbloods in Marakyn at the moment that I know of, which is too bad for you—you'd be better off having another charmblood to take you through the ins and outs."

Influencing or goading people didn't seem much better to Driskell. Maybe even worse. "Why does that matter? Don't all the powers all work the same?"

Danton ruffled a hand through his hair. "Sure, at a basic level. But as you get better at using your powers, you'll find that there are certain tricks unique to yours—ways of thinking—that can help give you more control. With my powers, it helps if I imagine the light as something I gather, rather than create, and then do something with. Most simply, of course, I can make that light actual light that you can see, and I don't even think about that anymore.

"But for something more complicated, like illusions, in my head I'm taking that light and sort of...painting it over the area I'm changing." He waved his hand across the room as if he were, indeed, painting it with a wide brush. "But that's nonsense to Thrax, who's a fireblood. To hear him talk, it's all raw power—burn this, burn that." He hesitated. "I'm not sure how a charmblood envisions using their powers."

This power sounded a little ethically grey to him. What in the abyss was he going to do with it that wouldn't make him feel *wrong* inside?

Another thought came to him. "Can you use your powers by accident?"

Danton wiggled his hand back and forth. "Someone like you, maybe. If you've had *any* amount of real practice with your powers, not really."

Great. So he could be influencing someone and not even *know* it?

"But now that you know what it feels like to burn aether, you'd know if you were doing it."

Oh. Well. That was a relief.

Danton clapped him on the shoulder. "I can see you need some time to think about this. Give me a few days. I'll do some asking around about charmbloods."

"Thanks," he said. "I appreciate your help. And, um, maybe this goes without saying, but don't tell anyone?"

Danton laughed. "You have my word, though I'd like to bring Thrax into the loop, if you don't mind." At Driskell's look, he held up his hand. "Thrax is trustworthy. I promise. It's not that he's particularly versed in all the ins and outs of our magic, like maybe some of our researchers are, but among us, he's probably the one who's embraced his powers the most."

"All right," Driskell said. "If you think it'll help."

"He'll be *eager* to help, anyway. Together, maybe we can come up with a plan to help you take the first steps."

Driskell didn't know if he wanted to take the first steps. But he also wanted to feel like he was in control of this, rather than the other way around.

He had been carried along, helpless, by the flow of the events happening around him for far too long. This was his to own.

He wouldn't be carried along by this as well.

Chapter Thirty-Three

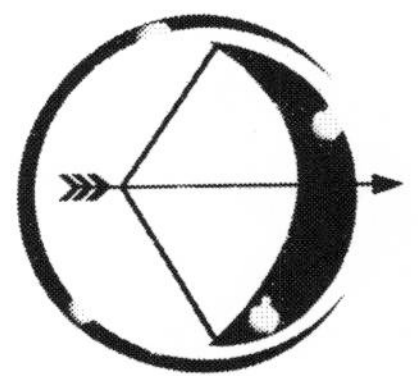

Silver, White, and Blue

Vaughn and Ivana stepped into a paradise.

A verdant plain stretched in front of them in all directions. Far to the right, picturesque, snowcapped mountains graced the horizon.

Vaughn glanced back. Directly behind them was the river, sedate and sparkling, reflecting the cloudless blue of the sky above.

The white fog still swirled, but it had retreated to the opposite bank.

He began to relax, but then he remembered Azaz's warning that they weren't completely safe here, either.

There was no sign of their new guide—Thaxchatichan's *xchotli*. "Do you think we should wait for a few minutes or start walking?" Vaughn asked Ivana.

"Let's see if this new *xchotli* shows up first. It looks pretty, but I..." She glanced back at the fog. "I don't trust this place, either."

No sooner had she finished speaking than something odd appeared in the sky. It looked like...a stairway?

He pointed it out to Ivana, and together they watched as the stairway lengthened, stretching out toward the ground. Before it touched the grass, a woman—or, at least, she looked like a woman, aside from the pale, almost luminous skin and disconcerting silver eyes—began walking down the stairs. She wore a shimmering white length of cloth fastened in a high collar around her neck, but it was sleeveless, so it merely draped down the front of her body. A silver cord snugged the loose-fitting fabric to her waist, and from there it hung to slippered feet.

Her hair hung unbound to her waist, glistening white, but her face was young.

She waited a few steps up for the stairway to finish resolving, and then completed her descent to the ground.

She stood in front of them. "Honored guests of Thaxchatichan?"

"Uh. That's us," Vaughn said.

"Excellent. Follow me."

She turned and began walking back up the stairway.

Well. Apparently, her robe was backless. The front was held in place by only two thin crossing strips of fabric, the bottom ends attached to the skirt of her robe, which began at her lower back, and the top ends attaching to the back of the collar around her neck.

All in all, it gave the impression that a wrong move or a catch of the fabric might cause the entire getup to come cascading off her.

"If this is normal attire in Thaxchatichan's court," Ivana muttered, "you, at least, won't be complaining about our visit there."

He *was* staring, wasn't he? He cleared his throat and tried to avert his eyes, but it was rather difficult since they were following the woman up an increasingly high stair with no banister or rail on either side.

"You know," he said indignantly, "I've been *exceedingly* good. Some might even say unnecessarily good."

"I see. So you *deserve* a little fantasy?"

He refrained from telling her that most of his fantasies of late involved her.

They continued to ascend. Vaughn turned to look behind them once and wished he hadn't: the stair was disappearing a few steps beyond where they had last trod.

Just when he thought they would be climbing for an eternity, the sky began to change. The crisp blue of a sunny day darkened into midnight blue, and pinpricks of light began to dot the sky above.

Then the palace rose before them. It was a blinding, glowing white against the night sky, with a full moon rising behind it, and the entire thing appeared to float in midair.

The sight was breathtaking. Indeed, the *xchotli* paused at the top stair and turned slightly to face them, a knowing look on her face, as if to allow them a moment to take it in.

"It's magnificent," Vaughn said, feeling as though she were waiting for some sort of praise.

Satisfied, she nodded. "We have reached Thaxchatichan's palace. I will show you to your room, where you may freshen yourselves. Then, Thaxchatichan will see you both and hear your inquiry."

That sounded promising.

The woman walked toward the palace across the sky itself.

Vaughn glanced at Ivana. She shrugged and put a foot out—and it held. She took the lead in following the woman.

Vaughn took a deep breath and cringed as he stepped out onto what was, by all appearances, nothing, but his steps fell on a hard surface, and now that he was on it, he saw that it glistened like glass.

He followed the woman and Ivana across the—courtyard?—and to the main door.

Everything about the palace was white and silver, with splashes of blue.

The walls were silver. The floor looked like white marble. Blue crystal chandeliers hung from the ceiling.

The gross extravagance made the palace in Cohoxta look like a hovel.

It was breathtaking at first, but after a while, his eyes began to hurt. These gods took their affinities seriously. Did *everything* have to look like the moon and water? Hopefully, whatever room they were staying in wasn't decorated the same.

The *xchotli* led them on through several twists and turns and another two staircases until they reached a white door. She pushed it open with a touch and stood aside.

"This is one of the rooms that was of old reserved for your kind." Her eyes drifted to Ivana. "Your…companion…may stay with you, of course." She inclined her head. "If you need anything"—her eyes slid over Vaughn, and he was certain she meant *anything*—"simply speak it."

With that, she left them alone, the door shutting gently behind her.

Vaughn looked around the room and let out a sigh of relief. It was almost normal-looking, except that apparently Thaxchatichan thought "his kind" preferred a setup more like the nomads south of Donia. And except that everything was oversized.

From the large sleeping pallet piled with furs in one corner to the oversized tub in the other corner to the overlarge, legless chaise that reclined next to a low table that would fit five or six. It was almost as if everything had been designed to fit two or three, or even four humans, rather than one.

Perhaps they had been.

He shrugged his pack off his shoulders and set it down next to the chaise. Then he turned to face Ivana.

It struck him that they were truly alone for the first time since she had inexplicably kissed him. Since then, they had either been in the company of others or in enough danger that they hadn't had time to think, let alone talk.

She didn't look at him. Instead, she paced the perimeter of the room, much as she once had at a set of rooms they had been given at Ri Talesin's estate, looking into every corner, opening every drawer.

"What are you looking for?" Vaughn asked. "It isn't as though I need to hide who I am here."

She finished her sweep. "I just like to know my surroundings," she said. "Especially when they're so unfamiliar."

He pulled off his boots, sat down on the chaise, and stretched his toes out with a sigh. "Well, we had a bit of a rocky start, but I'd say overall things have gone well?"

"We started in the abyss. I'd say that's more than rocky." She stopped in front of a long etching above the fireplace. "If Xiu hadn't rescued us, we would have been digesting in the stomach of a bloodbane before we even got started."

"But he did, and we aren't. And anyway, he seemed an amiable god, don't you think? If Thaxchatichan is anything like him, we'll be off to see Zily in the morning and home before dinner."

Ivana didn't answer. She was running her fingers over the etching. "Come look at this," she said.

He groaned at having to stand on his sore feet again, but he did as she asked and joined her at the wall.

"Look," she said. "What do you make of it?"

He studied the carvings. They looked as though they were depicting a scene, or several scenes. Small humans surrounded a large, radiant figure who looked like a much larger version of the *xchotli* who had brought them here—Thaxchatichan, he supposed. Some of the humans bowed down. Another spilled her blood into a bowl nearby. Two others fought, stark naked. One, also naked, reclined in front of Thaxchatichan, as if a piece of art to admire. All of this, Thaxchatichan appeared to preside over.

The blood in the bowl was silver, and while it seemed many objects around here were also silver, the etching had been done in full color.

"Banebringers," Vaughn said. "They must be. From the things Xiu and Azaz said, combined with the myths, I'm beginning to gather that there is actual truth to the legend that Banebringers would travel here."

Ivana frowned. "They look like they're being used more as slaves than 'honored guests.'"

Vaughn shifted. It did look like that.

Azaz had said there would still be danger, even on this side of the divide. He probably wasn't just being dramatic.

Ivana turned away from the etching to face him. "Don't get too comfortable," she said. Her eyes ran over him with a particular sort of irritated disgust that he knew well. "Or distracted."

"What was that?" he asked.

"What was what?"

"That look. Why'd I get that look? I didn't do anything!"

She sniffed. "I'm aware. I'm warning you *not* to."

"If you're suggesting I'm going to go calling our glowy-skinned friend for a quick romp in the sheets..."

"I doubt I need to fill in the details for you."

He frowned, affronted. "I'll have you know, I haven't had a

good *romp* in over a year."

"So you said."

"What, you don't *believe* me?"

She didn't say anything.

He folded his arms across his chest. He had tried to change. Because of *her*. And all along, she hadn't even believed he had made the effort? He didn't want to admit it, but that...hurt. "I thought you had recognized that I'm not that person anymore. I thought that's why you—" He broke off. He wasn't sure he wanted to bring up her unexpected advances.

No, damn it, yes, he did. He wasn't allowed to dally with women, but *she* could kiss him and then say nothing about it afterward? "Apparently, I'm not the only one who knows how to use people for their own pleasure."

Her eyes flashed. "You have never understood me. Don't pretend you do now."

"I could level the same charge at you," he snapped. "You think you hold the sole rights to being mistreated and misunderstood?"

Her jaw twitched multiple times. "You want to play a game of who had it worse off, is that it?"

He ran a hand through his hair. No, he didn't want to play that game. But he was so tired of these unwinnable arguments. "How long are you going to hide behind your past—any of it? When are you just going to let it go?"

"Let it go? Let it *go*?"

"Ivana, I just meant—"

"I need a hot bath," she said, then walked over to the tub.

She ran her hand into it, and it came up wet.

Vaughn blinked. Apparently, the *xchotli* hadn't been joking when she said they just needed to speak what they wanted.

Ivana unfolded a large screen and dragged it across the area with the tub so she was blocked from his view. A moment later, he heard the slosh of water.

He turned away, trying not to let his imagination run away with him.

"I need food," he said hopefully.

He spun around to the table, but nothing magically appeared. He frowned and opened a low cabinet nearby.

A plate of fruit and cheeses was within.

Now, had that been there before or after he'd said he needed food?

He set the plate on the table and plopped down on the chaise with a sigh.

Sweetblade was dead—that much was true. But that hadn't stopped *Ivana* from erecting a barrier around herself again. She didn't trust him, *refused* to trust him, whether due to principle or fear, he didn't know. If only they could get past this roadblock in their relationship, maybe...

He shook his head. It wasn't worth contemplating.

Chapter Thirty-Four

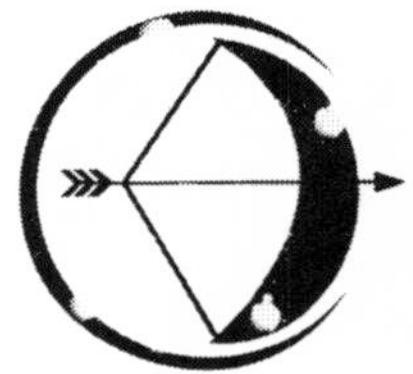

An Overdue Visit

Ivana had no clean clothes to change into. Unlike Vaughn, she hadn't come prepared for this journey. "I need clothes," she said as she toweled off after her bath.

Nothing appeared nearby, and she frowned. Back into her old clothes it was.

"They're out here," Vaughn said.

His shadow came nearer, and a moment later, he slung a garment over the top of the screen. Then his shadow retreated.

She sank to the ground, clutching her towel to her. Everything inside of her felt so out of control. A decade of carefully teaching herself to brick up her emotions—control every word, every thought, every feeling—had been for naught.

She was adrift at sea, alternating between desperately

clinging to anything that she might perceive as a rescue line and considering simply slipping off her driftwood into the depths and never resurfacing again.

Would she never find peace now that Sweetblade was gone? Was this her doom, her punishment?

She swallowed and stood up again. She had to get through whatever they had to do here and get back home. If she was going to let herself drown, she'd at least do it in her own pond.

She pulled down the garment and found it was two. One slipped to the ground, and the other she held up in front of her. She had been half afraid it would be a copy of whatever the moon-lady had been wearing; she was sure Vaughn would enjoy *that*. But it was an unremarkable white robe, one piece that she could slip her arms into, cross over her front, and belt. She bent and picked up the piece she had dropped. A shift for underneath.

She strapped her dagger to her thigh and then put on the shift and robe and belted it.

When she stepped out, she found Vaughn had changed into clean clothes himself, no doubt from his pack.

He was sitting on the chaise, a half-eaten plate of food in front of him. He shoved the plate toward her without looking at her.

She ate, and not a moment too soon, for as soon as she had popped the last grape in her mouth, a knock came on the door.

Vaughn rose to answer it. The moon-lady stood outside.

"Thaxchatichan will see you now."

Vaughn was filled with both trepidation and curiosity at the prospect of meeting his patron deity. Would she be a larger version of the moon-lady? Wear water as clothing like Xiu did fire? Was she abnormally tall as well?

And, of course, given the sole myth they had about her—in

which she was decapitated by her own brother—the most pressing question was: Did she have a head?

When he voiced the latter to Ivana, she gave him a look that reminded him that, in fact, the most pressing question ought to be whether she would be as amiable—or at least helpful—as the fire god had been.

On that note, some of the looks and comments of the respective *xchotli* filled him with a sense of foreboding rather than hope.

The moon-lady led them into a giant hall; it was twice as wide as it was tall, and the vaulted ceilings must have reached twenty feet at their peak. He'd imagined a hard room, all white marble and silver trimmings, but instead, the room was surprisingly soft. The plush light blue rug stretched the entire width and length of the room, and the walls, while they may well have been stone underneath, were draped in flowing silver fabric.

The far wall was made of pure glass, giving an unobstructed view into the starry night sky and of the full moon. Unobstructed, that is, except for the larger-than-life woman who reclined on a chaise on a dais.

She was wearing clothing similar to the moon-lady's, including the collar that encompassed her entire neck; she lay on her right side, revealing a generous amount of the same moon-white flesh on her exposed left side, except that it was tattooed with blue and silver markings, right down to the place where her robe covered her, beyond the hint of the curve of her left breast.

All he could think was that it seemed she had her head after all.

She was surrounded by at least a dozen attendants, both male and female, some who reclined below her chaise, and others who stood nearby, as if awaiting her command. All the attendants, male and female alike, wore the same fabric collar around their necks that she and her *xchotli* did.

She didn't rise when the moon-lady led them into the hall; instead, she rolled over onto her stomach. She had been absently running her free hand through the hair of one of her male attendants, as though petting a dog. She ran it through his hair one last time, giving a tug as she withdrew her hand that made the attendant wince, and then she propped her chin up on her hands and tilted her head to gaze at them.

"One of yours, my lady," the moon-lady said, "and..." She looked at Ivana. "I don't know what she is."

Vaughn rather took exception to being talked about as though he were a possession, but now was probably not the best time to voice his opinion—especially if he wanted the goddess' cooperation.

Chati—he decided she needed a nickname too—studied Ivana first, then turned her eyes to Vaughn.

"Thank you, Chara. You are dismissed." She looked around, as if noticing her attendants for the first time, and flicked her hand in annoyance. "In fact, all of you are dismissed." The attendants obediently rose and filtered out of side doors in the hall.

Once they were gone, Chati gestured to Vaughn and Ivana. "Come closer," she said.

Vaughn swallowed. She made him nervous. Perhaps it was the way she was looking at him as though he were a succulent piece of meat.

They walked up the long hall and paused in front of the dais. "Uh..." He glanced at Ivana, and then knelt. Best to show proper respect. Ivana rolled her eyes but followed his lead. "My name is Vaughn, my lady. And this is Ivana, my companion. We've come to request—"

Chati abruptly rose from the chaise, her eyes flashing with anger.

Uh-oh.

"It has been millennia since one of my own has come to pay me due homage. *Millenia.* And now you show up begging favors?"

"Begging your pardon, my lady. We didn't even know we could get here until a few weeks ag—"

She slashed her hand through the air and padded down the dais on bare feet. She *was* tall, taller than any human woman would be, but not as tall as Xiu. And it seemed, as she joined Vaughn at his level, that she shrank to a more normal size—though still taller than Vaughn.

He bit his tongue and waited. He had seen what Xiu could do; he had no doubt this creature—goddess, such as it were—could snuff out his life in an instant if she wanted to. Now was probably not the time for quips.

He wondered idly if he would still spawn a bloodbane in this world.

She gripped his chin in one silver-inscribed hand and yanked him to his feet, and then she turned his head from side to side, as if inspecting a prize horse. Then she ran her hands across his chest and down his arms before stepping back and tapping her chin thoughtfully. "Still," she murmured, "he is a handsome one."

Then, unexpectedly, she smiled brilliantly, the anger of a few moments ago gone. "What do you wish of me, *teotontl*?"

He blinked, her sudden shift in attitude leaving him momentarily confused.

"Come," she said, waving her hand. "Don't be shy. Ask whatever you desire."

He stirred. "Very well, my lady. As I said, we've come to request your help in gaining an audience with Zily. I mean, Ziloxchanachi."

She frowned. "Ziloxchanachi? Why in the heavens would you want to see Ziloxchanachi?" She laid a hand on his arm. "You're mine. He has no servants."

This talk of belonging to her was starting to wear on him. Had ancient Banebringers *really* voluntarily visited these beings?

"Not to serve him, my lady," he said quickly. "We need his help with some problems we're experiencing in our world. Or at least advice."

She pursed her lips and stared at him for a moment. "The Great Father sees no one. Not even his own children." She sniffed. "Enough of this nonsense. What do you truly want from me? Riches? Power? Weapons? I can open my treasury or armory to you, if you wish."

He blinked once again. Any of those things would come in awfully handy. Perhaps they *didn't* need to see Zily. But what was the catch? There had to be a catch.

She trailed a finger down his arm. "Or perhaps you would rather I teach you the delights of the body."

"Er...I'm pretty good with that already."

She laughed and pushed him lightly on the shoulder. "Oh, you mortals do amuse me. When I'm done with you, you would be a god of love in your world." She quirked one eyebrow up and gazed more deeply into his eyes. "I confess, that is what *I* would have you ask. Your tenure in service to me need not be tedious, after all."

She ran a finger along his jaw and then stepped in closer to him so that her breasts were right below his eye level. He pressed his lips together, determined not to let her distract him.

"Tenure in service, my lady?" he asked. That needed more clarification.

She dropped her hand, clearly annoyed that her proposal wasn't having the desired effect. "Yes, of course. Has your kind so soon forgotten our arrangement?"

"It's been millennia," he reminded her. "Perhaps you could

refresh my memory?"

She sighed heavily and pulled down her collar to scratch at her neck.

When she did so, he noticed a shimmery silver line running horizontally around her throat. It wasn't one of the tattoos; it looked like a scar.

All right. Maybe she had *lost her head at some point...*

"You give me one year in service, and I give you whatever you ask for when your service is complete. The same offer is open to all of our chosen, should they wish to take us up on it." She turned to the side and looked out through the glass wall, giving him an unhindered view of her exposed side.

That was deliberate, he thought. Also, there was no way he was going to give her, or any of the gods, a year of "service" for any reward.

Not only did he not have that kind of time, but given what the etchings on the walls displayed, he was beginning to understand what sort of service she meant.

They were nothing but favored pets.

"My lady," he said firmly, "we wish to see Ziloxchanachi. I have no desire to take you up on that offer at present."

She turned toward him again, her eyes flashing, and he thought she would strike him. But before he could flinch back, instead, incredibly, she ripped her own head off her body and flung it across the room. "Insubordinate, ungrateful wretch!" her mouth said, though her body still stood, headless, in front of him.

He gaped at the stump of her neck, his stomach queasy, and her headless body moved toward her head to retrieve it. "After all I have already given you," the head said, and she bent down to pull it up by the hair.

Gods have mercy, he thought. *She...can take her head off.* He was starting to feel dizzy. *Keep it together, Vaughn.*

She still held the head in her hand, and the eyes glared at him, as if daring him to mock her headless state.

He swallowed, steeled himself, and tried to pretend nothing out of the ordinary had happened. "All you've given me? Forgive me, my lady, but all I've received is hatred from my friends and family and the inability to lead any sort of normal life."

She scoffed. "Mortal scum," she said. "Who cares what they think?" She settled the head back on her neck, twisting it a little as though needing to tighten it down, and pulled the collar back up to hide the scar. Then, she stepped quickly closer to him. "The Great Father is an old dotard," she said. "He cannot help you." A calculating look came into her eyes. "I, however, may be able to. I have resources you don't realize. Allies in your world. I give this aid free, not as part of a contract."

He narrowed his eyes at her. Xiu hadn't seemed to know anything about what was happening in their world, but Chati did? That seemed...odd.

There was only one god he knew of who had a finger in their world, and that was Danathalt.

And Danathalt was somehow working with the Conclave.

What was it that crazy bug lady had said to him, the last time she had talked to him? That she didn't have anything personal against him? Or by that, did she mean Chati?

Were Danathalt and his patron friends, even allies?

He hesitated. What help, exactly, would she offer? Could she stop the Conclave from hunting them? Force them to abandon this war and leave the outer regions alone?

Or was this all a ploy to get him to reveal his purpose here so they could be stopped?

He needed to talk to Ivana. Get her take. She had had the advantage of being below the notice of the goddess and so could merely observe.

He, at least, didn't trust this creature. Xiu was borderline apathetic, but he had helped them get further on their journey, at any rate.

Chati seemed borderline insane.

No, he revised. There was no "borderline" about it.

He bowed to Chati. "My lady is generous, but I need to think on this offer. May my companion and I retire for the evening and speak with you again tomorrow? Our journey has been long."

Chati sniffed and scratched at her neck scar again. "You may. But leave your servant. I wish to speak with her further."

Vaughn blinked and glanced at Ivana. He didn't want to leave her alone with this crazy goddess; he had no doubt she could defend herself against normal foes, but one who could remove and reattach her head at will was beyond normal.

Ivana shrugged and jerked her head, indicating she didn't care.

So he let himself be led away by the moon-lady, who had reappeared.

Chapter Thirty-Five

Monster

After Vaughn and the *xchotli* had gone, Thaxchatichan turned her eyes toward Ivana.

Ivana wished she wouldn't.

Ivana was no stranger to gruesome sights, but someone literally taking off her head, throwing it across the room, and then picking it up and setting it back on again with nary a bat of the eye easily took top marks for the most bizarre.

She had been thankful that up until now Vaughn's patron had seemingly seen her as unimportant and had ignored her.

Even *she* was a little nervous as to what this creature intended now.

Thaxchatichan paced closer to Ivana. Was she going to attempt to seduce *her* now, having—incredibly—failed to seduce

Vaughn?

But the goddess stopped in front of her. "What are you?" she asked.

Ivana blinked. "My lady?"

Thaxchatichan flicked her hand. "You are mortal, but you are not one of my siblings' chosen, nor a *xchotli*. How did you enter the portal?"

"I don't know," Ivana said honestly.

That seemed to aggravate her. She walked around Ivana in a slow circle, looking her up and down. "You lie," she said in a low, dangerous voice.

"My lady, I do not. I had no intention of coming here, and I don't know how it happened."

Thaxchatichan continued to circle her. She narrowed her eyes. "Hmm. Very well."

Ivana relaxed. She was tired, wrung out, and she just wanted to sleep.

Thaxchatichan's lips twisted cruelly. "I'll find out what you really are, why you lie, and we'll have some fun in the process, won't we?"

Ivana's heart sank; she sincerely doubted that.

Thaxchatichan stepped back from her. *"Show me your secrets,"* she hissed, and then the lights went out.

Even the starlit backdrop was gone; it was pitch black.

Ivana swallowed and began stepping slowly backward. As long as she didn't turn, she could find the door. It was directly behind her.

Except it wasn't.

She took one last step back, and when she did, she could see again, and the entire room had changed.

She started. She recognized this place. This was the road outside Lord Kadmon's gates. She had been here before, recently, and a long time ago.

An illusion, of course. But it didn't feel like a mere illusion. She turned, slowly, in a circle. Gravel crunched underfoot. Cold air seeped through her thin garment.

The gates opened, and a carriage emerged.

It was only then that she saw the two figures huddled near the gates.

She stepped back again. It felt so real. But she couldn't be in two places at once. She couldn't be both the girl at those gates and the woman she was.

Not an illusion—she was hallucinating. She had to be. Chati had done something to her...

The taller figure stepped forward into the road, blocking the carriage.

Ivana's throat tightened. *No.* She couldn't live this again.

She couldn't hear the words from the distance she stood, but she didn't need to. They had been emblazoned into her mind over a decade ago, then buried—never forgotten, but rehearsed in her recent nightmares.

Gan Gildas—he hadn't been a Ri yet, then—stepped out of his carriage.

Her heart quickened. *Please don't make me live this again,* she pleaded inside, but she pressed her lips together. She wouldn't beg this crazy goddess for succor. She wouldn't.

Her father drew his ceremonial sword.

Despite her efforts, a whimper left her lips. "No," she whispered. "Don't. Papa. No."

Gildas ran him through.

Dream-Ivana threw herself on her father's body, and real-Ivana wrapped her arms around herself, unable to tear her eyes away, trying to hold back the pain seeping from old scars.

She could hear her own screams now, echoing in her ears.

Her fault.

The scene changed, and she breathed a sigh of relief.

Until she saw what it was now.

Dream-Ivana at night, alone in a clearing with Airell.

Ivana choked back a cry. Even this hadn't been in her nightmares.

The two embraced, and she threw herself forward to try to grab dream-Ivana, stop her from making the worst mistake of her life, but her hands went right through her.

"Stop!" she screamed. "You idiot girl! Stop!"

Dream-Ivana didn't stop.

Ivana sank to the ground and wrapped her arms around her knees, forced to watch this sequence live itself out again in front of her.

Her fault.

It changed to another moment. Dream-Ivana stood at the side of a wagon, wrestling with the bonds of her sister, knowing in her heart she would fail to free her.

She was close enough to see the betrayal in her sister's eyes when dream-Ivana begged her forgiveness and ran, lest she be captured herself.

The scene lingered long enough for real-Ivana to watch the tears flowing down her sister's face, a moment she had never actually seen.

"Ana!" her sister screamed again after the fleeing figure. "Ana," she whispered. "I hate you."

Ivana gasped and scrambled backward. She had no memory of that. Thaxchatichan was planting things in her mind, or her mind was making them up.

No. Thaxchatichan was dredging up her worst fears.

Even with that knowledge, hot tears were on her cheeks.

Her fault.

She sat alone in a tiny room, weeping in the dark.

She and her sister knelt at a family grave, her mother freshly laid out.

She held the body of a tiny infant, born too soon to live.

She stood above a corpse, at her feet the body of a man who had trusted her, and turned away, dead inside.

All her fault.

"Stop this!" she screamed, unable to take it anymore. "I beg you. Stop this!"

The scene flashed back to the first. Gildas got out of his carriage.

Real-Ivana ran forward and fell between her father and Gildas. "Don't do this," she begged her father. "This isn't your fault. This isn't your mess to clean up."

Gildas ran her father through, the phantom sword passing right through her own body.

Ivana, stood, paralyzed. Her father's body didn't fall this time. Instead, it turned to her, blood gushing from the wound, and looked directly at her. "What have you become, Ana?"

And her nightmare came to life. Bodies all around her. Her mother, her sister, countless nameless people rose from a lake of blood and surrounded her. "Monster," they chanted. *Monster,* they whispered.

She knelt to the ground, curled up in a ball, and covered her head with her arms. She wouldn't look. She didn't have to see. She could bury it; she had done it once before...

Monster. Monster. Monster.

"Stop this, please," she whispered.

"Enough!" a new voice boomed into the room. And then everything vanished.

Everything except the gaping, bleeding wound in her own heart.

She didn't look up to see who had spoken. She didn't even care who her rescuer was. She still knelt, trembling, on the ground.

"What purpose do you have here, sister?"

"Entertainment?" Chati's voice said, saccharinely innocent.

The new voice growled. "Leave playtime for your own," it said. "You won't learn what you seek to know from this one. Let her be." A rustle. "Take her back to her room."

Two hands on each arm dragged her away because she couldn't move on her own.

Monster. Monster. Monster.

Vaughn paced in the room, agitated. Whatever Chati had wanted with Ivana, it couldn't have been anything benevolent, and it had been far too long for his liking.

When the door opened, he spun. Two of Chati's attendants, but not the moon-lady, pushed Ivana into the room and shut the door behind her.

She stumbled and fell to her hands and knees, trembling.

Alarmed, he rushed to her side. "Ivana! What happened?" Had she been tortured? But to what end? She *appeared* unharmed, but...

She looked up at him. Her face was tight, and something almost savage flickered across her eyes. She pushed herself to her feet and unbelted her robe, letting it fall open to a clinging short shift she wore underneath.

Heat rushed through his body. Even so, he found himself backing away from her. There was nothing sensual or suggestive in her expression. She stalked toward him and then shoved him back against the wall, pressing herself up against him.

"You want me?" she said, her voice raw and grating. "Take me." She kissed him, her tongue immediately questing at his lips to part them, and then she pressed her thigh against his groin.

He groaned, and she kissed him again, this time so hard, his teeth bit against the inside of his own lips.

Something wasn't right. *She* wasn't right.

He took her by the shoulders and pushed her back.

"What's wrong?" she snapped. "Change of heart? Twinge of conscience? I won't resist. I mean it. Do whatever you want with me."

He didn't know what Chati had done to her, but she most definitely wasn't in her right mind.

He cupped her face in his hands and looked into her eyes. There was something manic there. Something desperate. "No," he said softly, and then he took an educated guess. "I will not help you abuse yourself."

She stared back at him.

And then she crumpled.

He caught her as she sank to the floor, one arm around her waist, her back against his chest, and when they were both on their knees, she began to sob.

He hesitated, then wrapped his other arm around her.

She grasped his arms and held them against herself, as if they were a lifeline.

And she wept.

Hot tears splashed onto his arm, her entire body shuddering and convulsing with sometimes silent, sometimes vocalized cries.

He swallowed and tucked her head under his chin. He had no words for her, didn't even know what had prompted this sudden breakdown, so he simply continued to hold her tightly to himself.

Eventually, her sobs subsided and her shaking stopped.

He held her until she pushed herself away.

He let her go and sat back on his heels.

She stared at the floor for what seemed like an eternity until finally, she lifted red, swollen eyes to his. "I just want to sleep," she whispered, her voice hoarse. She rose and wrapped her robe around herself again.

He didn't ask for an explanation. He merely nodded and stood.

She turned her back on him, kicked off her slippers, and curled up on top of the bed of furs.

He picked up one of the blankets and laid it over her.

She grabbed his hand as he withdrew. "Don't leave," she said. "Please."

He hesitated. Then he lay down next to her. After a moment, he wrapped his arms around her and pulled her back against his chest.

She didn't resist.

And for the only time in his life that he could remember, he fell asleep with a woman in his arms that he hadn't slept with.

Chapter Thirty-Six

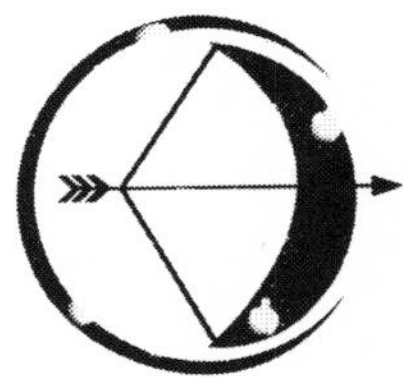

Uninvited Guests

A heavy pounding woke Vaughn in the middle of the night. Or at least, he *felt* like it was the middle of the night. He had lost all track of time in this place.

Who in the abyss is making so much noise? he thought in his half-awake state, and he rolled over to go back to sleep.

The pounding sounded again.

He groaned, and Ivana stirred next to him.

That, more than anything, stirred him to full wakefulness.

Ivana was next to him. They had shared plenty of rooms in their travels together, but never a bed.

More pounding.

The door, he realized belatedly. Ivana sat up, and he rolled out of the bed and pushed himself to his feet.

Before he even had the door open all the way, another almost-but-not-quite human pushed his way into the room—on the tall side of average, but still within a believable range. He appeared young—perhaps in his twenties—with flawless skin the color of burnished bronze that seemed to shimmer when he moved.

He kicked the door shut behind him, and Ivana was on her feet, her hand at her thigh in a split second.

The stranger held up his hands. "I mean you no harm." He glanced at Vaughn. "We must go—now."

Vaughn ran a hand through his hair and eyed the man. Compared to everyone else around here, he was downright casual, even normal. He wore a baggy V-neck shirt with pantaloons and a pair of practical leather boots. His eyes were what stood out. They were white, but not white like a bloodbane's. Vaughn could make out the location of his iris and pupils inside a slight ripple within the white, and then the irises where translucent, almost clear, with a normal black pupil in the center. "I'm sorry, but who are you?"

"A friend," the man said. "You're in danger. We must go *now*."

Vaughn glanced at Ivana, and she shrugged.

He could well believe they were in danger, but would they be in more or less danger by going with this stranger?

Steel rattled faintly in the hall, and then the door burst open. Half a dozen warriors clad in steel of Chati's colors—silver, white, and blue—streamed into the room.

The stranger waved his hand at the group, and they *disappeared*. He grabbed Vaughn's arm, yanked Ivana over to him, and a moment later began to emit a bright white light from himself.

More soldiers streamed into the room and immediately fell back, squinting as the light grew brighter.

Vaughn's eyes started to water, and he had to close them.

When he opened them, they were no longer in the guest

room.

In fact, based on the distinct lack of silver, white, and blue décor, he didn't think they were in Chati's palace anymore at all.

Instead, they were on a wide portico twenty feet up overlooking a grassy plain dotted with flowers of every color of the rainbow; the sun was shining and there was a light breeze in the air.

Had the stranger just...*moved* them to some other location, just like that?

Nearby, an enormous, brightly colored bird perched on the railing, and it cocked its head to look at them and then let out a loud trill.

The stranger strode over to the bird and flapped his hand at it. "Oh, hush," he said.

The bird hopped back and flapped its wings but didn't fly away. Instead, it squawked several times, followed by another trill and a decidedly defiant look at the stranger.

The stranger sighed. "So much for a discreet entrance," he muttered.

He turned to face the portico doors, seeming to steel himself for something.

Ivana sensed it as well, for she took a step back and hovered her hand near her thigh.

The portico doors swung open. Another too-tall-to-be-human man strode through; he looked Fereharian, with deep bronze skin like Ivana's and the stranger's—though it didn't shimmer. He wore a sleeveless tunic that hung to his knees and belted at the waist with a cord threaded through with the same brightly colored feathers that were on the bird, creating a feather skirt of sorts over the tunic. More of the feathers were woven into his white hair, which hung to his shoulders in braids. At his chin was a small, tapered goatee; the rest of his face was clean-shaven—

and bearing an expression of barely contained fury.

That didn't bode well.

The stranger immediately fell to one knee and bowed his head. "I beg your forgiveness, Great Father," he said before the other man could speak. "But I must speak with you—"

Great Father? As in, *Zily*? Exactly whom they wanted to talk to?

Oh, this *definitely* didn't bode well.

"You dare to come here again?" the white-haired god said, pinning the stranger with eyes that shimmered and rippled with constant changes of color. "I expressly forbade you from bothering me any further!"

The stranger winced. "Please, Great Father. I *must* speak with you."

The bird trilled again, and Zily turned his eyes on Vaughn and Ivana, but they lingered the longest on Ivana. "What are these that you've brought here?"

The stranger cleared his throat. "If you would let me explain—"

"Are these *mortals*?" He didn't give the stranger a chance to respond, one way or the other. "You've gone too far." He made a gesture in the air, and a half dozen colorfully dressed guards burst through the portico doors. They were human in appearance, but Vaughn doubted they really were.

Vaughn backed up, and Ivana drew her dagger, but neither gesture was of any use. With a cry of pain, Ivana's dagger fell from her hand, red hot and smoking on the ground, and one of the six guards had wrestled Vaughn into submission with superhuman strength before he could even think of a desperate plan. Disarmed, Ivana had fared no better.

As for the stranger, the remaining guards had surrounded him, though they hadn't laid hands on him.

"You'll rest in my dungeons for a time," Zily said to the stranger. "Perhaps that will teach you."

The stranger's eyes darted to Vaughn and Ivana. "The mortals," he said.

Zily considered them for a moment. "Prepare them for sacrifice."

"No!" Vaughn shouted. "Ziloxchanachi—Great Father—I beg you." Vaughn's guard dragged him toward the portico doors. "We came in good faith, seeking your aid."

Zily ignored him.

"It's about Danathalt!" Vaughn threw out desperately.

Zily whirled around and held up his hand, staying his guards. "What did you say?"

Vaughn seized on the opportunity and spoke quickly. "He's working with the Conclave—a religious group in our world—and they're trying to destroy us—Banebringers, *teotontl*, your chosen."

Zily pinned Vaughn with his swirling eyes for a moment, and then he sneered. "Why should I care about the playthings of my children?" He flicked his hand at them. "The sacrifice will be after-dinner entertainment."

And with that, the guards dragged Vaughn and Ivana away, the stranger walking behind, his shoulders slumped, with his escort.

Vaughn was blindfolded, stripped, dressed in a thin tunic that hung to his knees, and, after a short walk, shoved. He stumbled forward, ripped his blindfold off, and whirled around—but the clang of iron behind him was enough to tell him where he was, even if it hadn't been pitch black.

Again.

He walked toward the sound of the clang, and his outstretched hands found bars.

"Ivana?" he whispered. *Please be here.*

"I'm here," she said.

He moved slowly in the direction of her voice—and almost tripped over her foot. He reached out toward her to regain his balance, and she pushed him away. "Don't touch me."

He sighed. *All right. So now we're back to this again.*

They hadn't had the opportunity to talk about last night. Given her reaction just now, he doubted she *would* talk about it.

He moved around the room, cautiously, feeling for walls, doors, anything.

It confirmed that they were in a small cell, barred on two sides, stone walls on the other two. He felt no objects of any kind, so he found a wall and slid down to the floor.

The sound of dripping came from somewhere.

So. This was how it all ended. After all they'd gone through in their own world to get here, then through the abyss and rescued out of the clutches of his crazy patron—only to be sacrificed to the very god they had set out to find. The irony didn't escape him.

Well. At least he wouldn't have to overthrow Airell and subject himself to the misery of being Ri. Being dead was *almost* better than that.

Almost.

He tried to muster some hope for rescue, but they were being imprisoned by what was likely the most powerful entity in the universe. Their only "friend," the person who had brought them here, was locked up himself somewhere and obviously didn't have the power to stop Zily, or surely he would have.

"Is this really how you want to spend our final hours?" he said into the darkness. "Angry at me for something I *didn't* do?"

A shuffle, a bump. Then she slid down the wall next to him.

And...silence.

He closed his eyes and listened to the *drip, drip, drip* of whatever was leaking.

He tried to burn aether to reach out for the water, hoping by some miracle his magic was working again, but nothing happened, as he already knew would be the case. It was too dark.

He sighed and laid his head back against the wall.

"Regret not taking me up on my offer now?" Ivana asked. There was a bitter tang to her voice.

He turned his head toward her, though he couldn't see anything. "If I had," he said, "you would have loathed me for all eternity."

"Yes, probably."

"And then I'd *really* not have had a chance when you are in your *right* mind."

"How pragmatic," she said drily. "And here I was about to believe you when you said you'd given up such ways."

He noted that she didn't say he didn't have a chance anyway, or that she already loathed him. Were they making progress? A little late. "Burning skies, woman, I didn't say I'd sworn myself to celibacy," he said. "Only that I was trying to avoid casual encounters with random women."

"I see," she said. "And I'm neither casual nor random?"

Casual and random? Ivana? She was anything but. So much so, that as much as he wanted her, the prospect of having her also terrified him. He hadn't meant to imply that. "Not random, anyway," he muttered.

She made a low noise in her throat, and he was glad he couldn't see her face. "But as it turns out, all eternity wasn't going to be very long."

"Knowledge of that wouldn't have changed anything," he said. He shifted. Half of his rear was going numb. "I know you're determined on principle to hate me, but I'm not *that* bad of a guy."

Drip. Drip. Drip.

Determined on principle to hate him?

Once again, Vaughn could not have been more wrong.

She didn't hate him. In fact, it had been a long while since she had hated him. Oh, he could be irritating from time to time, but then again, so could Aleena.

No. It wasn't Vaughn she hated. It was herself.

She had hated herself before for the choices that had ruined her life, and then she had been able to bury those feelings.

But they had never gone away, had they? And now she had even more to hate herself for.

Monster.

It would have been better if she had died on her flight to Cadmyr so many years ago, rather than have to suffer this torment for a second time.

And these were the thoughts she had to keep her company in her last hours, alone in the dark. How fitting.

Yet that wasn't quite right, was it? It had been more than a decade since she had fallen to pieces like she had tonight. More than a decade ago, it had been a regular occurrence.

Every time, she had been utterly alone, and so her pain had fed upon her loneliness and her loneliness upon her pain in a vicious circle until she simply could not take it anymore. Until she had found herself at the point of being willing to do anything, *anything*, to make it stop.

Tonight...she hadn't been alone.

She hated that Vaughn had been there to witness the depth of her weakness, and yet at the same time, she had been glad for his silent presence and strong arms.

What difference would that have made, all those years ago?

She would never know. But she didn't have to be utterly alone now.

Ivana's voice was strained when she at last spoke. "I don't hate you."

Vaughn snorted. "Well, that's progress. Maybe next time, you could try to sound like it's not agony to admit that."

"I'm also not angry at you."

He rubbed at a sore spot on his knee from where he had stumbled onto the stone ground of the cell. Should he press? Would she tell him why she had broken down like that? "I don't suppose you want to tell me what happened after I was escorted out of Chati's throne room?"

Ivana sighed. "She seemed to think that I had some inside knowledge on how I managed to bypass the rule that only Banebringers can enter the portals. I haven't the faintest idea, of course. She became angry, and best I can figure, did some god-magic on my mind to attempt to get me to tell her anything I was hiding. Didn't help her much since I don't know what she wanted to know, and anything else I wasn't telling her was far less important than other secrets I hold, apparently."

Other secrets? "And...this turned you into a complete wreck because...?"

Drip. Drip. Drip.

"She made me literally relive all the worst moments of my life," Ivana said at last. "And then some."

The number of times Ivana had woken in the night recently with a cry or in a sweat came to his mind.

She cleared her throat. "Eventually, our erstwhile, if failed, rescuer intervened—I didn't see him, but I recognized his voice—which is probably the only reason I'm still sane right now." She paused. "He called her 'sister.'"

"Interesting," Vaughn mused. He had guessed that their rescuer might be another of the deities. "Another god?"

"Used loosely, I suppose."

Vaughn stood up abruptly. That wasn't Ivana's voice. In fact, it sounded like...

A dim light flickered into existence, and Vaughn squinted in its direction.

The stranger sat in another cell, sitting on the ground, also leaning against the wall, his arms draped over his knees.

The light was coming from him—literally. His entire body was lined in a whitish glow, making his bronze skin look almost actually metallic, now.

As soon as Vaughn could see clearly, the stranger smiled at him. "Taniqotalin, at your service," he said. He wiggled his hand in the air and squinted an eye. "Or maybe not so much."

Vaughn racked his brain. "Taniqotalin...Danton's patron?" He exchanged a glance with Ivana.

Taniqotalin furrowed his brow. "If you say so."

Ivana stood up and walked over to the bars of their cell. "Were you sitting there the whole time, listening to us talk?" She sounded affronted.

He shrugged, not at all abashed. "I wanted to understand you better." He leaned forward. "You understand, you're the first mortals I've talked with in millennia."

Ivana frowned. "So this was all some sort of grand experiment to you? Perhaps we should have taken our chances with Thaxchatichan."

He shook his head vigorously. "No. Trust me. Better to be sacrificed to the Great Father than forced into service to

Thaxchatichan. She's *crazy*."

"Easy for *you* to say," Vaughn said. "You're just going to be held here for a little while, if what Zily said was true."

"Zily?" Taniqotalin asked, seeming amused. "I wouldn't call him that to his face. I doubt he'd appreciate it."

Ivana was still frowning slightly. "You don't seem very god-like."

Taniqotalin snorted. "They used to call us 'gods.' Some of your people still do—well, not the ones who look like *you*, mind you. But some of the others."

"You're saying you're not actually gods?" Vaughn asked.

"Having incredible power and wielding it to force the weak to bow doesn't make you a god," Taniqotalin said. "Only a tyrant."

Ivana took a step closer to the bars. Vaughn recognized that look in her eyes. She was becoming curious. "What are you, then?"

Taniqotalin rubbed his jaw. "What are *you*?"

"Mortal? Human? Female?" she responded.

"And I am immortal, *chitqi*, and..." He shrugged. "Whatever."

Vaughn didn't know what any of that meant, but a feeling of dread was growing in him. "Wait. Please don't tell me this means that Yathen and Temoth and Rhianah *are* the real gods?"

Taniqotalin tilted his head. "I don't know those names."

Vaughn frowned. If anyone ought to recognize the names of other...powerful beings...he felt like it ought to be one of the supplanted heretic gods. "Well, this is all fascinating, but why did you rescue us, then?"

"Ah, now we come to it." He put his hands behind his head. "A fair exchange. Tell me why you went to all the trouble to come to our world to see"—he chuckled—"*Zily*, and I'll tell you why I rescued you."

"Wait, first, can I call you 'Tani'? You all have really long, complicated names."

Taniqotalin shrugged. "I'll take no offense."

Vaughn glanced at Ivana.

"Don't see how it matters," she said, "seeing as how we're hours away from being executed by the god we were seeking aid from."

"Good," Tani said. "You mentioned the Conclave. Some religious group in your land. That they're working with Danathalt?"

"We think so," Vaughn said. "They appear to have had control over Danathalt's Banebringer—er—one of his *teotontl*, for a little while, anyway. Or at least she was working with them."

Tani's eyes narrowed. "One of Danathalt's *teotontl*?"

"Yes. The first one we'd ever run across."

Tani frowned.

"Anyway, for a long time, they've used what we call 'Sedation' as their method of keeping us Banebringers under control, and recently, we..." He cringed. "We unmasked that they were using our aether to do magic while claiming we were servants of the heretic gods." He inclined his head. "Uh, sorry."

Tani waved his hand. "Go on."

"And now they've launched a coup and taken over the capital, have control of the king and, more importantly, the army. And are possibly trying to create an army of bloodbane. And they're trying to not only take over Setana but systematically eliminate all Banebringers—or at least, keep us as milk cows. So when we learned that once upon a time Banebringers used to come through these *portals* to visit the gods, we thought, if we could make one work, maybe we could persuade Zily to do something." He ran a hand through his hair. "Of course, we didn't realize we'd end up in the abyss and Zily would want absolutely nothing to do with us. To put it mildly."

Tani sat back. "The Great Father has had nothing to do with

anything or anyone for millennia," he said.

"The curse?" Ivana interjected.

Tani nodded. "After Danathalt tried his little coup, Zily was done with all of us. Flew into a fury. Probably went a little overboard—the curse reeks with, 'You like fighting? I'll give you fighting. You can fight till it comes out your nose.'"

"Fighting," Ivana mused. "We met Xiuheuhtli in the abyss. We would have been torn to shreds right through the portal had it not been for him. He mentioned that you all had to fight. What is that about?"

Tani leaned back again. "For millennia, we fought, but we all fought each other. Oh, it was grand, the games we used to play. We're immortal, see—so it's difficult to permanently *hurt* each other—"

Vaughn raised his hand. "Uh, my patron's head comes off."

"I said difficult, not impossible. But it reattaches, right? No permanent damage."

Gods have mercy. Some other gods. Any other gods.

Tani went on. "Anyway, it was a grand era. Schemes and murder, feasting and drunken orgies—when we weren't killing each other."

"Yes. Sounds like a great time," Ivana said.

"At one point, some of us got bored and figured out how we could reach your world through the portals. We started experimenting with mortals, so they could come visit us—and by 'visit us,' mind you, I mean *entertain* us. Serve us. In return, they received rewards and a measure of our own power and were treated as *teoton*—demi-gods—in your world. It was a beneficial arrangement for all involved."

He rolled his eyes. "Then *Danathalt* had to go ruining everything with his little coup. Zily got his knickers in a knot, and now we're stuck fighting only our most hated rival, all the time, in

Danathalt's realm. Oh, sure, we can take respite here for a while, but it *just* isn't the same. Zily even messed with the portals so mortals would end up in the abyss if they tried to come through. They soon learned not to try anymore."

Vaughn digested all of that. "So there's no rhyme or reason to why you *beings* choose Banebringers," he stated flatly. "It's all a game to you."

"Blame Zily for that," Tani said. "We used to pick mortals who seemed most suited to our affinities, and those who seemed most likely to take us up on our offers."

So. Probably the greediest and most power-hungry of mortals, then.

"But Zily's curse broke the whole system. It's not even under our control anymore. It just happens, like the magic is running rampant in whatever dimension exists between your world and ours, breaking through when your sky burns once a year and the barrier is at its weakest."

Vaughn felt his heart sink. He didn't know why. He was going to die anyway. But it was doubly discouraging to know that all of this had always been in vain. "So, not only do you not care what's happening to us, you can literally do nothing about it because you're forced to be too busy fighting with each other."

"That about sums it up."

Vaughn looked at Ivana. "I'm sorry that I dragged you into this," he said. "I had no way of knowing it was a pointless trip."

Tani held up his hands. "Whoa, whoa, whoa. Let's not jump to conclusions."

"You just said—"

"Now we come to the bit where I tell you why I'm interested in you."

Vaughn fell silent, his ears perking up.

Tani stood up. The light around him brightened. "We—

everyone but Zily—are sick of this curse. Some of us have been trying to push Zily to do something, and he's insisted there's nothing he can do about it. In cursing us, he also cursed himself, see. He's locked to Danathalt, only in Zily's case, by terms of the curse, he removed himself from our doings. So Danathalt can't do anything, either—including trying to overthrow Zily again.

"But then you showed up. You and this"—he waved his hand at Ivana—"non-*teotontl,* which ought to be impossible. Xiuheuhtli rescued you because he was intrigued, not because he cared about your fate. No mortal has attempted to come through the portal since a few centuries after Zily locked it to the abyss. He delivered you to my sister because he had to—she was within her rights to demand it—but he also informed me.

"When I found out Thaxchatichan had you, I knew that was bad news."

"Why? Other than the obvious," Ivana asked.

"Because Thaxchatichan has long been an ally of Danathalt. And those of us who've been watching have known for some time that Danathalt is up to something. As it turns out, we're right." He nodded to Vaughn. "With what you've told me, my guess is he's trying to influence events in your world through a *teotontl* he shouldn't have. What does that portend? How did he even manage to exert enough control for that? I'm not sure, but he surely means no benefit to your people—and any scheme of Danathalt's can only make things worse for us here."

"This still doesn't explain why you rescued us," Vaughn said.

"If Thaxchatichan and Danathalt wanted you, then I knew they couldn't have you. It's been decades since I attempted to speak with the Great Father, and I thought this warranted his attention. We all thought..." He looked at them speculatively.

"Thought what?"

"That maybe this was a sign things were about to change."

Vaughn rubbed at his exposed kneecap. "Well, sorry to disappoint you. Nothing's going to change other than right now we're alive, and tonight we won't be."

"Hmm," Tani said. "I'm not so sure. I think if you can make the right argument to Zily—before he orders your blood drained, of course—he might hear you."

"Why?" Ivana asked. "He said it himself: He doesn't care about your mortal playthings."

"No. He doesn't. But I think after all this time, he's become tired of being idle. He's tired of hearing our whining. He might even be getting a little lonely. And he's suspicious that Danathalt is going to try something again. If the troubles you're experiencing are a result of Danathalt's meddling, he may be more interested in helping you than he lets on."

The jangling of keys echoed down the hall.

"Hold on," Ivana said. "You transported us here—instantaneously."

"Yes."

"Can't you transport yourself—or us—out?"

Tani laughed. "Perhaps," he said. "He might have been able to stop me. He's not called 'Great Father' for no reason—he's the most powerful among us. Though I wouldn't take you, if I could. That would only enrage him further." He shrugged. "Zily had a small tantrum this time, so I'm letting him feel like he punished or humiliated me. He could have done much worse to me." He shuddered. "I certainly don't want to end up like Thaxchatichan."

Two guards emerged from the hallway. One of them opened Tani's door. "The Great Father requests your presence at dinner."

"See," Tani mouthed to Vaughn and Ivana. *"Lonely."* And then he disappeared in a flash of light. Literally.

Vaughn was guessing it wasn't because he'd turned invisible.

The other guard opened their door. "Out," he grunted. "And

don't try anything."

Chapter Thirty-Seven

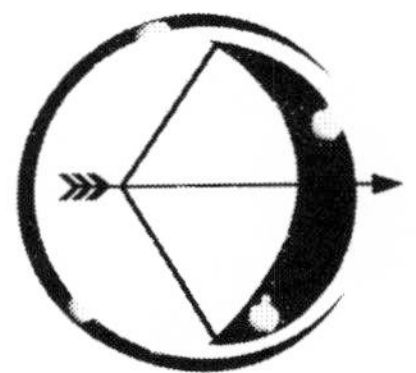

Greatly Honored

They didn't try anything.

As if they could have. The guards may have looked mostly human, but they had inhuman strength. Ivana and Vaughn were blindfolded again, so Ivana strained her other senses, waiting for an opportunity to exploit, but in the end, she was forced to conclude that even if, by some chance, one of them managed to escape...where would they go?

She didn't even know how to get home.

Their blindfolds were removed. They stood inside the doors of a great hall; it made Thaxchatichan's look like a child's playroom.

The walls were lined with servants clothed in an array of bright, solid colors, but each only sporting one color—which matched the color of their hair.

A dozen more of the large birds they had seen on Zily's portico perched around the hall, and at the end, Zily sat atop a throne of dyed bones.

Well. That was encouraging.

A large stone basin stood at one side of the hall; three steps led to the top.

It was to this that the guards directed Vaughn and Ivana.

They were jostled together as they walked.

"Turns out you don't have to kill me for getting us into this," Vaughn whispered to her.

"If by some chance there is such a thing as an afterlife, and we end up in it together, I will never forgive you," Ivana said.

"There's a cheery last thought. Haunted by you in life and death."

One of the guards poked Vaughn in the back with the butt of his spear. "Quiet," he said.

Once they had reached the basin, Zily stood to address them directly. "You are greatly honored," he said. "I haven't sacrificed a mortal in my own throne room in millennia."

Interesting, Ivana thought. Had some of the Banebringers *agreed* to be sacrificed? To what end? Perhaps the heretic gods had promised them something more than demi-god status in this life.

Vaughn stepped forward. "Great Father, please grant one last petition."

"No," Zily said.

Vaughn blinked, as if he hadn't expected that.

"The nattering one first," Zily said.

One of the guards shoved Vaughn up the stairs and forced him to his knees. "Fine, then I'll talk anyway!" Vaughn shouted. "Danathalt tried to overthrow you once, and he'll try it again!"

Zily snorted. "He'll fail, then."

The guard pushed Vaughn forward so that his upper body fell over the basin, and then grabbed Vaughn's hair and forced his head back, exposing his throat.

"He's meddling in our world, our politics, our religions. He's trying to find a loophole in the curse. Is there a loophole, Great Father?"

The guard pulled a curved knife out of a sheath at his waist and put it to Vaughn's throat, presumably waiting for some signal from Zily, who was idly stroking his giant bird and watching Vaughn with his swirling eyes.

He was remarkably calm for someone seconds from death. He was no coward, whatever else he might be.

Or pretend to be. Once again, Ivana found herself grudgingly admitting that there was more to this man than appeared.

His eyes flicked to hers, desperation there. His jaw and throat were tight. He was clearly out of ideas.

It wasn't always true that she didn't want to die, but she certainly didn't want to die here. And she didn't want Vaughn to die, either.

She wrenched her arm out of the grasp of her guard, who had let his hand loosen in inattention, and stepped forward. "Danathalt has a Banebringer!"

Zily held up his hand to stay the hand of Vaughn's guard. He held the position while he silently studied Ivana. "What?"

"A Banebringer," Ivana said. "A *teotontl.*"

"Impossible," Zily said, but it was more musing than a declaration. Still, he stared at Ivana. His gaze was starting to become a little disturbing. "He's forbidden from doing anything that would knock our rivalry out of balance."

Someone cleared their throat from a place on one of the walls. Tani stepped forward. "Is that true, Great Father? Do you even know what's been happening, secluded up here in your palace?"

"He spoke to me," Vaughn said. "Through his...*teotontl*. She wasn't normal."

That drew Zily's attention away from Ivana. He gestured to the guard, and the guard let go of Vaughn's hair and put his knife away. Vaughn swallowed and rubbed his throat.

"What did he say?"

"He told me his name, and he said he didn't have anything against me personally." He paused, and Ivana was certain it was for dramatic effect. "My patron is Thaxchatichan, who, as you know, has long been an ally of Danathalt. We don't know what he's scheming, but you can rest assured it won't be good for any of us. Perhaps we can find a way to help each other. Will you hear more?"

Ivana was...impressed. Vaughn sounded like he knew what he was talking about, despite having only the limited information from their brief conversation with Tani.

Zily's eyes swirled with color. "Release them," he said. He glanced around his throne room. "And leave us, all of you. No, not you, Taniqotalin."

The guards turned and left. So, with a nod of encouragement from Tani, Vaughn and Ivana hesitantly made their way over to Zily's throne.

There they stood, face-to-face with Ziloxchanachi, head of the heretic gods, and he had finally granted them the audience they'd sought.

"Tell me what you know," Zily demanded.

Vaughn related everything he could remember about Danathalt's doings in their world. About the crazy bug-lady who'd turned out to be his Banebringer and her shenanigans. About the unnatural corpse-thing that was—perhaps—under her control, and in turn controlled bloodbane. About the Conclave, what they had been doing for the past hundred years, and how Vaughn had heard them talking about being in league with Danathalt—and how they were apparently making more corpse-things. About their coup, and their actions in the past eighteen months, how they'd been trying to eliminate or enslave Banebringers and bring the rest of Setana firmly under their control. About the bloodbane that had been seen congregating around Weylyn City. And, finally, about Donia, and Xambria, and the Conclave threat on their border.

"Your petty fights don't concern me," Zily said when Vaughn had finished.

Tani broke in. "No, but Danathalt's attempts to directly intervene in their world ought to give you pause." He hesitated. "You know your curse better than I. Is it indeed *possible* that he could have his own *teotontl*?"

Zily stroked his goatee. "The curse demands that balance must be maintained, but it isn't precise—I have none; he might be able to get away with one. But to directly influence, and perhaps even speak through, that *teotontl*, suggests a level of unprecedented control. If anyone could do it, it would be he—since the places of weakness in the barrier are linked to his realm." He frowned, and then spoke more softly, as if to himself. "I fear I may have given him this tool myself."

"Do you think he's trying to find a way to subvert the curse?" Tani asked.

"I would not be surprised." Zily tapped his bone throne with his index finger. "I've been idle too long, and it may be my undoing."

"Help us," Vaughn interjected. "And perhaps we can find out what he's up to. Maybe even find a way to stop him." Truth be told, Zily was hardly the epitome of the benevolent dictator, but of the two of them, Zily seemed to have less interest in their world, which was better in the long-term for mortals, as far as Vaughn was concerned.

But Zily merely chuckled. "Stop him? You? Mortals? No, the only way to stop him would be to undo my curse so I could directly intervene. As it is, as long as he does nothing in our realm to affect the balance of power, I can do nothing."

"You...cursed yourself in your own curse?"

Zily winced. "I may have been overzealous."

Tani was right. These beings weren't gods. They were overpowered immortals with the same whims and desires as mortals. Which made them doubly dangerous.

"Can you cut off the portals all together so he can no longer reach us?"

He shook his head. "The weaknesses in the barrier are not my doing. They belong to something older than me."

Even Tani looked startled at that proclamation.

"So...undo the curse."

"I cannot," Zily said.

"What do you mean, you can't? You did it. Can't you undo it?"

Zily seemed troubled. "No. And if I increase my power in order to stop him, he will do the same."

Vaughn slumped back. It seemed they were at an impasse. He doubted Zily would help them if Vaughn could offer nothing in return. It turned out the heretic gods didn't care about them enough for that.

"However..." Zily turned his shifting eyes on Vaughn, and then to Ivana, once again. "There has always been a connection between this world and yours. My children must fight. Do you see a similar effect in your world?"

Vaughn frowned, but Ivana was the one who spoke. "Yes," she

said slowly. "The aether of *teotontl* who have rival patrons affects aether of the rival. It fights to the death when combined, or at least until it's rendered ineffective. It's how the Conclave has controlled captured *teotontl* all these years."

Zily nodded. "It is possible that, similarly, you may be able to affect our world by what you do in yours."

Vaughn blinked. "What? Really?"

"If you could bring unbalance to the curse in your world, it may be enough to unravel it in ours as well."

"But I thought there *had* to be balance."

"Among us, yes. That has nothing to do with mortals. Therefore, you may be able to affect it when I cannot."

"There are an awful lot of *maybe*s here."

Zily shrugged. "I hardly plotted out all the ramifications of my curse in advance."

Ivana sighed and put two fingers to her forehead, as if that were the worst thing she'd heard all day.

Vaughn continued with the more salient point. "What are we supposed to do? Defeat the Conclave? We can't. That's the whole problem. That's why we risked our lives coming here. To get your help to defeat them."

"Danathalt may have made a critical error by interfering in your world because now I may interfere as well. I will create for you one of my own *teotontl*."

Vaughn's heart fell. A single Banebringer? *That* was what Zily offered?

Tani broke in. "Aren't we playing into Danathalt's plans? Doesn't he want the curse to be broken, so he can try again?"

Zily stroked his beard again. "I don't think that would occur to Danathalt. He is narrow-sighted and small-minded. No, he's doing what he's doing to try to subvert the curse, not unravel it. If we unravel it without his knowledge, I have the advantage. If, however, he finds a way to subvert me with the curse in place...I may be unable to stop him." Zily stood up, his face firm. "No, this is the best plan." He flexed his fingers. "I feel invigorated. Perhaps this will be a nice change of pace."

Vaughn raised his hand. "Uh. Okay. This is all nice, but how is one Banebringer—er—*teotontl*—supposed to help us defeat the Conclave?"

Zily's eyes swirled hues of red and orange. "Danathalt may be my rival, but *I* am the most powerful of our kind. Use that to your advantage. You will also find out what Danathalt's plans are and report back to me."

Vaughn felt cheated. Like he'd come here asking for aid and ended up being enlisted in a war between two powerful entities instead. And what in the abyss were they getting in return? A single *Banebringer*?

But it seemed they had little choice. He'd successfully changed Zily's mind—and Vaughn wasn't certain it was going to make a difference anyway. "And how do I report back to you?"

Zily seemed surprised. "Why, next year at the sky-fire, of course. This time I'll have Taniqotalin waiting to escort you directly here."

"A *year* from now?" Vaughn spluttered. "There are Conclave forces on the borders of Donia *now!*"

"You mortals have always been resourceful," Zily said. "It's why you make such good entertainment."

"Can't you at least give us some sort of super-powerful weapons?"

"You have them. They are called *teoton*." He waved his hands. "Now get out of my sight before I change my mind. I *was* looking forward to after-dinner entertainment. Taniqotalin, find a tear in the barrier and take them to it."

But there was still one more question. "Wait. Who is your

teotontl? How do we find him or her?"

Zily made a dismissive gesture. "I cannot reach through the barrier to your world outside of the sky-fire any more than any of my children. It was fortuitous that you brought a non-*teotontl* with you. Her obvious connection with me puzzled me at first, but now I understand."

Vaughn started. He turned to look at Ivana in horror.

She, for her part, was staring at Zily. "*What*?" she asked.

"Well, I certainly couldn't choose the male. He already has a patron." He clapped his hands. "Now, *leave me*!"

Tani put one hand on the small of each of their backs and pushed them away from Zily, down the hall, and out of the room. Only when the giant doors thudded shut behind them did he turn to look at them. "We'll have to go back to the abyss, so stay close to me."

Vaughn swallowed. "How do you find a tear?"

"Why, we find a bloodbane that's drawn to it and you'll follow it out."

Vaughn felt faint. "*Follow a bloodbane out of the tear?*" He took a deep breath. "Look, before we do that, are you sure there isn't anything else you can give us? Even advice? What will...?" He looked at Ivana, who was stone-faced and silent. "His Banebringer be able to do?"

Tani frowned. "I doubt even Zily knows that. He's never had his own mortals."

"But his affinity?"

"Everything and nothing. The cycle of death and rebirth. Time, or perhaps destiny, itself." He studied Ivana with his odd, clear irises. "I think we may have answered our question as to how she was allowed here. It's possible a *teotontl* of the Great Father had and has and always will have his imprint upon them. Time is and was and will be again, after all."

Vaughn stared at him, baffled by what sounded like nonsense to him. "Great. That makes perfect sense."

Tani glanced back at the doors. "Now we must go. The longer you tarry here, the more chance that Danathalt will discover where you are. And believe me, we don't want him to stumble across us in the abyss." Tani shuddered and put a hand on each of their shoulders.

White light whisked them away from Zily's palace.

Chapter Thirty-Eight

Teoton

Vaughn and Ivana reappeared in the far-too-familiar wasteland of the abyss, Tani at their side.

Tani glanced around, frowning. "This will be easier if I can quickly search on my own. Don't go anywhere."

Panic choked Vaughn's throat. "Wait! Don't *leave* us!"

But it was too late. Tani had flashed out of visibility, leaving them standing on a rocky cliff in the middle of the abyss, a yawning cavern behind them.

Vaughn swallowed and looked around. Wasteland it might have been, but it was not empty. Dark shapes moved on the plain below them, and the skittering of tiny feet echoed in the dark behind.

If they were torn to shreds by bloodbane at *this* stage in their journey...

But before he could contemplate further on what the skittering could be, Tani flashed back into existence and the skittering abruptly stopped.

Tani now carried a large bag—large to Vaughn, anyway. "I shouldn't be doing this," Tani said, "but your plight has me intrigued. I would see you succeed." He withdrew a smaller bag and set it on the ground. "You lost anything you came with, and I understand that you may need supplies for your return trip. Food, water, and more suitable garments." His eyes swept over the two of them, making Vaughn conscious that they were still wearing the flimsy sacrificial tunics they had been dressed in. "Change quickly."

Tani made no pretense at giving them privacy—but he also ignored them, gazing out over the plains of the abyss with narrowed eyes, as if watching or waiting for something.

Vaughn rummaged in the smaller bag. There were two sets of identical clothing that consisted of a short-sleeved, thigh-length tunic that pulled on over the head, billowy pants, a belt, and boots. They were remarkably normal-looking for garments given to them by a god, though the cloth was strange—sturdy, supple, and soft—the belt was engraved with symbols he didn't recognize, and the boots were light as air and absurdly comfortable.

He tossed Ivana the set of clothes that looked smaller. Then, he turned his back on her and changed.

When he turned back, she was tugging on her boots.

Tani craned his neck to look into the cavern behind them, as if the skittering feet might have eyes. "I have one more gift for you," he said, and then withdrew an already-strung silvery bow and accompanying quiver and handed them to Vaughn, followed by a dagger and sheath for Ivana. "It's all I could do in a pinch. A millennia ago, you would have left with much, much more."

Vaughn slung the quiver over his shoulder and accepted the bow. It was unlike anything he had ever seen before. Though it looked like silver, it didn't feel like metal, and it was the lightest bow he'd ever held.

Ivana strapped the dagger in its sheath to her belt so that the sheath lay angled across the small of her back. Vaughn had almost never seen her wear her dagger this way—she seemed to prefer a thigh holster—but he doubted Tani had noticed such details. Then she picked up the bag.

"Now," Tani said. "I've found a candidate close to where you entered, which I do believe you would prefer?"

That hadn't even occurred to him. That they could return, for instance, on the other side of Setana.

"Yes," Ivana said firmly before he could reply. "That would be necessary."

Tani surrounded them in white light.

When they reappeared, it was in the middle of the plain again.

Vaughn took a step back. Two bloodwolves were fifteen, perhaps twenty feet away. But they appeared, at present, uninterested in Vaughn, Ivana, and Tani. They stalked toward the same spot from opposite directions and then began circling.

Nothing happened for a few minutes, other than Vaughn feeling more and more like he was going to vomit. *Just follow them out. Right.*

The air split. Rather than black flames licking out of the tear, blurry, colorful flames licked out—like the land racing by on the back of a horse.

"When I say so, start running and hurl yourselves through that tear. Don't worry about Danathalt's beasts—I'll take care of them."

Easy for you to say, Vaughn thought.

The bloodwolves snapped and snarled at the air, pacing back

and forth, waiting for the tear to grow large enough.

"Now!"

Vaughn took a deep breath and sprinted toward the tear, Ivana only paces behind.

The bloodwolves, intent on the tear, didn't see them until they were almost on the tear. One of them growled and lunged at Ivana.

Vaughn grabbed Ivana's arm and together they jumped right past its snapping teeth. The distant sound of yelping was the last thing Vaughn heard—and then they burst through to the other side.

They crashed into the ground—and a moment later, one of the bloodwolves burst through after them.

Vaughn scrambled backward, bow already in his hand.

The bloodwolf leapt at Ivana.

Ivana barely had time to complete the roll she had fallen into after their inelegant entrance back to their world and raise one arm as a feeble shield against the teeth of the bloodwolf. Her new dagger was already in her other hand, but it was too late.

"No!" she shouted, and the chill of fear coursed through her veins. She cringed back, and—

...no teeth sank into her flesh.

She opened one eye, then immediately scrambled backward, both eyes wide.

The bloodwolf was suspended in midair, as if hanging by a puppeteer's strings, its mouth open, razor-sharp teeth gleaming and ready to tear out her throat, its eyes burning with white fire.

She whirled around. Everything had just...stopped. A bird stood like a statue on a branch. The trees were unnaturally still. Even the tear had ceased mending itself, halfway there, though black flames still spouted forth, likewise frozen.

Everything except her was frozen.

Including Vaughn.

He stood, caught in a single moment, his mouth open as if to shout, bow drawn, arrow already set to the string.

Even as she stared at him and his bow, she could trace the arrow's future trajectory. Not through calculations or even a reasonable guess. She just *knew*. It would have been deadly accurate, as usual, but too late.

What in the abyss had just happened? Was she hallucinating again?

She became dimly aware of the ice still flowing through her veins—what she had written off as fear—because it felt so cold that it was hot, boiling even.

It didn't precisely hurt, but it wasn't comfortable, either. And she was starting to feel lightheaded.

Burning skies. This wasn't a dream, a hallucination, or some new machination of the heretic gods.

She had done this.

She spun again. She was *still* doing this.

And if she knew anything about the way Banebringer powers worked—which she did—if she didn't stop, she would kill herself.

Think, Ivana. She knew how to burn aether outside her body. She'd done it many, many times. It just required direction.

She backed a good distance away from the bloodwolf.

Stop, she thought. *Stop this!*

And just like that, everything began again.

The burning in her veins also stopped, and she fell to her hands and knees, gasping, as if someone had kicked her in the back.

Beyond her, Vaughn's shout was given voice, and

simultaneously, there was a hard *thwack.*

Silence. She sat back on her heels. Vaughn was staring at the dead bloodwolf, which, incredibly, now had an arrow-sized hole clean through its head, and then at his arrow, which had buried itself all the way to the fletching in a tree beyond the bloodwolf. An impossible feat.

"How in the abyss did you do *that*?" she asked.

At the same time, he turned to her and asked, "How in the abyss did *you* get over *there*?"

Vaughn and Ivana stared at one another for a moment.

He didn't know how he had done that. He had done nothing out of the ordinary, felt nothing out of the ordinary other than that the bow had been easier to draw than normal. Had it been the bow, then, perhaps? If so...*damn.*

Ivana, likewise, didn't answer him. She just shook her head. "Where are we?"

He glanced around to take note of their surroundings—a small clearing surrounded by forest. Nearby, a tiny hut sat nestled amongst the trees, and in front of an open door lay an old man.

Ivana walked over to him and nudged him with her foot. "Dead," she said. "Banebringer?"

"I'm guessing," Vaughn said. "Must have been hiding out here—wherever 'here' is—and died of old age or some other ailment."

Ivana swiped a hand across her brow and made to wipe it on her new tunic, but instead, she stopped and stared down at her hand.

He didn't look at her hand. He looked at her forehead.

She had a cut there, likely gained when they had crashed

through the portal and onto the rocky ground, still oozing red blood.

But the trickle running down her forehead and into her eyes was hardening into silver.

Zily hadn't been lying. Ivana was his new Banebringer.

Her throat constricted and she lowered her hand, then looked away from him and back down to the man lying at her feet.

Her hand clenched into a fist and her jaw jumped.

He took a few hesitant steps toward her. "I-I'm sorry," he said. "I know how it feels to realize...that you're one of *them*—us—now."

She lifted her head and turned toward him. "You think I care about that?" she said through clenched teeth.

He blinked. "Uh—most people do?"

She snorted. "I don't give a damn about what color my blood turns. What I give a damn about is that now I'll be nothing more than a tool to your Ichtaca." Her nostrils flared. "I didn't ask for this. I went along with your little scheme out of some...misguided desire to know more about my parents."

He hadn't known that. He'd thought he'd just annoyed her enough that she'd given in.

"And now I'm embroiled in this, whether I wanted to be or not. And to be clear, I didn't."

Birds chirped in the trees overhead, filling a moment of silence, a moment during which his chest tightened, and his hands began to sweat. "You...*are* going to help us, aren't you?"

"Do I have a choice?" she spat.

"I won't stop you if you run," he said softly.

Something flickered across her face other than anger. But it was gone before he could identify it. "Then you're a fool," she said. "Because given how important this could be, you ought to have already tied me up and be dragging me back, kicking and screaming."

She was right. He would be a fool to just let her go. But he wouldn't, *couldn't* force her to do this. He knew what it was to be poked and prodded, interrogated, treated as if his only value, his only identity, was in that of being a Banebringer. How much more so, for her? "You're fond of telling me how much of an idiot I am," he said. "So does this surprise you?"

She rolled her eyes, and he moved to stand in front of her.

He touched her jaw and turned her head to face him. "I won't force you to do this. But I would very much like it if you would."

He held his breath at her moment of silence, but it didn't last.

She pressed her lips together. "Of course I'm going to come back with you," she said, sounding downright grumpy. "You dragged me this far. What in the abyss—or out of it—else would I do now?" She glanced back down at her silver-stained hands. "Do you know what I just did? I didn't mean to—but somehow it happened anyway."

He shook his head.

"I froze everything except myself. That's how I moved. You, the bloodwolf—it was like you all turned into statues."

He blinked. "That's...different."

"Yes. Thanks for that observation. Pretty sure I also could have easily killed myself since I had no idea what I was doing."

He exhaled and glanced around, his eyes lingering once again on the arrow that had drilled straight through the bloodwolf's head and into the tree beyond. "All right. Well. We'll figure that out when we get back to Marakyn. Let's find a place where we can see the lay of the land and figure out where exactly we are."

Chapter Thirty-Nine

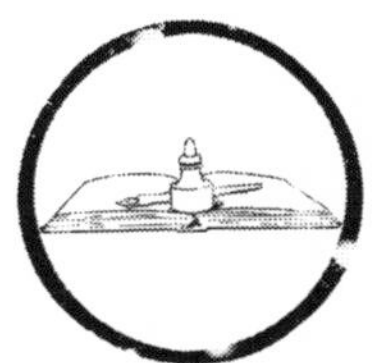

Ethically Nebulous

Driskell closed his eyes and imagined a giant bubble expanding from himself. The effort was costing him; he had already become familiar with the feel of the aether "burning" in his blood—that peculiar boiling ice sensation—and he was burning more than he should have been at once.

Still, he continued to push at the bubble until it enveloped Danton and Thrax, both just a few feet away from him, and then stopped expanding it.

He slowly backed off on the amount of aether he was burning, bringing the boil down to a simmer, and then the lazy trickle of the tiny, pre-simmer bubbles.

He held that for a moment until he felt as though it were stable, and then he opened his eyes.

Danton and Thrax were doing their best to ignore him while playing a game of tapolli on Danton's little table.

"I'm thirsty," he said. "Anyone want to go get me a drink?"

Danton moved one of his stones forward, and neither of them responded to his plea.

Driskell sighed, and the bubble popped.

He slumped forward and put his forehead in his hands. "I'm never going to get this."

Thrax pushed his chair back from the table and put his hands behind his head. "I might have felt a tingle in my fingers that time."

Driskell lifted his head to glare at Thrax.

Danton swept the red and black stones into a pile, disrupting the imaginary game. "I told you, this isn't going to work on us. We know what you're doing. *All* the information, anecdotal or otherwise, we've managed to find on charmblood powers—"

"I *know*," Driskell said. He ticked points off on his fingers. "They don't work well on people who know what you're doing. They don't work as well if the person even knows you *could* be using your powers. Subtle suggestion works better than direct commands. And it's at its best when you're working with assumptions, beliefs, or desires the person already has and just nudging them along a little."

"Yes. In other words, you need to practice on someone else," Danton said.

Driskell was already shaking his head, but Thrax broke in before he could protest.

"Look, head to one of the shops where you've been meaning to buy something. Use your mind powers to get a better deal. They won't be the wiser, and it'd be the perfect situation to practice on."

"That's like...cheating!" Driskell said.

Thrax groaned and slapped his palm over his entire face.

Driskell gave Danton a plaintive look. He hated this. He couldn't practice on Danton and Thrax because they knew he was doing it, and so it wouldn't work. He didn't want to practice on anyone else because it felt unethical. Aside from that first suggestion he had made to Linette, he had yet to influence anyone to do anything.

Danton sighed. "Do you at least feel you're making progress with controlling the flow of aether?"

Driskell shrugged. "I don't know. Maybe? I think I went a little too fast at the beginning, but once I had it stabilized, it felt more in control."

"I mean, that's definitely better than passing out every time you try to do this..."

Driskell winced. "I don't think I'm cut out for this. I can't think of a scenario in which I would feel comfortable using these powers on people."

"So don't use them *on* people," Danton said. "Do that thing where you supposedly enhance yourself instead."

"That's still—"

"There you go," Thrax said. "Perfect. Next time you're with that girl of yours, throw a few love-beams her way and..." He wiggled his eyebrows.

Danton snorted. "Love-beams?"

"I will *not!*" Driskell said.

"I'm not suggesting you get her to do something she wouldn't already want to do," Thrax said. "I'm just saying, you could make it a little more fun if—are you blushing?"

"I don't—we don't—that's not—" Driskell stammered.

Danton elbowed Thrax hard enough that he made a small *oof.* "Shut it, idiot. They're, you know, not *there* yet."

"Rhianah help us," Thrax said. "Of *all* the people to get stuck with *these* powers, and we get straight arrow here."

Driskell bit his lip. "Look, I'd rather not have these powers at all. And if I had to be destined for something, I don't know myself why it couldn't have been fire or ice or—or *anything* less ethically nebulous."

"'Ethically nebulous,'" Thrax repeated. "That's a phrase you don't hear every day."

Danton tried again. "Driskell...I know you don't like this. But think of it this way: that Conclave representative who's always skulking around, trying to find some evidence that we're doing something underhanded? If you could learn to control this, you could use it to mislead him, persuade him, or otherwise buy us more time here and there. Is that any more unethical than using more conventional means of doing those things?"

Driskell chewed on his lip. "I mean...I don't know. I guess not."

"We're overthrowing the entire established order," Thrax grumbled, as if he hadn't heard any of that, "and he's worried about being *ethically nebulous*."

That was it, though, wasn't it? Everything around Driskell was shifting sand. What had been unthinkable a few months ago was now happening, what had been wrong, right—how far did it go? He had no control over anything else, but whether or how to use his powers, he did. He needed *some* anchor in his life.

Even so. Danton had a point. He could be useful. Helpful, even. But he would have to *practice*.

"I get it," Danton said. "I really do. If I seem like I'm in trouble a lot, it's because I'm terrible at saying *no* to all the bad influences in my life"—he threw a pointed look at Thrax, who crossed his eyes in return—"not because of my own inclinations."

"How about this?" Thrax said. "Burn aether at the most miniscule level you can manage, as regularly as you can manage. Go about life. Do what you would ordinarily be doing. Except keep projecting those love-beams. See what happens. You don't have to specifically try to persuade or manipulate anyone. You're practicing your efficiency, that's all. Just don't overdo it and pass out."

Driskell turned that over. That didn't seem so bad. "That's...I could do that. I could try that." *But not around Tania.*

"There, see? I can be helpful," Thrax said.

There was a knock at the door to Danton's room.

Danton stood up and opened the door.

One of the newest-arrived Banebringers—a middle-aged Arlanan man named Huiel, and one of Yaotel's inner circle who had been elsewhere—stood there. "Dal Driskell? Lady Nahua is looking for you. You, too, Danton."

"Uh-oh," Thrax said. "What'd you do now?"

Huiel threw Thrax a sharp look. "The Conclave army is moving."

Later that day, a crowd spilled out of the gates of Marakyn, a thousand eyes on Driskell and the group assembling just outside the city walls.

Driskell stood next to his horse, holding the reins and waiting for the signal that they should leave, trying to ignore the murmur of the crowd behind him.

"Driskell!"

He turned, startled, to see a lone figure dashing out of the crowd. Tania.

He had said *goodbye* to her earlier, giving what explanations he could—but there was no denying or hiding that a Conclave army was marching toward Marakyn.

She drew up in front of him. Her brow was knit in worry.

"Tania. I thought you were needed at work?"

"Did you think I wouldn't come to see you off? I've heard so many rumors—" Her breath caught in her throat. "You will be careful?"

Driskell tried to school his face as well as Nahua or Tanuac might. "It's just a diplomatic envoy."

"But why is the Conclave's army still here? Tanuac *did* meet their demands, didn't he?"

Driskell swallowed. His stomach was churning as much as Tania's own probably was. He could allay her worries. He had the power within him to potentially convince her that they were for no reason.

"*Didn't* he?" she repeated.

No. He wouldn't begin that. Where would it end? What was the line? He already hated lying to her. He hated it with every fiber of his being and had since all of this had started. And he already had to do it again. "Of course. Which is why there's nothing to worry about. I'm sure it's just some misunderstanding."

She studied his face. She knew him too well. She knew he wasn't being entirely truthful. She knew it was because he was in a position of confidence and simply *couldn't* tell her everything.

He took her hands in his own, lifted her right hand, and kissed the back of it. "And when I get back, we have your grandmama's birthday celebration to look forward to." He tried to smile. He didn't know if he was successful. That was another matter. His planned proposal was looming, and he still didn't know what to do about it.

She nodded, but she didn't smile. Instead, she drew close to him and buried her face in his neck. "Driskell," she whispered. "I know this isn't what it seems. I know you can't tell me what's really going on. But promise me, please..."

He turned his head to breathe in her hair. He blocked out the gaze of a thousand people, not caring in that moment. Who knew when his secret might be found out? Who knew if she'd ever let him hold her again, once it was? "I'll be careful," he said softly.

"Driskell," Nahua said from behind him. "It's time."

He started back, feeling guilty—as though he had given away more than he should have, even though he hadn't technically said anything incriminating.

Tania reluctantly let go. She inclined her head to Nahua. "My lady," she said softly.

Driskell stepped back, and Nahua gave Tania a warm smile. "Tania. I know you're worried, but please don't be. I can assure you your Driskell would not be among a group destined for more than diplomacy."

Driskell wasn't sure whether he ought to be offended at that, despite the truth of it. He was no soldier. He'd be more likely to harm himself than someone else if he tried to use a weapon.

"Yes, my lady," Tania said softly.

She exchanged one last look with Driskell and returned to the crowd.

"You're so good at that," Driskell said, wishing he could speak half-truths so naturally.

"It's all in the wording, Driskell," Nahua said. "I spoke no untruth. You're here as my aide, and nothing more. It makes it easier to lie when you're also telling the truth." She flashed him a half-smile. "All the same, I'll be glad when the truth is the truth again."

Driskell pondered her words as they mounted their horses and their envoy moved out. Perhaps that was the trick to using his charmblood powers. The information Danton and Thrax had dug up had been that the likelihood of success was higher if he was working with what the person already wanted or believed to be true. Perhaps it was also more likely to succeed if what he said was still technically true as well.

He glanced up the line. Tanuac had sent over a hundred soldiers as well as Nahua's personal guards to accompany her...and himself.

The Banebringer team—Danton, Yasril, Linette, and another moonblood who had just arrived with Huiel's group—that would infiltrate the Conclave's camp and steal their aether had started on their way earlier that morning.

Driskell took a deep breath. Nahua was right. He was here as her aide. In truth. He wasn't part of the infiltration team. They were here under the banner of peace. Even if talks went sour, for the Conclave to attack Nahua and himself would be entirely inappropriate.

Right?

Right.

They spotted the vanguard of the Conclave army a day and a half out from Marakyn, where the forest began to peter out into the hilly plains of Donia.

Nahua gathered a dozen soldiers and her guards and rode out to meet, once again, Bherg and a small contingent of priests, while the rest of the men stayed behind in the temporary camp they had erected the night before.

This time, there were no refreshments. There was their group of mounted soldiers and the priests on foot.

Nahua held up her hand to their group. One of her guards hoisted the Donian flag with the white cloth of peace tied underneath, and they met Bherg on the plain.

She didn't dismount.

"My lady," Bherg said, bowing low as his party approached. "I—"

Nahua cut in. "*I* demand to know the meaning of this." Her gracious demeanor of the last "negotiations" had evaporated. "We have complied with your demands and bent over backward to accommodate your 'representative.' And yet your army has remained on our border for weeks, and even now marches toward Marakyn. Did our last tax payment not reach your coffers? Have you other charges to unfairly levy against a region that has faithfully submitted to Setanan rule for centuries?"

Driskell stared at Nahua in amazement. She was a holy terror, and Driskell had never seen her like this before.

Even Bherg quailed for a moment before regaining his composure and sneering in return. "Where is your father, girl? Why does he continue to send out his puppy to negotiate?"

"I was given legal authority long ago to represent Ri Tanuac whenever he deems it appropriate," Nahua said, "as you surely already know. And as his representative, I demand an answer on his behalf for your actions."

"Very well," Bherg said. "We received word that your Xambrian ambassador was spotted in the city not three days ago."

"Impossible," Nahua returned immediately, not missing a beat. "He was soundly ejected, per your stipulations."

"You would say that, of course."

"Your spy probably can't tell one Xambrian from another," Nahua said. "We have a Xambrian trader who makes an appearance on occasion, fluent in Setanan per the law."

On occasion was stretching the truth. Driskell couldn't remember the last time a Xambrian trader had come to Marakyn.

"In addition," Bherg said, "our representative feels that you have not been fully including him in all matters of business."

"Nonsense," Nahua said. "He has attended every council meeting, has had access to all our files, once again, per your stipulations."

"He believes—"

Nahua seemed to grow. "He *believes*? You're threatening my city with an army because your spy *believes* we've failed to comply with your demands? And on that meager evidence you plan to what? Slaughter our people and raze the city to the ground, perhaps? Is this the new standard under Conclave rule? I think you'd best turn your eyes toward home if so because you'll soon find revolt in your heartland while you gallivant around the Empire inventing reasons to intimidate the outer regions."

There was a long pause in which Driskell slowly came to realize that Nahua had struck a nerve.

Perhaps things weren't as tidy back in the core of the Empire as the Conclave wanted everyone to believe.

Was there a struggle to hold on to their power, perhaps?

And then an idea began to form in his mind. Perhaps he could...help.

Could he? Was he capable of doing so?

This wasn't Tania or a random innocent person. This was someone determined to destroy Donia for whatever slights, real or imagined, it had committed against Conclave sensibilities.

He twisted one of the reins around his wrist, uncertain...

No. He *could* do this. He might fail, but no one would know.

He burned aether. He tried to do it slowly, to come to that almost-simmer at first rather than after an initial furious boil, and it sort of worked, but there was still too much on the front end.

Even as he did so, he had to keep himself from shrinking back, as if Bherg might somehow *know*.

Bherg ignored him.

He stabilized and stretched out his bubble toward Bherg, who was rallying himself to another verbal assault on Nahua's reasoning. Driskell encompassed himself and Bherg in the bubble, and he didn't hear Bherg's next spoken words, nor Nahua's next rejoinder.

Driskell suddenly had the hunch this was a grasp at power. That they were striking out to bully the outer regions into behaving out of fear, rather than because they believed Donia was planning to revolt, and they had seen Donia as an easy first target.

Tanuac had guessed as much, but Driskell suddenly felt it, *knew* it to be true.

The irony, of course, was that they *were* planning to revolt.

He repeated Nahua's words back at Bherg in his mind, feeding off the fears Driskell was already certain were true. *While you linger here, what's happening back home? Should you be spreading your army so thin?*

"Setana has more than enough troops to protect itself while also devoting resources to its outer regions," Bherg said.

"Devoting resources? Is that what you call it? Perhaps a better word would be *wasting*," Nahua rejoined.

Driskell continued to project words of doubt. *Wasting resources better used on solidifying your hold on Setana, perhaps?*

Yes. That felt right. Were Bherg's masters even now growing antsy at this side trip? Had they been clamoring for results?

His aether was burning faster than he would have liked, and he wasn't sure why, other than that he wasn't good at this. He had no idea what he was doing. He didn't even know if he was helping or throwing nonsense into the wind.

Even so, he took another chance. What would a man like Bherg be after personally?

Almost immediately, the answer came to him.

If you fail here, how will that lower your esteem in the eyes of whatever masters you serve? Perhaps more caution should be in order...

"How *dare* you insult my honor in such a manner!" Bherg burst out. Driskell had missed the inciting words, but Bherg was obviously becoming too agitated. Driskell didn't know if it was because of Nahua's words, his own influence, or both. But he sensed the soldiers behind him straighten up, and Bherg's own men grow tense, and he worried Bherg might do something rash to stop the onslaught. Maybe this had been a bad idea.

No need to panic! Just withdraw for a bit to think it over! he threw out desperately.

At the same time, his head began to spin.

Oh no.

He withdrew the bubble instantly, but it was too late.

Blackness passed over his eyes.

When Driskell woke next, he was no longer on the ground, no longer on the plains, no longer outside even.

Instead, he was on his back in a strange cot in a strange tent.

And there was someone else in the tent with him.

He turned his head. It was Nahua.

She sat in a chair next to the cot, watching him. His spectacles rested in her hands.

He sat up. Based on where he had awoken, he half-expected to feel dizzy or pain, but other than feeling a little stiff and achy, he felt fine. He flushed, remembering his rather dramatic episode. What had happened? Had the Conclave army left? "My lady. What...?"

She handed him his spectacles. One of the side arms had broken, and someone had then taped it together. "Dal Yaotel assures me that you are *not* the Banebringer already among our staff that he spoke of some time ago, and that he had no idea. Further, Danton assures me that, rather, this just happened at the recent sky-fire. Even so...why didn't you tell at least me?"

Driskell settled the spectacles back on his face, but a pit

opened in his stomach. He lowered his gaze to his hands.

Silence.

When the silence became unbearable, he looked back up at Nahua. "I just couldn't. I was afraid."

"Afraid? Given the current treaty?"

"No. Afraid that—afraid I'd lose my job. Afraid you or Ri Tanuac would think less of me. Afraid—" He swallowed. Afraid the wrong person would find out. Afraid of his own powers. Afraid of the fact that his blood turned silver. Afraid of what he would lose.

Afraid that everyone was wrong, and this meant he was damned. "I don't know. Just afraid."

"Oh, Driskell. I had hoped you knew me better than that."

Relief washed over him, but also guilt. "I'm so sorry."

She sighed. "Who else knows?"

"Danton. Thrax. And anyone you've told."

"Yaotel, my father, and Linette," she said. "Not Tania?"

He wrung his hands together and shook his head, ashamed to admit he hadn't even told the woman he hoped to marry. "How did you find out? What happens to me now? And...what happened to the Conclave army? Did we get the aether?"

She held her hand up. "One question at a time. You passed out while we were *negotiating* with Bherg. You slid off your horse, your hand got tangled in the reins, and your horse bolted. He only dragged you for a few seconds before you came free, but when I got to you, you were out cold. You were lucky not to be injured worse than you were."

"I was injured? I don't feel injured."

"Linette worked on you. Mostly bruises. Your wrist took the brunt of it." She nodded toward his hand.

He flipped his hand over. His wrist was bruised and red. And there were still the remnants of what looked like healing scrapes, some still flecked with bits of silver.

Well. That explained how she knew.

"I got to you first. Wrapped your wrist. No one else saw."

"Thank you," he whispered.

"You can trust me, Driskell."

"Danton—" he began.

"He didn't betray your confidence. I felt I needed to inform my father and Yaotel and asked Danton to help."

Driskell swallowed, then nodded. This was it, wasn't it? Now, he would have to join the Ichtaca and work for them instead.

"Why do you look like you've swallowed a rotten egg?" Nahua asked.

"I-I don't want to join the Ichtaca," he blurted out. "I want to continue in the position I'm in."

"Good. I was hoping you would say that."

He blinked. "My lady?"

She gave him a gentle smile. "You're invaluable to me, Driskell. I wouldn't let go of you so easily."

Tears stung his eyes, and he blinked them away. "How long have I been out?"

"About two hours. We're back at the camp."

"The Conclave?"

"After your incident, Bherg withdrew. He..." Her brow furrowed. "He seemed on edge. Said he needed to contact his superiors back in Weylyn City before proceeding with further...*discussions*. It was rather unexpected. I half-expected him to give his army the order to attack then and there."

Had it worked? Had he made a difference? Goaded Bherg into an alternate course of action by manipulating his own anxiety and fears?

"Did Danton say anything more? Like about what I could do?"

Nahua shook her head. "He only said you must have passed

out overusing your magic. Why? What can you do? What were you *trying* to do?"

He took a deep breath. "I'm...apparently a charmblood."

Nahua sat back. She knew the basics of what that was. She had read all his notes and charts.

"You were trying to get him to leave us alone," she said softly.

He hesitated, then nodded. And then looked down at his hands. It was awful, wasn't it? What he had done. Using someone like that. He felt sick, even knowing it was the "enemy."

"Driskell, look up. You might be the only reason we've bought ourselves some time. It may not be much. Once they discover their stock of aether has been replaced with less combat-oriented aether, I imagine there will be no further negotiations. But it's still time."

"They succeeded?"

"They did. We were waiting on you to wake up to get back to Marakyn."

He drew in a deep breath. "Then we need wait no longer."

Chapter Forty

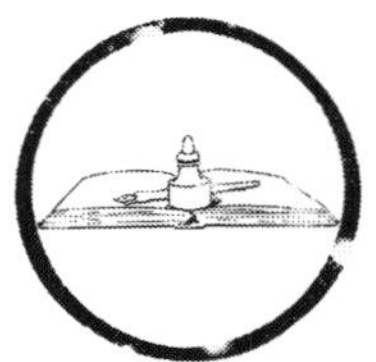

A Worthy Ally

Driskell clattered down the steep stair leading underneath the civic hall. He tugged open the heavy metal door at the bottom. It wasn't locked, but there was a guard on the other side.

The guard nodded to Driskell and let him through. He continued through the windowless tunnel leading away from the hall and into the side of the mountain.

But Driskell wasn't headed far in. In the years right before Setana subdued Donia, one of the rooms had been converted to a war room.

It hadn't seen any use since then—or, perhaps, even then. He could almost imagine his ancestors huddled around the gigantic map of Donia and surrounding regions, debating the difficult decision of whether they would resist Setana or simply give up.

He stopped in front of that door, knocked, and then stepped inside.

The gigantic map was still there, and today, Tanuac, Nahua, General Gyano, and two of his senior officers huddled around it, along with Yaotel and Huiel. Driskell had since learned that Huiel had previously been overseeing training Banebringers—new and old alike—out in Venetia somewhere.

They'd been trickling in over the past few weeks. Yaotel had put out a call for Banebringers who could get there in time, letting them know they had protection in Marakyn if they were willing to help repel the Conclave's force.

The group around the table ignored him as he slipped in and quietly shut the door. They were used to him coming in and out, delivering messages and, sometimes, more wine.

"...contacted me yesterday," Yaotel was saying. "And her report not only corroborates what Vaughn ran into but makes it clear that there is no reason to wait."

"Excellent," General Gyano said. Driskell was still impressed at how the aging general had taken the news of their alliance with Banebringers in stride. He was pragmatic, and his pragmatism served them all well, because he recognized the asset the Banebringers could bring and immediately began to brainstorm ways to utilize them without making their presence known. "But what about Vaughn?"

Yaotel shook his head. "That's the only problem. I haven't heard from him."

Driskell cleared his throat, and everyone turned to look at him. He gave a short bow. "My apologies, but I have a warning and two urgent messages." The first message was verbal and directly relevant to what they were discussing, so he led with that. "Dal Vaughn and Da Ivana just arrived back in Marakyn. I kept them both at the consulate for now because I know you've been waiting for Vaughn's return."

Yaotel's shoulders visibly relaxed. "Good," he said. "How recently did they arrive?"

"They showed up at the seventh-tier gates about an hour ago. And, looking rather rough, I might add." He raised an eyebrow. "Should I send for them immediately?"

"Yes," Tanuac said. "With apologies. You had a second message?"

He walked a sealed envelope over to Tanuac and handed it to him. "A Fuilynian messenger arrived bearing this."

Though no one had been speaking, the entire room stilled.

Tanuac broke the seal, unfolded the piece of paper, and read it silently. Then he nodded, looking grimly satisfied. "Ri Leito sends word. They have decided to accept their Xambrian Ambassador's offer."

General Gyano slapped the table. "Excellent," he said again.

They had been waiting on word from Fuilyn since the Xambrian ambassador had shown up. Venetia had already pledged their support, but Fuilyn had been an unknown until now—geographically, it would be the most vulnerable of the regions if their alliance with the Xambrians took a downward turn.

Grins broke out on the senior officers' faces. "We might do this, General," one of them said.

"Not so fast," Tanuac warned. "There's still the issue of Ferehar."

The grins slipped off every face, and then the room was quiet again.

Ferehar was a problem. Mezzo had been clear that all four regions needed to agree, and Ferehar was especially important due to its proximity to Xambria. But they had yet to hear anything from Ri Airell. They had sent three messengers so far, and the first two had returned without even being admitted, Airell having refused to see them; the third had not returned at all yet. His cooperation wasn't looking promising, and yet Ferehar was necessary for their plans.

Yaotel glanced at Driskell. "You said you had a warning?"

"Oh. Uh, yes. That priest is lurking around again. It took me so long to get down here because he was pestering me." He had tried to subtly suggest to the priest that he ought to go elsewhere—with the help of a little aether—but it seemed to have little effect on him. Perhaps because it was too out of line with what the priest wanted to do, and Driskell wasn't skilled enough to figure out how to work that to his advantage.

Tanuac rubbed his chin. "He's been even more persistent since you arrived back. We're running out of time."

Considering the Conclave army was now camped within half a day's ride from Marakyn, that was an understatement. As of yet, they seemed content merely to wait—presumably for orders from Weylyn City as to what they should do. But the moment they discovered the aether they had wasn't useful...

"Thank you, Driskell," Tanuac said, "you may go retrieve Dal Vaughn now."

He bowed and left the room.

Vaughn wanted nothing more than to sleep. He didn't think they had been on the other side more than four or five days; it felt like a year. And in that time, he had had exactly one actual night of sleep, and it had been interrupted. Then it had taken four days to pick their way back to Marakyn. The portal had spit them out south of the city, up in the foothills of the mountains and seemingly in the middle of nowhere. With no shelter, no bedrolls, rationed food and water, and only the clothes Tani had provided, the journey back hadn't been an easy one.

So, when Driskell had appeared shortly after they had presented themselves at the seventh-tier gates and told them to wait in the consulate rather than going directly to Vaughn's room, he couldn't say he was altogether pleased.

They waited in a small suite of rooms where they could bathe, change, or take some refreshment if they wished. Driskell had informed them that Yaotel was in a meeting, but he would return with instructions in a bit.

"A bit" turned out to be sooner rather than later. They only had time to track down the bag Ivana had unintentionally left at the shrine and the others had brought back with them, wash their faces, and eat a light meal before Driskell returned.

Vaughn felt the weariness pulling at him even more as they followed Driskell through the civic hall, down a back stair, and into a damp tunnel. He had no idea how Yaotel would react to any of the news he brought back, and he doubted it would make a difference to Yaotel's plans for him in the short-term.

He did know he didn't have the energy—or patience—for arguing.

Driskell stopped in front of a thick wooden door, and then his eyes ran over Vaughn, lingering on the bow and quiver still slung on his back. "Do you want me to take your bow back to your room, or...?"

Vaughn exchanged a glance with Ivana. For his part, he wasn't just going to hand off this incredible bow to an acquaintance. They had tested it on the way back—several times. It was so light, it could have been hollow, yet it seemed indestructible. Even more notable, it could be left strung without damaging the bow, and Vaughn was able to pull and hold a draw with complete ease for minutes at a time.

And it could punch holes through trees. Literally.

Nothing a weaveblood—the rarest Banebringer in their records—had made had ever come close.

"I'll hang on to this for now," Vaughn said. "It's, uh, special."

Driskell didn't even ask about Ivana's dagger, though whether that was because it was less conspicuous than a bow sticking out over her head, or because she had once saved all their lives, Vaughn didn't know.

Driskell bowed and then knocked on the door. He popped his head in. "They're here."

There was an affirmation from inside the room, and he pushed the door open. "Go ahead."

Vaughn stepped into the room, Ivana just behind.

They were greeted by seven or eight faces, most of whom Vaughn recognized, but not all.

Yaotel's face went rigid as soon as he saw Ivana. Vaughn could tell he wanted to say something, but he had bit his tongue.

Would his attitude change when he found out she was a Banebringer now too? And if so, for better or worse?

Vaughn stepped up to the table, the surface of which was an enormous map, and Ivana stepped back against the wall. "So," he said, "anyone notice there's an army camped within a day's march of Marakyn?"

Yaotel didn't seem to appreciate his attempt at humor. "Is there a reason you didn't contact me to tell me what in the abyss you were doing—since you're obviously not dead?"

Vaughn cleared his throat. He felt smugly satisfied about what he was about to drop on Yaotel. "About the abyss. My qixli didn't work there, and then we were forced to leave all our stuff behind in Thaxchatichan's palace right before Ziloxchanachi had us arrested." He tapped his chin. "And while Taniqotalin gave us enough supplies to get back here, he didn't retrieve my things. So, see, I couldn't have contacted you."

There was silence in the room. General Gyano, whom Vaughn had only met a few times, looked confused, along with the two men Vaughn presumed were senior officers. Yaotel was staring at him like he'd sprouted a third eyeball. Tanuac's brow was furrowed, and Nahua was looking at him speculatively. Huiel gave a little roll of his eyes, as if positive this was exactly what would happen when Vaughn showed up again.

"You mean to tell me," Yaotel said, "that you *actually* made that damn door work?"

"Didn't Danton and Thrax give you a report?"

"Yes," Yaotel said. "They said you disappeared in a ball of fire." He jerked his head back toward where Ivana leaned against the wall. "Along with her. What was I supposed to make of that? No body, no bloodbane, so we were reluctant to pronounce you dead—"

"Therefore, you obviously should have concluded that it worked," Vaughn said. "What's the issue here?"

A muscle jumped in Yaotel's jaw. Vaughn was certain that, had they been alone, he would have had an earful by now. As it was, he was grateful for the presence of Ri Tanuac and his people to keep Yaotel's frustration in check.

"As you have astutely noted," Yaotel said evenly, "there's a Conclave army camped a day's march outside Marakyn. Did you gain anything of immediate use in your travels? Something that will dramatically sway our course of action?"

Vaughn pressed his lips together. A single Banebringer, two super-powered weapons, and some incredibly comfortable clothing hardly seemed of any importance in the face of an army. Long-term, what they had learned could change everything. But they wouldn't survive long enough for him to figure out Zily's cryptic mission if they didn't win *now*.

"Then I'm in no mood for your mouth," Yaotel said,

interpreting his silence correctly. "I brought you here immediately because you're needed."

Vaughn gritted his teeth. "And I just risked my life ten times over on a crazy chance that not only worked, but *did* bear results of long-term importance. I'm happy to regale you with the full details later, but I'm exhausted and cranky, and *I'm* in no mood to be scolded. I'm back, and as promised, I'm now at your disposal." Grudgingly.

Yaotel exchanged a glance with Tanuac, and to Vaughn's surprise, stepped back and deferred to the Ri.

Ri Tanuac drummed his fingers on the map. "Gyano. Take a break. Dal Huiel, your assistance has been invaluable already—we'll call on you again soon."

The general and his two officers filed out of the room, followed by Huiel. Driskell started to follow, but Tanuac stopped him. "No, stay this time, Driskell. It's time you were brought into the loop. I may later need your reflections."

Vaughn raised an eyebrow, and Driskell slowly drew out his notebook and sat down in one of the chairs next to Yaotel.

When the wooden door had shut with a heavy *thunk,* Tanuac leaned forward on his hands, splaying his fingers flat against the map. "We have a problem," he said.

No kidding. But Vaughn bit his tongue. Mouthing off to Yaotel was one thing. Mouthing off to the Ri of Donia was another.

The side of Tanuac's mouth quirked up. "Let me revise that. We have many problems. But there's only one problem you need to concern yourself with, Dal Vaughn. The army outside Marakyn is not it."

Vaughn didn't want to hear what was coming next. He didn't want to *do* it. He had hoped, beyond hope, that it wouldn't come to this, that maybe Yaotel had come up with a different plan while he'd been gone.

"Ferehar," Tanuac said, "has steadfastly refused to cooperate."

That wasn't news. "With all due respect, Your Excellency," Vaughn said, "I told you that would be the case. My brother is a power-hungry ass."

"A dangerous combination, agreed," Tanuac said. "Therefore, we're done attempting even the finer points of diplomacy." He glanced at Yaotel and then, for some reason, at Driskell, before looking back at Vaughn. "Yaotel assures me that even a charmblood would likely have little success with persuading Ri Airell to relent. No, ultimately, Airell needs to go."

Vaughn clenched his teeth, but he said nothing.

Tanuac laced his fingers together. "Both your experience and your comrade Da Aleena's time in Ferehar have confirmed that Ri Airell's position in Ferehar is tenuous. We don't believe it would take much to topple him, but we need someone sympathetic to our cause to put in his place." He raised an eyebrow at Vaughn. "Yaotel told me he's already spoken to you about this."

Vaughn had no choice but to acknowledge the Ri's statement. "He has. But"—he raised a finger—"I still maintain that the idea that they would accept a Banebringer as their Ri is insane. And even if I weren't a Banebringer, why in the abyss would they want yet another member of my tyrannical family in charge?"

"It makes a certain amount of sense," Ivana said softly.

Both Tanuac and Yaotel turned to look at her, but Ivana addressed Vaughn. "Worship of the heretic gods is not dead in Ferehar," she said. "If there would be anywhere a Banebringer could get away with usurping power, it would be there. And as to the family connection, it puts you in a perfect position to challenge him. Here in Donia, it wouldn't work. But in Ferehar, the people are used to the dynastic way they handle the position of Ri. Better to hand it off to the kinder, less oppressive brother and see what happens than have another bloody civil war."

The puppet brother, you mean, Vaughn thought bitterly. Ivana was right. Vaughn had already had these arguments with Yaotel—and lost.

Tanuac gave her a nod of acknowledgment. "And if it works," he said, "not only can you then agree to the Xambrian terms, but we will have accomplished something bigger than all of this. A Gifted as the Ri of one of our allies might lend us credibility as we push to integrate the Ichtaca into Donian society publicly."

"Or it might make everyone afraid another Banebringer will stage a coup here—because we're just that evil," Vaughn said darkly.

"Perhaps. But we're out of other options."

Vaughn folded his arms across his chest. "Just tell me what you want me to do."

"What we want you to do," Yaotel said, "is assemble a core team of people you can trust and who would be valuable to you. Contact Da Aleena and form a plan to oust Ri Airell with as little fanfare as possible. Then get to Ferehar as quickly as you can and do whatever needs to be done." His eyes darted to Ivana, but he didn't call her out.

Vaughn could almost feel the shackles slapping around his ankles as they spoke. He tried one last time. "I don't want to be a Ri."

Yaotel sighed. "Look. This is a temporary situation. As soon as all of *this* is over, as soon as we have some stability...do whatever you want. Hold elections or pass it on to someone else who can do the job. Take your wealth and disappear. I don't care, Vaughn, but we're in the middle of planning to defend Marakyn against a siege, yet we *must* have Ferehar or it won't matter. We can't spare an army to do this the brute-force way, and I don't want to draw attention to what we're doing anyway. I'm handing this off to you to handle in whatever way you see fit." He paused and met

Vaughn's eyes. "Do you understand?"

Vaughn tried hard to keep his eye from twitching. "I understand. May I go sleep now?"

Yaotel rubbed his temple. "Yes. Get some rest. And after you've done so, I do want to hear about the long-term solutions you think you've gained from..." He shook his head. "Your trip."

Vaughn gave him a mock salute, turned, and left.

Ivana pushed herself off the wall and followed.

Vaughn strode down the hall as if with some purpose, but the moment the door closed, he stopped and pressed his forehead to the cool of the stone wall. "What I would give to be able to get drunk right now," he muttered.

Ivana snorted. "Well. I'm sure you could find some pretty woman instead."

Burning skies, it was tempting, and he was *not* in the mood to hear her sanctimonious sentiments on that.

He turned to glare at her. "You want to know what you can do with your self-righteous opinion about my *former* vice?"

She rolled her eyes. "Not particularly."

He was tired, he was frustrated, and he'd had enough. "You can shove it. You have no idea what I've been through—no *right* to judge me."

Her jaw tightened. "What *you've* been through?"

"Oh, I'm sorry," he said, sketching a mock bow. "I forgot. You're the only one in the world who has ever had *everything* taken from them. Forgive me for my gross insensitivity."

"You don't understand in the *least*—"

"I understand enough," he snapped. "And you know, the rest of us have managed to get by without having to create an alter identity to murder people in order to cope. Because *that's* somehow less monstrous than the occasional consensual fling?"

Silence. She locked icy eyes on his.

She was probably contemplating murdering *him* now.

Instead, she shoved past him and stormed down the tunnel, leaving him alone.

He sagged back against the wall. *Smooth, Vaughn.*

And yet, it was true. She'd turned herself into a gods-damned cold-blooded killer rather than have to face the pain of her past. He wasn't going to pretend his way of dealing with life was great, but *burning skies*, it had to be better than that, right?

He swallowed. Sleep. He needed sleep.

"Because that's somehow less monstrous than the occasional consensual fling?"

Infuriating, insufferable man! Ivana thought.

He had no idea. He had never understood. He—

She sank onto a bench on the streets outside the civic gates.

He was right.

Monster.

And a coward. A weak-willed coward who hadn't been able to escape from her problems in any way other than to hurt other people to dull her own pain.

She could almost hear Aleena now. *Give yourself more grace,* she would say. *You can't go back. Only forward.*

No, she couldn't go back. But neither could she move forward. She was stuck in the present, a present in which she was still too keenly aware of her past, and a present that despaired of being able to ever have a future.

Why did Vaughn's words hurt so badly? Why in the abyss did she care what he thought?

Because he's one of the few who has ever tried to look deeper. Who has ever seen *deeper.*

And in the end, it turned out he saw her for what she really was, too.

That's not what he meant, and you know it.

She clutched her arms around herself. She felt as though she were being suffocated. Would that she had died long ago on the trip to Cadmyr, or on the streets, or by her own hand.

"Miss?" a voice said from above her.

Ivana jerked her head up.

It was a random stranger, a woman, maybe fifty, sixty years old, concern on her face. "I'm sorry. But you looked ill. Is there anything I can do?"

"No," Ivana said. "I'm just tired. Thank you."

The woman nodded and moved away.

That was it. She was tired. Exhausted in every way imaginable. Physically, emotionally, mentally. Sleep would do her a lot more good than wallowing in despair on a bench.

She stood up. She had to pull herself together. She was sliding back into a familiar pit, and if she hit bottom again...

She didn't know what might happen this time.

There was a moment of silence after Dal Vaughn and Da Ivana left.

Driskell swallowed and glanced down at his notes, some of which were written in a rather shaky hand.

He couldn't believe they were going to *take* Ferehar. Just *take* it, just like that.

"Dal Yaotel," Tanuac said, and Driskell looked back up. "Are you certain Dal Vaughn is the appropriate person for this? I understand his familial connections give us an advantage, but..."

"Yes," Yaotel said without hesitation. "Despite appearances, I can assure you he's competent and resourceful."

Tanuac exchanged a glance with Nahua. "Not exactly what I meant. If you say he can get the job done, I trust you. He just seems a bit..."

"Insubordinate? Independent? Stubborn? Yes. He's all those things and more besides. Which is what makes him especially suited for this."

Tanuac tilted his head to the side. "I'm afraid I don't follow."

Yaotel nodded toward Driskell's notes. "Your attaché has the right of it. This could far too easily evolve into something neither of us intended. A grab for power. The start of a new Empire, perhaps? Donian—or Ichtacan."

Driskell spread his hand over his notes, horrified that Yaotel had seen any of what he had written.

Tanuac held out his palm to Driskell without taking his eyes off Yaotel.

Driskell looked at Nahua, and she lifted her shoulders.

He swallowed and handed his notebook over to the Ri, raw, unfiltered opinions and all, and then bit his lip.

Tanuac looked down at his scrawl for a few moments. Then, he handed the notebook over to Nahua and addressed Driskell. "Concerns about how this makes us any better than Setana, Driskell?"

"Your Excellency," Driskell said, "I don't mean to imply that—"

"No. You're right to ask those sorts of questions. Someone needs to." Tanuac rubbed a hand over his face. "Yaotel, I'm going to guess at your meaning: this Vaughn will comply with what we want for now, but ultimately, he's not going to be controllable."

"Just so," Yaotel said. "And more likely than not, he's going to do this in a way neither you nor I would have chosen, and since I've cut him loose to do it..." He put fingers to his temples. "Gods help me, we're going to have to live with whatever he does."

Tanuac nodded curtly. "I think...perhaps you and my attaché are correct. Best not to tempt ourselves with putting someone who could too easily become a puppet in place."

Yaotel inclined his head. "He's a good man, Your Excellency. I promise you that. And if we both manage to pull off our respective missions...he'll be a worthy ally."

Nahua slid Driskell's notebook back over to him.

Driskell let out a breath and flipped the notebook to a new page immediately as he chose another chair. "Pardon," he said, "but are you sure...you don't want me to go with him?"

Yaotel shook his head. "I appreciate the offer, Dal Driskell. But you're far too new to your powers to attempt that level of manipulation. You'll better serve here."

"And *I* need you here," Tanuac said. "If for no other reason than to keep me on the right path." He flashed Driskell a rare unfiltered smile. "How is your training with Huiel going?"

"I'd say well, Your Excellency," Driskell said. "While I mean no offense to Danton and Thrax, Huiel's obviously better at training. I feel more confident in my level of control now." Huiel had started by working on his stamina and control. Driskell could maintain a constant burn of aether, just a trickle, for hours now before he began to feel even a little dizzy. He'd started taking Thrax's advice and going about his daily life burning it. Not trying to *do* anything, just practicing letting it become second nature.

Even without *trying* to do anything, he could tell the difference in how people reacted to him. It made him uncomfortable, so he tried not to do it when he'd be around people.

Huiel said that was missing the point of his powers, but it still felt *wrong*.

Yaotel chuckled. "Danton and Thrax. Along with Vaughn, it's

like the trifecta of headaches right there. Shall we call for General Gyano and continue where we left off?"

Chapter Forty-One

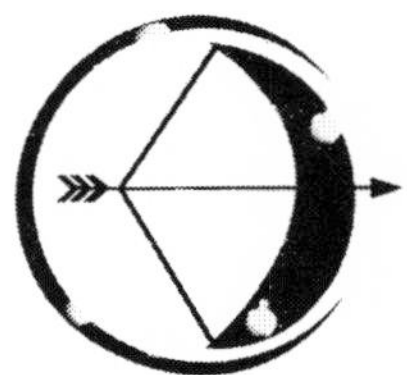

Planning

Three days later, Vaughn sat in the room he shared with Danton in the new Ichtacan headquarters, along with Danton and Thrax. Danton sat on his own bed, Vaughn on his, and in the space between the door and the beds, Thrax sat wedged on one of two chairs they had dragged in.

The other chair was empty.

His potential team. The people he trusted with his life were few and far between.

Thrax jiggled his leg up and down. "So...who are we waiting on?"

"Ivana," Vaughn said. "Maybe."

Thrax raised an eyebrow. "Maybe? Is she or isn't she coming?"

Vaughn had no idea. He had been to her room at the inn three times, and she hadn't been there any of those times. Or at least, she hadn't answered the door. The last time, he'd slid a note under the door with the details of the meeting and requesting that she be there, hoping that she hadn't decided to run. "I don't know. Hence, *maybe*."

Thrax gave him a smirk. "Lovers' quarrel, eh?"

Vaughn rolled his eyes. "We're not lovers."

"No judgment here, friend," Thrax said, holding up his hands.

"We're not lovers."

"Oh...*right*. You don't do the whole long-term thing. Or mid-term. Or even short-te—oof."

Danton had smacked him with a pillow. "Thrax, knock it off."

Vaughn closed his eyes and drew in a deep breath. Was this how Yaotel felt sometimes? He ought to apologize sometime for being such a pain in the ass. It was a little different when the roles were reversed, wasn't it?

A few nights of decent sleep in a decent bed had cured him of physical exhaustion, but mentally...

"I'm sensing an elevated tension level in this room," Thrax said. "When do we get to find out what's going on?"

Vaughn opened his eyes. "We can go ahead." Ivana already knew most of this anyway.

There was a knock on the door. Thrax leaned his chair back on two legs to a precarious point, reached behind him, and tugged the door open.

Ivana stepped in.

Vaughn let out a silent sigh of relief. It would have been a prayer of thanks, but he hadn't prayed *before* going to visit the gods. He certainly wasn't going to start now.

Thrax nudged the empty chair. "Good timing," he said. "Vaughn was about to enlighten us as to what all the mystery is about."

She shut the door and sat down, her arms folded across her chest, her face blank.

Thrax pushed his chair back on two legs again. Danton leaned forward, his elbows on his knees, expression attentive.

Here goes nothing.

"So, you already know the present Conclave threat to Marakyn, which will ultimately mean a threat to Donia—and her allies. You already know about the Xambrian proposal. And you already know that Ferehar isn't cooperating. To my continuing dismay, Yaotel has tasked me with dealing with the final problem."

"Let me guess," Thrax said, "you're about to in turn task us to help you deal with the final problem."

"Yes." He shrugged sheepishly. "Sorry."

"So, what's the plan?" Danton asked.

"That's partially what we're here to decide. But the big picture is that we oust Airell and I take his place."

Thrax's chair came back down on all fours with a thud. "*What*?"

Danton blinked a few times, then comprehension dawned on his face. "*That's* what all this business with Ferehar was about..."

Ivana remained silent, neither body language nor face betraying her feelings on the matter.

"Ferehar's resistance has little to do with the people and everything to do with who's in charge. Put a different person in charge, the whole story changes." Vaughn sighed. "This is coming from Yaotel and Ri Tanuac. I have absolutely no desire to be Ri of Ferehar or anywhere else, but Yaotel thinks my family connections will make it easier for me to usurp the position and maintain my hold on it."

"And then you'll immediately agree to the Xambrian alliance on behalf of Ferehar, of course," Thrax said, rubbing his index finger on his trousers, a thoughtful expression on his face.

"That's the idea."

"So, we're what, some sort of strike team?" Danton asked.

"Sort of. Tanuac isn't sending an army. He's sending us. Well, he's sending me, and I'm *asking* you to help me." He looked around. "You can say *no*."

Danton and Thrax exchanged a glance.

Danton spoke first. "You know I'm with you, Vaughn."

"Sounds like fun," Thrax said, grinning. "The coup here was getting a little boring, anyway. Too much talking, not enough action."

"You just want to set things on fire," Danton accused.

"Yes!" Thrax said, pointing at Danton as though he'd solved a difficult mathematics problem. "There has been absolutely *no* excuse to burn things here. Bor-ing."

"Let's not get ahead of ourselves," Vaughn said. "I can't guarantee kindling in Ferehar either, Thrax. In fact, I'm hoping to avoid a fight."

Thrax groaned and slapped his palm to his forehead. "Shoulda asked before agreeing..."

"You think your brother's just going to hand over the position to you without a fight?" Danton said.

"No, Airell won't. But"—he glanced again at Ivana, who might as well have been a statue for all the insight she was giving into her thoughts—"Aleena's been in Ferehar for three weeks now, gathering intelligence, and her initial report confirms what I already knew: nearly everyone except his own circle of friends hates him. I'm still personally dubious that they'll hate a Banebringer any less, but those in charge are willing to take that chance."

"So what do you need us for?" Thrax asked. "Have him offed." He made a slicing motion across his throat. "Done. Simple."

Vaughn dared to sneak another glance at Ivana. Still nothing. "I mean, that's one option."

"One *option*?" Thrax asked. "Without an army, what other option is there?"

Vaughn frowned at him. "Assassination is simple on the surface, sure, but it sets a dangerous precedent. I still have to hold the position without someone offing me in turn. It's not like I'm someone already there who's been groomed to gracefully slide into an open position, and as you noted, I'm not bringing an army with me." He exhaled. In fact, he was certain that Yaotel had that first "option" exactly in mind. Especially since they were all acquainted with a former assassin who could do the job nicely. But after mulling it over the past few days, he'd decided that would be a last resort. "Besides that, I would prefer…" He ran a hand through his hair. "Let's contact Aleena. She should be waiting."

He leaned over and picked up his qixli from the bedside table, held it between two hands, and waited.

A moment later, the impression of a face pressed up against the silvery aether. "Aleena. It's Vaughn. I've explained the situation and everyone's here."

Aleena's voice came through the qixli, metallic as usual. "Great."

"So, let's have it," Vaughn said. "We know everyone hates Airell and things aren't stable. What are we looking at more specifically?"

"I've been able to ingratiate myself to some key palace personnel, and 'not stable' is an understatement. Airell hasn't even been back to the palace in weeks, and apparently that's normal."

"Confirms the rumors I heard," Vaughn said.

Aleena made a sound that might have been a grunt of acknowledgment. "His Gan are furious. Less because they disagree philosophically with his policies and more because he isn't *doing* anything and so they have to pick up the slack."

"So what's he been doing, if not Ri'ing?" Thrax asked.

A tinny cough. "Lazing about at his country estate spending Ferehar's coffers on alcohol and women, if the accounts of him are to be believed. And making absurd demands when it suits him, like raising taxes for no reason—at least, no reason he's explained to the populace."

Vaughn raised an eyebrow. "And with this extra money...?"

"I've managed to get a peek at his books," Aleena said. "He's been funneling a good bit of it to Weylyn City."

Vaughn straightened up. "Now *that's* interesting. More than the normal percentage?"

"Much more."

Vaughn glanced toward Ivana. "So. It seems reports that Airell has thrown himself in with the Conclave aren't without merit."

"Oh, those are no rumors," Aleena said. "Airell's made no secret of the fact that he's the Conclave's favored Ri. He struts about boasting about the rewards he's going to reap when 'the rest of those disloyal dogs get what's coming to them.'"

"Wow. What an ass," Danton said.

That roused a muttered remark from Ivana. "That's an understatement."

And he had been certain she was planning to sit there in stony silence the entire meeting.

"He's almost universally hated," Aleena said. "Worse than Gildas. Gildas was hard—but from what I could gather, he at least had a gift for administration. He kept things running smoothly."

Vaughn nodded at that. "My father was...not a nice man," he said, "but he was also competent."

"Well, Airell is both not nice and incompetent," Aleena said. "Though I've heard he can be charming when he wants to be."

"Yes, he can," Vaughn interjected, "and don't be misled into thinking his ineptness is borne of stupidity." He ran a hand through his hair, remembering all the times Airell had deliberately gotten Vaughn and his other two brothers into trouble just to be malicious—and wheedled his way out of any responsibility himself. No, he was a snake. A selfish, indolent snake. "He's just self-centered, arrogant, and cruel. He uses his natural charisma to get what he wants, but once someone's no longer useful to him, he won't hesitate to discard them—or worse."

Ivana shifted. He supposed she understood too personally how true that was.

"That makes sense of some reports I heard of him, then," Aleena said. "Initially, he persuaded everyone he'd be good for Ferehar. But it didn't take long for that charade to be exposed. By all accounts, the affairs of Ferehar are in complete disarray, and it wasn't hard getting people to talk. His own servants—right up to Gildas' steward, whom Airell relieved of duty—are overflowing with frustration and are happy to have an understanding ear to vent to."

Vaughn shook his head. "As long as he continues to get what he wants, he won't waste effort pretending that he gives one whit about anything other than himself."

"An attitude that works for breezing in and out of a town to charm all the young ladies out of their virginity and businessmen into bad deals," Thrax said. "Not so great for holding a long-term position of power. How is he still Ri?"

"Fear," Aleena said. "There've been some rumblings of protest, but from what I can gather, right now people are too afraid of what he and his lackeys might do if they tried to challenge him. He's surrounded himself with like-minded people who tell him what he wants to hear and do what he tells them to do as long as he gives them what *they* want."

Thrax snapped his fingers and tore a tiny spark from one of the lamps in the room to dance on his fingertips. "So. What's this all leading to? What's your grand plan?"

"I intend to take Ferehar legally," Vaughn said. "By forcing Airell to hold the elections he never held, running against him, and winning."

Thrax groaned and Danton's eyebrows shot sky-high. "Pretty sure putting a Gifted in power would still be considered illegal to the Conclave, whether or not you win," Danton said.

"I don't care what the Conclave thinks," Vaughn said. "Considering I'm going to declare Fereharian sovereignty, it doesn't matter. I just want it to seem legitimate to the people. To *be* legitimate to the people. If that's even possible as a Banebringer."

Thrax wasn't impressed. "Burning skies, all you people are *so* upright, it's almost disgusting. We're in the middle of a rebellion here! If that isn't an excuse to get a little 'ethically nebulous,' I don't know what is. Live a little!"

Vaughn sighed. "Look. I know you all think I'm crazy. But if I have to be Ri, I want to start right. Seizing power through brute force would be completely normal in Ferehar—even expected. But Setanan law dictates that the next Ri be chosen by the appointed representatives, *not* handed down to the closest relative. Airell's seizure of power is illegal. If I can come in and win an election, no one can then further challenge me—legally—and I will have done something that no Fereharian Ri in recent memory has done, setting me apart from my own family's corrupt history." Which was something he was eager to do. He wasn't his brother, he wasn't his father, or his father's cousin before him. He wanted to be different.

"I think Vaughn's plan could work," Aleena put in, "if we can get Airell to hold elections. But how are you going to *force* him to do that in the first place?"

"Send a letter," Thrax said. "March up to the palace and demand he relinquish his title and hold elections. I'm sure *that* will go well."

Vaughn was starting to get a headache. He didn't need to hash out the entirety of his plan right now; he just needed Danton and Thrax to know what they were getting into. "I have an idea, but I'm still thinking it over."

"Think fast, Vaughn," Aleena said. "Last time I talked to Yaotel, he said he wants this done as quickly as possible."

"Yes, I'm aware. Thanks, Aleena."

He set the qixli aside and tossed a wry smile at Ivana, hoping to chip away at some of her stone. "Bet Yaotel'd love it if we could zap ourselves there like Tani and not waste the time in travel."

Ivana tilted her head to the side. "Maybe we could."

Vaughn blinked. "What?"

Ivana pointed to Danton. "Taniqotalin is Danton's patron."

Vaughn sat back. "You...think he could do the same thing?"

Ivana shrugged. "No idea. But it's worth exploring, isn't it?"

Danton looked back and forth between Vaughn and Ivana. "Try what? What could I do?"

"So, Taniqotalin," Vaughn said. "Your patron. He could zap himself—and others with him—instantly from place to place."

Danton's eyes widened. "You *met* Taniqotalin? Was he...nice? I mean..."

"The nicest of the lot," Vaughn said. "Though maybe still a bit full of himself. At any rate...what if you could do the same thing?"

Danton bit his lip. "That seems like an awfully incredible feat."

"Well, experiment with it if you get the chance. It could come in handy, even if you can't take us all instantly to Ferehar."

Danton nodded.

A knock on the door made him jump.

They all looked at each other.

"You expecting someone else?" Thrax whispered.

Vaughn shook his head. He stood, wiped his hands on his trousers, squeezed through the gap between Thrax's and Ivana's chairs, and opened the door a crack.

It was Dal Driskell.

Vaughn opened the door. "Come in. Sorry. Had no idea who it was."

Driskell stepped into the room and closed the door behind him. "I'm sorry. Am I interrupting something?"

"We were planning," Vaughn said. "For my takeover of Ferehar. But we're pretty much done."

"Oh. Uh. Yeah." He hesitated. "I was looking for Danton."

"You've found him," Vaughn said, gesturing at Danton.

Danton rose. "Is this private?"

"No, no. I wanted to invite you to, um, Tania's great-grandmother's birthday celebration tomorrow afternoon. If you're not otherwise busy." He looked around. "Of course, all of you are welcome. There will be plenty of food and drink to go around."

Danton grinned far too wide for the occasion. Did he *know* Tania's great-grandmother?

"I wouldn't miss it," he said.

"And I'm always ready for free food and drink, if you really don't mind!" Thrax said, slapping his knee.

Driskell shook his head. "Don't mind at all." He flashed them all a smile and turned to go.

Danton left with Driskell, and Thrax soon after. Ivana seemed almost as if she wanted to linger, casting a glance at the still qixli, but ultimately she, too, started toward the door.

Vaughn stopped her. They hadn't spoken since their...argument...three days ago. "You were awfully quiet. Any thoughts?"

She turned and contemplated him for a moment, then shook her head. "I understand what you're trying to do, but you're relying on Airell's compliance. He's not going to give a damn about holding an election. What's your idea?"

Vaughn paced back and forth in the only available space in his room, right in front of the door. "I'm not relying on Airell's compliance. Everyone hates Airell. Exceptionally so. Even his own household staff, according to Aleena. There's no loyalty there; I can use that."

"All right...how?"

"When a Ri is absent, his steward or closest living relative, if no steward was appointed, governs in his stead. Airell discharged my father's old steward, as you recall. That makes my mother Gildas' closest living relative. *She* is the one who should be acting as regent before a lawfully elected Ri is installed, not Airell. Therefore, *she* could unseat Airell temporarily and call for elections.

Ivana gave him a dubious look. "Why has she not already done so, then?"

"I doubt it's even crossed her mind. No one holds elections in Ferehar. What my brother did is in keeping with generations of practice; her asserting herself would do nothing...unless, of course, there's someone else to challenge Airell."

"And you think she'll help you?"

"She helped me once before."

"Helping you escape torture is a little different than helping you overthrow Ferehar—especially when one of her other sons is at the helm," Ivana said.

True. And yet... "I have no way of knowing for sure until we ask her."

"That's a bit shaky."

"I know." A heavy ball settled in Vaughn's stomach. The fate of hundreds of thousands of people not only rested on him coming up with a viable plan but succeeding.

But he was resolute. This would be Plan A. "But I'm committed to trying this."

She said nothing.

He hesitated. "You're really with us on this?"

She shrugged. "Did you tell Yaotel about me?"

"Yes. I gave him a full report." He eyed her. "Well. A full report of anything relevant, anyway."

"Not that I personally care, but he's given his blessing to me—Zily's only Banebringer—going with you?"

Vaughn rubbed the back of his neck. "I haven't asked. He told me he was giving this over to me to plan and execute, and I think he means it."

It *was* a valid question—whether Yaotel would want someone who could become important to their long-term plans out from under his purview. But it didn't really matter; Ivana wasn't someone Yaotel could control. If she wanted to help, she would, and if she didn't, she wouldn't.

"All right, so tell me, what else am I going to do? Sit around and wait for your researchers to track me down and demand I provide them with pints of blood to experiment on? For Huiel to track me down and demand I start training my new powers?" She snorted. "For *Yaotel* to try to tell me what to do?"

He exhaled. "This means going back to Ferehar again."

"Thank you. I'm aware."

"It almost certainly means running into Airell."

"You think I can't handle it," she stated flatly.

"Well, I mean, the last time we were in Ferehar, you did sneak off to murder an old enemy, getting me captured and endangering our timetable."

She grunted. "And I also rescued you, didn't I? From Airell's own estate house. And did I stop to murder him, too?"

"You know, I was never certain what you might do." In this case, she had controlled herself, thank the gods—no, strike that—thank...

Not having actual gods to swear by was sort of inconvenient.

"I'll be *fine*," she said. "And if it turns out you need me to off him, all the better."

Vaughn studied her face. Any trace of a lost, confused, hurting, or even angry woman was gone. She was now calm, collected, confident. "You really want to do that?"

She gave him a mirthless smile. "Kill Airell? Are you seriously asking me that?"

He shifted. He liked her not being confused. He wasn't sure he liked the return of the cold killer. "I thought Sweetblade was dead. I thought you wanted her to stay that way."

"Are you paying me?"

"Uh...no...?"

"Well, then. There we go. Sweetblade only took money."

"Right. I forgot. Ivana murders people for the fun of it."

Her eyes flashed, and he regretted the words as soon as he said them, remembering her reaction a few days ago—but she merely flicked her hand at him. "You exaggerate. It was *only* one person, and it was *revenge*, not fun."

"You do realize that normal people don't sit around congratulating themselves on how they *only* murdered one person last month, right?"

She blinked, opened her mouth, and then fell into silence. Then she stood up. Her face was hard.

Wrong thing to say—again. "Ivana... Look, about the other day. I'm sorry for what I said. You know I didn't mean—"

"It's fine."

"But—"

"An apology assumes I felt offended. Since I don't care in the slightest what you think of me or my decisions, I wasn't."

"Oh, come on. You were obviously angry."

"I was *tired*. Are we done here?" She moved toward the door.

He caught her arm. "Are we really doing this again, after everything we've been through? Are you ever going to let me in and let me *stay* there?"

She shook her arm out of his grasp. "Awfully serious for you, Vaughn."

"I-I'm concerned about you. You seem—"

"Then you're wasting your mental energy." She gave him one last indecipherable look, then left.

Chapter Forty-Two

Normal People

Ivana's throat was tight as she made her way back to her room at the inn.

"Normal people don't sit around congratulating themselves on how they only murdered one person last month..."

He was right, of course.

Which meant she wasn't normal.

Despite the gorgeous day, the world seemed to darken around her. The dagger, now at her thigh again and hidden under the wrap at her hips, suddenly seemed heavy. She had chosen to wear the traditional warm-weather garb of Donian women—a calf-length wrap and loose-fitting blouse that ended below her bust—when out and about because it made it easier to hide her dagger, and it was less conspicuous than wearing trousers and a cloak in the middle of summer. Was that a normal reason?

She passed the inn and kept walking, leaving the government tier behind. She soon came to the sixth tier, which boasted mostly the larger homes of the city's wealthiest residents. The streets were sparsely populated until she reached the end closest to the gate down to the fifth tier. There was a bustling commercial district, where high class establishments catering to those same wealthy individuals had sprung up.

She paused to run her hands over a bolt of silk hanging on a display outside a clothier. A rather normal thing to do. The callouses on her hands weren't—at least callouses in her particular arrangement.

The door to the shop was open to let through the breeze, and the shopkeeper moved quickly out to greet her. Ivana didn't look at her, but she could feel the woman appraising her—her class, how much she was likely to spend, where she should direct her attentions for the best sale.

Something about her must have convinced the woman she didn't have the money for silk; probably the bronze of Ivana's clearly Fereharian skin. Fereharians weren't known for being wealthy. "Lovely, isn't it?" the woman asked politely. "That's just in from Venetia, and from there, Yunqi. I'm not sure the color is right for you, however. May I direct your attention to this lovely laquen? It comes from the southern nomads, so it's just as exotic, without the exotic price tag."

It was ironic that, despite her appearance, Ivana could likely buy not only a length of that silk, but the entire bolt without dipping too deeply into her coffers—savings built up and invested from a decade of a lucrative business.

And 50,000 setans from her father.

That was hardly normal, either.

The woman held out a length of the laquen. "Touch it," she

urged. "It's incredibly soft."

Ivana obliged her, running her fingers over the fabric. "It is soft," she said honestly. "How much would it be to have a simple ciuhan made from this?" she asked, naming a popular Fereharian garment for women. If she was going back to Ferehar for what was essentially a covert operation, she might as well look the part.

The woman looked her over with a critical eye. Ivana could almost hear her calculating the best price she thought she could get out of someone like Ivana—an unknown Fereharian woman walking the wealthiest tier in Marakyn, in the guise of calculating measurements. "I'd say about ten setans," she said. "Eight for the cloth, and two for the labor."

Ivana produced a carefully calculated wince. "Eight seems inflated. I think I may have seen this same cloth down on the fourth tier for two setans less." She gave the woman a dubious look, as if to ask her if she were cheating her.

The woman seemed horrified at the very thought of her going to the fourth tier for this cloth. "Seven for the cloth," she said quickly. "And if you need additional alterations, I'll throw them in for free."

"I'd also like a second one made in this one," she said, fingering a cheaper muslin bolt for everyday wear. "I'll pay you nine for both—plus the two for labor—if you can have both done by this time tomorrow."

"Done," the woman said.

Ivana nodded, satisfied. "Excellent."

The woman whipped out her measuring tape from her apron on the spot, and while she took down Ivana's measurements, Ivana considered that it was also not normal to file every bit of detail about someone during a mundane purchase of cloth for a dress.

Ivana slipped her pick-up slip into her pocket, thanked the shopkeeper, and continued on.

No, there was no doubt about it. Nothing about her was normal. Discarding a name hadn't changed the essence of who she was inside.

Someone who still wore a dagger hidden at her thigh, and who could take life with hardly a second thought.

A decade of training and practice had deadened her to such things, and yet the pain of her youth, the pain that had led her to mold herself in that way, still existed, was still trying to claw its way to the surface of her psyche at every opportunity.

She had gained one without losing the other.

In other words, now that she no longer had Sweetblade, everything she had done, everything she had become, was meaningless.

It was easy to look at herself with an objective eye right now when the sun was shining, when confronting Airell was theoretical, when she wasn't so frightened of who or what she might be that she was ready to drown herself in the oblivion of a few moments of pleasure she might regret, when she felt nothing more than restless and suffocated. It was easy to think that she had everything under control.

But deep inside, she was frightened of herself. Of what she might do, of how the unholy marriage of apathy and agony might lead her to act when she was stretched to her limit—when she lost control.

Vaughn was right to be nervous.

She was anything but normal.

And she hated this new version of herself as much as any other.

Chapter Forty-Three

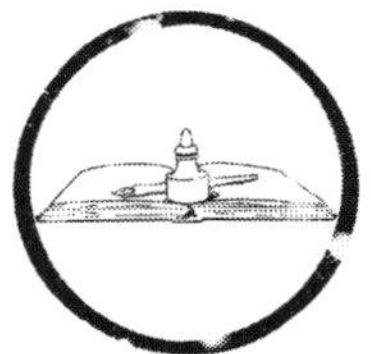

An Odd Pastime

The sun was shining. The grass was green. The sky overhead was blue. It was a bit on the warm side, but that only meant that, under the shawl draped over her shoulders, Tania had donned a blouse that ended below the bust, baring her midriff at the sides. Food and drink were set out in the clearing for the celebration that would start in about an hour, but guests hadn't arrived yet. Tania had asked Driskell if he wanted to take a turn around the garden, and so there they were.

Driskell should have been deliriously happy on a day like today, hand-in-hand with the woman he loved, the woman he had hoped to marry before the year was out. He had been planning for months to ask her today. Now. Everything had fallen into place exactly as he had hoped. Even the weather had cooperated.

It was *perfect*.

Except that he felt sick to his stomach.

They walked in the garden on the fourth tier. They weren't alone, but the garden was large and sprawling and designed to afford some privacy to wanderers.

He had to tell her. He *had* to. They'd been speaking of marriage, unofficially, for months. She would say *yes*. Waiting until she found out in some accident was not an option. Yet if he told her, there was more at stake than their own relationship. What if she turned him in? The Ichtaca could most likely protect him now, but if it became public, he might lose his position. They'd be forced to let him go, right? Yet if he didn't ask today, her father would wonder why. For that matter, her own great-grandmother would wonder why. She had been the one who'd insisted she share the attention on this day.

Unsavory political opinions aside, they were genuinely nice people.

As long as one wasn't a Banebringer.

"So quiet," Tania said softly. "What are you thinking over there, my little analyzer?"

He swallowed. "Oh, I don't know…" he said evasively.

She pulled him a little closer, removing her hand from his and instead sliding his arm around her waist to rest on the bare flesh there, and then she snugged herself against his side.

Would she be sighing in such contentment if she knew his hands contained blood that would turn silver?

And even if she could somehow stomach it—what of her family?

"Mmm," she said. "You're lying."

He couldn't tell her yet. But how could he ask her for her hand if she didn't know? That seemed unfair. Even if… Even *if* she was content with his being a Banebringer, she had to know what she was getting herself into. What might happen to him, if he were caught. Especially if he were caught outside Marakyn. What might happen to *her*.

"Your uncle was making jokes about drowning Banebringers again this morning," he said. "While I was helping him bring food up."

She laughed lightly. "Oh, Driskell. This again?" She pulled away and stopped walking so that they could face one another. "I wish I knew why this bothers you so."

"It bothers me because—" His breath caught in his throat. "Because people talk that way. We all do; we all have at some point. And yet, at any sky-fire, any one of us could be changed. Your *father* could be. Would he still talk that way? Why is there such animosity over something that seems so...random?"

The smile slipped off Tania's lips. She studied his face with those beautiful soft brown eyes, the eyes that would crinkle at the sides just so, the eyes that had looked at him shyly—and mischievously—under lowered eyelashes that first day of class and had made him fall in love with her.

"The priests say it isn't random," she said quietly. "That only those with wickedness in their hearts would be chosen."

"That's what the priests *say*," Driskell said in a lowered voice, "but those same priests are the ones who staged a coup in Weylyn City. Who, by some reports, were using the Banebringers' own magic. How can we trust what they say?"

Tania looked down and then around quickly. "I-I don't necessarily disagree with you. But you can't deny that Banebringers are still *dangerous*."

Driskell looked past her shoulder, into the bushes behind them. "Aren't we all, in some way?" he said quietly.

Tania put a hand on his cheek, bringing his attention back to her. "Driskell. What's this about?"

He bit his lip. "I-I just—I've been thinking about it a lot lately. First the Conclave coup. And then for a while we had a Xambrian ambassador, and, Tania, he didn't seem so bad—and your family keeps harping on it. It's as though they need to have someone to hate, for the sake of it. Can't we just give everyone a chance? As individuals?"

She ran a finger down his cheek and across his jaw and then drew him into an embrace and buried her face in his neck. She didn't say anything else for a long time.

Normally, he would have appreciated that. But now, he was keenly aware of the minutes ticking closer to the start of the party. Even now, he could hear voices. He was supposed to have already asked her by now. Gods...

"Who do you know that was changed this sky-fire?" Tania asked at last, breath tickling his neck.

His stomach dropped out from him. Why did she have to be so perceptive? There was no point in denying that something of the sort had happened. He turned his head to put his face in her hair. "I can't tell you that. I...I just can't." He bit his lip. "And it kills me that I can't," he whispered.

She pulled back and cupped his face in her hands. "Driskell, I love you. And I understand."

He blinked. "You...You do?"

"Yes. And...I don't want to know. I don't want to be put in the position of having to decide what to do. I don't want to put you in the position of breaching a confidence. If at some point, I find out... We'll figure it out then. Just don't say anything to my relatives, okay?"

He gave a shaky laugh. "As if I would." He studied her. "Do you hate Banebringers as much as they do?"

She sighed. "I don't know what to think or what to believe. But I do agree that...well, their talk makes me uncomfortable. I don't like it, either. Is... Is that enough?"

He pushed a lock of hair out of her eyes, and those sincere, sweet eyes completely undid him. "Will you be my wife, Tania?" he asked.

Her lips curled into a smile. "Finally," she said.

"Is that a *yes*?"

She laughed. "Driskell, don't be an idiot." And then she kissed him.

His heart thudded wildly, at the press of her lips and at the fear coiled in his gut.

She might accept him. But would she ever forgive him?

Vaughn turned the corner of the long row of hedges, Danton and Ivana behind him, and drew up short.

Driskell and his lady friend were embracing ahead.

He cleared his throat. "My, what a lovely day," he said loudly.

Driskell pulled back, a flush creeping up his neck. "Oh," he said. "Uh...hello. Tania, these are—"

"Your new friends," she said, smiling. She curtsied. "I remember you told me you invited them. I'm so glad you could make it. The party is this way."

She moved farther down the row of hedges, and they all followed her.

Danton caught Driskell's arm and pulled him back. "Well?" he whispered.

Driskell flashed him a smile and nodded.

Danton slapped his back and they disappeared around another corner of the maze, leaving Vaughn and Ivana alone.

She slowed her steps. "Why did I let you and Danton talk me into this?" she asked. "Danton is Driskell's new friend. He only invited us because we were there, and I'm sure he thought it would be rude not to."

Vaughn shrugged. "So? Thrax is right. Free food and drink, dancing... Why in the abyss would you pass up an opportunity to party?"

She frowned. "I can think of many reasons."

"Come now. I've seen you appear to be the perfect socialite before."

She flashed him a wry look. "Appearances can be deceiving."

He grinned. "So you're saying the *real* Ivana is a dour-faced fun-hater who wouldn't know a party if it hit her over the head?"

Her frown deepened. "I...can have...fun." She didn't sound sure of that.

"What a resounding affirmation," he said drily. "Can you really?" On a whim, he grabbed her hand and twirled her around, and then pulled her close. Before she could inevitably push him away, he dipped her backward. "Are you diverted yet?"

"Put me down!"

He dropped her gently to the grass.

She scowled at him, stood up, and brushed herself off.

"You're not making your case very well," he said, wagging his finger at her.

She folded her arms across her chest. "My idea of entertainment is not an afternoon making inane conversation with people I don't know."

That didn't surprise him. "Fair enough," he said. "Then what *is* your idea of entertainment? Name it, and we can do that instead."

She opened her mouth, closed it, and then opened it again.

He raised an eyebrow at her. "I'm waiting."

Danton appeared in the hedges. "Hey, you two. Are you coming? Party's getting started." He gave them a meaningful look—except Vaughn had no idea what the meaning was supposed to be.

The rapid change on Ivana's face was incredible. "Of course," she said, smiling. "We'll be right there."

So she *could* still act if she wanted to. Apparently, she just didn't care around Vaughn. He supposed that was a good thing?

He nudged her in the ribs and leaned over to speak in her ear. "You're saved for now. But I'm still waiting for a good answer."

She glared at him.

He gave her a charming smile and offered his arm.

She spurned it and marched ahead.

By the time Vaughn and Ivana had slipped into the back of the clearing where the food tables were set up, most of the guests had arrived—including Thrax—and were gathered together, facing a sharply-dressed middle-aged Donian gentleman standing with a *very* old Donian woman. Her back was bowed, her dark brown Donian skin lightened and spotted with age, and she clutched a cane with thin, bony hands, but her sparkling eyes told Vaughn she still had her wits.

The man held a rope in his hand, and he gestured toward Driskell and Tania.

Tania looked confused as Driskell pulled her to the front.

The man nodded at the old woman. "You all have gathered here for my grandmother's one hundredth birthday." The crowd cheered with abandon, and the man waited until the noise had died down before continuing. "What few of you know is that what you have *in fact* gathered for is also..." He moved to stand behind Driskell and Tania and suddenly looped the rope over the two and pulled it tight. "A celebration of my daughter's pending marriage to Driskell!"

Vaughn guffawed. He glanced at Danton, who was beaming

at his new friend. Obviously, Danton had already been in the know.

Tania's mouth dropped open, and then she grinned and swatted playfully at Driskell. "You oaf," she said. "I can't believe you. What if I had turned you down?"

He grinned stupidly.

"Then it would have been just my birthday celebration," the old woman said, a crooked smile on her gnarled face.

"Kiss! Kiss! Kiss!" chanted the guests.

Tania unwound herself from the rope and leaned over to give the old woman a kiss on the cheek. "Grandmama," she said. "You're a dear."

The guests laughed and booed, and many took up the chant again while others broke off to find more food and drink.

"Burning skies," Ivana muttered when Tania and Driskell obliged the remaining crowd. "I need a drink."

Her oddly out-of-place disgust amused him. "You know it won't do anything, right?" he whispered.

She groaned and instead filled an empty plate from one of the many platters set up on small round tables around the clearing. "Then I need to stuff myself until I burst and put myself out of this misery."

Music started up nearby. Thrax waved to them and joined the impromptu dancing.

Vaughn shook his head. He hoped Thrax didn't get too excited, forget himself, and start juggling fireballs. "What's wrong? Not one for a little romance?"

She turned murderous eyes on him, but before she could retort, Danton bounded toward them, a goofy grin on his face. "She had no idea!" he proclaimed. "*Everyone* knew. Her parents, her grandmama—everyone was in on it!" He inclined his head, as if in response to some imagined objection. "Well, not *everyone*, of course."

"Poor Driskell," Vaughn said. "It would have been pretty embarrassing had she turned him down."

Danton waved his hand. "Eh, she wasn't going to turn him down. They've been talking about marriage for months."

Vaughn raised an eyebrow. "You sure know a lot about our new friend."

Danton shrugged, seeming uncomfortable. "You know. We have a lot in common. We kinda hit it off." He leaned in toward them conspiratorially. "Did I tell you I tried out that instant transportation thing?" he whispered. "I can actually do it."

Vaughn raised an eyebrow, partially at the obvious change of subject, and partially because he was surprised Danton had figured it out so quickly. "Really? How far?"

"All I've done is a few feet. More than that, I pass out. But I think if I keep practicing, I could go farther." He flushed. "On the negative side, I'm certain I don't have time to be of any use to, uh, the thing you suggested it for, but..."

Vaughn glanced at Ivana to see her reaction, but she wasn't paying attention to their conversation. Instead, she was watching Driskell and Tania, who had begun a dance and drinking game with some of the guests. As he watched, Driskell downed a glass and set it aside so his hands were free for his bride-to-be.

"Boy has quite the constitution," Ivana commented softly. "That's the third glass he's had in the past ten minutes, and he seems none the worse for wear."

"Wha...?" Danton said, looking confused. Then his eyes widened. "Excuse me," he muttered, then threaded his way through the crowd toward Driskell.

"No," Vaughn said. It couldn't be. Driskell would have said something, wouldn't he have? What with the Ichtaca under Donian protection now...surely...

Ivana shrugged. "Just making an observation."

Uproarious laughter sounded from nearby, and the tail end of a conversation drifted to their ears—and everyone else in the clearing.

"Then I said, why not take all the demonspawn out on a boat and toss them overboard?"

Someone slapped the speaker on the back. "Always thinking, Pop."

Vaughn turned away, clenching the drink he had plucked off a tray in his hand. Now he remembered why he hated social occasions ever since becoming a Banebringer. Suddenly, the joyous occasion seemed too loud, too bright, too happy, too full of people who would never have to know the fear he constantly lived in.

It'd been such a long time since he'd done anything like this, and he had been feeling so unusually unhated in Marakyn, among normal people. But then again, they had mostly been allies.

And he was going to put himself forward as the Ri of Ferehar? It was insane. Even if they succeeded to that point, the people would never accept him—no matter how many orphanages he opened or setans he poured into the region.

Driskell had heard the statement too. The smile slipped off his face. Just for an instant before he plastered it back on again. It was enough for Vaughn to confirm the guess.

Tania glanced at Driskell and then frowned in the direction of her father.

Did she know? And she'd still agreed to marry him?

The festivities continued unhindered by the careless statement, but Vaughn no longer felt like celebrating.

Someone took up the chant again until there was a critical mass. "Kiss! Kiss! Kiss!"

Tania laughed, kissed a flushed Driskell again, and then called out to the crowd. "The next time you do that, we're picking two of you at random to kiss instead!"

They cheered. Apparently, the threat had fallen on deaf ears.

"What's wrong?" Ivana whispered in his ear. "Not one for a little romance?"

"Some people seem to have all the luck," he said, his eyes still on the almost disgustingly sweet couple.

Her reply was laced with amusement. "*Luck*? Because *you've* been dutifully cultivating commitment all these years?"

"That's not what I meant," he said, his throat tight. He turned toward her. "Perhaps I never mentioned how my former fiancée turned on me?"

The tiny quirk that had lifted one corner of her mouth faded. "You might have mentioned it," she said.

She met his eyes and held them. He took a deep breath. "Are you enjoying this?" he asked.

"It's one of the most miserable things I've had to endure all month," she said, plastering a smile on her face that belied her words. "And that's saying something."

He jerked his head toward the exit. "I don't think anyone will notice if we slip out."

They had almost made it to one of the entrances back into the hedge maze when the crowd took up its chant again.

Then, above the noise, he distinctly heard Danton's voice. "Those two!"

Vaughn turned, startled. *What in the—?* he started to mouth at Danton until he noticed that everyone had looked where Danton was pointing.

Everyone cheered. Driskell looked apologetic. Danton was grinning from ear to ear.

Burning skies, kid can't even get drunk, and he's still acting stupid,

Vaughn thought. Ivana was going to kill Danton. Possibly him as well, even though it wasn't his fault.

"Kiss! Kiss! Kiss!"

He rolled his eyes and turned toward Ivana. He didn't expect her to be at all inclined to give in to the peer pressure, which was why he was shocked when, instead of another murderous glare, he found her lips on his.

He stumbled backward a bit, but then he caught her against himself and dutifully, he felt, kissed her back.

The crowd cheered again, obviously pleased at his apparent shock and recovery.

Her lips curled in a smile against his own, and only then did he realize what she was doing. He obliged her, and together, they gave the crowd quite the show—so much so that the cheering died down and someone coughed uncomfortably. Only then, did she pull back and *bow*. He saluted the crowd and pulled her out of the clearing.

Once they were out of sight and hearing, Ivana collapsed against one of the hedges in a fit of laughter. She was losing it. It was as though she could feel her sanity slipping away beneath her fingers.

"I take it back," Vaughn said. "You entertain yourself by making crowds of slightly inebriated people uncomfortable. A bit of an odd pastime, but, you know, whatever works for you."

"Idiots," she said savagely. "Serves them right."

"Hey," he said, "seems *I'm* the victim here. Could have warned me."

She snorted and raised an eyebrow at him. "As if you minded."

Vaughn pulled her out of the hedge by one hand, and then he wrapped the other around her waist, drawing her close to him again. "Fair enough," he said. "But, damn, Ivana, if you're going to keep throwing yourself at me like this, I'm going to start getting ideas."

Her breath caught in her throat as his eyes slid to her lips. "Ideas?" she said, unconsciously letting her lips part and tilting her head up toward him.

He stared down at her for a moment, the raw longing creeping into his eyes making her entire body ache. And then he took her silent invitation, touching his lips to hers once more, this time more gently, not even a true kiss, just the barest, intoxicating brush.

"Yes," he whispered, without pulling back, letting his breath tickle her lips. "Ideas like maybe I'm not the only one who still wants this."

Yes, every part of her body cried. *I want this.*

Did she? And what would that solve? Would it make her understand what she was supposed to do, who she was supposed to be now? Would it push back the boundaries of encroaching darkness?

His voice was low. Raw. "Do you want to...go back?"

Even with the hesitation, his meaning was clear enough.

Maybe for an hour, the voice whispered. *Maybe for a moment, you could let it all go. Not be the woman you once were, not be a dead woman, not be the wreckage left behind—not be anyone or anything. Just be.*

And would she be someone who would regret a choice made in an irrational moment of passion, or someone who would relish it?

Her vision blurred. *I just want to be,* she screamed. Did she always have to make it so complicated?

She didn't even realize tears had spilled over her cheeks until Vaughn pulled back from her and had cupped her face in his hands, brushing the drops away with his thumbs, his brow furrowed.

"Whoa," he said. "I-I'm sorry. Forget I said anything."

She raised her hands to clasp his wrists, pushing back his hands, pushing back the tears, pushing back her weakness.

She was a disaster. Not someone who could make rational decisions about such things.

She looked up into Vaughn's eyes, hoping he would let it be.

He turned his hands to grasp her own in his and held them. And then he spoke words that cut straight through all her pretenses, all her lies. "The loss of Sweetblade has been hard on you, hasn't it?" he said.

She swallowed. Her inclination was to pull away, to shut him out.

"Are you ever going to let me in and let me stay in?" he had pleaded with her. He didn't understand what he was asking. But maybe...

She had to swallow twice before she could choke the single word out. "Yes," she whispered.

He nodded. "Can I do anything to help?"

She blinked, startled. This was not the same man she had met over two years ago. Was it possible for someone to change in so short a time?

Perhaps he had never been as bad as she had thought. Perhaps that had always been her own blindness getting in the way, choosing to see his own defenses and façades as the totality of who he was.

"I don't know," she said.

"All right. What do you say we head down to Huiel's makeshift training area. Have you had *any* practice yet?"

She shook her head.

"You should. Even if only to make sure you don't accidentally kill yourself." He raised an eyebrow. "I'll tell Huiel to stay out of it unless we need him. Promise."

She hesitated. She hadn't even touched the aether that now ran in her blood since those few moments outside the portal—not out of fear of killing herself, but to avoid facing yet another issue she had to deal with at some point.

But he was right. The last thing she wanted was to be caught unaware again.

Maybe it would be a welcome distraction. So at last she nodded. "Maybe that's a good idea."

Chapter Forty-Four

Practice

As it turned out, they needed Huiel: try as they might, they couldn't get Ivana to replicate what she'd done outside the portal.

Huiel stood in front of Ivana and Vaughn down in the large room in the tunnels they had converted to a safe place to train, his arms folded across his chest, a slight frown on his lips. "So you say you froze everything."

"Everything except myself," Ivana said. She was beginning to wonder if she had been hallucinating after all.

But she hadn't hallucinated being in a different location when she had unfrozen everything.

"And your patron is Ziloxchanachi himself? I thought he didn't do anything."

"He doesn't," Vaughn said. "But that's by choice, not because he has no powers. But Tani said he's god of, let me see if I remember this correctly: 'Everything and nothing and the cycle of death and rebirth.'"

"That's quite the litany," Huiel said, one eyebrow raised.

"I can burn the aether from my blood," Ivana said. "I can feel it, like before." And it continued to be a strange feeling. "It just doesn't appear to do anything."

"Even when you direct it?" Huiel asked.

"I've tried thinking about freezing everything again. Nothing happens."

Huiel tapped his thigh. "What was it you thought moments before everything froze?"

"A bloodwolf was about to tear out my throat. I wasn't thinking. I was reacting."

Huiel scratched the side of his neck. "I see." His eyes flicked down to the dagger at Ivana's thigh, and then he stepped over to the single weapons rack in the room. He selected a club and walked back over to them.

Then without warning, he swung the club at Ivana's head.

She didn't even have time to duck. Just like with the bloodwolf, she threw up her arm and...

Everything froze.

She slowly lowered her arm and backed away from Huiel.

Yes, just like before. Huiel stood as though he were posing for a portrait, club in the grip of an outstretched arm, and Vaughn's eyes were wide, one hand in the process of being raised. Like before, when she focused on it, she could feel the trajectory of that club, where it would have landed on her had she not stopped him.

It was...insane.

To see if she could change something other than herself, she moved around to the side of Huiel, pried the club out of his hand, and put it back in the weapons rack. Then she turned to look at Huiel again. Her feeling about what would happen changed. He would stumble forward without the weight in his hand.

And then, like before—and with no difficulty—she directed everything to start again.

Huiel stumbled forward.

Vaughn shouted.

She stood to one side, her arms folded and her mind whirling.

Huiel spun and stared at her for a moment. Then he nodded. "It worked?"

"It worked."

"You're used to reacting quickly with whatever's at your disposal," Huiel stated.

She couldn't deny that. "Yes."

"There's got to be a way for her to use it at times *other* than when someone is about to clobber her," Vaughn said.

"Unless that's some sort of specific characteristic of Ziloxchanachi's magic, I agree," Huiel said. He looked at Ivana thoughtfully, and then pointed at her dagger. "A tool," he said. Then he tapped her on the side of the head. "A tool." He touched the vein in her wrist. "One more tool in your arsenal. I'm guessing that it's not a power that can be accessed just for the fun of it." By demonstration, he made a tiny whirlwind spin around on his hand for a moment and then clapped it out. "Rather, when you *need* it for something."

A tool. She frowned. "All right. I suppose that might make sense." She hesitated. "There's one other thing that happens. I thought maybe the first time it was a fluke, but I was able to replicate it. If I focus on something, I can tell what would have happened if I hadn't frozen everything. This time, I did something that would change that, and then I knew what the change would make happen. And sure enough, it did."

Vaughn clapped a hand to his forehead. "Burning skies."

"What?" Ivana said.

"Zily isn't only god of everything and nothing, death and rebirth. He's the god of *time*. Remember Tani's theory about why you were able to go through the portal?"

"Yes. It made no sense to me."

"Me either, but it had something to do with you being Zily's Banebringer"—he cast a quick look at Huiel—"er, Gifted, in the future, which somehow affected the present...I don't know, but either way, again, *time*."

Ivana digested that. "So, I'm not freezing everything. I'm...stopping time?"

Huiel's eyes widened. "And seeing and changing the future by what you do."

They both turned to look at her. "Wow," Vaughn said. "That's pretty intense. I mean..."

Huiel shook his head and held his hand up. "Before we get carried away, let's remember that most of us can only burn the smallest amount of aether for a few hours at a time before becoming fatigued. I'm sure this power will have uses that will become more apparent with practice, but I'm guessing they'll be fairly limited in scope." He turned to Ivana. "You should train more—see what you can and can't do. The only way we learn those sorts of things is by practicing and experimenting."

Here it went. Huiel would want to drag her into some sort of training regime...

"We're leaving in a day or two on a task for Yaotel," Vaughn said. "So that'll have to wait."

Ivana flicked her eyes his direction and gave a tiny tilt of the head, which she hoped he would interpret as gratitude.

Huiel pursed his lips. "All right. Well, some parting advice then. Since you've already been burning aether externally for some time, I doubt control or efficiency will be an issue for you. However, stamina is a different matter. I'd practice burning that low level of aether, even if it doesn't do anything. That's what I've had Dal Driskell doing, and it's—"

Vaughn cut in. "So, he *is* a Bane—Gifted!"

Huiel paused. "I…figured Yaotel would have told you that since you've been in on a lot of the meetings…"

"I haven't talked to him in a few days," Vaughn said.

"Anyway," Huiel continued, "that's what I've had Driskell doing, and it's considerably lengthened the amount of time he can burn his aether before tiring." He hesitated and then said hopefully, "I don't suppose you'd give it one more try before you go, though?"

Ivana could appreciate his thirst for knowledge, so she nodded.

A tool. What else could she use it for? What was something she *needed*? Something that having a little more time might help her accomplish?

She glanced around, and her eyes lit on a book that lay open on top of a small table shoved into the corner. She walked over to it and put her hand on top of it. *Time to study,* she thought, and then she burned aether.

The flame in the lantern on the wall froze. She glanced behind her. Vaughn and Huiel had also frozen, both looking in her direction curiously.

She perused the book, which looked like a manual someone had put together for the various types of Banebringers. She stopped at the moonblood chapter, curious, and read all about Vaughn's powers of invisibility, dark vision, and water manipulation. About the best way to train a new moonblood. Even a summary of the myth where Chati lost her head.

She did this until she began to feel dizzy, and then she let go. "Do all Gifted have a passive ability, like moonbloods and dark vision?" she asked without turning, as if nothing had happened.

There was a moment of silence, and then, "No," Huiel said, "but some do. Beastbloods, for instance, have especially strong constitutions. Don't get sick and are harder to kill." A pause. "Did you read that whole thing?"

"No, just looked at some of it."

"See the future at all?" Vaughn asked.

She turned and raised an eyebrow at him. "What, in a book? No. Nothing stood out to me."

He rubbed his jaw. "All right. Thanks for your help, Huiel."

They walked away from Huiel, silent until they reentered the tunnel leading out. "Do you want to practice more, or...?" Vaughn asked.

"I think I've had enough for one day." It had served the purpose of distracting her from her whirlwind of emotions. "I have a few garments to pick up from a dressmaker." And prepare for yet another long journey.

The sedentary year she had spent in Fuilyn had been nice in some respects.

Vaughn studied her for a moment and then nodded. "I'll let you know when and where we're meeting to leave," he said. He grimaced. "It'll be soon."

"As always," she said. "I'll be ready."

Chapter Forty-Five

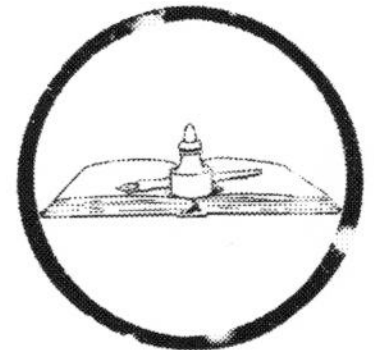

A Pretentious Chamber

There was a yawning and rather pretentious chamber in the civic hall where the Ri, at one point in time, had held audience with his nobles, heard grievances, and received foreign dignitaries.

It had sat empty for decades.

The Ri of Donia no longer received foreign dignitaries, grievances were handled much more efficiently than a long line of would-be petitioners out the civic hall doors, and they met with their nobles—their advisors—in the conference room, not an echoing stone hall meant to intimidate and cow.

It had been used, on occasion, for balls, but Ri Tanuac, being a rather practical man, wasn't given to elaborate parties.

Now, the layers of dust had been wiped from the chandeliers;

the drapes laundered, rehung, and pulled back to let in the sun; and the stone floor, which was inlaid with tiles in a large diamond mosaic, mopped and polished.

Guards stood at regular intervals down the long carpet leading to the front, where Ri Tanuac stood in front of an ornate chair that wasn't *quite* a throne, flanked by Nahua on his right and Yaotel on the left. Further, the four Gan stood at the front as well, two on each side, and behind the chair, looking rather grim, were all three of Tanuac's personal bodyguards. General Gyano stood at the ready nearby.

Driskell, on the other hand, stood in the back, having just arrived—and feeling rather overwhelmed by his first sight of the chamber in all its glory.

Nahua caught his eye and nodded to him.

Driskell straightened and smoothed his formal tunic and focused on his destination, rather than the dozens of minor nobles and other persons of status gathered in the hall, whom he was certain were watching his lone procession up the carpet to the front.

They probably weren't, considering there was a low buzz in the room as everyone waited for the dignitary who was the reason for the overhaul of the chamber and the theatrics.

Driskell took his place behind Nahua, notebook ready.

None too soon.

Dal Bherg swept into the chamber, accompanied by four other priests—making their number five, considered to be a holy number in the Conclave's religion.

A trickle of sweat ran down Driskell's temple, and he flicked it off.

"Steady, Driskell," Lady Nahua whispered.

I can't do this, he wanted to plead. It had been a mere eighteen days since the sky-fire, sixteen since he'd told Danton his secret, and thirteen since he had started training with Huiel. He had only the barest idea of what he was doing and what he was capable of.

But he had already agreed to do his best; therefore, he would.

He burned his trickle of aether, the kind that projected "love-beams," as Thrax called them. That, at least, he had been practicing constantly.

Bherg didn't waste words on pleasantries. He halted in front of the platform and surveyed the group there before his eyes settled on Tanuac.

"Ri Tanuac," he said, the emphasis on "Ri" a bit sardonic. "We meet at last."

"Holiness Bherg," Tanuac said. "Be welcome."

"Welcome? As my representative was welcome when you barred him from the government tier four days ago and subsequently ejected him from Marakyn itself?"

"He was causing trouble, Holiness," Tanuac said, at complete ease. "Stirring up discontent and spreading dangerous rumors. I cannot allow that—which you would have known had you not in turn refused to receive my message explaining myself."

Driskell expanded his bubble toward Bherg and his priests. Rather than any particular suggestion, which Huiel informed him was more advanced—Driskell projected into the space contained by the bubble a general feeling of calm.

"Dangerous rumors, indeed," Bherg said. "Dangerous, and true. Is it not true that you have held multiple closed councils with your Gan, as well as other officials—such as General Gyano—without the presence of my representative?"

Tanuac said nothing.

"Is it not true that in these councils, you plot against the Setanan Empire?"

There was a murmur in the room.

Bherg was calm enough. As calm as a frozen lake. Not exactly what Driskell had been aiming for. He changed from calm to contentment. It was a fine distinction, and he didn't know if he was skilled enough to make it, but he tried anyway.

"Is it not true that in your plots, you collude with none other than demonspawn?"

Driskell was so shocked that his bubble popped. Bherg...*knew*? *Oh, no.* He struggled to school his face.

Tanuac still seemed completely at ease. Perhaps Driskell's love-beams were affecting the wrong person. Not that Tanuac being calm was necessarily a bad thing...

"Holiness," Tanuac said. "What evidence have you for any of these outlandish accusations?"

"I have my sources," Bherg said.

All right, not contentment. Happiness? No, far too radical of a change. *Back to calm.*

"Would one of those sources be Dal Dax, who less than two months ago attempted to assassinate one of my new advisors and his friends?" Tanuac asked.

A triumphant smile spread over Bherg's lips. "Dal Dax. Yes. Yes, it would. And he had some interesting stories to tell us, believe me."

"He's a traitor with his own motivations, and therefore unreliable."

"He was a fool," Bherg said, "thinking to manipulate us to his own ends. You can rest assured your traitor is now safely Sedated, as he ought to be."

Yaotel looked as though someone had socked him in the gut. He recovered quickly, but the pain Bherg's statement had caused was evidenced in that split second.

Tanuac's tone, which had, up until now, been warmer than would have been called for, went cold. "Sedated or kept somewhere so you can drain his blood for your own purposes?"

Bherg took the accusation without comment. Calm. But Driskell doubted that it would matter, at this point, how calm Bherg was. It would end the same way.

"Is it not true, Holiness, that you and your Conclave have betrayed your own teachings, using Banebringer magic yourselves? Is it not true that you experiment on bloodbane, seeking to create abominations that allow you to control them for your own purposes? Is it not true that the vise-like grip of your hand even now slides around the throat of Setana, seeking to squeeze anything left of it that the Empire has not already taken?"

Oh, dear.

Bherg drew a long syringe out from under his robes—calmly. "Perhaps we should test this on your new advisor, and see what happens?"

He made to move toward Yaotel, but Tanuac blocked his way. "You will not touch him."

Bherg made a motion with his hand, and his five priests began chanting.

After a rather elaborate-sounding recitation and some waving of hands...

Nothing happened.

Bherg frowned. He whirled around to face his priests. They, to a man, looked mystified.

Bherg whirled back. "You did this," he stated.

"Did what, Bherg?" Tanuac asked, dropping the priestly honorific.

Feeling rather desperate, Driskell threw out a suggestion. *What if you're mistaken?*

Bherg hesitated. His brow wrinkled. And then it smoothed. "I bring a message from the seat of the Empire in Weylyn City." He began to recite. "Donia is now considered in violation of the terms of the agreement reached with the Empire's duly appointed representative—myself. Ri Tanuac will surrender his title and position and allow the Empire to appoint a replacement—or face the consequences."

There was a stillness in the room as those there collectively held their breath.

His suggestion falling flat, Driskell expanded his bubble of calm as far as he could. *Ri Tanuac is a good man. The Conclave is evil,* he inserted for good measure.

Other than Bherg and his companions, Driskell doubted a single person there believed anything otherwise. It wouldn't hurt to reinforce it, would it? His gut twisted, all the same.

"Over my dead body," Tanuac said. Calmly. Almost pleasantly. "Guards, please see Bherg and his party out of Marakyn. General Gyano, please have your soldiers round up every Conclave priest in the city and eject them—without harassment, please. As of this moment, I reject Conclave rule of the Empire, and therefore I'm afraid I must as a result declare Donia a sovereign state once again."

"Very well," Bherg said. "Consequences it will be." He shook off the hand of one of the guards. "That won't be necessary, Dal. I can see myself out."

He turned on his heel and strode out of the audience chamber, the priests on his heels.

Gyano jerked his head and half a dozen guards peeled off to follow them.

The audience chamber door slammed shut with a resounding thud.

When the echoes had stopped ringing off the walls, Tanuac turned to face those remaining in the hall.

Driskell scanned the faces. Some were shocked, some fiercely proud, some resigned. Only a few looked disgusted or angry—Gan Dillion being one of them.

Driskell let go of his aether.

Cheers broke out. No more calm.

Driskell swallowed. Would they still be cheering when they were staring down an army set on tearing down Marakyn's walls?

He doubted it.

Driskell decided he would visit Tania that night. He wanted her and her family to hear the news of what had happened that afternoon before the special newssheet had been run and distributed—or rumors reached their ears.

As it turned out, they were *all* gathered at her house by the time he had a moment to spare—her mother, father, siblings, cousins, aunt, uncle, and of course, grandmama.

And when he stepped into the room, it fell silent.

His gut coiled. Apparently, the news had run ahead of him.

He sought Tania's eyes first. He couldn't bear the penetrating gaze of her father, the red eyes of her mother, the curious expressions of her younger siblings, and worst of all, the accusatory look from her uncle.

In response, Tania rose from where she had been sitting, a little apart from the others, went to his side, and took his hand. "Let's walk," she said. "We'll be back in an hour," she added to the room in general before pulling Driskell back out into the night.

They walked hand-in-hand down the empty street, lit by the moon and stars and light from windows. She didn't say anything for a long while, and neither did Driskell.

When she broke the silence, her voice was soft and her words to the point. "You've known this was going to happen for a while, haven't you?"

Driskell bit his lip. What was the point in lying about it now? But would she be angry? Disappointed? "Yes," he said.

She slid her arm through his own and drew him close to her. "I'm sorry."

He blinked and craned his neck to look at her. "*You're* sorry? For what?"

"That you've had to bear this burden alone." She laid her head against his shoulder. "I...wish I could have helped."

"I wish I could have told you," he said truthfully. "You're not angry?"

"Angry? Driskell. Surely you know me well enough by now..."

He did. He should have. But he still couldn't help worrying, mostly because she still didn't know all of it.

"Your uncle looked disgruntled," Driskell said.

"He's irritated that you didn't say anything. Give them some warning. I told them all you couldn't, how that wasn't fair. I think my father gets it, but my mother is..."

She drew up short and turned to face him. "How bad is it, Driskell? Mother is worried sick. She's certain the Conclave is going to do to Donia what they did to Venetia."

Driskell took a while to think about that question. How bad was it? Tanuac was confident that, having disabled their battle priests and with the help of the Ichtaca, they could stave this army off. Marakyn's fortifications were second to none in Setana. But there were other cities, less prepared, less defensible. How long would it take for the Conclave to threaten them? How far did Donia's resources stretch alone?

In the end, Donia could not win against the might of Setana by herself. With Venetia and Fuilyn fully in, they *might* have a chance, but it would be a long and costly war—in lives as well as resources. What they needed to guarantee their victory and ultimate sovereignty was Xambria—and Ferehar. And Ferehar was now in the hands of Dal Vaughn, who was on his way there at this moment. "Ri Tanuac wouldn't have done this if he didn't think we could win," Driskell said.

"You're being diplomatic," Tania said, her eyes searching his own. "What do *you* think?"

Driskell bit his lip. "I think the army currently threatening Marakyn will be handled," he said. "I don't know beyond that." He spread open one hand. "But is there ever any certainty in situations like these? Tanuac saw a chance, and he took it. It's been in the hearts of most Donians for centuries, Tania. But we've always been too afraid to do anything about it."

A tiny smile curled her lips up. "Listen to you. You'll be a Gan before you know it."

He didn't even know if that was a realistic goal anymore. Nahua didn't seem to care, but what of everyone else? Would an entire quarter of Donia follow the lead of a Banebringer one day?

"But...surely, there's no truth to the rumors about the Ri working with Banebringers, is there?" Tania asked.

He drew her against his chest so he didn't have to look into her eyes when he lied.

The city was quiet as Driskell made his way back from his walk with Tania; he hadn't bothered returning to her house.

Tanuac had ordered a citywide curfew, which would go into effect at midnight each night. From then, citizens were to stay inside until daybreak.

Driskell took a detour to the retaining wall on the seventh tier before entering the gates to the civic quarter.

The wall here was chest-high. Driskell leaned on it, looking out over the plains.

His heart dropped into his stomach. The Conclave army had, in the time Bherg had left, already encamped around Marakyn.

Tanuac expected an attempt at a siege rather than an outright attack upon the walls—which would have been foolish. But though the Conclave apparently knew they had Banebringer help, and though Bherg now knew his supply of aether was fake, Bherg didn't know that Tanuac had been preparing for this for months. The city was well-stocked with supplies, and it had its own underground water supply, as well as a back way out for escape—or in for more supplies—through the tunnels, which cut all the way through the mountain, parallel to the aboveground pass, and emerged in Ferehar. Indeed, Vaughn had been apprised of this closely kept secret, and his own team had been instructed to take the tunnels to avoid being hampered by bloodbane on the way across the pass.

They could hold here for months. Tanuac hoped they wouldn't need to.

Even so, the sight of the Conclave camp spread out across the plain, surrounding the city, was daunting. The sky glowed faintly red from the collective light of their lanterns and torches and cookfires, and in the distance, Driskell could see the long, snaking line of the army's supply train, stretching to the horizon.

He doubted he would be able to sleep tonight. He had no responsibilities by way of the army itself—he was no soldier. He would perform as he always had: at Tanuac and Nahua's side, taking dutiful notes for later study—and possibly posterity.

Tanuac had praised his exceptional ability to keep everyone at the meeting that day unnaturally calm—and in the event of riots or protests, he would be deployed to deescalate the worst of them.

Why, then, did he feel so on edge? He scanned the horizon again, but nothing had changed.

He turned to look to the northwest, toward the mountains, toward Ferehar. If he knew what gods to believe in anymore, he would pray.

He supposed he'd just have to live with good, old-fashioned hope.

Chapter Forty-Six

Not at all Suspect

The gardens on the grounds of the palace in Cohoxta, the capital of Ferehar, were a pretty bit of land, and though they were well-maintained, Ivana had the impression that they also didn't see much use.

Other than by, apparently, Vaughn's mother.

Askata sat on a stone bench that was nestled against three flowering trees; she faced Ivana across a small pond, but Ivana was hidden in the shadows of another small copse of trees and shrubbery.

Askata was also preoccupied. She faced an easel set in front of her. While Ivana couldn't see the subject of her painting, by the trajectory of Askata's eyes, she guessed it was the mother duck with her four babies that were presently swimming placidly around the pond.

Ivana stepped out of the trees, pulled down her hood, and waited.

Askata was so absorbed in her work, it took a minute for her to notice Ivana.

When she did, she did a double-take, then gently set her paintbrush down on the ledge of the easel, below her canvas, folded her hands in her lap, and waited.

Ivana skirted the edge of the pond and sat down next to her. "Askata," she said, nodding to the woman.

Askata didn't even favor her with the tiniest of fake smiles. "Your presence here cannot be a good omen," she said, then she picked up her paintbrush again. "What do you want?"

Askata was a practical, down-to-earth woman who didn't mince words.

Ivana was beginning to like her. "I'd like you to come with me and have a chat with some of my friends—who would be more than happy to tell you all about what they want."

Askata looked at her askance. "*That* doesn't sound at all suspect."

A rare genuine smile tugged at the corners of Ivana's lips. "It does," she admitted. "But in this case, I'm perfectly serious. More importantly, whether you like what they have to say or not, you may return home unharmed and unthreatened.

Askata studied Ivana. "Where is my guard?"

Askata's "guard," Ivana had learned from Aleena, was there not to protect Askata, but to keep an eye on her. A gift from Airell after their little incident a couple of months ago. "He became ill and is currently confined to his quarters." She let her eyes drift out over the pond, feigning indifference to Askata's response.

Askata put the finishing touches on the fourth duckling. "Is...*he* with you?" she asked quietly.

Ivana didn't need to ask whom she was referring to; it wasn't the guard. "Yes."

There was a visible tremor in Askata's hand as she set down her pencil and sketchbook on the bench. Then she stood. "Then let's make this quick. Airell left our estate in Qichio shortly after I did, along with his..." Her upper lip curled. "'Advisors.' I've been back at the palace for several days, so he should be arriving any day."

"I know." Ivana stood as well. "But, to be on the safe side, we can leave without anyone seeing us." She held out her hand. "You'll have to trust me because I don't have time to explain."

Askata pressed her lips together, nodded, and took Ivana's hand.

The ease with which even someone like Askata decided to trust her—even if it was because Ivana held the promise of seeing her son—was astounding. What must it be like to be able to trust so easily?

Ivana slid her hand into her pocket and burned Vaughn's aether, cloaking them both from sight. She had to admit it was nice that she was able to use Banebringer aether now without having to subvert the system by mixing it with her own blood.

"Don't let go of my hand," Ivana said.

Vaughn paced in the room they'd rented at The Ancient Drum, a clean, tasteful inn in a quiet part of the city. Aleena, Thrax, and Danton were with him, but they seemed far more at ease than he felt.

Of course, they were just accessories to this plan. None of *them* was going to challenge Airell's claim to the position of Ri. None of *them* had to explain to their own mother why she should turn on one of her own sons to help another.

The door opened, and Vaughn turned to face it.

It closed a moment later of its own accord, and then Ivana and his mother flickered into view.

He breathed out. So, she had come. That was a start.

Askata's eyes flicked around the room at the other faces, then rested on Vaughn. "Teyrnon," she said. "You're back." Her eyes roved over him from head to toe.

Vaughn clasped his hands behind his back, bearing her scrutiny. He looked different from the last time she had seen him, when he had been a bloody, filthy mess.

"You look well," she said.

"Well enough," he said.

There was a silence in the room that quickly turned awkward until Aleena thankfully cleared her throat and stepped forward. She inclined her head. "Askata," she said. "A pleasure to meet you at last."

Askata's brow furrowed, but she made no reply. Instead, she turned back to Ivana. "I've come with you in good faith," she said. "Now will you tell me what you want?"

Vaughn took a deep breath. If his mother decided not to help, he still didn't know what he would do. Prudence would dictate that they detain her until after Airell was dealt with. But imprison his own mother?

He didn't know if he had that in him. "I intend to challenge Airell for the title of Ri," he said. "And I need your help to succeed."

Askata's eyes widened.

It felt as though everyone in the room had simultaneously drawn in their breaths and were holding them, waiting for Askata's response.

She looked down at her arm and pushed up the sleeve. There were yellowing bruises in the shape of fingers.

Vaughn gritted his teeth to keep the swell of anger in check.

Askata stared at her arm. "Will you hurt him?" she asked quietly.

Vaughn shifted. He had to be honest. "He'll be imprisoned. But if all goes according to plan, I imagine he'll ultimately be executed for treason."

There was another long silence. Then she shook her sleeve down and looked up, her eyes now hard. "Just tell me what I need to do."

Two hours later, Vaughn and Danton left to accompany Askata back to the palace and Thrax went to find food. That left Ivana with Aleena in the room.

Ivana hadn't had a chance to talk with Aleena alone yet—so she was grateful until Aleena strode across the room and startled her by enveloping her in an enormous hug.

"I'm surprised you came," Aleena said—pulling back before Ivana could push her back—and gripping her arms instead.

Ivana returned the grasp. That was much more comfortable. "If I had stayed in Marakyn, I'd have just ended up being an object of fascination for the Ichtacan researchers." She let go and turned away to feign picking through her bag.

There was a pause. "Why would that be?"

She looked back over her shoulder. "Vaughn didn't tell you about our trip to the abyss?"

"He mentioned it briefly, but I only talked to him through the qixli once alone," Aleena said.

For some reason, Ivana had assumed Vaughn would have told Aleena. "Since I was the only available option, Zily picked me to be his first and only Banebringer." Ivana pulled out her new ciuhan, stood, and turned to face Aleena again.

Aleena's eyebrows shot up. "That's unexpected."

She snorted. "Tell me about it."

"And...you're all right with this?"

Ivana shrugged. "I don't care, except inasmuch as eventually it's going to mean having to deal more and more with the Ichtaca. I'm sure I slipped away far too soon for Yaotel—before, at least, they were able to draw a few pints of my blood. Fortunately, he's a bit preoccupied right now."

"He still holding a grudge?"

"Like a bloodbat holds its prey." She laid the skirt of the ciuhan out on her pallet, then the shirt next to it, and then the sash that tied it together. She crouched down and rubbed the fabric of the skirt between her fingers. It had been a long time since she had worn one of these. The last time, if she recalled correctly, had been at a wedding for one of the townsfolk in her hometown. In lieu of the latest Setanan fashion, traditional clothing sufficed for such occasions.

Aleena joined her at the pallet. She touched the fabric as well. "Soft. You doing okay?"

"I'm sorry?"

"I mean, back in Ferehar and all. Last I left you, you seemed a little...off."

Last Aleena had left her. That seemed like eons ago.

Off. As she recalled, she'd gotten drunk. Well. *That* wasn't an option anymore. Banebringers couldn't get drunk.

That year of ignorance before Vaughn had tracked her down again had been blissful, hadn't it? It had been nice believing she could leave everything behind and move on, just like that.

It had been a lie, all of it. Like her entire life.

Why this line of thought now? "I'm fine," she said. The words sounded hollow in her own ears. They would certainly sound hollow in Aleena's.

"Uh-huh," Aleena said. "You want to talk about it?"

She straightened up. "I'm tired. It's been a long couple of weeks." Try a couple of months. A couple of years. Damn, it'd been a long life, hadn't it?

It was starting to wear a little thin.

Vaughn and Danton walked Askata back to the palace in silence, all three invisible. They avoided the main thoroughfare, which ran from the southern gates at the river, straight through the city, and out the northern gates. Instead, they detoured through less busy streets, circling around the hill below the palace where the wealthiest nobles had their city estates and through the smaller, eastern gate in the palace wall that led to the extensive gardens behind the palace.

Danton was going to be her new "guard." They had needed to have one of their own on the inside before attempting to, essentially, seize the palace—in addition to Askata and Aleena's contacts. Someone to unlock doors, guide people away from where they shouldn't be, and make sure Airell stayed put.

The plan wasn't without risks. There were five of them: Vaughn, Danton, Aleena, Thrax, and Ivana. Vaughn had to stay hidden until the last moment, Thrax had to be cautioned not to accidentally burn the whole place down, Aleena wasn't a fighter, and Danton would overuse his magic in the wrong place at the wrong time in order to be helpful if he wasn't thinking.

And Ivana? Ivana had to be kept away from Airell.

She would kill him if she had an easy opportunity, and he had to be kept alive long enough to have their election. Otherwise, this was just one more violent coup in Ferehar's long history of violent coups.

It was still essentially a coup, but Vaughn didn't want it to be violent, and the election had to be real.

At least, that was what he told himself. If Airell won...

He shook his head. If Airell won, after all the trouble he went to in order to make this a legal transfer of power, he'd have some difficult decisions to make.

No, this plan was not without risks, and the weaknesses of their team were, frankly, the least of their concerns.

They were also relying on information that everyone at the palace hated Airell so much that they wouldn't resist, and they were relying on his mother, who was siding with one son over another. In the end, would she be able to carry through?

He wished he were more certain of anything.

He left his mother and Danton in the garden where Ivana had retrieved her a few hours ago.

"Teyrnon," Askata said before he let go of her arm.

He turned to face her.

"I'm sorry," she said.

He blinked. "For what?"

"For never doubting your father's word. For not seeking you out once I knew you were alive. For..." Her throat constricted. "For the fact that, even had I known...I don't think I would have been ready to accept you as you are until now."

The confession stung, but he schooled his face. "Then I suppose it was just as well that you didn't know."

She hesitated. "I...I don't pretend to understand Banebringers. But I'm willing to learn. I'm willing to try. And I will help you do this." The hand on his arm tightened. "But promise me...if it is at all within your power to find a way to do this without hurting Airell..." Her face tightened. "I can't lose another son."

He studied her face. "If it's within my power," he said. "And that's all I *can* promise."

She nodded. "Then good luck." She let go of his arm.

The look on her face changed from astonishment to wonder as, having broken contact, Vaughn no doubt blinked out of sight right in front of her.

Danton, who had been standing at a discreet distance, moved in closer at Askata's reappearance.

Vaughn, however, moved away. But he stopped at the edge of the area to study his mother. The eleven years since he had left home had been kind to her in some respects; she looked younger than her age and still carried herself with all the grace and even slight arrogance of a woman molded to be a noble. If she wanted to remarry, she would have no trouble finding willing suitors, even though she was an older widow.

And in other respects, the years had been unkind. The slump of her shoulders, the tremor in her hand, the wary look in her eyes.

The bruises on her arms.

He clenched a fist. No, *he* wouldn't hurt Airell. But that didn't mean Airell wouldn't pay.

Chapter Forty-Seven

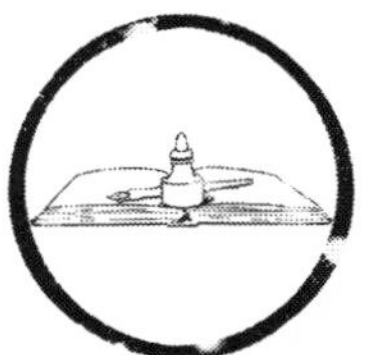

Marching Orders

Driskell patted the packet in his pocket one more time. He had just spent more money at one time than he ever had before—on a custom-made pendant he would give to Tania at their wedding. It had been tempting to use his powers to negotiate a better deal, but he had resisted. It simply wasn't right. His constant low-burn of aether he kept going any time he was around strangers probably made the jeweler more favorable to him anyway.

Even so, Tania would kill him if she knew how much he had spent. He wanted to get the pendant back to his room and safely hidden away.

Raised voices in the square he was headed toward caused him to slow.

A man stood on the raised stone edge of a fountain, and a crowd had gathered around him.

Uh-oh. A protest?

"Ri Tanuac is a good man," the man on the fountain said, his voice raised to be heard above the general commotion of the street. "He's given us a chance to be out from under the Setanan thumb."

Or...not?

"My sister's family lives in one of the towns around Ipsylanti!" another man shouted from the crowd. "What is Tanuac's plan for keeping those people secure?"

There was a general murmur of agreement.

"I am certain the Ri has plans—" the man on the fountain began.

"Easy for us to say, safe behind Marakyn's walls!" a woman called out. "How do we know he's not clinging to power at our expense?"

"You're too used to the way Setana does things," the man on the fountain said earnestly. "If he rolls over and lets the Conclave put someone in charge, that's the end of it!"

There was another murmur, some nods, some shaking of heads.

One man in the back caught Driskell's attention. His eyes gleamed, his lips turned downward in a snarl of disgust.

Silver flashed then disappeared into the palm of the man's hand, and then he moved around the edge of the crowd.

What? Oh...no.

Driskell glanced around desperately, looking for a Watchman, but there were none around.

So, heart pounding, he moved to intercept the man.

He grabbed him by the arm when he reached him.

The man turned to him angrily—and Driskell began burning

more aether and expanded his bubble to encompass both of them.

"You don't want to do that, friend," Driskell said.

The man spat on the ground. "Why don't you mind your own business, *friend*?"

Driskell waved a hand around the area. "Will you turn the inside of Marakyn to violence when there hasn't even been any on the outside yet? What do you think will happen? You'll chance inciting a riot and end up at the end of a hangman's noose, and for what? To prove a point to yourself?"

The man hesitated.

Driskell projected calm. *Don't be foolish,* he thought at the man. *This is a foolish man's path. Think, friend,* think.

"You're...right," the man said at last. "I was being foolish in my anger."

Driskell blinked. *It worked? It actually worked?*

The man put a hand on his shoulder. "Thank you. You saved me a lot of trouble."

"I'm, uh, certain the Ri would be happy to hear a petition," Driskell said.

The man nodded. "I'll go to the palace to lodge a complaint tomorrow."

Then he turned away.

Driskell watched as the man left the crowd, which was now calmly dispersing, still taken aback that his little stunt had worked.

So far, they had been lucky. No riots, a few non-violent protests, but generally the morale of the city was high.

That would change the longer the siege went on.

There would be more of the malcontents, more restlessness, more fear.

"Dal Driskell!" a male voice called from behind him.

Driskell spun, searching for the person who had called him amongst the press of people and spotted Deloro, his friend and a clerk from the civic hall—waving to him from across the square. Sweat trickled down his temple.

Driskell glanced around and then hurried to meet him.

"I've been all over the city looking for you." Deloro dabbed at the sweat with a handkerchief. "Tanuac needs you."

Driskell frowned. Had he missed a meeting on Tanuac's calendar he was supposed to be at? He had thought he had a few minutes to take care of picking up the pendant. "I'll be right behind you," he said.

Deloro nodded and dashed off.

Driskell found Ri Tanuac sitting at his desk in his private study, which was curious in and of itself. Typically, he didn't call on Driskell there.

But more than that, Driskell was surprised to find Yasril, the moonblood, there.

Driskell bowed to the Ri. "Your Excellency," he said, then nodded at Yasril.

Driskell's hand drifted to the pouch where he kept his notebook and pencil, but Tanuac stopped him. "No, Driskell. No notes today. I have a task for you both."

He stood, rounded his desk, and leaned against it. "Yasril has been in and out of the Conclave camp several times now, providing me intelligence on numbers, makeup of troops, and so on. As Yaotel feared, that bloodbane abomination they've brought with them has started gathering bloodbane in the vicinity. They're hiding in the forest and are mostly docile—which Yaotel tells me must mean they're under the control of that thing." Tanuac passed a hand over his face. "This isn't unexpected, but it is concerning. A normal assault, Marakyn can withstand. But bloodbane that can fly—and carry those that can't—right over the walls, among other possible uses for them?" Tanuac shook his head.

Driskell imagined dozens of bloodhawks harassing people on the streets. Hundreds of bloodbats finding their way into homes. Bloodhawks dropping bloodcrabs or bloodwolves. Bloodspiders climbing right over the walls. *Mass panic,* Driskell thought. And certainly, mass bloodshed and destruction.

The strength of Marakyn's defenses was in its walls and tiered structure. If those were essentially nullified...

He shuddered.

Tanuac acknowledged his reaction with a nod. "However, Yasril's discovered something else in his spying. Their troops are restless. Some are merely bored, tired of waiting. Some are nervous about the possibility of assaulting Marakyn. But in hushed conversations when they believe no one is listening, Yasril's also heard mutterings about the bloodbane. They terrify the average soldier, and many have reservations about using them at all. The Conclave has not done well—at least in this army—at selling their mission."

Tanuac pushed himself off his desk and looked directly at Driskell. "So. Driskell. This is where *you* come in..."

Chapter Forty-Eight

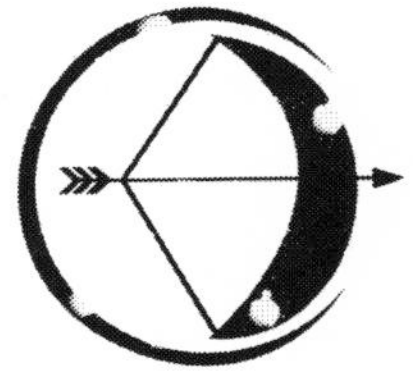

The Ri of Ferehar

Vaughn clenched the reins of the horse tightly in his right hand and let his left rest casually at his thigh. At least he was *trying* to make it look casual.

Try as he might, he couldn't loosen his grip on the reins. And it wasn't because he was nervous about maneuvering a lotli, the small chariot nobles and other important persons used in Ferehar.

No, what he was nervous about had nothing to do with his mode of transportation and everything to do with the fact that hundreds of eyes were watching his progression through the city and up the wide boulevard that led to the palace.

Not just hundreds. Thousands. And the number was increasing as many curious onlookers decided to trail behind the procession to find out what was going to happen.

At some point, a runner broke free of the growing crowd and sped up the street ahead of them. A messenger to warn Airell of impending guests, no doubt.

"Relax," Thrax whispered from where he walked at his right. "You look like you're about to vomit."

"Easy for you to say," Vaughn retorted.

"Just be thankful you're not the one sweltering in armor under the summer sun," Thrax said.

It was true.

They had decided to make a visual statement with their arrival, and not only by arriving at the palace in a lotli. Thrax was dressed in traditional Fereharian armor, a full suit of which was called a "xixchpil." The xixchpil wasn't used at all by Setanan regulars but was occasionally donned by Fereharian reserves when they were called upon by the United Setanan army. It consisted of quilted cotton two-fingerswidth thick and hardened with brine underneath a thick one-piece, long-sleeved leather shirt that buckled in the back, topped with a colorful and highly decorated cotton tunic. Vaughn could only imagine how hot Thrax was.

There was nothing ceremonial about the sword at Thrax's side, but that wasn't his real weapon anyway.

Vaughn, however, felt exposed in nothing but his fine Fereharian clothing. Frankly, he couldn't remember a time when he had donned the traditional garments for men: a knee-length skirt, sleeveless vest—worn unbuttoned—and a short cape. While the garments for women had evolved only a little over time and continued to be worn side-by-side with Setanan fashion, the garments for men had all but been discarded except on special occasions.

The outfit kept him cool; he would give it that.

He kept his eyes on the road ahead of him, ignoring the whispers behind him. He ought to be smiling and waving and ingratiating himself to the people, but there was only room for one goal in his mind right now, and that was manipulating his brother.

He wasn't cut out for this sort of thing. He didn't know how to play these games.

He was supposed to be the third son, an archer in the United Setanan.

Vaughn and his "guard" stopped at the gates to the palace, which were open to allow the easy flow of workers about their business throughout the day.

"Breathe," Thrax muttered, then he stepped forward to meet the gatehouse guard. "Lord Teyrnon would speak with his brother, Lord Airell," Thrax said, pitching his voice loud enough for everyone nearby to hear.

Vaughn had to stop his eye from twitching at the title *Lord*.

The guards at the gatehouse—whom Askata had made certain were men sympathetic to their cause and loyal to her—didn't need to respond because Airell himself was already striding toward the open gate. "*Ri* Airell." He sneered. He stopped just outside the gate and then looked Vaughn up and down. "Teyrnon," he said. "You have nerve, showing your face around here again."

"Airell. You have nerve, being here at all," Vaughn replied.

"I beg your pardon?" Airell asked, one eyebrow raised.

"You have taken on the mantle of Ri unlawfully," Vaughn said. "Or did I miss the elections?"

Airell's face, which previously had been rife with arrogance, flickered with a bit of uncertainty, and then disbelief. But the look was gone in an instant, and his face darkened. "You will address me as 'Your Excellency,'" he said. "Now get out, or I'll toss you out."

"Do you really wish to treat the laws of Ferehar with such flippancy?"

"Bah," Airell said. "The Conclave approved my position here."

The horse harnessed to the lotli stamped its foot, swished its tail, and tried to bow its neck to graze on the bits of grass that had straggled through the gaps between the paving stones. Vaughn handed the reins to Thrax, stepped down from the platform, and walked up to his brother. "In front of all these people," he said, turning his profile to the crowd and waving his arm expansively in that direction, "you dare to spurn the laws of Setana in favor of the Conclave? Do you come at their beck and call now, a dog to dogs?"

Airell surveyed the silent crowd behind Vaughn, and then any trace of the anger that had been building in him melted away. Instead, he favored Vaughn with an indulgent smile. "You have no right to speak to me of the laws of Setana. By their laws, you should be in an irreversible coma right now...demonspawn." He added the final word casually, but there was a hint of triumph in it, as though Airell believed identifying Vaughn as a Banebringer would quell any doubts Vaughn might have been raising.

A murmur *did* run through the crowd at Airell's words, but Vaughn merely returned his brother's smile. He'd been hoping Airell would bring that up. "Then why, when you captured me some months ago, didn't you send for a Hunter to Sedate me? Why did you keep me alive to torture me instead, risking the lives of your entire estate for the pleasure of your new masters? No, brother, it is *you* who will not speak to *me* of laws because the Conclave cannot even keep their own."

The crowd fell silent again. Vaughn's accusations of the Conclave were accusations everyone had heard and few disbelieved—but one still didn't speak of them openly.

He wasn't worried. Aleena was out there somewhere watching the crowd for threats, and Ivana was out there somewhere watching *him*. If someone—a Conclave priest, for instance—made a sudden move, she would be ready to use her own magic to stop it—literally.

Unless, of course, seeing Airell again had distracted her. He would have left her back at the inn to be on the safe side, but he needed her, and she had promised she'd behave.

No matter what happened, the hundreds who had trailed along hoping for some excitement were about to get it.

Airell eyed him silently for a moment, no doubt weighing his options. Finally, he raised his hand in the air and brought it down in a chopping motion, as if that were the end of it. "Guards. Arrest both of them."

Two of the guards moved forward warily.

"Before you do that," Vaughn said to the guards, though he pitched his voice loud enough for anyone nearby to hear, "you might be interested to know that all those excess taxes Lord Airell has been levying are going straight to those same Conclave traitors."

The murmur was back, and as those in the front passed Vaughn's words to those at the back, it swelled with an angry undercurrent.

Airell's voice took on a patronizing overtone. "Now, brother. How could you possibly know that?"

Vaughn ignored him. "And if that's not enough to convince you," he continued, still speaking to the approaching guards, "you might consider that Lord Airell is not even the lawful regent. That title belongs to another."

The guards halted and exchanged a glance with each other, as if uncertain of what they should do. Then one of them turned to look at Airell.

Airell eyed the rustling crowd again. "You have no authority here," he said at last. "I am Gildas' closest living kin, and as such, even should I relinquish the title of Ri, I am still in charge. And I say you are demonspawn and will rot until a Hunter can be called. Or do you intend to take my palace by force with your paltry honor guard?" He raised an eyebrow at Thrax, lips curled up into a smile.

Vaughn didn't expect Airell to surrender, which was why he had a hidden card—if it decided to play itself.

And then it did.

The crowd parted. Askata made her way through the gaggle of servants watching from the courtyard on the other side of the palace wall, trailed by Danton in his role as her personal guard. Her bearing was regal, her chin held high, and her eyes flashing—and a maid scurried in her wake. She was a sight to behold—Thaxchatichan herself might have trembled before her.

She spoke only four words, and they carried naturally across the square. "Whose palace, my son?"

Airell's face paled.

The crowd hushed once more, all eyes on Askata. "Since you relieved my husband's original steward, by law *I* am his closest living kin, and *I* am the one in charge."

She glided farther forward. "And *I* say there will be an election, and my third-born son, Teyrnon, and his attendants will be welcome at the palace—and under my protection—until the matter of the next Ri is decided."

It was only then that Airell realized what was happening. "*You* intend to challenge me?" He laughed, high and shrill. "A *Banebringer*? What sane person would elect a *demonspawn* over *me*?"

At this, the crowd went eerily silent, possibly more silent than Airell would have liked.

"This man is a Banebringer," Airell said to the crowd, disbelief coloring his voice. "Demonspawn!"

A voice near the front of the crowd shouted out, "Pot, meet kettle!" There was an answering wave of agreement, no longer a murmur.

Vaughn felt, rather than saw, the crowd press in closer behind him, and Airell took a step back.

A bead of sweat trickled down Vaughn's back. *Come on, Airell. Just give it up*. He did *not* want this to become a mob execution.

Then at last Airell held up his hands with a laugh and a shake of his head. "Very well, very well. I will relinquish control to Lady Askata, the rightful regent." He eyed the crowd once more. "In fact, as a measure of good will, I will *surrender* to Lady Askata and allow myself to be imprisoned until such a time as I can be cleared of all accusations by winning the...election."

Vaughn stepped in toward him and spoke softly so that only Airell could hear him. "Saving your neck by forcing our mother to protect you? Wise move." He met his brother's eyes. "But let's be clear about something. You seem to think I'm the cowardly child who fled that night. Who had no idea what was happening to him. Or even the man you managed to subdue and keep at your whims, not so long ago.

"You were right to keep me constrained then. Because you have no idea what I could do to you, do you?"

"Demonspawn scum," Airell growled, a barely contained sneer hidden beneath the veneer of congeniality he'd pasted on his face for the benefit of the crowd.

"I could have simply marched in here and squeezed your heart until it popped," Vaughn went on. "Ripped out your veins. Even broken your bones, one by one. With a thought." He tapped his head. "With. A. Thought."

Airell's throat constricted.

"But I didn't because I won't stoop to your level and that of our ancestors, in flesh or spirit. I'm going to do this right."

He stepped back and nodded to his mother.

Askata gestured toward the two guards who had previously been headed toward Vaughn. "Piaz and Omo," Askata said, "please escort Lord Airell to the dungeons and place him under constant guard."

Piaz bowed immediately to Askata. "Of course, Lady Regent," he said.

The guards bound Airell's hands behind his back and led him away.

Vaughn jerked his head slightly at Danton, who followed the guards.

Once Airell had been taken back into the palace, Askata turned to address Vaughn. "Lord Teyrnon," she said, her voice carrying across the square. "Welcome home."

Chapter Forty-Nine

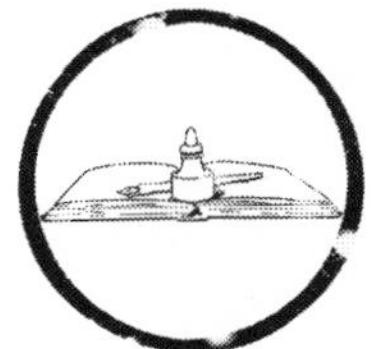

Love-Beams

Driskell stood in the middle of the enemy camp, surrounded by soldiers.

Soldiers eating. Soldiers sharpening blades. Soldiers arguing, talking, and laughing.

He was struck by the uniformity of their home region. They were mostly Setanan. A few Fuilynian faces. No Fereharians. No Donians or Venetians that he saw. The United Setanan was supposed to be just that—an army of combined forces between the seven regions to deal with external threats or further expand the Empire, when the king, ostensibly, deemed it time.

This division had obviously been formed specifically to deal not with external threats, but an internal one.

With sweaty hands and a pounding heart, he expanded his

bubble farther, encompassing all the soldiers in the immediate vicinity—a dozen or so sitting around a cookfire, eating their midday meal.

He'd done this going on ten or eleven times today so far. Yasril, the poor man, had been holding Driskell's clammy hand for hours.

Yasril hadn't complained. Well, he hadn't said much of anything, considering people could still hear them, despite both of them being invisible. Instead, he'd followed Driskell around as he found groups of soldiers who were not preoccupied.

Driskell took a deep breath and closed his eyes. *Those bloodbane out in the forest,* he inserted casually into a natural break in the conversation, as though he himself were part of it. Even though they couldn't "hear" the actual words, the general idea of it would bleed through.

That was the idea, anyway.

They sure make me nervous. As he thought it, he exuded a slight feeling of agitation. A trick he and Huiel had been working on—making sure to include the *feeling* along with the thought.

Several of the dozen soldiers sitting around the cookfire shifted and looked around nervously, which was Driskell's cue that his influence was doing something.

Gods, I hope the commander knows what he's doing. What if they lose control?

No one started talking about bloodbane, but a general sense of unease began to radiate from the group.

How could they even think of using *such creatures, anyway? Is it right to loose monsters on a civilian population? Will they do the same to my hometown if we do something to upset them?*

All were tidbits of conversations Yasril had overheard among the soldiers on one of his many excursions into the camp to spy for Tanuac.

Many of the soldiers were now looking in the direction of the forest, where most of the bloodbane were being gathered. No one said anything for a few moments, and then nervous conversation started again.

As the last time he had expanded his bubble, Driskell started to feel dizzy. He'd expended more aether today than he had in a short time before. Huiel had warned him not to overdo it. He probably was on the edge of that.

He let the bubble go, nodded to Yasril, and pointed toward Marakyn with his free hand. Time to go. This wasn't the first trip they had taken into the enemy camp, trying to slowly build up a sense of unease, restlessness—possibly even mutiny.

He had to admit, he was relieved to be done for the day. This was always a terrifying experience.

They wound their way silently through the camp, avoiding the more traveled paths lest they accidentally bump into someone.

They had almost reached the edge of the camp when a red-faced, mustached officer came barreling backward out of a tent along the path, shouting at someone else inside.

Right into Driskell and Yasril.

Driskell was knocked backward, and Yasril tried desperately to keep his grip on Driskell's sweaty hand, but it slipped away as Driskell went sprawling on the ground.

Panicked, Driskell scanned the area frantically, looking for some sign that Yasril was still there, but the officer had turned to see whom he had bumped into before Yasril could have taken any action.

"I'm so sorry, I—" He blinked, then his eyes swept over Driskell. "Who are you?"

Driskell's mind whirled. His deep brown skin marked him as obviously out of place in the camp. There were no Donians among the Setanan troops in *this* army. "A-A messenger."

Driskell stuttered, rising to his feet.

A young, clean-shaven soldier turned onto the path and stopped when he came upon the scene.

Driskell's eyes darted to the younger soldier and then back to the mustached officer. He took two careful steps back. "From, um, Marakyn." Driskell tried to reinforce his words with aether, but his bubble kept popping.

The mustached officer narrowed his eyes at Driskell and took a step toward him. "Is that so? Well, then. Let me escort you to the commander, and you can give him your message."

Driskell backed away. "Uh, no, I've already delivered it. I'm just going to—"

The officer jerked his head toward the younger soldier, and together they grabbed him, immobilizing his arms with their bodies.

Driskell struggled in vain. *Let me go!* he tried to scream at them, but the only thing he succeeded in doing was making his head swim.

He gave up, stomach in his throat, and let them lead him away.

The officer brought him to the center of the camp, where there was a large tent in the middle surrounded by several smaller tents. He halted outside the larger tent and spoke quietly to the two guards outside while Driskell fought his increasing anxiety and tried to appear calm. Maybe he could really play like he was a messenger. Maybe if he could convince them, they'd let him go. He burned aether again, the low-level he reserved for constant enhancement of himself.

"You may enter," one of the guards said. He stood aside to allow the officer and Driskell into the tent. The younger soldier sketched a quick bow to the officer and went his own way, while the officer drove him inside from behind.

Driskell blinked a few times, waiting for his eyes to adjust to the lesser light.

Across the tent from him, bent over a large table surrounded by other officers, was not Bherg, but a broad-shouldered, burly Setanan man with a pock-marked and scarred face. When the mustached officer and Driskell entered, the man straightened up and clasped his hands behind his back. "Treybon," he said, nodding to the officer. His voice was a smooth tenor, a startling contrast to his rather fierce outward appearance. "What is this?"

"A Donian spy, Commander," the officer named Treybon said without hesitation. "I found him skulking about the outskirts of the camp."

Driskell glanced around and swallowed. Every eye was trained on him. None of them looked friendly. "I'm not a spy," he tried. "I have a message." He burned a little extra aether and slowly expanded his bubble.

The commander raised an eyebrow. "Is that so? Why was I not informed that a messenger had arrived, then?"

Driskell's heart sank, and he cast about for some reply. "Where is Holiness Bherg?" he asked.

"Bherg is on his way back to Weylyn City," the man said. "I am Commander Gered."

That was...interesting news. Had Bherg been relieved of duty because of his bungling of the battle priests? Had they sent the priests back to the city, too, now that they were useless?

Commander Gered was tapping his right index finger on the table, watching Driskell.

Driskell continued expanding his bubble, not too fast, not too desperate, just an easy increase of aether, bit by bit, until it encompassed the entire table and Gered behind. Then he, just as slowly, withdrew the aether, until it was as low of a burn as his personal enhancement, but leaving the bubble intact.

Phew. He'd done it before, but never under such pressure.

"Forgive me, Commander," he said. "Might I ask what happened to Bherg? Was he relieved of duty?" *I'm safe,* he projected into his bubble. *I'm a friend. You can tell me.*

Commander Gered hesitated. It was a hesitation Driskell was coming to associate with his magic doing *something*. "Yes," Gered said at last.

Several heads swiveled in Gered's direction, not a few eyebrows raised.

Nerves skittered across Driskell like rats on a corpse. His bubble shrank a bit, but he steadied it. *I'm safe,* he projected again, though he wasn't sure if it was for his own benefit at this point or Gered's. *I'm a friend. You can trust me.*

One of the other officers at the table stirred. "If he's a messenger, where is his message?"

I'm a friend, Driskell thought again. *You can trust me*. "My message is verbal," he said. "I-I need to speak to Commander Gered alone." He was improvising now, his only thought being that if he could get everyone else away, he might have a chance to escape. He wasn't brawny, but he could sprint. If Yasril were anywhere nearby, the man could grab him, and they could sneak out.

"Why are you wasting words with a spy, Commander?" the officer pressed. "Execute him or torture him—but have done with it so we can get back to the matter at hand."

No, I'm not a spy! I'm a friend. You can trust *me.*

At that moment, a foot soldier skirted into the tent, over to Gered's side, and whispered something in his ear.

Gered nodded, his face giving away nothing of what he had been told, and the soldier left. "What is your message, Dal? You can speak it now, or not at all."

Driskell's mind whirred. "I've come to beg you to reconsider using bloodbane on Marakyn. Setting a hoard of monsters on a city of innocents is an extreme measure." *I'm a friend. You can trust me.*

Gered hesitated. "There are no innocents in Marakyn."

He hadn't denied it. Oh, gods, he hadn't denied it. Was that their plan? The way they'd take Marakyn? What an awful, despicable—

"Not least of all, you, Dal Driskell."

He'd been recognized. Panic squeezed his chest, and the bubble popped.

It's fine, he assured himself. *It doesn't matter.* Surely, the commander wouldn't think that Tanuac would have sent his attaché as a spy. He gained control and expanded the bubble again, a bit too rapidly—but stabilized it at the end. *It doesn't matter,* he thought at Gered. *I'm still a friend.*

"I cannot imagine that Tanuac would have sent his attaché," Gered began, and Driskell's heart lifted, "as a simple messenger."

As quick as it had soared, his heart crashed.

"I wonder," Gered said, tapping his chin, "how badly Tanuac wants you back?"

Oh, no. He struggled to maintain the bubble. He had to get out of here. *I'm a friend,* he projected desperately, burning aether at far too quick a rate. *You can trust me.*

Another officer spoke. "I imagine if he doesn't return, Tanuac might be rather put out."

Gods help me, Driskell prayed to no one in particular. What he would give right now to be a moonblood, able to disappear, or a fireblood, to set something on fire as a distraction, or...

"But would he be put out enough to do something rash? And if so, is that to our benefit or detriment?"

"Worth considering further," the officer said.

Driskell focused on the nameless officer instead.

I'm a friend, he projected at the officer. *Let me go.* "I can assure you," Driskell said to him, instead of the commander. "Tanuac has half a dozen other clerks who could take my place."

The officer nodded sagely. "He has a point, Commander. He's merely a glorified clerk."

Gered frowned. "Hmm," he said again. "But if that's true, then Tanuac certainly won't mind if we dispose of him to be on the safe side."

Driskell's breath caught in his throat. *No, you definitely don't want to do that.* He was starting to feel dizzy.

Gered nodded once. "Detain him while I think about it."

*He couldn't be taken prisoner. Oh, no...no...no...*What if they tortured him for information? He didn't know if he could withstand that sort of thing; he was no hardened soldier, nor a trained spy. He was just an attaché.

One of the guards came forward and tied his hands behind his back, and Driskell was helpless to do anything about it.

"Have you nothing further to say, Dal?" Gered asked, eyeing Driskell curiously, as though he truly expected something interesting to come out of Driskell's mouth.

Driskell thought furiously. What did Gered want from him? He didn't understand. "I'm not your enemy," he said. He wasn't. None of them were. *Give this up. Leave us alone... I'm not your enemy.*

Gered nodded, as if he thought so. "No. A...friend, perhaps?"

And then it dawned on Driskell. All this time, he had been projecting to Gered that he was a friend, and it had worked. Except Gered had taken it in a different way.

He thought he was literally a friend.

A traitor to his people.

Panic squeezed Driskell's chest, and it seemed, his aether

right out of him, out of control, reduced to nothing in one blast of heat.

He sank to his knees, his head swimming, spots dancing in his eyes.

Darkness.

Chapter Fifty

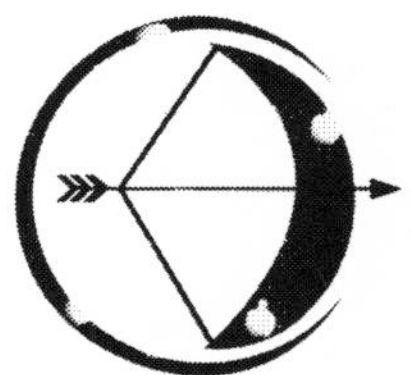

Company

The sun was setting, and Gildas' old office in the palace was shadowed, but amber light spilled through the window behind Gildas' desk, which was directly across from the doorway.

It was an impressive space: Gildas' workspace, personal library, and separate seating area complete with bar for casual meetings. Gildas had spent most of his time in this room, and, by all reports, Airell had spent little to no time in it—so hadn't changed it at all.

It drudged up old memories of the three times Vaughn had been in this office.

The first time had been when he'd been a boy playing hide-and-seek with his brothers. Airell had lured him in here to hide on a dare and then left him long enough that it was Gildas who'd ended up finding him. He had dragged Vaughn out from under his desk and had him whipped on the spot.

The second time, it had been with his old tutor, the one who Gildas had...relieved of duty. Having heard the rumors of the tutor's illegal language lessons for Vaughn, Gildas had summoned both of them here and then demanded that Vaughn corroborate or deny the rumors. They had stood right in front of that same desk, and Vaughn had been too terrified of his father to lie.

The third and final time had been when Gildas had introduced him to Cheris. Vaughn could still see her standing there, just in front of Gildas' desk, turning to greet him with a coy smile the moment he'd darkened Gildas' door, as he did now. He had been immediately smitten.

It was his only positive memory of this room, yet even that had been robbed of any happiness by the events that would later transpire.

He stepped across the threshold, leaving the door open, and walked to his father's desk without lighting a lantern, despite the lessening light. He didn't need one.

He ran a hand along the dark and luscious wood—rysta, an import from Cadmyr. It had been so well-polished that the golden beams of sunlight shattered and glistened on its surface like a placid lake. He moved behind it, but he couldn't bring himself to sit in the chair. Not yet.

The light from the hallway changed, and Vaughn looked up.

His mother stood framed in the doorway. "I haven't been in here since your father died," she said. "Airell didn't use the room other than to raid the liquor collection." She paused. "Do you normally stand in darkness?"

He lifted the glass shield of a lamp on Gildas' desk with one hand, rubbed the fingers of the other against a sliver of fireblood aether, and then touched them—and the residue of the aether—to the wick.

It lit instantly, and he set the shield back into place. "I don't need light to see."

She moved into the room without comment, coming to stand in front of the desk.

Then she handed him several sheets of paper.

He accepted them cautiously. "What's this?"

"I took the liberty of arranging your schedule for the next two weeks."

Vaughn blinked and looked down at the top sheet. He hadn't even spent a single night in the palace and his mother had already drawn up a *schedule*?

But sure enough, there before him, written in her neat hand, was a list of the next fourteen days. There were dinners, meetings, appearances...

His head spun, and he set the stack down on the desk.

"I've already made the official declaration that there will be an election in two weeks," his mother said. "Election law requires five days to allow time for the representatives to gather, but, though I know Ri Tanuac is anxious to move forward, I believe you will benefit from some additional time." She glanced at an old newssheet lying on Gildas' desk. "The announcement will be in the morning newssheet as well as proclaimed by criers. I've also sent runners to notify the representatives across Ferehar, and I imagine the first of those will begin arriving within days."

She tapped her finger on a line on the schedule. "Now, the most notable item is one week from today, when most of the representatives should have arrived. I've arranged an informal gathering and extended an invitation to both the representatives and any additional nobles who wish to come. All the Gan will certainly be there. This will be a time to introduce you to the representatives formally as well as offer you the opportunity to mingle with them around light refreshments. You will, of course, want to have a formal speech prepared, but you should also spend time considering your goals as Ri and how you want to express them. The representatives will be curious about who you are and what you have to offer."

Vaughn's eye twitched. His goals as Ri? His goal as Ri was to sign the Xambrian alliance so Yaotel would be happy, survive for a few years, and then find a way to disappear again.

"I've also scheduled a number of appearances around the city," his mother continued. "It would be good for you to hear and express an interest in the concerns of some of the major leaders—the factory guild's chief, as one example. Obviously, they won't have a vote, but popular opinion will no doubt play a role in the vote of undecided representatives. Remember, they may hate Airell, but they can always abstain rather than vote for an unknown." She paused. "Or a Banebringer. On that matter, it would probably be best if you downplay that aspect of yourself for now. It may intrigue some, but many will be uncomfortable with it, and a few will be set against you because of it." She flicked her eyes to the lantern he had lit earlier. "You need to show you're normal—let that aspect fade out of their minds, as much as possible."

Yes, that's right. Play a role. Be someone other than who you are. Vaughn's gut twisted. *"Stop crying." "You're too sensitive." "Why can't you be more like Airell?"*

"However, you should also keep in mind that your biggest advantage is that you are *not* Airell. You need to be what they expect yet also not. Under the schedule, you'll find notes on the Gan and any of the representatives that I am well enough acquainted with to know how they might be swayed. I've noted what their likely initial reactions to you will be, how likely they will be to vote for you, and what they want to hear. You can do with that information what you will."

Burning skies. Someone save me.

His mother gave him a stern look, as if she could hear his thoughts. "You can, of course, do what you wish. But I would strongly suggest to you that if you want to take on this role, you must do your part."

Even now, after such a trying day, his mother looked the picture of elegance—the perfect noble wife, with not a hair out of place, not a wrinkle in her royal blue gown.

"Are you sure *you* don't want to run against him?" Vaughn asked.

She smiled, and it was only then that Vaughn saw the strain. "Even if Fereharians would elect a woman, I would much rather do what I've always done."

He raised an eyebrow at her. He hadn't the faintest idea what she'd always done, other than attempt to keep her husband's temper directed away from their children.

She shrugged her slight shoulders, even that casual gesture graceful. "Damage control."

He leaned back against the window and folded his arms across his chest. "I appreciate *your* vote of confidence."

She studied him for a moment and then turned her back to move toward the bar. "I haven't the faintest idea what to expect from you. The boy I knew was sensitive, empathetic, and timid."

Yes. He knew. So-called flaws in his masculinity that his father had attempted to squash out of him—and had ultimately led to what Vaughn had then interpreted as the only positive attention he'd ever received from his father: the "gift" of a beautiful fiancée.

It turned out Gildas had merely been concerned for his own reputation. Cheris had made certain he'd known exactly what she had been promised in exchange for seducing his third youngest son. Wealth and power—neither of which Vaughn could offer her as a demonspawn and a fugitive.

Ironic that if he won this election, that was exactly what he would have, and once again, as seemed to be his fate, it was a twist to his life he had never wanted or asked for.

His mother straightened up from her search for anything left under the bar and faced him again. "That boy would have been eaten alive in this role. And yet here you are with questionable friends in tow, challenging your brother, lighting lamps with your fingertips, and handling a bow that looks like it was bequeathed to you from the heavens themselves."

Oh, if only she knew how accurate that was.

"I don't know who you are now and what you might do. Is there anything left of that boy, Teyrnon, or did Gildas drive it out of you?"

I don't know, he wanted to say. But as much as she no longer knew him, he also no longer knew her. She had helped him twice now; it was enough to convince him she was an ally, but not enough to answer her probing question—a question he hardly dared to explore himself. Besides, he had hardly had time to take her full measure, and he was not in a position where he could afford naivety. She was a noble's wife, a noble who had been able to survive and thrive as the wife of Gildas. Could she have an agenda of her own with all of this?

So instead, he said simply, "I prefer to be called 'Vaughn' now. Did you need something else from me?"

It came out harsher than he had intended, but if the words had hurt her, she didn't show it. She glided back toward the door. "I also wanted to see you. It's been eleven years...Vaughn."

She stopped in the doorway again, as if waiting for him to say something else.

He did, in case the words *had* hurt her. "Thank you," he said. "This would have been a different day without your help. A much bloodier day." He swallowed. "And it's good to see you again."

The clock on Gildas' desk ticked in the silence that followed as she stood there, her back still to him. And then finally, she spoke. "If that boy is still in there," she said softly, "I think it's clear the man he's grown into would not be eaten alive, despite his own misgivings. And I would fight to see *that* man as the Ri." Her voice hardened. "The gods know Ferehar could use someone with a little compassion in charge for once."

She nodded toward the paper that still lay on Gildas' desk. "Check your schedule. Your first meeting is in about an hour."

She swept out of the room.

Askata had kindly arranged for temporary accommodations in the palace for all five of them. The gods knew there was enough room; the palace had an entire wing devoted to guest rooms, and with Airell's "advisors" permanently ejected, the wing was empty.

Even though there were enough spare rooms for all of them, Aleena had offered to share a room with Ivana. Ivana still wasn't sure why; perhaps Aleena thought she needed company—or perhaps she thought she might do something rash and wanted to keep an eye on her.

Either way, Ivana had declined. She was more than happy with her solitude.

Or so she thought.

She now sat in an armchair in front of the fireplace in her room. It would have been cozy if it were winter, but it was summer, so the hearth was cold and dead.

She worked her dagger out of the sheath at her thigh and

turned it over in her hands. What was she supposed to do now? Twiddle her thumbs? Go back to Marakyn and let them experiment on her?

Ugh.

There was a knock at her door. She slid the dagger back into its sheath but kept hold of the hilt. One could never be too careful. "Come," she said, turning her head toward the door.

One of the many maids scurrying around the manor entered the room and curtsied. "Your pardon, Da, but Lady Askata asked that we make sure our guests are settled in comfortably. Is there anything I can get you? I can draw a bath, if you wish, or bring you food or drink."

"I'm well situated," Ivana said. "Thank you."

The maid shifted from one foot to the other. "Are you certain? Ri—I mean—Lord Airell always wanted to be sure his guests' needs were well-met."

Ivana studied the woman. She was staring intently at a spot over Ivana's shoulder. "What sort of needs?"

"Well—anything you might want, really." She glanced at Ivana and then quickly looked away. "Usually, his guests were male, but I...begging your pardon, that's—that's fine."

Ivana pressed her lips together. How many guests had this poor maid had to *entertain*? "Fortunately, I'm not a guest of Lord Airell," she said softly.

The maid flushed. "Just so, Da. I'm so sorry to have disturbed you. I'm just...used to certain protocols, I suppose."

"No apologies necessary, Da." She paused. "Have you stopped at any of the others' rooms yet?"

"Only Lord Teyrnon's, but he wasn't there."

She nodded. "Well, none of us are guests of Lord Airell, so I think you can safely dispense with normal protocols and do precisely as your lady asked you and nothing more."

The maid curtsied again, looking relieved. "Yes, Da."

She left and closed the door behind her.

Ivana slid her dagger out of its sheath again. "Bastard," she muttered under her breath, and then she clenched the hilt and brought it up to the light. It was a good thing that from her vantage point in the city earlier that day, she hadn't been able to clearly see Airell's face. Hearing his voice again had been bad enough.

She hissed and stopped herself from stabbing the arm of the chair just in time. Instead, she stood up and snapped the dagger back into its sheath. She could have killed him, right then and there, and been done with it. Maybe she should have.

But the person who would do that is dead, remember?

Well, that was a pretty lie to tell herself. If she had been close enough to do it easily, she probably would have, promise to Vaughn notwithstanding.

It was late. It had been a tiring day. And who knew what the next would bring? She paced back and forth along the window a few times, trying to shake off the dark mood that had descended on her. She had thought she wanted to be alone, but now solitude meant she was alone with her thoughts, and the thought of trying to sleep agitated her more, for then she would have dreams she couldn't control. The void inside her yawned wider, taunting her with whispered memories, and she didn't want to listen.

What was Vaughn doing, if he wasn't in his room?

Maybe he wouldn't mind company.

Vaughn closed his eyes and breathed deeply of the cool night air.

Well, "cool" might have been an overstatement, but it was certainly cooler than it had been during the day—and less stuffy than inside the palace. Perhaps he ought to sleep here on the roof, as commoners sometimes did on hot summer nights.

Commoners. Listen to himself. One day in the palace, and he was already thinking of himself as a noble again. This place was poisonous. No matter what happened, he would not fall back into that. He had fled from that life and since seen it for what it was. Toxic. He would play Yaotel's game for now, but at the first chance of getting away from here...

He would what? Abandon them all? If there was going to be a war, Yaotel would need him.

His chest squeezed. Sometimes he missed flitting about killing bloodbane. It had been lonely, but it had also been simple. This was still lonely, and now complicated.

"I thought I might find you here."

He jumped. "Gods, Ivana," he said, turning. "You nearly startled me right off the roof."

She moved to his side and looked over the edge, three stories down. "That would have been unfortunate."

He took a step away from her. "Unless, of course, that was your intent..."

She raised an eyebrow at him, bemused.

"Well, who knows what someone might have offered you?"

Something flickered across her face, but she snorted. "If you think—"

He held up a hand. "I don't. I was teasing."

She studied him with those dark, implacable eyes for a moment, and then turned to look out across the palace grounds. "You should be more careful. You jest, but you're making yourself an easy target." She glanced behind them. "You ought to at least have a guard on the stairs—or Danton or Thrax, if you can't trust any of the guards yet."

He cleared his throat. Damnation. It wasn't that such things hadn't occurred to him—no, he was painfully conscious of how little he could trust anyone but his own little circle of friends. But he wasn't used to taking guards with him everywhere he went. "Thanks," he said. "Any other free advice?"

"Yes, since you asked. One of the maids stopped by my room to offer me her 'services,' which are extensive." She quirked an eyebrow up, and Vaughn took her meaning. "Apparently, this was standard protocol when your brother was Ri. If you win, I suggest you do something about that."

He chuckled. "Why do I feel like that suggestion has the ring of a threat about it?"

"She stopped by your room, too, which was how I knew you weren't there."

"You *asked* if she stopped by my room?"

She shrugged. "I was curious what you would do when offered your old vice on a platter."

"Was she pretty?" he quipped, offering her a half-cocked smile.

She frowned. "Not amused."

He ducked his head, duly chastised. "Sorry. Poor taste. I'm kidding, of course."

She made a soft sound in the back of her throat. "Of course."

He looked over at her, but she said nothing more. Her hair was still bound back at the nape, but strands had come free. He didn't know why he always found those loose strands that tickled her neck so irresistible, but there it was.

He took a deep breath and looked away. "Did you need something, or did you seek me out merely to cheer me up with ominous warnings?"

"I thought you might want company."

He raised an eyebrow. "She who would prefer the companionship of a rock to a human being offers me this? How uncharacteristically generous."

She put her hands behind her back as if standing for inspection. "If you don't, I can leave."

An owl hooted from somewhere across the palace grounds. Company. Such a simple concept, wasn't it? "I never mind your company," he said softy, though he suspected her offer had to do more with her own frame of mind than her concern for his. He'd never get her to admit that, though.

"I appreciate you not killing Airell today," he said.

She said nothing.

"If it makes you feel any better, he's locked up in the dungeon." He pulled out the key he had put on a chain around his neck by way of demonstration. "And I confiscated the only key because I don't know who might be loyal to Airell. Is that sufficient foresight for you?"

Neither the jailor nor his mother had been happy about handing over the key, but he didn't even know if he could trust his mother, let alone the jailor.

His stomach clenched again, and he pushed it away.

Sadly, Ivana failed to praise him. "I'll feel better once he's dead."

He tucked the key back under his shirt. "Will you? That doesn't seem to be your experience."

She said nothing.

They stood in silence for a while, she in her at-ease position, and he slouched over with his hands in his pockets. A warm breeze occasionally lifted the still hot air, and crickets took up a chorus in the palace gardens below. Beyond the palace walls, the city of Cohoxta stretched out on all sides. To the south, the Atl River glistened in the moonlight; to the east, the Fereharian Mountains rose above the horizon, blocking out stars.

In that moment, it seemed surreal that he was staying at the Fereharian palace, when not even two years ago he had been on the run from the Fereharian Ri, his own father. That his mother seemingly accepted him, had even sided with him over her firstborn. That he would attempt to wrest the title of Ri from his own brother, who, knowing the way the rule of law tended to work in Ferehar, would likely be executed for treason if Vaughn won.

"What am I doing here, Ivana?" he asked softly. "I spent the past hour courting three of the four Fereharian Gan for their votes and support. My mother seems pleased with how it went, but I was never raised for this."

"I'm sure Yaotel and Tanuac will provide you with some quality advisors."

His mouth twisted at the taste on his tongue. "Yes. You're right. I'm here to do what I'm told, aren't I?"

"You want to do something else?"

"No, I—" He exhaled, frustration bubbling up. "I was the third son of Ri Gildas, and then a Banebringer—to Yaotel, an asset, and to the other Ichtaca, a member of their 'club,' as you like to put it. They want me to be Ri? Fine. I can be whatever identity they want to slap on me. I've plenty of practice, after all." His words caught audibly with a hitch in his throat, and he pressed his lips together to stop the bitter barrage.

Ivana shifted.

"I know," he said. "What sane person complains about being handed one of the most powerful and affluent positions in the Empire?"

"That was," she said softly, "not at all what I was thinking."

"No?"

"No."

He waited. She didn't elaborate.

"What were you thinking, then?" he prodded.

There was a long silence, and then she turned to face him.

"That perhaps you and I have more in common than I originally suspected."

He gave her a wan smile. "Yes. Except while I'm dying to be known as the person beneath my layers of identities, I rather think you're hoping just the opposite for yourself."

She didn't return his smile, which wasn't surprising. What *was* surprising was her response to his observation. "We're both a mess," she conceded.

A warm breeze blew again, and loose hairs flitted into her eyes. He reached out to brush them away before she could, but instead, their hands collided.

He caught her hand in his, and she didn't pull away. Instead, she intertwined her fingers in his own and looked up at him. Her face was implacable no longer; instead, it was strained with what he could only describe as grief.

He almost never knew what was going on in that head of hers because she rarely told him. But he knew how his own isolation ate at him, and he knew that somewhere inside she was still hurting deeply.

He hesitated, and then he drew her against himself, untangled his hand from hers, and wrapped his arms around her.

She stiffened, but he held her tightly. Bit by bit, the tension drained out of her, and she at last slid her arms up his back and relaxed into his offered embrace.

Ivana buried her face in Vaughn's shoulder. He was wrong. He was so, desperately wrong. She wanted to be known more than anything. She wanted to be just Ivana, without anything else complicating her life. The problem was she didn't know who that person was anymore. She had lost herself three times over, and the shattered pieces of the person who had been left behind were more than just a simple mess—as if a sturdy broom could swiftly sweep them up or a skilled hand could untangle the knot.

No, her deepest fear was that she was irreparably broken.

She had never truly healed from her shattered past; she had never learned to cope in any other way than running, literally and figuratively.

She had never faced herself, and therefore now she no longer knew herself.

But she did know that right now, she didn't want to be alone, and so she let Vaughn hold her, drank in the simple comfort of another's solid presence.

The thought of going back to her room and lying in the darkness...

Aleena would welcome a change of mind. But Aleena would also ask her questions. Prod and pry at her, even if only with those *eyes*. And Ivana didn't want to think, she didn't want to reflect—she wanted company, not a counselor.

After a moment, she whispered, "Can I stay with you tonight?"

He pulled back to look at her, one eyebrow quirked up.

"Just...in the room."

He brushed her cheek with the back of his hand. "You can stay with me."

Chapter Fifty-One

Just to Be

Vaughn's suite was bigger than Ivana's, with a separate bedroom from the sitting area as well as a private bath, so it turned out she would have plenty of space to "stay in his room."

He unlocked the door and held it open for her, and then he crossed the room to light a lamp.

She sank down onto the couch in the sitting area. A weariness that went beyond physical fatigue pulled at her.

"Do you want something to drink?" Vaughn asked, holding up a bottle of wine that was on a side table. "It looks like a good vintage. By that I mean, it might even *taste* good, even if it can't offer anything else to us."

She glanced at the bottle. "Where did that come from?"

There was a tag around the neck of the bottle, and he flipped it over to read it. "A gift from my mother, apparently."

She sighed. "I'll pass. And so should you."

He looked at the bottle in his hand and then set it back down. "It's from my *mother*. Are you suggesting that my own mother would try to poison me?"

Ivana felt that he shouldn't rule out that possibility, but he probably didn't need that thought implanted in his head right now. "So the tag says. Have you confirmed that?"

He rubbed at his jaw. "Oh. Right."

Gods, sometimes he still seemed so naïve. "Do you think anyone would be interested in a pool for how long you last? I'd go for two months."

He plopped down next to her on the couch. "You know—"

"I'm joking."

"Are you?"

She turned her head to look at him, considering the matter more seriously. "Well, you're a Banebringer, so that's a slight deterrent. An assassin would be wary of taking such a job, and that information is public knowledge, so a client couldn't hide it in your case. Still, that doesn't rule out poison and 'accidents.'" She tapped her chin. "Also, since *most* clients wouldn't want to unleash a bloodbane in the middle of the palace, you'll need to be the most concerned when you're traveling or out of the city."

"Most?"

She shrugged. "There are always those people who just want the world to burn."

He muttered something under his breath.

"All things considered, if you continue on your current path of naivety, I'll give you four months. Six, if I'm being generous, and I'll grant a year if I'm overestimating how many people might take the more blunt-force method of getting rid of you."

"Ivana—"

"We still haven't addressed those who will seek to depose you in other ways—more subtle ways. Such as framing you, hurting people you care about, or, since a strong point in your favor over Airell is that you're generally a 'nice guy,' slowly eroding your reputation through gossip and rumors, or forcing your hand in less 'nice' ways to destroy trust. Granted, it's hard to get rid of a Ri, but someone could certainly negate your influence or make life miserable enough for you that you just give up and run."

"Ivana!"

She stopped. "Yes?"

He rubbed his temples. "I am perfectly aware of the sort of games people play in these circles. Why in the abyss do you think this is the last place I want to be?"

"Ah. I assumed—"

"That since I seem to have a knack for being reckless with my own welfare, I don't know anything else?"

"You *did* say you weren't raised to this."

"I wasn't. Airell was. Ironically, Airell squandered the opportunity. But I *know* what's out there. I just won't be a natural at navigating it." He sighed. "I thought you wanted to stay here because you needed companionship, not to give me a list of all my potential problems."

Huh. He had a point. "Well. I suppose if I'm focusing on solving your problems, I'm not thinking about mine."

He brushed the back of his hand against her cheek. "How about," he said, "we not talk about problems right now?"

"Fair enough," she said.

He exhaled through his nose, and his face softened. Then, after a moment of hesitation, he scooted closer to her, put his arm around her shoulders, and drew her against him.

Her instinctual reaction was to pull away, to stiffen, to reject his offer of comfort.

But she fought it because if she didn't stop to *think* and just let herself *be*...this was...nice.

She forced herself, as she had earlier, to relax against him. She closed her eyes, and they were silent for long enough that she started to drift off.

"Ivana?" he asked abruptly.

"Mmm...yes?"

There was a long pause, long enough that the pause itself roused her.

"What are you going to do after all this is over?"

"I thought we weren't talking about problems," she said.

Another pause. "Is that question a problem?"

She turned it over in her mind. "Sort of. Because I don't know."

"You could stay here with me."

She drew back. She told herself that it was only so she could see his face, but inside she felt more like a bird that had fluttered away from something that had startled it.

The latter must have shown on her face, because he rushed to explain. "I mean—I could use someone around who thinks the way you do. To remind me not to do stupid things like drinking anonymous bottles of wine given in gifts." He rubbed his jaw. "Temoth, I could even give you an official title. Like, 'Advisor of Keeping Vaughn Alive.'"

She had to smile at that. "Doesn't that normally fall under the purview of bodyguards?"

He waved his hand. "Oh, I'm sure eventually I'll collect some burly men I can trust for that purpose. But that's not what I meant."

"Ah. You meant more like an Intelligence Advisor."

"Fine. Your version wins." He flashed her a smile. "Besides, long-term, it will be easier to figure out how we're supposed to use your powers to fight Danathalt if you're here. This would give you something to do in the meantime."

She turned the possibility over in her mind. "Does the official title come with pay?"

"Official titles normally do."

If he was serious, there was a certain appeal to it. It would be a way to use her skills to protect someone she cared about rather than hurt someone she didn't. "I'll consider it."

"Really?" he asked, looking genuinely surprised.

She was rather surprised herself. Especially that she had listed Vaughn in a category of people she cared about. When had *that* changed? "Yes. But maybe you should get elected before you start spending Ferehar's money."

"Fair enough," he said. "As long as you promise that you don't turn me down and then end up working for someone else—like Yaotel. Because then I might become disgruntled."

She snorted. "That is *not* likely to happen."

"What if he paid more?"

She rolled her eyes. "Even were it possible for Yaotel to match the coffers of Ferehar, I would make a horrible 'Intelligence Advisor' for Yaotel because I don't like him enough to care about what happens to him—not to mention he doesn't like me enough to ask."

There was a long pause, during which all that happened was Vaughn's small smile grew until it stretched from ear to ear.

She frowned. "What are you grinning about?"

"You just admitted that you like me."

"I said no su—" Gods help her, she sort of had, hadn't she?

She sniffed and looked away. "All that means is I like you *enough* that I'd be willing to keep something from happening to you. For pay."

"You," he said, putting his hands on either side of her face and forcing her to look back at him, "are a big, fat, liar." His smile had returned to more normal proportions, and a playful twinkle was in his eye.

She had no response for him because he was right, and they both knew it. She could no longer deny it: She *had* grown fond of him.

She pressed her lips together, shoved his hands away, and glared at him. "Well...don't let it go to your head."

He was not to be deterred. He poked her nose. "You don't scare me in the least."

She swatted at his hand and let out a breath. "Temoth, I know. I never have. It's *so* irritating."

His smile grew again. "If you haven't discovered by now that my biggest talent is being a pain in the ass..."

Her own smile was back; it welled from her core and filled her wholly. But it was more than a smile: it was the warmth of shared friendship, and more—the breathtaking, impossible-to-dismiss evidence of life inside what she thought was only a dead and empty husk.

It was overwhelming.

Vaughn's smile fell away. She didn't know what he saw, but he lifted his hand to her face to trace her forehead, her eyes, her nose, her cheeks, her jaw, following his own fingers with his eyes—as if he were committing every line to memory—until his fingertips brushed her lips.

Fire shot through her, burning away her smile and bringing into sharp awareness her danger.

Vaughn dropped his hand and met her eyes at last.

He didn't move, but he didn't have to. She could read his thoughts in his eyes, could feel his kisses and caresses warm on her skin before he had even touched her.

Danger melted into desire, and in that instant she lost—or won?—whatever battle she had been fighting these past months. In giving him her smile, her friendship, she had freely offered him a glimpse into whatever was left of *Ivana,* and she had no energy—no desire, even—to manufacture further pretense or excuses right now.

She was tired. She wanted to live in the present for once. Not the past. Not the future.

She just wanted to *be.*

Vaughn sensed the change in Ivana when it happened. It was the sound of a key turning in a tiny lock, audible only to those who were listening for it.

And he was. He was drinking in every pore of her skin, every mark in the brown of her irises, every line of her face, and wondering when she had become so absolutely beautiful to him, in a way that went far beyond the warmth of her skin or softness of her lips.

He ached from his fingertips to his toes to imbibe her fully, but he didn't dare.

Until he heard that soft *snick.*

He couldn't pinpoint what was different; it wasn't the first time her lips had parted at his touch and her eyes reflected his own longing.

But when he tentatively reached out once more to touch her face, and she visibly shuddered...

He wrapped his other arm around her back, drew her close, hesitated a hairsbreadth from her lips...and then kissed her.

Once. Twice. Three times—and she returned it all without hesitation.

His lips left hers to find her jaw, her neck, her throat, her collarbone, the V of her chest left by the ciuhan blouse she had donned for that day.

A soft rush of air left her lips, and she tilted her head back. Thus encouraged, he pulled back one side of the fabric to continue as far as the cut of the blouse would let him, just until the firmness of bone gave way the soft rise of her breasts.

There, he was stymied. No buttons, no drawstrings—the blouse of a ciuhan was designed to slip on and off over the head, but after their multiple stops and starts, he sure wasn't going to attempt that without her expressed consent.

So, though he longed to gorge himself on the sight of her, to touch and kiss every part of her, he returned to her lips, and settled for sliding his hand under the neckline of her blouse, along her bare shoulder, and down as far as the neckline of the blouse would let him.

She caught his hand.

He pulled back from her lips enough to meet her eyes. *No. Not again!* He'd thought it was different this time. He'd been so *sure...*

It doesn't matter, he berated himself. If this was it, this was it. He could not, would not, demand more than she was ready for again.

But though she held his hand in place, she didn't push it away.

No, her eyes were burning, which only made him ache all the more.

"You told me once," she said, still close enough that he could feel her breath on his own lips, "that we were the perfect lovers because we could enjoy each other without irksome things like attachment and assumptions and hopes."

"I did say that," he acknowledged, his heart hammering. He had convinced himself at the time that it had been true.

"Is that what this is?" she asked, reaching up with her other hand to run her thumb along his jaw.

Attachment. Oh, he was far beyond mere attachment. But she wasn't ready to hear that—and he was nowhere near ready to say it. That made this even more dangerous for him, but right now, he didn't care.

"If you mean is this *more* than that, then..." He turned his head to kiss the fingers she had just brushed along his lips, intensifying the ache. "I think you know me well enough to know the answer to that."

She didn't reply, but her eyes flicked to his lips again.

"But if you mean is this *less* than that..." He gave a strangled chuckle. "I am, shall we say, more than ready to indulge your every whim. Tonight. Tomorrow, and for as long as we both want."

She ran the back of her hand along his cheek again, and then the jaw, and then turned her hand to touch his lips again.

At the last, her fingers trembled against his lips, and when he met her eyes, he saw there a naked vulnerability he hadn't seen since that night below Gan Barton's manor, and he remembered once more what she would be giving him. "If...you really *do* want this," he said.

She held his eyes. Time slowed as he waited for her response. He could hear her breathing and nothing else, and the eternity held in that moment about killed him. It had been so. Damn. Long.

At last, she cupped his own face in both her hands and drew him close. "I want this," she breathed against his lips, and then she kissed him again.

It was all he'd needed to hear. Fire burned through him, and all that remained was bare skin against skin, and caresses, and the consummation of his long-arrested desire to *know* her.

Knowing, all the while, that for him, at least, this was so much more. It was something he hadn't done since Cheris.

To make love.

Chapter Fifty-Two

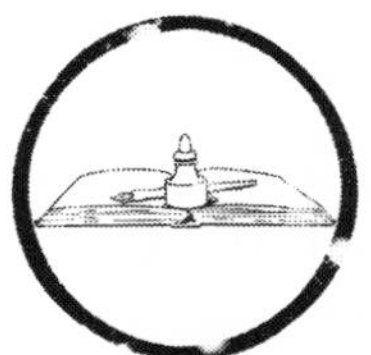

The Commander

When Driskell opened his eyes, it was dark. He jerked upright, his heart immediately going into full pattering drum mode.

He hung his head and clenched his fists together.

His first mission, and he had failed. There was no other way to look at it. But that didn't mean he had to stay here and wait for them to torture him.

He organized his thoughts into a list. Take stock of the surroundings. Identify his situation. Identify likely escape routes. Identify potential resources. Make a plan and follow it.

There was only the faintest bit of light filtering in through the closed tent flap, so it was difficult to see his surroundings.

This wasn't starting well.

He closed his eyes. He had more than his eyes, after all. His arms had been tied behind his back and around what felt like a wooden stake in the ground. He gingerly stood up.

Yes. Just tall enough that he wouldn't be able to get his arms over the top, even if he jumped.

He pushed his back into the stake a few times. Solid. Probably no yanking it out or pushing it over, either.

Well, drat.

No one was around that he could see—and he felt as though if someone were hiding in the dark and had seen him wake up, they wouldn't be letting him test his bonds.

The tent flap opened, and the orange light of a cookfire outside filtered in. There was a hushed conversation, and then Commander Gered stepped into the tent holding a lantern.

He set the lantern carefully on the dirt ground and gave Driskell a onceover. "I see you've been surveying your situation," he said.

Driskell sank back to the ground, silent. *I'm a friend?* he projected hopefully.

Gered glanced back through the flap, as if checking to be sure no one had followed him in, and then settled down onto the ground himself. "I'm curious, Dal Driskell. Did you know Dal Dax?"

Driskell eyed the man warily. "No, Commander. Not well."

"Hmm. He, too, came to us—or, rather, my predecessor—as a traitor to his people."

Driskell really *had* inadvertently convinced the commander he was here as a turncoat.

There had to be a way to capitalize on that.

"Unfortunately, my predecessor was, among many things, a shortsighted man, and failed to utilize such a resource when it fell into his lap. Instead, after sucking what knowledge he could out of it, he destroyed it out of religious zealotry." Gered nodded to Driskell's arm.

Driskell looked down. There was a tiny prick there. A prick with a single, silver dot.

His cursed blood went cold in his veins. They had tested him while he'd been out. They knew.

The danger he was in went far beyond torture.

"Don't worry. I have no love for Banebringers, but I'm also a pragmatic man. Dax was burning with hatred, for all of us not like him; I sense something more subtle out of you." He paused, as if giving Driskell a chance to confirm.

Yes. Subtle. That's right. Um... How much did Gered know about Banebringers? Did he understand or know anything at all about the different profiles? Would he want to know what powers he had, use them for his own purposes? Or was he like most of the masses, who had no real idea what Banebringers could do, aside from wild bedtime tales used to scare children?

His mind whirled furiously, trying to come up with some suitable response. What would a man like Gered respond to? He *was* practical if he didn't care that Driskell was a Banebringer—or, at least, he wasn't a religious zealot. Driskell reached out with his aether, trying to understand the man better, but right now, all he sensed was vague curiosity.

I'm a friend, Driskell projected again. It couldn't hurt to keep reinforcing it. "I'm afraid," Driskell said. "I-I respect Tanuac, but I think he's gone too far. He shouldn't have broken away from Setana. I had hoped that you might give him leniency, give Marakyn leniency. When we realized you planned to use bloodbane...I despaired. I knew I had to do something. You weren't supposed to find out about...about me."

There. That was believable, Driskell thought. It even included elements that were true. His fear. His respect for Tanuac. His despair. With a little encouragement from the aether bubble he had now expanded around the two of them...

Gered nodded. "A perfectly reasonable response, son," he said. "But what do you have to offer me in return for this leniency? Information on a peaceful way to take the city, an offer to open Marakyn's defenses at the right time? Further plans of Tanuac's we can thwart and use against him? A better target?"

"I..." Driskell hesitated. He did the only thing he could think of. He projected his own despair and genuine confusion. Gered seemed to think him a young, naïve person who might still be of use to him.

Let him continue to think that.

Gered's face softened. "You remind me a bit of my own son," he said. "Not Donian, of course."

"Commander," Driskell said, trying a different tactic. "If you don't care that I'm a Banebringer, why are you working for the Conclave? You don't seem to share their vision for Setana." *I'm a friend. You can trust me. I'm like your son, after all...* he added for good measure.

Gered chuckled. "So earnest, so naïve. My prediction is that the Conclave will burn itself out in a bid for control of the land. And when they do, someone needs to be there to step into the void of power left behind, yes?" He clenched his fist in the air. "What better person than a commander currying their favor and therefore close by when the fall occurs, concerned only for the stability of the land, and the strength of mind and body to give it?" He gave that telltale hesitation, no doubt unsure as to why he was sharing so much with this unknown "traitor."

I'm a friend. I'm like your son.

Gered's face relaxed. "I'll give you some time to think on it," he said, standing up. "If you think of some way in which you can be useful to me, call for a guard." He glanced down at Driskell. "I like you, Driskell, though I can't put my finger on why. But my patience is limited. If you can't be useful to me, I will have no choice but to neutralize you." He nodded, as if agreeing with his own statement, and left.

Driskell sank back against the wooden stake. *Gods have mercy.* What had he gotten himself into?

Chapter Fifty-Three

Echoes of Silence

Ivana lay against Vaughn's chest, her eyes closed. To look at her, one might think she was simply contentedly soaking in the residue of consummated desire that still clung to her.

Really, she was hoping that if she didn't open her eyes, she wouldn't have to confront the churning frenzy of emotions within her.

Vaughn's heart was beating normally now, but she knew he wasn't asleep, because he was tracing light circles on her shoulder blade with the hand that cradled her against him.

It was...so...tender. Despite the strength of his passion, he had been a gentle lover, as eager to please her as to slake his own lust. Perhaps even more eager to please her than to slake his own lust—though certainly there had been plenty of that as well.

He splayed his hand against her skin and his chest rose and fell in a quiet sigh. He shifted so he could see her face, and she tilted her head back to look at him. He was smiling at her, that same gentle smile...

Her throat tightened. He studied her, and then the smile faded. "You're...not having regrets, are you?"

She blinked, startled. "No—no, not at all."

His brow furrowed.

"I just...I need to process. This is..." She closed her eyes, and then turned over so her back was to him. She couldn't explain it to him. He had slept with so many women for pleasure over the years that, even though their own agreement wasn't exactly the same, he couldn't possibly understand what this had been for her. How much she had had to give, and give up, to give herself to him.

He had touched her in ways that no man had touched her—that she had *allowed* no man to touch her—for almost fifteen years.

Despite her manifold experience, none of it had been like this. None of it had mattered. It had all been a means to an end—at best, tolerable, at worst, unpleasant.

None of it had ever made her feel this way inside.

Not even Airell.

She hadn't expected the raw vulnerability she had felt. She hadn't expected how that tearing away of every layer to simply *be* would be at once so satisfying...and so painful.

At once exhilarating and terrifying.

She had no words to describe that. She was afraid to even try.

After a few moments, Vaughn slid his hand over her waist and across her abdomen and drew her close to him again. "I know," he said softly.

His simple statement startled her. He did?

This was…not the same man she had almost given herself to once before.

Far from reassuring her, that realization only added to the frothing whirlpool within her.

She leaned against him, her back to his chest, and tried to simply rest in the warmth of his body against hers. Tried to push away everything else and just *be* again.

It wasn't working. She opened her eyes to look across the room at the discarded clothing, evidence of their liaison. Her dagger in its belted sheath lay on top of the blouse and skirt of her ciuhan. He had discovered it underneath her skirt, belted to her thigh as usual, and undid it himself. It had felt like he'd stripped away an entire layer with that one action.

His own shirt and trousers were in another pile, also ornamented—with the chain that held the key to Airell's cell.

She frowned and closed her eyes again. She did *not* want to think about that bastard right now. So instead, she replayed every moment of the past hour in her mind until she fell asleep.

Ivana bolted upright with a gasp and in a cold sweat. She shook her head, trying to fling away the vestiges of the nightmare, but it didn't work. Her heart was still pounding, her stomach still clenched in revulsion and terror.

She could still see Airell's face in her mind, hovering over her, tearing at her clothes and demanding that she give him what he wanted.

Taking it—forcefully.

She closed her eyes and concentrated on breathing deeply, in and out, until her heart had stopped thrashing about in her chest.

She looked over at Vaughn's sleeping form to try to center

herself, to remind herself of the pleasurable evening she had just enjoyed.

Instead, she saw the lines of Airell's face in his brother's profile.

Bile rose in her throat and she stumbled out of the bed, afraid she would vomit. She landed on trembling hands and knees and choked it back. Tears stung at her eyes from the effort, and panic closed her throat once the vomit was back where it belonged.

Stop it! she screamed at herself, and her panic turned to rage, rage that she was unable to control this, rage that Airell still haunted her and could ruin this peaceful night.

Even in her dreams, he was a bastard.

She looked down and saw where she had landed.

Vaughn's clothes lay beneath her, the key to Airell's cell glimmering in a shaft of moonlight that peeked through a crack in the closed curtain.

She stared at the key, her mind churning.

No, a tiny voice said inside. *No, Ivana.*

But it was too late. Whatever doors to her inner self had been opened that night slammed shut, one by one, the sounds echoing inside as though down an empty hallway. The voice chased the doors, growing both more insistent and less influential, but the heat of her rage turned cold, and she scorned the voice, daring it to stop her, until finally the last door closed, and she heard nothing but silence.

The cold, spiteful silence of a trained killer.

She closed her hand over the key.

Vaughn was startled awake by…something not immediately apparent.

He groaned and rolled over to go back to sleep.

But something was wrong. He frowned. He was facing Ivana's side of the bed, and she wasn't in it.

He sighed. Apparently, she wasn't ready to stay with him all night. It didn't surprise him, even if it was disappointing. He had hoped to wake up with her by his side.

All the same, he shifted over to bury his face in her pillow and breathe in her smell. He then rested his cheek there and closed his eyes, preparing to go back to sleep.

And then his eyes sprung back open.

He was staring at his pile of clothes in the dark.

He sat up. Hadn't he left the chain with the key to the dungeon sitting on top of his trousers?

He scooted out of bed and pulled back on his undergarments before rooting around in the pile. He picked up his shirt and shook it out, and then his trousers. Nothing fell on the ground.

He felt in the pockets. Nothing.

He turned to the bedside table. Maybe he had put it there.

Nothing.

His frown deepening, he lit the lamp on the table. He opened the drawer to the bedside table, but it was empty. He looked behind it, but there was nothing there.

He shook out his clothes one more time, and still nothing.

Where in the abyss could it have gone?

He got down on his hands and knees and looked under the bed. Still nothing.

He sat back down on the bed and ran a hand through his hair. Ivana's clothes were gone, obviously. Maybe it had somehow stuck to her skirt and—

He froze. Or had she taken it?

No.

His chest tightened.

No!

He had to be wrong. He *had* to be. He would go to her room and find her, prove himself wrong.

He threw his clothes back on, left his room, and hurried down the hall to Ivana's room.

He banged on the door. There was no response. He glanced down the hall. It was dark and empty, of course—given the time of night. He banged again, and still there was no response. He tried the door handle, and it opened.

He pushed it open and peeked his head inside.

It was only one large room: a sitting area, a fireplace, and a bed, and Ivana wasn't in it.

Aleena. She must have gone to stay with Aleena.

He strode to the next room over and knocked.

After a few moments, the door opened. Aleena stood there, groggy and rumpled in a robe she had obviously hurriedly thrown on over her nightshift. She blinked at him. "Vaughn? What in the abyss? It's the middle of the night!"

"Is Ivana with you?" he asked.

"What? No. Why would she be with me? Isn't she in her room?"

His heart sank. Gods, *no!*

He sagged against the doorframe. His heart was squeezing so hard, he thought he would collapse.

"Vaughn? What's going on?"

Priorities. He could deal with the betrayal later. For now, he had to stop her.

"I think she took the key to the cell where we're keeping Airell," he said, turning to head down the hall to the next room. He banged on the door.

Aleena stared at him and then disappeared back into her room. She reappeared, dressed, just as Danton opened his own door. "Vaughn?" he asked blearily. "It's the middle of the—"

“Yes, I know. Get dressed and meet me at the dungeon—*now.*”

He didn’t wait for Danton, but Aleena joined him as he strode down the hall.

“All right, explanation,” she said, hurrying to keep up with him. “How did Ivana get the key?”

He had to swallow three times before he could speak with a steady voice. “I assume she took it off the top of my pile of clothes, where I left it.”

She grabbed his arm and dragged him to a halt. “Your pile of—” There was a long silence in which she stared at him and Vaughn assumed she was making connections.

“Yes,” he said simply. It was all he could manage.

She closed her eyes. “Oh, Ivana...”

Vaughn didn’t respond, and Aleena said nothing more.

They started back down the hall toward the dungeons.

Chapter Fifty-Four

Always, Yet Not

The Cohoxta palace dungeons consisted of a single large, circular room. Four metal doors with a slot at the floor were set into the walls; two had barred windows, two did not. In the middle of the room was a table with four chairs, three of which were occupied by guards tossing dice.

Ivana came back down on the flat of her feet from where she had been standing, tip-toe, to see through the small barred window into that very room. One last time, she checked the pouch tied to her belt to be sure she had everything she needed. She had stopped by her room to quickly change into something more appropriate for murder and flight, and to gather a few supplies.

She glanced at the guard to her right, who, unlike the three inside the dungeon, stood at attention next to the door.

However, much like the three inside the dungeon, he stood stock-still, unmoving.

Frozen in time.

She plucked the keys off his belt, unlocked the main door to the dungeon itself, then put the keys back.

Then she sprinkled a bit of crushed paltic into his mouth. In a few minutes, he'd be fast asleep and wouldn't hear a thing.

Just to be on the safe side, she burned moonblood aether before entering the dungeon and shutting the door behind her.

Ignoring the cells for now, she dosed the three guards at the table with paltic as well, then shrank against the wall, stopped burning her own aether, and waited for the drug to take effect.

She heard the first guard collapse outside the door first, with a soft thud and a quiet grunt.

The three at the table looked up—one even had time to rise to his feet and draw his sword before they all met the same fate.

She stepped back out into the room and surveyed the unconscious guards.

That had been painfully easy.

Ivana circled the room to peek into the two cells with barred windows. One was empty, the other held a figure huddled on the ground, against the wall, head down.

She lifted the key that now hung around her own neck, unlocked the door, and dragged it open.

The figure scrambled to its feet, and the light of the lanterns from the dungeon flickered on his face as he lifted his head to peer toward the door.

Him.

That same half-cocked grin spread over his face. Self-assured. Cocky. Even in his situation, having the gall to let his eyes rake over her as though she were a serving girl he intended to proposition—or worse.

She had prepared herself for rage. Perhaps even pain—an opening of old wounds. The things that had driven her here in the first place.

Instead, and not for the first time that night, she was unprepared for what she felt.

Cold. Bone-chilling cold that seeped out from within, freezing the cursed blood in her veins—the embodiment of the bitter, empty place of death and despair that had been caged inside of her for a decade, covered over with contempt at worst and cold apathy at best.

And whatever strides she thought she had made in understanding herself evaporated. She no longer did.

"Hmm," he said, his eyes sweeping over the sleeping guards. "Are you here to rescue me? I actually would rather you leave me here until things settle down."

Though she half-expected her breath to fog the air when she spoke, she didn't shiver. "Oh, I'll leave you here, don't worry." She stepped inside.

His smile faded, and now he searched her face. "Who are you?" he asked.

She faced her tormentor for the first time since he had left her alone with her confusion and broken promises.

She had him at her disposal, with no interruptions, and all of a sudden, she no longer wanted to lunge at him to slit his throat.

He was the reason her family was dead, her life destroyed.

He was the reason she'd hated herself then and hated herself still.

She wanted to make him bleed. Suffer. Crumple to the floor screaming soundless screams at the knowledge that his own miserable wretchedness had brought him to this place.

All the things she denied herself in the dead of the night when the bars of the cage rattled and whispers seeped into her dreams.

"An old acquaintance." She tugged the cell door closed behind her, and, using moonblood and iceblood aether, gathered water and froze the lock. Then, hand close to her thigh, she approached him. "I wouldn't expect you to remember me, of course, but I would like it if you could *try*. It would enhance the experience so much more."

His eyes darted back and forth between her face and the hand now fingering the hilt at her thigh. "All right. So—I offended you somehow, once upon a time. Look—I don't know—"

"Offended me somehow? Even your own father remembered me, you bastard."

His mouth worked, open and closed, as if struggling to remember. "A name?"

"Ivana," she said. "I would give you the name of the daughter you paid me to dispose of, but she didn't live long enough to bother naming her." She drew her dagger.

"Ah," he said. "Well, that narrows it down to about half a dozen women."

She struck him across the face, hard enough that blood trickled from the side of his mouth. "I'm not amused," she hissed, pressing the flat of the dagger against his throat. He backed away from her until he ran into the wall, then stared at her.

She realized that he hadn't meant the quip to be humorous; he had been thinking out loud. Wholly unlike his brother in that regard.

The stray thought of Vaughn pierced and cracked her cold shell like an unexpected arrow from the dark. The shock of the blow made her reel, and the realization of what she had done trickled out of that crack like the blood trickling down Airell's neck.

She had grasped at light, tasted freedom. Yes, she had had a chance to start over...and she had thrown it away.

She was no different than she had ever been. She was just a killer who had learned how to have a good time in bed.

Despair choked her throat.

Airell must have seen something change in her face because he dared to mock her. "What's wrong? Can't do it?" He gave her a patronizing smile. "Don't feel bad. You should only expect a whore from a backwater town to be worthless at murder, hmm?"

She stepped toward him, brandishing her dagger again, and he snapped his mouth shut, his face going pale.

But he needn't have worried. All she'd heard was "whore."

Once a whore, always a whore. Couldn't stop with just one brother?

All desire to torture him had evaporated. Only one questioned remained now. Which way did she point the dagger?

Vaughn burst through the door to the dungeons, followed closely by Aleena.

He skidded to a halt inside the chamber, his gaze taking in the unconscious guards, just like the one outside the dungeon door. All the cell doors were closed, and he heard no voices.

For one panicked moment, he thought he was too late. But why would she have shut the cell door when she'd left? Maybe she hadn't come after all; maybe she had changed her mind...

Aleena darted to the first cell door and peered through the small barred window. "Damn..." She tugged on the door, but it didn't budge. She turned to Vaughn. "It won't open."

Vaughn hurried to the door and looked through the bars himself.

Airell, his face both bloodied and pale, plastered to the wall, a trickle of blood running down his throat.

Ivana was in front of him, dagger in hand, close enough to finish the job.

"Ivana!" he shouted.

She didn't move.

He tried to grab the water in her body, but, strangely enough, it didn't seem to work—not like in the abyss, or when Airell had kept him drugged. As if it were...resisting. A passive ability of Zily's Banebringer?

Good thing he had found a backup in the supply room outside the dungeon—if he could get in the cell to use it.

He tugged on the door himself, but just as Aleena said, it wouldn't open. He touched the metal lock. Ice cold.

He cursed and ran a hand through his hair, looking around the room for a solution, while Aleena stood at the door attempting to rouse a response from their wayward assassin. "Ivana?" she called. "Ivana, come on! It's Aleena."

He'd burn his hands trying to melt it with one of the lanterns on the walls, so first, he tried force. He backed away from the door, rammed his foot into the lock, and then tried the door again. Still frozen shut.

It took a few kicks, but the ice holding the lock in place and the door shut finally shattered and broke. With Aleena's help, they managed to wrest the door open.

He darted into the cell and skidded to a halt, surveying the scene.

"Ivana, *stop!*" he said.

He didn't know if it was the urgency that had infused his voice, or if she hadn't been ready to draw the dagger across Airell's throat.

Either way, she neither moved away nor acknowledged him.

"Ivana," he said, taking a step closer. "Put the dagger down."

She barely flinched. She stood unmoving, almost as if frozen, but it wasn't his doing.

He cautiously approached. "I need him alive," he said. "You

know that."

She stirred. "You seem to think I care."

His throat tightened. No. He knew she didn't care. Had she ever cared about anything? He moved closer. "You will *not* destroy everything we need to accomplish here on a quest for personal revenge." And yet, if she wanted to kill Airell, she could do it. Now. She didn't even need to stop time to accomplish her goal before any of them could do anything about it, with her blade already almost at Airell's throat.

And yet she hadn't—yet. What was stopping her, after all of this?

It didn't matter; he couldn't take the chance that she would give this up on her own.

Before she could reply, before he moved into her peripheral vision, he slid a syringe out of his pocket. Hoping to the gods the label on the bottle he'd filled the syringe from was correct about the bottle's contents, he gathered himself up and sprung.

The needle sank into her arm, and Vaughn dispensed the contents of the syringe before she shoved him to the side and whirled on him instead, outrage on her face.

Vaughn scrambled to put himself between Airell and Ivana. "Put. It. Down," he said through gritted teeth.

He knew instantly that she tried to burn aether, because she reeled and staggered back, one hand to her head. Even so, she didn't let go of the dagger.

Fortunately, even though his water magic didn't work on Zily's Banebringer, it seemed the old-fashioned method Airell had used on him still did. Frankly, he was impressed that she had managed to stay on her feet. He remembered well what that felt like, and how often he had passed out trying to burn aether while the substance had been in his body.

She regained her equilibrium, and a bitter smile twisted her lips. "You think I won't hurt you?"

"No," he said softly, his heart thudding painfully. "I know you will."

She met his eyes. Her jaw twitched. She said nothing.

"But I'm a Banebringer," Vaughn said. "You won't chance killing me."

Something flickered in her eyes then. And for a moment, he wasn't as certain about that as he had felt only seconds before. *"Some people just want to see the world burn."*

He saw Aleena move cautiously into the cell out of the corner of his eye. "Aleena? She won't kill me, will she?"

There was a long silence. "I'm ninety percent sure," Aleena said.

"I'll take those odds," he said.

"But I won't," Airell said. "So while you two argue about who is or isn't going to kill whom—" He lunged for the now open cell door.

The room exploded in a flurry of activity.

Vaughn, Ivana, and Aleena all leapt toward Airell.

Vaughn took a punch to the gut, and then stars flashed as he was kneed in the groin, but he wasn't sure who had done what.

Airell grunted, Ivana let out a feral growl, and when the dust had settled, the situation had changed entirely.

Ivana's attempt to get to Airell first had been more like a drunken stagger, and she had paid for the sudden movement. Her head was pounding, her vision blurring.

The situation in the cell had changed. Danton had arrived during the scuffle. Airell had been backed into the corner of the cell. And Aleena had spread her body over his like a net, facing Ivana, who now stood before both of them with her dagger.

"But I'm one hundred percent certain she won't kill me," Aleena said grimly, locking eyes with Ivana.

Damn her! "Aleena," Ivana said. "Please." It was taking everything she had not to collapse.

Aleena said nothing.

"I thought you were on my side."

"I *am* on your side. But more importantly, I'm your friend."

Ivana gave a short, slightly hysterical laugh. "And now I suppose you're going to give me some trite statement about how you're doing this for my own good?"

"No. I wanted you to know that even though you're my friend, some things are more important than friendship."

Ivana stared at her. There was nothing she could do. Aleena was right. Ivana wouldn't hurt her.

The rage, the cold, the despair of earlier had dissipated. She was left with nothing. Emptiness. She shoved her dagger back into the sheath on her thigh, a little harder than necessary.

Aleena shook her head and pointed to the dagger, wiggling her fingers.

Ivana clenched her teeth, drew it again, and surrendered it to her *friend*.

Who promptly surrendered it to Vaughn. They filed out of the cell, and at the point of her own dagger, Vaughn, with Danton's help, marched Airell into the next cell over, just in case the lock had been compromised on his, and locked him in it.

Only then did he turn toward Ivana. "Search her, Danton," he said, his voice hard, his eyes not leaving her face.

Danton moved forward and ran his hands lightly over Ivana. "I'm sorry," he said, "I-I really am."

"I don't have any other weapons," she said.

Danton glanced uncertainly back at Vaughn.

Vaughn rolled his eyes. "For Temoth's sake—" He stepped

forward and searched her himself.

He wasn't rough, but neither was there anything gentle in his touch. He was just thorough. He skimmed his hands down her thighs and her ankles, made her take off her boots, and then patted down her entire upper body.

His eyes never left hers while he did the latter, and she couldn't help but remember how those same hands had slid against her skin so tenderly only hours ago.

She looked away.

He found her pouch of aether and the packet containing the paltic she'd used on the guards, and retrieved the stolen key, but she truly had no other weapons. Nothing but the weapon in her own blood, but she couldn't use that without, she suspected, passing out.

Vaughn stepped back and handed the three items to Danton. "Now lock her up in another empty cell."

Aleena started forward. "Vaughn!"

He spun on his heel to face her. "She broke into a secure area, incapacitated four guards, and attempted to murder a critical prisoner. She will stay locked up until I decide what to do with her."

Aleena's brow furrowed, and she glanced at Ivana and shrugged. "Sorry. If I had known he would lock you up..."

"Why in the abyss is everyone apologizing to *her*?" Vaughn said, his voice rising. "As if she's some sort of victim? She let her personal feelings get in the way of what I'm trying to accomplish here."

"I don't think she's the only one letting personal feelings get in the way," Aleena muttered.

Vaughn tossed her a sharp glance. "Lock her up," he repeated, and then he spun on his heel and left the room.

Even if Ivana could have used her powers, all the time in the world wouldn't allow her to break down the heavy metal door to the cell Danton had reluctantly locked her in.

She'd been in worse conditions for far longer, but given her churning mind, splitting headache, and roiling stomach, she doubted sleep would come easily.

The dungeon was damp and chill, so she sat against the wall, drew her knees to her chest, and wrapped her arms around them, trying to conserve body heat.

The cell was also dim. Airell was now in the other cell with a window, so the only light she had was from what filtered through the food slot at the bottom of the door.

She was alone in the dark and cold.

A familiar and fitting place for her.

If she had only been more decisive, she could have been in and out before they had found her.

And gone.

Gone from this place, from the memories, from Vaughn, and Aleena, and everyone and everything she had left in the world that she had, against all odds, come to care about.

And she would still be alone in the cold and dark.

She pressed her forehead to her knees. If she didn't move her head, the room didn't swim as much. But that didn't stop her thoughts from swimming.

Once upon a time, she had chosen a different sort of life in a deliberate effort to block out the misery of her former one. To master the art of control of herself and her emotions, to numb herself to pain and death—both that of others, and the painful and dead places inside herself.

It had worked.

Until Vaughn had first cracked, and then breeched, and finally torn down the walls that had protected her for so long.

That person no longer existed as she once had. And neither did the person before that one—the shattered, suffering, slightly-less-naïve girl.

And yet vestiges of both were still inside her. She could not undo the things she had done and seen. She would carry those memories with her forever, along with the blood-stained hands that still moved too easily toward violence, and the conditioning she had inflicted on herself that, to this day, still made hurting people a viable option.

Meanwhile, she could not undo the events that had transpired to bring her to that place. And the pain that she had buried for years, that she had beaten into submission and caged and walled in until it was no longer a threat, had never gone away. If anything, it was stronger than it had ever been.

The only person whom it seemed no longer remained was the one who knew none of these things—pain and suffering, bloodshed and death.

That was the only person she ever remembered being happy as, and she could never go back to her.

She could never escape this struggle. She would always be Sweetblade, and yet not, and never the person she had been before, either.

The struggle to be something different and new, without knowing what that could realistically look like, *how* to even make that person come to be, was tearing her apart.

She closed her eyes and drifted into the place between wakefulness and sleep.

She was tired.

So tired.

———

Ivana jerked awake to the sound of the cell door opening and then closing again. She sat up, groggy, trying to blink past the haze in her eyes to see who had entered. She was afraid to try burning aether; though the headache had lessened to more of a dull pounding than someone trying to stab out her eyes, the sudden movement still made the ground pitch as if she were on the deck of a ship in a storm.

She laid her head back against the wall and tried not to move.

"Vaughn let me bring you some things," a voice said.

Her mind caught up. Aleena.

She stood in front of the closed door, as if waiting to be invited in, holding a bulging satchel to her chest with one arm and a lantern in the other hand.

Ivana blinked at her. Her tongue felt like cotton.

Aleena also had a bedroll slung across her shoulder, which she unrolled for Ivana. In the middle was a chamber pot, which she set to the side along with the lantern.

Then she settled down next to Ivana and silently unpacked the satchel.

Two blankets. A change of clothes. A book, a notepad, and a pencil. A candle and holder. A clean towel, a hairbrush, and a chunk of soap. Some fresh fruit, a skin of water, and a skin of wine.

Sadly, the wine would no longer help.

When the satchel was empty, Aleena folded it up and set it on her lap. She folded her hands on top of the satchel. "This is the last time I'm allowed to come see you," she said. "Vaughn doesn't want to keep you drugged or chained. But he says that means the door can't be opened once the initial dose he gave you wears off."

Smart. Once she was able to use her aether again, all that had to happen was for someone to open the door, and she could simply stop time and walk out

Aleena nodded toward the slot in the door. "The guards will give you your meals after this, and Vaughn's instructed them to let you have anything reasonable you want and that can fit through that slot."

"How generous of him. How long does he intend to keep me locked up?"

Aleena spread her hands flat on the satchel. "He only wants to keep you away from Airell, so I imagine he'll let you go after the elections—whatever the result."

Two weeks, then. It was logical, and she couldn't blame him, but she ground her teeth together in frustration all the same.

She supposed it could have been worse. "He's not so angry that he's going to let me rot down here forever?"

There was a long pause. "He's not angry, Ivana. He's hurt." Aleena tried to catch Ivana's eyes, but Ivana looked away, refusing to be subject to that piercing gaze.

"I told him I couldn't be trusted. He never could believe me. It's his own damn fault."

Aleena's voice was hard. "Bullshit."

"I-I'm sorry?"

Aleena turned her entire body to face Ivana. "You were carried away by your desire for revenge. None of us are perfect."

Ivana snorted. "Yes, except when I'm *not perfect,* as you say, the result is a little more extreme."

Aleena sighed. "Be that as it may...you aren't the same person you used to be."

Her words hit too close to her thoughts from earlier. "Aren't I? It's our actions that reveal who we are, and in the moment that counted..." She swallowed, her throat dry. She knew what that moment had been. "What did I do? Exactly what *she* would have done."

"You didn't kill the guards," Aleena pointed out.

Ivana chuckled darkly. "Great. A pat on the back for not murdering or maiming anyone. I'm making real progress."

"Our actions can also *shape* who we are." Aleena touched Ivana's chin and forced her to look in her direction. "Perhaps you need to stop waiting to feel different and simply *be* different."

Aleena had caught her in those perceptive, penetrating eyes, and they drilled through whatever was left of Ivana's shell to her soul, spitting out the detritus of her own self-loathing and fear as they went.

"But what if I can't?" she found herself saying. "What if I try, and I fail?" *Again.*

Aleena held her eyes for a moment longer, and then nodded. "That's the first true thing you've spoken since I got here," she said quietly.

And with that, she gathered up her satchel and the lantern and left.

Alone, cold, and in the dark.

Ivana folded one of the blankets up to use as a pillow, drew the other one over her, and curled up on the bedroll on her side, staring into the darkness.

Chapter Fifty-Five

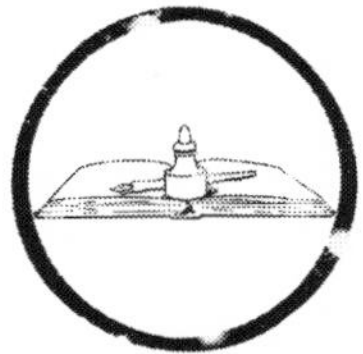

The Abomination

Commander Gered burst into Driskell's newly constructed "cell"—a simple shack made of rysta wood so he didn't have to be tied up anymore. The door slammed against the wall, making the entire structure shudder, and then slammed shut again.

"Time's up," Gered said. He seemed...agitated.

I'm a friend, Driskell projected immediately, also beginning his low burn of self-enhancement. He had continued to reinforce it over, and over, and over. He had no idea if his magical influence would wear off on its own eventually, and if so, how long that would take, so he figured it was better to be on the safe side.

"Commander?" Driskell asked.

It had been three days since Driskell had been captured. He

didn't know what Tanuac thought. Had they tried to rescue or retrieve him? Probably. Obviously, it hadn't worked—or Gered had told Tanuac something that had stopped him from trying.

That he was a traitor, perhaps?

Driskell had a hard time believing *Nahua* would believe that of him.

Maybe Gered had told them he was dead—or Sedated.

He shuddered. Poor Tania. He sincerely hoped she knew nothing about it. There was still hope he could get out of this alive and intact, and he hated to think of her suffering for no reason.

"I've been patient with you, Dal," Gered said, "though at times I find myself wondering why. It must be the way you remind me of my son."

Driskell swallowed. He had tried to reinforce that, too, since Gered had brought it up.

"Now the time has come for you to prove your worth to me. Do you know a Vaughn? Thrax? Danton?"

"Uh...yes. Friends of mine." No reason to lie. The more honesty he could inject into his manipulation, the easier it went over. He had learned a lot in those three days. Even so. "Former friends of mine," he revised. *I'm your friend now.*

"Good. I've been given new orders." His eyes flashed, and his annoyance was strong enough that it seeped out into Driskell's bubble. "And you're going to tell me everything you know about them and their plans on the way."

Driskell felt queasy. "On the way to where?" he asked, though he knew the answer already.

The shack door opened again, with less force this time.

The bloodbane abomination stepped in, a sinuous sort of grace about its movements.

Driskell stepped back into the wall of the shack. That...*thing.*

Gered shifted, and Driskell *felt* his shudder in the aether bubble.

At least he wasn't the only one who found it disturbing.

"What is it?" Gered snapped.

"You called for me," it stated.

Driskell started. For some reason, even though it resembled a human, he hadn't expected it to *speak*.

Driskell focused on Gered, determined to ignore the thing.

"A moment." Gered turned back to Driskell. "I've just received word that Ri Airell has been effectively ousted by your Banebringer friends while the Conclave's back was turned. Because this army is the closest, we've been ordered to head to Cohoxta to take back control."

Oh, no. Marakyn could withstand a siege. The capital of Ferehar? Not so much.

"The entire army, Dal?" *I'm a friend. Tell me your plans.*

Gered snorted. "To subdue a tiny rebellion in Ferehar? Of course not. We'll leave behind most of the army to continue the siege."

Turn it into a list, Driskell, he told himself. He had to be calm. He had to stay in control. He had to find out all the details in the event he could escape and send a message.

"I see," he said. "If I may presume, you seem agitated." *I can help. You can tell me. I'm a friend.*

Gered hesitated.

A good sign. It meant Gered was speaking so freely because of Driskell's magic, which meant it was still working.

"I was meant to subdue Marakyn," he said, "not some backwater city that barely qualifies for the moniker. But the Conclave wants me on this because they know I'll do what needs to be done, and, frankly, because my second is as competent as I am and can handle things here."

That sounded ominous. "What needs to be done, Commander?" The abomination moved, and Driskell's eyes drifted to it again.

Its head was tilted slightly to the side and turned in his direction, as if staring at him with those white, pupil-less eyes.

He shivered and quickly looked away.

Gered gave Driskell a fond smile. "Take heart, son. You came here to prevent needless bloodshed in the city you love? You've succeeded. In the interest of speed and efficiency, instead of a whole army..." He rose and jerked his head at the abomination. "We're taking this thing."

Driskell's stomach dropped out from him.

Chapter Fifty-Six

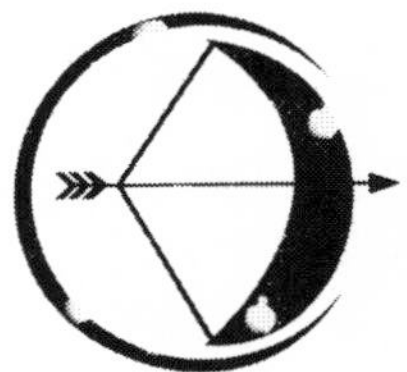

Barriers

Vaughn stood at the window in Gildas' office, leaning back against it with his arms folded and gritting his teeth together to prevent himself from biting anyone's head off.

"Look," Thrax said from where he sprawled on one of the loveseats, rolling a ball of fire up and down his knuckles. "All I'm saying is he should get out there and do something, you know, charitable or something. He doesn't have much time to prove he's less of a prick than his brother, and since he's Gifted, he's starting with negative points."

"Don't disregard the work he's been doing meeting directly with the representatives and other key figures," Askata said, frowning at Thrax. "Overall, I think those meetings have gone well, provoking curiosity rather than contempt, and I have high hopes that the reception tomorrow evening will be a success."

Vaughn tried hard to keep his face neutral. Meetings. Dozens of them. This Gan, that Gan, this noble, that noble—he had to be on his best behavior, playing the part of the noble perfectly—and despite how keenly interested everyone was in him, none of it was *him*.

He was dreading the reception.

"Regardless," Askata went on, "I have a more hopeful view of his starting 'points,' as you put it. Airell is starting on poor footing as well. They hate him. They hate Banebringers. Teyrnon—I'm sorry—*Vaughn* probably won't have to do much to prove he'll be better, even as a Banebringer."

"Maybe," Danton said, wiggling his hand in the air. "But with all due respect, my lady, you haven't lived as one of us. You don't know how bad it is. You hear the mutters, but you haven't been on the other side of a ravenous mob out for your blood."

Vaughn wished, not for the first time in the past week, that he had some sort of magical ability to turn his ears off. He could turn invisible, but he'd still *hear* them. Besides, then they'd notice he was gone.

"Well, he can't stay holed up in the palace," Thrax reasoned. "The whole of Cohoxta probably thinks he's in here sacrificing babies to the heretic gods or something."

Askata's musical laugh rang out. "Really, Dal Thrax. I think you exaggerate."

There was silence in the room. No one other than his mother thought Thrax was exaggerating. "Well," Vaughn said. "Some of the heretic gods might be pleased with that."

Thrax snapped his hand over the ball, extinguishing it. "Yeah. You probably should leave that out of any speeches you give."

Temoth, he missed Ivana. She had a level head. She'd be sure to offer some practical advice embedded in a healthy layer of sarcasm.

He clenched his hand into a fist, digging his fingernails into his palms.

He turned around. "Aleena, what do you think?"

Aleena was, by all appearances, intent on picking dirt out from under her fingernails. She shrugged. "Whatever you do, take some guards with you before you go wandering around the city."

He sighed. She was still irked at him for keeping Ivana locked up. "Thanks. That was helpful."

"Vaughn, your qixli is glowing," Danton said, nodding toward the device sitting on Gildas' desk.

What now? He'd already advised Yaotel of the situation. Yaotel was... Well, he obviously would have done things differently. The uncertainty of Vaughn winning the election combined with a hostile army living outside the walls of Marakyn had made Yaotel less than enthusiastic about Vaughn's plans, but to Vaughn's surprise, he hadn't tried to order Vaughn to change them.

Vaughn picked up the qixli and waited. A moment later, Yaotel's voice came through. "Vaughn, you have a problem," Yaotel said without preamble.

"Tell me about it," Vaughn muttered.

"One of Tanuac's scouts just checked in from the pass. Looks like a unit has broken off the main army and is headed your way."

Vaughn groaned. Well. That hadn't taken long. Someone must have sent a pigeon to Weylyn City. Probably one of those damned guards who had been loyal to Airell whom Askata had let go. Or, even more likely, a Conclave priest. "When you say 'unit,' how many are we talking?"

"Scout estimated about two thousand."

Two thousand soldiers. That wasn't *too* bad. Cohoxta's walls were hardly the wonder of Setana, but against a force that small, they shouldn't have a problem defending them. They had more than a quarter that number of Watchmen alone, thousands more able-bodied men within the city who could be called upon, and reserves from the closest towns if need be.

What was this, then? A test of their defenses in preparation for a larger assault? That wasn't a comforting thought, but there was nothing he could do about it at present.

"How long?" Vaughn asked.

"They're marching double-time. I'd say you have a week, week and a half, tops."

He looked at his mother. "Who's in charge of the Fereharian reserve?"

She winced. "At the top? No one right now. Airell fired Gildas' security advisor, and his own was useless, like the rest of his so-called advisors. Obviously, forming a new cabinet should be one of your first tasks."

Vaughn frowned. "Suggestions? I need someone competent, obviously, but they need to be able to work with Banebringers." He glanced out the window, which provided a spectacular view of the southern city gates, the bridge across the Atl River, and the large settlement beyond. "We should be able to handle this, but the last thing I need is our defense commander deciding to throw in his hand with Airell and sabotaging our efforts."

There was a long hesitation, and he raised his eyebrow at his mother.

"Vaughn, this army... It's a unit from the United Setanan. These are our people," Askata said.

Vaughn snorted. "They're not *my* people. Donians are more my people than these Conclave dogs. Besides, what would you have me do, open the gates and welcome them in? Surrender?"

Askata pressed her lips together.

Come on, he silently pleaded with his mother. She *knew* this would happen eventually. They had hoped later rather than sooner, but...

"I have the perfect man in mind," she said at last.

"Good," Vaughn said. "Can you find him and bring him here?"

Askata nodded, whirled around, and left the office.

It was only then that Vaughn realized the qixli was still glowing. "Vaughn, there's more," Yaotel said.

Vaughn turned back. "What?"

"We've been keeping tabs on that bloodbane abomination the Conclave has with this army."

"Yes, I know."

"It's not with the main army anymore."

The brisk efficiency and confidence that had characterized Vaughn's feelings toward this matter evaporated, and his stomach dropped into his toes.

"Maybe there's another explanation," Yaotel went on, "but you'd better be prepared for the possibility that they sent it with the unit headed toward you."

Two thousand men was one thing. Two thousand men with a corpse-thing? That was an entirely different matter. "Do you know how many bloodbane this thing can control?"

"Last count we had, there were over a thousand of various sorts swarming around the forest, and that number was growing."

Burning skies.

"Vaughn, you've *got* to keep them from taking back control," Yaotel said. "You go down here before we even get to your little election..."

Vaughn swallowed. "Yes. I know. I don't suppose you can offer any assistance yet?"

There was a long silence, and then: "If it's true that we no longer have to contend with a possible massive bloodbane attack against Marakyn…" A sigh. "I'll send a few healers and I'll ask Tanuac if he can spare some troops to help secure the area—assuming you can hold them off for a few days." A wry tone entered Yaotel's voice. "And assuming your mother approves."

Vaughn grunted. At this point, he didn't care what his mother approved of. He was more concerned with surviving long enough for Tanuac's assistance—which would be too late to help with the initial defense—to do any good. "She'll be fine with it. Appreciated."

The qixli stopped glowing. Vaughn put it down and looked around at the remaining faces in the room with him: Thrax, Danton, and Aleena.

Thrax leaned forward. "Vaughn, we've barely been here a week," he said. "Maybe you get this commander your mother has on your side, but what about the men? Will they be willing to fight for you?"

"Fortunately, they aren't fighting for me. They're fighting to defend their home."

"Against an army that's coming because *you* showed up," Thrax pointed out.

There was that, but the Conclave didn't *have* to send an army. Other than existing, Vaughn wasn't doing anything illegal. "Anyone who's been paying attention knows what my becoming Ri would mean for Ferehar," Vaughn said. "In fact, many are counting on it."

Fereharians felt less Setanan than Donians did. The promise that Vaughn would break them away from the Empire might be enough on its own to overcome reflex prejudice. At least all signs from initial meetings pointed that way.

Now he had to prove he could defend it.

"And what are you going to tell them?" Thrax asked.

"That Setana has turned on us and we intend to take back our country; we can rely on anyone who rallies to that call." He cracked his neck. What a way to start this. "Danton," he barked, and Danton sat up, startled.

"How's your zip-zap thing going?" Vaughn asked.

Danton scratched his chin. "I transported myself a full mile the other day without too much trouble, and I can now make multiple hops in a row with only a short rest between. I think I could do more, but I'm trying to increase it incrementally so I don't accidentally kill myself doing too much."

Good enough. "Smart plan. Now would be an especially bad time to accidentally kill yourself." He flashed a forced smile at Danton. "I'm going to need you to keep an eye on the road and surrounding area as the army gets closer. I want to have as much warning as possible. For now, take a look at the city defenses and let me know if you see anything that needs repair." Walls alone wouldn't keep out bloodbane because some of them could fly—or climb. But it was a start.

Vaughn turned to Thrax, who was already sitting up, his eyebrow cocked, awaiting his own orders. "Thrax, I want you to liaison with this commander my mother has for us. You were at Gan Barton's estate when only a fraction of this number of bloodbane attacked us." And Vaughn was certain they had won only because Ivana had killed that corpse-thing controlling them. "Make sure he understands what we're dealing with and that we need to think beyond the walls in our defense strategy. In addition, make sure he knows your and Danton's skillsets and plans to use them to full advantage." Damn, he wished he had a beastblood. "For now, go with Danton. I'll send for you when my mother returns."

Thrax gave him a lazy salute, and he and Danton left together.

Aleena was now the only person left in the room with him, and she was watching him with her piercing eyes, all pretenses at fingernail-cleaning set aside.

"All right," he said. "You win." He unclipped the second key from the chain around his neck. "Go get Ivana and bring her to me here." They would need her, for multiple reasons.

Aleena stood up and held out her hand for the key.

He hesitated. "I can trust you to do this, right?"

"I know how important this is, Vaughn," Aleena said. "And she will too."

He wasn't sure about that, but he gave her the key anyway.

It was hard to judge time without the sun, but Ivana determined by meals that it had only been about a week when her cell door opened again.

She didn't bother trying to burn aether, partially because she was curious to see who it was and why they had come earlier than expected, and partially because, after a week alone with her thoughts in the dismal chamber, she was mentally and emotionally drained. She just didn't care. Where would she even go, what would she do, if she ran?

It turned out to be Aleena.

She didn't move into the room. Rather, she stood in the doorway, holding the door open. "You're being released," she said.

Ivana stood and stretched. Her body felt as though it had been curled into a ball for weeks. "Already?"

Aleena flashed her a grim look that made Ivana uneasy. "You're needed enough to take the chance, I guess."

That wasn't in any way ominous.

"I'm supposed to take you to Vaughn." She hesitated. "I told him you'd come."

Ivana shrugged, feigning nonchalance. "Fine." She followed Aleena back to the central dungeon chamber, up the stairs, and then through the halls of the palace, past the audience hall, past the ballroom and grand dining room, and into the area where the real business of running Ferehar took place.

They stopped at Gildas' office, and Aleena knocked.

"Come," Vaughn said, his voice muffled by the door.

Aleena opened the door for Ivana, and she stepped inside.

Vaughn was sitting behind a massive desk, the side of his head resting in the palm of one hand while he scribbled on a piece of paper.

"Ivana's here," Aleena said.

He didn't look up. "Thank you, Aleena."

It was obviously a dismissal, but Aleena hesitated. She glanced at Ivana, and Ivana jerked her head at her, and then rolled her eyes up slightly. Aleena, no doubt understanding that she wasn't to go far, nodded and left.

It came as a sudden revelation how much of a partnership she and Aleena had formed. She had always been Ivana's right hand, but now, she was a trusted ally and friend.

No doubt Ivana would find some way to screw up that relationship as well.

"I see you've settled into your not-quite-official role already," she said, taking in the well-appointed room.

Vaughn pressed his lips together. "I thought about having Aleena bring you to the audience chamber in an attempt to intimidate you," he said, still writing. "But then on second thought, I realized that probably wouldn't work, and..." He put the pen down and passed his hand over his face. "Frankly, I'm not in the mood for games."

He looked up, but at something over her shoulder. His face was grim and pale.

"Aleena said you had something important you needed to see me about," she said.

He looked back down at the note he had been writing. "Yes. I'm releasing you because there have been some changes in our circumstances."

"Changes in our circumstances?"

He drummed his fingers against the desk and stood up. Walking around it, he leaned against it to stand in front of her, though he still didn't meet her eyes. "There's a unit from the United Setanan on its way to Cohoxta, two thousand strong. We estimate it'll be here in a week or a little more."

No wonder he looked so anxious and tired. He had few real resources right now. He wasn't Ri yet; he was relying on his mother to do what he wanted until he was official.

He'd have been better off if he had brought his own army with him.

Even so, two thousand men? Surely, they had enough Watchmen and militia to deal with that threat.

Vaughn was staring at the ground, and he roused himself to speak again. "It's possible they have the corpse-thing with them."

Oh. *Oh*. "Damn," she said softly.

"Askata is calling in the reserves, Thrax is going to be working with our new defense commander, and Danton is surveying what defenses we have. Given both your training and your magical talents...your aid would be invaluable." He looked directly at her at last. "I'm begging you to help us, just this one last time, even though I think it's clear you are going to do whatever you want, regardless of what I do, or don't do, or would wish you to do."

The final words were laced with bitterness. And they hurt, because she couldn't protest that they weren't true—that he had misjudged the quality of her character.

There was silence. Neither of them broke the gaze. The moment stretched into several moments, and it seemed to Ivana that her own fatigue increased considerably in those few heartbeats.

What did he want her to say? That she was sorry?

She was. She regretted her decision to steal that key with every fiber of her being. She felt it like a rot eating at the corners of her emptiness. It wasn't a pleasant feeling.

But the words wouldn't come. Apologizing was admitting one more failure, one more mistake, one more black mark on her record.

Whatever hope she had had of starting over, whatever they had shared—she had ruined it.

"I came here to help you," she said, breaking the gaze. "That hasn't changed. Just tell me what you want me to do."

"As soon as I know, I will."

There was another long silence.

She swallowed. "If there's nothing else right now...can I go back to my room? My normal room, that is?" she asked. She desperately wanted a bath, and a change of clothes, and to sleep in a comfortable bed again.

He passed a hand over his eyes, and then rubbed at his chin. He started to say something, and then stopped. "There is something else, if you'll stay another moment."

He walked over to the sitting area, sat down in one of the armchairs, and then gestured for her to sit across from him.

She did, tentatively.

He leaned forward and clasped his hands together.

Ivana waited.

"Look, I..." He ran a hand through his hair. "I don't know how to have this conversation. This isn't my strong suit. But I can't... I don't want this hanging over my head, with everything else. So I have to know. Was any of it real? Or was that night all one big con to you?"

She blinked and stared at him. "Is *that* what you think?"

"I don't know what to think." He looked up at her. "I've tried to explain it in my head in a thousand ways and it's the story I keep returning to."

She could hardly blame him. She was perfectly capable of doing what he suggested, in theory—though she didn't think she was *that* good. She herself had even told Aleena that he'd been stupid for trusting her.

Yet it still hurt.

Why had she allowed him so close to her that this hurt? As if she needed more sources of pain in her life.

"There was no con," she said. "I happened to wake up, and I saw the key lying there. It was just too easy."

"*Easy*?" He shook his head. "No, Ivana. 'Easy' would have been when we first came to the palace, and he was out in the open. 'Easy' would have been not having to figure out how to break into the dungeon." He ran a hand through his hair again. "You gave up the 'easy' option, only to—" He broke off.

His voice had lost its measured tone and was now tight—with anger, hurt, betrayal? She didn't even know.

Her own throat tightened, and she clenched her hands together in her lap. "You asked me a question, and I told you the truth. Whether you choose to believe me is your business. I certainly wouldn't blame you if you don't. And I certainly wouldn't blame you if you hate me now." She stood up, ready for that to be the end of the conversation.

He gave a half-laugh. "Hate you? If I could hate you, this would be much easier to deal with." He gripped his knees. "I just want to understand."

How could she ever make him understand the panic, the revulsion, the rage—the way *She* had come to the rescue at exactly the wrong time?

Ivana could have left it at what she'd already said. But his face was drawn, his eyes searching hers for some other answer—and she had enough regard for him that she didn't want to leave him with yet another burden to bear.

"You want to understand?" she asked, her voice tight. "Then understand this: I hate him almost as much as I hate myself. So when I woke from a nightmare that *involved* him—" She would not, could not tell him the details. He was smart enough to figure it out. "I was distraught." She gave a short, humorless laugh. "You of all people should know what that looks like." Her fingernails were digging into her palm. "I saw the key, all I could think about was revenge, and *she* was more than happy to take over."

She met his eyes. "I swear to you that every moment of that night up until then was real to me." Every touch, every kiss, every caress—

Gone, just like that fleeting ray of hope.

A moment of clarity came to her. She had thought there was nothing left of the person she had been before all of this had started, but she'd been wrong. Without *her,* she was just as much of a screw-up as she'd ever been.

She drew in a sharp breath. She was going to cry. She was barely holding it in, and she didn't want to be here in front of him anymore. "Are we done?"

His eyebrows were knit together as he studied her face. "I told my mother you were away on personal business. You can say the same if anyone asks."

She had no words left, so she nodded tightly…and fled.

Vaughn sat in the armchair, unmoving, for longer than he should have when there was so much to be done.

"I hate him almost as much as I hate myself." Present tense.

He had always wondered what went on in that mind of hers.

He stared down at his hands. He didn't know if it made him feel better or worse to know that their night together had been genuine for both of them, not just him.

Yes, he had seen her break down before. He could understand now what might have transpired.

Why hadn't she woken him?

But he also knew that. She may have given him her body, but that was where it ended, wasn't it? She had never willingly let down that barrier into the deepest parts of herself.

He could still see the blood dripping off her dagger in Lord Kadmon's bedroom, hear her laugh bubble up in a rare moment of shared friendship, feel her tears dripping on his arm as he'd held her in the abyss, and the warmth of her skin as she'd moved against him in the night.

She was, in so many ways, more raw than he had ever known her to be, and at the same time, even more closed off to him—because she never told him what spawned these decisions, what she felt inside that made her act in such drastic ways.

Could their already shaky friendship recover from this? Could he even trust her to be reliable anymore? Unfortunately, there was no time to find out either answer right now. He had something more urgent to deal with than his personal problems.

There was a knock on the office door. "Come," he said.

Danton peeked his head in the room. "I'm back. Do you want to hear my report?"

Not really. He stood up. "Let's have it."

Chapter Fifty-Seven

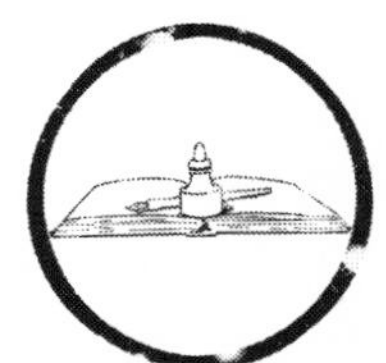

A Dangerous Game

"Dal Driskell," a man's voice said. "Commander Gered wants to see you."

Driskell slid the knife he'd been sharpening back into the sheath at his waist. He didn't know why he bothered. He wouldn't know how to use it if the time came. But Gered had told him to choose a weapon, and he'd figured a knife would be more generally useful to have on him than a sword or club if he escaped.

Driskell followed the man who had spoken, one of Gered's personal guards named Paran. Driskell had made sure to burn extra aether when interacting with any of the soldiers Gered kept close, and Paran was no exception.

Indeed, he was already burning the aether in his blood to

enhance himself. Even with the strides he'd made since the skyfire—especially since being dragged along with this army—he still wished he were better at it. Given the way Gered had come to trust him for no logical reason at all, he had a feeling he could have the entire unit dancing to his tune if he *really* knew what he was doing.

They were within half a day's march from Cohoxta and had settled into a deserted stretch of woods, ostensibly to rest. In reality, it was so the abomination could collect and organize all the bloodbane it had been gathering in one place.

They had left behind the most common bloodbane that it had already gathered near Marakyn—letting them scatter where they would—but there were many that it had kept control of, and those had trailed behind the army the entire way. In addition, it had begun calling more bloodbane from the pass, the mountains, the forests, as they marched.

Now, any bloodbane that had been tailing them—and more—had started to flow into their camp.

Driskell had lied as much as he felt he could to Gered. He'd told him that Vaughn, Thrax, and Danton had different powers than they did. He gave Gered the wrong descriptions. Encouraged him to attempt to parley, because Vaughn might listen to reason.

Those were easy lies because Gered didn't have any contrary information and already believed Driskell.

The moment Gered suspected Driskell had been manipulating him, Driskell's ability to do so would become more difficult. And if Gered had any actual *evidence* that Driskell had lied? It would drop to impossible.

It had been a good decision not to fabricate more than necessary. Gered had sent out scouts to nearby villages on their way to collect rumors, and already, rumors had confirmed what they already knew: that Ri Airell's Banebringer brother had challenged him and was in residence at the palace with Lady Askata's blessing. Driskell held his breath every time a scout came back, hoping someone didn't have a contradictory rumor about the Banebringers' powers, but apparently they hadn't been flaunting them publicly, because no one seemed to know.

But manipulating Gered was only part of what Driskell had been doing. Since Gered was no longer keeping him a prisoner, he had decided to continue his original mission: influencing the troops themselves—far beyond those in Gered's inner circle like Paran. Any opportunity he had, he beat waves of anxiety and discontent and doubt in the troops' direction. Inserted subtle suggestions into overheard conversations. Even tried to plant thoughts of desertion in the minds of those who seemed most outwardly receptive to his magical influence.

Unfortunately, while he could influence humans to a yet-unknown degree of success, he could do nothing to bloodbane.

He glanced to his left, where a pack of three dozen bloodwolves was lying sedately among the trees, panting with tongues lolling over their enormous razor-sharp teeth in the hot sun as though they were domesticated dogs.

If domesticated dogs were scaly and black and the size of small ponies.

One of them turned its head to look at him now, and it seemed to Driskell that its white, pupil-less gaze held a barely contained malevolence, as if what it wanted was to tear out Driskell's throat, but it was being prevented from doing so.

In fact, he supposed that was exactly the case.

He shuddered and looked away. What if that *thing* keeping them under control...lost control?

Their little army would be shredded.

Paran glanced at him. "I know," he said. "They give me the

jitters too." He straightened up and set his jaw, as if to prevent his own shiver from manifesting.

Driskell burned a bit more aether and imagined the invisible bubble that helped him control the projection. He made it bigger in his head until it encompassed Paran. "Yeah," he said. He leaned closer to Paran, moving his bubble with him. "I have to admit, I know these Fereharians are rebels, but being torn to pieces by one of these monsters is a wretched way to go."

Paran nodded his head in agreement. "It is. But hopefully they'll just surrender."

The downside to his ability was that if he was using it, Driskell could never tell if someone truly agreed. Paran *appeared to* agree, but later, he might wonder why he ever thought that way. Or maybe he did agree. Maybe he was an ally. And Driskell would never know because he couldn't afford to take the chance.

Commander Gered was standing on a ridge looking out over a sprawling vineyard. Some of their soldiers were moving through the rows of vines, gathering food for the troops. It was a bit early yet; the grapes wouldn't be as sweet and plump as they could be—but even a small army needed more food than they could carry for the march, especially since they had no baggage train. They were moving at double-speed. They would rest and feast when they arrived and won. That was the theory, anyway. Meanwhile, any farmers they passed suffered for it, while they stripped their fields on the march.

Driskell took a deep breath and held his aether at the ready. It was a strange feeling, like keeping the blood in his veins just below boiling. "You asked to see me, Commander?"

Gered nodded. He pointed out over the vineyard and beyond. "A hard four-hour march will bring us to Cohoxta." Gered drummed his fingers on his thigh. "Are you sure you're ready to do your part?" Doubt crept into his voice.

His part. Once they were in the city Driskell was tasked with finding Vaughn—and Danton and Thrax, if he could manage it—and leading him to Gered under the guise of friendship.

Of course, he was going to do no such thing, but Gered didn't know that. Driskell burned aether and expanded his bubble. "Yes, Commander. These dogs will never know what hit them. I'm beginning to be sorry we were unable to do the same in Marakyn."

Gered nodded and patted his shoulder. "All in good time, son. I know you're eager to oust those traitors. And you'll be rewarded for it."

Driskell wondered, not for the first time, how much Vaughn knew about the makeup of this army. Tanuac had scouts on the pass, and Yaotel had a spy in the original camp, so Driskell had to assume Vaughn knew they were coming, and that he knew they would have bloodbane with them.

Gered continued. "We'll use Acalli as a base. My scouts tell me that the town has been all but deserted, with most of the townsfolk fleeing into Cohoxta." His lips spread into a tight, cruel smile. "They probably should have fled elsewhere."

There was something in Gered's tone that sent a chill down Driskell's spine. "Commander?" he asked.

The hand on Driskell's shoulder tightened. "It's none of your concern, Driskell. Do your part, and all will be well."

Driskell started. *What?* Oh, no, no, no. That wasn't good enough. He *had* to know what was happening. It was relatively easy to manipulate emotions by suggestion, but he found forcing someone to talk when they didn't intend to a little harder. He burned a little more aether. "If I'm going into a situation, I ought to know what I could face. What if I'm captured and can't get out? What will that mean?"

Gered studied him.

Driskell straightened up. "I've betrayed my people for the greater good of Setana, Commander. You owe me this."

"Perhaps you're right, son. Perhaps you're right. Well, there's not much to say. Once we have their ringleader and have secured the palace, my plans are to immediately conduct a series of mass executions—as an example."

Driskell was so shocked, he almost lost his bubble. "Commander?" he asked, incredulous. "Mass executions?"

Gered pressed his lips together. "This order comes from above me. Cohoxta has harbored Banebringers. There's only one penalty for that. We can't slaughter the entire city, of course, but enough to ensure there will be no thoughts of grass-roots resistance."

"Commander," he said, trying to infuse reason into his voice along with additional burned aether. "That seems a little harsh, doesn't it?"

Gered swung his eyes toward Driskell. "Are you having a change of heart?"

Why wasn't it working? Drat it all. He turned the aether inward, making himself more appealing rather than working on the other person's emotions. "No, Commander," he said with a curt bow. "I am ready to do whatever is necessary."

There was a moment if Driskell wondered if it all was lost.

But there was the hesitation. And then Gered nodded again. "I knew you'd come through. You're a good lad, Driskell. A credit to Setana."

He let out a silent breath. The first moment he could escape from this madman, he would take it.

"May I be excused, Commander?"

Gered waved his hand. "Of course, of course." And then he turned back toward the fields to watch his troops strip the poor vineyard owner's land clean.

Chapter Fifty-Eight

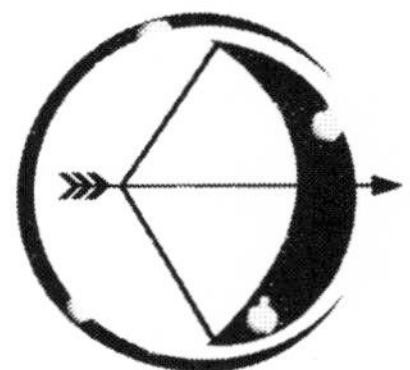

Leading by Example

Vaughn's qixli glowed, and the small group of people surrounding him fell silent. He snatched the qixli out of the pouch at his waist, his heart pounding.

"They're seven or eight miles out," Danton said over the qixli. "Right now, they're just camping."

"The bloodbane?"

There was a long silence. "I'd say more than the scouts said, and definitely more coming."

Vaughn swore. His first scouts had counted maybe five hundred, far fewer than Yaotel's initial report. But then rumors had reached them of bloodbane swarming out of the hills and forests, ignoring terrified villagers and townsfolk as they streamed toward Cohoxta with a bizarre singlemindedness—unless someone got in their way. It was much like those early reports coming out of Weylyn City.

Refugees from those villages directly in the path of the army and who heard about the danger ahead of time were still cramming themselves into Cohoxta—behind the ostensible safety of its walls.

"Keep me updated," Vaughn said. "If they start to move, I want to know immediately. Meanwhile, see if you can get a better idea of how many of each type of bloodbane we might be dealing with."

"Will do," Danton said.

Vaughn drew in a deep breath and set the qixli down. He glanced through the window in the main conference room, out over the city, and toward the southern gates—for what seemed like the hundredth time in the past week. The river glistened under a blue summer sky, but nothing moved on or beyond it. Acalli, the large town across the river, had been fully abandoned three days ago, and the southern road and bridge was deserted, aside from a few Watchmen scurrying about a barricade they'd erected across the width, closer to the city.

"My lord?" Commander Moqel asked.

Vaughn shook himself and glanced at the older man his mother had chosen for the job of organizing their defense. He was Fereharian, through and through, and his deep bronze skin was leathered by many summers and winters alike spent outdoors. "Forgive me, Commander," Vaughn said. "You were saying?"

Askata's skirts rustled next to him in a disapproving manner. He hadn't known skirts could rustle disapprovingly until he'd had to work so closely with his mother.

"My men have begun enforcing a curfew," Moqel said, "but we're having a problem with the number of refugees from the villages along the southern road. The inns and hostels are full. Those who would extend hospitality have done so. We're running out of room."

"If bloodbane controlled by that thing get into the city," Thrax put in helpfully, "anyone on the streets will be torn to bits."

"Yes, thank you, Thrax," Vaughn said. The idea, of course, was that bloodbane *wouldn't* get into the city. That Ivana would take care of the corpse-thing before it got that far. But Vaughn wasn't willing to take that risk.

He turned to Gan Anque, who was the only one of the four Gan not already hiding in his city manor. Vaughn had no doubt there was some political calculation to Anque's move of remaining to advise the regent. However, he *was* the Gan who seemed most positive toward Vaughn.

Vaughn hoped he wasn't about to ruin that. "Your Grace," he said. "What would you say to opening your manor to any refugees who still need a place to stay? It'd be temporary, of course."

Gan Anque stroked his short goatee. "My wife will have a fit," he said. "But that can sometimes be entertaining. Yes. I am willing."

"Excellent. We'll inform the other three Gan that they, too, will be opening their manors to refugees."

Askata's skirts rustled. "Lord Teyrnon," she said. "That may not be the wisest—"

"We'll lead by example, of course," Vaughn said, interrupting. "Dal Calpix." Vaughn turned now to the new steward his mother had chosen, an older Fereharian gentleman with silver in his hair and a strong sense of proper protocol and etiquette. "Please prepare the palace to receive guests."

The steward's eyes widened. "My lord?"

"They don't need private rooms, Dal. We just need somewhere to put people until we get through this. If by some chance the bloodbane make it through the city walls, hopefully they won't make it to the palace walls." He turned to his mother. "Children and their mothers or caretakers are priority, followed by elderly."

"My lord," the steward protested. "This is a kind gesture, but you'll have every beggar and good-for-nothing taking advantage of your generosity along with those truly in need."

"Well, I suppose we don't want beggars ripped to shreds by bloodbane, either, do we?" Vaughn asked, pinning the man with his best stern gaze.

The steward's mouth flopped open and shut a few times like a fish out of water, and then he turned to Askata. "Regent?"

Askata had deliberately tried to step aside during the past week, allowing Vaughn to take the lead when decisions needed to be made, but in the end, she was regent, and the final say was still with her. Vaughn held his breath. Would she contradict him now?

Askata sighed. "Do as he says, Dal," Askata said. "I won't make value judgments on whether someone deserves to be left to the bloodbane at this late hour."

Dal Calpix gave a short bow to Askata and left the room.

"I'll take my leave as well," Gan Anque said. "I would be happy to inform the other three Gan?" And he did, indeed, seem almost delighted at the possibility.

Vaughn nodded to him, and the Gan whisked out of the room.

"Calpix can prepare the palace," Askata said, "and the Gan their manors, but we'll need someone to gather those who still need a place to hide."

Aleena exchanged a glance with Ivana, who in turn gave her the briefest of smiles. "Lady Regent," Aleena said. "Da Ivana and I would love to take on that task."

"At least until I'm needed elsewhere," Ivana added.

"Good, Da," Askata said. "Take a few of the maids with you

also. They'll know the city best; we don't have a lot of time."

That was an understatement. If the army started moving immediately, it could be there in as little as four hours.

Aleena nodded, and then she and Ivana left the room.

"Commander Moqel?" Vaughn asked. "Is everything else ready?"

"As ready as we can be, my lord," Moqel said.

Hopefully, that would be enough.

Ivana stood in the grand entrance hall of the palace, surrounded by frightened women and crying children. She held one of the doors open, ushering them inside, trying to keep order.

She glanced at the sun and then through the open palace gates and down the main boulevard. It was dark, and people were still coming. The palace courtyard was swarming with hundreds waiting their turns to be let in.

Aleena stood farther in, sending the group she had just arrived with off throughout the palace with household staff. She saw Ivana looking at her and shouldered her way over.

"How's it holding out?" Ivana asked in a low voice.

"There's still some room," Aleena said. "But it's getting tight."

Vaughn's offer of opening the palace to refugees had indeed been taken advantage of by more than they had imagined. But they weren't beggars and good-for-nothings—the surplus, beyond refugees, were mostly women, children, and elderly who simply didn't feel safe in their own homes. The manors of the four Gan were also crammed full. She was certain the Gan were thrilled.

The qixli that Ivana held in her hand started glowing. Heedless of the half-curious and half-horrified looks around her, she gripped it and waited.

It was Danton. "They're about three miles out, coming at a good clip." She could hear the strain in his voice even through the tinny sound of the qixli. "I've already let Vaughn know. He said it's time."

"I'll be right there," she said, then put the qixli away. She glanced toward Aleena and hesitated.

Aleena put a hand on her shoulder. "Go," she said. She grinned. "Do what you do best." And then she turned and started barking orders.

Chapter Fifty-Nine

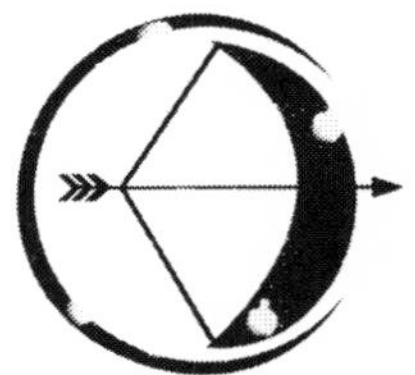

The Calm

The streets of Cohoxta were empty. Most people were closeted in their homes—in cellars and safe rooms, if they had them. Others huddled in the community safe rooms beneath the Watch posts. And, of course, a good number were packed into the palace and manors of the four Gan, counting on the safety of another set of walls.

Askata and Aleena were at the palace, Commander Moqel by the gates.

Vaughn, however, was huddled with his small group of friends in the middle room of the southern Watch tower, where guards spent their break time.

Thrax was unusually sober-looking; he didn't even have his customary ball of fire. Danton leaned back in his chair on two legs, trying to appear nonchalant, but Vaughn could see the fear in his eyes.

Ivana was standing, propped up against one of the pillars nearby, her arms folded, her face unreadable.

"The Conclave army will be here in about a half hour," Vaughn said. "You all know your roles, but let's go over it one more time. Thrax, you're working with Commander Moqel. Light things on fire. Bloodbane, preferably. If they get through the walls, they'll almost certainly head for the palace. Delay them."

Vaughn ran a hand through his hair. Damn, he wished he had more beastblood aether.

"Danton, you're our eyes and ears." His ridiculous mobility made it easy for him to pop around to various locations to see what was happening and report quickly to Commander Moqel or Vaughn if need be. "But if you see where you can confuse a group of soldiers with lightblood magic, don't hesitate—just do it."

Danton swallowed and nodded. Vaughn worried about him the most. He was too young to have the burden of such decision-making on his shoulders, but Vaughn had no choice.

All of this would be fine if they were just dealing with soldiers, of course. If that were it, they'd be fine.

But then there were the bloodbane. The thousand plus bloodbane Danton had identified could obliterate the city without human help. And the palace. Damn, if the corpse-thing wanted to, it could make that army of bloodbane obliterate all the villages and towns within fifty miles.

Mortals survived alongside the horrific creatures only because they *didn't* attack in coordinated groups of thousands at a time, and many types stuck to their favorite haunts away from civilization.

He turned to Ivana.

"Ivana. You have the most important task. Find the corpse-thing."

Thrax guffawed.

Vaughn frowned at him. "You have a comment?"

"'Find the corpse-thing'? I mean, if you're going for dramatic effect, that really kills it."

"I'm not going for dramatic effect, firebrain. I'm telling her what she has to do."

Ivana sighed. "Yes. I'm going to find that...strange humanlike intelligent bloodbane that seems to be able to control the other bloodbane—"

"'Corpse-thing' *is* more concise," Danton whispered to Thrax.

Ivana glared at them both. "And I'm going to—"

"Kill it?" Danton put in.

"Disable it," Thrax suggested.

"*Neutralize* it," Ivana said.

"Oh, that's good," Thrax said. "She's good."

Dear gods, help me. But not you, Chati.

"People, get it together. We have about twenty minutes until we are the only thing standing between this city and the abyss," Ivana snapped.

Danton seemed appropriately subdued, but it failed to sober Thrax up. "She's way better at the dramatic one-liners than you," he whispered to Vaughn.

Vaughn ignored him. He was beginning to suspect the more nervous Thrax became, the more jokes he made. "Once Ivana neutralizes the corpse-thing, I'm assuming the bloodbane will go rogue. That's better than being guided by a semi-intelligent mind, but it's still going to be chaos. Some of them will run off. Some will try to destroy the city anyway. I've divided the beast-blood aether we had between you; don't waste it."

He drew a deep breath. "I'm going to be honest. The odds are not as good as I would like. We've done the best we can, but it may not be enough. You all know the damage a half-dozen bloodbane running amok in a city can do; there are a great many more than that accompanying two thousand soldiers intent on capturing this city, whatever it takes. We're rightly focused on the small picture tonight, but we can't lose sight of what happens if we fail to hold our position here—beyond the many innocent lives that will be lost. If we lose Ferehar, the Xambrians won't sign the alliance. The Conclave will destroy Donia, Venetia, and Fuilyn. And if you thought rule under the old Setanan Empire was bad—"

Thrax clapped him on the back. "You know, you're a great guy, Vaughn, but motivational speaking isn't your thing. If we win here, you might want to have someone else write your speeches."

Vaughn ran a hand back and forth through his hair. "My point is... We may have our quirks, but if anyone can pull this off, this team can. I know I can count on every one of you to try." He didn't look at Ivana as he said that. He *thought* he could count on her. He couldn't see what advantage she had in copping out now, other than self-preservation. And if that were going to be the case, she could have left days ago.

"Nope," Thrax said. "Still needs work."

Vaughn sighed and stood up. It was much more fun being a pain in the ass to the one in charge than the other way around. "All right. Let's get to it."

Chapter Sixty

The Storm

Commander Gered had insisted Driskell march with the vanguard as they approached the barricade that had been erected across the bridge in front of Cohoxta. Driskell would have preferred to have been left behind in Acalli—not least so he could slip away when he had the chance.

A second reason might have had to do with the six bloodgiants that lumbered along in front of them, living siege weapons controlled by an intelligent mind.

Instead, here he was, even though he would fall back with Gered to Acalli once the fighting started—until it was his turn to do what he was supposed to do, anyway.

It was almost as if Gered were keeping an eye on him, which was rather disconcerting.

Driskell kept the tiniest bit of aether continuously burning to maintain his self-enhancement. The last thing he needed at this moment was Gered to realize he had been manipulating him all this time.

They crested the rise to the middle of the bridge, and Gered held up his hand to bring the train to a halt.

From what he could see between the bodies of the bloodgiants, the city looked, by all accounts, to be asleep. Which it ought to have been, at this time of night. Only the Watch tower at the gates had a light flickering in the window facing south.

Gered waved Driskell back. "I don't want to chance anyone recognizing you."

Then why did you bring me? he projected, hoping by some miracle the commander would order him back to Acalli.

No such luck.

Vaughn waited in the Watch tower, looking through the southern window. He held his qixli in one hand, ready to contact Danton, who was keeping watch on the bloodbane in particular—lest some of them sneak off, cross the river farther down, and circle to the north gate or another section of the wall—which a concerted effort by enough bloodgiants could make short work of.

And they could send bloodhawks across *anywhere,* which set Vaughn particularly on edge. They had little beastblood aether—enough to make only a few dozen tipped arrows divided among their best archers. A number in turn limited to those who would allow blood to be drawn and mixed with aether so they could use it; the inadequate amount of time they had to explain such a thing to people who'd previously thought aether was cursed made that task even more difficult.

Vaughn ran his hand over the silvery sheen of whatever otherworldly material his bow was made of. And despite all this, his job was to be *useless.*

The army had seized Acalli not even a half hour ago. Ivana had already begun her hunt for the corpse-thing while he waited for the army to make its move. They expected some sort of parley, after which *he* had to fall back to the palace.

So everyone told him, anyway.

You're the reason this army is here, his mother had said to him when she had caught him stringing his bow. *Rather than chancing your life on the walls, why not surrender and save us all the trouble?*

Her sarcasm was not appreciated, but he took her point.

He cast his eyes toward Acalli, but it was too far for even his dark vision to tell him if the army was amassing in the shadows of its buildings.

He leaned forward. *Wait.*

Yes, there. Movement on the bridge.

Vaughn gripped the qixli and activated the aether. "I see them," Vaughn said quietly.

"Yeah," Danton said. "They're definitely moving. Some bloodgiants at the front, and some near the back. The bloodspiders are right at the edge of the bridge, bloodhawks... Circling around. They've got the bloodwolves split into two groups; not sure what that portends."

Vaughn stared out the window. He saw the bloodgiants at the front now; he didn't like that they were holding some back. "I have to go. I need to give Thrax a heads-up, and after that...well."

There was no acknowledgement. "Danton?"

"Temoth, there's a lot of them, Vaughn," Danton whispered.

Vaughn's free hand tightened on his bow. "Remember, if we pull through this, and I'm the next Ri, you get to bask in my glory as one of my closest friends," he said, keeping an eye on the group of soldiers that was now forming up beyond the barricade. The bloodgiants were spreading out along it. The hastily erected barrier wouldn't last long against the brute strength of bloodgiants, but every minute was another minute Ivana had to find and eliminate that abomination that was controlling them. If she could do it before the walls were breeched, they'd be okay. Probably.

"You mean that?"

"Huh?" Vaughn asked, bringing his mind back to Danton. "Sure. What do you want? Wine? Feather beds? I'd offer women, but I'm too enlightened for that now, sorry."

"*No.* That I'm one of your closest friends."

"Oh." Vaughn had the urge to reach out and ruffle Danton's hair, but one could only do so much through a qixli. "Of course I mean it. And you're going to be fine. Just keep your head about you and remember that you can literally make them all—even the bloodbane—look like they're dressed in only their undergarments. Now, I need to contact Thrax—"

"I know. I'm out."

Silence. Vaughn thought of a different contact. "Thrax," he said. "You ready?"

Ivana lay on her stomach on the roof of the tallest building in Acalli, peering over the edge, burning moonblood aether to keep herself invisible.

Even so, she had to be careful. The corpse-thing at Gan Barton's estate had been able to see through Vaughn's invisibility, and that had been his own native aether.

Where was the damn thing? She had passed hundreds of soldiers and bloodbane streaming over the bridge, and Acalli was still swarming with them.

If the corpse-thing acted anything like how the other one had acted, it would stay back while directing the bloodbane, rather than wading into the fray. It could be in any of the buildings in the town, shielded from view, and nothing about the movements of men or bloodbane seemed to suggest to her which one. She just had to locate it.

Vaughn climbed down from the Watch tower and joined Thrax and his mother atop the wall.

Beyond the bloodgiants, soldiers stretched out the length of the bridge. They had lit lanterns along the way, and now he could plainly see the bloodspiders scurrying around near the back, and white, pupil-less eyes punctuated the darkness beyond, like tiny white orbs floating in the night.

Vaughn glanced down the wall. The archers were ready, but he saw more than one jaw clenched and knuckles tight around the bows. The light was a tactic to inspire fear, no doubt, since there was no other reason to give their archers well-lit targets.

A group of three soldiers moved to stand next to the bloodgiants.

The nearest one's claws twitched, and for a moment Vaughn thought it would rip the soldier's head off. But it controlled itself.

Or, rather, that thing controlled *it*. Was that a good sign? That Ivana was even now distracting the thing, perhaps? Or maybe it had its limits and had finally reached them.

Either way, the longer they could keep them talking, the better.

The center man, surely the commander, held up his hand, and the man on his right held up the flag of parley.

The commander eyed Vaughn, Thrax, and Askata. "We are emissaries of the Conclave in Weylyn City," he shouted into a horn.

Vaughn made a point of looking at the soldiers arrayed behind him. "A rather odd-looking diplomatic party," he shouted back.

"We're not here on diplomacy," the commander said. "This city is under judgment for harboring not one, but multiple Banebringers."

Thrax snorted. "Well, that's a load of crap," he said. "Maybe the Conclave ought to be under judgment for being damn hypocrites."

The commander pinned his gaze on Thrax. "Perhaps if you can take us to their ringleader, one Dal Vaughn, I'll spare you."

Thrax flashed him a toothy grin. "Sure. You heard him, Vaughn. He's gonna spare me. That was easy."

The commander's eyes narrowed.

Vaughn smiled at him.

"I offer you terms, Dal Vaughn," the commander said. "Your unconditional surrender in exchange for us sparing the city the slaughter that is sure to come."

"Regent," Vaughn said. "What do you say to those terms?"

"We will not surrender," Askata said immediately, holding the commander with a cold stare. "We confess to no crime that the Conclave itself has not already committed, other than, apparently, that of following Setanan election law."

Was it Vaughn's imagination, or did some of the soldiers behind the commander look uncomfortable at Askata's words?

The commander seemed uncertain of what to do, as if he hadn't expected that answer. "Well enough. I didn't want to negotiate with demonspawn or their allies anyway."

Vaughn made a shooing motion with his hand, and his mother stepped away from the edge.

"All riiiiight." Vaughn said, drawing out the words to allow her bodyguard time to take her arm and lead her down the stairs. "Well. I have a message for you to take back anyway." He waved his arm expansively over the assembled army in front of them. "Take your troops and go back to Setana. Tell the Conclave they're no longer welcome in Ferehar. You're happy, I'm happy, no one needs to get hurt. Deal?"

The commander cast Vaughn a look of pure hatred and then stepped back into the ranks of the soldiers behind the bloodgiants.

Vaughn raised his bow, but Thrax took his arm. "Get back to the palace," he said firmly. "Now."

Vaughn gritted his teeth but acquiesced.

The thudding of bloodgiants pummeling the barricade began before Vaughn had even put his foot on the first step down. It took only until he had reached the bottom to hear the crash of the stone collapsing, followed by the plunks of the debris raining on the river below.

His last glance back before he disappeared—literally—down the street showed him bloodhawks bursting from the darkness and diving toward the archers on the wall.

Ivana, what are you doing?

Ivana crouched in a swath of overgrown weeds between two tall, narrow buildings and watched the town square through the leaves. She had found the corpse-thing, and only because it had finally emerged from, of all places, the tiny town shrine.

It stood now by the well, its hands clasped behind its back, staring toward Cohoxta and looking for all the world like some sort of military commander.

The effect was only enhanced by the hundreds of bloodbane that still surrounded it: mostly bloodwolves, at this point, as the bloodhawks had suddenly taken flight from their perches around the town and flown as one toward Cohoxta, and the bloodgiants, bloodspiders, and bloodcrabs had moved elsewhere.

The Conclave was improving. From the side, the corpse-thing looked almost human. Even the pallor of its skin had improved, as though the corpse had been to a mortician this time. She hoped that didn't also mean it was even more intelligent.

It glanced her way for only a moment, and she cringed. It still had those white, pupil-less eyes.

Its white eyes turned in their sockets, scanning the area. A frown touched its colorless lips, as though it knew something was off, but finally it turned back to staring toward the city.

A hundred bloodwolves was quite the shield. Under normal circumstances, trying to reach that thing right now would be suicide.

Unless one could simply stop time, of course.

It might still be suicide, in more than one way. Should she wait for a more opportune moment to reveal itself? But every moment she wasted was another moment that the rest of those bloodbane could be breaking through the gates of the city and allowing the soldiers to pour in. Then again, it wouldn't matter how much time she had saved if she struck at the wrong moment and failed.

Ivana fingered the hilt of her dagger in one hand and a sliver of moonblood aether in the other.

Before she could burn her own aether, the corpse-thing straightened up as if hearing or seeing something.

Its lips drew back tightly against its face in a satisfied smile, which made it look even more like a cadaver.

As one, the bloodwolves rose around it.

They congealed into a frenzied mass of black scales, sharp

teeth, and white eyes, growing more and more frantic, as if building tension within themselves.

Then, with a crescendo of noise, the bloodwolves broke free of their leashes while the corpse-thing remained in place.

Ivana drew in a sharp breath. That didn't bode well for the city, but it would make her task that much more likely to succeed.

She waited.

Driskell lingered near the middle of the unit while Gered was talking, continually projecting doubts about the legitimacy of this mission to those around him. The soldiers shifted and looked around, especially when Thrax accused the Conclave of being hypocrites.

Hypocrites, Driskell thought at them, seizing on Thrax's words. *You're following the lead of hypocrites and rebels. Usurpers. Warmongers. Powerful people who don't give a damn about you.*

A moment later, Gered strode back into view, flanked by two personal guards: Paran and a second Driskell couldn't remember the name of.

Gered looked satisfied. "Come," he said to Driskell, and Driskell had no choice but to follow him back along the lines of men. "Well," he said as they walked, "they didn't surrender, Driskell. Shall we return all the way to Acalli and wait for Cohoxta's walls to fall, or do you want to wait by the bridge, as eager as you are to get into the city as soon as possible to ferret out the traitors?"

Driskell blinked. He didn't need to burn aether to hear the sarcasm dripping from the commander's voice.

Something was wrong about this. Gered's eyes had taken on a glint Driskell had not seen there since the first time he'd met him.

Yet he didn't move to apprehend Driskell. He still walked, his hands behind his back. As if waiting for something.

Gered and his guards stopped at the end of the bridge and waited. A terrific boom sounded from the direction of the city.

Driskell winced and swallowed.

Another boom. The column on the bridge started to move. Driskell couldn't suppress a shudder as hundreds of bloodspiders and bloodcrabs scuttled by, followed by more soldiers.

The booms were coming at more regular intervals now. Like a giant pounding on a gate, demanding to be let in. Yes, yes, exactly like that, in fact.

A terrific crack split the air, and shouts turned to screams. Driskell's stomach churned. He had to get out of here. He had to—he didn't even know what. What could he do against this?

Gered glanced at him. "You seem unsettled, Driskell. Why would that be?"

"Commander, I should think anyone would be unsettled by these things."

A cacophony of noise rose faintly from the direction of Acalli. It might have been animals, but Driskell had a sinking feeling that it was, rather, the rest of the bloodbane moving out.

Gered's eyes flicked up toward the town. "Mmm. No, I think it's rather more than unsettled, I'm afraid."

Driskell took an involuntary step back. *Gods help me.* Gered knew. But *how*?

"Did you know that my pet bloodbane can sense your Banebringer magic? It knew immediately what you were doing once it got near you, but it took it a little while—being rather limited in intelligence, despite appearances—to figure out the implications. Once it did, it informed me of your little manipulations."

The second of Gered's bodyguards moved behind Driskell, so he couldn't continue to back away. His heart started to pound.

The little knife at his waist seemed a mockery.

"You were good. You had me convinced, despite the sheer ridiculousness of the scenario. Even had me growing fond of you."

He was going to die. Or be Sedated, which was just as bad.

Worse, they were *all* going to die. Despite weeks of trying to at least sow confusion amongst the army, none of it was going to matter; none of it had made a difference. He looked around. Gered had waved in a few more men, and Driskell was now surrounded.

"I almost had you Sedated as soon as I found out, but then I realized you would be more useful alive, then and now. Can you imagine what someone like me could do with a power like yours?"

Driskell blinked. "If you think I'm going to *work* for you—"

"I know what the Conclave does with their aether. I can do it too."

No, he wasn't going to die. He was going to be kept prisoner, an aether cow for Gered to use to slowly eke out his own place of power.

While everyone *else* died.

Despair clouded his mind. Who had he thought he was? Some sort of hero out of folklore or legend? Just because he had some magical powers? What, he would save the day by making a few soldiers feel guilty about their orders?

He was nothing. Just a naïve attaché with dying dreams of more.

Aleena stood outside the palace, surveying the palace courtyard. There were still far too many people milling about in the open for her liking.

She strode over to the nearest group. "You need to be *away* from the gates!" she shouted. "Get inside!"

Then a few people started screaming and pointing.

A single bloodhawk spiraled over the palace walls, shrieking—and then fell to the courtyard stones with, not an arrow, but what looked like a *hole* punched through its chest.

She spun to see Vaughn striding toward her, bow in hand and a grim look on his face. "I don't suppose you've heard anything from Ivana?" he asked.

She shook her head. "And I don't dare contact her in case it ruins whatever she's doing."

He nodded and looked up at the sky. "They had half a dozen bloodgiants that I could see, and Danton told me there were even more." He shook his head. "If she doesn't take that thing out soon, more than bloodhawks will be in the city, and at *that* point, we're in serious trouble."

His qixli started glowing. Vaughn snatched it out of its holder and held it out.

Thrax's voice came through. "Vaughn, the bloodhawks and bloodspiders have kept the men on the walls from being effective, and the gates are buckling. Commander Moqel is falling back and mobilizing the street units for killing bloodbane. He predicts once the walls have been breached, the soldiers will head straight for the palace and attempt to seize it. He'll do what he can to harry them, but with the bloodbane—"

There was a distant rumble, not through the qixli, but from the direction of the river. "Strike that," Thrax said. "The gates are officially down. Gotta go."

Vaughn swore. "Thanks." He put the qixli back into his pouch. "Get the rest of these people inside. Looks like we're in serious trouble."

Paran took Driskell's arm. Was it his imagination, or did the soldier look a little reluctant? "Dal Driskell," he said. "Come with me, please."

But Driskell wasn't even burning aether. He didn't even have his useless self-enhancement going.

Paran leaned toward him. "For what it's worth," he said under his breath, "I'm sorry. But duty is duty."

Driskell stared at him.

No. It *had* worked. If Paran was reluctant, then how many others would be as well?

Driskell jerked his arm out of Paran's hand.

"No," he said.

Paran looked nervous, and Gered laughed. "Come now, Dal, do you really think to—"

"*No!*" Driskell screamed, and as he did, he pushed the energy of burned aether outward, not in a blast, not in a rush, but he forced that tiny trickle as though through a hundred tiny holes.

All half dozen soldiers around him drew up short, including Gered's own bodyguards.

Gered stopped laughing.

Driskell backed away. "You will not touch me," he said through clenched teeth.

The soldiers stared at him. Paran said soothingly, "Of course we won't, Dal. If you'll just come—"

He kept pushing that trickle through those holes. "You will let me go."

"I don't know, Commander," another soldier said. "I think we ought to let him go."

"Seize him, idiots!" Gered snapped. "He's using his demonspawn magic on you."

Still, all the soldiers hesitated.

Gered's eye twitched. He growled and lunged at Driskell

himself.

Driskell darted out of the way and fled the only direction open to him: the now-empty bridge toward Cohoxta.

Vaughn stood at a window overlooking the palace courtyard with his mother. Beyond the walls, the street below the palace appeared to be in flames.

But right in front of him, the courtyard stones were awash with blood and bodies. A bloodgiant had smashed down the palace gates a few minutes ago, and bloodbane were everywhere. It took only a glance to realize they were working together like a well-trained squad, allowing each other the space to capitalize on their strengths and leaving their own soldiers alone. It was intelligent behavior when the brains of those demons had none.

Vaughn didn't see the offending creature that was lending its intelligence to these beasts. He could only hope Ivana was close to her mark, or this would be over soon. Even as he watched, a pair of bloodhawks broke off from harrying a half dozen soldiers into a corner—to let the advancing bloodwolves take over—and spiraled upward toward an upper-story window. One of them slammed into the window, and the glass cracked. It flew back, spiraled up, and then dove back down toward the same window.

"That's it," Vaughn said, swinging his bow off his back. "I'm going out there. I should have been out there a long time ago."

His mother grabbed his arm. "Teyrnon—"

He shook her off and strode away. He could *help*. He didn't know if it would be enough to buy Ivana more time, but at this point, it hardly mattered. If they lost Cohoxta, which seemed likely at this point, this was over, and he was dead.

He pulled out his qixli as he walked. "Thrax," he said. "Are you nearby? I'm done hiding."

"Vaughn—"

"I'll be out in the palace courtyard in about two minutes. I could use you."

He shoved the qixli back in the pouch and kept going.

Aleena was in the entry hall, trying to soothe the panicked people crammed into it.

She gave him a salute as he passed, and he nodded tightly in her direction.

At least some people understood.

The hundreds of terrified faces made him even more determined. This was, in a very real way, all his fault.

If he died doing penance for it, so be it.

Thrax must have been nearby because he was waiting by the palace doors by the time Vaughn marched out of them.

He made his way to Vaughn's side. "Orders?"

"Focus on the bloodbane. Take them out," Vaughn said. "All of them. Just try not to get any of our own soldiers caught up in it—and for Rhianah's sake, do *not* set the palace on fire, or you'll do their work for them."

"Got it, captain," Thrax said. He conjured a tiny fireball in his hand and took off running.

Vaughn burned aether and turned invisible, surveying the situation. He noted the broken wall and gauged his ability to climb the detritus to the top.

He could do it. He slung his bow onto his back, ran across the courtyard and over to the wall, dodging bloodbane and soldiers as he went, and began climbing.

At the top, he gained his footing, and without hesitation grabbed his bow again and sighted the bloodhawks that were working on breaking through the palace windows. It was too far for the accuracy he needed—with a normal bow and arrow.

He let loose one of Tani's arrows.

The arrow pierced the bloodhawk through and still flew for a few feet on the other side until it hit the wall of the palace and, thankfully, its journey was arrested.

The bloodhawk fell to the ground and didn't move again.

He let go of his invisibility, threw out a hand, and grabbed the water in a second bloodhawk's body in midair.

It flapped its wings and struggled against his hold. "You want me?" Vaughn shouted. "Come and get me!"

At the same time, Thrax let a fireball go. It slammed into the head of a bloodwolf—knocking it clean off.

The screams of humans and shrieks of unnatural beasts quieted as every living creature in the courtyard momentarily redirected their attention to either Thrax or himself—bloodbane and human alike.

It was as though they had received new orders: eliminate the greatest threats.

A bloodhawk that had made it into the palace burst back out of the broken window and flew directly toward him. A half dozen of its companions joined him on the way.

And on the ground, any bloodbane near Thrax turned to face him instead. He grinned savagely at them, and a moment later, his entire body was wreathed in flame.

Soldiers—enemy and ally alike—ran from him.

Vaughn reached for another of Tani's arrows and turned toward the demons headed his way, its jaw set. He lined them up. And with some instinctual burst of aether, he let it go.

The arrow tore holes through three of the bloodhawks before losing its momentum.

Vaughn blinked. *My gods.*

He drew another arrow and did the same to another three—

and at the moment the seventh had almost reached him, a fireball flew through the air and knocked the bloodhawk down to the ground in a flaming mess.

A row of ornamental bushes lit on fire. Vaughn cursed, pulled water out of the nearest source he could feel, and doused it. "Watch it!" he shouted to Thrax.

"Sorry!"

But there was no more time for words.

A bloodgiant had turned his way.

He pushed against the water in its body, keeping it from drawing closer, drew another arrow, and sent it through its skull.

His quiver was emptying faster than he would have liked, so he slung his bow on his back, grabbed another bloodhawk swooping toward him, and flung it hard into the side of the palace.

It fell to the ground, dazed, and went up in flames a moment later.

He blinked and shuddered. The aether literally felt like it was boiling within his veins—without the heat.

And yet, incredibly, he still had more.

He looked up at the sky, down at the ground, and selected his next target.

A red glow lit the night sky, and Driskell was racing right toward it in an effort to lose Gered.

He almost came barreling out directly into the middle of a street brawl.

He backpedaled and hid around the nearest corner, then peeked out.

Some of Cohoxta's Watchmen were in the street fighting

Gered's soldiers. The building behind them, which looked like a guardhouse for a manor beyond a well-kept lawn, was alight and already crumbling.

He felt sick. Hopefully no one had been inside.

What was worse, the flames were spreading. Even as he watched, a breeze blew several burning brands to the next rooftop, which began to burn, and glowing embers floated down to the grass. The blades caught, flared, and died out with a wisp of smoke, but there were more embers coming.

The manor had its own walls and gates, but they were decorative rather than defensive, and the gates already lay broken on the ground—and ineffective to stop sparks floating on the breeze, functional or not.

Driskell swore under his breath, feeling paralyzed by his inability to help here, either. What good had escaping done if he couldn't help? What could he do, charm the flames into submission?

Vaughn could use water, and he wasn't here. Suddenly, there was a flash of light, and Danton appeared next to him.

Driskell stumbled back, startled.

Danton's face broke into a grin. "Driskell?" He staggered a little, and then shook his head. "I saw someone who looked like you, and I thought it had to be my imagination! Yaotel said you'd been captured."

"I was. And brought with the army. I just escaped."

Danton clasped him on the shoulder. "I'm glad to see you. But why are you *here*?"

"It's the direction that happened to be available." Driskell glanced around, looking for Gered, but the commander was nowhere in sight.

"It's good you chose this street," Danton said. "Three streets over, there's a bloodgiant stomping down the street and smashing anything in its path." Danton stared in the direction of the aforementioned street, his jaw twitching. "Bloodbane are running amok in the city. Another bloodgiant just smashed the palace walls down, and enemy soldiers have surrounded it. I assume they're waiting for bloodbane to kill all our soldiers defending the palace before moving in to seize it. It doesn't look good."

"But what happened? Did the enemy army start a *fire* in the city?" Gered was planning on mass executions, but, burning skies, he hadn't said anything about burning the entire city to the ground!

Driskell shook his head. "Believe it or not, it was *bloodbane.* I saw them from on top of a nearby building. A dozen bloodhawks flew in with burning bloodspiders in their claws and dropped them on random rooftops. This entire *street* is going up in flames, not just this guardhouse. I can only assume it was a tactic designed to keep our soldiers away from the palace and distracted, but if these flames get out of control..."

There wouldn't be a city left to defend. "What can I do?" Driskell whispered.

Danton surveyed the burning buildings. "I'm no soldier. I can hold my own in a fistfight, but this is a little beyond my ken. I've been trying to keep an eye on what's happening around the city for Vaughn and the commander and report back. Then I saw the fires start." Danton jerked his head toward the manor behind him. "This street is just below the palace and has all four of the Gan's city manors. I don't give one whit about the Gan's fancy houses, but there are hundreds of families packed into them—mostly refugees from surrounding villages. I say we need to figure out a way to deal with this fire."

"Can you bring buckets of water from the river, quickly?" Driskell asked.

Danton shook his head. "Already thought about that. I'd never get ahead of it, and going back and forth that quickly so many times would kill me." He looked at Driskell. "Ideas?"

Driskell looked at the men fighting in the street. One of their own soldiers ran one of the enemy through, and Driskell had to look away. It was madness. All of this was pure madness. To think what they could accomplish if people put as much effort into useful applications as they did into slaughtering each other...

Yes. What they could accomplish, if only they put their minds to it.

He knew what he could do.

Driskell set his jaw and marched out into the street.

"Driskell? Driskell!" Danton shouted.

Driskell could hear the panic in Danton's voice, but he closed it out, lest he lose his nerve. He gathered in his aether, held it till it boiled, and halted in the middle of the street. Then, just like he had before, he pushed it out—controlled, tiny streams through tiny holes—and shouted. *"Stop!"*

To his utmost surprise...they did.

Enemy and friend alike stopped what they were doing to look at him.

He hadn't planned this out. He had only the vaguest notion of how to do what he wanted to do. But he knew what needed to be done, and the manpower was literally scattered across Cohoxta to do it. He poured more of his aether into his bubble and expanded it farther than he had ever dared. *"Put down your weapons. Can't you see there's a fire that needs dealt with?"*

About half of the men, mostly those closest to him, looked at the now two burning buildings. The other half seemed puzzled.

"What are you, idiots?" he shouted. "Why are you having a street brawl when a city is burning down around you?"

Was it his imagination, or were the buildings on the *opposite* side of the street starting to burn as well?

He shoved down his panic and pointed down the street. "Those here to defend, make a water line to the nearest well that way." He pointed the other way. "Those here to attack, make a water line that way."

The friendly troops moved to act, while the enemy started at him, even more befuddled.

"What if this were your town?" he pleaded with the enemy troops. *Your homes,* he suggested silently. "What kind of monsters are you?" *Your families.*

The flames appeared to spread even farther, though, curiously, Driskell felt no additional heat.

Some of those closest cried out in panic and dropped their weapons. They began to respond to Driskell's order, some of them even shouting at the ones who were still standing still to get moving.

"Would you want to go home and find your home in ashes?" Driskell continued. He pushed even more aether into the words, playing off everything he'd been speaking to these soldiers for over a week. "Your families slaughtered in the streets? Why are you even here? Who told you to come? Commander Gered? The Conclave? Some noble who doesn't care if you die here today? Do you even care about this cause, or did they tell you there were demonspawn here?" One of the homes melted into ash. He could have sworn he heard screaming and pleading.

He decided to inject a little fear into those who still hesitated. "I have news for you. The only demonspawn here are those who allow this senselessness to continue. Maybe the gods will choose you next for slaughtering innocents."

And then, there was a split in the air. Black flames licked out, and a horrendous monstrosity of the abyss stepped through and pinned the enemy soldiers with a stare.

That did it. The last of the soldiers standing in that street dropped their weapons and the lines began to form.

The bloodbane vanished.

Driskell spun to look back toward where he had been standing with Danton.

Danton gave him a huge grin and a thumbs-up.

A little theatrics, apparently, to help him out.

Danton took one line, and Driskell took the other—Driskell using his charmblood aether to encourage them to keep going by any means necessary—and Danton using illusions to terrify some of them into working harder.

The water started coming.

Other soldiers, both friend and foe, eventually arrived in the street. Driskell expanded his bubble again, pressing silently the urgent need to *put out this fire.* He scattered it on the wind like chaff, sent it swirling through the city.

Stop fighting and come and put out this fire.

No one else who arrived questioned it.

The corpse-thing walked slowly behind the charging army of bloodwolves, its hands behind its back.

It passed Ivana's position in the alley, and as it did, she burned aether and leapt.

It spun, impossibly fast, and dodged her attack.

She rolled, came up in a crouch, and stared at it. *What?*

It cocked its head at her, as if merely curious as to what sort of creature might be attacking it.

Ivana rose and took a few steps back, wary. Had she not stopped time?

But no. There was no night breeze, no sound of animals. The

bloodwolves she could see had drawn to a halt.

She returned her attention to the corpse-thing, mind racing for Plan B.

She slid her boot knife out of the sheath at her ankle, already pretreated with beastblood aether, and in one smooth motion, launched it at the corpse-thing.

It caught the knife, then it held it up to the moonlight and turned it in the air, examining the silver sheen.

It lowered the knife, and this time the look it gave her was less neutral, and more calculating.

Why wasn't it frozen? Why was everything else around her frozen, but the one thing she wanted to *kill* wasn't?

"What game do you play?" it asked.

She stared at it. She hadn't expected it to speak, but the one at Gan Barton's had spoken, hadn't it? Would talking to it work? It certainly hadn't with the last, but this one didn't seem the same. "Call back your bloodbane," Ivana said. "Or at the least, let them free. Do you want to serve human masters?"

Its eyes glimmered. "Human? My master is both human, and not. And even if I wished to do otherwise, I have no ability to act on a will contrary to that of my master's. My orders are to break through those gates and then cause mass confusion and terror so the human soldiers may seize the palace without resistance. Therefore, that is what I shall do."

"That's not a good plan," Ivana said. Actually, it was, but...

"Oh?" It looked her up and down. "What master do you serve?"

"I don't... I serve no one," Ivana said.

"Then why put your life in danger by helping these humans?"

What in the abyss? It was now reasoning with *her*? "I *am* human," she said.

"Mmm," it said noncommittally. "But you could be so much more, couldn't you?" It gestured toward the dagger she still held in her right hand.

Something about its voice was...compelling. She didn't know why. A part of her brain said it was foolish to listen to it. And yet she found herself listening all the same. The hand holding the dagger dropped to her side unconsciously. "What do you mean?"

"'Banebringers,' they call you, don't they? Once upon a time, you were gods." It walked toward her, and the closer it came, the more compelling she found it.

"You could be a god again," it whispered.

Images floated into her brain, images of people bowing down to her, doing her bidding.

This was wrong. These weren't desires she had ever had. They weren't coming from her own brain. This didn't make sense.

The corpse-thing stopped in front of her. "Give it to me," it said, pointing to her dagger.

She hesitated. Why in the abyss should she hand over her only remaining weapon to the thing she was supposed to kill? That made no sense. And yet it felt like the right thing to do.

She stared at the corpse-thing. Its eyes had changed. They were still pupil-less, but red swirls began to twist through them.

Wait. Something was trying to push through her clouded mind. She had seen this before. It was what had happened when that other corpse-thing had seemed to absorb any magic thrown at it and use it back against them.

But she hadn't done anything other than stop time, which it apparently was able to absorb? Reflect? She didn't even know.

Men, lounging around her, half-dressed, waiting on her every whim.

She blinked, and the image shattered. That had been the wrong temptation to implant in *her* mind. Her brain rejected it soundly as false, and whatever the reason for the corpse-thing's newfound abilities, *she* now felt more herself.

"Give it to me," the corpse-thing said again.

Even out from under its spell, she felt as though she ought to do it. She tilted her head. *What? Why?*

She looked at her dagger, and then at the corpse-thing. She felt that same sense of precognition she'd felt with the trajectory of an arrow or the swing of a club, except with no clear sense of what would happen if she did it.

Her aether expenditure had to be pressing to its limit. This was the longest she'd ever kept her aether burning at a time, and though her endurance and control had increased dramatically, she had started to feel dizzy with less before.

Even so, she pressed the feeling harder, deliberately burning a little more aether for it.

She saw the dagger cut along her own cheek, tipped in her own blood.

She pressed harder.

Her dagger embedded in the corpse-thing's stomach.

She pressed harder.

Spots flickered in front of her eyes, and she withdrew the extra aether. The spots disappeared.

You can't give your dagger to that thing. It makes no sense. But something other than sense beat against her.

So, against all common sense, she handed the dagger to the corpse-thing.

It took it and ran its dead finger along the flat of the blade. "It's as I suspected," it trilled, as if delighted. "You've been to visit the gods."

It ran the point of the dagger along her cheek and then held it up in front of her eyes, her blood turning silver on the tip before her eyes. It frowned. "But what are you? I don't recognize you."

Ivana changed tactics. She let her eyes go glassy. "Your words are...tempting."

It lowered the dagger. "Of course they are. What human doesn't want to be a little god, after all?"

"None," she said. "Not a single one of us…"

It held out its other hand to her. She had no idea what taking its hand might do, but she doubted it would end well for her. She didn't dare press her aether again to *see*.

"I can show you how," it whispered, its eyes almost completely red now.

She started to reach out her hand…and at the last moment, instead grabbed its wrist—the same wrist that held her dagger—and shoved it toward its own stomach.

The dagger plunged in about a half-inch—not far enough to kill it—before the corpse-thing resisted with its super-human strength.

But then its eyes went wide in a human-like expression of shock. The color left them. It staggered backward and then slumped onto the ground, motionless, its hand sliding off the dagger and flopping to the ground.

The dagger fell out, and Ivana let go of her aether.

She fell to her hands and knees, darkness swimming in front of her eyes. She knelt there for a moment, waiting, waiting.

The feeling faded quickly.

She crawled over to the corpse thing and stared down at it. That had *not* been a deep enough wound to kill anyone, let alone a bloodbane.

Silver blood leaked out of the small puncture her dagger had made, and its chest continued to rise and fall. It wasn't dead.

Silver blood. The abyss. Danathalt's creatures. Danathalt, Zily's rival.

Her aether could Sedate bloodbane. Of course it could. It made perfect sense. But she never would have imagined that a bloodbane *could* be Sedated until now.

But their blood was silver, just like Banebringers, wasn't it? That was the reason Banebringers were called demonspawn.

She drove the dagger into the corpse-thing's heart, just to be on the safe side, and waited until it stopped moving.

She sat back on her heels and glanced back toward Cohoxta.

A red glow lit the night sky from the direction of the palace, and smoke curled up against it.

Well, damn.

She yanked her dagger out, burned moonblood aether, and sprinted toward the city.

The front doors of the palace thudded. The women and children in the front hall drew back.

Aleena stood between them, holding her tiny knife in a sweaty hand.

Realistically, there was nothing she could do. She had a small supply of aether of various kinds that she had made with her own blood before this had all started, but she had little experience in using it, and not enough to matter against the army of demons outside the door anyway.

Still, she planted her feet and stood.

The door cracked inward.

A bloodgiant turned before Vaughn had a chance to react. It thundered toward the wall. Vaughn drew an arrow, but not before the creature slammed its entire body into the wall under Vaughn.

The wall heaved, then cracked, and then disintegrated beneath his feet.

He threw himself at the next section of wall but only

succeeded in not falling off. Instead, he slipped and slid and crashed down the rubble in stages.

The bloodgiant gave him no time to react. It picked up the nearest piece of the wall and hurled it. Vaughn rolled out of the way just in time—and turned invisible.

The bloodgiant roared in frustration. Vaughn put an arrow through its open mouth.

He stumbled to his feet, his chest heaving, and spun around to survey the grounds.

His stomach fell. Despite the dent he and Thrax were making in the bloodbane, there was no way it would be enough. The two of them alone couldn't hold off this hoard. Satisfied that a few dozen at a time could handle the two Banebringers, most of the bloodbane were now supporting enemy soldiers in fighting through the few remaining Watchmen to reach the palace. He heard the crash of a window on a lower level and screams from inside.

His head spun—perhaps because he had hit it, possibly because of the amount of aether he was burning—or maybe because the screams and shrieks and crashes and blood were suddenly too much.

He lifted his bow and sighted multiple possible targets, and none of it seemed enough.

They were being overwhelmed. The Conclave would win.

Despair choked his throat.

He lost his invisibility. A bloodwolf caught sight of him and hurtled toward him. He lifted his bow, felt for an arrow. Only one left.

He let it loose just as the wolf lunged at him—into the soft part of its throat.

It yelped and landed just shy of him, and then lay still.

A half dozen more had surrounded him.

Well, Zily, he thought. *Whatever hopes you had for using us to fix your little problem...*

Then something changed.

One of the bloodwolves knocked into another, and the offended wolf turned on its companion, teeth at its throat.

Another lunged at one of the enemy soldiers.

The others seemed to forget about Vaughn and turned to join the fray.

A hoard of bloodrats went skittering and squeaking by him, over the gap in the wall, and into the city.

A bloodhawk in the sky circled above but didn't land.

He almost collapsed in relief. Ivana. She had done it. She had killed the corpse-thing.

The bloodbane had returned to their normal, stupid—albeit dangerous—selves.

Vaughn heard Thrax roar with satisfaction somewhere on the grounds, and the sound of yelping grew louder until Thrax burst into view, a flaming ball chasing three bloodwolves, two of which were on fire.

The wolves, rather than turning and attacking, fled toward the nearest exit—a gap in the wall. Vaughn doused them with water as they went, lest they cause more problems.

And for some reason, all the human soldiers—enemy and ally alike—had disappeared at some point during the fray. He couldn't account for that, but not having to deal with humans trying to seize the palace was a relief.

Thrax gave him a thumbs-up from across the courtyard, and, feeling energized again, Vaughn darted around, ripping any intact arrows from fallen bloodbane he could find. *He* didn't need beastblood.

But they weren't out of danger yet. The bloodgiants never wanted anything but death and mayhem, and there were three of them left—one of which was attempting to bash down the palace's massive front door.

"Hey, pea-brain!" Vaughn shouted. He picked up a brick that had been dislodged from the ruined walls and hurled it at the bloodgiant. It bounced off the giant's thick hide, and it didn't even turn to look at him.

The door went down.

The door crashed to the ground, and a bloodgiant stood in the doorframe, staring at Aleena. It turned its mouth in some hideous mockery of a smile, tore off a shattered half of one door to use as a giant club, and swung it at her.

She flung herself out of the way, and the wood crashed down just behind her.

Screams. Shouts. Burning fire in her side. She thought it had missed!

Blackness.

Vaughn ran toward the bloodgiant that had just stepped into the palace after ripping half the door off. He burned aether and let one arrow loose.

The arrow burrowed into its back, completely disappearing, and it fell forward with a crash. He loosed another, just to be on the safe side. It spasmed and didn't move again.

Satisfied, he turned—and was immediately disheartened. Still so many...

They were scattering, and no longer working together—and some had fled—but there were still too many seeking to do as much chaotic damage as possible.

He set his jaw, pressed his lips together, and held his aether ready like a pot of boiling oil.

He wouldn't go down without trying.

Ivana arrived at the palace to find complete chaos—and a battlefield strewn with the bodies of humans and bloodbane alike, though there were still far too many of the latter living.

In the distance, she saw what she could only assume was Thrax—because it looked like a flaming man.

And then there was Vaughn.

She blinked.

Was he...*glowing*?

She had never seen him loose arrows so fast. They flew at lightning speed, skewering one bloodbane after another, streaks of silvery mist dissipating off them as they went. And the same silvery mist clung to Vaughn's bow—and Vaughn himself. As if the aether he was burning was steaming off him like sweat on a cold day.

She shook her head and took stock of the rest of the grounds. Where could she help? Her dagger was also a gift from the gods, but to use it would require getting close to bloodbane.

If she could get close to the bloodbane...she could apply her own blood to the blade and Sedate them.

Vaughn and Thrax seemed to have the outside of the palace under some semblance of control, if there was any order to a battlefield, but she saw too many broken windows in the palace itself—and the front door had been smashed in, a bloodgiant lying motionless on top of the remains. Were there more bloodbane running amok inside?

She took off toward the front door, burning moonblood aether to avoid any bloodbane that might notice her on the way.

When she got there, she stepped around the hulking figure of the dead bloodgiant and—

There was a group of women huddled around a prone figure on the floor. Ivana pushed her way through. "What's—?"

She drew to a halt as if she had run into a wall. Aleena lay there, a large splinter of wood run straight into her stomach.

No. Gods, no.

She moved her feet and fell to Aleena's side. "Aleena!" she shouted, shaking her.

Her eyes fluttered open. "Ivana," she whispered, a smile touching her lips. Then her eyes closed again.

Heart in her throat, Ivana pressed her fingers to Aleena's neck. Her heart was still beating—for now.

Ivana gritted her teeth and stood, rage pulsing through her. "Are there more in here?" she asked the group around her.

One shook her head. "I don't think so," she said.

But there were more out there, and if Aleena died, Ivana would be damned if it were for nothing.

Ivana slid her dagger against her palm, wetting the blade with her own blood. And if she had to, she'd bleed herself dry trying to make sure that didn't happen—before she ever got to damnation.

Vaughn felt for an arrow, and his quiver was empty again. He had tried to continue collecting as he went, but there was nothing more around him.

Too bad Tani's magical bow didn't come with a magical quiver that never ran out.

A hand grabbed his and pressed a handful of arrows into it.

He turned. Ivana stood next to him, looking not at him, but at the dozen or so bloodbane stalking their way.

"You're glowing," she said, not looking away from the

bloodbane.

"Yeah," he said. He had noticed the wisps of what appeared to be silvery, shimmering steam trailing off his arms just a few minutes ago. "Weird." He looked down at his hand. Three arrows.

There were a dozen bloodbane stalking their way, and those remaining were joining them.

And he was finally, *finally*, starting to feel dizzy. He was afraid if he kept going...

"You haven't seen Thrax, have you?" he asked.

"A few minutes ago."

There was no sign of the flaming man now.

Ivana frowned. "Why aren't they attacking?"

She was right. The remaining bloodbane had crowded around, pacing back and forth—some even circled them—but none were attacking. It was almost as if... "You did take care of the corpse-thing, right?"

"Yes. It's dead. Positive." She paused. "Vaughn, they're afraid of you."

"*What*? That's insane. Bloodbane aren't afraid of people, they're—"

"Look at them. Really look at them."

He did. The five bloodwolves were pacing back and forth, snarling and snapping, their ears lain back, but their eyes rolled in their heads like terrified horses.

The three bloodcrabs danced on their needle-legs, as if eager to stab them both through, but they skittered forward, and the instant Vaughn moved, they skittered back again.

A pack of bloodrats shrieked and ran around them in a wide circle, first closer, then farther.

One of the bloodwolves took a step toward them.

Vaughn took a step toward it, holding out his steaming arm

as if about to throw something at it.

It slunk back, tail down.

He looked down at himself, and then back at the bloodbane.

"That's because you're not merely human anymore, are you?" Ivana said softly.

Vaughn swallowed. He had no idea what was happening to him, but at the moment, all he cared about was using it to their advantage.

"I'm nearly spent," he said. "We don't make it out of this alive if they attack together."

"I know."

"And whatever my body is doing that's scaring them, it could stop at any time," he pointed out.

"You could be right."

"So. Here's my desperate plan. We stay together. I walk toward them. You stab them when they're distracted. One by one. As fast as we can."

"That's your plan?" she asked incredulously.

"You have a better one?"

"Yes," she said. "You distract them."

And she took off running.

"Ivana!" he shouted.

The bloodwolves turned from Vaughn to easier prey.

"Distract them," he muttered. He ran toward the whole group, and they scattered.

Ivana jumped toward the closest bloodwolf and burned aether.

Time stopped. It froze as it turned toward her, its mouth opened. She sailed through the air, grazed it with her dagger, and then unfroze time.

It collapsed behind her.

She wet her dagger with the stream of blood trickling down her palm and jumped again.

Vaughn hardly registered what was happening around him. Ivana appeared to be disappearing and reappearing at random all over the place, leaving the corpses of bloodbane in her wake. The bloodhawk that had been circling finally gathered up its courage and dove at him.

A moment later Ivana was there—the bloodhawk frozen, claws outstretched, about to rip his face off. She swiped it with her dagger, glanced at him, and it fell to the ground.

He hardly had time to register that she had included him as an active part of her time stop. When had she learned that?

What in the abyss was she *doing*?

He grabbed an entire pack of bloodrats that was scurrying toward him and flung them in different directions.

The dance continued. He spun and whirled, flinging bloodbane when he could, distracting them when the dizziness came back, while she darted around felling bloodbane in strange starts and stops.

At some point, Thrax joined them again.

Another bloodwolf dove toward Thrax.

Thrax let loose a jet of fire.

Ivana stopped time.

The fire was going to miss.

Vaughn grabbed the bloodwolf and shoved it into the fireball's path.

Ivana let go.

The bloodwolf landed in a smoking husk.

And then there was nothing but silence.

Up and down the ranks they went, more and more men joining, ignoring the lines of friend and foe to focus on the task at hand. Driskell tried to keep count—he estimated some five hundred men between the two sides were now working on the burning buildings.

Little by little, the flames diminished. The buildings along the street in either direction were all but charred timber, but they had finally gotten ahead of the flames and managed to keep the fire from spreading farther into the city.

Driskell didn't even notice that dawn had come until the last flame had simmered into a smoldering, smoking ember, and there was still light in the air.

Rest, he projected. The soldiers all began to drop to the streets almost gratefully, exhausted from their frantic labor.

Driskell didn't know where the remaining soldiers from either side were. Many were likely dead.

He decided to try something new. Instead of a bubble, he imagined his influence as a mist on the breeze, carried far beyond his sight to whomever might be in its path.

Come, he said to the wind. *We're done here. Rest.*

A few minutes later, they began to trickle in. Wounded and uninjured, friend and foe—they came at his call. They seemed confused, but he caught them under his bubble once he could see them, reiterating the command. *Rest.*

Someone drew another bucket of water and passed it around. Soldiers took drinks; they poured water over their heads. They laughed.

Driskell could feel his aether running thin. He was starting to get dizzy. He closed his eyes and slowly brought back in the bubble but left the mist—almost as if his aether were slowly evaporating, rather than burning at a clip.

"What in the name of all the gods is happening here?" a sharp voice cut through the rising murmur.

Silence fell.

Driskell opened his eyes. Commander Gered stood at the other side of the street, his sword drawn.

He strode into the street, and then paused. He looked at his soldiers, frowned, shook his head, and then spotted Driskell.

Panic rose in Driskell's chest.

"*You,*" Gered said, spittle flying out of his mouth.

A murmur traveled through the exhausted soldiers.

Driskell tossed a tendril toward the commander. "I was trying my best to find a peaceful resolution to this."

Gered didn't bite. Instead, he spat. "*Peaceful.* I'll have peace when every last demonspawn and their allies are rotting in their graves."

He strode toward Driskell.

Driskell stepped back. The evaporating aether dissipated, and he threw everything he had at Gered. "Stop!" he shouted.

His head spun. It wasn't working.

Danton was now standing in Gered's way. He conjured a believable-looking bloodwolf, snarling at his side, but Gered ignored Danton and walked right through it.

Driskell drew his tiny knife and held it in a shaking hand. "Go home," he tried one more time. "You aren't wanted here."

Gered laughed. "That won't work on my anymore, boy." He tucked his hand inside a leather pouch at his side and came out with a syringe. "I was saving these for the ringleaders. Thought you might be of some use to me, but I think I'd be better off putting you down."

The last thing Driskell heard was Danton shouting, Gered

sneering, and his own hysterical pleading.

And then everything stopped. He felt himself crumple to the ground, almost as if watching from the outside. He tried to move, but he couldn't. Nothing worked. He couldn't see, couldn't hear, could speak, couldn't move.

And then, last of all...

He was no longer aware of anything.

Vaughn, Ivana, and Thrax stood in the middle of pure carnage—bloodbane lay everywhere, smoking, bleeding, still.

And then there were the human bodies. Hundreds of them. Fereharian and otherwise. Mostly dead, though they'd have to check them all in case anyone could be saved.

Vaughn staggered back at the thought of sorting through all those bodies, feeling dizzy. Hundreds slaughtered, first by each other, then by the bloodbane...

And yet he, Thrax, and Ivana had taken out the remaining bloodbane—or at least those that hadn't fled into the city—by themselves.

What kind of creatures had they become?

Ivana was right. No mere human stood a chance.

Thrax cleared his throat. "Bad news. I discovered while chasing some bloodbane out of the dungeon that Airell's cell was broken into. He's not there."

Vaughn passed a hand over his face. *Great.*

Thrax whistled. "Say, did you know that both of you are *glowing?*"

Vaughn looked at Ivana. Thrax was right; she was steaming too.

Ivana looked back at the palace, then over Vaughn's shoulder. "I'm going back inside," she said. "Aleena's hurt. But you might want to turn around. The city is smoking."

Danton stood over Driskell's crumpled form, rage and grief warring in his chest.

"He'd barely been a Banebringer for two months," he shouted at the enemy commander. "You monster! You fucking monster!"

The words were nonsensical. The commander didn't care how long someone had been a Banebringer, nor did he think he was the monster.

But it was so unfair. Driskell didn't deserve this. None of them did. *None* of them did.

"Don't worry," the commander said. "I have plenty to go around."

He tossed aside the empty syringe and produced another.

Run, Danton's mind urged him. He could be gone in an instant. He doubted the commander even realized that.

But he couldn't. He couldn't leave Driskell there to be dragged away and stuffed in a hole somewhere.

He had nothing. His illusions could do nothing to protect him.

So he drew his short sword and took a step back. It was perfunctory. He could handle the weapon, but not against someone like this.

"Come, boy. Put it down and surrender. Face your crimes."

A hard voice spoke from across the square. "He's committed no crime, and no one is surrendering but you."

Vaughn?

The enemy commander sneered at Vaughn and raised his syringe in defiance.

Vaughn burned aether and pushed him back.

He stumbled backward, and Danton darted out of the way.

"I'm done with this," Vaughn said. "I told you to get out. This city is under my protection. Indeed, the entirety of Ferehar is under my protection. Take whatever remains of your troops and go back and tell the Conclave that."

The commander spat. "You'll rot in the abyss, demonspawn."

Thrax, who had stumbled into the square on Vaughn's heels, growled and moved forward, but Vaughn motioned him back.

Vaughn seized the commander's body, keeping him on his feet but unable to move.

Whispers traveled around the square. The soldiers gathered there were staring at him.

He was still "steaming," though it was beginning to slow down.

"I've already been to the abyss," he said. He looked at his hands and waved them around a little to make the steam swirl. "And I'm definitely not rotting."

Some of the Fereharian soldiers' mouths had dropped open.

"Demonspawn scum," the commander mouthed.

Vaughn swallowed. He twisted his hand, snapped the commander's spine, then let his body fall to the ground.

He pushed aside the wave of nausea that threatened to overwhelm him and turned his eyes away from the broken body to sweep over the soldiers sitting there. "Let's try again. Any other takers for my message?"

As one, the enemy soldiers rose to their feet. One, a low-ranking officer judging by the stripes on his sleeve, organized them into ranks and then came to stand in front of Vaughn. "I-I think I'm the highest-ranking officer left, my lord," he said. The officer was young and bruised and coated in soot, and his voice shook. "And on behalf of our unit, we unconditionally surrender."

"I don't want prisoners," Vaughn said. "I mean it. Go back and tell the Conclave to stay away."

The officer pressed his lips together and gave a curt nod.

"Thrax," Vaughn said, "take the rest of our men and see that these troops find their way out of Cohoxta without causing further damage. Keep an eye out for any bloodbane still in the city."

Thrax nodded and began rounding up the rest of the soldiers.

Vaughn waited until the square was empty of all but himself, Danton, and the unfortunate Driskell.

He knelt next to Driskell's prone form and stared at him. "What am I supposed to tell Tanuac and Nahua?" he said, sensing Danton's presence above him.

"That he did this. All of it." Danton waved his hand around the square. "This city would likely be ash if he hadn't intervened." He ran a trembling hand through his hair. "He was my friend."

Vaughn stood, though weariness threatened to keep him down, and put a hand on Danton's shoulder. "Let's get him back up to the palace."

Chapter Sixty-One

Cursebreaker

Vaughn closed his eyes and drew in a long, deep breath before walking through the door in front of him.

Thrax and Danton were already there. He had passed Sanca in the hall coming from the room. Yaotel had sent her as one of the promised healers along with a couple hundred of Tanuac's soldiers, all of whom had been welcome relief to the weary remnants of the Cohoxtan Watch.

Sanca merely shook her head and gave him a sad smile.

Thrax sat in the corner, his face drawn. He was abnormally sober.

Danton stood by the side of the bed, his arms folded tightly around himself.

Driskell lay on the bed before him. His eyes were closed. His chest rose and fell slowly. He could have been asleep.

He wasn't.

Nothing they could do would wake him.

"I didn't know him long," Danton said, "but you know how sometimes you meet someone and you know—" His voice broke. "You know you're meant to be friends?"

Vaughn crossed to the bed and put his hand on Danton's shoulder in silent sympathy.

After a few minutes, Vaughn spoke. "It's been four days. We should let his family know. And Ri Tanuac. And...his fiancée." He'd been delaying the inevitable amid trying to bring some semblance of order after the chaos and destruction of the attack—part of which involved personally hunting down any bloodbane still terrorizing the city.

"She doesn't even know he's a Banebringer," Danton whispered.

"Cruddy way to find out," Thrax said somberly.

Vaughn reached for the qixli in his pouch. "I'll do it," he said.

"No," Danton said. "I...I know Tania, a little. And she should hear it first."

Vaughn shrugged and held the qixli out to him.

Danton pressed his lips together and shook his head. "I've been practicing. I can do this." He took a deep breath and closed his eyes.

Vaughn's eyes widened. "Danton, no—!"

It was too late. Danton disappeared in a flash of light.

Vaughn ran a hand through his hair and stared at the spot where Danton had been. It was one thing to pop around a few miles. Marakyn was three hundred miles away! Even if he did it in stages...

"Let it be, Vaughn," Thrax said. "I know he seems goofy sometimes, but he's not the sixteen-year old you saved anymore."

"What's this?" he said. "Thrax, playing the sage?" He gave Thrax a small smile.

But it was sapped of any real joy by the prone figure lying in front of them.

Vaughn and Thrax kept a silent vigil, waiting for Danton to return. Vaughn rubbed a hand back and forth through his hair. He couldn't believe Driskell had been with the enemy army this whole time. Tanuac had given him up for lost. And yet, from Danton's recounting of the events, Driskell had played a large part in containing the chaos four nights ago. He could have run or hidden, knowing he had no combat skills. Instead, he'd risen to the occasion.

And paid the price.

There was another flash of light, and Vaughn turned toward it. To his shock, it wasn't just Danton who had returned. It was Danton...and Tania.

Danton gasped, staggered, and collapsed to the floor.

Vaughn's shock turned to alarm, and he fell to his knees next to Danton.

"Danton!" he shouted, shaking him.

He didn't move, didn't even breathe, for fifteen long, terrifying seconds. And then he groaned, and his back heaved as he pushed himself to his hands and knees. "Good. I'm good. I'm okay."

"You idiot. Were you *trying* to kill yourself?"

He sat back on his heels, looking a little unsteady. "She wanted to see him. I...I had to try."

Vaughn looked up at Tania. She was frozen to the floor, staring at Driskell's motionless form.

Vaughn helped Danton to his feet.

"He's... Are you sure he's not just unconscious?" Tania asked, her voice unsteady.

"We're sure," Vaughn said gently.

She moved forward, hesitated, and then took his hand. She brought it to her forehead and closed her eyes. Tears gathered on her eyelashes. "He tried to tell me," she whispered. "I...I thought he was talking about someone else." She opened her eyes and looked around at the rest of them. "He was such a good person. I... How could this have happened?"

"Do any of us seem like bad people?" Danton asked.

She looked at each one of them in turn, then shook her head silently and turned back to Driskell.

Vaughn didn't know if that was an answer to Danton's question or a denial of the truth.

There was a knock at the door, and then it immediately opened.

Ivana stepped inside. "I thought I would..." She halted when she saw Tania. "Where did *she* come from?" she asked quietly.

Vaughn jerked his head toward Danton. "Danton brought her here."

Ivana's mouth dropped open. "I thought he couldn't do that?"

"Apparently, he's been practicing. Damn near killed himself doing it, though."

Ivana didn't move any farther into the room. She just crossed her arms over her chest and watched. "She didn't know he was a Banebringer," she observed after a moment.

"No."

"She doesn't appear to care."

It took Vaughn a moment to answer. "It does seem that way." He could still vividly remember, on the other hand, the smirk on his own fiancée's face and her accompanying words: *"You thought I loved you?"*

He tucked his hands in his pockets. No. No, she never had.

He glanced at Ivana, and there was a frown on her face as she stared at Driskell and Tania. No, not Driskell *and* Tania. Just Driskell. "Ivana?"

There was something...odd about Driskell. She couldn't see it. But the moment she had focused on just him, she could feel it.

A wrongness hung about him like a tattered cloak. Was that something Banebringers could feel? She hadn't seen someone who had been Sedated since she herself had been changed. She glanced at Vaughn. "Do you sense that too?"

"Sense what?"

"He just doesn't seem *right*."

Vaughn gave her a funny look.

All right. So it was just her.

Almost without thinking, she moved closer to him. The sense of wrongness grew. She put a hand to his forehead, and as a test, she burned a bit of her own aether—not to stop time, but just generally.

She jerked her hand back almost immediately. His body was alight.

No, not alight. She still couldn't *see* anything, not with her eyes. But when she touched him and burned aether...

She tentatively put a hand back out to touch his head.

Yes. She could see it, just not with her eyes. Every vein, every artery burned with conflict. She could feel the enmity between the types of aether, she could feel the triumph of the foreign aether, the hopelessness of the native.

She poked at a blob of foreign aether with her mind, willing it to retreat.

It jerked back as if burned but didn't do as she ordered. So she poked again, this time infusing her touch with more aether—and snapping whatever invisible hold it had on the native aether.

And it worked. The native aether twitched.

So she did it again, to another aether-bug, and then a few more, and then a dozen, and as she sifted, she became faster, until she was running every drop of blood in his body through her touch, freeing the native aether, breaking the foreign.

The foreign drew back, subdued. His bodily systems working again. Cleaning the blood. Absorbing the foreign contaminants. Creating new charmblood aether. Until there was nothing left but what ought to be there—for a Banebringer.

A gasp jerked her from her trance—and she realized she had closed her eyes, because now she opened them...and found Driskell staring up at her, confusion on his face.

She dropped her hand and backed up, past Tania, past Danton, past Vaughn and all the way to the door.

Driskell sat up.

"My gods..." Thrax said, his eyes wide, while Danton gaped soundlessly first at Ivana, then at Driskell.

"Driskell?" Tania cried.

He rubbed his temple. "How did you get here?" He looked around. "And...where is *here* anyway? What happened?" His brow furrowed. "I thought for sure—"

"Driskell!" Tania threw her arms around him. "Oh gods... They said... I thought... I don't even care."

He returned her embrace, but he was still obviously confused.

"Wh-What did you *do*?" Vaughn asked, his own eyes wide.

What Ivana had done was monumental. Unheard of. Impossible. "I just...broke the hold the foreign aether had over the native. It was easy, once I got the hang of it."

"You reversed Sedation. That's not... That's not possible."

Ivana looked pointedly at Driskell, who was holding Tania's

hands and talking. "And yet."

"Temoth, Ivana. Do you know what this means?"

"I can think of many implications. But can we hold off on breaking into Weylyn City and—"

"No, no, not that. I mean, maybe, eventually. But no. What I meant was—*you broke the curse.* You made it so there was no curse in his body. You did what Zily couldn't do because he himself is subject to his own curse. But you're not, are you? You can do what he could do but is restrained from doing himself? He told us that—he told us that, didn't he?"

Ivana stared at him, stunned. That sort of made sense.

"This could be bigger than being able to bring back Sedated Banebringers. This could be...so much bigger. What else can you do with that aether?"

Danton and Thrax's eyes were also on her; they didn't understand what Vaughn was talking about—Ivana barely understood Zily's cryptic instructions herself—but they knew she had just done the impossible.

She almost excused herself, uncomfortable under their scrutiny, when there was a knock on the door again.

Askata's new steward, Dal Calpix, cracked the door and poked his head in. "The final tally is in," he said, his face deadpan.

The room stilled. Everyone looked at the steward. Vaughn's stomach was in knots.

Once news of their defeat of the Conclave force had spread—once it was safe—once everyone realized what had happened—once the rumors had taken hold...

The representatives had asked Askata to go on with the election, despite the chaos, even though Airell had disappeared and had not shown himself again. Most of them just wanted it to be over.

Today, the votes had been cast; they had just been waiting to hear the results.

Calpix slid into the room, Askata on his heels, and closed the door behind them.

Calpix's somber expression cracked. "You won. It was close. Seventy-two to sixty-nine." He hesitated, then bowed. "Your Excellency."

Vaughn stared at him. He'd...won?

Thrax whistled. "They elected a Gifted to be Ri. I'm shocked. Pleasantly shocked, but shocked all the same."

Askata nodded at Thrax. "It seems your performance in saving Cohoxta from the Conclave sealed it. After that, any representatives who had been on the fence went to your side."

Calpix turned to Vaughn. "Your Excellency, if you're open to advice, you might wish to speak to the representatives before they go back to their respective homes."

Vaughn put his hand against the wall. *Your Excellency*. This had all been theory until now.

"Oh, no," Thrax said. "And you haven't had time to find a speechwriter yet. This could be the beginning of the end."

"Your Excellency?" Calpix queried again. "Your first orders?"

Ugh. *Ugh*. "They know what I plan to do, don't they?"

"Obviously, there has been no official statement."

"They aren't fools, Teyrnon," Askata put in. "And what you said to the enemy commander has been repeated and spread until the entire city knows it verbatim. They may well be hoping for it."

Vaughn sighed. "I'll address them in the morning. But before I do that, there's something more important I need you to do for me, Dal Calpix."

Calpix straightened up. "Of course, Your Excellency."

"First, stop calling me that," Vaughn said. The steward's eyebrows knit together in disapproval, but he said nothing. "Second, bring me a stationery set and the Fereharian seal. Third, find me some sort of example in the archives of an official declaration, statement, or some such, on the part of the Ri. I just need a template to work with."

"Your Excellency," the steward said, a defiant lift to his chin. He bowed, then left.

Askata inclined her head to Vaughn. "Congratulations," she said. "Is there anything I can do to help at present?"

"Find out which of the Gan voted for me."

She inclined her head again, approval in her eyes, and then followed Calpix out the door.

Vaughn cast his eyes around the room. Everyone was looking at him. Even Ivana, who looked faintly amused.

"Danton, I feel as though news like this deserves to be relayed in person. Do you feel up to zapping yourself back and letting Ri Tanuac and Yaotel know what's happening?"

Danton saluted. "At your service." He smirked. "Your Excellency."

"You'd better disappear now, before I smack y—"

Danton flashed out of sight before Vaughn could finish.

Vaughn exhaled and rubbed his temples. He glanced at Driskell and Tania, who were sitting close together on the bed, their hands clasped together. "When Danton gets back, do you want me to see if he thinks he can take you back?" he asked Tania.

She pulled Driskell's hand into her lap. "No. I'm never leaving him again."

"O-Okay. Well, you're welcome to stay here with Driskell as long as both of you plan to be here. For now, why don't we leave you two alone."

Vaughn stood up and jerked his head at Thrax. He didn't

bother with Ivana. She was already headed to the door.

When the door had closed behind all three of them, Thrax gave a mock bow. "Your Excellency," he said. Then he stuck out his tongue at Vaughn and strolled down the hall.

"Real mature, Thrax," Vaughn called after him.

That left him with Ivana.

He cleared his throat. "Let's find some time this week to discuss this…thing you did to Driskell," he said.

She shrugged. "Okay. Just let me know."

He watched as she walked away. Something ached within him, watching her go, and it wasn't his loins.

There had to be a way to salvage that situation. There was a completely reasonable unspoken agreement hanging between them that what had happened between them was over. Whatever intentions either of them may have had beyond that night…

Well, she had betrayed his trust, after all. And he had locked her up. Was there really any going back from that? Yet he felt as though he'd lost so much more than a potential lover.

He'd lost the only person who had ever seen him.

Chapter Sixty-Two

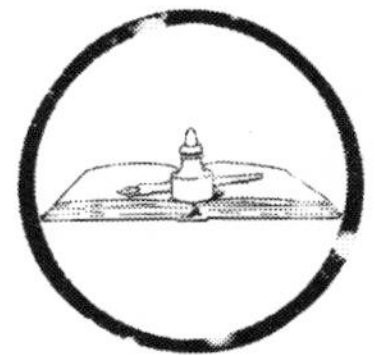

Choices

Driskell sat with Tania on a bench on his room's balcony that night, the remnants of their light dinner on a silver serving platter.

Tania had scooted close to him the moment he'd set the platter on the ground, and she now leaned against him, his arm around her shoulder.

It was a beautiful view. The sun was setting in brilliant splashes of reds and oranges to the west, and since his room faced north, he couldn't see most of the destruction of the city.

Danton and Thrax had told him his stunt with the soldiers had likely saved Cohoxta from burning down; and that it had certainly allowed Vaughn, Ivana, and Thrax to successfully defend the palace against the rogue bloodbane without having to worry about the enemy sneaking in behind their backs.

He still marveled that it had worked. Danton had said it was probably because he'd been preparing the soldiers beforehand, continuing to feed them distrust and anxiety until they were easily manipulated at the end.

Manipulated. He still didn't like that word. "You really don't care?" he asked Tania for the dozenth time that day.

She laughed lightly and nudged him with her body. "Driskell. How many times do I have to tell you *no, I don't* before you believe me?"

"Would you have felt that way if I had told you when it had happened, instead finding out when faced with the prospect of losing me?"

She was quiet for a long while. "I think," she said at last, "that it might have taken me longer to process." She pulled away from him, faced him, and took his hands. "But, Driskell, I love you. Your-Your...*change* hasn't made me question my love for you. It just makes me question everything I thought I knew about Banebringers."

He bit his lip. "They prefer to be called 'Gifted.' Just...so you know."

She furrowed her brow but nodded.

He searched her eyes. "I was so worried."

She put her forehead to his and said nothing more.

A light tapping at the balcony door made Driskell turn.

Danton was standing at the open door to the balcony. He held out a qixli to Driskell once he had his attention. It was already glowing. "Sorry to bother you, but Ri Tanuac wants to speak with you."

Driskell took the qixli tentatively. "What do I do?" He'd never used one himself before.

"Hold it in one or both hands," Danton said, "and burn the

aether in it. It kinda takes care of the rest."

"Thanks." He did as Danton instructed, and a moment later, the glowing stopped and a tinny version of Tanuac's voice came through the device.

"Driskell?" the voice said.

"Um, hello, Your Excellency?"

"It works. It works," the voice said, almost as if talking to someone else.

Driskell glanced at Danton.

"Yaotel had him make his own," Danton whispered. "I think this is the first time he's used it."

Ah. That would explain it.

"Driskell," Tanuac said. "To say I'm relieved to hear your voice would be an understatement. We had all assumed the worst when you disappeared."

"I'm so sorry, Your Excellency."

"Sorry? Good gods, son, don't be sorry. I've already been briefed on everything that happened, and—Well. We can talk when you get back. I just wanted to let you know that, as soon as you think you're ready for the trip, I could use you back in Marakyn. I've got Ambassador Mezzo already hovering at my door, an army to get rid of, and there will be meetings—"

"Your Excellency," Driskell said, interrupting. "I understand. I think Dal, er, Ri Vaughn is going to make a speech tomorrow, and then I'll be ready." He glanced at Danton. He wondered if Danton could take them back.

"Is he going by 'Vaughn'? I'm told his birth name is Teyrnon."

"Um...I don't know, Your Excellency. But I can find out," Driskell said.

"Can you also let him know we're formalizing the alliance tomorrow morning?" Tanuac asked. "And that I'll be contacting him personally sometime tomorrow afternoon."

"Yes, Your Excellency."

"Very good, Driskell. And..." Tanuac paused. "We'll be glad to have you back."

Ivana stopped by the wing of the palace that had been turned into a medical ward for the injured, as she had every evening for four days.

Sanca gave Ivana a broad smile as she entered the large hall at the top of the stairs, which Sanca had set up as her "office." "She's awake," she said.

Ivana let out a slow breath. *Thank the gods*. "Can I see her?"

"You have fifteen minutes," Sanca said. "She needs to rest."

Ivana rolled her eyes. "Fine."

Sanca ushered her down the hall and into one of the private rooms, and then she left, closing the door behind her.

Ivana walked over to the bed where Aleena lay. She was partially propped up on pillows but not quite sitting.

She smiled at Ivana as she pulled over a chair to sit next to the bed. "My second visitor today," she said.

Ivana raised her eyebrow. "Second?"

Aleena nodded. "I'm told Vaughn stopped by earlier to see how I was doing, but I wasn't awake yet. I've also been told *you've* stopped by every day."

Ivana studied her face; color had returned to it, but there was still strain in her smile.

"They say I'll live," Aleena said gently. "So you can stop worrying."

Worrying. That was what she had been doing, hadn't it been? She cleared her throat. "Good. I'm glad to hear it."

Aleena snorted. "Ever the expert in understatement, aren't you?"

Ivana laced her hands together. "Thank you," she said.

Aleena tilted her head. "For what?"

"For risking your life to help with this whole mess. It's even less your fight than mine, and I'm sure Vaughn is appreciative of your support."

Aleena started shaking her head before Ivana had even finished. "Look, I like Vaughn and all, but I didn't do it for him, or the Ichtaca, or any other reason than that you said to me, 'Aleena, we have people to save.'"

Ivana interrupted. "I didn't say that."

Aleena ignored her. "Don't you know by now I'd do anything for you?"

Ivana gave a little laugh. "What? Why?" She was hardly worthy of such devotion.

"Because you saved my life."

Ivana snorted. "You were pretty beat up, but you would have lived. I just helped you recover faster."

"No. No, I wouldn't have. Sure, maybe I could have eked out another day, another week, another month, but my life was over. I'd already decided that. Until you found me. Until you found me, and you *saw* me."

Aleena held Ivana's eyes long enough that Ivana became uncomfortable and looked away with a shrug.

"I can never repay you for that," Aleena added softly.

"That's ridiculous," Ivana said, looking back over. "You don't have to repay me. Whatever you may think, you owe me no debt. I was just—"

"I know," Aleena said, a small smile on her lips. "Doing what you do."

Words from long ago echoed in Ivana's mind. *Saving people.* "Temoth, not that again."

"Let me tell you something." Aleena struggled to sit up more, and then she put a hand on her stomach and winced once she had achieved her goal. She looked around, even though they were alone in the room, then spoke more quietly. "Sweetblade was an anomaly. A hitch in the trajectory of your life. You can call it a mistake, you can call it a path you were forced into by circumstances—whatever. But she was never who you were meant to be, never the path you would have taken."

An *anomaly*? "She was more than a *hitch*. I lived as her for more than a decade. You can talk about paths and choices and mistakes all you want. I am not and cannot be the person I was before that *hitch*. It *was* the path I took, and to continue with your ridiculous analogy, if you take a different path, you end up at a different destination, whatever you may have intended."

"Or maybe you just get lost for a while."

Lost. That was what Vaughn had said, too. She frowned. She didn't like it when the people closest to her agreed on her problems.

"That doesn't mean you can't find your way back," Aleena continued. "Or maybe you find a new path just as promising as the first." She shrugged. "So maybe you won't be the same person as when you started, but are any of us, after a decade or two of life?"

Ivana closed her eyes briefly. "I wish I could believe any of that."

Aleena took Ivana's hand, squeezed it, and then let go. "That's okay. You don't need to. I can believe for you until you're ready to believe for yourself."

Ivana gave Aleena an incredulous look. How could anyone be so eternally hopeful? "That is the most ridiculous sentiment I have ever—"

There was a knock on the door, and Sanca poked her head in. "Time's up," she said. She bustled over to the bed. "What are you doing sitting up?"

Aleena groaned and winked at Ivana, who moved the chair back where it belonged and out of Sanca's way.

"Thanks, Sanca," Ivana said, amused. She had the feeling that Sanca was thoroughly enjoying her new role. "For taking good care of her, that is."

Sanca gave her a stern look. "Out," she said.

Ivana obeyed. She stepped into the hall, closed the door behind her, and then leaned against the wall. *"Maybe you just find a new path."*

She wanted to continue arguing with her old friend. *And what would that be, Aleena? Do you have suggestions? Because the only possibility I had I've almost certainly ruined.*

The only problem with arguing with Aleena in her head was that she knew Aleena well enough that she could also fabricate her responses. *Almost certainly? I still hear room in there for possibility,* she would say.

And then Ivana would stop arguing because it would only lead to Aleena telling her to go talk to Vaughn and see what happened. And she didn't want to. She was...

She clenched her hand. She was afraid. Afraid that her assumptions and fears would be true. Afraid that she had forever shuttered the only glimmer of light, the only tendril of life, she had seen in herself for years. For a moment, she had dared to hope.

It was so much easier to go on believing the worst than having it confirmed.

It might be considered ironic that her entire adult life had been built around taking risks, and now she balked at what seemed to be such a simple one on the surface. But that was different. Her life had been built around *calculated* risks. Risks she could mitigate, plan for, even control. And if it were too risky—she didn't do it.

She couldn't mitigate anything about this risk. She couldn't have a Plan B or C. She couldn't control anything about it other than what she herself said or did. In her world, that meant she didn't do it.

"Maybe you need to stop waiting to feel different and just do something different."

Burning skies, Aleena was annoying when she was right.

She looked out the window across from her. It was fully dark. Which meant it was getting late, at this time of the year.

Ivana walked around the interior of the palace—she didn't think walking outside at night was a good idea right now, with the occasional bloodhawk still seen flying over the city—six times before she decided to seek out Vaughn.

She had a feeling she knew where he would be, after the afternoon he had had. Sure enough, she found him on the roof again, this time sitting cross-legged a few feet back from the edge. A sheath of paper was next to him, a large rock holding it down in case of a stray breeze, no doubt, and he crouched over a lap desk, pencil in hand, profile to her.

He didn't hear her come up the stairs, which didn't surprise her. He was intent on whatever he was doing, and people rarely heard her approach. So she watched him for a moment. He scribbled something on the paper, paused, and then scratched it out.

"Predictable," Ivana said at last. "At least this time you've had the foresight to leave Thrax at the bottom of the stairs."

He started and turned to look at her. "You *have* to stop doing that," he said.

"Good practice for you. You need to learn to be more aware of your surroundings. Even when you're absorbed in something else." She nodded toward his stack of paper.

He looked out over the palace grounds, his face perfectly schooled, as if to assess the progress on damage clean-up and repair.

It was a different view than the last time they had spoken on the roof. Thrax had managed to burn down half the gardens, there were at least three gaping holes in the palace walls, and smoke from the bonfire that had been kept for two days straight to burn bloodbane bodies still lingered in the air to the south, close to the river. The lawn would have to be replanted. It had been churned into a muddy—and bloody—mess. And beneath the many hardened silver patches, the stones in the courtyard were stained red.

Of course, that was minor compared to the real work he had ahead of him.

"It's this damn speech. I've tried dozens of variations, and nothing seems right." He ran the hand not holding the pencil through his hair. "I mean, what am I supposed to say: 'Hello there, I'm your new Ri. I didn't want to be Ri, but the head of a secret group of Banebringers told me I had to take Ferehar so we could leave the Setanan Empire and be safe from the coming Xambrian war.'" He threw down his pencil. "Because *that* works."

"Maybe you should have Thrax whip you something up," she said.

He snorted. "Right. If I want it to be full of dick jokes." He rubbed at his eyes. "Sorry. Did you need something?"

She hesitated. He was obviously tired. It was late. Maybe...Maybe this conversation could wait until tomorrow, after he had his speech out of the way. Or it wasn't too late just to forget the whole idea—

"Ivana?"

A coward? You, *Ivana?*

Shut up, Aleena.

She walked closer to him and settled herself down at the edge of the roof, putting her back to the knee-high railing around the edge and leaning against it.

He watched her movements but said nothing.

"Yes," she said. "Two things, perhaps. Unless you're too busy."

He set his lap desk aside. "I could use a break."

She forced herself to meet his eyes. "First," she said, and then halted. Burning skies, why was it so hard to say two little words? She had already acknowledged that she had made a mistake.

She swallowed. But to apologize was more than admitting a mistake, wasn't it? To apologize was to extend a hand, hoping it would be clasped in return rather than spurned.

It was to seek something from another she couldn't even extend to herself.

Forgiveness.

She exhaled and tried again. "I'm sorry," she said, her voice barely above a whisper. "For what I did. For betraying your trust. For hurting you. For almost ruining everything you've worked for. If I could go back, I wouldn't do it." She swallowed again, her throat dry. "I-I'm sorry."

Vaughn studied Ivana's face, which was uncharacteristically nervous.

He believed her. He even understood.

That didn't mean it didn't hurt, of course. It did. When he thought of that moment when he realized what she had done, it *still* sent a pang through him, even knowing she hadn't used him to do it.

Did he forgive her?

Yes. Yes, of course he did. He already had.

———

After a few moments of silence, Vaughn moved over to sit in front of Ivana. "And...I'm sorry for locking you up."

She blinked. That had not been what she had expected. "What?"

He shrugged. "I overreacted."

"It was an entirely logical thing to do, given the circumstances."

He looked over her shoulder. "Perhaps. But I didn't do it because it was the logical thing to do. I did it because I was angry, and I could use logic as my excuse." His eyes flicked back to hers. "Even if the outcome would have been the same. I'm still sorry for my motivation."

"I... Okay." She was still confused, but if it made him feel better... "It's fine. Really."

"Good. And I forgive you."

"Wait—it can't be that easy." It *couldn't.* He was lying. He had to be. Why he would do that, she didn't know, but it just...*couldn't* be that easy.

He raised an eyebrow. "It can't?"

"I-I *betrayed* you. I hurt you."

"Yes? I mean—I'd be lying if I said I wasn't still a little hurt. But in hindsight, it might have been naïve of me to show you the key to Airell's cell, knowing you. And your past."

Even so. He had every right to reject her apology. To spurn her. She closed her mouth and stared at him.

"You had a second thing?" he asked, as easily as if they had just decided on how to redesign the unfortunate gardens.

Ivana stood up, feeling unsettled. "I was wondering if your offer is still on the table."

He blinked. "Offer?"

"The one where I get to be 'Advisor for Keeping Vaughn Alive.'"

"Oh," he said, smiling faintly. "That one." And then he looked at her. Long. Hard. As if to see past any façade or game.

"Of course, I understand if you'd like to decline now. After all, you need someone you can trust in that position."

Still, he said nothing. Instead, he stood up and walked over to the edge of the roof. "Dal Calpix had the bar in my father's office restocked," he said. "Do you think I can trust him?"

Was that relevant? "You'd best hope so, or you have more to worry about than if he poisoned any of the liquor you probably won't drink."

"Yes. Yes, that's about my feeling on it too. He seems a good man. My mother certainly likes him. But can I *truly* trust him?" He sighed and turned to face her. "The fact is, Ivana, aside from, perhaps, Danton and Thrax, you're one of the people in my life I trust the most."

"I think you need new friends."

He met her eyes. "You risked everything to help us when you could have run. I can't dismiss that."

She shifted. "I was bored."

"You're not selling yourself well," he said, a small smile on his lips.

She crossed her arms over her chest. "Is the offer still there, or not?"

"Why do you want it?"

She cast him a side eye. "It sounds not-boring."

"Do you have any more enemies from your past still living that you might abandon your duties to seek out personal vengeance against?"

She turned the question over in her mind. "I mean. Airell's out there somewhere. But other than that…I don't think so."

"See," he said. "The fact that you gave that serious contemplation is why I still think I can trust you."

She raised an eyebrow. "That makes absolutely no sense."

"If someone in that position were going to betray me, nine out of ten of those people would be doing it for money, power, or status. I happen to know that you care little for those things, which makes you more inherently trustworthy than most people."

"That's ridiculous," she said. "What if I'm in that ten percent?"

"I agree with you that an attempt on my life, reputation, or position is certain within the next year. Frankly..." He shrugged. "I'll take those odds."

"But—"

He raised an eyebrow. "You're the one who asked me if the offer is still on the table. It is. Do you want the job?"

She hesitated. She *was* the one who had asked. Because...it had seemed a good opportunity to start over. And, well, she supposed it still did. "Yes."

He nodded. "Then it's yours."

Silence. The breeze blew, and those irritating strands of hair that always worked their way loose from her tie tickled her neck.

Vaughn's eyes flicked to them. And then to her lips. And then back to her eyes.

She fought back against the rush of heat that swept through her. Their friendship might have been repaired, but that didn't mean—

"Ivana," he said, and the word itself felt as though he had reached across the space between them to caress her cheek, though he didn't move.

She swallowed. "I'll see you in the morning," she said, but her body didn't turn.

"I'd like to try again," he went on softly, as though she hadn't spoken.

He moved closer to her, close enough that he *could* reach out and touch her face if he wanted to. "This is a lonely life. And it would be nice to know that, every once in a while, I don't have to sleep alone."

It would. "And when our fling ends?" she asked. "Then what? Do I still have a job?"

"Of course." He shrugged. "That's the beauty of it, remember? No assumptions. No expectations. No hopes." He met her eyes and smiled. "It won't matter."

She had to give him credit. He was so close to achieving the perfect air of nonchalance with that smile.

But not close enough, and the realization sent a chill through her.

He's lying. It would matter. How much, or in what way—she didn't know. But it would definitely matter.

She should have called him on it. If nothing else, she should have refused, on principle, because of it. But she wanted what he offered too much—as much as she had before. Maybe more, now that she had tasted it and knew it was possible.

She didn't want that to be their last night.

She stepped closer to him. *This can't end well,* a tiny voice inside warned her. "I...I think I would like that," she said.

He slid his hand around her waist and drew her against himself, trailing a finger down her cheek, across her jaw, and then met her lips with his own once more.

He had just moved his hand beneath her shirt and up her back when someone cleared their throat from across the roof.

Vaughn pulled back and frowned at the interloper.

Ivana turned to find Driskell standing there.

"Uh," Driskell said, fumbling with his hands at his waist, looking rather mortified. "Your Excellency, I'm, uh, I...I'm *so* sorry to interrupt, but..."

Vaughn's right eye twitched slightly. "It's all right. Am I needed?"

"Just a message," Driskell said. "I heard from Ri Tanuac. He's talked to the Xambrian ambassador and they're finalizing the alliance tomorrow morning. He'll be contacting you sometime tomorrow afternoon. Oh, and, um, he wants to know if you're going by 'Ri Vaughn' or 'Ri Teyrnon.'"

Vaughn looked pained. "Formally, 'Ri Teyrnon,'" he said. "But *please*—among friends...I'm still 'Vaughn.'"

Driskell gave a short bow. "Of course, Your Excellency."

"Driskell."

"Yes?"

"I consider you a friend."

"Oh. Right. Sorry. Your Ex—Vaughn. I'm...not used to being informal with a Ri."

"Me, either," Vaughn muttered, then he cleared his throat. "Thank you. Tell Ri Tanuac I'll be expecting his contact. And that..." He tossed Ivana a wry look. "I know what I'm going to say in my speech tomorrow."

Ivana disengaged herself from his arms. "And you still have that speech to write," she said.

Vaughn made a small sound of protest in the back of his throat.

No need to scandalize poor Driskell any further. "If it's not too late when you finish, feel free to bring it by and I'll..." She raised an eyebrow at Vaughn. "Have a look. Dal Driskell, I'll walk you down."

Chapter Sixty-Three

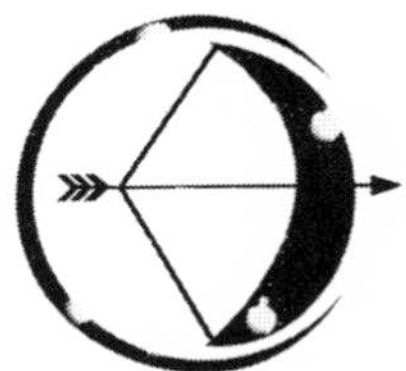

A Long Tradition

Far more than just the representatives showed up to hear Vaughn's statement.

In addition to the approximately one hundred and fifty representatives from across Ferehar, as many of the citizens of Cohoxta as could squeeze themselves into the courtyard outside the palace were there. They spilled out the open gates and into the boulevard beyond.

Thankfully, it wasn't raining, though it could have been a little cooler.

Well, at least, *Vaughn* would have liked for it to have been a little cooler, dressed as he was in full formal wear: three layers of silk and linen topped with a stiff jacket, and Dal Calpix had insisted he wear *gloves* of all things.

From his place on the large balcony built into the front of the palace designed for this purpose, he glanced enviously at regular folk. Some of the men were dressed in common Fereharian garb for the warmer months: loose, billowy pants that gathered at the knee and a sleeveless tunic.

There was an occasional breeze that he couldn't even feel through his layers. Too bad he couldn't convince Dal Calpix that he ought to put back on the vest and skirt he'd ridden into the city wearing. Of course, he could have worn whatever he wanted if he had insisted, but he figured there would be more important matters to argue with his steward over in the coming months.

Gan Anque had been chosen to speak for the representatives, and he now stepped forward from his place next to Vaughn. "Ri Teyrnon has asked the representatives to pass judgment on Lord Airell. We have consulted and come to an agreement." He cleared his throat. "Lord Airell has been found guilty of the charges of treason. If he returns to Cohoxta, his life is forfeit, and he will be executed by hanging."

There was a smattering of applause and one loud *whoop* from the crowd.

Vaughn swallowed. He had known that would be the verdict. At least he hadn't had to be the one to pronounce it.

"Shame," Ivana muttered under her breath from where she stood to one side with Danton, Driskell, Tania, and Thrax. "I was hoping for castrated, tarred, feathered, then drawn and quartered. Then again, I'm not nearly as magnanimous as you."

Vaughn flashed her a tight smile and then glanced at his mother, who stood next to the three other Gan. She was stiff and unmoving, her face tight, her lips pressed together, her jaw locked. She said nothing and looked nowhere else other than straight ahead.

The grief she was suppressing must have been enormous. At

least she didn't have to see another son die today. She would just never see him again.

Gan Anque seemed to feel he had enough order and quiet to continue. "Our new Ri has asked to address the representative body before we disperse."

There was a murmur of assent.

Vaughn swallowed again, his throat dry, clutching the clean copy of his speech in sweaty palms. This was it. Oh, gods, he wasn't meant for this.

Anque looked at him. "Your Excellency?"

Ugh. Ugh, ugh, ugh.

But he stepped forward all the same. Looked out on the sea of faces.

So many of them. There was curiosity, hope, awe, and yes, there were more than a few faces layered with disgust.

So he looked back toward his friends. Driskell, arm in arm with Tania, gave him an encouraging smile. Danton winked. Thrax stuck his tongue out.

And Ivana.

Ivana, whom he had woken up beside this morning, who had returned with him to his own rooms and stayed with him while he'd attempted to put something in his stomach, listened to his nervous ramblings, and convinced him not to rewrite his speech at the last minute. Who had eventually decried him as altogether "ridiculous" and marched off in irritation.

She met his eyes. She didn't smile, or wink, or stick her tongue out. But she *looked* at him.

He took a deep breath and turned back to his audience. He fingered his speech. He had tried to memorize it, but he didn't trust himself without the words in front of him.

"Ferehar is part of a long tradition," he said. "A tradition of struggle, of bloodshed, of power changing hands and sometimes being taken. Even before Setana, Ferehar joined its neighbors in its squabbles over who the next chieftain would be. Setana, for all its faults, introduced a system that, in theory, could have mitigated some of this power struggle." He ran his eyes over the crowd. "We all know that for the lie it was. I stand before you as not only the son and brother of two previous Ri, respectively, but as a descendant of a line of corrupt, selfish, and often downright cruel leaders. When my father, Ri Gildas, usurped the position from his predecessor—a distant cousin—none of you cheered. And yet none of you dared to challenge him, either. Just as none of you dared to challenge Ri Airell when he seized upon the opportunity that the disappearance of Ri Gildas afforded him."

The crowd was still and silent.

"But I did." He took a deep breath. "And unlike my predecessors, I challenged him not because I wanted to, but because it was what needed to be done.

"I am only half-Fereharian in heritage. But my mother and her family are Fereharian. I have Fereharian friends. I lived here for the better part of my childhood—until I was driven out. I know what it means to be Fereharian, in my own way: to be mocked, disdained, hated, through no fault of my own." He pressed his lips together. "And just like Setana cares nothing for me and my kind, you *know* that Setana cares nothing for Ferehar, other than the wealth it can give it.

"You have, incredibly, elected me to be your new Ri. Yet my very existence is illegal in the Setanan Empire. This puts us in a bit of a bind, doesn't it?

"I can only assume I'm standing here because I represent something that you want. A change." He shrugged and veered off his script. "Either that, or rumors of my glowing during the recent battle have you so terrified of me that you didn't dare vote differently."

There were a few titters, but most people shifted as though uncomfortable. Too soon for jokes, apparently.

"As your Ri, I have sworn to do what is best for Ferehar."

The only sound was the chirping of birds. Well, here went nothing.

"And what is best for Ferehar is that we reject the oppressive thumb of the new Setanan Empire, now under control of the Conclave. I will not serve masters who preach that my kind is born from demons and who would seek to bring a city to its knees simply for us being amongst you. I will not serve hypocrites, who do these things with one hand and with the other use us as objects to further their own power. Together with Donia, Venetia, and Fuilyn, we declare independence from the Setanan Empire." He took a deep breath.

"We don't expect this decision to go unchallenged by Setana. We will be supported by the Xambrian Empire, with whom Ferehar will be formalizing an alliance as soon as our new Xambrian ambassador arrives." He swept his eyes over the crowd, gauging reactions. There was shock on many faces. Even the representatives hadn't realized that much. And yet there were others who were nodding slowly, as if they'd realized the necessity of the decision. "I know that many of you are unsure about this decision. I know many of you, though it's what you want, are unsure about my leadership. I know some of you, despite the protection demonstrated by myself and my companions this past week, still harbor hatred and misunderstanding about my kind and will whisper about the new demonspawn in charge of Ferehar at the tavern tonight.

"I hope in the coming days and weeks and months to gain your trust. To prove the lies of the Conclave about Banebringers wrong. To show you that while we are, at heart, just like you, we can also offer more—to Cohoxta, to Ferehar, and to our new allies."

He drew in another breath. "Yes, there will be changes. Some welcome. Some difficult. But I promise I will do my best, as long as I am Ri, to administer Ferehar with equity and compassion." He looked at his mother when he said the last. She gave him the tiniest of nods. "Thank you."

There was no thunderous applause as he stepped back to the side, but when Gan Anque stepped back to the front, he nodded in Vaughn's direction. "Ri Teyrnon. Thank you."

And there was a murmur of agreement.

For now, that would have to be enough.

That night, Vaughn sat at a long table in the private dining room. His mother, Ivana, Danton, Aleena, and Thrax sat around it; Driskell and Tania were preparing to return to Donia.

He cleared his throat and stood. "Since I can't get drunk, I'll try to act properly so for the occasion," he said, smiling at them. "We're here not only because of me, but because all of us together did this. So I have an announcement. Henceforth, we're no longer to use the term *Banebringer* around here, which I admit, I myself have continued to use. From now on, we will use the term most of the Ichtaca prefer: 'Gifted.'"

Thrax grunted—which Vaughn took to be a sign of approval.

"We have a lot to figure out about what happened to Ivana and me when we went to the abyss," Vaughn said. "About her powers."

"Why you were glowing?" Thrax offered. "Seems unfair that the rest of us can't glow."

Vaughn shook his head, smiling. "About how to distill some of Danton's newfound skills to be more beneficial. We also have external and internal pressures. I have no idea what's going to happen going forward; tonight we feel hopeful, but none of us are stupid or naïve. We know this is only the beginning, a small victory at the start of a rather desperate-looking long view." He raised his glass to them. "But I'm glad that all of you are at my side."

They all raised their own glasses. "Hear, hear," Thrax called loudly, clinking his fork against his glass.

"Thrax, all of us are listening," Danton said.

"I've always wanted to say that," Thrax said. "Sounded good, didn't it?"

Vaughn sighed. Since when had he become the responsible *and* mature one?

If nothing else, that was a sign his life was falling apart.

He looked at Ivana. She gave him a small smile.

Everything except her.

For now.

Epilogue

A little way down the Atl River, Airell took shelter under an old fisherman's lean-to. The lights of Cohoxta could be seen in the east; otherwise, the night was dark and still.

He clenched his fist as he stared at the lights of the city that should have been his. The city that was still, by all rights, by every Fereharian tradition, his.

He was still fuming over the news one of his contacts inside the city had smuggled him two mornings prior. That upstart brother of his—a *demonspawn* of all people—had stolen the position of Ri right out from under him, and now Airell was in exile from his own home.

He had underestimated his brother and his resources.

"Lord Airell," a soft voice said from behind him.

Ri Airell, he wanted to spit back, but he refrained. Instead, he turned and faced the newcomer with a congenial smile. No, *newcomers*. Bherg had a cloaked and hooded friend with him.

"Holiness Bherg," Airell said, bowing slightly. The priest, who had returned to Weylyn City after being relieved of his position with the army outside Marakyn, had immediately travelled to Cohoxta once news of Teyrnon's little rebellion had reached his circle of Conclave higher-ups. There, he had found Airell already imprisoned, coordinated a rescue during the chaos of the battle, and then given him instructions to stay in hiding and meet him in this place, on this date, if the election results didn't turn out favorably.

Bherg didn't smile. "I didn't know whether you would show."

"Ferehar is mine," Airell said, keeping his voice pleasant. "It was promised to me, and I will do whatever it takes to get it back."

"Then our purposes align," Bherg said. He stared at the city for a moment himself. "That commander had the gall to suggest to my cohort that I was doing an inadequate job of handling Marakyn. And then what did he do? Botch the job and get himself killed anyway."

The Conclave needed Ferehar. Airell wanted Ferehar. Bherg wanted to restore his reputation.

It was a strange but hopefully profitable partnership for all involved.

"Are you going to introduce me to your friend?" Airell asked Bherg, nodding toward the other man.

"No," Bherg said. "I don't think just yet. Suffice to say that he claims to have a vested interest in our success."

Airell raised an eyebrow at the mysterious man.

"The woman," the man said softly, "that the new Ri has at his side. She'll need to be dealt with before you can succeed."

Airell chuckled. "That whore who couldn't even manage to kill me when she had the chance? How in the abyss—?"

"Don't underestimate her," the man said, his voice cold as ice.

That drew Airell up short. Well. He wouldn't make the mistake of underestimating someone again. "Very well," he said. "And how do you suggest we deal with her?"

"Don't worry about that," the man said. He turned his eyes on the city as well. "I'll take care of her."

ABOUT THE AUTHOR

Carol lives in the Lancaster, PA area with her husband and two energetic boys. She loves reading (duh), writing (double-duh), music, movies, and other perfectly normal things like parsing Hebrew verbs and teaching herself new dead languages. She has two master's degrees in the areas of ancient near eastern studies and languages.

Also available:
Banebringer (The Heretic Gods #1) – May 2018
Sweetblade (A Stand-Alone Heretic Gods Novel) – Dec 2018

Coming soon:
A World Broken (The Chronicles of the Lady Sar #1) – Q2 2020

Stay up to date with me via
Twitter: @parkcarola
Facebook: facebook.com/parkcarola/
My Website: carolapark.com
My Newsletter: carolapark.com/newsletter-sign-up/

Made in the USA
Middletown, DE
21 May 2022